Angelica

SHARON SHINN

2003
50TH
ANNIVERSARY

ACE BOOKS, NEW YORK

ANGELICA

An Ace Book
Published by The Berkley Publishing Group,
a division of Penguin Putnam Inc.,
375 Hudson Street, New York, New York 10014.

Visit our website at
www.penguinputnam.com

First edition: March 2003

Library of Congress Cataloging-in-Publication Data

Shinn, Sharon.
    Angelica / Sharon Shinn.— 1st ed.
        p.   cm.
    ISBN 0-441-01013-X (alk. paper)
    1. Samaria (Imaginary place)—Fiction.   I. Title.

PS3569.H499 A85 2003
813'.54—dc21
                                        2002027775

PRINTED IN THE UNITED STATES OF AMERICA

10   9   8   7   6   5   4   3   2   1

To my cousins:

Mike, who bought much of the early music,
and still plays guitar while the rest of us sing;

Kay, who is equally comfortable singing
in front of a campfire or at Carnegie Hall;

Karen, who provided Susannah's voice and
her ability to harmonize with any piece of music;

and Kathy, whose gift was not music,
but a friendship that began the day she was born.

SAMARIA

MANADAVVI

MT. SUDAN
MONTEVERDE

VERDE
DIVIDE

GAZA

PLAIN OF SHARON

GALO

WINDY POINT

SEMORRAH

CAITANAS

DESERT

BETHEL

SINAI

CASTELANA

BREVEN

THE EYRIE

VELORA

JORDANA

CORINNI MOUNTAINS

GALILEE RIVER

MT. EGYPT

HELDORAS

LUMINAUX

CHAPTER ONE

Susannah lay in the tent alone, dreaming.

It was the same dream, the one she had had since she was so young she could not remember her age. She was in an immense place of light and hushed mystery, with unexpected gleams of silver and strange, sparkling tapestries laid against the walls. She floated through this space like a sea creature moving effortlessly through the suspended weeds and reefs of her domain, inhabiting an alien element but feeling perfectly at ease. She lifted a hand to touch one of the glittering patterns hung before her, but her fingers felt nothing but a glass coolness. In her dream, she put her fingers to her cheek, and it was just as cool, as porcelain, as unreal.

This time, the voice accompanied her as she walked through her magical realm. "Susannah," it said in its deep, unearthly tone, and then it spoke unintelligible words. She nodded and smiled and continued on her tour of the white-and-silver room. She could tell that the owner of the voice liked her, was welcoming her to this place. She just could not tell what it was he wanted her to understand. Sometimes he talked to her for hours as she wandered through her dream; sometimes he just spoke her name once, then let her move about in silence. Although he always addressed her by name, he never supplied his own, and never, while she slept, did she ask it. It was only after she woke that she would wonder why she never thought to extend the courtesies that, in her waking life, she would extend to any stranger who invited her into his home.

Sometimes he left off his incomprehensible speech and addressed her in sentences that made absolute sense, and then she would converse with him as she would with any friend. Today was such a day.

"Susannah," he said.

"I am here," she replied.

"It is almost time for you to leave the Edori," he said.

"No, my friend. I will travel always with my tribe."

"You will travel farther than you know."

"I do not mind the travel," she said. "But I like to always return to the place I know."

"And the people you know," he said.

"My people are my place," she said.

"Your people, and your place, are about to change."

She smiled at him. "No, my friend," she said. "For I am not a changeable woman."

"Susannah," he said again, but his voice had changed, had grown smaller and thinner and more insistent. *"Susannah."*

And then that white space tilted under her, and the world spun a quarter of a turn, and she opened her eyes to find herself being shaken by the shoulder.

"Susannah," the young, thin voice repeated. "Are you going to sleep forever? It's time to be waking up."

She blinked a few times, trying to readjust her mind to reality. She had been so deep inside her dream that she felt she was climbing from a dark, narrow cavern onto a hillside of much light and wind, so that she was having a hard time keeping her balance. She put a hand up to shield her eyes, though the light filtering in from the open hole at the top of the tent was scarcely strong enough to hurt her eyes.

"Amram?" she said in a questioning voice, though she knew perfectly well who was beside her. "Is something wrong?"

"No, nothing is wrong, it is just that you have been sleeping so long and I wanted you to wake up."

Thus the purely selfish and unself-conscious reasoning of her lover's sister's son, who was ten years old and had not seemed to realize yet that people might have emotions and needs and experiences that did not relate to him.

"Well, I am awake now, but it will not do you much good, since I do not intend to get up," Susannah said cheerfully. She resettled herself into a slightly more comfortable position on her pallet and smiled up at the boy. Like his mother, Tirza, and his uncle, Dathan, he was dark-skinned and dark-haired and dark-eyed, a true Edori of absolutely unmixed blood. He was also frowning.

"But I *want* you to get up," he said. "You were going to go berry-picking with me today."

"I still may. Or I may do it tomorrow."

"But you promised me!"

Susannah yawned and tucked her hands under her cheek. "I do not recall any promising," she said. "And to be quite honest, I don't feel much like going berry-picking or doing anything with someone who won't let me sleep."

He sat back on his heels, a look of mutinous disbelief tightening all his fine features. "But then—you mean—you're not going to get *up*? And even if you got up, you wouldn't go with me?"

She yawned again, this time covering her mouth with her hand because the yawn was so big. "Not today," she said, closing her eyes and snuggling more deeply into her sleeping roll. "Maybe tomorrow, if you don't disturb my rest."

"But that's not *fair!*" he exclaimed.

A shadow darkened the tent door; she could feel it even through her closed lids. "You. Out. Go trouble somebody else," she heard Dathan's voice say. She smiled but did not open her eyes as Amram whined again about the injustice of the world, and Dathan repeated his commands, and the two of them changed places. Once Amram was outside and Dathan was inside, the light against her eyelids grew subtly darker, as Dathan tied shut the tent door. She felt him moving through the scattered pallets to come stand beside hers, and then he lowered himself slowly next to her on the ground.

"You're not really asleep, are you?" he whispered. "This late in the morning?"

She did not open her eyes, but she could not repress her smile. "Well, I was, until Amram so rudely shook me from my dream. Why, how late is it?"

He pulled up the blankets covering her, brought his body in next to hers, and let the blankets fall over both of them. Instantly, the heat of his body flushed every inch of her skin; he was as warm as a fire, and just as beautiful. "Late," he told her. "Everyone has had their morning meal, and Claudia has gone off to the river for water for the second time. Bartholomew is trying to get a group together to go into Luminaux tomorrow, so everyone is counting their coppers and debating what they might have to barter. Very busy it is in the camp this morning."

Susannah shifted so that Dathan could slip his arm under her shoulder and draw her closer. She loved the feel of his hands, one in her hair, one pressing against her back. She loved the scent of his skin, newly washed this morning in the ice-cold river but smelling of Dathan still for all that. She loved the silken fall of his long black hair across her cheek. She still had not opened her eyes.

"I'm not hungry," she said. "No reason to get up for a meal. And I can go to the river later to bathe and wash out yesterday's clothes. And I have nothing to barter in Luminaux, so I've no need to get up and start looking through my bundles."

"So you're just going to stay in the tent all day, sleeping?" Dathan asked. His face was so close he merely had to lean in a little to kiss her on the corner of her mouth.

She smiled, squeezing her eyes shut even tighter. "I might stay in the tent all day," she murmured, "but I do not mind if I am not sleeping."

No one bothered them for the next couple of hours, as they lay entwined on the sleeping pallet and played at love. Every one of the six tents in their camp was communal, and seven slept in their tent most nights. Privacy was a thing they had to work into the day—but they never had trouble finding time for each other. None of the Edori did. It was an understood thing that a man and a woman would need time alone together; and if a couple had sought out that time, well, others were ready to take up their responsibilities for a few hours. There were other elders to watch the children, other hands to tend the fires. There was no need to rush. Time was plentiful and the seasons were slow. This was one of the many joys Yovah had given them, the love of one for another, and it was a joy to be savored.

Even so, Susannah had not thought to fall back asleep in Dathan's arms and so still be lying in the tent when the noon hour spiked its golden head into the bright blue of the summer sky. Laughter woke her this time, laughter coming from the other side of the tent walls, and she recognized Tirza's sweet voice.

"Not a sound from them for hours," she said cheerfully. "I don't want to go in and check on them, but perhaps I could pull down the center pole and have the whole tent collapse. That might bring them out in a hurry."

"I shall have to tell Adam how long they have lain together," Claudia said with an amused voice. "Perhaps he will try to prove to me that he, too, can lie abed for an entire morning. Even if we are only sleeping, I think I would enjoy such a day!"

Now Susannah did open her eyes, blushing in the half-dark of the tent. Dathan was still deeply asleep, so she kissed him on his rough cheek and came to her feet, careful not to disturb him. She changed quickly into day clothes—not particularly clean ones, as she intended to change again as soon as she had bathed in the river—and stepped outside.

"Well! Look who has woken up!" Tirza exclaimed with exaggerated surprise. "I thought perhaps you had drifted off to the arms of Yovah and we might never see you walking among us again."

Susannah smiled. "And I'm sure that would be delightful, too, but I have spent my last hour or so far more pleasurably," she said audaciously. The other two women laughed, and Claudia came forward to lay her hand on Susannah's belly.

"Still much too nice and flat," she said. "What are you waiting for? It's too long since the tribe had a little one."

"She is waiting for Dathan to be a little less reckless, which means she'll never have a baby," Tirza said. "But I think maybe she'll tame him. He is so settled around this Tachita girl! I never thought to see my brother so calm."

Susannah made a face. "Settled! Calm! I don't think those are the words I would ever use for Dathan. No, and who would want a lover like that? You make him sound like an old man."

"Dathan will not be an old man even when he is an old man," Claudia said dryly. "But someday you may see the advantages of stability over charm." Claudia was at least fifty years old, more than twice the age of Susannah and Tirza, and often she made similar dreary predictions based on her own years of experience. Tirza and Susannah exchanged glances, then burst out laughing. Claudia smiled with them and raised a hand in a casual benediction.

"Yes, you will, and I won't be around to remind you of it," Claudia said. "You'll be settled around the fire, thanking the god for your good man who remembers to hunt when he says he will and who is always there to strike the tent, and you'll say to yourself, 'Claudia was right, as she was about so many things. This is the kind of man to have after all.' "

"Well, Eleazar always remembers to hunt and he is always there to help me when I need him," Tirza said. "And when Amram was born? You could not have found a better father. I thought I would have to steal the baby while he was sleeping and find another tent, that's how much Eleazar wanted to hold his son."

Claudia leapt in with her own story about a past lover and his virtues. Susannah did not pay much attention, though she kept a pleasant smile on her face. Claudia and the other older women of the Lohora tribe seemed very quick to point out Dathan's faults to Susannah, faults that she would have been a fool not to have noticed for herself and faults that she did not care about one bit. Yes, it was true, Dathan could be lazy—and there were days when he simply could not be inspired to help with the packing or the cooking or the washing, whatever the chore was—and he had forgotten, at last year's Gathering, that he had arrived with Susannah and owed her the courtesy of not flirting with women from other tribes, at least while she could see him.

But, sweet loving Yovah, Dathan was magnificent. The handsomest of all the Edori men, the most charming, the sweetest tempered, the most loving. Anytime he stepped into view, from an absence long or short, Susannah felt her heart speed up and an involuntary smile reshape the pattern of her lips. His laughter could brighten the most miserable day, a sullen word from him could throw her into despair. He had been her world for four years, since the first Gathering at which he had noticed her and come to sit with the Tachita tribe for two days while he wooed her in the most obvious fashion imaginable. He had written a song for them to sing together at the great bonfire, and he had drawn her aside, away from the clustered campfires, to practice its intricate harmonies and rhythms. He had not even tried to steal a kiss from her those first two days, and she had been in an agony of uncertainty, not sure if he was courting her or just being nice to the tall, serious young woman who was the sister of a new-made friend.

But when he had kissed her, that first time, then she knew.

She had not been prepared to follow him after that first Gathering—she was only twenty at the time, though some women left their parents' tents earlier than that to follow their lovers to their own tribes, and it was not her youth that had held her back. Her mother was sick, and her younger brother was afraid, and she could not bring herself to abandon her family at a time when it seemed so fragile. But she had wanted to. She had wanted to shed all responsibilities and trail after this dangerous and seductive man, and go where the Lohora tribe went, and call herself one of them, and love this man for the rest of her life.

She had not gone, and she had later come to approve of that hard-won decision. Her mother had died that fall, needing every minute of care her daughter could provide. Her father, so dependent on the woman he had lived with for thirty years and by whom he had had three children, seemed as lost as a blind man or a man stricken by dumbness, incapable of caring for himself. Susannah had been mother and sister and caretaker for her father and brothers. She had been so busy that she only had time to wonder, once or twice a day, what other serious women Dathan of the Lohoras might be charming into laughter while the months spiraled past.

But then the Tachita clan fell in with the Morosta tribe and traveled with them for two months, and Susannah's older brother went courting himself. Soon enough, he brought home a shy but smiling Morosta girl who slipped into their tent as easily and happily as if she had lived with them her whole life. She took over some of the cooking chores, she teased Susannah's father out of his grief, she played with the younger boy and made moon-eyes at the older. Susannah knew that, if tardy spring ever arrived again, if she lived long enough to attend another Gathering, and if the sweet-voiced Lohora man came wooing her again, she could now leave her father's tent guiltlessly and begin her life as an adult woman.

She had worried about it, though. One did not have to know Dathan well to realize that he was a habitual flirt, a lover of women, a carefree man with such charisma that he could not be held to ordinary standards. He might only have been playing with her, that last spring when he kissed her by moonlight; he might have loved her at the time but, during the intervening year, forgotten her pensive smile and severe cheekbones. He might have fallen in love elsewhere—more than once—with a hundred different women, all of whom were dreaming of him at night in tents crowded with family members. Susannah would not count on him remembering her when they arrived at the Gathering in the spring.

That winter had been hard, and the spring had come so late that even the patient elders of the tribe had wondered if, this year, Yovah had forgotten the turning of the seasons. Travel across the ice-hard mud of the lower plains had been slow, and the Tachita clan had been among the last to make it to the Gathering. As always, there were others ready to welcome them, to take their horses, to direct them to a campsite, to offer food or any assistance the weary travelers might require.

And there was Dathan, standing a little apart from the initial greeters, stationed there at the outskirts of the great camp, as if waiting for each new tribe to walk up so he could scan their faces and commit them to memory. When, in all the bustle of arrival, Susannah finally noticed him standing there, she saw that he had spotted her long ago. His gaze was fixed upon her face; he was not smiling. She felt her body go cold, then hot. She felt her blood run with burning ice. She felt, in that one long exchange of glances, every contour of her world change.

That had been three years ago. She had left with the Lohora tribe and had followed them ever since. A few times, the erratic and easy-going travel pattern of the Lohoras had brought them in contact with the Tachitas, and then she would spend a few happy days with her father, her brothers, and her two new nephews. But most often, her visits with her family were restricted to the times of the Gathering, when all the Edori clans came together for a brief period of celebration. There, they all shared news, and recited events of the past year, and lifted their voices in joyous worship of the great god Yovah. Those days were too short, those days with her family and the members of her clan, but Susannah was not prepared to mourn the life gone by. She was too happy in this one.

The river was breathtakingly cold. Susannah flung herself into it before she could think about it too long, and surfaced, gasping for air. How could a southern river be this chilly this late in the season? Still, once she was used to it, Susannah did not mind so much, for the summer afternoon was hot and the contrast of temperatures felt good against her skin. She dove under the water again, soaping her body, soaping her hair, and rinsing herself off in the cold, clear water.

Once she was both clean and dry, she turned to the task of washing out the soiled clothes from the past few days. A few of Dathan's were mixed in with hers, which made her frown a little, but she went ahead and washed them. He had, after all, been hunting three times

this week with the other men of the clan. He may have been too busy
to attend to his own washing. Often, Susannah found Tirza washing
out some of Eleazar's shirts, and when Susannah taxed her with it,
Tirza merely smiled.

"Oh, I do not mind a few other pieces of clothing in my pile,"
Dathan's sister said. "When I was a young girl, and my mother was
sickly, I washed for the whole tent! Ten of us! But it's an easy enough
chore, and I make up songs while I'm soaping the clothes, and when
I get back to the camp, someone else has always made dinner. And
you know I am just as happy if I do not have to cook! So the arrangement suits me fine."

And Dathan is Dathan, Susannah thought to herself now as she
scrubbed the dirt off of a particularly fine blue shirt that belonged to
her lover. As well scold the crows for scavenging as to scold Dathan
for skimping on his duties.

It was late afternoon by the time she finally returned to the campsite, a bundle of wet clothes in her arms. She pegged these out to dry
behind the tent, then went to investigate the status of dinner.

Anna and Keren, Eleazar's sisters and two of the others who slept
in his tent, were stirring a pot over the fire. "That smells good!" Susannah exclaimed. "How lucky I am to live with women who are such
excellent cooks!"

It was something she said often, but her words always made the
other two smile. Anna was a good ten years older than Susannah, a
shy and quiet woman who had lost a lover five years ago and never
taken another. She had followed him to his clan, but returned to Eleazar's tent upon her lover's death. Keren was the only flighty member
of Eleazar's family, a small-boned and pretty girl who never forgot
how lovely she was and who had broken many hearts at the Gathering
and on the road. Tirza could not wait for her to fall deeply in love
and follow some other man's clan, but so far she had shown no signs
of wanting to leave the comforts of her own family. Still, she did her
share of the work and was generous with possessions, when she had
any, so Susannah could not help loving her.

"Yovah's hand guiding you," said Anna, who was so pious that
even a mock-serious question would elicit a religious response. "But
we were fortunate also to have him bring you to our tent."

Keren ignored all this. "Susannah! Are you coming to Luminaux
tomorrow? It will be so much fun."

Susannah stole a piece from a loaf of bread cooling beside the fire. "I have nothing to sell or barter," she said. "And I promised Amram I would go berry-picking with him tomorrow."

"You can take Amram berry-picking any day," Keren scoffed. "Besides, he will want to go to Luminaux. Everyone is going. You do not need to have anything to sell! You just need to have eyes that want to look around and see how beautiful the city is."

"I do love Luminaux," Susannah agreed.

"And you could sell something," Anna said. "You have finished that embroidered shirt you were working on all winter. That would fetch a nice price in the marketplace."

"Yes, but I made that shirt for me!" Susannah exclaimed, laughing. "I wanted something beautiful to wear at the next Gathering."

"Make another one," Keren said. She, of course, had no idea of how many hours went into such a project, since she would never sit still long enough to attempt such a thing. "The next Gathering is more than six months away."

"Well, perhaps I'll bring it with me, and see if there is anything in Luminaux so precious that it makes me want to trade my shirt," Susannah decided. "Is everyone really going?"

"No, of course not," Anna said with a repressive look at her sister. "I think there are ten or eleven who said they wanted to go. Bartholomew and all of his tent. Dathan and Keren. Thaddeus and Shua. And a few of the children. I, for one, am not up to the long journey there and back in a single day, and I know Claudia is not, either. We will make a feast dinner so that you can eat heartily and tell us of all the wonders you have seen in the Blue City."

"I will wear my emerald dress," Keren said dreamily. "And my long gold earrings. I will look quite beautiful as I wander between all the blue buildings of Luminaux."

Anna looked over at her sister in sharp irritation, but Susannah burst out laughing. "That is the true beauty for you," Susannah said, her voice admiring. "One who judges how she will look as she stands in a green meadow or beside a gray mountain. What dress to put on and how to style her hair. . . ."

Anna was frowning still, but Keren smiled, completely unoffended. "One has to be aware of these things," she said.

"One has to be aware of when she's making a fool of herself," Anna said. "Be glad it is only Susannah here to hear you say such ridiculous things."

"*Only* Susannah," Susannah repeated, but she laughed again. "Do not mind her for my sake," she said to Anna. "I will be happy to go to Luminaux and see how beautiful she looks there."

Susannah stayed near the campfire, helping the sisters cook and filling the remaining hours of the afternoon with idle chatter. Claudia came over to borrow some spices and agreed with Anna that Susannah should sell her embroidered shirt. Bartholomew dropped by on some pretext, though Susannah suspected it was merely to speak to Anna. He was a big man, strongest of all the Lohora tribe, and not given to much laughter. But they all looked up to him, and took their problems to him, and if there was a quarrel in the clan, he was the one most likely to solve it. His lover had left him two years ago, following a man of another tribe, and he had grown even quieter since that defection. Though all the Lohoras privately agreed that he was better off without her, since she had been as mercurial and unreliable as Keren, without Keren's ready smile and willing hands. Susannah hoped that he had noticed that Anna was fashioned the way a woman should be for a serious man. Or rather, she was pretty sure Bartholomew had realized it, and that he was waiting for Anna to make the same discovery.

"What time do you leave for the Blue City in the morning?" Susannah asked him, after he had tasted the stew and pronounced it very good. "My tentmates have persuaded me I should join your party."

"Excellent! We will be glad to have you," Bartholomew said. "I had hoped to leave early, for it will take us two or three hours to get there, and I would like to have a little time to shop and buy."

"Early?" Keren said innocently. "But—Susannah—could you rise with the sun, do you think? This morning you lay abed till almost noon."

"Yes, and Dathan—wasn't he sleeping late as well?" Anna asked, her eyes wide and guileless. "Maybe neither of you will be able to rise in time to join Bartholomew's party."

Bartholomew was grinning, but Susannah blushed furiously. "Yes! I am sure! I am quite rested from all of my sleeping and will be ready to join you as soon as dawn breaks!" she said. "And as for Dathan— well, I will kick him a few times when I rise, and if that does not wake him, he can stay behind."

They were all laughing at this. "Bartholomew, I am sure there are delicious stews brewing over your own fire, but we would be happy to have you here at ours," Keren said. "You know my sister is a very good cook."

That was generous of her, Susannah thought. But then, Keren had sharp eyes for love, and she had no doubt seen what Susannah and Claudia and many of the other Lohoras had seen. Bartholomew shook his head regretfully. "No, my sisters have already finished the evening meal, and I know they are expecting me," he said. "But perhaps in the morning—a nice hearty meal to fortify me against the day's journey—"

"We would be happy to feed you in the morning," Anna said. "I don't want to go on this trip into the city, but I'll make sure you set off well fed."

Bartholomew turned to look at her. "You won't come with us? Is there anything I can pick up for you in the Blue City while I am there?"

Anna frowned and stirred the pot. She was blushing a little. "I am sure you have plenty of commissions to carry out for your sisters. No need to worry about me," she said.

"Nonsense. One can never have too many friends for whom to be doing favors," Bartholomew said.

"Purple dye. Didn't you say you wanted some of that?" Keren asked. "The other day, when you were sorting your threads."

"Yes, some purple dye would be welcome," Anna admitted, a little embarrassed by the attention. "But not if it is any trouble to track down! Only if you come across it in the market."

"I will find it if I can," Bartholomew promised. "And I will be happy to sit at your fire tomorrow morning and eat."

When he left, Keren and Susannah exchanged meaningful glances, but Anna busied herself with the meal. There was no time to talk of women's idle concerns anyway, because Dathan and Amram and Eleazar were back from their day's excursions. Tirza was close behind them, fresh buckets of water in her hands. The night was suddenly filled with much talk and merriment, as a night should be. Susannah sat next to Dathan in the circle of light created by the fire, and ate her excellent stew, and smiled in the dark for happiness.

Early the next morning, a party of twelve left the Lohora campsite, heading south to Luminaux. There were few enough taking the short journey into town that there were sufficient horses to go around, and so they all rode. Amram's yearling behaved so badly that Bartholomew offered to exchange mounts with him, but Amram was too vain to be seen on a ten-year-old who was too placid to start at the sound of a boy's high-pitched yell. So they made it rather haphazardly into the city, two or three of the men throwing a watchful circle around the youngest member of their tribe as he rode in on the restive animal.

They left all the horses at one of the stables on the edge of town and walked into Luminaux. It was the bright lapis gem of Samaria, this small city on the southernmost edge of Bethel. It had not been part of the original settlements that had been founded, a little more than two centuries ago, when Yovah first brought the angels and the Edori and the other mortals to this world of Samaria. No, most of the colonists had clustered together on the plains of Bethel and in the gentle slopes of the Velo Mountains. The Edori, of course, had been wanderers right from the start, and they had investigated every hill and valley, every riverbed and coastline of the small continent that had become their new home. Soon enough, the Jansai and the Manadavvi and the more adventurous of the farmers had also spread out into the other regions of the country, into the provinces they named Jordana and Gaza.

But Luminaux had been founded by none of these. It had been settled early on by the artisans of the new community, who had found a rich trove of treasures in the earth nearby: stunning and variegated blue marble, mineral veins under the ground bristling with gems and metals, everything an artist might need to create items of great style and beauty. First the quarries were set up, then the town, in a welcoming little triangle on the western bank of the Galilee River. Long after the mines were exhausted, the city continued to thrive, itself a work of art and a treasure of fragile beauty.

It was named Luminaux but called the Blue City because of that gorgeous stone cut from the ground and set into the shapes of buildings and monuments and fountains. All the earliest structures had been made of that turquoise or cobalt or azure stone; and even now, most new buildings had a lintel or a walkway or a front porch carved from a piece of some elegant marble. Anything in the city that didn't come naturally blue achieved that status artificially, as residents painted and dyed and stained their surfaces to achieve a lustrous skyline glow. Fountains seemed to run with blue water; blue flames appeared to burn in the street torches at night. It was a conceit, but a joyous one, and no one ever came to Luminaux without falling in love with the city.

"How long shall we stay?" Bartholomew asked, as they quickly covered the half mile that led them from the outskirts of town to the heart of the city. Everyone had acquired an itchy restlessness; it was clear this group would not cohere for long. "Where shall we meet when all our shopping is done?"

"At the stables," Eleazar suggested. "In four hours."

There was much protest at this. "Five hours?" Bartholomew said.

"Make it six," said Keren. It was now a couple of hours before noon.

"A very long day for very young ones," Bartholomew warned.

"It will be light until quite late," Dathan said carelessly. "One of us can carry Amram before us if he falls asleep in the saddle."

"I won't fall asleep! I never sleep!" Amram declared.

"I can attest to that," Susannah said.

"Six hours, then," Bartholomew said, and they all agreed. And in a few moments, everyone had scattered into the plentiful attractions of the city.

Susannah at first had thought she and Dathan might walk together through the delights of Luminaux. But, "Eleazar and I have to go to the ironmonger's and look for new braces," Dathan had said in a very important voice. That particular tone always meant he was lying, though he did not seem to be aware others knew. Susannah guessed that they might spend half an hour at the ironmonger's, and then the rest of the afternoon at some of the taverns, sampling the excellent wine of the Luminaux vintners.

"Yovah guard you," she said with a faint smile, and let them go on their way. She did sigh a little as she watched them go.

As for herself, she had no real chores to accomplish, and no burning desire to sell her single item of some value, so she just wandered at random across the blue cobblestoned streets. She spent a great deal of time moving through the open-air market at the heart of the city, fingering the fine silk cloth and wondering how anyone could ever create garments so beautiful. She knew without a doubt that Bartholomew would purchase some purple coloring for Anna, but when she happened upon the dyemaker's shop, she could not resist going in and seeing if there were any pink or cinnamon or cerulean color samples she could buy with the few coins she had in her pocket. She could not resist a very bright yellow dye that was being sold at a discount because of some flaking in the cake, and the shopkeeper gave her some hints on how to mix it with other colors to make garments of many hues.

At lunchtime, she stopped at a bakery run by an Edori woman and her daughters. Frida refused to let Susannah pay for her meal—

"Except in gossip," the baker added. So they spent a wonderful hour talking about all the friends they had in common. Frida's shop was busy, though, and Susannah did not want to take up too much of her time, so she did not linger long. Wandering back out into the streets, she continued her slow, happy tour of the city. When she grew tired, she rested in one of the many small parks lining the lovely boulevards, and when she grew thirsty, she drank some of the colored water spuming up from the fountains. It tasted like springwater, only bluer. She hoped it would not tint her mouth, and she bent down to take another swallow.

The day passed slowly but in magical contentment, and Susannah could not believe it when the hour came around to meet the others at the stables. She hurried to arrive on time, but she was not the last one to put in an appearance. Eleazar and Dathan showed up a few minutes after she did, while Bartholomew grew impatient and the other women in the group showed one another their day's purchases. The two late-comers were laughing and happy, and when Dathan kissed Susannah, she could taste the wine on his breath. But he was so cheerful and affectionate that she could not be angry at him, and so she smiled and kissed him back.

"Good. We're all together. Let's waste no more time here," Bartholomew said, and in a very few minutes they were back on the road.

Susannah brought her playful mare alongside Dathan's, and they rode next to each other for the first few miles. "And did you have a successful day?" she asked him. "Were the ironmongers helpful?"

Dathan laughed. "Yes, indeed! You cannot imagine how much time it took us to barter for the best metal at the best price, and naturally we had to examine each link and joint for any sign of weakness, but I am sure that we came away with good material that will serve us well."

"And then, of course, you had to spend some time celebrating your new acquisitions," she said.

"A man must celebrate life's simple joys," he said.

She tried asking him a few questions that were more serious, but the replies he gave were nonsensical or incomplete, and she gave up. He rarely drank while the Lohoras were on the road, though when they camped for a few days he would take wine with his evening meal. And at the Gatherings—well, there was many an Edori, male and female, who imbibed too much at that great festival. This was not such a gross transgression. She really did not mind.

She ranged ahead of him to check on Amram, who sat quite de-
terminedly in the saddle and swore he felt no fatigue at all. She inter-
rogated him rather more closely, for she knew his father had not
watched him all day, and she wanted to make sure he had gotten in
no trouble and had fed himself a noon meal besides. But he answered
satisfactorily, and even showed her some pipes and whistles he'd
bought at a music academy, and so she concluded that he'd spent his
day at least as profitably as the rest of them.

She kicked her mare forward so she could ride with Keren for a
while when Bartholomew, who was in the lead, pulled his horse to a
sudden stop. Perforce the rest of them halted behind him. They were
about an hour outside of the city by this time, and a thin twilight had
washed the sky with gold, but visibility was not perfect. Bartholomew
squinted a little and pointed with his left hand.

"Campfire? Over there? Did we pass another campsite on our way
into the city?" he asked.

Susannah looked and, sure enough, she could see gray smoke rising up from a central point about half a mile away. It did not look
like smoke from a campfire, she thought, though she was not sure why.
Perhaps because it did not curl up in one smooth tendril, but seemed
to rise from an area so broad that no one would build a campfire that
big, not even at the Gathering.

"Perhaps another clan arrived while we were in the city," Eleazar
said. "The Corvallas come this way sometimes in the summer."

"And the Chicatas," Thaddeus added.

"Good news, then!" Dathan said recklessly. "Let's go invite them
to our camp for the night. We have traveled alone for months now. It
would be good to have some company at the fire."

It annoyed Susannah, just a little, that he would say such a thing;
Dathan was never so happy as when he could meet a stranger. It was
as if the familiar and the beloved were never quite enough for him.
But she strangled her resentment and quickly added her voice to the
general murmur of approval that ran through the group.

"It might not be Edori," Bartholomew warned. "It might be Jansai." That silenced them a bit. The gypsy Jansai clans were almost as
mobile as the Edori, though most of them returned from time to time
to their single permanent settlement, a city called Breven, which was
set up in the desert region on the far eastern edge of Jordana. The
Jansai were merchant traders, and not always strictly honest, and they
treated their women like rare possessions that must be hidden from all

outside eyes. In general, the Edori could not fathom the Jansai and the Jansai lifestyle—and at times, for no real reason, the Edori feared the Jansai, just a little. The Edori were always wary when they came across the gypsies.

"Even so, let us see who is camped here," Thaddeus said. "If it is Jansai, we do not need to linger."

"But it is probably Edori," Dathan said.

"I would like to see the Chicatas again," Keren said.

They all began to move forward, a little north of their true route, to go say hello to whatever clan might be found camping here on the southern plains.

But they never did learn what tribe the Edori were from, or even if the travelers were Edori and not Jansai. For when they got close enough, they could tell that there was indeed something amiss about the fire—and, closer still, they could tell that it was not a campfire at all.

But it had, at some point, been a camp. And a fire.

Silent, shocked, hardly able to credit what they were seeing, they came closer to the burning ground. A circle of tents or wagons had been formed here on the plains, travelers settled in the middle, horses no doubt tethered just outside. But all of that was gone. Now there was a great scorched circle of grass and canvas and bone, as if a sudden conflagration had erupted in the middle of a peaceful campfire and incinerated everything in seconds. There was almost nothing recognizable in the blackened remains, even now still flickering with remnants of fire. Here what might be a charred body—there the outline of a cart, crumbled into coals on the smoldering grass.

They looked at one another in horror, several of them mouthing prayers to Yovah because they could not trust themselves to say the words out loud. Jansai or Edori, no one deserved to die like this. They still could not guess what could have caused a tragedy both so comprehensive and so contained. Nothing they knew of burned so rapidly that no one standing nearby could escape it—and then burned itself out, leaving a tidy circle of destruction behind.

They could not keep themselves from glancing from side to side, looking for the wounded child, the smoke-sick survivor. But nothing living remained here at this prairie campsite. Even the carrion birds, quick to scent disaster, had passed by this place.

CHAPTER TWO

Gaaron laid his voice against Esther's pure soprano and held the tenor note so long she gave him a quick sideways glance. Smiling, he modulated down the required scale, note for note skipping under her voice by a series of minor thirds. The *Argosy in F Major* was not much of a showpiece for either of the singers, but it had been, after all, designed to display the woman's part to its best advantage, and Gaaron needed to pay more attention to Esther's styling and take his cues from her. He made a little grimace, intended to convey "I'm sorry," since he could not pause to speak the words. She shrugged, and smiled, and lifted her voice in the octave leap that was the only impressive moment in the whole score.

It was dawn, and only the really luckless would be awake to hear them mauling this sacred piece, but still. Whenever you raised your voice to Jovah, you should do it with as much skill and enthusiasm as you possessed. Here at the Eyrie, the angels and the mortals made a point of singing to Jovah every hour of every day, so that there was never silence in the hold, and the god knew they were thinking about him, raising their prayers to him, without ceasing. Naturally, at least two singers must be employed at a time, for the central principle of their lives was harmony. Only if the god saw that the races of Samaria existed in harmony would he continue to love and protect them—and harmony never failed here at the Eyrie.

Only recently had Gaaron begun signing up for the very early duets, but he had discovered that he liked to be abroad at this hour. Almost no one was awake, and the whole stone complex was quiet. Here in the little cupola at the top of the Eyrie—the open-air chamber that had been constructed more than two centuries ago to suit just such singers as themselves—he could look over the whole complex, and half of Bethel besides. Situated at the very top of the Velo Mountains, the Eyrie was a vast and labyrinthine complex of beige-quartz stone that housed all the angels of Bethel and the mortals who resided with them. From this vantage point, the highest in the Eyrie, Gaaron could look down on the small town of Velora at the foot of the mountains, and at the summer-green plains that spread southward from the mountains as far as the horizon would allow him to see. Except for their singing, there was no sound in the world. The sky was a hazy white just now starting to deepen into blue. Everything seemed new-made, unused, sweet with possibilities.

Esther finished off the *Argosy* with a pretty little "Amen," then sent her voice down on a series of half notes till she hit a new key she liked. Gaaron only had to listen to the first few notes before he recognized the *Fiat* by Lochevsky, and he added the tenor underpinnings that would anchor the soprano notes in place. Esther was a polished though not particularly imaginative singer, a matronly mortal woman with high-piled white hair and a sharp-edged face that always appeared on the verge of a frown. Although Gaaron was usually a traditionalist himself, he preferred it when one of the younger residents of the Eyrie joined him on these dawn watches. They were more apt to try some of the more difficult contemporary pieces, which they sang with gusto even when they missed some of the more unlikely notes. Esther didn't have much flair even on the pieces she had been singing since she was a child.

But that was unkind. Gaaron was never unkind. He told himself to be more generous, and to pay more attention. When Esther's voice tumbled from G-sharp to the tricky B-flat, Gaaron's was right there on the F to bolster her up. She smiled again, pleased at the ringing harmony. He smiled back.

Bolstering people up was what the leader of the Eyrie's angelic host was best equipped to do.

They had made it through most of the *Fiat* before their replacements showed up at the cupola's narrow door, yawning their way through their first sentient hour of the day. Zibiah and Ahio were both angels, both young—and both, Gaaron would have sworn, had been up fairly late the night before. Still, you never missed a harmonic if you had signed up for it on the previous day. No matter what adventures your evening might have led to, if you were expected just after sunrise, then you had better be prepared to sing just as the sky turned blue.

Zibiah joined her voice to Esther's on the last chorus of the *Fiat*, while Ahio brought in the bass line just under Gaaron's. The final few measures were done in a very robust three-part harmony that made the piece, briefly, seem truly sacred. As the four of them held on to the final notes, Ahio gave Zibiah three downbeats with his head. Then the two of them burst into a flurry of careless arpeggios that seemed to laugh the morning sun above the prairie. Gaaron could not help a smile. Ahio was a composer, of a sort, though you had to be an energetic and quick-witted singer to be able to romp through any of his pieces. Gaaron nodded a good morning at them, then followed Esther out of the cupola and down toward the main plateau of the Eyrie.

Esther was shaking her head. "That girl's as silly as they come," she said. "As silly as any mortal girl come up to the hold to try to snare an angel lover. Some days I don't know what to do with her."

Since Esther was the de facto steward of the entire hold, the one who handled most of the housekeeping problems and was everyone's first ear to complain to when anything went wrong, she had some basis for saying that. But Gaaron frowned anyway.

"Don't do anything with her," he said mildly. "She's young, and a little flighty, but she always meets her responsibilities. Whenever I've sent her out to take care of a petition, she's gone willingly and done a reasonable job. The farmers like her—all the mortals like her."

Esther snorted. "The mortal boys, maybe."

Gaaron smiled again. "Well, that's not such a bad thing."

"And your sister, Miriam," Esther pursued, as if he had agreed with her, "she's another one. She's even worse than Zibiah."

"I don't think Miriam's very happy these days," Gaaron said.

"She would be if she would just do as she's told!"

Gaaron tried another smile, but he could feel that on his face it looked sad. "I think she feels that if she does what I want her to do, she will be even less happy than she is now."

"But you know what's right for her!" Esther exclaimed. "You know what's right for everybody! You're to be Archangel!"

And that, Gaaron thought, was the root of the problem.

"I certainly don't know what's right for everybody," he said, still in that mild tone of voice. "And I'm often wrong in Miriam's case."

"Since your mother died—" Esther began, but Gaaron cut her off.

"Since longer ago than that," he said. "Don't trouble yourself about Miriam. I will deal with her."

It was a relief, after this, to enter the wide, well-lit tunnels and separate. Esther headed down to the kitchens to meddle in someone else's life. Gaaron turned to the hallway that led to his chambers, hoping to escape to a few moments of privacy.

It was a faint hope, and it died when he came to his room and found the door standing open. Nicholas was waiting inside, staring out the triple window, and toying with the laces of his shirt. He was dressed for flying, in leather trousers and vest, and his long, narrow wings fell to thin, elegant points on Gaaron's blue rug.

"Nicholas," Gaaron said civilly, coming inside and letting the door stay open behind him. Nicholas was a tall, lean, restless young man who always made Gaaron feel even bigger and more solid than he was. For the older angel topped the younger one by almost a head, and his shoulders were twice as broad. And his wingspan—of which he tried not to be vain—was glorious, a lush snowy expanse of feathers and muscle that could unfurl to practically fill the room. Nicholas had said once that Gaaron was a mountain while he, Nicholas, was a spire, and Gaaron had never been able to forget the comparison. Though Nicholas had probably forgotten it as soon as the words left his mouth.

"Gaaron! Lovely harmonics this morning. That was Esther with you, I take it?"

"Yes."

"Impossible to mistake her voice," the younger angel said irrepressibly. "Or her selection of music."

Gaaron crossed the room to pour himself a glass of water. The singing had made him thirsty. "I assume there's some reason you've sought me out so early in the day?" he asked. "And made yourself welcome in my room?"

Nicholas waved off the last remark. "I knew you wouldn't mind."

"I thought you were down south," Gaaron said.

"I was. Yesterday. Flew back all night."

Gaaron glanced over at him appraisingly. Ah, so then the flying leathers were a holdover from a night journey, and not a preparation for the activities of the day. He should have known; Nicholas was not habitually an early riser. "And did you solve the weather crisis by the Corinnis?" Gaaron asked.

"Yes, but that was simple. A few prayers," Nicholas said impatiently. "But Gaaron, I heard a strange thing while I was there."

"In southern Bethel?" Gaaron asked with faint humor. "They are all farmers and miners there. They don't trade in strange things."

"Yes, that's what I thought, that's what made it stranger," Nicholas said. "And I heard it from more than one man—and they all looked sober as Esther at the crack of dawn."

Gaaron frowned at the joke but motioned Nicholas to continue. "What they told me—all three of them—was that they'd seen a unknown man in the fields one day. He was far enough away that they couldn't really see his features, but none of them recognized him, and he didn't have a horse nearby, and no one had seen him traveling in that direction, though the land's so flat you can see a man approach from twenty miles. And they all said that his skin was very dark, darker than an Edori's, black almost. And he was wearing strange clothing, very tight to his body, like an angel's, only it looked like it was made out of a shiny material. And when one or two of them decided to approach him, to see if he needed something, he disappeared."

Gaaron waited a moment, but apparently that was the end of the story. Nicholas watched him with a blazing excitement in his eyes. He was blue-eyed and dark-haired, and any emotion painted a ruddy flush across his narrow cheeks. "He disappeared where?" Gaaron said politely.

Nicholas waved his hands. "That's it! Disappeared! To nowhere! One moment he was there, and then he was gone, and not one of them saw where he went."

"Well, I'm sure he—"

"Gaaron, they took me to the place. It's a level field of crops with no treeline, no hills, no little dips and valleys that a man could duck behind. I mean, you have to walk for half an hour before you're out of someone's line of sight. One moment he was there, and then he was gone. They all said the same thing."

Gaaron considered, but he could not think of any good responses. It seemed unlikely that a strange visitor really had disappeared from the full sight of three hardworking, no-nonsense Bethel farmers—but then, it seemed unlikely that any such men had banded together to make up this story just to confound the angels. "Had they ever witnessed a thing like this before?" he finally asked.

Nicholas looked impatient. "No! And I'd be bound to say no one else has, either! Gaaron, a strange man just showed up on the Bethel plans and then *un*-showed up a few minutes later! Don't you find that miraculous? Don't you find that terrifying?"

"Well, I don't know what I can be expected to do about it, since he's gone now," Gaaron said placidly. "What did you *want* me to do?"

"I don't know," Nicholas said with a black frown. "I just thought—you know *everything*. You would know what to do now."

"I hardly know everything," Gaaron said. "But I can't see what good it will do to get frantic over this, when we don't know what it means, we don't know if it will happen again—we don't even know for sure what the farmers saw."

"Well—but you could go there, couldn't you?" Nicholas asked. "You could fly out there today and see for yourself. Maybe he'll appear again and you can talk to him. He'd hear what *you* have to say."

Again, Nicholas' statement of utter belief in Gaaron's powers. Gaaron felt a momentary weight settling across his shoulders, as he so often did in Nicholas' company. "I could do that," Gaaron said. "I need to go to Mount Sinai today or tomorrow, but after that I could head to southern Bethel if it would make you happy."

"Yes! But you should go now, first, and then go see Mahalah after you have returned," Nicholas said eagerly.

Gaaron could not help smiling. "I think the order in which I do things doesn't matter so much," he said gently. "But I will head down there in a day or so. You can even come with me if you like."

Nicholas started to reply, but before he had gotten a few headlong words into his next sentence, another visitor stepped through the open door. It was Miriam, and she looked stormy. As always, Gaaron was struck by how unlike him she seemed, both in temperament and looks. Nonetheless, they were full brother and sister, not half, like so many children of angelic descent. She was mortal, while he was angel—small-boned where he was big—a lustrous blonde, while he had short, light-brown hair of no particular style or beauty. All they had in common was bark-brown eyes, deep and still and watchful.

Her eyes, at the moment, were also smoldering with fury. "I thought I told you not to interfere with my life," she said the instant she stepped inside the room.

"What have I—" Gaaron began, but Nicholas interrupted.

"Don't talk to Gaaron that way!" the young angel exclaimed. "He's the one who—"

"I can talk to him any way I want, and I don't need you here to tell me what to say," Miriam shot back. "So why don't you just leave?"

"I was here first! And I'm not done talking to him."

"Well, what *I* have to say is more important."

The weight of dealing with Miriam settled on Gaaron's shoulders right on top of the weight of Nicholas' hero worship. For a man who was still two years away from thirty, Gaaron thought, he was accumulating burdens at an exceptionally rapid pace.

"Quiet. Both of you," Gaaron said in his deepest, sternest voice, and even Miriam paused in her tirade to listen to him. Most people did, when he employed that tone. He tried to resort to it rarely. "Nicky, we'll talk later. Go to the kitchen, get something to eat, and then go to bed. Miriam, why don't you close the door behind him, and then you and I can talk in privacy—and, I hope, with some civility."

All these directions were followed in absolute silence. Gaaron crossed the room to the small table by the window, and pulled out a chair. Specially designed to accommodate angel wings, the chair featured a narrow back that he could lean his spine against while his massive wings piled on the floor on either side of him. Miriam closed the door with some force behind Nicholas and strode across the room.

"If you think—" she began hotly, but Gaaron interrupted.

"Civilly," he said. "And rationally. Sit down. I'll listen."

Unwillingly, Miriam sat, then crossed her arms like a pouting child. She had pulled her beautiful hair into a knot on the back of her head, but some of it had come loose and tumbled across her cheeks. To Gaaron, she looked very young and very beautiful. Two more ways in which she did not resemble him at all.

"If you think I am going to spend the summer with the Manadavvi just so Neri and her angels can watch over me, you are quite mistaken," she said in cold, precise tones. "I won't go."

Gaaron raised his eyebrows. "Who told you that's what I was planning to do?"

She looked even angrier. "So it's true?"

Gaaron shook his head. "It's true that Lucas Karsh did extend the invitation, and that Neri forwarded it on. But I had made no decisions one way or the other. I was going to ask you if you were interested."

"Why would I be?" she demanded.

"Well, why wouldn't you be?" he said somewhat humorously. "You're not happy here. I thought you might enjoy a change of scenery."

"But at *Lucas Karsh's* holding?" she exclaimed. "With Neri flying in and out every other day just to spy on me?"

"I can't imagine Neri would have time to spy on you more than once or twice a month," Gaaron said evenly. Neri led the host at Monteverde in Gaza, and the demands on her time were just as taxing as those on Gaaron's. "She's pretty busy."

"Well, she and old Lucas are great friends, and I know she's in and out of his estate all the time," Miriam said sullenly.

"She values his opinion, that's true. I still don't think she would be bothering you quite as often as you envision. She thought—I thought—and I'm sure Lucas Karsh thought you might enjoy a chance to get away from the Eyrie for a while."

"And what would I do there, anyway?" Miriam burst out. "There's nobody there my age, except his daughters, and they don't like me. I don't like them. I don't like Lucas Karsh, either, when it comes to that. Stuffy old man."

"Well, then, you don't have to go," Gaaron said pleasantly. "So how else have you been spending your time, besides eavesdropping on other people's conversations just to find out things that will make you angry?"

That, of course, was calculated to make her even more furious. "Eaves—I was not! Esther came up to me and was scolding me for being out late last night, and looking so smug and stupid that I wanted to hit her, and I said she couldn't tell me what to do and she said, 'Things will be different when you're at the Karsh estate,' and then I made her tell me the rest of it. And I don't know why you have to talk about me with Esther, or anybody else, for that matter, when you don't even talk to *me* about me."

Naturally, Gaaron did not approve of hitting anybody for any reason, but he was in accord with Miriam at this moment; he would have liked to slap Esther himself. "I try to talk to you about you," he said, keeping his voice gentle with an effort. "Usually, you're the one who is withholding secrets."

Now she looked guarded and alarmed. "What kinds of secrets? I don't have any secrets."

"Then you *haven't* been singing down at that little place in Velora—what's it called? Sordid."

"I can go to Velora if I want," she said belligerently.

"I never said you couldn't."

There was a moment's silence while she stared at him, trying to read his thoughts. "Well, and I can sing at Sordid if I want to," she said. "You can't stop me."

He opened his eyes wide, exaggerating his sense of surprise. "Do you really think I can't?" he said.

She jumped to her feet and began pacing. He merely watched her. "Well, you shouldn't, then! You shouldn't interfere in my life! I'm old enough to know what I want to do and I—"

"You're nineteen," he interjected.

"And I can make my own decisions."

"If you made good ones, I might agree with you," he said. "But singing at a place called Sordid is not a good decision."

"Nothing's ever happened to me there," she flung at him over her shoulder. "No one's taken any liberties or tried to hurt me or—or any of the other things I guess you're afraid of."

"And why do you think that is?" he asked.

She came to a halt, staring at him. "What? What have you done?"

He shrugged. "I'm leader of the host here. I'll be Archangel in less than a year. I would expect that, if I were to talk to the proprietor of any establishment in Velora—or, indeed, any inn or tavern or club from here to Luminaux—he would pay strict attention to anything I had to say. And if I asked him to take particular care that nothing untoward happened to my sister—I would think he would do everything in his power to keep her safe."

Miriam whirled away from him and began pacing in even more agitation. "I hate you!" she cried.

"I don't understand why."

"Why! Because I—because nothing I ever do can be done away from you! Because you watch over me every single second! Because you're always *there!*"

And you should be grateful for that, since my being there *is all that's kept you alive more than once,* Gaaron thought somewhat grimly. Some of the sternness of his thought was translated to his voice as he said, "And I expect I will continue to watch over you until I'm certain that you're doing a good enough job of watching over yourself. So far, you haven't convinced me that you can take care of yourself."

She glared at him from those deep, dark eyes, which right now looked like wellsprings of hatred. "I never will convince you," she said, her voice low and intense.

"I hope you do," he said quietly. "Someday."

She glowered at him another moment, and then she spun away and stalked off. She slammed the door behind her as she left.

Not so good, Gaaron thought, listening to the silence resettle in the room after the sound of her footsteps disappeared. *Esther was right. I have to do something about Miriam.*

That afternoon, giving up hope of solving the problems he was having with his sister anytime soon, Gaaron took off for Mount Sinai. The day was sunny and fine—warm on the ground, but cooler the higher he flew, and he cruised at the upper altitudes that his body could stand. Here, the cold was an actual presence, a pressure on his back and shoulders, an icy mantle laid over his outstretched arms. The air itself was thin, hard to breathe, and sharp; it was like inhaling razors. But Gaaron loved it. He loved the effort he could feel from each of his muscles as he powered through the resistant air. He loved the sweep and plunge of his great wings, the brief vacuum created by the forced upswing, the strength and energy in the hard thrust downward, so powerful it scattered the separate molecules of the wind before him. He was a big man, tall in stature and thick in body, and he was always aware of this when he stood on the earth. He tried, when he was near mortals or even other angels, not to take advantage of his size and never to strike an intimidating stance. But high above the world, alone on the currents of air, he could savor his sheer brute power. He could battle the cold and the wind and the ungenerous atmosphere, and he could wrestle out an exultant victory.

It took nearly three hours to fly to Mount Sinai, located about one hundred and fifty miles due east of the Eyrie in a mountain range of its own. Although petitioners could reach it by way of a snaking, narrow path up the mountain, Gaaron had it much easier. He circled once, to get a proper perspective, then eased down to land on the small stone apron at the entrance to the mountain retreat. He came down lightly, wings outspread to their fullest until he had reabsorbed all his weight on his feet. Then he folded the big wings back, ducked his head to enter the threshold, and stepped inside the corridors of Mount Sinai.

It was a place of cool gray stone and calm silences, heavy with the accumulated prayers of holy people. Here, two hundred and forty years ago, when men and angels had originally settled upon Samaria, the first oracle had taken up residence. And every day since that day, oracles had lived here, communing with the god, consulting with their priests, training their acolytes, and guiding the spirituality of their people. Oracles also lived at Mount Sudan in Gaza and Mount Egypt in Jordana, but this was the oldest retreat, the first one established, and it had, or so it seemed to Gaaron, a special quality of piety and peace.

An acolyte came up to greet him as he stepped into the common room where a handful of petitioners waited to see Mahalah. "Angelo," she said in a low voice. "We were not expecting this honor."

He smiled at her and nodded his head. "I am content to wait until the oracle is free."

"She will want to see you immediately," the acolyte said.

Gaaron gestured at the four people already waiting. All of them recognized him, of course, and none of them looked prepared to resent the fact that his claims might supersede their own. "I will take my turn," he said. "It will be a pleasure to sit quietly in a quiet place and listen to the clamoring of my thoughts."

She bowed her head. "I will tell the oracle what you have said."

Once she left, Gaaron glanced around the room and picked out the only chair that might suit him, a backless stool with sturdy legs. The three men and one woman sitting in the room glanced his way, nodded or murmured "Angelo," and then returned their attention to their own concerns. Wherever else one might socialize while awaiting a service, the anteroom of the oracle's chambers was not it; here, no one would approach him casually or stoop down by his chair to ask a favor. He had spoken truly to the acolyte: He would enjoy an hour or two to merely sit and think without fear of importuning or interruption.

Actually, it was less than an hour before the anteroom emptied and another female acolyte came to fetch Gaaron for his audience with Mahalah. He followed her down the quiet corridors, hearing the *shush-shush* of his wings as they brushed both walls behind him. These hallways were smaller and narrower than the ones at the Eyrie. They were perfectly adequate, yet he always felt as if he should lower his head or hunch his shoulders more closely to his body, as if he was too big for the space or it might close up on him unexpectedly. It was something of a relief to make it to the large open chamber at the end of the corridor and step into the heart of the oracle's world.

Mahalah was sitting in a wheeled chair at a table near the center of the room. She smiled when Gaaron entered, but did not rise. Indeed, she could not rise. She was elderly and frail, and her bones would no longer support her. Gaaron had asked her more than once if she was in pain as well as being weak, but she had always dismissed that as a matter of no concern. He supposed that she was.

"Gaaron," she said, holding out her hand as he crossed the room. Her fingers were small, stubby twigs encased in loose, hot folds of skin. Her arms were covered in layers of flowing blue silk, but enough of the fabric fell back from her hand that he could see the fragile sticks that constituted the bones between her wrist and elbow. Her round, wrinkled face was wreathed in wispy gray hair, and the skin on her cheekbones was layered with age. Still, her eyes were a glittering black, snapping with intelligence, and there was some power in the pressure of her fingers. "An unexpected pleasure to greet you here today," she said.

"I have been meaning to come for the past few weeks," he said, accepting the chair she indicated. She brought her chair closer, till only a small table separated them. "To inquire after your health, if nothing else. Are you as strong as ever?"

She smiled; it was something of a joke. "I will outlive you," she promised. She turned to the young acolyte and requested food and drink to be brought to them. The girl bowed and departed.

"I have never seen any but young women serving you here," Gaaron remarked. "Is that because you find young men too rowdy and high-spirited, or because you think they cannot be trusted to serve the god with the attention he requires?"

Mahalah smiled, then sighed. "No, it is because of a stupid decision made fifty years ago, and I would very much like to reverse it. It happened around the time I came to be oracle here and Isaac stepped into the post at Mount Sudan. Before then, all the oracles had accepted both boys and girls as acolytes, but there had been some trouble at Mount Sudan. Too much intermingling between the sexes, with the result that—well, there were some unwanted pregnancies and a few young people sent home in disgrace. I am not a prude," she added quickly, "but two of those girls were barely fifteen. So Isaac decreed that he would only induct boys at Mount Sinai, to prevent such trouble in the future. And I immediately said that I would accept only girls here, just so the god did not perceive any favoritism among us. But I am a little sorry sometimes. I love my girls, but I miss the energy and chaos that boys can bring."

Gaaron grinned. "Take it from me, girls can bring just as much chaos if they put their minds to it."

She smiled back. "Which leads me to ask, how is your sister?"

Now he grimaced. "Miriam is . . . Miriam. She is not very happy with me these days. I interfere too much in her life."

"It wouldn't matter if you didn't interfere in her life at all. She would still be restless and turbulent. That is the nature of the woman who bears such a name."

Before he could reply, the acolyte entered again with a tray of refreshments. She set it on the table between them, bowed, and left the room soundlessly.

Gaaron absently filled his plate; his mind was on the last thing Mahalah had said. "Her name has a meaning? I thought it was just one of the names from the Librera."

"As is mine, and yours, and everybody's," Mahalah replied. "But, yes, most of those names did at one time mean something. You, for instance. Gabriel Aaron. Your names mean 'God is my strength' and 'mountain of strength'—so you see, you were very well named. Mine isn't so clear in translation, some texts say it means 'dancer' and some say 'harpist.' And Miriam—well, the name means 'rebellion.' Of all of us, perhaps, she was the most aptly called."

"I thought the names were just . . ." Gaaron shrugged, then smiled. "A collection of pleasing syllables."

"Yes, we have forgotten much in the centuries since we have been on Samaria," Mahalah said in a regretful voice. "We came to this place knowing a great deal—about the world our people lived on before, about the way we arrived on this world, about the order of the stars and the planets above us. We've lost all that. We've lost our history." She snorted. "We've even lost our language, to some extent. Can you read the Librera? Not one in five can. Maybe not one in ten. Our language has changed, and some of the words in the great book are lost to us. How much more will we lose as the centuries roll on? Two hundred years from now, what else will we have forgotten?"

Gaaron listened, frowning. "But what have we lost? We know that Jovah carried us away from the world where our fathers lived because there was such hatred and dissonance there that he feared we would all die in a fire of self-destruction. And that he brought us here to Samaria, and bid us live in harmony—as we have done. And because technology brought about the weapons that led to the ruin of our old world, we have chosen to do without technology on our new one. What else is there to know? What important parts have we forgotten?"

She leaned forward, her black eyes intense. "How did he bring us here? Through what method?"

Gaaron sat back, perplexed. "He carried us here in his hands. So the Librera says."

"And can you read the Librera?" she shot back.

"I—a few words—not whole chapters," he said.

"So you cannot translate the passage about how his hands wrapped about us and ferried us through the stars to this planet. But don't you wonder about that? Just a little? How his hands held us? There were hundreds in that first settlement. Whose hands are big enough to hold that many lives at once?"

Gaaron smiled a little. "Oracle, are you speaking blasphemy?"

She settled back in her wheeled chair and shook her head. "No, I am sighing over the ignorance of the world," she said. "I am a devout woman, but I have always had a lot of questions. It amazes me that more people do not have the same questions."

"Most people are too busy trying to organize their lives to trouble themselves with questions of theology," he said.

"Questions of theology are far more interesting, in most cases," she said dryly.

"Well, I come to you today with my own question that I hope you—or the god—can answer," Gaaron said.

"You will be Archangel in eight months, and you want to ask the god who your angelica should be."

He nodded. "If that would not be too much trouble."

She took hold of the wheels of her chair and turned herself away from the table. "No trouble at all. Perhaps we should have attended to this matter sooner, but there has seemed to be no rush. With everything so peaceful in the realm, the choice of angelica has not seemed to be such a pressing concern."

"It is a pressing concern to *me*, since I will marry her," said Gaaron, rising and following her as she rolled over to the far side of the room. She came to a stop before a glowing blue plate set into the wall. It was surrounded with knobs and buttons, all offering to perform mysterious functions that only an oracle would understand. Gaaron stood back respectfully. Through this interface, as it was called, Mahalah would communicate with the god. She could ask the god any question and have an answer returned—though not always, so Gaaron had been led to believe, an answer that was easy to decipher.

Mahalah twisted a few of the knobs and then skimmed her fingers over some of the buttons in quick, decisive motions. "I should first ask you," she said over her shoulder, "if there is someone for whom you have a preference. A Manadavvi girl, for instance, or one of the mortals living at Windy Point."

"Not at the moment," Gaaron admitted, casting his mind over the wellborn women of his acquaintance. No one of that group, in particular, whom he would choose as a lifemate—but none so dreadful that he would stand here and hope Jovah did not announce her name. "I have had little time for—for forming attachments since my father died. The responsibilities of running the hold and watching over Miriam have kept me pretty well occupied."

Mahalah looked up at him with a sly grin, an unexpected expression on such a wise old face. "Still, that doesn't mean some enterprising young woman wouldn't have decided to make you her main occupation," she said. "In fact, I'm surprised to learn there aren't mobs of eligible girls throwing themselves at you. To be angelica to the Archangel! That's a goal worth pursuing, even if the man himself isn't exactly to your taste."

"Thank you," Gaaron said politely. "I will now look with suspicion upon any woman who seems to show the slightest interest in me."

Mahalah laughed and fiddled with more of the controls. The colors on the iridescent plate flickered and changed, and strange characters began to scroll slowly down the screen. Not, apparently, words or sentences that Mahalah had any interest in, because she kept talking. "What about Zebedee Lesh's daughter? She seemed awfully attentive to you last time I saw you both at Windy Point."

"She's very nice," Gaaron said, a little surprised. "I didn't notice that she was particularly attentive."

"She came to the dinner all but naked to attract your attention," Mahalah said. "But it appears she failed in that goal. Oh, and what's her name? Stephen's daughter, at Monteverde. She's the daughter of an angel. She knows what life at a hold is all about."

Gaaron dutifully summoned up an image of Neri's niece, a dark, sleek girl with unfathomable eyes. "Chana," he supplied. "Yes, she seems very likable. Quiet, I think. I haven't talked to her all that much."

"Not for her lack of trying, I'd guess," Mahalah said. "So you can't come up with any preferences on your own?"

Gaaron was watching the screen, where the scrolling letters had, for the moment, stopped. A tiny dark blue light in the corner of the screen flashed a constant quick signal, seeming to adjure the two of them to wait a moment while the god considered possibilities. It reminded Gaaron of someone tapping his finger while he paused in thought. "I didn't think the god took into account the preferences of the parties involved," Gaaron said. "I had always heard that Jovah chose angelicas and angelicos at his own discretion, and did not consult the Archangels as to where their hearts might be given."

"That is generally true," Mahalah acknowledged. "But in my experience, if the oracle informs Jovah—in a very neutral way, of course—that the Archangel already has emotional ties somewhere, Jovah might weigh that fact when he makes his selection."

Gaaron smiled. "So then, when Adriel was named Archangel, you or one of the other oracles told the god that she was already attached to Moshe? And that is why Jovah declared him to be angelico?"

"That might have been how it worked," Mahalah said. "It was more than twenty years ago. My memory is not so good."

"Your memory is perfect," Gaaron retorted.

"In general, however, you are right," Mahalah pursued. "The god is less interested in the state of your heart than in the state of the realm. He chooses—or so they say—someone who is your exact opposite in many ways. If you are cold, she will be warmhearted. If you are arrogant, she will be humble. If you are a doubter, she will be a fanatic. He is interested in balance."

"I am a pragmatic man," Gaaron said. "Does that mean he will choose for me an irresponsible spendthrift? That does not sound so promising."

Mahalah laughed. The blinking light had stopped, and now she was busily keying in more strange hieroglyphics. "Perhaps I didn't say it just right," she said. "Since you are a levelheaded and, practical man, who does not even notice when women are throwing themselves at you, perhaps she will be a dazzling creature of so much loveliness you cannot look away. Or perhaps she will be hideously ugly but with such luminosity in her soul that she forces you to reevaluate your standards of beauty. There will be something about her that will change you fundamentally, but in a good way. That is what the god achieves when he chooses a spouse. He stirs you up. He brings you forth." She hit a

key, then waited expectantly. "That is the theory, anyway. We shall
see what he offers *you*."

A few words came up on the screen, a small scrawl in the middle
of the gleaming glass. Even Gaaron could read the words, for they
were just a handful of names.

"Susannah sia Tachita," Gaaron said out loud. Then again, "Susannah sia Tachita . . ."

There was a long pause before Mahalah swung her chair around
to face Gaaron. Even her wise face looked shocked. "She's an Edori,"
the oracle said.

Gaaron nodded. "So it would appear."

"Do you even *know* any Edori?" Mahalah asked.

He shook his head. "I've met a few. Here and there, mostly in
Luminaux. There have always been a few tribes at the Gloria, so I've
talked to a few of them there. They've always been friendly. But—they
don't really seem to need much from the angels, or from anybody.
Even the Jansai we trade with on a regular basis. But the Edori . . ."
He shrugged. "They are strangers to me."

Mahalah was watching him. "Perhaps that was why Jovah chose
her, then," she said. "So that you could bring them into the fold. Make
them a bigger part of our lives. Help us understand them."

He nodded again. He felt numb, a little unreal. He had expected
to be surprised by the god's choice, but this was more than surprising.
This was catastrophic. Yet he was a servant of the god. He would not
question and he would not defy. "Has she—but I suppose she must
have been. I did not think—"

"What?" Mahalah said. "You're making no sense."

"Has she been dedicated to the god, then?" he said. "I did not
think the Edori ever were."

Involuntarily, his hand went to the acorn-sized crystal in his right
arm, high up under his biceps. The Kiss of the god had been installed
there shortly after he was born, as it was for all true believers and their
progeny. It was by these Kisses that the god could track them, knew
if they were well or ailing, could gauge the states of their hearts. Some
of the more romantically minded said that when true lovers met for
the first time, their Kisses would light with a frenzied fire, but Gaaron
had never known anyone who claimed such a thing had happened to
them. Of course, perhaps no one he knew had ever found their true
love.

"It is rare for an Edori to be dedicated," Mahalah admitted. "But not unheard of. Particularly among Edori who intermarry with other mortals, more devout ones. They often dedicate their children."

"And so this Susannah—she is a product of such an inter-marriage?" Gaaron said. It was impossible to make it sound as though he was not speaking with an effort.

Mahalah tapped a few more knobs and scanned the text that appeared before her. "Not according to this," she said. "She appears to come from a long line of pure-blooded Edori. Perhaps as far back as the founding of Samaria." She glanced up at him, smiling. "Perhaps she is one of the original descendants of Amos Edor himself."

"Who?"

She shook her head. "One of the first colonists. Never mind. What matters now is that you find her fairly quickly and explain to her the honor in store for her. She might not be as thrilled as a Manadavvi girl would be to learn she is to become the wife of the Archangel."

"And where do I find her? Does Jovah tell me that?"

"No. I do not think the Kiss imparts information that we might find helpful but for which the god has no particular use. He can only tell us her name and her lineage, not where she is right now."

"Then I have a challenge before me."

"I'm afraid you do. But you have time—to find her, anyway, if not to woo her. That may take even longer."

"Sweet Jovah singing," Gaaron said under his breath. "Well, let me set out then on my appointed task—to go about the wooing of my Edori bride."

CHAPTER THREE

But Gaaron did not immediately get an opportunity to set out looking for his bride. He did not return to the Eyrie until very late that night, for he stayed at Mount Sinai to have dinner with Mahalah and some of her more senior acolytes, and then he insisted on flying home instead of staying till morning. Even more than flying at high, risky altitudes, Gaaron liked to fly at night. The sky was a blackness before him, generously spread with sleet-sized drops of icy starlight. The earth was a blackness below him, lit at distant, irregular intervals by sharp points of light—the clustered candles of a small village, the few winking lamps of a lonely farmhouse, the bright warm circle of an Edori campfire. More than once he was tempted to swing down to that Edori camp and introduce himself, inquire after the women of the clan and ask if any of them could point him to the Tachitas. But it was late. And he was tired. And such a midnight visit would make him feel like a fool.

He would feel like a fool by daylight, too.

It was not far from dawn when he touched down on the Eyrie's broad plateau, pausing a moment to savor the blended harmonies of the singers taking this late shift. He could not positively identify either of the male voices, but the soprano was definitely Miriam. And why wasn't she lying quietly in her bed, innocently sleeping? He was too tired to go and ask. He spared a moment to try to remember if he had signed up for any singing sessions tomorrow, particularly any morning ones, and was relieved to recall that he had not. He went straight to his room and directly to bed.

The morning was consumed by tasks he had eluded by leaving the premises the day before—a conference with Esther, the perusal of a note from Adriel, a meeting with one of the angels Neri had sent down from Monteverde with some trifling piece of news that could have waited for a month to be shared. He found a few minutes to look for Miriam, but she was still sleeping and he did not want to wake her.

He realized, in a moment of brief and somewhat helpless humor, that his life was bounded by women. The Archangel—the leader of the host at Monteverde—his steward—his sister—his oracle—all were women. And now that he must bring a wife into the hold, he would be adding one more female to the mix.

Lucky for him, he considered himself levelheaded enough to understand their logic, cut through their emotions, value their insights, and accept their gifts. Most days . . .

He had barely finished breakfast in the formal dining hall when Nicholas came bounding in, all dark glancing energy and slim, quivering wings. "Gaaron! You're back! You haven't gone to southern Bethel yet, have you? Not without me?"

Gaaron rose. "I wouldn't think of going without you. I had hoped to go this afternoon, but I'm afraid there is a tangle of things to cut through today. Would tomorrow morning suit you?"

"Yes, and Zibiah as well." At Gaaron's look of surprise, Nicholas rushed on. "Well, I told her about it! And she said she would like to go and see this disappearing man for herself."

"If he really has disappeared, I doubt any of us will see him, but she is welcome to come along," Gaaron said. "Anyone else you would like to add to the party?"

"Not so far," Nicholas said with a grin. "I'll ask around."

Before Gaaron could answer, a small storm of boys burst into the dining room like thunderclouds exploding. Four of them appeared to be chasing two others, and the yelps and shouts and threats of violence were accompanied by the crashing of chairs and tables as they trampled through the furniture arrangements of the room. Esther, never far off when a crisis beckoned, darted into the room and began adding her own strident tirade to the noise, but the boys paid no attention.

The four bigger ones had cornered the two smaller ones and Gaaron saw, to his dismay, that it appeared to be angels versus mortals, four to two.

"Give that back! You stole that from the storeroom yesterday, and I looked for it all day! Give that back and get out of here, you rotten children!"

Esther's voice had no effect at all, nor did Nicholas' easy admonition of "Quiet down, now, can't you see people are eating still?" One of the mortal boys let out a shrill shriek of apprehension.

Gaaron was on his feet and across the room before any of the young angels realized he was even in the room. "Jude. Zack. All of you. Stand back," Gaaron said in a stern voice.

There was sudden and immediate silence in the room.

All six of the boys cowered back from the shape of the avenging angel so unexpectedly appearing before them. Jude and Zack, who were big and bulky for thirteen-year-olds, tried to show defiance, but a momentary spike of fear tightened both of their young faces. The mortal boys were only nine or ten, small-boned and delicate as so many of the full-blooded humans were. Gaaron felt even more huge next to them.

But he was, for one of the rare occasions in his life, deliberately using his size to his advantage, and he made no effort not to look imposing.

"What's going on here?" he said in a slow, ominous voice.

"Nothing," Zack said sulkily.

"I said," Gaaron repeated even more slowly, "what's going on?"

"They took something of ours," Jude said.

"Did not!" one of the young boys burst out. "It wasn't yours! You stole it!"

"Yes, yesterday they were down—" Esther's voice started in, but Gaaron flung up a hand to stop her. She fell silent.

"Zack?" Gaaron asked, keeping the weight of his gaze on the black-haired boy, the biggest of the group, and the most consistent bully of the hold. "What happened?"

Zack hunched his shoulders. "We was down in the—"

"We were," Gaaron interrupted.

"We *were* down in the storerooms yesterday, and we found some stuff, and it didn't look like nobody was using it—"

"It didn't look like anybody was using it," Gaaron corrected. His voice was unshakably patient; he knew he sounded as if he was willing to stand there all day, hearing the stupid story, enforcing rules of grammar and manners as well as addressing larger ethical issues. In fact, he would have preferred to spend his time almost any other way—but this, too, was one of his duties, and he would perform it as painstakingly as the task required.

"So we took it," Zack finished up.

"And what did you take?" Gaaron asked. "Show me."

"Don't have it anymore," Zack said. "Silas took it."

"Tell me, then."

Zack looked down, looked up, looked down again. "Flute," he said.

Gaaron hid his surprise. He had been expecting something much more reprehensible. "Why?" he said.

" 'Cause he's stupid, and he takes things just because he *can*," Silas burst out.

Gaaron transferred his gaze to the mortal. He knew he shouldn't despise the small pale boy for his size and fairness, but he'd never liked Silas. Too whiny, too fragile. "I believe I asked Zack why he took it," Gaaron said, and Silas fell to studying the scuff marks on the toes of his shoes.

" 'Cause I wanted it," Zack said. He tossed his dark head. He was half brother to Nicholas, though neither acknowledged the connection. His mother had been an angel-seeker, one of the women who frequented the hold hoping to catch the attention of an angel and, with any stroke of luck, bear an angel child. Nicholas' mother, by contrast, had been a Manadavvi heiress who didn't believe in consorting with such inferior persons, and wouldn't allow her son to do so, either. Gaaron sometimes wasn't sure which of the three parents most disgusted him by their behavior.

"Wanted it to—?"

Zack shrugged. "To play it, maybe. Some people do."

Gaaron nodded and turned back to Silas and his compatriot. "And why did the two of you want the flute?" he asked.

"We didn't want it! We were bringing it back!" Silas protested.

Gaaron tilted his head to one side. "And can you think of other ways you might have resolved this problem?"

"Huh?" Silas said.

Zack loosed a crack of laughter. "He means why didn't you snitch on me, you big baby, instead of stealing it yourself like the little thief you are."

The pair of insults forced Silas to launch himself across the other three angels and go for Zack's throat. He was too quick for Gaaron; he connected and wrestled the bigger boy down with a pretty creditable show of fury and skill. He didn't have the upper hand for long, for Zack flipped him to his back and started pummeling him in the chest.

Gaaron glanced at Nicholas, who watched with a certain enjoyment, as if he'd have been willing to cheer the combatants on if there hadn't been more sober company watching. But catching Gaaron's gaze, Nicholas nodded, and they waded into the fray to separate the fighters. Gaaron hauled Zack to his feet with an almost effortless lift, and Nicholas caught the squirming Silas in his arms.

"It's his fault! He started it!" Silas was wailing.

"I don't care who started it," Gaaron said calmly. "As far as I'm concerned, you're all equally guilty and you all deserve an equal punishment."

"Hey! We didn't—"

"Be quiet," Gaaron snapped, and they all shut up. "I know Esther has some boxes she needs hauled from the upper levels to the storerooms. You'll help her for the rest of the day, and tomorrow, if she needs you, and you won't complain about it once."

"Oh, I've got lots of boxes," Esther said.

"And if you give her any trouble," Gaaron said, "I'll think of some additional chores that need to be done."

"It's not fair," Jude muttered. "Not my fault."

"Well, it is your fault, and would you like me to explain it to you?" Gaaron asked pleasantly. "One, you chose to associate with companions who would rather steal than request permission to use something that they would happily be allowed to borrow. Two, you didn't inform any elder that a theft had taken place. Three, you joined in an unfair fight against opponents who are smaller than you, younger than you, and outnumbered by you and your friends. Frankly, I can't see that your behavior has been anything but abominable."

"Well, I didn't do anything," Silas said.

"You're a jerk," Zack burst out.

"You chose to steal instead of informing an adult, and, if I guess correctly, you took the flute back not to return it to its place, but to annoy Zack. Not exactly a commendable motive. Sometimes we're judged by our intentions as well as our actions."

"Yeah, but I—"

"One more word from any of the six of you and I'll add to your duties," Gaaron said. "I know Enoch has some cleaning that he needs done down in the food pens. Would you like to help him?"

They all looked mutely up at him. Jude shook his head.

"Good," Gaaron said briskly. "Then you all go with Esther. Except you, Zack," he added, raising his voice slightly.

The other five turned away, Silas with a malicious and triumphant gleam in his eyes. Zack stayed behind, chin up, defiance in every line of his body.

"And you'll take on an extra task," Gaaron said. "You'll go find Ahio, wherever he is, and tell him you need to learn a song."

"A—song?" Zack said, clearly caught off balance.

Gaaron nodded. "On the flute. Tell him you'll need to be proficient enough to perform at least once piece in public in eight months."

"But I—I can't play the flute," Zack said.

"Well, no, I suppose you can't right now. But you will in eight months. You'll perform at the Gloria, after we've sung the mass."

Zack looked pale. "I haven't—I can't—I don't—"

Gaaron smiled and patted him on the shoulder. "You'll do just fine," he said. "You have a long time to get ready. But not today. Or tomorrow. You've got boxes to move."

So there was the morning gone; and the afternoon consisted of another bitter encounter with Miriam and the writing of a reply to Adriel. And then he had to make time to see some of the petitioners who had arrived yesterday, only to find him gone. Some required a simple adjudication of a dispute between themselves and a neighbor; others had more pressing concerns that took more time to consider and settle. The problems that involved weather imbalances were the easiest to correct. All Gaaron had to do was promise to send help and then hunt up a couple of angels to go sing the necessary prayers that would bring rain or sunshine. He felt a little envious as he watched the small cadre take off. He would have liked to have had nothing better to do than sing to Jovah and make the world right again.

He ate a late dinner that Esther put together for him after the formal meal was over and the kitchen was more or less closed. And he rounded off the day by climbing to the cupola high above the Eyrie to join in the harmonics. He hadn't signed up for this shift, but it had been almost two days since he had sung at all, and he felt the lack of music in his very blood and bones. Runners and other athletes described a sense of malaise if they missed a day or two of vigorous exercise; they explained that their muscles felt crampy and their moods grew black. Gaaron experienced the same symptoms, as well as something strange and constricting gathered around his chest. It was as if his lungs forgot to breathe, if they were not filled with air to be loosed in song. It was as if his ribs tightened up, shrank down, if they were not expanded by the glory of music.

Naturally, there was already music floating down from the stage, a rather maudlin lullaby that someone must have thought suited the advanced hour. Three others were already gathered in the open room at the top of the Eyrie—Ahio, Sela, and Miriam. His sister gave him a cool glance but moved closer to Sela to make room for him. He could see the calculating look that passed between the other singers, the quick assessment of who could sing what part now that a fourth voice would be added. Ahio and Gaaron were both tenors, but Ahio had a deeper range than Gaaron and could slip into the bass part without much trouble. Sela was technically a second soprano but often sang alto parts, and Miriam had a soaring and energetic soprano that could, on her best nights, send any audience into transports. Four-part harmony—that was the best, that was what every singer really lived for. They all started smiling in anticipation.

Gaaron hummed along with the song in progress just to get the feel for the ensemble and to be ready to segue to the new piece once it was chosen. Ahio raised his right hand, finger extended, to signal that he had a composition in mind, and the others all nodded to him. When their mournful lullaby came to a close, Ahio waited about two beats and then offered up the opening melody of the *Lorelei Cantata*. It was an exquisite piece of constantly shifting harmonies and lead lines, and Miriam laughed with delight when she recognized it. They let him do the opening measure as a solo, and then they all came in on their parts with utter precision.

Gaaron felt that familiar little shiver run down his back at the resonant beauty of those perfectly realized minor harmonies. He saw Miriam close her eyes and take a step backward, putting her hand out to the wall behind her as though to keep her balance. The rest of them watched Ahio, who did casual directing, moving his finger through the air to give them the beat and to signal them to swell in a crescendo at the first key change. Gaaron's favorite part was the section in the middle when the tenor voice was twinned with the alto line in a series of changing staccato intervals. It was a complex and demanding interlude, requiring quick sips of air and absolute confidence in your partner, and both he and Sela were grinning broadly when it came to its conclusion. Miriam's voice swooped in to wrest the melody back, and Ahio added a rhythmic counterpoint in a resonant bass. They finished the piece in a triumphant swell of major chords that would surely have the whole compound sitting up in bed and wondering why nobody felt sleepy.

Miriam had her hand up, requesting the next selection, and Ahio pointed at her as if to give permission. But her choice surprised everyone, most of all Gaaron. She sang the opening line of the *Davinsky Alleluia*, which by rights was Gaaron's solo, as the whole piece was written to show off a tenor voice. The other two murmured their approval, for this was a beloved piece among angels at the Eyrie, and they looked expectantly at Gaaron. He was watching Miriam. She nodded and abruptly shut her mouth, and he picked up the line without missing a beat.

It was one of his favorite selections, a sunny and hopeful composition written as part of a celebratory mass. He felt his voice pour from his mouth, warm and rich and textured with pattern. His chest filled and emptied, filled and emptied, but he never felt breathless or drained; swirls of silk seemed to coil in his lungs and unroll. The music sounded so effortless it almost did not feel like it was coming from him. It seemed as though it was spontaneously generated by starlight and contentment and goodwill. The voices joining his in harmony supported him with an actual physical sensation; he felt their lift and buoyancy catch him at his knees and elbows and elevate him the barest millimeter off the floor.

They were not completely through the *Alleluia* when Sela was fluttering her fingers, asking for the next turn. Gaaron motioned her to add harmony to what should have been his solo "amen," and then he dropped his voice away so that she could begin the next piece. It would be their last one for the night; other singers had already arrived at the doorway, ready to take their places. Sela motioned them in and then launched into a much quieter but very pretty choral piece that sounded better with every voice added. They all sang along happily, modulating down from the ecstatic heights of the *Alleluia*. It was, Gaaron thought, about the best way anyone could hope to end a day.

When the shift was ended, Ahio and Sela lingered, though Gaaron turned to go. He had a long flight ahead of him tomorrow, and he

was still a little tired from last night's midnight journey. He was somewhat surprised when Miriam chose to exit with him. He waited till
they were out of range of the singers before speaking.

"I enjoyed that a great deal," he said. "Thank you for choosing
the *Alleluia*."

All her animosity of the afternoon seemed to have melted away.
She smiled at him in the flickering gaslight that lit all the corridors and
open spaces of the Eyrie. "I like you best when you are singing," she
said. "And I wanted to like you for at least part of the day."

"Well, that's encouraging," he said. "I, of course, always like you,
even when you're driving me to lunacy."

"I hear you're flying to southern Bethel tomorrow," she said.

"I suppose you got that from Nicholas." Gaaron had thought for
quite some time that his volatile sister and the erratic angel were destined to fall in love, since they were so similar in temperament and so
obviously the worst possible partners for each other. But although the
two had always been good friends, nothing warmer had ever developed
between them. "You can come, if you like. We can hand you around
between us when one of us gets tired of carrying you."

"No, thank you," she said prettily. "But if you hadn't asked, I
would have insisted on going."

He smiled in the semidark that shadowed the open plateau. "Let
me know, sometime," he remarked, "if I ever stumble upon the trick
of handling you right. If I ever figure out even the smallest detail."

She laughed at that and slipped into the corridor ahead of him.
"You're the best brother ever," she said over her shoulder, "which
makes me have to be the worst sister ever. I don't see why you can't
understand that."

"Do you want me to bring you anything back from southern
Bethel?" he asked.

She snorted. "Is there anything there *worth* bringing back?" she
asked. "An interesting story, maybe. Bring that."

"I'll see what I can do."

They walked along in a rare companionable silence till they
reached the fork in the hallway that led to their separate chambers.
" Night," she said, but he stopped her with one big hand on her shoulder.

"You're my heartache and my joy, and even if you hate me for
it, I'll watch out for you till I die," he said quietly, and kissed her on

the top of her head. She looked up at him, dark eyes shining in the gaslight, and he thought he could read the reply circling in her head. *And as long as you feel you have to watch over me, I shall make your life hell.*

But she didn't say it. "Good night, Gabriel Aaron," she said instead. "Come see me when you get back."

They left shortly after breakfast, though that required Gaaron affecting deafness when a few people called his name as he left the dining room. Zibiah and Nicholas were already awaiting him on the plateau, Zibiah giggling in her foolish manner over something Nicholas had said. She was pretty in an unremarkable way, with short brown hair and lively green eyes, but it was really her animation that gave her any charm at all. She and Miriam were friends, of course; the less sober someone was, the more likely Miriam was to be drawn to that person.

"Ready?" Gaaron asked, though they clearly were. "Let's go."

The flight to southern Bethel would take longer than the flight to Mount Sinai, particularly since Nicholas and Zibiah seemed inclined to dawdle along the way. Gaaron let them set the pace, knowing that few angels could attain the speed he could generate with his massive wings. They were not in a hurry, in any case. No rush to hear earnest, thoughtful farming folk tell an incredible story.

They stopped once for lunch, and for Zibiah and Nicholas to trade insults, and then they were on their way again. Nicholas took the lead when they got close to the site he'd visited before, since there were a number of different farming settlements in this part of the country and Gaaron was not entirely sure which one had witnessed the miracle. Finally, almost six hours after they'd set out, Nicholas folded his wings and made a precipitous descent toward a cluster of buildings that appeared to comprise a farmhouse, a silo, and a few other necessary structures. Zibiah promptly imitated him, neither of them unfurling their wings till they were so close to the ground it could have been deadly. Gaaron followed at a more sane and leisurely pace.

Two men and a woman had already gathered in front of the farmhouse by the time Gaaron touched down. He saw both farmers tilt their heads back and try to judge his height, a thing other big men always did when they found themselves confronted with someone even bigger. They were weather-beaten and sunburned, so their ages were hard to tell, but Gaaron guessed them to be father and son by the similarity of their broad faces and ruddy hair. The woman standing beside them, smiling in a somewhat bemused fashion as if she did not often entertain angels, was probably the wife and mother.

"Hi there, you remember me," Nicholas said with his usual careless charm. "This is Zibiah, she's from the Eyrie, too. And this is Gaaron."

The name confused them; it was not how he was formally known. "I'm Gabriel," he corrected Nicholas, shaking the woman's hand, then the older man's, then the son's. "They call me Gaaron. I hear you have an interesting story to tell."

And it was interesting, but there was not much more to learn than Gaaron had gleaned from Nicholas' recital. The farmwife insisted on serving them refreshments before they tramped out into the field to see the exact spot where the man had first appeared and then disappeared. Angels hated to walk, and Gaaron could see that both Zibiah and Nicholas were dying to say "Meet you out there!" and take off for the back acres. But Gaaron gave them a level look, and they dropped into line behind him and the farmers, and they all made their way through the muddy earth to a spot that seemed to be dead center on the property.

The older man pointed out various sites of interest ("Here's where we first saw him, here's where we was, here's where he just sorta vanished"), but Gaaron paid little attention. Nicholas had been right. The land stretched out, flat and utterly boring, for miles in all directions. They were standing in the middle of acreage planted with some low-growing crop, beans or tubers, nothing you could disappear into if the mood happened to strike. Where had the stranger come from? Where had he gone?

"Have you seen him again?" Gaaron asked.

"No, and we've kept a lookout," the son replied.

"Has anyone nearby seen him? Or noticed anyone unusual in the area? Where's the nearest town? Have you inquired there?"

"Was up there yesterday," the older man said. "Asked around a little. Sounded like a fool, so I quit asking. But nobody else seen nothing—at least that they was admitting."

Gaaron nodded. "I appreciate you telling me, though. I don't think you're a fool. But I don't see that there's much I can do for you unless this—this disappearing man comes back. I would like you to inform me if you see him again—or if anyone does."

"Be happy to do that," the farmer said. "Be happier if we don't have to."

Gaaron smiled at the rough humor. "Thank your wife for the delicious cakes," he said. "Let us know if you learn anything else. Now, I'm sorry, but we've got to go. We have a long flight ahead of us."

The farmer nodded. " 'Preciate you coming out, Archangel."

Gaaron, flexed on his feet in preparation for takeoff, was startled enough to relax his stance. "I'm not Archangel yet," he said.

"No, but you will be soon, and we're all glad for it," the farmer said. "You're a good man. We was all happy when you was chosen."

"Thank you," Gaaron said gravely, trying not to look at Nicholas' grinning face. "I'll do my best to earn your trust."

And he nodded again, tensed his calves and his shoulders, drove his wings down in one forceful sweep, and took off. The temperature of the air changed rapidly across his skin as he climbed quickly through the sun-warmed air into the higher, cooler altitudes. At first he could hear Nicholas and Zibiah behind him, laughing and talking as they ascended, but within a few minutes he had left them behind. He still did not go as fast or as high as he would have had he been alone, but he did level out at an altitude he was pretty sure they would stay below. He did not particularly want to leave them behind, but there was no insistent reason to stay together. They all knew their way back to the Eyrie.

He flew at this pace for maybe an hour, trying to shake off the vague, disturbing sense of unease he had felt as he stood in the farmer's plowed fields, hearing a flatly impossible story. Add the mystery of disappearing men to his long list of chores to deal with, and his duties were beginning to pile up to almost unmanageable proportions. And he had not even begun to whittle away at one of them: the search for his bride-to-be.

At that point in his musings, it occurred to him that he should be paying more attention to the land below him, looking for signs of Edori. Actually, and he knew it, he should be looking for other markers as well: plague flags raised by travelers or small villages, weather-related disturbances such as flood or drought, signs of blight on otherwise prosperous communities. Any angel who crossed any wide swath of land was trained to watch for these indications of trouble. Gaaron dropped a few hundred feet and slowed the pace of his wingbeats even more, and scanned the ground below for anything out of the ordinary.

They had flown perhaps another hour when Gaaron spotted smoke on the horizon. He dropped even lower and glanced behind him, to see Nicholas and Zibiah as rather indistinct specks in the distance. He slowed to what was almost hover speed and dropped a few more feet, wanting the two of them to see him as he angled in the direction of the smoke. Campfire? It was late enough in the afternoon that some travelers, having come across a friendly spot, might have decided to end their journey for the day and set up their tents. But the smoke seemed too black and heavy for a campfire. It looked more like it rose from the mass burning of clothes and furnishings that some groups practiced after plague or other sickness—a cleansing fire, but a sign of trouble.

Gaaron glanced back again to find Nicholas and Zibiah closer and following him. Nicholas raised his hand to signal that they, too, had seen the smoke and interpreted it as Gaaron had. Gaaron descended another few yards but picked up the pace. A fresh sense of worry prickled through his veins and drove him forward faster.

What he saw from the air made him miss a wingbeat and drop even closer to the ground in a sickening tumble. Or maybe the fall wasn't what made his stomach clench and roll. Absently, he righted himself, flicking his wings in a slow, steady motion, holding himself above the burning circle, and stared down.

It had been a campsite, well enough. Even now, from above, Gaaron could see the charred remains of a few wagons, the blackened clumps of rubble that bore the shapes of men and horses. But that was all that remained, the bones of men and the cinder ribs of wagon struts. Everything else, flesh and wood and metal, appeared to have been annihilated in an unimaginably fierce conflagration.

He heard a gasp behind him and then a muttered prayer. Zibiah and Nicholas had arrived. He said nothing, did not even look at them, but remained where he was, hovering above the camp, looking down. His heart felt small and his wings felt weary. He did not even know the words to describe such devastation.

"Gaaron." Nicholas was the first to speak in an urgent, frightened voice. "Gaaron. What happened here?"

"Are those—I think I see—are those bodies down there?" Zibiah asked, her voice little more than a whimper.

"I have no idea what happened. Yes, they look like bodies to me," Gaaron said grimly. "Men and animals."

He heard a small sob escape from Zibiah, then a coughing noise, as if she was fighting back the urge to vomit. He still did not look at her, only down at the burning camp. Not burning for much longer now, though, for there was very little left for the fire to consume. Another hour and even the smoke would be gone. They would have missed this sight entirely had they passed through much later.

"Edori, do you think?" Nicholas asked. "Or Jansai?"

Gaaron pointed at one of the shapes he thought had been a horse-drawn conveyance. "Jansai. Edori usually don't travel with wagons. Probably traders."

Nicholas was silent a moment. "Should we—should we go down there and see if we can find something? To identify them, I mean. So we can tell someone in Breven?"

"I suppose we must," Gaaron said. "Not that I think we'll find anything. A little jewelry, maybe. I don't know what might be left."

"You don't think anyone—anyone survived, do you?" Nicholas said.

At any other time, Gaaron would have felt sorry for Nicholas, such a light and careless young man trying, in this crisis, to be responsible and decisive. But he couldn't feel sorry for anyone except those strangers below. Their deaths had probably been quick, though, Gaaron thought; that was something to take comfort in. Had the fire not been instantaneous, there would have been some sign of that. For one thing, some of the individuals would have survived, escaping from the fast-building bright enemy. They would have run for help, or rescued their fellows or, at the least, died in a fanning circle away from the burning campsite, their own clothes on fire as they raced from the central disaster. But none of that appeared to have happened here. It was as if all the travelers, all their horses, had been engulfed in flame in a single moment, flame so hot that it instantly consumed their flesh and they turned into ash where they stood.

"No. No, I think they're all dead," Gaaron said slowly. "But I think we should do an air search of the area. Who knows, someone may have been off gathering firewood or hunting for dinner when—when the blaze started."

Zibiah, who had drifted some distance away, either to be sick or to compose herself, now floated closer. Gaaron heard the soft flutter of her wings before she spoke. "What do you think—how did the fire start?" she asked in a quavering voice.

Gaaron shook his head. "I don't know. I can't imagine. I've never seen anything like this."

"Come on. Gaaron wants us to look for anyone who may have survived," Nicholas told her. Then, aiming his words back at Gaaron, the younger angel asked, "Should we split up?"

"Yes," Gaaron said, and then, a second later, "No. We don't know what happened here. We should stick together."

And without another word, Gaaron led them away from the nightmare camp. He spread his wings to their fullest and coasted low to the ground, watching for signs of life. A little summer river could be found just north of the campsite; anyone who had left to get water would have gone in this direction.

But they arrived at the water's edge, and skimmed up and down its banks, and found no one.

Gaaron went farther. A hunter could have ranged five miles from the camp and even now be on his way back. Or a whole contingent of merchants could have fallen half a day behind, doing last-minute business in a farm community while the rest of their caravan moved on to make camp for the night.

But they made a broad circle a few miles out around the perimeter of the camp, and they saw no tired, happy men making their way back with unexpected bounty.

Farther out, then? Someone who had been absent from the camp when the calamity came, but close enough to see that disaster had struck, and smart enough to run away? Gaaron banked and headed back to the river. Any Jansai, any Edori, separated from his group, would know he had no chance of solitary survival unless he stayed by water. Gaaron heard Nicholas' voice behind him, calling his name in a questioning voice, but he flew on anyway. They would search north along the river for a few more miles, and then they would search south. And then, if they saw nothing, they would give up.

They had gone about two miles up the river when Gaaron spotted a piece of red cloth lying in a patch of tall grass.

He pointed so the others would see it, then drove his wings hard for speed, tilting his shoulders down so he would drop as low to the ground as he could without crashing. A bitter disappointment coursed through him as he got nearer, for the scrap of red fabric appeared to be just that—a shirt, a shawl, some garment discarded by the side of the road. He landed on his feet and walked closer, pushing through the waist-high weeds to the spot of color in the grass.

And the red shirt twisted, and resolved itself into a small girl, who began shrieking at the top of her lungs.

Gaaron froze mid-step as the girl kept screaming. She looked to be about ten years old, small-boned and underfed, with the smooth skin and long sleek hair of the Jansai. Except that skin was scratched and bloody from some headlong and treacherous flight. The veils around her head, the type worn by every Jansai woman and girl to hide her face from strange men, were ripped and ragged, and her dress appeared muddy and torn. She backed away from him, still screaming wordlessly, trying to draw the remnants of her veil around her face, covering her cheeks with her hands. She was the very picture of lunatic terror.

Gaaron felt rather than saw Zibiah and Nicholas approach overhead. He pointed twice, once to the left of the Jansai girl, once to the right, and the two angels landed behind her just where Gaaron had indicated. Now if she turned to run, one of them could stop her.

She could not have heard them land, for they came to earth soundlessly as falcons, but some suddenly developed feral sense allowed her to feel them arrive and know herself surrounded. She whipped her head from side to side, her howls intensifying, and then she wound her arms around her head and dropped to the ground, weeping.

Gaaron stood where he had stopped, unwilling to terrorize her further, absolutely at a loss. Clearly they could not leave her here, but just as clearly, she would be hysterical as long as they stayed. He looked over at Nicholas, whose eyes were as wide and shocked as the girl's, and the younger angel spread his hands if to answer an unspoken question. The question had been, *What can we do?* and Nicholas' reply had been, *I don't know.*

And then Zibiah, silly Zibiah, began to sing.

It was a lullaby, a pretty, soothing song that mothers sang to their fretful babies, and Zibiah sang it in a soft, comforting voice. She was into the second verse before the sobbing child began to quiet, and by the time she reached the chorus, the sounds of weeping had ceased altogether. Zibiah took a step closer to the cowering girl, and began the song over again at the beginning.

Nicholas glanced at Gaaron again, eyebrows raised. This time the question was, *Do we join in?* But Gaaron shook his head. Jovah knew, the Jansai girl had every reason to be hysterical at the approach of strangers, but maybe some of her fear could be attributed to the fact that Gaaron was male. The Jansai were fiercely protective of their women; not only did they keep the women cloaked from the eyes of strangers, for the most part, they kept the women hidden away entirely from the outside world. It was said that a woman might speak to only three men in her entire life: her father, her brother, and her husband. This child might have been traveling with the caravan, but she had no doubt been kept inside one of the wagons, under the watchful eye of her mother, and it was likely she had never spoken to a strange man in her life.

And Gaaron, even he had to admit, was a big enough example of maleness that a sheltered girl might find him terrifying in the extreme.

Zibiah continued to sing and continued to move closer to the girl, taking small, unalarming steps. When she glanced at Gaaron for direction, he merely nodded. This was out of his hands. Neither of the men would be able to get close to the girl without sending her into shrieking panic.

Nonetheless, Gaaron held his breath as Zibiah drew near enough to kneel down beside the shivering, silent bundle of red misery. But there was no renewed outburst. The little girl seemed to shudder, and then turned herself into Zibiah's embrace. The angel drew the Jansai onto her lap and leaned her head down, singing even more softly into the child's ear. Her lacy wings folded forward, enclosing the girl in a white net of safety, shutting her off from the sight of men. Her head bent even lower, till her face, too, was hidden by the feathered weave of her wings. They could hear her voice still crooning.

Gaaron stepped back a few paces and motioned Nicholas over. "I don't want to make camp for the night," Gaaron said, "but I don't know if she'll be able to travel."

"If Zib carries her—" Nicholas began.

Gaaron shook his head. "But what if flying sets her off again? A lot of people are frightened when they're taken up in an angel's arms."

Nicholas glanced at the sky. Late afternoon, and they had at least a three-hour flight ahead of them. "We don't have any camping gear," Nicholas said. "Not even a blanket. We don't even have much food between us."

"I know. There are a few farms not far from here—twenty miles at the most. You could get provisions while I stay to guard them. We could spend the night, take off in the morning when she's calmer."

"If she's calmer," Nicholas said.

"I know," Gaaron said soberly. "She might never calm down as long as you and I are nearby, and we can't leave Zibiah alone."

"Gaaron," Nicholas said, his eyes wide with a new thought. "We can't camp here. We can't build a *fire*."

Gaaron's head swung up, his expression arrested. "No, of course we can't," he said slowly. Not unless they wanted to guarantee that the girl would grow crazy with fright again. "You're right. We have to go back tonight."

"Should I go on ahead?" Nicholas said. "Warn the Eyrie?"

Gaaron shook his head. "I'd rather we stayed together if we're flying. Just in case—I don't know. Just in case."

They returned the few paces to where Zibiah sat, half concealed in the tall grass, rocking the child on her lap. She put her finger to her lips to enjoin silence.

"I think she's sleeping," the angel said. "But your voices might alarm her. She's afraid of men."

Gaaron nodded, but secretly he was pleased that Zibiah had reached this conclusion on her own and had made all the other corresponding deductions—that she would have to be the one to carry the girl, and communicate with her, and essentially control the rest of this expedition. He spread his wings and extended his arm, then raised his eyebrows with a question. *Can you fly?* he meant to ask. *All the way to the Eyrie? Tonight?*

Zibiah nodded and rose somewhat unsteadily to her feet, the girl in her arms. "I don't see that it will do us any good to wait," she said. "And maybe she'll sleep through the flight. If we can get her to the Eyrie and put her in a room before she sees any more men, maybe she'll calm down a little."

Now Nicholas waved his hands to get her attention, holding up his canteen and then mimicking eating a bite of food. Zibiah smiled.

"I'm not hungry," she said. "And I have plenty of my own water. I gave her some, too, before she fell asleep. I think we're ready to go."

So Gaaron nodded, the signal to ascend, and as slowly as their wings could manage the separation from the earth, they lifted themselves into the air. Gaaron waited for the howl of anxiety to come from the abandoned child, but she did not waken—or, if she did, she did not cry out again. Staying as near to the ground as he could so that the Jansai girl was not buffeted by cold air at the higher regions, Gaaron led them back to the Eyrie. Zibiah fell in place behind him to coast as much as possible on the drag created by his passing, and

Nicholas flew behind her to be ready to offer assistance if she needed it.

It was the longest, slowest flight of Gaaron's life. He had never been so happy to see the serrated range of the Velo Mountains come into view, or to touch down on the wide, cool stone of the landing at the Eyrie.

CHAPTER FOUR

The Lohoras had been traveling as fast as they could, northwest from Luminaux, when they fell in with the Tachita clan. As always when two Edori tribes came together by happy chance, there was great rejoicing at the opportunity to visit together, tell stories, and share campfires.

Susannah was particularly overjoyed to meet up with the Tachitas, and she spent that first evening at her brother's campfire, catching up on family news. Paul, her older brother, was looking so much like a settled man, so much like their father, that she could not help but laugh at him and tease him about the extra pounds he had gained. Linus, who was now nearly sixteen, she scarcely recognized, for he was taller than she was and could lift her off her feet with a strength he had not possessed even six months ago. Her nephews, aged two and one, at first were shy of her, but then consented to sit on her lap, both at one time, as long as she jogged her knees up and down and pretended to give them pony rides. The older one in particular was quick to respond to her voice and her laugh, and he readily tilted his little face forward when she leaned in to rub noses with him. She thought maybe she should wait no longer; it might be time for her and Dathan to have a child after all.

"You all look so well and happy," she said to Ruth, Paul's wife, who stirred the supper pot while Susannah amused the children. "I commend you for the care you have given all the men in my family."

"They are easy to care for," Ruth said, ducking her head shyly and smiling in a bashful manner. Susannah was not sure, but she thought she saw a thickening around Ruth's waist. Another baby on the way so soon? There must be a great deal of love in this tent. "They miss you, but there does not seem to be any other great sadness in their lives. Even your father is better these days. He is able to talk of your mother and tell me many happy stories about her. For so long, he would not even mention her name."

"That is good to hear," Susannah said. She absently leaned in and kissed the two-year-old on the top of his head. He squirmed in her lap and she let him jump up and run away, though she kept her eyes on him to make sure he did not wander too near the fire. "For Amariah is such a pretty name."

"I have asked Paul, and he thinks it would be a good idea," Ruth said, her soft voice rushing over the words. "If the new one is a girl— and I'm sure it is—he thinks we might name her Amariah. Unless it's the name you want for your own daughter, when you have one?"

Susannah laughed gaily, though she was a little amazed that Ruth had picked up on both her thoughts—that it was time for her to have a baby, and that Ruth herself might be pregnant again. "You're welcome to the name, for I'm still not sure when I might want a baby," she said. "I think the news will make my father happy as well."

Indeed, when the men returned a little while later, Susannah was deeply pleased to see for herself the truth of Ruth's words. For her father seemed whole again—older, a little slower, not quite as quick to smile—but not the hurt and grieving man he had been for so long after Amariah's death. He sat by her during dinner and described their wanderings since the Gathering, their sojourn in Breven, their camp at the Caitana Mountains not far from Windy Point. The Tachitas rarely moved out of the Jordana province, having many contacts among the merchants and petty farmers there. The Lohoras, on the other hand, knew no boundaries and traveled pretty much where they would.

"We haven't been by the Caitanas for a year or more now," Susannah said. "I might mention it to the others. That's pretty country and I'd like to see it again."

Paul looked over at her from across the fire. "You've seen other interesting sights, and far less pretty ones, from what I'm hearing," he said.

Susannah glanced at her nephews, not sure how much to say in front of them. Ruth, holding the younger one to feed him, nodded as if to say she could speak freely. "We came across a campsite burned beyond recognition," she said softly. "We couldn't even tell if it had been Edori or Jansai camped there—or, who knows, a band of farmers traveling to Luminaux. It was a very frightening place, and we did not linger long. We moved our own camp out that very night, late as it was."

"I wonder what could have caused such a thing? Bartholomew described it in a great deal of detail," Paul said, glancing at his older son.

"And I wonder if any other Edori have seen something similar," Susannah added. "You need to spread the word among the other clans you meet, and we'll do the same. Bad enough if it happened once, but what if it happened other times, in other places?"

"We'll pass along the news," Paul said solemnly.

After that, the talk turned to happier things, campfires they'd shared with other clans since the Gathering, funny words the boys had learned to say. Linus offered to wrestle his older brother, to prove to Susannah how strong he had grown. Their father turned to reminiscing, recounting a tale that involved their mother and some ill-advised additions she had made one night to the cook pot. He had them laughing so hard that Susannah's stomach actually hurt. But it was good to laugh with her father and hear stories about her mother. The pain was welcome.

After the meal was over and the dishes had been done, they gathered up the sleepy boys and made their way through the thicket of tents to the biggest fire outside Bartholomew's tent. Here the others were already taking their places, turning this fortuitous meeting into a mini-Gathering, a coming together of far-flung Edori souls. Someone passed around sweetbreads still hot from the fire. Dathan offered a skin of wine to Paul and other men of the Tachitas. Some of them accepted it; Paul did not. Her brother then turned a sideways look on Susannah. She kept her gaze on the fire and pretended not to see.

Most of them had shared their news casually over intermingled fires, so there was no need, as there was at the true Gathering, for clan members to get up one at a time and recite the events of the past few seasons. So after everyone was settled, and Eleazar had built up the fire a little more, no one moved or spoke for a few minutes until Claudia came to her feet.

"Greetings to you all," she said formally, smiling around at the assembled company. "Praise be to Yovah for bringing you to our campfire tonight."

And she lifted her voice in a simple song of thanksgiving that everyone immediately joined. The quick surge and rumble of voices filled Susannah with a deep and visceral satisfaction; she felt, if such a thing could be said to exist, a fierce contentment. She lifted her own voice in harmony, sliding her rich alto under the plain melody line. They sang it through twice before any of them were willing to let the song die.

Then Anna came to her feet and stood beside Claudia, and the two sang a traditional Edori tune in the old language that almost none of them used anymore, except when singing. After that, Linus jumped up, eager to show off his new tenor range, though his voice broke once or twice on the higher notes and caused Susannah to cover her face to hide her smile.

"Sing with me," Ruth said, turning to Susannah. So the two of them stood before the fire and performed. The first year that Ruth had lived in their tent, before Susannah had left the Tachitas to follow Dathan, Ruth and Susannah had sung together all the time. They had perfected their pitch and their timing so that, on a few songs, at least, they could produce amazing harmonies and dazzling leaps of interval. When they had finished their first composition, members of both clans called out for an encore, so they offered two more pieces.

"Susannah! Don't sit down! Come stand by me!" called another Tachita when Ruth was finished, so Susannah obligingly moved over a few paces. She had been the only reliable alto in the group, back when she lived with the Tachitas, so she had been in high demand on any song for which harmony was required. Which suited Susannah just fine. She did not particularly like to carry a melody line. She liked to listen to the music, get a sense of its tone and mood, and then make up her own harmonies, which often differed radically from the ones the composer might have intended. It was her only true musical ability.

But it was in demand, at least on this night. Keren was on her feet before the final notes had sounded in this latest duet, and she called Susannah over. Keren had a showy soprano that never sounded as good as when grounded by Susannah's reassuring low counterpoint, and the Tachitas praised her extravagantly when the song came to its conclusion. Throwing Susannah a droll look, Tirza then came to her feet, determined not to be shown up by her lover's vain sister.

"Susannah. That piece about the winding river. Sing that with me, won't you?" Tirza asked. So they launched into that one next, a wistful ballad about lost love and redemption beyond the grave. Everyone sighed when they were done, and no one leapt quite so readily to his feet.

"It seems all the clans have grown tired," Bartholomew said in an amused voice. "Perhaps one more prayer to Yovah would be in order, and then it is time to seek out our tents."

Everyone murmured agreement with this sensible plan of action, and the whole group joined in on the final song of the evening. Susannah's journey from singer to singer had brought her halfway around the fire, and not until then did she notice that Dathan was sitting quite close to a Tachita girl by the name of Cozbi. Neither one was singing this final prayer, which was scandalous in and of itself. They were talking in low voices, until Dathan paused to take a drink from his wineskin. He spilled a few drops down the corner of his mouth, and Cozbi laughed at him, rolling her eyes.

Susannah did not think it was so funny.

Once the prayer ended, Susannah made her way back to where Ruth sat cradling her sons in her arms. "Let me carry the little one," Susannah said, and took him carefully from Ruth's hold. Ruth rose a little unsteadily to her feet and smiled.

"It was so good to sing with you again tonight," Ruth said. "Every time I offer a prayer to Yovah, I miss the sound of your voice next to mine. The Lohoras stole a greater treasure than they knew when they took you from us."

"They did not take me—I chose to follow them," Susannah said, smiling. "What have you been feeding this boy? He is as heavy as a sack of rocks."

"We have been feeding him rocks," Paul said behind her. "That is the best diet for babies."

Linus came up on her other side. "Stay in the tent with us tonight, will you, Susannah?" he begged. "I want to wake you in the morning by tickling your ribs."

"And what makes you think *you* would be awake first?" she scoffed. "Perhaps I would leave my dreams early just so I could tickle *you*."

"Yes, stay with us," Ruth pleaded. "All these boys in my tent every morning! I need a woman's calm voice next to mine to assure me that I am still sane."

"She may tell you that, but that will not make it true," Paul said, and Ruth freed one hand from her hold on the baby to slap him on the arm.

"You see what I mean?" Ruth said piteously. "I am friendless without you."

"It had better be a girl you're carrying this time," Paul said. "Or you will have no allies at all."

Susannah thought of Dathan, leaning over Cozbi and smiling down into her speculative eyes. If she went back to sleep on her own pallet, she would know if Dathan came back late this night—or not at all.

"I would be happy to share your tent tonight," she said. "But Linus has to sleep outside. I think it may rain tonight."

They wrangled happily for the next half hour as they disposed themselves on the tent floor and traded the usual insults. Susannah found herself wedged between Linus, who slept closest to the outer edge of the tent, and her older nephew, who lay in the middle. All around her, the breathing was deep and even, with the occasional questioning cry of a baby hushed to instant silence. She had forgotten the rhythmic sound of her father's quiet snoring, proof that he still lived. How she had listened for that sound in the days and weeks after her mother's death. How it comforted her now.

She lay awake longer than she wanted to, remembering Dathan's face and Cozbi's smile, and telling herself that it was just the wine and the excitement of new company that had planted Dathan so firmly at the pretty girl's side. She would not have thought Cozbi was the type to flirt so readily with another woman's lover, though. She had always seemed thoughtful and clear-eyed, back in the days when Susannah lived with the Tachitas. Well, everyone changed, she supposed; she herself certainly had. Why not Cozbi?

She finally fell asleep, and then quickly was dreaming.

She was back in the room of white and silver, moving effortlessly between the strange hard walls. The screens and tapestries stretched out before her blinked with a gorgeous array of lights, and she paused before each new vista, delighted at its marvelous, mysterious patterns. The voice that was so familiar, but so incomprehensible, seemed to call her from a distance, so she tried to find its source, stepping through unfamiliar hallways of smooth, arching white material and gleaming circular lamps.

"Susannah," it called, and she paused before two doors, one on either side of the corridor.

"Where are you?" she called back. "I'm lost. I can't find you."

"Susannah," it said again, its tones low and urgent.

She tried one door, but it was locked, so she turned to the other one. It fell open as soon as she laid her palm across the smooth surface. She stepped inside, but this room was even stranger than the last one, all in darkness, with hidden shadowy shapes catching faint reflections from the light outside. One entire wall, floor to ceiling, appeared to be a window opening onto a view of the night sky. Constellations pressed against the glass like children peering into a candy shop. There were so many stars she could not count them or sort them out. And they were moving, revolving around her, above her, like a picture panel circling a candle and throwing fantastical designs behind it.

She took a step backward, feeling small and strange and dizzy. "I don't like this place," she whispered. "Take me back to the white room. I am afraid here."

"There is nothing to fear. You are perfectly safe," the voice responded, mercifully speaking in words that Susannah could understand.

"Take me back," she said again, even more softly.

"Come visit me," the voice said. "Very soon."

Susannah closed her eyes, to shut out the shifting, disorienting view. She put her hands out and felt behind her for the door, then stepped backward, one careful pace at a time. Once she was in the hallway, she shut the door before opening her eyes again. Back in the white corridor, an alien enough place, but not so strange as the place she had just been.

"Susannah," the voice said. "Come visit me soon."

"Not now," she whispered. "I want to go home."

She woke with a start, taking a quick gulp of air and feeling her body jerk so hard she elbowed Linus in the head. For a moment, she did not know where she was, and she was washed with a quick wave of panic, but then Paul sat up across the tent from her, and she remembered.

"I'm all right," she breathed, before he could speak and wake anyone else up. "Go back to sleep."

He did not lie back down, but peered at her through the darkness,

tilting his head so he could see her past the tent pole. "Another one
of your dreams?" he asked quietly. "You still get them?"

She nodded. "Sometimes. Usually they are pleasant enough. This
one was just a little strange."

He resettled himself on his pallet, but she could sense his eyes on
her even through the darkness. "You can tell me about it in the morning," he said.

She laughed softly. "By morning I will have forgotten it."

But she had not.

Sometime the day before, between sharing meals at the campfires and
singing in front of Bartholomew's tent, the Lohoras and the Tachitas
had agreed to travel on together for a few days. So when camp was
struck with its usual quick efficiency, Susannah elected to walk on
beside Ruth and the babies instead of keeping company with her own
tentmates. Paul and Linus occupied themselves with the packhorses,
and Susannah's father had joined up with the old men of the Lohora
clan, so Ruth and Susannah were able to talk freely without any eager
ears overhearing their observations. Ruth whispered news about Tachita girls, gossip about who was pursuing whom, and Susannah relayed
similar stories from clans she had encountered on the road. It was very
satisfying talk, although not always good-natured, and they both giggled and glanced around guiltily every time they repeated something
just a touch unsavory about someone else they knew.

"And then after all that, she chose to stay with a trader who works
along the river cities!" Ruth ended up one tale. "Moved into a house
there in Castelana and says she's not traveling with the clans ever
again. Can you imagine?"

"No," said Susannah. "But did she love him?"

Ruth shrugged. "He had a lot of gold and he brought her bolts
of the most beautiful silk cloth," she said. "I think she just loved the
idea of the luxury of the life she could have with him. She loved what
he could bring her, not the man himself."

Susannah nodded. "Well, she's part allali, isn't she?" she asked,
using the Edori word that meant "city-dweller"—or, in fact, anyone
who was not Edori. "Her mother was only half Edori, if I remember
right. Maybe part of her has always longed for a more comfortable
life."

"I don't think I would find it comfortable to be trapped in one
small house my whole life and see only the same view every day from
my windows," Ruth said. "But last I heard, she was determined to

become an allali in every respect. She was going to marry this man—"

"No!" Susannah exclaimed.

"Yes, and she was going to be dedicated to Yovah. And she had already begun calling the god 'Jovah,' as all the allali do. It sounded very strange, coming from her mouth."

Susannah lifted her hand to her own Kiss in her right arm, symbol of her dedication to the god nearly twenty-five years ago. "I did not know an adult could choose to be dedicated," she said slowly. "I thought only infants and children were given the Kiss."

Ruth shrugged. "Well, who knows about things like that? You and your brother are the only ones I ever knew who bore a Kiss, and it didn't seem to change your lives much. Do you think it makes you closer to the god? I find it hard to believe. He is so close to us already."

Susannah swept back her heavy black hair to expose her right ear, though Ruth had seen this particular revelation before. "Oh, but I am even more special to the god," she said in mock solemnity. "For I have another Kiss set right here on my skull."

Ruth paused a moment to inspect the sight, a second crystal node implanted right behind Susannah's ear, smaller than the one in her arm and completely colorless. "Well, I have always thought that must be such a bother," she said. "Doesn't it get in the way when you comb your hair? And doesn't it *hurt*?"

Susannah let her hair fall. "Oh, I can't feel it at all. I forget it's there for days at a time."

"I still would not want one," Ruth said. "Or a Kiss in my arm. I think they're very strange things."

Susannah shrugged. "They're gifts from Yovah," she said. "I don't mind them."

The baby, who had been riding in a sling against Ruth's stomach, woke just then and began to fuss. Ruth shushed him and began to rock him, crooning a soft lullaby. Susannah dropped back a few paces and then waved at Ruth, an offhand promise to hunt her up later. She cut through the slow parade of walkers and searched through the moving camp to find her tentmates.

Keren was nowhere in sight, but Anna and Tirza were easy to find, chatting amiably among the stragglers in the rear of the group. Anna did not move very fast, and sometimes Eleazar insisted she ride one of the horses, especially when the terrain was rough. But today, with two clans mingled and so many children to watch out for, the whole company was moving at a very sedate pace, and it did not matter how slowly Anna chose to walk.

"There you are! I thought you had decided to turn your back on the Lohoras now that you were with your true family again," Tirza greeted her.

"The Lohoras are my true family," Susannah said with a smile. "And I doubt any of you minded having one less body in your tent last night, though my brothers complained of how much room I took up. I! With my slim figure!" And she pirouetted quickly between one step and the next, and then laughed at her vanity.

Anna and Tirza exchanged quick glances. "Oh, you were in your brother's tent," Anna said. "Well. That is a good place to be."

Susannah felt her nerves flutter with apprehension. "Why, where did you think I was? Sleeping out by the fire like one of the old men? No, thank you, I do not wish to wake up with dew all over my face."

"Of course that's where we thought you were," Tirza said, sending a warning look at her lover's older sister. "I told Anna and Keren that you were tired of their cooking and had gone back to Ruth for something more nourishing."

"You said no such thing!" Susannah exclaimed.

They bantered a while longer, but Susannah felt her unease spread from the surface of her skin inward, until it knotted all her muscles and kinked up all her veins. When Anna stepped away to go look for Claudia, Susannah turned to Tirza.

"Tell me," she said with quiet determination. "You thought Dathan and I had left the tent together last night, didn't you? You thought that because he, too, was missing from the tent."

"I hoped you were with him," Tirza said.

"But you did not really think so," Susannah said. Her own voice was hard with the anger she was trying to hold inside. "You thought your brother was probably out all night with some pretty young girl from the Tachita tribe."

"Dathan is Dathan," Tirza said. The look on her face was sad, but the tone of her voice was pleading. As if she did not want Susannah to be angry enough to leave Dathan, as if she wanted Susannah to understand. "He is drawn to pretty girls. He always will be. That doesn't mean he does not love you, because he does. I never thought to see my brother so settled as he is with you, so content. Before he met you—every month, he was at some new girl's side. At every Gathering, at every chance-met campfire, he was flirting with the loveliest girl he could find. He was true to no one, till he met you. Susannah, he talked of you for an entire *year* after he first fell in love with you, and he didn't see you once between those two Gatherings. Do you know how amazing that is? For Dathan? I know he makes mistakes sometimes, but I believe he truly loves you."

Susannah said nothing during this entire speech, but merely walked along beside Tirza, biting her lip and staring down at the ground beneath her moving feet. It was true; she knew Dathan loved her. But she did not know if he loved her enough. She did not know if he loved her as much as she loved him, or if his feeling for her was fitful and fanciful, a brief high fire that burned even more brightly when it was fed foreign and exotic fuel. She did not want to share Dathan with all the pretty girls he would meet from now until his last Gathering. She did not want to share him with even one of them.

"Come back to the Lohora camp this evening," Tirza said in soft, persuasive tones. "I'm sure Dathan will be in our tent tonight."

"Are you?" Susannah said, more sharply than she intended. "He has not looked for me once today, which is strange since he must think I know where he slept last night. He must know I am not happy with him. Why hasn't he come to charm me out of my anger?"

Tirza looked dumbly back at her, and they both knew the answer to that. Because he was off somewhere with Cozbi, roaming ahead of the slow-moving caravan, on horseback maybe, or pretending to be off on a hunt. If Dathan realized he had something to apologize for, he seemed to think he had a few hours' grace before he needed to speak his piece.

Susannah put a hand out to Tirza's shoulder, a gesture of comfort. "Don't look so stricken, Tirza, this is not your quarrel," she said. "This is something Dathan and I must sort out ourselves. If we can."

"But Susannah—" Tirza said, but Susannah made a sharp gesture with her hand to cut her off.

"Not your quarrel," she said again. "Let's talk of something else."

It was late afternoon, and Susannah had returned to Ruth's side, before Dathan rejoined the clans. Susannah had not confided her troubles to Ruth, but the other woman could sense that something was wrong, and they had walked in silence for the rest of the journey. Paul had joined them once, when Bartholomew called a halt and they all took refreshment, and he had watched Susannah with concerned, narrowed eyes. But Ruth had shaken her head at him, so he had said nothing.

Ruth was the first one to spot Dathan, picking his way through the scattered walkers, clearly looking for someone. "There he is," she said quietly.

"Who?" Susannah said and, looking up, spotted Dathan. "Oh. I guess he's back."

"Give me the baby. He'll want to talk to you alone."

"Maybe I don't want to talk to him."

Ruth lifted the sleeping child from Susannah's arms. "Maybe you do," she said, and dropped back a few paces to leave Susannah striding along, angry and solitary and easily seen.

Dathan located her and quickly angled through the line of walkers to make his way to her side. She would not look at him, just kept putting one foot down in front of the other, and focused her eyes on the flat vista ahead. It would be time to camp in another hour or two. The days were long, this time of year, and they could go farther than they might during the winter months, but none of them liked to tax their strength so far. They had old ones and young ones in their group; there was no need to push themselves too hard.

"Here you are," he said, sidling up next to her and putting his arm around her shoulders. He bent down a little to peer into her face, which she kept averted. "I've been looking for you. Have you been walking with the Tachitas all day?"

"Except for the hour I was walking with your sister, when you were nowhere to be seen," Susannah said coldly.

"When was this? Earlier today? I was with the horses."

So they had gone off on horseback. Dathan was usually careful to use part of the truth any time he told a lie. Susannah said nothing.

"Have you been playing with your nephews? I saw you holding one a few moments ago. I know you miss them."

"Yes, very much," she said.

He squeezed her shoulder. "You could have a baby of your own, you know," he said. "Then you would not miss them so deeply."

"Or I could live with the Tachitas again, and then I would not have to miss them at all."

"No, no, I would not like that," he said softly, leaning in to kiss her on the cheek. "It would be much better for you to stay with the Lohoras and bear your children for my clan."

She came to an abrupt halt, and he stumbled and dropped his arm and came around to face her. "But not with you, Dathan," she said clearly. "I would not choose to have your children until I was sure that you would be prepared to be a good father to them, and a faithful lover to me, and I do not think that day will ever come—when I am sure of you."

"Don't say such a thing, Susannah," he said. "You can be sure of me. There is no one and nothing I love as much as I love you."

"Dathan, you spent last night in the arms of another girl!"

"That's not true!" he said swiftly.

"You did not sleep in your own tent."

"And neither did you!" he shot back.

"Oh, yes! I slept in the tent of my brother's providing. Four others can testify to that. But your sister cannot tell me where you spent the night—and I don't think you have the nerve to."

"I didn't want to tell you because I knew you would be angry! But we were drinking—I was, and some of the Tachitas, and a few Lohoras, but not very many. And the hour grew late, and we were embarrassed to crawl back to our tents, smelling of wine, so we slept under the stars and had rocks under our ribs and woke in the morning feeling very sorry for ourselves. And it is not a very responsible thing to have done, but it is not as bad as what you believe of me!"

She stared at him a long time, trying to read his face, trying to gauge how much of the story was true. No doubt his evening had ended under the stars in the company of the revelers, but how had it begun? Where had he gone once the singing stopped and everyone left the communal fire?

"Cozbi is a good girl, and a truthful one," she said slowly. "If I ask her something, she will tell me. Shall I find her right now, and ask her where she spent her evening? Are you at all afraid of the answer she might give me?"

Dathan flung himself away from her and began following the rest of the caravan, now a good twenty yards beyond them. "I don't care! Ask what you like! But you shame me and yourself by proving to everyone that you don't trust me."

She followed him more slowly. Was that a bluff? Did he really think she would not ask? Or was he truly innocent, this time, truly willing to have her know every detail of his evening?

And even if he was telling the truth, this time, could she bear to spend the rest of her life questioning his activities every time he was out of her sight? Was that any way to live, suspicious and hard-hearted and angry? But was it possible to live without him?

She strode on alone for a few moments in a state of blind despair.

She had not gone very far when Dathan fell in step beside her, having waited for her after all. She glanced up at him, giving him a small, unhappy smile. Neither of them said anything, but neither of them pulled away.

That night, to soothe everyone's frayed nerves, Susannah's two families set up their tents side by side and shared a common campfire. Bartholomew joined them just for the company. Anna and Tirza insisted that Ruth sit still and tend her baby while they made the meal for both tents, and Keren was unexpectedly charming as she entertained the two-year-old. The men built up the fire, and Susannah's father and Eleazar held a grave discussion about the proper way to strike a tent in the middle of a rainstorm. Susannah thought, as she looked over the whole busy group, that she wished they could travel together forever, all the people she loved in one small caravan. That would truly be the god's paradise on earth.

They had just settled themselves down to eat dinner, all of them laughing as they crowded close around the fire, when they heard a ripple of wonder run through the whole mingled campsite. It was low and instantly silenced, for the Edori did not believe in showing much astonishment, but the attention of the whole camp was soon directed upward. The adults tilted their heads casually toward the sky, and a few children pointed, but they were determined not to be amazed at the apparition forming overhead.

And rapidly descending.

It was an angel, a man, oddly dressed in scanty leather flying gear and appearing, from this angle, twice the size of any ordinary human. His wings, spread to their widest to cushion his landing, looked big enough to wrap twice around a standing tent. The sun was behind him, so it was hard to see more of him than his graceful, gorgeous shape, like something out of a legend or a ballad. "And then an angel of the god appeared and said, 'Do not be afraid . . .' "

And Susannah was not afraid, not exactly, but a little thrill of apprehension ran along her veins. Never in her life had she seen a sight so imposing and so magnificent as this: an angel landing beside her campfire at sunset and stepping forward, out of the mystery of his own shadow, to resolve into a grave and earnest man.

CHAPTER FIVE

The little Jansai girl had told them nothing. That whole slow, weary flight back to the Eyrie, she had slept in Zibiah's arms, waking once in a while to utter a few whimpering cries, and then sleeping again when the angel offered her a soothing lullaby.

It was past midnight when they landed on the Eyrie's plateau and Zibiah, exhausted, laid her burden on the stone itself. Gaaron said to Nicholas, "Get Esther."

"She'll be asleep," Nicholas said.

"Wake her."

Esther, when she arrived, looked even more sharp-featured and irritable than when she hadn't been woken from a pleasant dream, but she quickly took charge of the situation. "We'll take her to that little room down the hall from Miriam. No one's using it now, and I know the linens are clean. I'll bring her some food and water and stay beside her tonight."

"Zibiah, you stay as well."

Zibiah turned to him with her eyes wide and smoky with fatigue. "If you want," she said.

Gaaron put a hand on her shoulder as if to offer her some of his own strength. "She trusts you," he said gently. "At least a little bit. You can sleep while she sleeps. Just—stay with her for now."

Zibiah nodded mutely and stumbled down the hall after Esther.

Gaaron went to his room and composed a note to Adriel, describing what they'd found and why they'd gone to southern Bethel in the first place. The Archangel might have better theories than he had—or more information about similar bizarre occurrences in other parts of Samaria.

Next he headed up to the cupola, where four voices were performing a quiet cantata, and waited till the current song ended. Then he motioned to Ahio, the only angel in the group, and drew him a few feet away so as not to disturb the other three singers, who stared after them in frank curiosity.

"Are you rested enough to start out for Windy Point tonight?" Gaaron asked. "Or have you been up all day and night, as usual?"

Ahio grinned. He was a relaxed and easygoing young man who seemed to get along effortlessly with everyone in the hold, male and female, angel and mortal. A little lazy, Gaaron had always thought him, though he never appeared to be shirking his duties or shifting his responsibilities to others. Perhaps it was his casual approach to everything that gave the appearance of indolence.

"I've slept well and deeply in the past day, thank you very much for your concern," Ahio replied. "I can easily start off for Windy Point. Do you need to await a reply from Adriel?"

"Yes, I'm sure she'll want to send one."

Ahio cocked his head to one side. He was fair-haired, dark-eyed, and strongly built. Gaaron had always thought he looked like an angel straight out of the Librera, except for the cheerfulness of his face. Librera angels always came across as stern and wrathful, meting out the justice of the god.

"It must be something fairly important to send me off to Jordana in the middle of the night," Ahio said. Not asking outright, but making it clear he would like to know the story.

Gaaron hesitated, then shrugged. Not a chance that Nicholas and Zibiah would not spread this story to everyone in the hold within the half hour. "We went to southern Bethel today—yesterday, I guess—to find some farmers that Nicholas said had seen a strange man appearing and disappearing."

Ahio nodded. "Seemed like an unlikely tale."

Gaaron snorted. "I agree, but the farmers held to their story, and I have to say, if it was true, it's an alarming one. Because there's nowhere in those fields where someone could hide."

"And this is what you want to tell Adriel?"

Gaaron shook his head. "No. Well, that's part of it. As we flew back, we came across a campsite that had been . . ." Gaaron spread his hands, unequal to finding the right word. "Annihilated. Burned beyond recognition. Men, horses, wagons, everything. I cannot imagine what kind of fire caused that kind of destruction. And then, not far from the campsite, we found a Jansai girl, maybe ten years old. Zibiah carried her back here. I'm assuming she was a little distance from the camp when it was destroyed, and maybe she can tell us what happened. But—at least so far—she won't speak to us. Maybe in the morning, when she's calmer. But I'm not so sure. In any case, Adriel needs to know."

Ahio nodded. "Let me pack some food, and I'll leave within the hour."

"Thank you," Gaaron said gravely.

Ahio flashed that easy smile. "I am happy to be of service to the Archangel-elect."

And that sort of flippancy, Gaaron thought as he made his way down to his own quarters, *is exactly the sort of thing that makes me doubtful of Ahio.* But perhaps he had meant it. Perhaps, like Nicholas, he was proud to be a member of the hold that could boast the next Archangel of Samaria. And perhaps he also admired the angel who would lead all the hosts and guard the entire realm for the next twenty years. Gaaron had admired his own father, in the moments he hadn't hated him. Admired him for his decisiveness, his strength of purpose, his unswervable will.

Hated him for almost everything else.

Gaaron pushed open the door to his room, half expecting some other crisis to be perched in one of his chairs, awaiting his arrival. But no, the room was blessedly empty, mercifully quiet. Gaaron stripped off his flying leathers, gave his face and upper body a cursory wash in the water room, and fell into bed. He did not have another thought till morning.

He woke to find Miriam curled up in the big armchair under his window, reading a book. The sunlight fell in through the open shutter as if it had tripped over the sill in astonishment at the sight of her pretty face. It lit her blond hair like a restless wick and made a moving flame of her head as she glanced from side to side.

When she saw Gaaron's eyes were open, she jumped up and went to sit on the edge of his bed. She looked very young and extremely pleased.

"Gaaron! When I told you to come back from the southern farms with an interesting story, I did not really think you would succeed so dramatically," she said.

He smiled, and lifted a hand, briefly, to touch that blond hair. Once she moved out of direct sunlight it was not quite as lambent but still full of its own self-important luster. "So you've heard the news," he said. "How is the little Jansai girl this morning?"

Miriam grew instantly serious. "Not so good. She's refusing to eat and she won't let anyone but Zibiah near her. Poor Zib is just exhausted, but the girl won't stop clinging to her, and, of course, Zibiah won't leave her side."

"Good for Zibiah," Gaaron said, sitting up in bed and reaching for a glass of water. Sweet Jovah singing, he was tired. "What about Esther? Isn't she helping out?"

"The Jansai girl hates her," Miriam said with a certain smugness. "Screams every time Esther comes in the room."

Gaaron could not help but grin at that. "And you? Have you tried to take a turn?"

Miriam nodded. "Yes, and she let me stay in the room, at least. She actually slept a little bit when Zibiah and I sang a couple of lullabies. And she drank some water. But she won't eat. And she won't talk. Gaaron, what happened to her?"

Gaaron told his version of the story, though he was pretty sure she had gotten accounts from both Nicholas and Zibiah already. "And if she were just any ordinary girl, no doubt she would be traumatized and unable to speak for a day or two, but a Jansai . . ." He shrugged. "I doubt we'll ever get her to tell us what happened."

"What are you going to do?" she asked.

He yawned mightily, unable to stop himself. If he was this tired, he could only imagine how Zibiah must feel. "As soon as Ahio comes back from Windy Point, I'm going to fly out to Breven and see if I can convince one of the Jansai to come back here," he said. "Surely she'll talk to one of her own people. Maybe we'll learn something then."

Miriam smiled. "That's what I told Zibiah," she said.

"You told her that I would fly out to Breven?"

"No, I told her that you would know what to do."

Gaaron regarded his sister helplessly for a moment. She looked completely sincere. So many souls relying on him—Nicholas, Ahio, Miriam, Esther, everyone in the hold—so many truly believing that he knew, he always knew, exactly what to do all of the time. He felt that familiar weight settle onto his back, and he straightened up in bed to help him catch his balance.

"Well, all I want to do right now is get up and put on some clothes," Gaaron said. "So out you go. I'll check in with you later."

She scooted out the door, and he slowly rose and dressed. It was a day in which not much could be accomplished; certainly he could not expect a reply from Adriel before tomorrow. It would take Ahio eighteen hours or more to fly to Windy Point, and he would have to rest both on the way and before he attempted the flight back.

It occurred to Gaaron only after breakfast that he did not have to await the Archangel's reply before he set off for Breven to make his own inquiries.

He paused in his eating to consider this. Adriel might have similar tales to tell him, of random fires on the Jordana plains or strange men flickering in and out of view right on the edge of the Caitana Mountains, but he could not imagine that, even if she did, she had interpreted these events any more definitively than he had. And he needed to get to Breven as soon as he could, to inform the Jansai that one of their own was even now recuperating in the Eyrie hold. Adriel's reply could wait upon his own return; he need not waste any more time.

Therefore, as soon as he finished his meal, he called to Esther and asked her to fix him a pouch of traveling rations. She looked disapproving, for she never liked it when he was gone from the hold overnight, but all she said was, "How many days will you be gone?"

Two days to fly to Breven—a few hours there—a night of rest—two days to fly back. "At least two days' worth. I'll get food for the return journey there," he said. "I'll leave within the hour."

Then he had to seek out Miriam, to tell her where he was going, and inform the other angels that he would be gone a few days; they must take turns greeting the petitioners who arrived, looking for mediation. It was a matter of a few minutes to pack several changes of clothes, for he required no formal wear to visit with the Jansai. He slung a pack over his shoulder, carefully fitting the strap between the joints of his wings and cinching it around his waist so that it did not inconvenience him while he was flying. He flexed his shoulders. The fit was perfect.

Once he had picked up his food, he was off. The morning was clean and as sweet-scented as freshly washed laundry, and the air felt as soft against his skin as well-worn cotton. He was traveling alone; he could fly as high and as fast as he liked, which, today, was very high and very fast. His skin prickled with the cold of the upper atmosphere, but the sensation invigorated him. Most of his life, he was too warm. Like all angels, he had hot blood designed to withstand the frigid air at high altitudes—and he, with his big body and bulky muscles, had an even higher temperature than most. It was always a relief to him to plunge upward, into the icy reaches of the heavens, and it was even better when the unfriendly color of night enhanced the illusion of chill. He preferred the winter feel of starlight on his skin.

He flew on for hours without stopping, crossing the Galilee River before he even considered touching down for a rest. A quick break for food, then he was aloft again, winging on toward the coast, just south of the Caitanas and a little east of the mountain range that turned this edge of Jordana into a desert. He was feeling strong and relaxed, well into his easy rhythm of downbeat and upswing, and thought perhaps he could fly straight through to Breven without stopping for the night. But that was stupid. He would arrive dull and tired and incoherent, and a man always needed his wits about him when dealing with the Jansai.

So he dropped down to cruising altitude and began to scan the ground below him for a pattern of lights that would indicate a town big enough to boast an inn. He found one about an hour later, though it wasn't much of a town or, in fact, much of an inn. The proprietor, a thin and balding older man, wore a calculating expression that just now was overlaid with awe at the angel's arrival.

"My best room—that you'll have—my very best room," the man chattered, scrawling something down in his desktop ledger.

In lieu of payment, Gaaron flashed his bracelets, universal currency for angels on the road. They were thick gold bands set with a triangular pattern of sapphires—the blue gems to represent the Eyrie, the pattern to signify Gaaron's lineage. The Eyrie would accordingly be charged for Gaaron's stay. "I would prefer that no one wake me in the morning," Gaaron said. "But you may not see me anyway, since I will be on my way early."

"Very good. As the angelo wishes. This way, please."

The room was small, the bed lumpy, and the heat high. Gaaron cleaned himself up and then lay down gingerly, seeking an easy place to rest his spine so that his wing joints did not dig into the mattress. There appeared to be no comfortable spot on this bed. He groaned, turned to his side, and prepared to spend a miserable night.

He was up with the sun, ate a quick breakfast in the tavern adjoining the inn, and was on his way again forty minutes after opening his eyes. Bright sunshine made the flying pleasant, especially when he rose high enough to escape the sun's heat, but once he crossed into the desert, even the upper atmosphere became oppressive. His wings slowed and he lost altitude, seeking a brisker current of air. None to be had. He coasted into Breven feeling hot, sticky, and about fifty pounds heavier than when he'd started out.

And Breven was not a sight to gladden any man's soul. They called it a city, but it was little more than a collection of wagons and canvas huts and open-air markets, all looking as impermanent as an Edori camp. The Jansai were wanderers, gypsies, merchants, and peddlers, as well as thieves and cheats, and when they returned to the place most of them considered home, it was only for a brief visit. So there were few buildings more durable than shacks thrown together from a few planks of wood, and a large outlying band of wagons and campsites encircling the heart of the city for about ten miles deep.

Gaaron came to his feet in what passed for the business district, the collection of awnings and canopies that made up the most varied and cutthroat market of the three provinces. Vendors called to him, smells assaulted him, small boys darted past him shouting out unintelligible words. This close to the sandy soil, the air was unbearably hot. The heat rose through the leather soles of his boots and burned his feet.

Gaaron strode to the closest merchant's stall and did not bother to engage the vendor in polite chatter. "I'm looking for Solomon," he said brusquely. "Is he here?"

"Good Angelo, you have traveled far—you must be hungry. Here, a nice dish of spiced-wine stew—only a few coppers, the best you've tasted—"

"I'm not interested in food," Gaaron said. "I need Solomon immediately. Where is he?"

"A glass of wine, then, or flavored water? I assure you, nowhere in Breven will you find a more—"

Gaaron slammed a fistful of silver coins onto the vending table. "Solomon," he said flatly.

The man jerked his thumb over his shoulder. "The big tent at the far southern edge of the market. Blue-and-white stripes."

"Thank you," Gaaron said with an edge, and pushed himself through the crowd in the direction indicated. All the buyers were men, of course—all the vendors as well. Not a woman to be seen anywhere on the hot, dusty streets of Breven.

At the blue-and-white tent, Gaaron had to introduce himself to a villainous-looking old man guarding the entrance, but his name was actually good enough to gain him a quick entrée. He ducked his head to step through the canvas door, into the welcome coolness of shade, and then stood there a moment to get his bearings. The interior of the tent was at least as big as his two-room suite at the Eyrie, though not partitioned into separate chambers. It was filled with exotic furnishings—rugs of animal fur, chairs of stretched leather, glass globes of light hanging from highly figured bronze poles. Half a dozen people lounged around on brightly colored chairs and pallets, dressed in flowing robes of gaudy colors. All were covered in rings and necklaces and bracelets of thick gold; all were men.

One of them broke free of a conference and waddled over to the angel's side. "Gaaron!" he exclaimed, holding out a meaty hand and smiling up from the folds of fat on his broad face. He was even more brightly dressed than the other men, in clashing colors of scarlet and lavender, and he wore jewel studs in his ears next to big hoops of gold. "What brings you all the way to Breven from your inhospitable mountain hold?"

Gaaron smiled briefly and shook the gypsy's hand. A shrewd, cunning, and not altogether honest man, Solomon was the richest of the Jansai and the closest thing they had to a leader. Gaaron didn't trust him at all, but he could never bring himself to entirely despise the man. He had a greasy charm and swift flashes of insight that made him, when he chose to be, a formidable ally.

"News that you might not hear from any other source for days or weeks," Gaaron said. "And a question."

Without asking how private the information was, Solomon turned toward the others in the tent. "Out," he said, waving his hand in one grand sweeping gesture. Without a word of protest, the others filed from the tent.

"Water? Wine? Refreshment of any kind?" Solomon said, leading the angel back to an arrangement of furniture in the middle of the tent. Gaaron chose a backless stool covered with dyed leather. Solomon sunk into a wide, soft armchair that looked as if it had been crafted especially for him. "You are my guest. There will be no charge."

This was said with some sarcasm. Gaaron could not help grinning. "Then, yes, I would like a chance to sample your hospitality."

Solomon poured them both drinks, something sweet-tasting and wonderfully refreshing after the long flight and the hot city streets. "And what is your news?" the gypsy chieftain asked.

"I was with some other angels flying over southern Bethel a couple of days ago," Gaaron said somberly. "We spotted a Jansai campsite— completely destroyed by fire. Impossible to tell how many were in the group, and there was nothing left that I could bring back as a clue for you to learn the identities of the travelers. I believed it was Jansai because the embers appeared to be shaped like Jansai wagons."

Solomon was silent a moment, absorbing that. His broad, shiny face seemed remotely sad. "So. Another one," he said at last.

That jerked Gaaron upright on his stool. "Another one? You mean other Jansai camps have been destroyed like this?"

Solomon shrugged. "Jansai—Edori—who can say? There were not even shapes left in the cinders for us to be able to judge. But everything was burned, and no one was left alive." He looked over at Gaaron in the dim light of the tent. "Some of our people found a site like that five days ago not far from Luminaux. Who knows how long ago it happened?"

"Would you have any idea what caused such a thing?"

"No. Would you?" the gypsy shot back.

Gaaron shook his head. "No. But there may have been a witness at the site we found. A Jansai girl, about ten years old. We found her not far from the camp, hysterical. So far she will not talk to us."

"And she should not ever talk to you, if she is a good girl," Solomon said. "One of our women among the men of the Eyrie!"

Gaaron brushed this aside. "She's a child. And she's afraid. And we need the information she has. I thought you would be willing to send someone back to the Eyrie to question her."

"If it is so important to you to get answers from her, why did you not bring her with you today?"

Gaaron smiled somewhat grimly. "She barely survived the flight to the Eyrie in the arms of a female angel. I did not think she could endure a flight of several hundred miles in my arms. Terror would have struck her dead."

"As modesty should have," Solomon muttered.

"But it did not, and I believe she has been spared for a purpose," Gaaron said sharply. "Will you send someone? As quickly as you can?"

Solomon eyed him speculatively. "And if I do? What is such a service worth to the man who will be Archangel?"

Gaaron smiled again, a more feral expression this time. "I imagine, what it would be worth to *you*," he said gently. "Information about any man or creature menacing travelers upon the road would have to be of interest to the Jansai."

Solomon stared back at him a moment, and then gave a gut-deep laugh. "You can't blame a man for testing his limits," he said genially, and poured more liquid into both their glasses. "But I doubt she will be able to tell us much."

"I hope you're wrong," Gaaron said. "For if there have been two such attacks—you know of only one other?—two such attacks, we have to assume there may be more. We need to know what we are facing."

"I have told the Jansai to ride with care. I assume the Edori are likewise spreading the news among their clans."

"If they even know of it."

"They know," Solomon said. "We saw tracks of Edori horses by the burned campsite."

"And the river merchants? Have you told them the story?"

"All the Jansai are carrying it across the provinces. Before the week is out, I would guess every farmer from here to the north edge of Gaza will have heard the rumors."

"I would appreciate," Gaaron said, "being apprised of all such occurrences in the future. Anytime something untoward happens, anywhere across Samaria, I would like to be told of it."

"Certainly, Gabriel," Solomon said, his eyebrows raised high.

Gaaron smiled. "And for that, I will pay a service fee. When the goods are delivered."

Solomon smiled back. "Ah, now we understand each other, Archangel-elect. I will be happy to do business with you over the next twenty years."

• • •

Gaaron did not linger in Breven; he could not imagine anyone ever did. He did offer to fly a Jansai interpreter to the Eyrie, but Solomon laughed at him.

"And how would this Jansai return to Breven without horse or wagon to sustain him? And how would you carry both a man and a woman all that way from the desert to your mountain? And do you think we would really allow any of our women to be held so close in a man's arms for any purpose whatsoever? Gabriel! I thought you understood us better than that."

"I was merely thinking of the time I could save," Gaaron said, coming to his feet and preparing to exit. "I apologize if I said something offensive."

Solomon followed him to the tent door, where the coiled heat was waiting to hiss and strike. "Time is not something about which the Jansai worry greatly," Solomon said. "We will be there when we arrive."

With that promise, Gaaron had to be content. He flung himself aloft, anxious to shake the actual dust of Breven from his wings, and struck a course that was almost due west over the mountains. He would not make it back tonight, but perhaps, this time, he could break his journey at Castelana or one of the other river cities, someplace that boasted accommodations a bit more civilized than the inn he'd slept in the night before.

However, he did not cover the miles as quickly as he'd hoped. The sultry desert air dragged on him, made his wings clumsy and sluggish, and once he got over the mountains, things did not improve much. A storm was brewing over the Jordana prairie, and the combination of wind and humidity made the flying both tricky and slow. By the time he got clear of the bad weather, he was tired and sunset was not far away. And he was nowhere near the Galilee River.

He banked and descended a little to scout the ground below for signs of a settlement, though he could easily fly another hour or more before he had to look for shelter. This part of Jordana was fairly well populated, since it was on the direct trade route from Breven to the river cities, and Gaaron was certain he'd find something acceptable before true night came on.

What he found, and what, on impulse, he dropped down to investigate, was an Edori campsite. Mysterious fires and lost Jansai girls should not combine to make him forget that he had another mission to complete in the near future. He landed softly, rocking forward to shift his weight from his wings to his feet, and strode forward to see what he might find at the camp.

CHAPTER SIX

Children ran forward to greet Gaaron, and the adult Edori came to their feet, looking mildly curious but completely welcoming. "Angelo, Angelo!" the children cried out as they came close enough to touch. One or two of them actually put their fingers out to his feathers, and Gaaron twitched his wings away, folding them back as tightly as they would go.

"Children," a voice admonished, and Gaaron found himself face-to-face with one of those indistinguishable Edori, all tan skin and long black hair. This one was male, and bigger than most, though not Gaaron's size or height. "Apologize for your rudeness. You would not stroke a strange woman's hair just because it was of an unfamiliar color. Do not touch the angel without his permission."

"Sorry, Angelo," came from a chorus of voices, and the children stepped back, though they did not disperse. Gaaron smiled at his rescuer.

"Thank you," he said. "No angel enjoys having his wings tugged on and poked."

"No, and I would not like anyone to pull on my beard, either," the Edori replied. "Despite the roughness of our greeting, we are happy to see you here. May we offer you dinner? A place to stay for the night? We are just settling down for our evening meal and would be happy to have you join us."

He had never broken bread with the Edori before. Until Mahalah had named his bride-to-be, it had never occurred to him to try it. But, unless he was luckier than the laws of chance generally allowed, this would not be his last foray into an Edori camp, so he had better get used to the customs.

"I would be happy to share your meal," he said formally. "I regret that I have nothing to offer to share."

The Edori laughed. "Your company, Angelo, your company! And, if you choose to stay afterward, your voice as we sing around the campsite tonight. That would be a splendid gift."

Was he serious? Did he really expect the Archangel-elect to lead a few Edori ballads after the meal was over? Then again, perhaps none of these people recognized him. It was a fact he'd never seen any of them before. "My name is Gabriel Aaron, and I lead the host at the Eyrie," Gaaron said. "People generally call me Gaaron."

"Then that is how I shall introduce you," the other man replied. "I am Bartholomew of the Lohoras. I am eating with friends tonight. Let me take you to their fire."

So Gaaron followed Bartholomew to a big fire where there seemed to be a dozen people gathered together, all cooking and talking and trying not to stare at the angel in their midst. Bartholomew gave all their names, but Gaaron only caught one or two, and could not have assigned them to the relevant face if he had been quizzed five minutes later. One of the women was named Susannah, and for a moment his heart leapt up, but she was holding a baby that looked like her, and she was here with the Lohoras. Gaaron did not think Jovah would have chosen for him a woman who was already wife and mother.

"Sit, please, Gaaron, and someone will serve you. Will this chair do for you? No, I suppose not. I do not know how you can be comfortable with those wings dragging behind you, but I suppose—ah, yes, thank you, Eleazar, that stool looks like just the right thing—"

In a few moments, Gaaron was seated on a rickety stool before the fire, a battered metal plate on his knees and a circle of smiling Edori faces watching him from around the fire. Someone sang a quick prayer of grace, and then they all began eating. The food was surprisingly good.

"I would compliment the cook, whoever she is," Gaaron said to the young woman sitting beside him. She was pretty and smiling, and he wondered if all Edori sat so close to their friends around the fire, or if she had deliberately drawn her own chair as near to him as she could get.

"I am one of them," she said with a sideways look and another smile. "I like to cook. What do angels generally eat? I can make almost anything."

"Oh—we eat what I imagine everyone eats," Gaaron said. "Meat and vegetables and bread. Cakes and pastries."

"I love pastries—those wonderful, sweet cherry-and-nut breads that you can get in places like Luminaux," she said wistfully. "You have to live in the city to get such luxuries."

He could not help but smile. "And do you like luxuries?"

"Oh, yes!" she exclaimed. "Every single one of them."

"Keren is a Luminauzi at heart," said a woman on the other side of the lovely girl. This one, he was pretty sure, was the one named Susannah. "She loves beautiful things. Craves them."

"I would live in Luminaux if everybody else would," Keren said, something of a pout on her full lips. "But no one else will stay, and I do not want to be the only Edori in the Blue City."

Susannah lifted a hand to stroke Keren's fine black hair. At a guess, Gaaron would put the young Keren down as a vain and shallow flirt, but this Susannah seemed to feel a genuine affection for her. "And what would we do without you if you chose to stay in Luminaux?" Susannah asked her gently. "You must live with the Edori always, and pick up such luxuries as you may upon the road."

Keren wrinkled her nose, then smiled and turned her attention back to the angel. "What kinds of luxuries do you have in the Eyrie?" she wanted to know. "Do you eat little pastries every day? Do you dine on plates of gold or silver? Do your women dress in silk?"

Involuntarily, Gaaron looked across Keren's head and met Susannah's gaze. The other woman smiled and raised her shoulders in a tiny shrug. *What are you going to do with the envious young?* she seemed to say.

"We have some extravagances, I suppose," Gaaron said. "Though we are nothing like the Manadavvi. Have you ever traveled north to Gaza? There some of the wealthy own so much land that a man cannot walk from one end of his property to the other in a single day. I have seen Manadavvi who use diamonds as buttons for their shirts. And, in fact, at a Manadavvi household I have eaten off of gold plates. But not at the Eyrie. We are too busy working to concern ourselves too much with niceties."

Keren seemed disappointed by the conclusion of Gaaron's remarks, though she had been enthralled with the description of the Manadavvi. Susannah stirred and looked more interested, though. "What kind of work do the angels do?" she asked. "I admit, I am not used to considering you engaged in hard labor."

He grinned at her over Keren's head. "Well, sometimes by the end of the day I feel that is exactly what I have been doing," he said. "But mostly I am just talking. The merchants and the farmers come to have me settle disputes. Sometimes there is a disagreement about who owns what land, sometimes they need a mediator to help them reach some kind of trading arrangement. The Archangel and the leader of the host at Monteverde send me news and questions. The oracles tell me of pronouncements Jovah has made. And, of course, any number of people can visit the Eyrie to ask for a weather intercession—"

But he had lost her attention. "'Jovah'," she repeated. "I have heard that is how you angels name the god."

He was utterly confused. "That is his name."

"We call him Yovah. All Edori do."

It was as if someone had told him his sister's name was not Miriam, or his own name was not Gabriel. He could not at first credit it. "That is—but how can you call him by a name that is not his?"

Susannah was smiling. Keren, on the other hand, looked completely bored. "I imagine Yovah has many names," Susannah remarked. "I imagine people see him in many different ways. But he is wise, and he knows who calls on him and what they need from him, and he never fails to answer a prayer no matter how he is addressed."

"To me the god has always been direct and unchanging," Gaaron said a little stiffly.

Susannah smiled again. "To the Edori, very few things are simple or unchanging," she remarked. "I am sure our way of life would be very strange for you—and your way of life very strange to us."

"I wouldn't mind learning the angel way of life," Keren interjected. "Even if you do work all the time. I would still like to see what the life is like."

"Would you?" Susannah asked softly. "I don't think I would like it at all. I would miss my family and my freedom if I were living in one of those stone holds. I have not been to Monteverde, but I have seen Windy Point. From a distance. From below. It is so high up you can barely view it from the ground. And it looks so cold and so unfriendly that it makes me shiver."

"Windy Point is placed rather inhospitably," Gaaron acknowledged, "though it is a welcoming enough hold once you get inside it. And, like Windy Point, the Eyrie is hard to reach, for an angel must fly you up to the very top. But it is quite a beautiful place, full of warmth and music. You might like it better than you think."

Keren had turned her big eyes on Susannah. "Not that you are any more likely to go to either one of those places than I am," she scoffed.

"True," Susannah said. "I just want to less."

Before Gaaron could think of an answer to that, the people sitting around the campfire began to shift closer together. He looked up and noticed that others were joining them from their smaller fires. Keren edged even closer to Gaaron, then smiled up at him when her arm brushed against his.

"What is happening now?" he asked her.

"Oh, everyone is coming together to sing," she said. "We have done so every night that the clans have traveled together. You could join in, if you like," she added naively. "Everyone's voice is welcome."

"Thank you," he said, and dared not look at Susannah at that point. But he could feel her smiling again. Or still.

Bartholomew was escorting the others over to Gaaron for their own introductions, so he rose to his feet and said polite hellos to a collection of men and women he would never recognize again. To their credit, he thought, they did not make much fuss over him. They treated him with the casual friendliness they might extend to anyone who happened to wander up to their campfire at night, angel or no. He could not decide if he found the lack of ceremony refreshing or just a little annoying.

The others reseated themselves, but Bartholomew stayed on his feet. "Let us thank Yovah for his many gifts this day," the Edori said. He offered a prayer in a language that Gaaron did not know, but he listened appreciatively to the simple melody and the fine voice that delivered it. A chorus of Edori voices came in on the amen, much as angel voices might have in the same situation, and Gabriel appreciated that as well. Perhaps he would have something in common with his Edori bride after all, if they both loved music.

Keren had jumped to her feet, tugging on Susannah's arm. "Sing with me," she demanded, and Susannah obligingly stood beside her. "That song that Ruth sang the other night. I will start it."

Keren's voice was high and full of emotion, though not particularly strong, and Gaaron settled himself more comfortably to listen to it. He did not know this song, either, but at least this time he could understand the words. And the melody was not difficult. By the time she had sung it straight through twice, he would have been able to match her on it, note for note, had he been so inclined.

But then she skipped into the next verse, and Susannah's voice joined to Keren's, and Gaaron lost all inclination to do anything but listen.

Susannah had a rich alto voice, and it wrapped around Keren's sugar-sweet voice like a decadent layer of cream. The song was a tale of lost love, found love, everlasting love, and the twined voices made the story seem tragic and then triumphant. Keren's thin soprano was given extra depth and texture by Susannah's smooth alto, though the lower voice never intruded on the brilliance of the higher, just filled it out and made it glorious. Gaaron listened, amazed. He hoped the song would never come to an end.

It did, of course, but instantly someone else called for Susannah to join in a duet. This time her partner was a young boy, maybe fifteen years old, whose reedy baritone could never have sustained any song all on its own. But Susannah, singing the harmony above the melody line, drew the other voice upward, lent it strength and range. Everyone around the campfire applauded heartily when the piece was over, leading Gaaron to suspect that this was one of the first times this number had been done in public, or at least successfully.

"Linus! One more!" someone called out, but the boy shook his head and quickly took his seat.

"Susannah! Over here!" a woman called, and Susannah stepped a few paces over. This new piece was more lively, and the other singer's voice was almost as strong as Susannah's, so it was quite dizzyingly beautiful to listen to. Their voices were nearly matched in range, so the harmonies were close, and at times the two lines became unison. The effect was of a length of bronze velvet folding and unfolding, revealing first one rich layer, then two, then just a single unbroken swatch of gorgeous color.

They finished the song on a few quick key changes, then burst into breathless laughter at the end. As before, the performance was greeted with acclaim, and the two women bowed at the crowd, then at each other, then at the crowd again, clearly enjoying themselves.

Gaaron turned to Keren as casually as he could. "Your Susannah appears to be much in demand," he said. "Of course, she has an excellent voice."

"Oh, everyone likes to pair up with Susannah, because she makes even the worst singer sound good," Keren said carelessly. "At the Gathering, all the old women with their cracked voices and all the little girls who can hardly hold a note, they all want Susannah to sing with them. I don't know what they do for harmony the rest of the year."

Bartholomew, who had moved to the angel's other side, now spoke up fondly. "Yes, the Lohoras can hear that lovely voice any night they choose, but the Tachitas must wait for happy fate to unite them again with their daughter."

"Tachitas?" Gaaron said sharply. "What do—are the Lohoras friends of the Tachitas? Do you travel together often?"

Bartholomew shrugged. "When we encounter them, which we do from time to time. It makes Susannah happy to be again with her brothers and her father. And her nephews. So we travel with that clan when we can."

"Susannah—she is originally of the Tachitas?" Gaaron demanded, feeling his face heat and his bones seem to swell. His tongue, too, had expanded, and made his words thick and stupid. "And—you say—she has nephews? No children of her own?"

"Not yet," Keren said softly. "But we all hope they will come soon."

I must speak with Susannah, Gaaron wanted to say. *I must tell her of the life in store for her.* But that sounded lunatic; he could not make such an announcement to Bartholomew. Sweet Jovah singing, he could not make such an announcement to Susannah herself. What would he say to her? He had given this particular conversation no thought at all in the past weeks.

"Susannah!" a lazy voice called out, and a beautiful young man came to his feet. "Sing with me."

His mind busy with his problem, Gaaron still had attention to spare for the drama going on before him. Was it his imagination, or did Susannah hesitate a moment before moving through the circle to stand at the side of this handsome creature? Did her face lose its smiling look as she gazed up at him? Was his own smile coaxing and hopeful?

Was this the man Keren hoped would someday father Susannah's babies? Who was he? Who was he to Susannah?

They began to sing, and for a moment, Gaaron forgot all his questions. Clearly these were two who had sung together often, for they caught each other's cues and line breaks. They laid voice against voice like palm to palm, with an equal, steady, pleasurable pressure. The man's voice was nearly as rich as hers; he sang like a sybarite, one who enjoyed any delight presented to him, the more physical the better. As they sang, the young man watched Susannah, teasing her, wooing her with his eyes, lavishing her with attention. Susannah tried to duck her head, to turn away, but that small smile reappeared around the corners of her mouth, adding a gaiety to her performance that the song, quite strictly, did not require. It was a courtship clear enough, and Gaaron felt a peculiar and unpleasant sensation curl through his stomach as he watched.

Why had Jovah chosen as his bride someone who loved another man?

When that song ended, Susannah sat down and steadfastly refused to sing again, though she had many additional offers. Other singers rose to their feet, alone or in pairs, and the music was agreeable, but not particularly memorable. Not only that, everyone was getting tired. Children had fallen asleep in their mothers' laps, and lovers were drowsing in each others' arms. Even the final singers sounded exhausted.

Bartholomew rose to his feet and a stir went around the campfire. "I'm for bed," he announced and the others murmured their agreement. "I will see you all again in the morning, my brothers and sisters."

Everyone rose and stretched and said good nights. Keren and a stern-looking older woman came to Gaaron's side. The older woman eyed him with a measuring look.

"I would like to be able to offer you the hospitality of our tent, but I'm not certain you would fit," she said truthfully. "We are crowded as it is, and if Susannah joins us tonight—"

"Though she might stay with Paul again," Keren piped up.

"And she might not," the woman snapped. "And if she sleeps here tonight with Dathan—"

Gaaron spared a moment to wonder how many men Susannah might be sleeping with at any one time.

"Then we would have no room for the angel, who, it seems to me, might need more space than we have to offer."

Gaaron grinned. "I do not want to be any trouble," he said. "I have slept out in the open before. If you have an extra blanket, I can make myself comfortable."

"Or we can have Eleazar pitch a tent for you," the older woman said. "We have a spare and it is no bother."

"Yes, but he does not want to sleep all alone," Keren objected. "Maybe Eleazar or Dathan would share his tent? Or Amram, even, he would be happy to."

What was this? Now he would have to take the overflow from this overfull tent into his own little shelter? Why did they not pitch enough tents to begin with, if they had spares lying around?

"Bartholomew, if we had thought to ask him," the older woman said thoughtfully. Then, to Gaaron, she said, "How many are you used to sharing your pallet with? I am sure we can find that many willing to spend the night at your side."

Gaaron opened his mouth, closed it, considered, and spoke carefully. "I am very sure you are trying to do me honor," he said gravely. "I don't entirely understand your customs. I am used to sleeping alone. I have two rooms in the Eyrie that are mine, and no one is there except at my invitation."

The two women stared at him as if he had said he usually painted his body blue. Actually, that statement might have earned him less shock. "You sleep alone—always?" Keren said at last. "By choice? But aren't you—how can you—but aren't you afraid in the night when you wake and hear no one breathing? When you cannot put out a hand and touch your sister or your lover or your friend? Don't you worry that there is no one in the world alive but you?"

"Such fears have not occurred to me," Gaaron said kindly. "But I am supposing that you all sleep together in bunches? For comfort?"

"Because that is how people *sleep*," Keren replied, and the woman beside her nodded.

"I appreciate your concern for me," Gaaron said. "I will happily sleep alone. If you wish to set up a tent for me, I will sleep there. Otherwise, I am quite content on a blanket before the fire. I would prefer that, in fact, since it is late and everyone is tired."

The two women exchanged glances, and then the older one shrugged. "I will get you a blanket," she said. "Tell Keren if there is anything else you require."

In a few moments, he was as settled as he figured he would ever be at an Edori campfire. They had found not just a blanket but

a good-sized pallet, springy and surprisingly comfortable. He had resigned himself to sleeping on the hard ground, something he despised,
but it was too late now to try and take off for civilization. Besides, he
had to stay. He had to at least talk to Susannah. Though what he
would say to her he still could not imagine.

The camp settled down around him while he lounged on his bed,
watching. There appeared to be two tents pitched by this fire, one with
Keren and her friend and various other Edori of a range of ages, the
other filled with a smaller family that included two babies. Susannah's
nephews, Gaaron supposed. He hoped that the "Paul" referred to earlier had been Susannah's brother, and that she had been sleeping
chastely in his tent to be near to these very same nephews. He wasn't
sure how he would ask her about that, either.

Susannah had not returned to either tent yet. Nor had the handsome young man with whom she had sung her last duet. Dathan, Gaaron thought his name might be. Dathan, with whom Susannah
sometimes slept.

Perhaps his thinking about them had conjured them up, for just
then the two appeared in his line of sight, walking forward slowly from
the darkness beyond the perimeter of the fire. Their heads were bent
low; Susannah had her arms crossed on her chest. Dathan reached
forward as if to put his arm around her, and she jerked away.

Clearly, they had been arguing.

Normally, Gaaron was not the type to eavesdrop on other people's
private conversation, but these two people, he reasoned, concerned him
deeply. So he kept his head down on the pallet and watched, trying to
guess what they were saying. They were not close enough for him to
overhear their words, but she was obviously furious about something
and he was trying to charm her out of her anger. She came to a sudden
halt, turning on him and loosing a low stream of impassioned words
that he tried in vain to stem. He reached for her again and she pushed
him away, stepping back. He flung his hands in the air, said something
sharp and short, and strode away. Here, to the campfire. He did not
so much as glance at the angel before ripping open the canvas door
and stepping inside the tent where Keren and the others from that clan
were sleeping.

Susannah stood indecisively where he had left her, staring after
him. The half-moon threw off enough light for Gaaron to make out
her face, more sad than angry, full of indecision and woe. After a few
moments, she, too, came up to the tents staked before the fire, but then

she hesitated. She paused before the one that Dathan had gone into, then she turned away and took a few steps toward the second tent. Then stopped, pivoted, and stood there, looking helpless and depressed.

Gaaron sat up on his pallet, shaking his wings out behind him. "Oh!" the Edori said, her eyes wide with surprise. She had been gone during the discussion of Gaaron's sleeping choices. She had no reason to know where he was lying now. "I didn't see—"

He put a finger to his lips and she fell silent. Two tents full of wakeful Edori not five yards away; they could not talk here. He came to his feet and gestured for her to follow him, away from the circle of fire. She hesitated a moment, then shrugged. He thought he could almost read her mind. She had no reason to return to either tent tonight; she may as well take a walk with a visiting angel.

They moved silently away from the camp, Susannah matching him stride for stride. She must spend most of her life walking, as the Edori moved their camp every day or so. She was probably in even better physical condition than he was. At any rate, Gaaron admired her free gait, her sureness of foot, even in the dark on the open land. She seemed like a very capable woman.

He decided not to lead with a comment on the scene he had just witnessed. Instead, he said, with a smile in his voice, "You're wrong about the Eyrie, you know. It's not cold and unfriendly. The Velo Mountains, where it is built, are made of a peculiar sort of reddish-tan stone. When the gaslight is on, the stone seems to glow, almost like low candlelight. It is a very warm and welcoming place."

"Yes, I'm sure it is," she said, her voice a little tight. She was still thinking about her argument with her lover, and not about Gaaron's words. "And you said—there is music there?"

"All day, all night," he replied. "Groups of people sing in a small open room so that the Eyrie is never without harmony. It is quite beautiful, actually. But there is more. When the Eyrie was built—when all the holds were built—the original settlers installed these incredible rooms. They're acoustically perfect music rooms, and they include these—machines—that play songs recorded by the early settlers. Hagar, the first angelica. Uriel, the first Archangel. Other angels of the time. It's the most glorious music I've ever heard. And anyone can listen to it."

She was intrigued by that; anyone who loved music would be. "Machines? That can play music? I never heard of such a thing."

"I don't believe such things exist anywhere except the angel holds. I should have mentioned those to Keren when I was listing the amenities of the Eyrie."

Susannah actually laughed at that. "She's vain and shallow, but she's a good-hearted girl. She is so young and pretty—who could not like her?"

"I have a sister who is young and pretty and difficult, but I love her very much," Gaaron said. "You do not have to defend Keren to me."

"Still, I admit she can be difficult. And Tirza wants to strangle her half of the time."

"Now, who's Tirza? I know I met each one of your friends, but I'm sorry, there were too many names and faces—"

She laughed again. "Tirza is the lover of Eleazar, who is Keren's brother. Keren and Eleazar also have a sister named Anna, who sleeps with us. And Tirza is sister to Dathan, who is . . ." She fell silent.

"Who is your lover," Gaaron said gently.

She looked off in the distance, though her pace did not slow down. "Who has been my lover till now," she said in a constricted voice.

"Something I don't understand," Gaaron said. "You all talk of 'lovers.' Does no one marry among the Edori?"

"No," Susannah said briefly.

He was amazed. "No? Never? But then how do you—I suppose there is no property to pass on, but—even among the angels, where there is a great deal of freedom between men and women, there is still marriage. It just seems strange to me," he ended up lamely.

Susannah shrugged in the dark. "The Edori believe in no false bindings. You stay with a man because he loves you and you love him, or you don't. If he no longer loves you, why would you want a legal binding to tie him to your side?" Her voice stopped short, then she shrugged again. "If you no longer love each other, you move on."

"But marriage is about more than love, isn't it?" Gaaron said. "The merchants intermarry to better their trade routes and their bargaining positions. The farmers marry to consolidate their land. Jovah alone knows why the Jansai marry, because they don't seem to possess the ability to love, but even they have such ceremonies. Sometimes it is a politic thing to do."

Susannah glanced over at him but kept walking. "Then why call it marriage? Call it a business transaction and draw up the papers. That at least makes more sense."

Gaaron didn't feel this discussion was going quite the way he wanted. "The angels marry for a variety of reasons," he tried. "They can only marry humans, of course, because Jovah does not permit angel to wed angel. Sometimes love is the reason for the marriage. Sometimes it is to promote closer ties to—oh, the Manadavvi or some other group." He took a deep breath. "And of course, every Archangel marries at the behest of the god."

"Really?" Susannah said in a voice of polite uninterest.

"Yes. The god searches all of Samaria for the perfect bride—or groom—for the Archangel, and there's usually some good reason for the choice, or so the oracle says—" He was getting bogged down in clauses here. He couldn't bring himself to say the next necessary thing.

"I wouldn't like that at all," Susannah said. "Having my husband picked for me. He would be sure to be old or ugly or—or something."

"Don't you trust your god a little more than that?" Gaaron said humorously. "Surely Jovah would take your tastes into account."

She lifted a hand and rubbed a spot behind her ear as if smoothing away a troublesome headache. "I trust Yovah on most things," she said darkly. "But this seems like something for people to decide for themselves."

She dropped her hand, and moonlight glittered for a moment in the Kiss on her bare arm. Gaaron knew he was changing the subject in a cowardly way, but he said, "You've been dedicated. That's rare among the Edori, is it not?"

She nodded. "Both my older brother and I were. We were born during a time when there was a priest traveling with our clan. I think he was with us for three years. I don't remember, I was just a baby. My mother and father were very close to him, and when Paul and I were born, he convinced my parents to have us dedicated. We were the only babies born to the Tachitas during that time, so no one else of our tribe received the Kiss."

"Why was a priest traveling with the Edori?"

She looked amused. "I don't know. Maybe he was running away from an unhappy marriage?"

"I don't believe the priests marry, either."

"Anyway, I don't know. I never met him. He gave me a second Kiss, here, behind my ear." She pulled her long hair back and he bent down, though in the moonlight he could barely see the small glass nugget tucked into her skull. "Did you ever hear of such a thing?"

"No, I never did. Next time I see Mahalah, I'll have to ask her if she has any idea what it means."

"Who's Mahalah?"

How was it possible someone could be alive in Samaria today and not know the names of the three oracles? "The oracle at Mount Sinai," he said in a cautious voice. "You—you're unfamiliar with oracles?"

"Oh, they're the ones who talk to the god, aren't they? I've never actually spoken to one." She gave him a quick, sideways look, droll and ironic. "We live a very simple life. You understand."

He took a deep breath. "I was visiting the oracle just the other day, in fact. Asking her—asking her whom the god thought *I* should choose to be my bride."

Now she came to a halt and swung around to face him. The camp was far enough behind them that he couldn't even see the fires anymore. Faint starlight and the gentle glow of the half-moon provided the only light by which to read her expression. "Why would the god need to choose *your* wife?" she demanded.

So they had not been familiar with his name. None of them had. Here he was, anonymous, in the one place it would make his life easier to be recognized. "Because I am the Archangel-elect," he said gently. "Next spring, at the Gloria, I will be instated as the new Archangel for the beginning of my twenty-year term. And before I take up that position, I need to find my bride, who will sing beside me at the Gloria on the Plain of Sharon."

Now her eyes were wide, easy to see even in the dark. "You? The next Archangel? But then—probably you should not be sleeping on the ground outside an Edori campfire. You should be in some angel hold, as Keren said, dressed in silk and eating off of gold."

He smiled. "I will be Archangel of all people of Samaria, the Edori included," he said. "I need to get to know them as well as I know the Jansai and the Manadavvi and the other angels."

"And is that why you descended to our camp tonight?" she asked. "To—to make friends with the Edori?"

He took another deep breath. Keep this up and his head would begin to spin. "Partly," he said. "But, in truth, I was looking for a specific Edori camp. One of the clans. One of your clans, in fact."

Now her eyes were, if possible, even wider. She was not stupid; she was capable of analyzing the whole conversation that had gone before and coming to the obvious conclusion. In a whisper, she said,

"The oracle told you that your bride would be found among the Edori?"

He nodded. "The oracle told me that my bride would be you."

She looked as if he had just flipped over to stand on his head. "*Me?*" she said in a completely different tone of voice. "*Oh.*"

Now he was the one confused. "Well—who did you think?"

She shrugged helplessly. "Keren, of course."

"*Keren?*"

"Well, she's young and beautiful and is fascinated by angels and was asking all about the holds and she seemed—"

"She's as young as my sister. She's almost a child."

"Plenty of men don't view Keren as a child," Susannah said in a knowing voice.

"That's beside the point," he said impatiently, feeling that the real point had been lost in anticlimax. "The god has chosen *you.*"

Now she started walking again. "No, thank you," she said.

Gaaron took three quick steps to catch up with her. "I don't think you can say 'No, thank you' to the god," he said.

"I didn't. I said it to you."

This was maddening. "I am repeating the god's words," he said sharply. "He chose you to be my bride. You cannot gainsay him."

She walked a little faster. "He did not say it to *me,*" she replied. "How do I know what *you* heard was a true pronouncement?"

"Because everything the god tells the oracles is true. Because it is through the oracles that we communicate with the god. Because if there is no truth on Mount Sinai, there is no truth at all," he ground out. He grabbed her arm and pulled her to a stop, and he hung on though she glared at him in the dark. "Susannah! I know it will take some time to get used to the idea, but you are destined to become the angelica. You have been picked out from all the women living in Samaria at this time. It is a cause for awe and rejoicing. Believe me, for it is true."

"I don't want to," she said.

He cocked his head to one side, feeling a certain anger rise. It was like arguing with Miriam. She seemed so sure of herself, and yet she seemed incapable of listening to facts and logic. "And what is keeping you here with the Lohoras?" he asked, knowing it was cruel. "Not Dathan, with whom you have been quarreling."

She jerked her arm away. "It is none of your business if we have been quarreling!"

"It is if you are to marry me," he shot back childishly.

"Which I am not."

"You would turn down the wealth and majesty of the angelica's life for a life at this Dathan's side? He's a handsome man, Susannah—is that what you were fighting about? How handsome he is, and how other women notice that?"

She took a sharp breath and her whole body tensed. For a moment, he thought she might strike him, big and menacing though he must look, winged creature of the god that he was. "You have no idea what lies between Dathan and me," she said in a low, hard voice.

"Perhaps not, but I—"

She spun on one foot and stalked back toward the camp at a rapid pace. Again, he had to hurry to catch up. "Don't talk to me," she said fiercely. "Archangel or no Archangel, you have nothing to say to me that I want to hear."

"You may not like me, and you may not like what I have to say, but I *will* say it," Gaaron said. "The god has chosen you as angelica. I live to enact the god's dictates. You will return with me to the Eyrie tomorrow."

She didn't answer, and her silence itself spoke of contempt. "So pack your bags tonight and be ready to leave in the morning," he added.

She walked even faster. Gaaron shrugged and let his own steps lag, let her outdistance him as they pulled closer to the camp. He was not so far behind her, however, that he did not see which tent she chose to go to: Dathan's.

He couldn't help thinking that she had gone to the Lohoras more to spite him than to gratify Dathan, and the thought gave him a peculiar feeling. As if he really did have some claim on her, an interest in her heart, and not as if he was making some sober alliance to satisfy the god.

He made it to his own pallet and draped his long body across its folds. So close to the fire, there was no need for a blanket. He lay on his side, facing the blaze so that he could fan his wings out behind him without fear of them getting singed. He closed his eyes and, to his complete surprise, fell immediately asleep.

In the morning, Gaaron was the second one awake. The first was one of the babies in the Tachita tent, who screamed to wake the dead just as the sun was beginning to stumble out of its own uncomfortable bed. Gaaron rolled to his feet, stiff and not entirely rested. He was on Keren's side, this time; he appreciated the luxuries of life, at this moment, more than he could say.

He made his way to the water tent that had been pointed out to him the night before, and cleaned himself up as best he could. It would be a relief to get back to the Eyrie tonight, back to his own bed, his own food, his own people. On this short trip, he had had enough of travel to last him for quite some time.

When he emerged, much of the rest of the camp was stirring. Bartholomew came over from his tent and exclaimed, "Gaaron! Would you be kind enough to join my sisters and my friends for breakfast? They would like a chance to visit with an angel."

"Gladly," Gaaron said, and followed the big man through a few closely set fires to a tent not far from the one where Susannah slept. Here he was reintroduced to a handful of women and two teenage boys, all of whom laughed when he offered to help with the meal or the fire.

"You could help us strike the tent, though," one of the boys said in a reedy voice. "That's a job I hate."

Gaaron looked up from his seat before the fire. "You're moving on today?"

Bartholomew nodded. "We've been here long enough. And, though it saddens me to say so, I think this is where the Lohoras and the Tachitas part ways. We're heading for Gaza—so beautiful at this time of year—and they want to visit the Caitanas. What else can we do? That is why the god made so many clans, so that Edori could travel to every corner of the three provinces. And that is why he decreed the Gathering, so we would never be parted too long."

Gaaron smiled. "A pretty sentiment," he said. "Jovah guard you in your wandering."

The breakfast was good—fruit, a coarse bread, and some kind of fried meat that he did not recognize. Gaaron shifted on his stool to try to get a view of the Lohora tent, but the way was obstructed by other tents and a constant stream of moving Edori. He thought he had seen Dathan duck out through the door a few minutes ago, heading for the water tent, but he had not seen Susannah emerge.

He thought he would have noticed her.

"And you, Angelo? Where do you go next?" Bartholomew asked.

"Back to the Eyrie," Gaaron said, shifting his attention back to his host. "I am as happy to be going home as you are to be moving on."

Bartholomew made a gesture that was almost placating. "To each the joys of his own life," he said.

Suddenly, the tent nearest to them collapsed with a breathless *whoosh* as the center pole was pulled rapidly out. A chorus of children's laughter and adult admonitions led Gaaron to believe this was not the way a tent was normally disassembled. Frankly, he did not care if it had been struck down by the hand of the god himself, for it removed the biggest obstacle between him and Susannah's tent.

Where, he could now plainly see, Susannah and Dathan stood face-to-face, engaged in heated discussion. They stood a little to one side of the tent, and he guessed they were trying to keep their voices low, but that they were having an argument there could be no doubt. The other members of their clans were huddled around the fire, faces turned elaborately away, expressions carefully neutral. It must be hard to live and love in such close quarters, so that every cold word, every unhappy gesture, could be witnessed by everyone else you knew in the world.

Gaaron came to his feet, making no pretense of not watching. Bartholomew said something to him, but Gaaron did not reply. He was intent on Susannah's face, Susannah's crisis.

Dathan said something that, if his tone matched his face, was harsh and unforgiving, and then he strode off into the tangle of tents still standing. Susannah stood there a moment, hopelessly watching him go, giving her head a series of tiny shakes, and putting her hands to her cheeks.

And then slowly, as if the power of his gaze had drawn her attention, or as if, all this time, she had known exactly where he was, she turned and stared at Gaaron. She dropped her hands; her expression became remote and unfriendly, but she did not look away. Her jaw set. Her chin came up. She watched him.

"Excuse me," Gaaron said, without looking again at Bartholomew. "I have greatly enjoyed your hospitality, but it's time for me to leave."

Making his way as quickly as he could through the crowded Edori campsite, Gaaron crossed the few yards separating him from Susannah. She met his eyes and watched him approach her, but she did not move, and she did not turn away. When he stopped in front of her, she said nothing.

Neither did he. In one quick movement, he bent to scoop her into his arms. Her hands went around his neck to help her keep her balance. He heard the cries and questions of the Edori camp falling away from him as he threw himself aloft, the Edori woman in his arms, and flew hard and fast in the direction of the Eyrie.

CHAPTER SEVEN

Susannah stood inside her room and wished she would die.

It was a pretty enough room, filled with green furnishings and white curtains and a bed she had yet to sleep on because it was too soft and yielding for her body. The double windows were accented by heavy shutters that she had folded back to reveal a breathtakingly beautiful sunny day and a lovely expanse of golden-red mountainside falling away from her view. She had been told that she could have anything else she desired to fill her room—rugs, furniture, pillows, artwork—but so far nothing had come to mind. She had never, until three days ago, slept inside a building, slept with a stone roof overhead and stone walls surrounding her. Even at night, she kept the shutters open, to admit the starlight, to admit the air, so she could breathe.

But it was not the close confines of the room at the Eyrie that had made her so miserable.

That long flight from Jordana to the Eyrie had been accomplished in almost total silence, though from time to time Gaaron had put his mouth to her ear to ask if she needed to stop, to eat, to refresh herself. And from time to time she had indicated yes, and they had come to a halt, and he had taken care of her needs with a dignified courtesy. She had not caused him any trouble, though she had not been able to meet his eyes and she had not volunteered any conversation. She had not even told him, each time he took wing again with her in his arms, how cold she was as they traveled so rapidly through the high, thin air, how her blood mewled and shivered in her veins, how her feet were so chilled she could not be sure she still had feet until she twisted her head and looked. She could feel his own skin, warm and reassuringly solid where she was gripped against him, and it was clear he was not bothered by the frigidity of the high altitudes. So she said nothing. She did not care if she was cold. She did not even care if she survived the trip.

But it was not the memory of the wretched journey that made her so unhappy now.

She took a few steps forward, and then a few steps to one side, and then stood there again, absolutely unable to fathom what she should do next. In camp, she would be watching the babies, or berry-picking with Amram, or stirring the pot, or skinning the fresh kills, or washing out soiled clothes, or any of a hundred other tasks that gave some shape and purpose to her life. Here, she had nothing to do, no way to fill the time, no one to speak to, nothing to think of.

But it was not idleness that made her walk to the tall window, and lean her elbows on the sill and stare out, wondering if she had the nerve to fling herself from this high place onto the stones below.

Dathan had lied to her. Lied to her the way she would have lied to a frightened child who saw monsters in the dark. Swore he had not spent the evening with Cozbi, when he had. When everyone knew he had. Susannah had lain abed late that last morning in camp, troubled by things the angel had said and Dathan had not said, idly listening to voices outside the tent. And Dathan had been standing by the fire, and Cozbi had come by and made some laughing remark, the kind of remark one lover makes to another, and Dathan had laughed in return. And Susannah had realized he had lied to her, and that he had probably lied to her in the past, and that he would always lie to her, and that she still loved him.

And she had wanted the angel to take her away so that she would never have to look at Dathan's face again.

But now that she was so far from him, hundreds of miles, maybe, likely to never see him again, she missed him so much and she hurt so much that she would really rather die than live.

The sill was not so high. She, who could climb treacherous mountain paths with a child in her arms or a heavy pack on her back, could easily swing up to the ledge and launch herself forward. The mountain face was steep here and she would probably fall a good distance. Far enough to break her neck.

She leaned her elbows on the sill and pillowed her chin in her hands and did not move for the next hour. Just stared out the window and imagined her fall.

When the chime sounded, she jumped back from the window and glanced around the room, unable to identify the source. She heard music here all day and all night, and she could not identify that source, either, but at least that seemed remote and unthreatening. This noise had been much closer and insistent. As if she was supposed to do something about it.

The chime called again and was followed immediately by a quick knocking on the door. "Hello? Are you in there? Can I come in?"

Susannah did not recognize the voice, a woman's, so she did not answer. Then again, she had met dozens of people during her short stay here, and she did not think she would recognize any of their voices if they called to her through a closed door. Gaaron's. No one else's.

"Please? Can I come in?"

Susannah shrugged. "Yes," she said finally.

Instantly, the door was flung open and a radiant girl stepped inside. She looked no older than Keren, but there the resemblance ended. Where Keren was night-dark as any Edori, this girl was fair as daylight, her hair a bright yellow and her skin flawlessly white. She wore Keren's same look of mischief, though, contained in one exceptional smile.

"Oh, I just got back from Gaza this morning and I could not wait to meet you," she said, tumbling into the room and looking around as if greedy for details Susannah may have imprinted on the furnishings in three short days. "I know I should have waited for Gaaron or Esther to bring me by, but once I heard the story, there was no holding me back. But you haven't come out of your room! It's nearly noon! I couldn't wait any longer."

Susannah, whose heart was breaking into two parts, actually felt a smile come to her face at this artless speech. "I am glad you have come to meet me," she said gravely. "I'm Susannah. Who are you?"

"But I'm Miriam, of course!" the girl said, coming closer so she could get a better look. "Gaaron's sister. He probably hasn't mentioned me—or if he did, he said such dreadful things about me that you were afraid to meet me."

Susannah's smile grew wider. "I think he did say your name once or twice," she said. "I don't remember any dreadful details."

"I'm the bane of his existence," Miriam said promptly. "But it's his own fault for being gone just now so he couldn't introduce me to you as he should have."

"Gaaron's gone?"

"Yes, Esther said he left this morning for—for somewhere first, and then for Windy Point. He should be back in about a week. But let's not talk about him! Tell me about you! Who are you and why are you here and are you really going to marry my brother? That's so romantic!"

"It doesn't feel very romantic," Susannah said. "In fact, right now I'm feeling—very alone and—scared and—lost."

Miriam came up and put a hand on either side of Susannah's face. Like Gaaron, she had warm skin, even in this chilly mountain hold, and her eyes were Edori-dark. "And sad," the girl said in quick sympathy. "But no one wants you to be sad. Tell me what's wrong."

Feeling the tears rise, Susannah stepped away, and Miriam dropped her hands. "I miss my friends—my family," Susannah said. "I don't know anyone here. And it's so . . ." She laughed softly. "How can you live this way, all separated from each other by walls and hallways? I am used to having everyone I love right at the end of my fingertips. I have never slept alone a single night in my life."

Miriam had crossed the room to the too-soft bed and plopped herself on it with a little bounce. She patted the covers in invitation, and Susannah settled next to her. It seemed much more comfortable when two people were sitting on it than when one person was trying to sleep in it. "Really? You all sleep in tents? With a lot of other people?"

Susannah laughed again. The action drove the tears a little farther away. "I don't know what you consider a lot. There were six besides me in the tent I shared with the Lohoras. Seven with the Tachitas."

Miriam's eyes opened wide. "All in one tent? How was there enough room?"

"Everyone curled up together like puppies."

"We could do that here, I suppose," Miriam said thoughtfully. "Though I don't think I'd want a bunch of us sleeping in one bed. But I'll stay in your room with you, if you want. And I bet Zibiah will. And Chloe and Sela. Oh, and the little girl—she follows Zibiah everywhere, she'll have to come."

Susannah was touched to the heart by this easy offer of companionship. "Miriam, that's so kind of you! But I can't take you up on such generosity."

"Zibiah and I sleep over all the time," Miriam said dismissively. "Nicholas and Ahio used to, too, but Gaaron put a stop to that and now they won't even when I ask them to, because Gaaron said so. Even if no one will find out. As if I—but that's Gaaron for you, everything has to be so strict."

Susannah was smiling again. This breathless girl seemed to have the knack for amusing her. "Who are all these people?"

"Nicholas, Ahio, Chloe, and Zibiah are angels. Sela's a mortal, like me. And they're my best friends, though Zibiah is my *best* best friend. And she'll do anything I ask, so I know she'll come sleep over with you, too."

"That's so kind," Susannah said again. "But I know it's not your custom to share quarters that way. And, I suppose, it's time for me to become used to angel ways."

Miriam leaned forward. "So it's true? You're really going to marry my brother?"

Susannah spread her hands in a gesture of complete uncertainty. "I suppose so. I—he said the god decreed it and—here I am. I guess I'll go ahead and do what he wants."

"No, no, no, no," Miriam scolded. "You can't just do what Gaaron wants! *Everyone* does what Gaaron wants! You have to be a little troublesome. It's good for him."

Susannah smiled. "Why does everyone do what he wants? Are they afraid of him?"

"Oh, no. It's because he's always right. It's very annoying. Nicholas and Ahio think he's practically the god himself, it's always 'Gaaron said this' and 'Gaaron said that,' and I can't stand it." Miriam's expression was of righteous indignation. "I mean, it's unbearable."

Susannah thought of Keren's fights with Eleazar, who was also an unimaginative and sober type, and she could completely understand. Even Susannah had found Eleazar a little hard to take at times. And Gaaron was even more strict and judgmental? The thought was too depressing. "Well, I don't suppose we have to marry right away," she said, trying to make her voice sound cheerful. "Maybe we can get to know each other a little first."

Miriam wriggled where she sat. "Make him woo you," she suggested. "Make him bring you flowers—and write you poems—and sing you love songs."

Susannah was amused. "Gaaron is the type to do those things?"

"No! That's why you must make him do them. It will be good for him to have to court you. It will make him less sure of himself. And then, when he falls in love with you, *then* you can marry him."

But talk of love instantly made her think of Dathan, not Gaaron. "As I understand it, there does not have to be love between the Archangel and his bride. Only a certain understanding."

Miriam rolled her eyes. "Well, of course he'll fall in love with you. It always happens. Even Hagar and Uriel were in love with each other, though the stories say they fought all the time."

"Who?"

"Hagar and Uriel—the first angelica and the first Archangel. Oh, never mind them. The point is, you will make Gaaron's life difficult, and he will fall in love with you, but you won't let him know you're in love with him, but your Kiss will light when he walks into a room, and his Kiss will light when you speak his name, and it will be very romantic."

"What's this? The Kisses will do what?"

"Don't you know *anything*? The legends say that Kiss calls to Kiss, that when true lovers meet for the first time, their Kisses light with fire and heat with flame. I've never seen it happen," Miriam added, "but I know it's true. And if the Archangel and the angelica aren't true lovers, brought together by Jovah, then who else could possibly be?"

"But I've already met your brother. And my Kiss behaved very well, thank you, and I'm sure his didn't send off any sparks, either."

Miriam shrugged. "Sometimes it takes a while."

"Oh, I'm sure. And sometimes it never happens at all."

Miriam smiled and jumped from the bed. "You watch," she said. "I'm starving. Let's go to the kitchen."

Susannah had eaten very little at the dinner last night, though Gaaron, sitting beside her, and Esther, bringing in five or six different trays to tempt her, had been most solicitous. She'd skipped breakfast this morning, choosing instead to stand at her window and contemplate death. She had not felt any stirring of hunger the whole three days she'd been here.

"I'm starving, too," she said, astonished to realize it. "I'd love to get something to eat."

• • •

Over their meal in the nearly empty dining room, Miriam bombarded Susannah with questions, only sometimes waiting to hear the answer before she asked another. She wanted to learn more about the Edori lifestyle, and Susannah's two families, and, once she heard his name, everything about Dathan. But she was quick and empathetic, in addition to being curious. When Susannah said stiffly that she would rather not discuss Dathan just now, Miriam instantly changed the subject.

"You sing, of course," she said, but even so, her tone was questioning. "Don't all the Edori get together and sing once a year at some kind of Gloria of their own?"

Susannah smiled. "The Gathering? Yes, singing is a part of it, though there is much, much more. It is a chance for all the clans to gather together, to share the things they've learned and experienced during the months that they are apart."

"Yes, but you *do* sing," Miriam repeated.

Susannah eyed her. "Yes, I enjoy singing. Why is it so important to you that I do?"

Miriam's brown eyes opened very wide. "Because you'll have to sing at the Gloria, of course. You'll have to lead the mass that everyone sings at dawn. The angelica always does."

"Me? All by myself? Singing the *Gloria*? I don't think I can do that."

"Well, usually just the opening section is the angelica's solo. I mean, all the masses are written for at least two voices, a man's and a woman's, and every mass has a choral response. So you aren't singing the *whole* thing by yourself, but—well, some of it!" Miriam smiled with a charming, mischievous dimple. "It's rude to ask, of course, but do you have a good voice? Because it's really important."

"I—my voice is fine, I suppose, but I—well, I don't know any masses! And when is the Gloria? In the spring?"

Miriam looked aghast that Susannah did not know the exact date. "Yes! The spring equinox, to be precise. So you have plenty of time to learn one."

"But a mass—that's formal music, isn't it? All I've ever sung are camp songs and ballads. I don't even—and I'm not used to performing solos—"

"What part do you sing? Most angelicas are sopranos."

Susannah looked at her helplessly. "I don't think so."

Miriam's eyes went even wider. "You're not a soprano? I don't know—*are* any of the masses written for an alto lead? We'll have to check. This makes it even more interesting."

"Maybe I can't sing, then," Susannah said hopefully.

"You have to."

Before Susannah could reply, a winged shape threw its shadow over them and then resolved itself into a young man. He was quite beautiful in a careless sort of way, Susannah thought, with an easy, negligent smile and a magnificently modeled body. "Are you talking about womanly things, or may I join you?"

"Ahio, are there masses written for alto leads?" Miriam demanded.

Seeming to consider the question itself an invitation, he pulled out a chair and reversed it, sitting so that his arms rested on the chair back and his wings spread out on the floor behind him. "Must be," he said. "I can't think of any offhand."

"Susannah's an alto."

He smiled over at her and she felt herself smile in return. "Congratulations."

"It seems to be a liability," she said.

He shrugged and his wings lifted and fell with a sweet sighing. "Rewrite the mass. Put it in a new key. Make the tenor part the descant. It's not very hard."

"Well, since I don't know any masses to begin with, it would be very hard for *me*," Susannah said with some asperity.

"Ahio is a composer. He'll help you," Miriam said.

"I'd have to know your range, though."

Miriam jumped up. "Let's go find out."

Ahio got lazily to his feet and Susannah more slowly rose. "You mean—go somewhere and sing—now?" Susannah asked.

"Unless you don't feel like singing," Miriam said.

Susannah hesitated just a moment. It was something to do, at any rate, and the more time she spent in Miriam's bright company, the less time she would have to spend alone in her room. "Why not?"

So they led her down through the winding, confusing corridors of the Eyrie to a small windowless chamber that was completely underground. The sensation of being buried alive pressed hard on Susannah; she found it a little difficult to breathe, here where no air could possibly reach. The room was well-lit and paneled on one wall with metal and glass cabinets that housed complex, indecipherable parts.

"Those are the music machines, you use them to play the old

masses," Miriam said as Susannah moved closer to the wall to examine them. "They're very strange, aren't they? When I was a child, I was afraid to touch them, but apparently they've been operating for more than two hundred years and they're impossible to break."

Susannah put a hand up to touch the glass, then the metal, cool and sleek and utterly foreign to her waking experience. And so unexpectedly familiar. "I've seen these before," Susannah murmured.

"Really? At Windy Point or Monteverde? I thought you'd never been inside a hold before."

Susannah shook her head. "In my dreams."

There was a polite silence behind her, and she turned to find Miriam and Ahio both looking quizzical. She spread her hands to indicate that she could not explain very well. "I have these—these strange dreams now and then," she said. "I'm wandering through a place that's all white and silver and glass. I've never seen anything that even resembled the place of my dream—except these machines. I know it sounds odd," she added. "It seems odd to me, too."

"Well, maybe your mother brought you to an angel hold when you were a little baby, and you saw these rooms, and your mind never forgot it even though you didn't *really* remember it," Miriam said.

"Or maybe somehow my spirit knew that someday I would be among the angels, and it prepared me for that moment with those dreams," Susannah said. "That's what the Edori would tell me."

"But it doesn't matter," Miriam said, already losing interest. "Let's practice something. What can you sing?"

Susannah named a few songs that they didn't know, and they named a few that she had never heard of, but eventually they compiled a list of three or four popular songs that all three of them were pretty sure they could perform.

"You start," Susannah said. "I'll come in on the chorus."

So Miriam, with complete unself-consciousness, opened her mouth and began singing. Her voice was high and sweet, pleasantly accented by Ahio's deep tenor, which he joined to hers in the middle of the second line. It was a silly little upbeat song, but their voices were very fine, extremely well-trained, and absolutely on the mark. It was a pleasure to listen to them.

Susannah dropped in as they swung into the chorus, harmonizing as she always did. It was as if her voice was a rich ingredient that she added to an appetizing stew, making the dish more flavorful, though the individual spices could not have been sifted out once they were all stirred together. To do this she always had to hear the other voices first, match hers to theirs, re-create their tones and rhythms with her own. It was as if her voice changed for every performance, became at least briefly an extension of someone else's. It was as if she borrowed those other voices, and embroidered them, and returned them more beautiful and ornate than they were.

She caught Miriam's startled look when her voice settled under the soprano part, and Ahio's smile. She didn't know what it was that made them react, whether she sounded worse than they'd hoped or better. In any event, they all kept singing, through the second verse, the third, and both choruses. Miriam lifted a hand to indicate that they should all hold the final note a few more beats, though Susannah could not resist fooling with the harmony, changing the chord from major to minor and back again while the others held the octave. A single downbeat and they all abruptly cut off their notes. A moment of quiet, then the usual laughter and quick catches of breath that followed nearly any song.

"But Susannah! What a beautiful voice you have!" Miriam exclaimed. "From how you talked, I was not expecting much, but—it's simply gorgeous!"

"Well, both of you are so much better than I am that I'm a little embarrassed—"

Miriam waved a hand. "Classically trained. Not better. And what was that harmony you did?"

"When?"

"On the second chorus," Ahio said. "Did you write that yourself?"

She had to think back. "Oh. I was just playing. I thought it would sound pretty."

The others exchanged glances. "You just made it up right then? As we were singing?" Miriam asked.

"Didn't you like it?"

"It was great, but—how can you do that? I can write harmony, but it takes me weeks to get it right," Miriam said.

"I don't know. I just hear it in my head. It sounds right."

Ahio was grinning. "The natural musician. Music comes to you unbidden. It's pretty rare."

Susannah shrugged. "It happens to me all the time."

"It comes to you in those strange dreams," Miriam suggested.

Susannah laughed. "I don't think so."

Ahio was more intent on the music. "Let's try the Galilee River song. Susannah, you lead this time."

She shook her head. "I can't. I don't . . . I don't like to hear my voice by itself."

"Well, you're going to have to—"

Ahio shook his head at Miriam, silencing her. "Not today. Let's just see what else she can do."

So this time he led off. The piece was a little more demanding in terms of pace and rhythm, but naturally neither of the hold-born singers missed a note and Susannah was determined not to, either. Ahio changed keys at every new verse, nudging them higher and higher until Miriam's eyes grew wide with reproach, though her voice never faltered.

"Stop that," the blond girl said at the end of the fifth verse before Ahio could go up another half-step. "You're making my throat hurt."

He gave her a lazy smile. "*She* can hit it, though," he said. "Her range is as good as Adriel's. Different octaves, but just as many notes."

"Well, that's good news," Miriam said. "Now we just have to find the right mass for her, and she can practice for eight months."

"I've never heard one of these masses," Susannah said somewhat cautiously, because the very word conjured up visions of grandiose and fabulously difficult musical arabesques. "You said you could play one for me? So I could hear it?"

"How about the Lochevsky *Magnificat?*" Miriam said with a little giggle, but Ahio gave her a quelling look.

"Something a little simpler, I think," he said, advancing to the wall of machines and studying some mechanical display. "Here. The *Orison*. It's a little tricky in spots, but she'll get the general idea."

Miriam promptly plopped herself onto the floor, so Susannah followed suit, crossing her legs under her and preparing for a long stay. "We don't have to listen to the whole thing," Miriam whispered. "But just to give you an idea."

"How long *is* a mass?"

"Two hours or more."

"Two hours! I can't sing for two hours!"

"Sshh," Ahio said, turning away from the machine and coming to join them on the floor. He sat down with one effortless movement, his wings spilling out behind him on the polished floor like bolts of dropped silk. "Don't miss the beginning."

And, indeed, seconds later, the chamber was filled with the eerie, disembodied sound of a woman singing. Her voice was so beautiful that Susannah was transfixed. It looped up and down the complex measures of the mass like a hand dashing color onto a canvas, and it was so gorgeous that it seemed to fill the air of the music chamber with additional layers of depth and texture. She was a soprano, but like no soprano Susannah had ever heard, and the Edori almost could not breathe for the first five minutes of the solo.

When the male voice joined hers in a minor duet, Susannah felt the skin on the back of her shoulders tingle with awe. She actually pulled her knees up closer to her body and drew herself into a tight hug, to make herself into one small, unmoving, listening creature. She had never heard anything like this; she couldn't imagine that such voices had ever existed. When the choral group came in on the first response, she actually gasped, and then she shook her head. She felt sated, as if she'd eaten injudiciously at a summer feast, and dizzy, as if she'd accompanied the meal with too much wine.

Ahio stretched up and turned off the music as soon as the chorus came to its end. They had been listening for less than thirty minutes; could it be possible that there was another hour and a half of that sublime music still to come?

"That's just the opening movement, but it gives you the general feel of it," Ahio said. "Pretty, isn't it?"

"*I* can't sing like that!" Susannah exclaimed.

Miriam laughed. "Well, of course you can't. No one can. That's Hagar and Uriel."

"The best voices of their generation, and, if you can believe the reports angels have left behind over the past two centuries, the best voices ever," Ahio observed. "Even Gaaron can't sing like Uriel, and I'd rather hear Gaaron than anyone I know."

"But I—I don't even think I can learn the *song,* let alone deliver it right," Susannah continued. "This is—I don't think seven or eight months is long enough!"

"You'll pick it up a lot faster than you think," Ahio said. "I'm not worried at all."

"Well, no, you don't seem like the type who worries about anything!" Susannah declared, which earned a burst of laughter from Miriam and a grin from Ahio. "And you're not the one who's going to be standing up there making a fool of yourself in front of however many hundreds of people show up for this Gloria of yours."

"Thousands, usually," Ahio said. "But we'll find the right piece for you. Don't fret about a thing."

And, indeed, over the next few hours, the next few days, Susannah found it easy to follow Ahio's advice. From the music room they went to the common rooms in search of Nicholas, and he was just like the other two, Susannah thought—careless, happy, and easygoing. The four of them lounged in Nicholas' far-from-clean room and talked the afternoon away, though later Susannah could not exactly pinpoint what their discussions had been about. Gossip about angels, living here or in the other angel holds—stories about trips they'd taken, weather intercessions performed, and small services rendered—shopping trips embarked upon, meals eaten, fashions mocked. None of it carried much weight. All of it seemed to elicit much hilarity. Susannah didn't contribute much to the conversation, but she laughed a great deal, and she felt energized with happiness when they all finally made their way down to the dining area for the evening meal.

Here they were joined by another angel, a soft-spoken dark-haired girl introduced as Zibiah. She was not nearly as flamboyant as Miriam, but just as relaxed and friendly as the others, and Susannah could instantly see how these four had become friends. At first Susannah felt a little shy, as if she was intruding on a circle of friendship that was already complete, but Zibiah seemed as happy with her company as Miriam and the men did, and so she quickly relaxed.

"How's your little girl today?" Nicholas asked as they toyed with their desserts, having eaten perhaps a little more than they needed to of the main courses. Susannah had eaten more than any of them, suddenly ravenous after her three days of near starvation, but no one had seemed to think that strange.

Zibiah shrugged. "Much the same. She's eating, though, which is good, and she lets me leave the room for a few hours at a time, as long as Chloe or Sela or someone else is with her. And that's *very* good."

"You have a little girl?" Susannah asked.

The others laughed. Zibiah made a face. "Not mine. I've inherited her. A young Jansai girl we found on the road about a week ago. She's terrified and she won't speak, and for a while she wouldn't eat, either, but she seems to be recovering a little."

"At first she wouldn't let Zib out of her sight," Miriam piped up. "Shrieked every time Zibiah would try to leave the room."

"And she *hates* Esther," Nicholas said with a grin. "But I figure that's a sign of her intelligence."

"How do you come to have a Jansai girl here at the hold?" Susannah asked. "They don't let their women roam alone."

"Found her by a burned campsite," Nicholas said. He made a big circle with his arms. "The whole place. Just ash and cinder. She'd apparently been out of the camp when the fire started, so she survived. But I guess she saw it, because—well, she's traumatized."

Susannah felt her heart grow chilled. "A whole campsite—just burned to the ground? All of it?" she said in a small voice.

Nicholas nodded. "Strangest thing I ever saw."

"Me, too," Susannah said. "We—my clan and I—came across just such a burned site a few weeks ago. We couldn't imagine what had caused such destruction."

Now Miriam and all three of the angels were staring at Susannah with sober alarm on their faces. "You mean—it's happened more than once?" Zibiah said. "But how could—surely something like that was some kind of bizarre accident—"

"Maybe it was the same site," Ahio suggested. "Where did you come across it?"

"A little north of Luminaux," Susannah said. "Maybe ten miles."

Nicholas shook his head. "We were in southern Bethel, too, but closer to the Corinnis. Couldn't be the same camp."

"But then—" Zibiah began, but Miriam cut her off.

"Did you tell Gaaron?" the mortal girl asked.

Susannah shook her head. "It didn't occur to me."

The others were nodding. "Gaaron will want to know," Nicholas said, and Ahio added, "We'll tell him when he gets back."

Susannah flicked a look at Miriam, for surely this was confirmation of her earlier assertion that all the angels thought Gaaron could solve any problem. But Miriam was nodding, too. Clearly, no matter how she aimed to rebel against her brother, she also turned to him for support and succor any time the need arose.

He must be a good man, Susannah thought, but even so she felt a dreariness coiled around the perimeter of her heart when she thought of trying to love such a man. She missed Dathan with his laughing ways, his happy manner, his easy charm. That was the only kind of man she could love, honor this Gaaron though she eventually may.

She nodded at the others and picked up her fork. "I'll tell him as soon as I see him again," she said, and finished off her plate of pie.

CHAPTER EIGHT

That evening, true to her word, Miriam brought a small cavalcade of women to spend the night in Susannah's room. In addition to Miriam and Zibiah, there was another angel named Chloe and a mortal girl named Sela. And a small Jansai girl who did not appear to have a name at all.

Miriam, Chloe, and Sela were the first to arrive. Sela was quieter and Chloe livelier than the others; that was about the only difference Susannah could see, since they were all young and pretty and full of laughter. All of them came bearing rolls of bedding so big they could scarcely see over the tops, and they filled the room with a new range of giggles.

"I brought wine from the kitchen. I don't think Esther saw me," Chloe announced, and the others squealed.

"I was in Velora today and I stopped at a cosmetics booth," Sela said in a soft voice. "So I picked up rouge and kohl and perfume— and this stuff—she said it would add streaks of color to my hair, but I don't know, it smells pretty awful—"

"Oh, I love that stuff!" Miriam cried. "My hair's so fair it doesn't do much for me, but it's great. We'll put some in tonight."

They unrolled their sleeping gear all around the room, talking without ceasing. Chloe slipped into the water room adjoining the bedroom. (Such a luxury, Susannah always thought, and such a waste—a place of continuously flowing water reserved for the use of one person!)

"I'd like lighter streaks around my face—do you think we could try that?" Chloe called from the mirror in the other room. "I don't want to end up looking like a skunk, though."

"What about you, Susannah?" Miriam asked. "Would you like blond shadings in your hair?"

They all clustered around her, stroking the long, silky length of her black hair and admiring its sheen and softness. "Oh, no, you can't streak Susannah's hair," Sela said in her gentle voice. "It's too beautiful."

"We could cut it," Chloe suggested, but the others cried out against that.

"Braid it, maybe," Miriam decided. "With ribbons and pearls. That would be pretty."

"How do you plan to wear it at your wedding?" Sela wanted to know.

"What are you going to wear for your wedding?" Miriam asked.

"When *is* the wedding?" Chloe demanded.

Susannah laughed and raised both hands to fend them off. "I don't know! I don't know! I've scarcely even seen Gaaron since we got to the Eyrie, and it's not like I exactly knew him before—"

"Plus she's in love with another man," Miriam supplied. "But she doesn't like to talk about it."

That news made Chloe and Sela croon out little *aahs* and crowd closer, as if to hear the tale or as if some of that doomed romantic glory might rub off on them. "Really—it's just that—actually, I *don't* want to talk about it," Susannah said, a little desperately.

"That's all right. We can plan your wedding anyway," Miriam said matter-of-factly. "We'll figure out what you need."

Before they'd made any headway on this promising activity, the chime sounded again. Zibiah entered, bedroll in her arms. She was followed by a small, wiry girl dressed from head to foot in dark, flowing robes. Her head was covered with a veil that draped over her face so that only her eyes were visible. But these were narrow, sharp, and suspicious, darting quickly around the room as if to seek out dangers. They instantly fixed on Susannah as the source of potential trouble, since she was clearly familiar with the other three in the room.

Susannah, seeing her, grew very still. So tiny and young she was to have witnessed such a catastrophic event, to have survived the death of what was probably her whole family. And then to be uprooted and replanted here, among angels and strangers. Well enough Susannah knew what that relocation felt like. She had a lot in common with this little waif.

Susannah took a few cautious steps closer to the Jansai girl, then dropped to her knees so that their faces were at the same level. Zibiah stood beside the girl, her hand on one frail shoulder, and spoke in a low voice. "That's Susannah. She just came here to live with us. She's an Edori. Have you seen Edori before?"

The girl nodded.

"Susannah's our friend, and she'll be very nice to you, just like Chloe and Sela and Miriam. She'll sing to you if you want—" Zibiah threw a quick questioning look at Susannah as she said this, and Susannah nodded. "And she'll stay with you sometimes when I can't. You'll like her, I think."

"Do you have a name?" Susannah asked quietly.

The little girl shook her head.

"She's never told us anything about herself. She hasn't talked at all," Zibiah said.

Susannah moved a little closer, sliding across the stone floor on her knees. "Can I call you *mikala?* It means 'young girl' in the Edori tongue," Susannah said.

The narrow eyes wrinkled up a little, as if behind the veil the face was showing a small smile. The girl nodded.

"I think she knows the word," Miriam said.

Susannah nodded. "She might. The Jansai know a lot of the Edori language. They travel as much as we do and go to the same places— sometimes we share words for those places. Isn't that right, mikala?"

Again, the wrinkled eyes. Again, the small movement of the head. Susannah smiled at her and edged closer. "You know what?" Susannah whispered into the girl's ear, leaning closer and pretending no one else could hear. "Jansai love luxury much more than the Edori do. Now this bed right behind me—it's too soft for my bones. I'm used to sleeping on the hard ground. But you—I bet you never came across a bed that was too soft for you. I bet you could sleep on five feather mattresses piled one on top of the other. I'm going to scoop you up and dump you on that bed, and I want to see you bounce."

And Susannah leapt to her feet and pounced on the little girl, who gave a muffled shriek that didn't sound at all frightened. Susannah whuffled into her hair and twirled her around in one big circle before dropping her from shoulder height onto the bed and then jumping on top of the mattress right alongside her.

"Bounce!" Susannah cried. "Up and down you go!" And the two of them bounced on the too-soft bed. And the little girl laughed out loud.

"That's a sound I haven't heard before," Miriam commented just a second before Chloe gave a little yelp and bounded across the room to land on the bed with the others. Moments later, all of them were on the bed, rolling around like maniacs and laughing like giddy children. Susannah positioned herself near the edge to make sure the Jansai girl didn't accidentally get pushed off, but everyone remained safely on, wonderfully happy.

"Ah, I knew this bed would be good for something," Susannah said breathlessly as she slid off the end and came to a seat on the floor, her back against the frame. The women behind her giggled. "And I didn't mean good for *that*," Susannah said over her shoulder.

"Well, it will be once you're married," Zibiah said.

"Or even before," Chloe added.

"Let's keep in mind that little mikala ears are listening," Susannah warned in a light singsong voice.

The bed behind her jiggled and swayed as various bodies righted themselves. "Your wedding," Miriam said. "We need to start planning that."

"Yes, let's take a look at your clothes," Chloe said.

Susannah came to her feet and looked somewhat doubtfully at the tall armoire across the room. She had her traveling clothes, of course, and Esther had made sure to supply a few rather nondescript dresses that seemed a little more acceptable in the angel hold, but Susannah didn't have anything that would pass for finery. "Probably not a very good place to start."

But they insisted on going through her wardrobe anyway, laying out her skirts and her dresses and exclaiming over the fine sewing on the handmade Edori clothes but making no other comment about their attractiveness. However, they all seemed to genuinely love the embroidered shirt that she had made last winter and that she had not had the heart to sell in Luminaux.

"You could pair this with a—let me think—a blue silk skirt and wear it on your wedding day," Miriam said. She laid it on the bed where the Jansai girl still sat and stood back to view it through half-closed eyes.

"I love it, too, but on her wedding day?" Zibiah said doubtfully. "Is it really fine enough?"

"It looks like a piece of Edori craft work, and Gaaron is marrying an Edori woman," Miriam said.

"I truly would not want to embarrass him by wearing something unsuitable," Susannah said. "But perhaps there would be another occasion—some dinner when we announce our betrothal—do you have such events?"

Miriam snapped her fingers. "The wedding breakfast," she said. "Held the morning after the ceremony. All the important guests will still be here, but it's not as formal as the wedding itself. It will be perfect to wear then."

The others agreed, which pleased Susannah. She liked the idea of wearing some token of her past life as she made the transition into her new one. "And where will I find this blue silk skirt?" she asked.

"Oh, Velora," the women answered in a chorus of voices.

"The little city at the foot of the mountain? But how can I get there?" Susannah asked. "I didn't think there was a way down the mountain."

"No, someone has to fly you down, but I can do that anytime you like," Chloe said. "Or Zib or Nicky or Ahio. Just ask us."

"Let's go tomorrow!" someone cried, and within minutes they were planning a shopping expedition for the following day. No one seemed to be worried about any duties they might be shirking here at the hold, and there was certainly nothing keeping Susannah at the Eyrie, so she was happy to be plotting future amusements.

The whole evening went like that, elliptical conversations punctuated by bursts of laughter followed by more discussion on some completely unrelated topic. They took turns sitting on a stool in the middle of the room and having Sela make up their faces. Only Chloe and Miriam were brave enough to try the hair-coloring product, and they walked around the room for the rest of the evening with silver knots in their hair and the pungent smell of chemicals drifting up around their faces. Between them, they drank three bottles of wine, even Susannah sampling some, although she didn't usually like it. But this was much sweeter than the bitter, raw wine they usually had in camp; it tasted more like dessert than alcohol, though its effects were much the same.

They discussed the men of the hold, angel and mortal, and who was attractive and who was not. They performed the same exercise for the residents of Monteverde and Windy Point, and tossed off the names of half a dozen young Manadavvi men and their varying critiques of their faces, their manners, and their potential. Zibiah curled up around the Jansai girl, stroking the little one's head, and spoke wistfully of wanting a child of her own someday. Chloe said flatly that she didn't want the responsibility. Miriam laughed.

"Well, if you have an angel child at an angel hold, you have no responsibility at all. Everyone's so delighted at the birth that you're practically pushed aside so that the elder women can raise the baby right."

Susannah had joined Zibiah and the mikala on the bed and was leaning her head against the wall to calm her dizziness. "Is that true?" she said sleepily. "That angel babies are so prized?"

There was a general chorus of agreement. "So much so," Chloe said, "that sometimes mortal children born to angels are not exactly welcomed."

Miriam jumped to her feet and took three quick bows. "As witness, me," she said.

Susannah focused on her. "Who didn't welcome you? Your parents? The others in the hold?"

Miriam sat down again and began pulling the silver rollers from her hair. Chloe said, "It's not ready yet," but Miriam kept removing them, one after the other.

"My mother was happy with me—she'd always wanted a girl, and so far she'd had only one child, and that one a boy," Miriam said. "And, of course, Gaaron was just nine years old—he didn't care one way or the other if I was born at all. But my father—oh, he hated me. My mother always swore that he never tried to leave me out in the cold unattended, or failed to feed me, but I always had the sense that he wished he'd gotten rid of me when I was young enough to dispose of easily. When I was a little girl, he would come up with tasks for me to do—impossible things—and then punish me when I couldn't get them done right. And he would scream at me. So loud everyone in the hold could hear."

Susannah sat up, disturbed and uneasy. Among the Edori, children were considered a rich bounty, and the whole clan shared the responsibility of caring for them. Unfit mothers and neglectful fathers would simply find their children appropriated, absorbed into some other family, some other tent. Abuse was not tolerated. "Is this true?" she asked, looking at Zibiah.

Zibiah nodded slowly. Her hand was still stroking the Jansai's head, though the little girl appeared to have fallen asleep. "Oh, yes. My family lived just down the hall. You could hear the yelling, sometimes for hours. My mother would take me to the very back room, and crawl under the covers with me and make a little tent, and she'd read to me, but she couldn't drown out the sound of his voice."

"But—why couldn't—why didn't anyone stop him?"

Miriam was combing her hair out and peering into a handheld mirror to see if the chemicals had had any effect. They didn't appear to have. "He was leader of the host here," Miriam said. "Everyone respected him—"

"Everyone was afraid of him," Chloe interjected.

"And everyone thought he was probably right," Miriam finished up. She set down the mirror and looked over at Susannah with an impish grin. "I was a pretty awful child."

"She was always in trouble," Sela said.

"What did you do?"

Miriam shrugged. "Stole things. Ran away. Hid out in Velora for three days so they couldn't find me. Lied."

Susannah thought of that big sober angel who had spirited her away from her clan and who seemed the embodiment of sound judgment. "And what did Gaaron say about all this?"

Chloe stood behind Miriam and began making tiny braids in the blond hair. "He was gone for a long time," Chloe said. "Fostering with Adriel and Moshe at Windy Point. I think it was one of the reasons Michael was so cross with Miriam. He missed Gaaron so much."

"Michael?"

"My father," Miriam said. "Plus, he hated Adriel and he didn't like the fact that she had Gaaron and he didn't. It made him very unpleasant."

"Why did he let Gaaron go to her, then?"

Zibiah rolled to her back and put her arms behind her head. Her wings spread out behind her, one of them drifting off the side of the bed and the other folding up against the side of the wall, the ragged wingtips making sharp serrated shadows against the stone. "It's a tradition," she said. "The young, promising angels are always sent for a few years to live with the Archangel, to learn what it's like to rule the realm. That way, if Jovah chooses them to be the next Archangel, they will have some idea of what they're getting into. Michael was sure Gaaron would be named the next Archangel. But Gaaron wasn't the only angel fostered at Windy Point. There were four or five others over the next few years who also lived there. No one knew which one the god would choose."

Susannah looked at Miriam. "Your father must have been very proud when Gaaron was chosen, then," she said.

"My father was dead by then," Miriam said in a voice of great satisfaction. "I think the god waited on purpose to make the announcement."

"Miriam," Susannah said in a voice of reproach. "Yovah is not so spiteful."

Miriam shrugged. "Not spiteful. Just."

"But things were better anyway, once Gaaron got back," Chloe said. She began plaiting the smaller braids together, looping a blue ribbon through the whole confection. "Michael was just a little afraid of Gaaron."

"Afraid of his own son? Why, how old was Gaaron?"

"He came back from Windy Point when he was nineteen," Sela said. "And he was big. Not quite as muscled as he is now, but just as tall. And his wings! Michael had always had the greatest wingspan of anyone at the Eyrie, and he was very proud of his appearance. But Gaaron had grown a foot in height and three feet in wingspan while he was gone, and when he stood beside his father, he made Michael look small."

"I had never thought Michael would be intimidated by anyone," Chloe said.

"What did Gaaron do?" Susannah asked. She was horrified and fascinated by the whole story.

Miriam laughed. "Oh, not much. Things were pretty quiet when Gaaron first came back. We were all getting used to each other again. And then, a few times my father would yell at me for some reason, and I think once or twice he hit me when Gaaron was in the other room, or maybe once when Gaaron could see him, but it was all very restrained. Not like it had been while Gaaron was gone."

She held up the mirror again to check Chloe's work. "Oh, I like that. Use more of that dark blue ribbon." She laid the mirror back down. "And then one day I'd done something—taken one of my mother's rings, I think, a gift that my father had given her—and my father started ranting at me. Slapped me once, went stalking around the room in a rage, slapped me again, stood in front of me screaming so loud that his face was red. And Gaaron walked into the room."

She paused for a moment, as if reliving that scene, and everyone else in the room was silent. "He'd been in his bedroom but he'd been able to hear every word, I suppose, every slap. And he stood there in the doorway for a long time, just looking at my father. And—I'll never forget this—my father's face had been so red, and now it turned completely white. He straightened up and stood there next to me, and he seemed to shrink and shrink, till he was almost my size. And Gaaron seemed so big, just standing there watching us.

"And then Gaaron walked across the room, really slowly, and he kind of fanned his wings out. I remember, because they seemed to fill the whole room, and they were so white and so bright that they made the entire room glow. And he knelt down beside me, and he put his arms around me, and then he folded his wings around me. And so then I couldn't see anything, of course, but I felt him turn his head so he could still look at our father. And he said, in the calmest voice you can imagine, 'Don't you ever touch her again.' And he picked me up and took me back to his room and we played card games for the rest of the night."

Miriam shrugged and picked up the mirror again. "Oh, that's good," she said.

"I thought about putting in some silver thread," Chloe said.

"No, I like it just like this."

"But, Miriam," Susannah cried. "What happened after that? With your father?"

Miriam laughed. "Well, he never did hit me again. And once in a while he'd yell at me, but Gaaron would just have to walk into the room and he'd stop. It was great—except that then Gaaron always felt like *he* had to point out my faults and tell me when I was doing something wrong. I never cared what Gaaron said, though. I went ahead and did exactly what I wanted to anyway."

Susannah let out a deep breath; she didn't realize she'd been holding it. "What a tale," she said softly. "But I like your brother better for it."

"Everybody likes Gaaron," Miriam said, looking in the mirror again.

From behind Miriam, Chloe put her two hands on the blond girl's face and turned Miriam in Susannah's direction. "So what do you think?" she asked. "A style you'd like for your own wedding?"

Miriam looked gorgeous, her hair a textured, colorful weave of elegance. "It's beautiful," Susannah said.

"Well, come here and sit down," Chloe said. "Let's see what I can do."

So for the next half hour, Susannah sat in the middle of the room while Chloe fussed with her hair and Sela tried cosmetics on her face. "Your skin is so dark, but it has these bronze tones," Sela murmured. "I don't know that I have the right colors here, but let me try this—"

"Do you have any gold ribbon?" Chloe asked. "Or maybe red. I need something really bright against all this black."

"Oh, I like that, I do," Miriam murmured, stepping back to get a look at the whole effect. But they wouldn't let Susannah even peek into the mirror until both makeup and coiffure were complete.

And then they let her stand and walked her over to the big mirror in the corner of the room, the one that was as tall as Susannah herself and could contain her whole body if she paused before it. But now all she looked at was her head and her hair. And she gasped.

"It doesn't even look like me," she said, turning from side to side to try to view every angle. Sela had brushed smoky rouge onto her cheeks and applied dark red lipstick to her mouth; she had rimmed Susannah's eyes with a faint black line, which made her dark eyes appear huge. Chloe had woven gold and crimson ribbons into the sleek black hair, turning it into a vivid tapestry of unrelated images.

"Bells," Chloe said, as Susannah twisted this way and that. "For her wedding day, little bells in her hair. Don't you think?"

Opinion was divided on that, but Susannah liked sound just as much as she liked color, and she thought she would like to try the bells sometime. "I look so *beautiful*," she said at last. "Thank you all so much! You make me feel so welcome."

An outcry at that—"Of course you're welcome among us!"—but they didn't really know what she meant. None of them knew what it was like to be so far from friends and family that you could not even imagine how to get back, and how lonely the company of strangers could be, even the company of well-meaning strangers. But these little acts of friendship mattered immeasurably to Susannah, slight and trivial though they were. Being alone was so much worse to one who had always been surrounded. And now she felt, just a little bit, covered up again by love.

They talked late into the night, drowsing on their bedrolls. Susannah drifted off to sleep more than once, convinced that the conversation was finally done, and then she would wake to catch a few more scattered words. Now and then, someone rose to use the water room, invariably tripping over some supine body on the floor, and then there would be smothered giggles and an exchange of insults. The little Jansai girl cried out once in the night, and Susannah stirred, but before she could even sit up, she could hear Zibiah's voice comforting the mikala in the dark.

It was as much like sleeping in an Edori tent as not sleeping in an Edori tent could ever be. In the morning, despite not having slept very many hours, Susannah felt as rested and as happy as she had felt since the last night she had slept in Dathan's arms, still convinced he loved her.

The next day they spent down in Velora, all except Zibiah, who had work to do in the hold, and the Jansai girl, who stayed with Zibiah. They spent a great deal of time in the open-air markets, fingering the merchandise and bargaining with the vendors, who seemed just a little wary of this explosion of girls into their midst. Although only Miriam, at nineteen, was really a girl, Susannah thought. Chloe and Sela were a couple of years older than she was, Susannah guessed, and Zibiah was somewhere in between. But they acted young, young as Keren, and Miriam's high spirits infected all of them. So perhaps the merchants were right to be wary.

In fact, Susannah kept her eye on Miriam, and watched her as she fondled gold bracelets or let the piles of semiprecious stones sift through her fingers. The look on Miriam's face was speculative, and Susannah remembered how, the night before, the blond girl had admitted that she had stolen things in the past. Miriam had a silver necklace in her hands and had been looking at it for the longest time, when she glanced up to find Susannah's eyes on her. Susannah shook her head, and Miriam smiled and put the necklace back.

After that, Susannah watched her even more closely.

They bought bolts of fabric, yards of lace and trim, handfuls of beads and sequins and bells. No one ever seemed to pay for anything, for Susannah saw no money changing hands, but all the women flashed their bracelets at the merchants as a sort of identification. Miriam, when asked, confirmed this; the Eyrie had an unlimited spending budget across Samaria, and all a resident had to do was show the coded bracelet to be able to make a purchase.

"You'll get one, too, when you are Gaaron are married," Miriam said, displaying hers to Susannah. It was a slim spiral of gold set at random intervals with three sapphires arranged in triangles. "It has to include sapphires in this pattern, but you can have them set in gold or silver, in a wide band or a narrow one—whatever you like."

"It looks very expensive," Susannah said.

Miriam laughed. "The Eyrie is rich."

Late in the day, the four of them were joined by Nicholas and Ahio, and, after much discussion, they settled on a small, dark, and clearly fashionable establishment in which to have dinner. The group including angels was escorted instantly to a table while other patient would-be diners had to wait a little longer. Susannah smiled an apology at the mere mortals as they passed, but saw no looks of recrimination on their faces. Apparently, being an angel was a pretty good excuse for any kind of behavior, rude or not. Or maybe it was youth that excused it.

They ate well, drank more wine than Susannah was comfortable with, and laughed even more than they had the night before. A man at a neighboring table had another bottle of wine sent over to them, so Miriam went to thank him and his friends and stayed a long time at his table. Chloe, Sela, and the men seemed to think nothing of this, but Susannah watched her, a little troubled. Miriam's open friendliness was one of her most endearing traits, the Edori thought—but maybe one of her more dangerous ones. Susannah was not so sure the young woman should be laughing so flirtatiously with men whom no one from the angel hold seemed to know.

"Excuse me," Susannah said to the others, and went to join Miriam and her newfound friends.

Miriam seemed delighted at Susannah's appearance. "Sit with us for a while! This is—wait, I can remember—this is Leet and Kasho and—and—Morvai! They've only been in Velora a few days, but they've already eaten at every restaurant and tavern in town."

"And we like this one the best by far," Morvai said smoothly.

The names were Jansai, Susannah thought; so were the faces, smooth and calculating, their skin oily with rich food eaten over a lifetime. They didn't wear traditional Jansai robes, so they weren't traders, at least not conventional ones. Probably in Velora to set up some kind of lawful business—a profitable one, of course, but nothing illegal.

Still, Susannah had the Edori's instinctive mistrust of Jansai, and she did not like any group of older men to be courting a nineteen-year-old girl, especially when those men had been raised in a culture that despised women.

Susannah pulled out a chair and sat down, letting her smile mask all her thoughts. "And where have you traveled from?" she asked.

Leet waved a hand. "Oh, from everywhere. Most recently Semorrah."

"Semorrah!" Miriam exclaimed, as if she had never been there, when Susannah knew for a fact that she had. "Is it as beautiful as they say?"

Leet laughed. "It is a strange city. They are building it on a rock in the middle of the Galilee River! No one can get to it except by boat. And you would ask, well, then, who would go there? But mark my words, that will be the city that everyone will want to visit. Because it is so rare, and so difficult, it will become precious."

"*I* want to go," Miriam said.

Morvai leaned closer to her. "We may head back that way when we leave Velora. You could travel with us."

"Could I?" Miriam said, with every appearance of delight.

"We would be happy to have you with us," Leet said, scrawling down something on a piece of paper. "Here is where we are staying. You could join us tonight or tomorrow to discuss travel plans."

"When will you be leaving Velora?" Susannah asked.

Morvai shrugged. "It's hard to say. Maybe in a day or so. Maybe in a week or two."

"When your business is concluded," Susannah said.

He smiled at her somewhat ferally. "You say that as if you doubt we have legitimate business here."

Susannah opened her eyes wide. "As far as I know, all Jansai are legitimate businessmen."

There was a little silence around the table, but none of the men denied their heritage. Leet examined Susannah a little more closely. "And what's an Edori woman doing so far from any Edori camp?" he asked. "Or did we miss your kinsmen as they pitched their tents somewhere near the city?"

"No, my clan is far from here at the moment," Susannah said calmly. "I am making my home at the Eyrie now."

"Yes," Miriam gushed, with just a shade too much enthusiasm. Not for the first time, Susannah suspected that Miriam was toying with the Jansai even more than they were playing with her. "She has come here to marry my brother."

"And your brother lives at the Eyrie, does he?" Morvai asked.

"Oh, yes. We were both born there."

"Pity to live in an angel hold and not be born an angel," Leet said. "Or so I've been told."

"Oh, but Gaaron is an angel," Miriam said, all wide-eyed. "He leads the host, in fact."

There was another silence, this one longer and more startled. "Gabriel Aaron?" Morvai said cautiously. "Who will be Archangel next year?"

"That's him," Miriam said happily. "He's *such* a good brother to me. I don't know that he'd really want me to leave and go to Semorrah without him."

There was another dead silence.

"I just had a thought," Susannah said smoothly. "Perhaps Gaaron would take you to Semorrah someday. Just for a visit. That way you could see the city, and he wouldn't have to worry about you being gone for a long time."

"Oh, yes, let's ask him tonight!" Miriam exclaimed. "That would be so much fun! Though I would like to travel with all of you," she added somewhat wistfully.

Susannah came to her feet. "Look, mikala, they've just brought over our food to our table," she said. "Say thank you to these nice Jansai for sharing their wine with us, and let's go join our friends."

Miriam stood up. "Thank you so much," she said prettily. "I hope your business in Velora goes *very* well."

The three Jansai grunted their good-byes, their eyes now smoldering a bit and their farewells sounding none too sincere. Miriam, on the other hand, was alight with sheer festive happiness as she and Susannah returned to the others and took their places.

"You're trouble," Susannah said in a low voice as she sat down next to Miriam.

The blond girl giggled and sent her a look of unadulterated mischief. "That's what everyone says."

"What, you weren't really worried about a bunch of old men like that?" Nicholas asked with disbelief.

"They're not so old," Susannah said with some heat. "*And* they're Jansai. *And* I don't think they're too afraid of angels or anybody else."

"Miriam's fine," Chloe said with a shrug. "She can take care of herself."

"I was only having a little fun with them," Miriam said to Susannah. "I really can take care of myself."

Susannah watched her thoughtfully. How to make this girl see reason without making her furious? No wonder her brother found her such a challenge. "No, you can't," she said softly. "Nobody really can."

The next five or six days passed in much the same way. Sometimes they shopped, sometimes they sang, sometimes they sat in the Eyrie and gossiped, but Susannah was always in the company of Miriam and her cadre of young, attractive friends. The first few nights, one or two of them slept in her room with her but, as she expected, that custom faded quickly. Miriam always made a point of coming to Susannah's room the last thing every night, to say good-bye and add, "Now, you won't be lonely, will you?" but after those first few days, Susannah's nights were spent alone. She tried not to mind.

The longer she knew them, the more Susannah was able to sort out the individuals in her new circle of friends. Ahio, for all his incredible good looks and lazy appearance, was the most serious of the group, a true musician with some passion for his calling. Nicholas, who was quick-tempered and volatile, was utterly good-hearted, quick to offer sympathy or support no matter how absurd the issue. Zibiah would do whatever she was asked, whether it was watch a lonely Jansai child or race another angel to the far side of the Velora market; she did not seem to have much independent conception of good or bad. Chloe had enough energy to inject even the quietest moment with hilarity. Sela had common sense when she chose to use it, which was maybe one quarter of the time.

And Miriam . . . Miriam was loving and defiant and intelligent and fractious and kind and aloof by turns.

Susannah could well understand why Gaaron had called his sister *young and pretty and difficult.* She could understand less well why he had not, from years of tearing out his hair in frustration, grown quite bald with the effort of raising her.

She wondered if she would ever get an opportunity to tell him that. She wondered if he would ever return to the Eyrie. He had been gone now for about a week, and she felt like she would never get a chance to know him, this angel whom she was to marry in a few months' time.

Surely, if Yovah had picked them for each other, he had meant them to interact a little more than this.

But finally one night, as she and Nicholas and Chloe and Miriam returned to the Eyrie very late, Miriam said, "Gaaron's back."

They were all disentangling on the open plateau where the angels landed. "How can you tell?" Susannah asked, looking around as if she had somehow overlooked Gaaron lurking in one of the nearby doorways.

"He's singing," Miriam said. "Can't you hear him?"

Susannah tilted her head to listen. From above came the choral voices of maybe a dozen singers—a large number to draw this late, for it was past midnight, but it sounded like a group of friends who had planned to stay up for an occasion and who were having a good time serenading the moon. The mix seemed weighted a little more toward female than male singers, and Susannah could not identify any single voices.

"I've never heard him sing," she apologized. "I can't pick him out."

"Well, it's him," Nicholas said definitively. "Think I'll go up and join in."

"Me, too," Miriam decided.

Chloe yawned. "I'm too tired! I'll see everyone in the morning."

Much as Susannah wanted to meet with her prospective bridegroom again, seeing him in a large group so late at night did not seem the ideal circumstance. She followed Chloe inside and said a sleepy good night as their paths verged in the gaslit halls.

Once she stepped inside her own room, Susannah found a note had been slipped under the door. It was from Gaaron and it was short: "I've been gone long, I know. Could you meet me for breakfast in my rooms tomorrow? If you can. Gabriel Aaron."

Susannah read this a couple of times, wondering if there was any tone to be discerned. Was he angry that she had been gone when he returned? Or had he come in so late himself that he just assumed any rational person would be asleep already? Was the opening line an apology? And why sign the note with both his names, which she had never used, which were only employed by the Jansai and the people who spoke of him as the Archangel-to-be? An implicit reprimand there? A reminder of his status and, by extension, hers?

Or simply the quick, negligent scrawl of a tired man who was not thinking too clearly as he settled back home after a long absence?

Nevertheless, Susannah slept fitfully, rose early, and took some care with her appearance. She put on one of the new skirts she had bought in the Velora market, but matched it with one of her old blouses, a beautiful purple-dyed cotton shirt that Anna had made for her. *My old life paired with my new,* she thought, *not that I really feel part of either world these days.*

Esther was just leaving Gaaron's room, pushing a wheeled cart before her. She greeted Susannah with a small sniff, as if surprised to see her awake so early or not surrounded by questionable company. Susannah grimaced as she sounded the chime on Gaaron's door. No need to wonder, then, if Gaaron had heard much of Susannah's activities while he had been gone.

But Gaaron, when she entered, did not seem to be thinking about anything so trivial as Susannah. He was standing before his triple windows, his face in profile to her, his great wings held stiffly behind him like shoulders hunched against pain. His face looked drawn and tired.

"Gaaron," Susannah said, and closed the door.

He turned his head to look over at her, and the sunlight threw every plane of his face into relief. He was not a particularly handsome man, but his features were strong, the cheekbones thick, the mouth generous. The brown eyes, so like Miriam's, looked utterly exhausted.

He smiled, though it appeared to be an effort, and crossed the room. "Susannah," he said. "It is good to see you."

There was an awkward moment when both of them wondered if they should shake hands or hug or merely just stand face-to-face, closer than strangers might, and then Gaaron put an arm around her shoulders and steered her over to the table. The gesture was comforting; she suddenly remembered the feel of his arms from that long flight to the Eyrie ten days ago.

The table was set for two. They separated to sit down. "And good to see you," she replied formally. "But you look tired."

He nodded and began serving himself. On the table were bowls of fruit and a cooked cereal and some spicy meats. His hunger was evident; he put a lot on his plate. "Exhausted and—uncertain. Not a good combination."

She waited a moment but he did not volunteer more. "Come," she prompted. "What have you learned in your long sojourn at Adriel's?"

He handed the serving spoons to her and waited while she put smaller portions on her plate. But he did not eat, even when they both were ready. "I don't know what's happening," he said at last. "Perhaps you've heard—I haven't had a chance to tell you—a couple of weeks ago, we came across a burned campsite down by the Corinni Mountains—"

"Miriam told me," she interrupted. "And I've spent some time with the little Jansai girl."

He showed a quick interest. "Has she told you anything?"

"No. She doesn't talk."

"Right. So we don't know what happened at the campsite, to destroy it so utterly. And then Adriel told me of another place, south of the Caitanas—also burned beyond recognition. Not Jansai this time, but—"

"Edori?" Susannah asked on a swiftly indrawn breath.

He shook his head. "No. A small farm settlement. A house, a barn, a dairy—each one completely leveled, charred to cinders. How, Adriel had no idea." He took one quick bite, but not as if he noticed what he put into his mouth. "I must get in touch with Neri at Monteverde and ask if she has come across any such devastation."

"I saw one," Susannah said in a small voice. "Down by Luminaux. We saw it—oh, a week or so before you came to our camp."

"Describe it to me," he said grimly, but he only nodded when she gave him the bleak details. "It sounds like the same site Solomon mentioned to me," he said. "But how can that *be*? What can cause such destruction?"

"And why?" Susannah asked. "I do not like to think it, but it sounds as if—as if a person—someone—had acquired the power to destroy other people. To destroy campsites and buildings this way—so precisely—it is not a random, unthinking act."

"It is not as if a lightning bolt came down and torched the earth," Gaaron said. "I know. I thought of that."

"Although . . ." Susannah let her words trail off as her mind started racing. "Although, angels *can* call lightning bolts, can they not? Or so I have always been told."

He looked at her sharply. "You think an *angel* did these things?"

"I was just—"

"No angel in the three holds would think to cause such destruction! Most angels never in their *lives* call down a thunderbolt, not for any reason! We know the prayers, yes, we are taught them, but these are not prayers we offer to the god! Don't say such things!"

"I did not mean to make you angry," she said quietly. "I just wondered if—if the type of destruction we saw is the kind of destruction that can be caused by a lightning strike from Yovah's hand."

He played with his cereal, now starting to grow cold. "I don't know," he admitted at last. "*I've* never called down a thunderbolt. I don't know if it burns cleanly or if it slices right down to the exact inch of ground you wish it to strike. I have always assumed it was a power not to be toyed with—that it might not be so precise as you might like and that you would have to be desperate to chance it."

"Maybe someone was that desperate."

Anger flashed in his eyes again. "I told you that no angel—"

"Perhaps it wasn't an angel," she said.

"Then who?"

She shrugged. "Angels are not the only ones who can pray to the god," she said. "The Edori lift their voices to Yovah every day, and he hears us and answers us. Perhaps some other mortal has learned these prayers that call down thunderbolts."

"Impossible," Gaaron said flatly.

"And why?"

"Because an angel would have to teach him those prayers! He could not learn them on his own!"

"I am learning masses sung by angels long dead, on machines that I did not even know existed," Susannah said. "Perhaps such machines exist elsewhere, in places you do not know of, and they contain more songs. More prayers. You don't know this isn't true."

"I don't know it," he admitted. "But it's a fanciful theory."

She gave him a small smile. "And your theory is—?"

"I don't have one," he said. "I can't even credit what is happening."

"There was another story," she said. "Nicholas told me. About a disappearing man."

Gaaron took another bite of his cereal and swallowed before speaking again. "An even harder one to believe! At least the circles of fire I saw with my own eyes."

"Has anyone else seen something like that? Did the Archangel say?"

"I did ask her. She hadn't heard it. Again, I'll ask Neri. Though a man would have to be very sure of himself to start telling such a tale. Most people would rather believe they'd been dreaming than that they really saw a man disappear."

"I think you should call down a thunderbolt," she said.

He gave her a quick look. "Just to see how it burns?" She nodded, but he shook his head. "A dangerous tactic. I would rather have Mahalah ask the god for information."

Susannah shrugged and addressed herself more attentively to her food. The meat was wonderful, better than anything she'd been served at the formal meals while Gaaron was gone. Like everyone else in the hold, Esther revered Gaaron; she would reserve any special treats for his return.

"So that is the tale of my last week," Gaaron said, trying to make his voice sound conversational. It still sounded strained. "How have you amused yourself since I've been gone?"

Susannah glanced up at him, a little smile on her mouth. "Surely you've heard that tale by now."

He smiled reluctantly in return. "You are said to have made friends with the all the youngest and wildest angels of my hold. As well as my sister, the youngest and wildest of all."

"She is a challenge," Susannah admitted. "But I love her already. I don't see how anyone can help it."

Gaaron lifted a glass of juice but did not sip from it, just sat there looking distracted. "I don't know what to do with her," he said. "She is, as you say, easy to love—but I fear for her, I fear where her inner devils will lead her. I don't think there is anything she would not try, just to try it—anything, no matter how bad it is. Just to see."

"If that is really true," Susannah said, "I don't know that you'll be able to stop her."

"I could lock her up in the Eyrie," he said. "Put out an interdiction that no angel can carry her off the mountaintop. That would curb some of her wildness."

"I don't think so," Susannah said, alarmed. "She would find a way down if she had to crawl through the rocks till her hands and feet were bloody. Even if the angels heeded your embargo—"

"They would," he said stiffly.

"She would elude you. And she'd hate you for it."

He ticked off experiences on his fingertips. "I've tried sending her to Adriel. Disastrous. I've tried sending her to the Manadavvi. She and some pampered heiress ran away—*disappeared*—for three weeks, and the Manadavvi girl has never been quite right since then. I've tried sending her to one of the river merchants in Castelana. She stole a valuable shipment—she swears she didn't, but I know she did—and caused an actual *duel* between two merchant partners, who are now sworn enemies. I have thought of sending her to Solomon—in Breven, you know—the Jansai know how to tame the spirit of the most rebellious woman."

"I think Miriam would lead a rebellion among the Jansai women instead," Susannah said. "Which, come to think of it, would not be so bad. Let's do that! Tell her why, and she'll go happily."

Gaaron smiled reluctantly. "And then she would be on the loose again. No, it does not seem like a permanent solution."

"I don't think you're going to be able to solve her," Susannah said softly. "I think Miriam is—Miriam is going to have to figure out who she is and who she wants to be. It is very hard to live up to a brother like you. She has to be a little outrageous to get any attention at all."

He grunted—an expression of surprise or acknowledgment, she could not tell—and finally sipped from his juice. "So! Aside from watching over Miriam, how have you spent your time while I've been gone?"

"By getting to know your young and wild angels, of course," she said immediately. "I know what you are thinking—these do not seem like the kinds of friends Susannah would make—"

Suddenly his eyes focused on hers, dark and intense. "I don't know you well enough to make that assessment," he said slowly. "You seem earnest and well-reasoned. You have been very calm in all your dealings with me. But somehow—I am not convinced that is who you are. You are like a Jansai woman—you wear a lot of veils and hide your true self."

Susannah smiled a little wryly at that. "There have been times in my life I have been so sober you would not have recognized my face with a smile on it. I am at heart a serious woman. But I am drawn to wildness, I will admit. Miriam—Keren—others in my life—" She faltered, but she would not name Dathan, she *would not*. "I am happiest when I am surrounded by that energy and that joy. It lifts me up. Without it, I sometimes find life—a little dreary. But I am not so unpredictable myself."

"There is not an ounce of wildness in me," Gaaron said. "I am the most practical of men."

"I know," Susannah said quietly.

There was a little silence.

"That does not mean," he said, "that we cannot forge a strong alliance between us. I find—I have an inclination to trust you. Your judgment is sound. I like to hear what you say in response to what I say. I realize that is not a—not an exciting relationship. I have not been accused by many women of being exciting."

She desperately wanted to ask him if he'd ever been in love, but she was too embarrassed. She would ask Miriam later, or the indiscreet Chloe. "I did not come here for excitement, as Keren would have," she said in a low voice.

"No, you came because your heart was breaking," he said unexpectedly. "I understand that. And I understand—perhaps I should explain—" He broke off, embarrassed himself. "If you find a search for excitement takes you elsewhere, among other men—angels do not find this—angels often sample the attractions of many," he ended in a rush. Then he became all formal again. "I do not know what conventions of fidelity govern the behavior of the Edori, but among angels no such conventions apply."

She had already been depressed by his earlier speech about forging an alliance. Now she thought her lungs would close up from a disinclination to breathe. "For the most part, Edori are faithful to each other as long as they love each other," she said quietly. "How much a brief infidelity matters to an Edori varies with the individual. I have never been the type of woman to love more than one man at a time." She made a helpless gesture. "But then, I have only really loved one man."

"And may not ever love again," he said. "Yes. But we can be friends, you and I, don't you think? Allies?"

Drearier and drearier, but what had she expected? She made herself look him straight in the eye. "Yes. Most excellent allies," she said firmly.

He held his hand out across the table and she laid hers in it. His hand was huge; it engulfed hers. He closed his fingers over hers with just enough pressure to make her think he could break every bone in her body without even meaning to. Edori men were strong, used to physical exercise and hard labor, but this man's strength was so implicit in every joint and muscle that it was almost frightening.

"I'm glad you're here, Susannah," he said.

She could not bring herself to say the reciprocal sentiments out loud. "Thank you," she replied.

It was a relief when the meal was finally over and she could escape to her room. Not knowing what she intended until she shut the door behind her, she leaned her head against the wall and started sobbing.

CHAPTER NINE

Gaaron had been shocked at the look on Adriel's face when he told her of the devastated campsite. A handsome woman in her mid-fifties, Adriel had always seemed to Gaaron the embodiment of reason and calm. He had greatly admired her when, as a teenager, he was sent to live with her for five years; she had been his model far more than his angry father or his timid mother had been. Then, of course, she had been in her prime, a strongly built, no-nonsense woman whose physical endurance was legendary. She could sing for hours, praying away rain or drought or plague, and never evince a moment's weariness. She was not the sympathetic, comforting sort, but everyone in the hold brought her their problems and told her their dreams, and trusted her completely to take care of them.

Gaaron had wanted to be that kind of leader. But he hoped he was never so shaken and at a loss as Adriel looked when he told her about the burned camp.

"Another one," she said, and told him her own tale of a ruined farm. As she spoke, she leaned her head against her hand. The black hair was graying already. The full, confident features looked thinner, as the features of a statue might look worn by the constant assault of time and weather. "Then, if there are two, there will be more. It cannot be accidental."

"There are three," he said, and he repeated Solomon's story. "But what can it be?"

She looked over at him and shook her head. "I have no idea."

The story of the disappearing man she found easier to dismiss, possibly because Gaaron did as well. So easy to write that off to too much wine or the power of imagination.

"But keep me apprised," she said. "Of any odd happenings that you observe. Perhaps if we see a pattern emerging . . ."

She shrugged and did not finish the sentence. *We can take care of it* or *We can ask for the god's help* or *We will know what to do.* She did not say any of those things. Clearly she could not think of what she, what any of the angels, might do to solve a problem so out of their experience.

For the first time, Gaaron realized that when he became Archangel, in less than a year's time, all these burdens would be his and his alone. Not even Adriel would be able to help him. Adriel was exhausted from her own twenty years of trouble.

Pray god Jovah had chosen wisely for him, then, when he named Susannah as his angelica, for he would need someone with whom he could confer and from whom he could solicit advice.

As if she had read his mind, Adriel changed the subject. "So I hear you have found your bride," she said, straightening in her chair and essaying a smile. "An Edori, no less. An unusual choice, but who can tell the mind of Jovah? What is she like?"

"I have only spent a few days with her," Gaaron said ruefully. "She seems—she seems to be a reasonable woman. Not given to emotional outbursts, at least so far. I think maybe she misses her Edori family. I hope she'll make friends at the Eyrie."

Adriel smiled more freely. "Reasonable and unemotional! What very dull words to use to describe the woman you will marry."

He smiled back. "They sound soothing to me. Someone passionate and unmanageable—like my sister—would be impossible to deal with. I will take placid and cool any day."

"I could kill your father," were Adriel's next unexpected words, but Gaaron could read the story behind the statement well enough. Adriel blamed Michael for every one of Miriam's misdeeds and now, apparently, for Gaaron's own stoicism.

"He is already dead," Gaaron said. "No need."

"He has much to answer for."

"Perhaps, but Jovah is the one who will review that with him," Gaaron said, rising to his feet. "I must go. It has been good to see you, Adriel. I would say that I look forward to seeing you again soon, except that I'm afraid such a meeting would mean more bad news from one of us at least."

"Perhaps not," she said. "Perhaps we will next come together to celebrate your wedding, and that will be a happy time. When is the event to occur?"

He looked at her blankly. "I don't know. We haven't discussed it. I suppose Susannah will have some thoughts on that."

Adriel drew his head down so she could kiss him on the cheek. "Yes, your calm, unemotional bride will probably have more thoughts on that topic than you would suspect."

He had left and set off, leaving Windy Point behind. It was situated in a high, lonely peak just north of the Caitanas, in the most inhospitable stretch of land in all of Samaria. Its sole geographical advantage was its nearness to the Plain of Sharon, the broad, open land where the people of Samaria gathered every year to sing the Gloria. But that was not enough of an advantage, Gaaron thought, to make cold, gray, inaccessible Windy Point an inviting place. Give him the Eyrie any day, with its warm walls and its constant music and its happy placement in the middle of Bethel.

It took him nearly two days to get back to his hold, during which time his last conversation with Adriel played through his mind more than once. Mahalah, too, had as good as accused him of insensitivity to the charms of women, but he supposed he could not help that. A man either responded to flighty, melodramatic, and flirtatious women, or he did not. He had to admit, he had had grave doubts about Susannah back there when they were at the Edori campsite, for every time he saw her, she was arguing with her lover. But she had been so quiet since he brought her to the Eyrie, so attentive when she listened to him, so thoughtful when she spoke. It seemed the god had indeed set out to find just the right match for the Archangel-to-be.

So it was something of a jolt to arrive at the Eyrie late one night and be told his chosen bride was not home, had not been all day, was probably still down in Velora carousing with the most high-spirited and aimless of the souls under Gaaron's care.

"Not a finger's width of difference between them, Chloe and Miriam and Susannah and that whole lot," Esther had said with a certain malicious zest. "And her seeming so quiet when she got here."

It had been with some misgiving that he had invited Susannah to join him the following morning, hoping she would not, after a few short days, appear debauched and reckless. But she had not. She had come into his chambers with an inquiring look on her face and the same pleasant demeanor he remembered, and he had been happy to see her. Not plunged into ecstasy, as a romantic new bridegroom might be, but pleased. He liked the strict, sober lines of her face, its dark complexion both exotic and restful; he liked the long black hair that she wore simply styled. It was so dark and so fine that, now and then, he found himself wanting to touch it, just to feel its shine against his fingers, as if a shine could actually have texture.

And he liked the way she talked about Miriam, as if she already cared about the impossible girl. And he liked how she listened to him, and he thought their chances of making a pretty acceptable match of it were better than good.

He had never really expected more than that from his angelica. It was, in some ways, a relief to get so much.

Having been gone more than a week, Gaaron found that there was much at the hold that needed his attention. First, of course, there were the petitioners who had waited for him all this time, taking hotel rooms in Velora until he got back, and exhibiting an inexorable patience because no one else's counsel or mediation was good enough for them. One of these was a merchant who claimed that Gaaron's sister had stolen three of his bracelets and demanded reparation. Gaaron paid it without even arguing.

Then, of course, there was the inevitable session with Miriam, who merely laughed when accused of her crime. "He *saw* me take those? I can't believe it. Susannah didn't see me, and she's been hovering over me like a bird of prey. I did it more to see if I could trick her than because I wanted the stupid bracelets."

"Then perhaps you'd like to return them to their rightful owner."

"I thought you said you already paid for them? Then why can't I just keep them?"

"I have a better idea," Gaaron said. "You will give them as gifts. To three people you may have insulted in the past few days."

She frowned mutinously. "What makes you think I—"

"Esther," he said, because it was a certainty that *something* she'd done in the past week had offended that prickly old soul. "Enoch." Esther's husband, a prissy and grouchy old angel, who had even less love for Miriam than Esther did. "And Susannah."

"Susannah! I haven't done anything to hurt her feelings. I adore her."

"You stole something to outwit her. I think that will make her feel bad when she finds out."

Miriam eyed him with disfavor. "And who will tell her that?"

"You will, when you give her the bracelet."

She argued a little more, but eventually gave in, and Gaaron was there at dinner that night when his sister presented the gift to his betrothed. He was watching Susannah's face when the little scene played itself out, wondering if this fresh evidence of Miriam's waywardness would turn Susannah against the girl. But it did not seem to. Susannah listened seriously to Miriam's quick, laughing tale, nodded, thanked her for the bracelet, and slipped it on her wrist. She said nothing more about it, and Miriam seemed a bit deflated, having no doubt primed herself with a lot of excuses to turn aside Susannah's wrath or sorrow. But when Miriam left their table to go lounge beside Chloe for a while, Gaaron saw Susannah watch her saunter away. The look on the Edori's face intrigued him. She was frowning, as if she was trying to solve a puzzle, but she did not look as though she despaired of figuring it out.

In addition to Miriam, there were other youthful troublemakers at the Eyrie who had considered Gaaron's absence a chance to behave badly. Zack, Jude, and their companions had disrupted the hourly harmonics one afternoon by coming through and yodeling completely dissonant and off-key music at the top of their lungs. They had stolen all the chairs from the dining room one night before dinner (though they were easily retrieved from the storerooms), and they had gotten drunk on the wine reserved for sacred ceremonies. All of these problems had been dealt with by Esther and Enoch, but Gaaron made sure to talk to the boys individually in the sternest voice he could muster, and he had the satisfaction of seeing Jude, at least, look a little scared.

Zack, of course, was impossible to overawe, but he did look a little apprehensive at Gaaron's threat. "If I don't see better behavior from you soon, I'll have to send you away," Gaaron said.

Zack sneered. "Send me where? To Velora? All my friends come there every day."

"Actually, I was thinking more like Breven," Gaaron said. The idea was borne of his conversation with Susannah. He could not *really* send Miriam to Solomon, but why not Zack? Or why not pretend he might send Zack? "The Jansai were just telling me they wish Windy Point was closer so that they could have easier access to an angel intercessor. Seems it was even drier than usual over Breven this summer, and they were hoping someone could be on hand fairly often to pray for rain."

Now Zack looked slightly alarmed. "I can't go to Breven! I can't sing prayers to Jovah!"

Gaaron arched his brows. "You can't? I thought you were studying your masses along with all the other boys your age."

"Yes, but—I haven't—not on my own I couldn't—and Ahio or Nicholas always sings with me."

"I'm sure you could perform the prayers," Gaaron said. "I'll come listen to you tomorrow to check on your progress."

"But I don't want to go to Breven!" Zack burst out.

Gaaron examined him with a look of interest on his face. "You don't? Well, you don't behave as if you want to live here."

There was a short silence. "Well, I do," Zack said sullenly.

"And why would that be?"

Zack hunched a shoulder. "All my friends are here. And—and I can do stuff."

"Get drunk and steal the chairs. I don't think I want you to 'do' that sort of stuff."

Zack flushed. "That's not what I meant. If I go to Breven, I won't be able to play the flute anymore. Who would teach me? I don't want to go."

Gaaron hid his surprise at this artless revelation. "Well, I'll think about it," was all he said. "But if you keep acting the way you have been—" He shrugged, and his wings lifted and fell behind him. "I'll have to do something with you. And you might not like what I choose."

Naturally, as soon as this conversation was over, Gaaron had to hunt up Ahio and find out if Zack really was coming to the older angel for flute lessons, and how those lessons were going. Ahio, whom he tracked down in one of the music rooms listening to a mass that Gaaron would have thought he would have long ago had by heart, nodded in his usual careless way when asked about Zack's progress.

"Good at it. A natural," Ahio said. "I never did think his voice was much above average, but he's got a feel for the wind instruments. I've tried him on the clarinet, too. I think you'll like what you hear."

"If I don't banish him before I have a chance to listen to him," Gaaron said.

"You can't really send him to Breven," Ahio said, though there was a faint questioning lilt in his voice.

"About a dozen people I'd pack off to Breven if I really thought it would do any good," Gaaron said with a sigh. "But, no, I can't. For one thing, he wouldn't stay. For another—" He paused and considered. "For another, I don't entirely trust the Jansai. I can't really say why."

" 'Cause they're a bunch of calculating and lying cheats," Ahio said without heat. He was fiddling with the chrome controls of the machine. "Susannah doesn't like them, either. And Susannah pretty much seems to like everybody."

"She said you and Miriam were teaching her some masses."

Ahio touched a button and the music that had been playing noticeably slowed, the singers' voices becoming low and elongated, as if their tongues had been stretched out and their throats had been choked. "What did you do?" Gaaron exclaimed.

Ahio grinned at him over his shoulder. "Cut the tempo. Way too much, but I'm trying to get the pitch to change."

Gaaron came a step closer. "I didn't even know you could do that. How did you figure that out?"

Ahio shrugged. "I spend a lot of time down here. Fool with the machines a lot. Did you know there are a couple of masses that you can play simultaneously? Note for note, beat for beat, they match up. You wouldn't believe the harmony you can get—eight-part, twelve-part—and these amazing fugues, interweaving between the two pieces. I've never heard anything like it."

"No," said Gaaron blankly. "I didn't know that. Could they be sung that way live?"

"Sure. Take a lot of rehearsal, but I bet you'd bring down the mountain if you tried that at a Gloria."

Gaaron smiled faintly. "It's the angelica's task to choose a mass for the Gloria."

Ahio nodded. "She knows. I'm helping her pick one out."

It was something the angelica was supposed to do on her own— by tradition, in great secrecy—choose the mass that would set the tone for the entire Gloria. In practice, of course, the angelica often an-

nounced her selection in advance so she and the Archangel could practice the piece well enough to make a creditable presentation.

"That's good," Gaaron says. "I'm sure she doesn't know the sacred music."

Ahio fiddled with the controls again, and the tempo picked up a
little, though not to concert speed. "And she's an alto *and* she doesn't
like to sing solos," the younger angel said. "We're going to have to
adapt something for her."

"But—all the masses open with a solo. Male part or female part.
All of them," Gaaron said.

Ahio gave him a swift, sweet smile. "That's why we're going to
have to adapt. Think you'll be opening on a duet for your first Gloria."

Gaaron didn't have much to say in response to that, so he left,
thinking it all over. Well, why not? There were only two unbreakable
rules of the Gloria. One was that it be performed every year, on the
Plain of Sharon, on the morning of the spring equinox. The other was
that it feature representatives of all the peoples in Samaria—angels,
Jansai, Manadavvi, Edori, and ordinary mortals. The Gloria was
meant to be proof to the god that all these individuals were living
together in harmony, that they had not—as the races on their home
world had—begun to war on one another with a ferocity that would
someday end in total destruction. As long as the Gloria was sung, the
god trusted that they were living their lives in some kind of peace. If
it was not sung, so the Librera told them, the god would send a thunderbolt to strike Mount Galo, the hulking peak that guarded the southern edge of the plain. If, within three more days, the Gloria was not
sung, he would destroy the river Galilee that flowed down the middle
of Samaria. If it was not sung three days after that, he would destroy
the world.

Naturally, since the time Samaria had been colonized two hundred
and forty years ago, the Gloria had never been overlooked.

In fact, as Gaaron had told Susannah, he had never even seen the
god unleash a thunderbolt, though he did indeed know the prayers
that would call one down. And he absolutely, in every sinew and tissue
of his body, believed that the god would smite them if they failed to
sing at the determined hour. But he didn't think the god would be
offended if the opening mass consisted of a duet. He thought the god
might indeed be pleased by that, more evidence of harmony between
races, between sexes, between Archangel and angelica.

He thought of Susannah's smooth, sumptuous voice, and realized that he was looking forward to his first chance to sing in harmony with his chosen bride.

All these conversations occupied Gaaron for the first few days of his return, and the succeeding days were taken up with the ordinary tasks of running the hold—flying off to the four corners of Bethel to ask for rain or check out a report of plague. He returned from one of these missions to find Miriam pouting in his room.

"I don't think it's my fault if I always get in trouble," she greeted him, her face stormy. "When you're *never* here to help me."

He stripped off his flying leathers and waited for doom to fall. "What happened?" he asked briefly.

She shrugged elaborately. "There were some men in Velora. I got to talking with them. I was just playing. Flirting a little. Usually when I mention your name, it makes them leave me alone. It's like a game. Only this time—well, either they didn't believe me or they liked the idea of making you mad. I don't know. And I think they were going to—going to—well, one of them grabbed my arm and he was pulling me along and I couldn't get free, I really tried, so I started screaming—"

He was standing in the center of the room, staring at her in pure horror. "What *happened*?" he said again.

"Well, I hoped that Nicholas or Ahio would be around, but they'd gone back up to the Eyrie after they dropped us off, but Susannah heard me and she came over—"

Making his blood run even colder. "Sweet Jovah singing. Did she get help?"

"No. She hit him with a rock," Miriam said with great satisfaction. "Right on the head. And he dropped my arm. There was kind of a crowd gathered by then, too, so the men just ran off."

"No one stopped them? Did anyone know who they were?"

"I didn't ask," Miriam said. "And Susannah was only paying attention to me. I don't know if anyone knew them."

Gaaron passed a hand over his eyes. "The god protect me," he said under his breath. "What am I going to do with you?"

"Well, if you were *here* ever, *you* could protect me," Miriam said. "Like you're supposed to. As my big brother."

He dropped his hand to stare at her. "If you would behave like a well-brought-up young lady, you wouldn't get in situations where you need protecting. Miriam! Do you realize what kind of danger you were in? Do you realize what those men could have done to you? Do you realize—do you know—what am I supposed to do with you? How in the world *can* I protect you? You don't want my protection. You want—" He stalked away from her to stare blindly out the window, where it was dark and there was nothing much to see. "I don't know what you want," he ended in a tired voice. "Maybe just my attention. Though when you have that, you behave even worse."

"I just want—I'm just trying to make the days more interesting," she said in a small voice. "Just trying to—just trying to figure it all out."

He whirled around so quickly that his wings flared up behind him, belling out and flattening down like a skirt caught in a breeze. "So what do I do now? Confine you to the Eyrie for a month? I think I have to. You know that all your angel friends will refuse to take you down to Velora if I tell them to."

She scowled. "Don't do that. I'll be good."

He shook his head. "You will *not* be good. You have *never* been good. I am out of ideas concerning you."

"I don't want to be cooped up in the Eyrie for a month," she said, her voice pleading. "Don't, Gaaron. I only told you the story because I knew someone else would. I thought you wouldn't be as mad if I told you myself."

"Well, you thought wrong."

"Don't lock me up here! I swear I'll jump out the window and kill myself."

He shrugged. "Solve your problems as well as mine."

"Don't, Gaaron," she coaxed. "Let me—I know! I'll stay in the Eyrie for a whole month—except for the times I go with you."

"I don't go down to Velora for fun," he said stiffly. "I only go out to make weather intercessions and offer other prayers."

"Yes, I know," she said eagerly. "Take me with you! I won't be any trouble. You carried Susannah for hundreds of miles when you brought her from Jordana. You can carry me anywhere in Bethel."

He frowned at her. This suggestion had come from nowhere. "Take you with me! To pray for rain or sun?"

"Yes, why not? I know all the music. I can sing harmony with you, and the god will respond twice as fast."

"You will be a distraction, and you will probably sing the wrong harmony on purpose just because it amuses you."

"I won't," she said. "I want to come with you. If I'm very good for the next week, and I don't leave the Eyrie at all, can I come? The next time you're called out on an intercession?"

He continued frowning at her, not sure how to answer. She sounded sincere, but Miriam could always be convincing. And why did she want to come with him? She had always been intrigued by the sacred music, it was true, and she had learned the pieces right along with him, even though, technically, only angels expected their voices to reach Jovah's ears. But that was because only angels could fly high above the world, close to Jovah, crooning their music directly to the god. If he carried Miriam in his arms, why could she not sing, too?

"I'll consider it," he said neutrally. "But if, in the intervening week, you do a *single thing* to make me angry or mistrustful—"

"I won't!" She jumped to her feet and came across the room to kiss him on the cheek. He was still disturbed enough by her revelations that he almost did not stand still for the kiss—but that much he had learned from his mother, who had had almost nothing to teach. Never turn away from a gesture of affection from someone you love, for you never know when that might be the last kiss you are ever offered. Miriam crossed the room, blew him another kiss from the door, and left with a jaunty toss of her hair.

He thought, No wonder both of our parents died so young.

CHAPTER TEN

It was impossible to speak to Susannah over dinner, for Enoch and Esther joined them and talked of mundane matters the whole time. Naturally everyone else in the hold also dropped by their table for a few minutes just to say hello. But Gaaron gave Susannah a meaningful look, and she smiled and nodded; she knew he wanted to talk, and she could guess the topic.

After the meal, Nicholas called for a musical game, and about half the residents of the Eyrie spilled out onto the plateau to play. It was a warm late-summer evening, the air as heavy as a shawl thrown across a woman's shoulders; the clean, spicy scent of mountain herbs flavored the breeze. It was not yet dark, but the sun had dipped below the horizon line, and the gold of the sky was tarnishing into black. It was a perfect night to stand outside and lift your voice to the heavens.

Nicholas was organizing the players into teams, to sing competing melodies that their opponents would have to then repeat in harmony, but Gaaron shook his head when invited to join. "Not right now," he said, and Nicholas nodded and went off to find other players.

Gaaron glanced around to find Susannah standing a few feet away, watching him. He smiled and joined her, and they strolled slowly around the perimeter of the plateau, between the mass of people and the rough rise of stone.

"You saw Miriam already, I take it," Susannah said. "Your face is lined with new worries."

"Jovah save us all," he said. "From her story, I was not sure— was she really in danger?"

"I wasn't sure, either, but I decided to act as if she was," Susannah replied. "We were lucky we were in the market, with so many people around."

Gaaron gave her a quick smile. "Did you really hit one of her attackers with a rock?"

"I did," she said calmly. "I've got a pretty good aim, too. I can hit a wolf at twenty yards nine times out of ten. I've even killed a rabbit or two, but that's been more luck than skill."

He shook his head. "You astonish me."

"You'd be surprised what you can do when you're driven by fear or hunger. Not that I think you've ever experienced much of either."

He thought that over. "Maybe not the kind you're talking about, but I admit to some fear over my sister. I absolutely do not know what to do with her."

"I think you were right the other day," Susannah said. "Send her away. Not to Breven, though. Luminaux, maybe."

"Luminaux?" he said, examining the idea. "What could she do there?"

Susannah laughed. "Almost anything she wanted, I would think. Luminaux has even more distractions than Velora."

"Then why would I want to send her there?" he demanded.

"Because you could apprentice her to one of the artisans there. Ask her if she wants to learn—I don't know—jewelry-making or shirt-dying or harp-building. She'll have to work hard or the craft master won't keep her—but I think she'll love Luminaux. She'll want to stay. So she'll work hard and try to do well. I think that's one of the things wrong with Miriam. She doesn't have anything to occupy her time or her thoughts. Learning a craft might fill those hours."

"Maybe," he said uncertainly. "But what if she said she would go, and be good, and then she got there and decided not to be good? Who would take care of her?"

"Maybe she'd just have to take care of herself."

He stared at her in the gathering dark. "She never has."

"She's nineteen. It might be time."

"I'll think about it," he said.

She nodded and made no more arguments. They walked on for a few minutes without speaking, listening appreciatively to the volley of music passing between the two lines of singers. Nicholas' team, which featured Ahio, Chloe, and Zibiah, among others, appeared to be more energetic—and louder—but the opposing team of older and more seasoned singers was more adept at catching each new melody and fashioning a reasonable harmony before batting it back. Most of the musical lines sounded as if they were being made up on the spot, though now and then Gaaron caught a few measures that sounded familiar. Tavern ditties and folk songs, of course; no one would play games with the sacred masses.

"You'd be good at this game," he remarked to Susannah.

"Maybe next time I'll join in," she said. "Or is it considered beneath the angelica's dignity?"

He laughed. "Not at all. But once it becomes clear to all the opposing players how good you are, they probably won't let you play again."

She smiled. "I see they didn't let you play. Is that because your voice is so good you shame all the others?"

He glanced down in surprise. "You have heard me sing?"

She shook her head. "The other night when a group of us came back late, Miriam said you'd joined the harmonics. But I couldn't pick your voice out."

"Well, then," he said. "Later tonight."

"What happens then?"

"You'll see."

They did not have long to wait before the melody game was over, and popular vote declared the older singers to be the winners. Then Sela stepped forward from the group and said, "I've been practicing this. Tell me what you think."

She sang a lovely ballad that drew light applause, and then Chloe joined her on a second song. Nicholas and Ahio performed a quick, demanding duet as soon as the women had finished.

Susannah turned to Gaaron with a smile. They had stepped forward to stand on the fringes of the group that had formed a circle around the singers. "It's like an Edori campfire," she said. "Anyone who wants to can sing."

He nodded. "Happens every once in a while. High spirits or good wine or, sometimes, a day of mourning, and suddenly everyone in the hold wants to gather together and sing. It's best on summer nights, like this one, but even in the winter we'll gather like this. Set up braziers around the whole plateau and stand out here till midnight, singing. It's probably what I love best about the Eyrie. About living with angels."

She gave him a sideways smile. "About living with music," she amended. "You do not need angels to sing."

He inclined his head in a stately nod. "My apologies, angelica," he said. "Indeed, you do not."

They listened perhaps another half hour before someone in the crowd called out Gaaron's name. Then the call was taken up by others, and someone from behind pushed him into the open circle at the center of the singers. He laughed and stepped forward, shaking his wings back and settling himself on the balls of his feet.

"No need for violence, I am happy to sing for you," he said. "Is there anything you'd especially like to hear?"

"The *Requiem*," someone called, but a chorus of boos led him to believe this was considered too maudlin for the time and place.

"One of the Grindel pieces," Ahio suggested, naming a composer whose upbeat and lively music was considered classical, though hardly sacred. "Oh, yes, sing Grindel," a few other voices concurred. Gaaron nodded and took a moment to review the music in his head. He looked for Susannah in the crowd but he had lost her somehow. He did not think she had left.

Tapping his left forefinger against his thigh to help him keep to the beat, he launched into the Grindel *Alleluia*. It was a fast and demanding number; if you once failed to catch enough breath on the rare quarter rests, you would never be able to make it through the rest of the piece. The timing was tricky, too, full of accented backbeats and unexpected sixteenth notes, but the whole thing was so headlong and triumphant that, even if you made a mistake, you found yourself carried along irresistibly to the highly ornamented conclusion. The applause broke out before he'd even made it through the final measure, a signal that he'd done the piece pretty well for not having practiced it in recent memory. He flung his hands out in a theatrical gesture as he held the last note for an extra few beats, then he dropped his head in a sweeping bow that made his wingtips brush the feet of the people standing behind him.

"Sing something else!" Nicholas called out.

"Sing a love song," Zibiah requested.

"Oh, Gaaron, sing that pretty one that you did last winter," Sela said, though he had no idea what piece she might be referring to.

"Sing one of the southern Bethel ballads," Miriam said. *She* had had no trouble locating Susannah among the onlookers, for she had the Edori by the arm and was pushing her into the inner circle next to Gaaron. "Susannah knows all of them. She'll sing harmony with you."

The crowd murmured its approval of this scheme, though Gaaron shot Susannah a quick questioning look. The newcomer might not feel so at ease singing in front of angels and other critical listeners. But Susannah merely grinned at him, shrugging a little as if to indicate that it was impossible to gainsay Miriam, and stepped close enough to speak to him in a low voice.

"Do you know 'Misty Valley Morning'?" she asked. "It's simple enough, we should be able to make it through without any rehearsal."

He nodded. "You don't have to do this," he said.

She laughed at him. "I'll enjoy it. You start. Sing the first verse, and I'll come in on the chorus."

He took a few steps over and turned to face her so that he could catch any bodily cues she might send—if she intended to hold a note an extra beat or two, if she wanted to slow the tempo. Then he began singing the first lines of the ballad. It was a pretty piece—simple, as she had said, but with a haunting, minor melody line that showed off the voice of any singer clever enough to pitch the song in his proper range. He saw Susannah smile with pleasure as he hit the high tenor notes, and he felt unreasonably pleased with himself. He began showing off a little, drawing out the notes more than they needed, adding little grace notes to the descending melody, making the music even more mournful. Someone behind him sighed, and he knew he was overdoing it but that nobody minded.

Susannah's voice joined his on the chorus, coming in with absolute precision a major third above his. Instantly, it was as if his own voice brightened, deepened, grew more resonant as it chimed against hers. He had sung with a hundred different singers, and no one had caught his timing and his tone as perfectly as she was doing. He remembered how her harmony had improved every singer she had sung with at that Edori campfire, how she had paired her voice with each of theirs and made both of them seem rich as treasure. It was as if her voice was absolutely pure, an undifferentiated well of virgin music, and it took on the characteristics of the singers around it. Yet it was better than that. More beautiful than that. He sang that simple song with all his strength, feeling the breath pour out of him from every inch of his body, feeling his toes curl and his shoulders lift and even his wingtips vibrate with the flood of music. And she matched him, note for note, never losing him, never overshadowing him, never letting him fall.

When the ballad came to its sad, riveting conclusion, there was a moment's silence. Gaaron actually had to catch his breath, something that usually only happened after one of the more demanding masses, and Susannah had time to glance around her as if to read the expressions on the nearest faces. And then the applause came, and Nicholas' whooping approval, and Miriam's high, excited laugh, and the cries for "Encore!" and "Another piece! Jovah demands it!" Susannah was laughing and smiling while the young, wild ones gathered around her to pat her on the back and exclaim over her first public performance.

"You've picked a fine one there," Enoch said, coming to stand beside Gaaron. "I wasn't too sure when you first brought her back, for an Edori angelica—? Well. But she can sing, can't she? That must have been what Jovah saw in her. Heard in her, more likely."

The condescending tone annoyed Gaaron, but he merely nodded. "I am certain Jovah listens to and approves of her voice," he said in a repressive tone.

He was more pleased when Ahio broke away from the group around Susannah and came over to give Gaaron a friendly slap on the shoulder. The younger angel was grinning. "I told you," Ahio said. "Give her harmony, and she'll bring the mountain down."

"We don't want the mountain to come down," Gaaron said with a little smile.

Ahio glanced back at Susannah. "It might come down anyway," he said, and laughed out loud.

Not for the first time, Gaaron found himself relatively happy with the woman Jovah had chosen to be his bride.

Two days later, the Jansai came.

Nicholas flew up from Velora to tell Gaaron that there was a delegation in the city looking for him. "Told me to say they were from Solomon," Nicholas said doubtfully. "And that you were expecting them."

"I am," Gaaron said. "Why didn't you bring them up here?"

Nicholas shook his head. "Because they wouldn't come. They said—the one man said—no Jansai goes anywhere under another man's power unless he's already dead. Plus there's a woman with them, and I don't think they would have wanted me to take her in my arms."

"No doubt," Gaaron said. "Where are they staying? What did you tell them?"

"They're camped out a little south of the city. I said I'd bring you as soon as I could."

Gaaron nodded. "Get Zibiah. Tell her I need her. Meet me on the plateau as soon as you can."

Gaaron went off in search of Susannah and found her with Ahio in the music rooms. For a moment he paused, just enjoying the sound of her singing along with a recording of Hagar, making even that fabulous voice sound warmer and more alluring. When the piece ended, she came to stand beside him near the doorway. Ahio glanced at them, then crossed to the controls to play with the tempo of the recording.

"The Jansai are in Velora to talk to the little girl," Gaaron said. "Do you want to come?"

"I certainly do," she said. "Now?"

He nodded. "Zibiah will carry her down. Nicholas will come with us, too, to give us some consequence."

She smiled. "As if the Archangel needed any consequence."

"You'd be surprised. Dealing with Jansai, you need any edge you can get."

"I wouldn't be surprised," she said dryly.

Ahio clicked off the music. "I'll come, too, if you want more wings around you," he offered.

Gaaron nodded. "Be on the plateau in a few minutes, then."

In about fifteen minutes, they had all assembled, Gaaron and Susannah taking a few minutes to change their attire. Gaaron had put on a white shirt and black pants, clothes that the Jansai recognized as formal. Susannah had changed into a bright blue shirt and a long black skirt with an embroidered hem—Edori clothes, Gaaron realized, which the Jansai would also recognize. She was making her own statement, he surmised, one that said, *I know you and you know me. Do not try any Jansai tricks.*

Or perhaps she just liked the colors, which flattered her dark skin and caused her black hair to flare with luster.

Zibiah was holding the hand of the young Jansai girl, who looked taller and thinner than Gaaron remembered. She peered out from under her veil with darting, suspicious eyes, and pressed closer to Zibiah.

"Does she know where we're going?" Gaaron asked.

Zibiah nodded. "I told her that her people had come to ask her some questions. She didn't say anything. She never does."

"Is she afraid?" he asked.

"I think she always is," Zibiah replied.

Gaaron glanced around at his group. Four angels, an Edori, and a little girl; perhaps the Jansai would not be impressed, but it was the best he could do on short notice. "Let's go," he said, and took Susannah in his arms.

The flight down the mountain and across Velora was short, but not so short that Gaaron did not notice how pleasant it felt to hold Susannah against him as he flew. Her long hair kept whipping into his face, tickling across his mouth and tangling with his eyelashes. "Sorry," she cried into the wind, a laugh in her voice as she tried to catch the wayward hair in one hand. But it was hopeless, the hair too long and the wind too wild. "Next time I'll braid it!"

They landed just outside the Jansai camp. There were two wagons, shaded by ribbed canvas coverings, and about ten horses. Gaaron counted four men crouched around the small campfire and guessed that one or two more might have gone into Velora for the day. Solomon had sent a show of force as well.

He set Susannah on her feet and strode forward. "I'm Gabriel," he said. "Thank you for coming."

"Covel," one of the Jansai said, standing to meet the angel. Not for the first time, Gaaron wondered where the Jansai got their names, since almost none of them seemed to be culled from the Librera. Perhaps they made them up out of euphonious syllables. His companions did not come to their feet, and Covel did not introduce them.

"I have brought the young girl who witnessed an attack on a Jansai camp," Gaaron said. "She will not talk to us, but Solomon graciously agreed to send a Jansai woman to ask her what occurred."

"My wife is in the wagon," Covel said. "She will ask the girl your questions. What do you want to know?"

So, pretty sure that Solomon had told Covel this whole story already, Gaaron patiently repeated the details of the burned campsite. What had caused it? Had the travelers been attacked? Had there been a strike of lightning? How had she escaped?

"And any other details she might remember," Gaaron finished up. "Though it has been more than two weeks now. She might not recall much."

"We shall find out," Covel said.

The Jansai turned to motion the young girl forward, either unwilling to speak to a female child or proscribed by Jansai law. But she buried her face in Zibiah's clothes and would not step forward.

Covel looked at Gaaron in irritation. "I can learn nothing from her if she will not talk to my wife."

Susannah stepped forward and bent over the little girl, murmuring something in her ear. The child looked up and allowed Susannah to detach her from the angel and take her hand. The two of them approached Covel, who had moved to the front of his wagon.

"I'll go in with her," Susannah said.

Covel turned his head and spit into the dirt. Then he looked at Gaaron. "She can't come in the wagon."

"I will go in with her," Susannah repeated. "We will learn nothing unless she is willing to talk, and she is not willing to go in there without me."

Covel looked again at Gaaron, who nodded. Muttering some Jansai imprecation, Covel pulled back the canvas flap that hid the interior of the wagon, and motioned them forward. Susannah helped the little girl in and then, making the awkward climb look easy, pulled herself inside.

Gaaron and the other angels were left facing the four Jansai men. Covel took the few short steps back to the fire. "Wine?" he asked. "Water? You may make yourselves comfortable while you wait."

Gaaron glanced back at his contingent. Zibiah seemed tense and uncomfortable, the lone woman now out of eight, but Ahio and Nicholas were looking about them with curiosity. None of them had spent much time with the Jansai outside of marketplaces where their wares were set up. It was interesting to see the arrangement of the tented wagons, the metal spit erected over the fire, the array of clay jugs and pans clustered in the shade of the nearest wagon. This camp was even more spare than the Lohoras', though Gaaron credited the Jansai with a greater sense of luxury than the Edori. Maybe because they had traveled far and fast, they had pared down their traveling gear to bare necessities.

"I do not know if you welcome women at your fire," Gaaron said gravely. "The rest of us would not be willing to take refreshment if she is not invited."

Covel snorted. "She may sit with us, if she likes," he said. "We are not interested in hearing her talk."

That was too ungracious an offer to accept. "Then—" Gaaron began, but Zibiah nodded her head. She was willing. Gaaron shrugged. "Then, we will be happy to take refreshment with you."

The eight of them disposed themselves around the fire, Jansai on one side, angels on the other, Zibiah carefully placed so that she was between the men of her party. There were no chairs, but the Jansai produced surprisingly comfortable leather-covered mats to at least shelter their clothes from the dirt. Gaaron spread his wings out behind him, unable to keep them from overlapping with Zibiah's, and hoped no small creature ran up from behind and skipped through his feathers.

One of Covel's wordless cohorts brought them clay cups filled with a steaming liquid. He handed two of these to Gaaron, so Gaaron passed the second one to Zibiah. Apparently the Jansai did not even want to risk accidentally touching a woman's fingers. Gaaron took a sip. It was fruit-flavored but heavily spiced with cinnamon and other seasonings, and it tasted marvelous.

"This is excellent," Gaaron said. "Thank you."

"A good drink for a long journey," said one of the heretofore silent Jansai.

Gaaron nodded at him gravely. "How did you find the roads between here and Breven?" The standard greeting to any traveler. The whole of Samaria was large enough that even angels from three holds, flying overhead constantly, could not monitor every mile of terrain. They often depended on Jansai and Edori for news of untoward conditions.

But the Jansai was returning a nonchalant answer. "No problems. The Galilee is high, but it has been higher. We saw no floods. No plague flags."

"Good to hear," Gaaron replied. "What villages did you pass through on your way?"

They continued making laborious travel conversation for the next half hour, while trying not to appear as if they were listening for any sound coming from the wagon. If the women were speaking at all, their low voices did not carry past the heavy canvas. Then again, it was possible that the child, who had uttered no coherent word for two weeks, was refusing to speak at all.

Finally, after another round of spiced juice and a discussion of the price of animal skins in the various city markets, the canvas flap folded back and Susannah appeared. She paused a moment, as if letting her eyes adjust to the brightness outside, then daintily stepped down. The girl did not follow her out.

Gaaron rose to his feet and she immediately came across the campsite to stand by his side. Her dark face was grave, and when she met his eyes, he saw that she had been crying.

"I take it she told you some of her story," he said, offering her his juice. She nodded and took the cup.

"It is a frightening tale," she said.

Gaaron pushed her to the inside of the angelic contingent, so that she was between Zibiah and his own body. "Tell us," he said.

She handed back the cup, then folded her hands across her up-drawn knees. "She had been traveling with her family and some of their friends. There were fifteen of them—only two of them men who were not related to her. She and her mother and her sister were in the wagon most of the time, though her mother would go outside to prepare meals. There were other women in another wagon—her mother's sister and her daughters. When the men left to hunt, the women would come out and tend the fire and clean themselves."

Susannah reached out for Gaaron's cup again and took another sip. "On this day, they had decided to camp overnight, so they were all feeling relaxed. The men had hunted the day before, so there was no need for them to leave. Many of them were merely sitting around the fire, drinking wine and telling stories. Kaski and her sister—"

"Who?" Gaaron said.

"Kaski. That's our little Jansai girl's name. She and her sister had to relieve themselves, so they slipped out the back of the wagon so that they would not expose themselves to the gaze of men." She glanced at Covel, who nodded. This, apparently, was common practice.

"They stayed out a while, running through the grass and trying to catch butterflies. But they were not far from the wagons and the fire. Close enough to hear had anyone called out their names or cried for help.

"When they grew tired, they headed back. They came in quietly, and bent low to the ground, so as not to draw the attention of the men. They were able to get very close to the camp and yet remain almost invisible. But they found they were not the only invisible creatures to come upon the camp by stealth. They were astonished to see three strangers—three black men—crouched in the tall grass a few yards from the wagons, watching the Jansai around the fire."

"Three black men?" Gaaron interrupted. "What does that mean?"

Susannah shook her head. "I couldn't tell. Were their faces black? Was their clothing black? Both? She just kept calling them 'the black men.' She kept looking at me, so perhaps their coloring was like the Edori."

"We do not call Edori black," Covel interjected. "Sometimes we refer to you with a word that means 'men of bronze.' Any child would know the difference."

"Still, my guess is that their skin was dark, and perhaps their clothes were as well," Susannah continued. "Other than that, she seemed to feel they were just like other men—shaped like us, like Jansai."

"And they were crouching in the grass before the campsite," Gaaron prompted.

"And while the girls watched, the black men stood up. They had— long sticks that seemed to be made of gleaming metal. She tried to describe them, but I could not understand what she was trying to say. The strangers pointed these sticks at the camp—and fire came out of the sticks—and the camp exploded with it."

Susannah hesitated a moment, either trying to picture that scene for herself, or remembering what Kaski had said in a small, trembling voice. "She said that there were just a few short screams from the people in the camp," Susannah went on slowly. "Like the fire caught them and burned them up so quickly they did not have time to call out in pain or terror. She said there were just those few short cries and then the sound of burning. Everything else was silent."

Susannah, too, fell silent for a moment. No one else stirred. "Kaski and her sister at first were too stunned to react. So they hid in the grass as the three strangers stepped forward and went to inspect the burning camp. They were speaking a language that made no sense. One of them bent down to pick up some of the cinders and rub it between his fingers, and he looked up and said something to his companions. All three of them laughed.

"And then Kaski's sister could stand it no more. She jumped to her feet and went shrieking into the camp, toward the laughing strangers. They whipped around and saw her running at them, and one of them aimed his fire stick and shot it at her. She burst into flame and crumbled into ash before Kaski could even say her name."

Another silence. Gaaron could understand why Susannah had been crying. Zibiah put her arm around Susannah and briefly pressed

her pink cheek against the bronze one. Susannah closed her eyes and
seemed to draw a moment's strength from the angel. Then she opened
her eyes, straightened up, and continued speaking.

"When her sister erupted into flames, Kaski flattened herself to
the ground and covered her eyes. She was sure the strangers had seen
her, so she was sure she would be the next to catch on fire. But though
she lay there for a long time, the strangers did not find her. They did
not aim their sticks at her. When she finally found the courage to stand
up and look about her, the strangers were gone."

Susannah lifted her eyes and gazed around the campfire at each
of them in turn, Jansai and angel. "And Kaski stood there a moment,
staring around her at all her dead. And she wondered when the black
strangers might come back. And she started running. And she ran for
two days before the angels found her. And she is afraid, even now, to
sit here in this canvas tent, knowing the black men could return again
with their fire sticks, and destroy every one of us, herself included. And
she thinks it will happen yet."

A moment longer Susannah held her head up, looking from face
to face, reading—as Gaaron did—horror in the angels' expressions and
nothing on the Jansai features. Then she dropped her head to Zibiah's
shoulder. The angel lifted her nearest wing and wrapped it around
Susannah, cradling the cramped body against hers. The dark head disappeared entirely under the folded wing, but Gaaron could still hear
Susannah's soft, bitter sobs.

"A grim tale to hear, but we needed to hear it," Gaaron said,
when he could find his voice again. "I take it none of you have seen
these 'black men' in your travels? You have talked to no one else who
has seen them?"

The Jansai all shook their heads. Except for Covel. "I've heard
about campsites that burned, but I never heard about black men
dressed in black."

"She's a child," one of the other Jansai said. "What she saw and
what happened might be two different things."

"Terrible thing like that, though, you tend to remember all the
details pretty clearly," Nicholas spoke up unexpectedly. "She's been
going over it and over it in her head, I'd guess. Seeing it every night
when she tries to fall asleep."

"Better for her if she had died," Covel said starkly.

"Perhaps now that she has been able to tell the story, she will heal," Gaaron said. "And now that she is among her own people again—"

"What? She stays with you," Covel said sharply.

Gaaron was astonished. Beside him, he felt Susannah stir and push herself up, though Zibiah's wing continued to stay half curled around her. "But—she belongs to you," Gaaron said somewhat blankly. "She is not happy with the angels. She needs to be among people she understands—"

"She has been tainted by contact with men," Covel said clearly. "We cannot take her back. If you do not keep her with you, we will leave her here beside the road. An impure woman is a disease in the heart of the camp, and will spread contagion throughout. She is dead to us. She is yours."

"But you—" Gaaron began, but before he could finish his sentence, Covel jumped to his feet and strode over to the wagon. He shouted out a few unintelligible Jansai phrases. There was a low moan from the tent, and a sharp cry that must have been Kaski's. Covel impatiently repeated his command, but nothing happened. Nimbly, he climbed up into the wagon, which rocked a little at his sudden weight, and disappeared into the canvas tenting.

A moment later, the little girl came tumbling out, shrieking and shaking and trying to turn around to scramble back in. Covel did not reemerge, but his hands thrust out through the canvas flap, pushing her backward with brute force. Twice more she tried to reenter the tent, crying the whole time, and twice more he repelled her. The second time, he shoved her with so much energy that she fell, somersaulting off the flat platform to the hard ground below.

Susannah was on her feet and running to the fallen girl before Gaaron could think to do more than stare. She knelt on the ground beside Kaski, gathering the girl into her arms and rocking her against her body. Kaski continued to twist and shriek in her arms, trying to get free, trying to make the Jansai keep her.

"You had better go," someone said in Gaaron's ear, and he looked up to find one of the other Jansai standing over him. "Take her or not, it does not matter to us. But she will not be coming back to Breven."

Gaaron nodded dumbly, enraged but powerless. He and the other angels came to their feet, Zibiah taking a few uncertain steps toward the huddle of sobbing girl and comforting Edori. Gaaron shook his head.

"I'll take them both," he said. "I don't think Susannah will let go of her. Let me get aloft first, and the rest of you follow."

It was five strides to the side of the wagon. Susannah looked up at him helplessly, but then she read the message on his face, and she nodded. She took a firmer grip on the writhing girl and rose to her feet, still watching Gaaron. He wrapped his arms around her, gauged the combined weight of the woman and the girl, and drove his wings down with one hard, muscular beat. In a few moments they were airborne, and ten minutes later they were back at the Eyrie.

CHAPTER ELEVEN

Miriam was bored.

All her friends were gone—*all* of them, even that sad, silent little Jansai girl—and of the hundred and fifty or souls who lived at the Eyrie, there was not a single one she cared to talk to. In fact, she'd had to leave the lunch tables early because Esther had spotted her from across the room and appeared to be coming her way, a purposeful look on her face. So Miriam had escaped out the side door and practically run down the halls, just to get away.

There was nothing to do in her room, so she wandered outside, up to the high peak that sheltered the singers performing their hourly harmonics. There stood Enoch and Lydia, older angels she never spoke to if she could help it. She hurried back down, crossed the plateau, entered the tunnels, and headed to the lower levels.

But two of the music rooms were in use, one of them occupied by that horrible boy Zack making monstrous music on a flute. Ahio claimed he had promise, but Miriam couldn't for the life of her hear it. She didn't like flute music, anyway—didn't care for any music except singing, really. Maybe she should listen to the masses, or, better yet, practice one of the pieces she might attempt to sing at the Gloria this year. Gaaron had not asked her to perform, but she knew it would please him if she presented some polished piece at the very Gloria where he was installed as Archangel. She had thought about having Chloe or Zibiah or one of the men practice a duet with her, but then she had decided this was something she should do on her own, proof to Gaaron that she could stand there with the world staring and show her love for him.

Of course, she had to admit she was enthralled by the picture—the slender blond woman, dressed perhaps in frilly white, perhaps in saturated blue, standing demurely before the crowd of thousands and singing some impossibly sweet and heartbreaking song. The impact was lessened somewhat when she imagined some of the angels standing beside her, overshadowing her with their very noticeable wings and their outstanding voices. No, it must be a solo.

She had not yet decided what this solo should be.

She stepped inside the music room and fiddled with the control panel a while, selecting a song at random, listening to a few measures, and then impatiently shutting it off. Another song, another dozen bars, another quick disconnect. None of them sounded exactly right. None of them created the mood she was going after. None of them made her seem like the wronged and misunderstood little sister who, in reality, wanted nothing more in life than to make her brother happy.

Maybe she should ask Ahio to write something for her.

Of course, Ahio wasn't here. Off with her brother on some mysterious mission Gaaron had not even paused to explain to her, even though she had told him how interested she was in knowing what he was doing at every moment.

It was enough to make even the calmest sister furious.

She shut off her most recent selection and skipped out of the music room. Sweet Jovah singing, what was there to *do* here? Making good on his promise, Gaaron had asked all the angels of the hold to refuse to take Miriam down to Velora for a solid week, and this was only the second day of that week. She thought she might lose her mind. Susannah had offered to teach her how to embroider and Zibiah had volunteered to play any game she chose, but Miriam had scoffed at both suggestions.

Anyway, they were both gone. With Gaaron, with Ahio, somewhere off the mountain.

Even Chloe and Sela had disappeared this morning, going up to the Lesh estate in Gaza on some errand. A favor to Neri, perhaps. There was no one here to talk to, absolutely nothing to do.

Miriam emerged back on the plateau and stood there, feeling as helpless as she ever had in her life. How did people live for months, for years, in Windy Point, with no distractions anywhere for miles around? How could they stand it? Why didn't they go mad and jump from the mountaintop, ending their tedious lives in one quick, exciting plunge to immortality?

She crossed to the far edge of the plateau, away from the entrance to the labyrinth, and started to scale the rough side of the mountain. In a thin, full-skirted dress, she was not attired for climbing, and she almost gave up the third time her hem caught on a sharp rock. But she and Sela had scrambled up this short wall of the mountain hundreds of times when they were children; she ought to be able to manage now that she was a full-grown adult.

She made it to the top of the rocky rim that outlined the plateau, and she looked down. From here, she could see Velora, less than a mile distant, nestled up against the side of the mountain like the Jansai girl in Zibiah's arms. It did not look so far. The side of the mountain did not look so steep. Perhaps, if she moved carefully and did not lose her patience, she could make it down.

A shadow fell over her from above and the shape of angel wings blocked the sunshine. She looked up quickly, but the face was in shadow. All she could tell was that the flier was not big enough to be Gaaron.

"What are you doing? Thinking about jumping off?" came the merry question, and she recognized the speaker. Jesse, one of the angels from Monteverde.

A friend of hers.

She cupped her hands around her mouth and shouted back. "Wishing I could fly! Nick and Zib and Ahio and Chloe are all gone, and I don't have a way to get down the mountain."

"Well, put your hands up, then," he said, and swooped down.

Giggling, she threw her arms in the air and leaned into his quick embrace as he snatched her from her rocky perch. Even more dangerous than trying to descend on foot, to allow herself to be plucked from unprotected high ground in that way, but she didn't care. Neither did Jesse, for he came at her in a flat-out dive and actually knocked her from her feet before he caught her up in his arms. They were both laughing.

"What are you doing here?" she demanded, crying the words into his ear.

"Message from Neri for your brother!" he shouted back. "But he's not here!"

"How long can you stay and play with me?"

He grinned. "As long as you like! Where to? Velora? Or some-place a little more exotic?"

For a moment she was tempted—really tempted—to say "Semor-rah," and then see if he would truly embark on such an ill-judged impromptu venture. She didn't have a damn thing with her, of course, just the impractical dress she was wearing, and there was always the chance Jesse would say yes. "Velora will do for now," she said.

"Velora it is," he said.

In another ten minutes, they were on the streets, walking through the bazaars and eating sweets. Miriam was so happy to be out of the Eyrie that she wouldn't have cared if they were walking the sinister boulevards of Breven, but as it was—on this sunny day, next to this attractive angel, strolling through the friendly streets of Velora—she felt she could not have been closer to pure contentment.

"Buy me a present," she commanded as they stopped at a little booth selling gloves and ribbons.

"Glad to," he said, and paused to look through the merchandise. He was a dark-haired young man of medium height and build, not so good-looking as Ahio or so volatile as Nicholas, and he had always adored her. She could never tell if it would terrify Gaaron or flood him relief if she decided to marry Jesse, and because she couldn't tell, she had always laughingly turned aside his protestations of affection.

Anyway, who would want to live at Monteverde, away from everybody in the world?

He held up a length of cobalt-blue ribbon, shot through with ran-dom gold stars. "That's pretty," he said. "Do you like that?"

"Oh, yes," she said. "I'll have Susannah use it to trim a shirt for me. It's so pretty!"

They strolled on, paused to buy another cake, stopped on a street corner to listen to a shirtless young boy sing a devastatingly beautiful song, turned another corner and instantly forgot him. They argued over the attractions of Luminaux compared to Semorrah, agreed that Adriel was looking old, wondered who might offer songs at the spring Gloria, and traded gossip about the other angels in their holds. This took them to dinnertime, so they asked for a table at an outdoor cafe and settled in for a meal, spending a long time looking over the menu because every single item sounded so good. In the end, they ordered half a dozen separate entrées, which they had decided to share, and a pitcher of beer. Which soon became two pitchers of beer. It had grown almost dark by the time they settled up their bill, Jesse flashing his emerald bracelets at the waiter and making the meal a Monteverde expense.

"Where to now?" Jesse asked as they walked out through a gate in the little wrought-iron fence that had enclosed their patio. "Unless you want to go back?"

"Go back? Oh no, it's hardly even dark yet."

"Fine with me, but I do have to talk with your brother," he said.

"Talk to him in the morning. He might not even be back yet."

"Where'd he go?"

She hunched an impatient shoulder, reminded of her grievances. "Does he ever tell me anything?"

Jesse grinned. "I don't know. Does he?"

She flounced forward, irresistibly drawn by the strains of music coming from around the corner. "No one tells me anything," she said over her shoulder. "What's going on up here?"

What was going on was a little street fair, a band of traveling musicians playing skirling music and a square of pavement set aside for a makeshift dance floor. Patrons were tossing a few coppers in a donation bucket and then pulling their partners under the gaily lit paper lanterns overhanging the intersection. The music was so fast that the dancers were twirling around in laughing, breathless patterns that often sent them careening into the shoulders of the onlookers.

Miriam clapped her hands. "Oh, Jesse, dance with me!"

He looked doubtful. "I'm not really a good dancer," he said. "The wings—they get in the way—someone steps on them or I swing around too fast and hit someone in the face—"

She pouted, instantly convinced the entire evening would be a failure if she did not get at least one opportunity to experience that music. "You'll do fine," she insisted. "Ahio can dance—he practices all the time. Just hold your wings back really tight—"

He shook his head. "Not in this crowd. Look at them! Bumping into each other every other step—"

"But I want to *dance*," she wailed.

"I'll dance with you, if your friend doesn't mind," said a voice at her side, and she turned quickly to survey the speaker. He was a middle-aged man, wealthy-looking, trim enough and vain enough to make an effort to hide his age. He didn't look reprehensible or Jansai, though, and with Jesse standing right here, what harm could come to her? She dimpled and extended her hand.

"He won't mind," she said, giving the merchant a mischievous look from under her brows. It was a look she had practiced a hundred times in the mirror and used whenever she was just about to get her way. Gaaron hated it. "And *I* would *love* it."

"I'll wait right here for you," Jesse called as she and her partner stepped onto the dance floor. The older man tossed a few coins in the bucket to pay their way, then swept around to face her and take her free hand in his. He bowed in a courtly way, and she dipped into as much of a curtsey as she could manage with her hands not free and her having no experience in curtseys.

The musicians had changed to a new song, but it was just as lively as the one before, so they were immediately caught up in the romp of dancers as they circled the rough pavement. Miriam was quite a good dancer when the ball was formal, but there were no particular steps to be following here—you just clung to your partner's hand and skipped from side to side and tried to maintain a forward motion. It was exhilarating, and Miriam laughed aloud. She even laughed when the couple behind them got too close, and the young man stepped on her gown so hard that she could feel it tear.

"Sorry!" he shouted over the music, but Miriam's partner turned her away before she could even tell him it did not matter.

"What's your name?" he asked her, leaning in so that she could better hear the words.

"Susannah," she said. "What's yours?"

"Elias," he said. "Why are you friends with angels, Susannah?"

She laughed up at him. "Because I'm supposed to marry one."

His eyes opened wide, and then he laughed, too. "The one back there?"

"I haven't decided."

They skidded through a few more figures of the dance, he was fairly adeptly keeping her clear of their neighbors, before he spoke again. "While you're deciding," he said, "I run a freighting business on the other side of town. I'd be happy to take you to dinner some-time."

She smiled. "You probably have a daughter my age."

He smiled back. "I do. That matters to you?"

She shook her head. "I would guess I'm not going to be back in Velora anytime soon. Or I might come by."

"I'll give you my address," he said. "In case you're ever free."

This time, when the song stopped, the musicians announced that they were taking a little break. The crowd gave a collective moan of disappointment, but many people cheered up when a barker started bawling out the cheap prices of his beer and wine. Most of the dancers moved in the direction of his refreshment cart as Miriam and Elias sauntered off the dance floor. The merchant was handing Miriam a card inscribed with his address when Jesse strode up to them.

"There, I'm glad you enjoyed yourself," he said, taking Miriam's hand out of Elias' and holding it firmly in his own. "Probably time we got back."

Miriam grinned up at Elias, suddenly her ally against all angels. "Why is it the minute I do anything just a little fun everyone turns into my big brother?" she wondered.

"Maybe because they think your ideas of fun are dangerous," Elias said. He seemed to be enjoying Jesse's frown of obvious jealousy.

Miriam opened her eyes as wide as they would go. "But they *never* are," she said.

Elias laughed. "I enjoyed meeting you, Susannah," he said. "Now go be nice to your angel friend."

Jesse's eyes cut over to her but he didn't say anything until Elias melted into the crowd. "Susannah? That's what you told him?"

Miriam shrugged with elaborate unconcern. "Well, I couldn't give him my real name. And besides, Susannah would have enjoyed dancing with him."

He shook his head and did not look as amused as he had when *he* was the once snatching her off mountaintops and encouraging her to misbehave. It was always that way. Even Nicholas, the most careless of men, would read her a lecture from time to time, and Sela could never be counted on to be as reckless as Miriam liked. Oh, everyone started out carefree enough when the adventure began, but someone would always draw back from a proposed escapade, and it usually ended with everyone but Miriam looking serious and thoughtful.

Even Susannah, who never moralized and who always seemed to understand exactly what Miriam was thinking, was not much of a companion for gaiety. It was very disappointing.

"Well, I don't know this Susannah of yours yet," Jesse was saying, "but she doesn't sound like the type to be meeting strange men at street fairs and promising to meet them for dinner."

Miriam flashed him a smile. "I didn't promise. In fact, I said I didn't think I'd be in Velora for ages and ages."

His eyes lit up. "Hey, now. That might be true. Why don't you come back to Monteverde for a week or two? Don't tell me your brother wouldn't be glad of a chance to shed you for a while, you *and* all the worry you bring him."

Miriam made a face at him. "Very funny. But Neri's worse than Gaaron."

"Come anyway," he coaxed. "I have to go back in the morning, and I never get to see you."

"You saw me for a whole day!" she exclaimed. "Just now!"

He smiled a little crookedly. "Not long enough."

She put her arms around his neck and gave him a look of sweetness. She could manufacture it on demand, and she knew how effective it could be. "Oh, Jesse, you're just the nicest boy ever. I don't know why you're so good to me. But I don't think that I should be coming out to Monteverde just to play around with you for a couple of weeks."

"Think about it," he said. "I won't leave till morning."

She put her hand up to touch the crisp dark hair on the back of his head. "I'll think about it. But you better take me back now."

He sighed a little theatrically and snatched her up. She gave a little shriek because he charged through the crowd with her in his arms, knocking aside the people standing around drinking beer and waiting for the musicians to start again. Once clear of the crowd, he tightened his hold and tore off racing down the center of the street. She screamed again and buried her face in his bare neck. She was scarcely aware of the transition between running and flying, so smoothly did he make it, but when she had the nerve to lift her head, they were airborne.

"You're a crazy man!" she cried into his ear, and he nodded.

"Crazy for you!" he called back.

In a few minutes, they were at the Eyrie, coming to a gentle landing on the deserted plateau. Jesse lingeringly set her on her feet, and she kept her arms around his neck.

"Are you spending the night?" she asked. "Did someone get you a room?"

He nodded. "I met up with Esther right before I spotted you. I'm all settled in. Although I'm feeling lonely—"

She laughed and shook her head. "I don't think I'm in the mood for company, but thank you very much."

He drew her closer. "Then give me a kiss good night? And think about flying back with me tomorrow. You'll have fun in Monteverde. I'll make sure of it."

"Oh—I don't know—" she said indecisively. And then, because she felt guilty for not giving him more encouragement, she stood up on her tiptoes and kissed him on the mouth. His arms tightened considerably and she felt his wings flutter and settle behind her. The kiss was nice, passionate without being painful, and she liked the feel of his mouth on hers. She let him hold the kiss a little longer than she should have, and when she pulled away at last, he looked down at her with absolutely no smile on his face.

"I do love you, Miriam," he said.

She slipped her hands away, pausing briefly to pat him on the cheek. "I know you do, Jesse," she said. "And it comforts me."

That didn't please him. His face clouded over, but he didn't say anything as she stepped backward a pace, freeing herself from his arms and his wings. "I'll see you in the morning," she said and, before there was time for any more discussion, turned away and hurried toward the hallway leading to her rooms.

It was then that she saw Gaaron standing there, just outside the doorway, watching her with an expression that was impossible to read.

She checked a moment, reviewed her conduct for the evening, decided it wasn't too bad, and continued walking. "Gaaron," she said coolly as she stepped past him into the hallway.

He nodded. "Miriam."

And that was all. He made no attempt to detain her as she quickened her pace and moved away from him. She thought, as she got deeper into the corridor, that she caught the sound of male voices behind her—Gaaron talking to Jesse, no doubt, and maybe not about the urgent message from Neri—but she just kept going. Down the gaslit hall, through the turn, down another hall.

Past her own door, down another hall, and straight to Susannah's room.

She knocked quietly, not wanting to wake anyone who might be sleeping, but there was no sound from within. But Susannah never locked the door. Quietly as she could, she turned the handle and stepped inside, pausing just across the threshold to let her eyes adjust to the darkness in the room.

It was not pitch-black, though; Susannah always left the window open, no matter what the weather, and a little watery moonlight drifted in. Enough for Miriam to make out the furniture in her path and the bed all the way across the room, where two shapes lay motionless under the thin cover.

Susannah and the little Jansai girl.

Miriam crept across the room, peeling off items of clothing and dropping them as she went. Pulling back the coverlet, she slipped into the wide bed next to the Jansai girl and drew the blanket up to her chin. She sighed and, for the first time all day, completely relaxed. She was asleep in five minutes.

In the morning, the room was deserted and she was ravenous. She rummaged through Susannah's clothes to find a skirt and blouse she liked and dressed quickly, hoping breakfast was still being served. It was, and that was good luck, but there was bad luck to go with it: Gaaron was lingering over his meal, and he saw her enter. He motioned her to come join him, so as soon as she'd filled her plate from the buffet, she warily crossed the room to his side.

"What?" she said, standing there with her plate in her hands as though she was on her way to some other table.

"Why don't you sit down?" he said pleasantly. "We can talk."

"You'll just yell at me," she said.

"What could I possibly want to yell at you about?" he asked.

She scowled. She hated it when he was smug; he was much easier to deal with when he was angry. "Because I left the Eyrie yesterday with Jesse when I wasn't supposed to."

"And why did you do that?"

"Because you left and didn't tell me where you were going, and you promised you'd take me with you next time you did an intercession! But you didn't, so I was mad, so it's your fault."

He nodded gravely, but she was furious to see he appeared to be biting back a smile. "Well, I'm going to do an intercession today, would you like to come with me?"

She dropped her plate to the table and plopped into a chair across from him. "*Really?* You'll take me with you? Where are you going? Is it a weather intercession? Too much rain?"

Now he was laughing out loud. "Yes, I'll take you. No, it's not rain. Western Bethel. But if you go with me, you can't go back to Monteverde with Jesse."

"I don't want to go with Jesse," she said instantly.

He tilted his head to one side, regarding her. "I know you don't. But I can't tell why."

For a moment, she scowled again, and then she broke into a brilliant smile. "Because I'd rather stay to torment you, of course. If I'm gone, you won't spare a moment to worry about me."

"If you're gone, I'll worry about you every moment without ceasing," he retorted.

She started eating as fast as she could. "When do you want to leave? I can be ready as soon as I eat and change clothes."

He was amused again. "Why change? I understand Edori clothes are very comfortable for travel."

She glanced down at the embroidered cotton shirt and the plain, full skirt. "They're Susannah's," she said.

"So I guessed."

"I spent the night in her room so I didn't have any of my own clothes with me."

"Oh, is that where you were?" he said innocently. "I did stop at your door this morning, but when there was no answer—well, I thought maybe you'd gotten up early. Since you so often do."

And that was meant to annoy her on a couple of counts, so she frowned again. "If you're hateful to me, I won't let you take me with you when you go sing prayers," she said with dignity.

"Well, then, I'll try to mend my manners, since I certainly don't want you to forsake me now," he said. He came to his feet, smiling down at her. It was like being smiled at by a mountain—it made you feel very safe, but it still made you want to jump off the peak just to prove you could. "Can you be ready in an hour? I have to write a note to Neri and then I'm ready to go."

She nodded, eating even faster. He turned to go, paused, and turned back long enough to lay his hand on the top of her head. She looked up at him, but he didn't say anything. Just pivoted away and left the room.

She quickly finished eating, hurried to her room, decided to keep on Susannah's clothes, though she would have to apologize for this before the day was out, braided her hair back, put on some warmer shoes, and rummaged around for a jacket. She had flown with enough angels to know that, no matter how considerate they were about staying at lower altitudes to keep their mortal passengers from freezing to death, the longer the flight, the colder she would be. Summer or no summer.

She was on the plateau a few minutes before Gaaron was. She could tell her promptness pleased him, because he smiled when he joined her. He had a canteen strapped over one shoulder, and a small leather satchel strapped over the other—food for the day, she guessed, though it hadn't even occurred to her to bring provisions.

"Ready?" he said and caught her in his arms. She bounced once from utter happiness, then squealed a little as he took off fast. That was to give her a little thrill, because he knew she liked the plunge and lift of a sudden takeoff. He was usually more sedate when he was carrying cargo. She snuggled against his broad chest and enjoyed the feel of the wind against her face, and the dizzying, exhilarating sense of great height and motion.

They had been flying in companionable silence for more than an hour before she remembered Jesse, back at the Eyrie awaiting her decision about flying to Monteverde. She supposed that once he realized she had gone off with Gaaron, he would have answer enough. She felt a little bad about it for all of ten minutes, and then she forgot about him in her undiluted happiness at the unfolding of the day.

They flew west and south for about three hours before stopping for a light meal. On their way again without much time wasted, continuing on in the same direction. When they finally dropped out of the high, chilly atmosphere for a layer of air that was more habitable, Miriam peered down, trying to make out landmarks. She couldn't imagine how angels could fly anywhere without getting hopelessly lost. To her, it all looked like the same stretch of rolling green land and undulating river, dotted with the occasional, identical range of squat mountains.

They were low enough now that she could make out a few buildings—a farming community, she thought, set in the middle of some of those legendary fertile acres of southern Bethel. There were a few silos, some structures that might be barns, a house or two, a patchwork quilt of fields and fences . . . and a plague flag, hanging dispiritedly in the faint wind.

"Illness?" she asked. "That's what you're here for?"

He nodded. "I don't want you to get too close—"

"Nonsense! I came here to sing with you and I'm going to sing."

"That's fine, but I still don't want you to get too close to anyone who's sick. I'm going to set you down here, go over and tell them I've arrived, and then come back to get you. We'll go aloft and sing, and you'll never have to be exposed to anyone."

She thought this over. "That seems a little rude."

"I assure you, they'll think it's practical."

"And I suppose they're not worried about you getting exposed. Or maybe they already know that angels never get sick."

He grinned as he came down in a perfect landing. "Yet another divine gift from Jovah," he said.

"Nothing in life is fair," she grumbled as he set her on her feet and waited a moment to make sure she had her balance.

"No, nothing is," he agreed. "Stay here. Move from this spot and I'll leave you here to be a farmer's sister the rest of your life."

Before she could think of a retort to this, he had stroked his wings three times and taken off for the farmhouses. She turned her face up to the sky and unbuttoned her jacket, hoping for a little of the sun's warmth to seep through to her skin. She felt chilled all over, her nose a little red block of ice, but she didn't mind, of course. She would have flown twice as high and twice as far, and not complained once.

Dropping to a seat on the thick grass, she took a moment to look around her. Pretty countryside here, if you were happy with only slightly rolling land covered with all manner of cultivated vegetation. There was a narrow line of trees visible in the distance, and the snaking brown contours of a road, but not much else to clutter up the view until you turned to look at the farm buildings themselves. The air was thick and still, laden with rich scents that made her think of variants of green. What little noise wafted her way seemed distant, unimportant, and peaceful—the droning of insects, the lazy calls of workers in the fields, an occasional cry from a passing bird. She pulled up a stalk of grass—or possibly a cash crop, she couldn't tell—and ran its long flat length through her fingers. It was such a rich satiny color she expected it to be smooth against her fingertips, but instead it was rough and sharp-edged, almost keen enough to cut her. She liked that; she pulled it through her fingers again.

Nonetheless, the charms of the still countryside paled within about five minutes, and she was thoroughly bored by the time Gaaron reappeared. "Jovah be praised, you're back," she said, scrambling to her feet. "I'd go mad if I was here very long by myself."

"Ah, then I know where to threaten to send you the next time you misbehave," he said gravely.

She smiled at him and raised her arms to be lifted up. "But I'm not going to misbehave anymore, remember?"

He caught her in an easy embrace and, with no effort at all, lifted both of them off the ground. "You remember the songs I taught you? Plague songs?" he asked as they headed upward.

"There are about a dozen of them, I think."

He nodded. "We need the piece that begins like this"—and he softly crooned a few bars. "Remember that one?"

She was starting to get cold again. To sing to Jovah, apparently, Gaaron needed to be even higher off the ground than he had to be when he was merely flying. "Perfectly," she said. "I am ready when you are."

He glanced down at her. "It's too high for you, isn't it? Sorry. We'll drop a little."

She protested, but he banked and descended into air that was only slightly warmer, though even that little bit helped. "*Now* are you ready?" he inquired. When she nodded, he began the song.

Miriam came in on the third note, balancing her voice above his as she would balance herself on a bridge over tricky water. All of the prayers had been designed to be sung as solos, by angels needed so desperately all over the realm that sometimes they were too busy to go off in pairs. Therefore, the harmonies were generally simple, uni-maginative descant lines designed more to please the ear than to rouse the god. Gaaron's voice was so strong that Miriam did not even try to match it; she just decorated it with pretty trills and graceful ascend-ing thirds. It was as if he were a deep-dyed purple robe, and she were bits of gold embroidery fashioned at the throat and wrists. Her voice made his more beautiful, but he was gorgeous enough on his own.

They sang for perhaps an hour, Miriam growing colder despite the lower atmosphere, before the prayer was answered. She could see the signs of Jovah's kindness, small colorful tablets pelting down like solid rain, showering all the land around the farmhouses with bright confetti. Excited, she pointed, and Gaaron nodded, but he did not stop singing until they had brought the prayer to its conclusion.

"Gaaron! Did you see? The god sent down medicine to make the farmers well again!"

"Yes, I saw," he said, amused. "It's a sight I have often seen, but it still remains amazing to me."

"I have seen you call sunshine and bring rain, but I don't think I've ever seen you ask the god for medicine before," she said. "I think I like these prayers best."

He quickened his wingbeats, which all this time he had held at a slow and steady hover, and then spiraled down. "I like the prayers for rain the best," he said. "For great crashing thunderstorms. Those are my favorites."

"Why are we going back down?" she asked. "Can't we just leave?"

"I promised I'd return to make sure they had gathered as many tablets as they needed," he said. "I'll just set you down right here again, but I'll be back in a few moments. And then we can go home."

She couldn't help a small pout, but she tried to suppress it. The day had gone so well for so long that she did not want to jeopardize good relations now. Still, it was with something of a flounce that she sat down again in the field, crossing her arms and staring stonily off into the distance as Gaaron headed back toward the inhabited buildings.

After a moment, she unfolded her crossed arms and tilted her face back up to the sun, which felt even warmer this much later in the afternoon. Maybe they should stay another half hour or so, eating a light meal here in the sunshine before taking off for the Eyrie again. Maybe then she would be able to face with equanimity the prospect of another long, cold flight.

She opened her jacket a little, then flopped down to lie on her back. Her knees were updrawn but the rest of her was flat against the ground. The grass was warm against her spine and the back of her head as if the green itself was radiating heat. She splayed her fingers on either side of her body and felt those rough-edged blades hold their tiny knives against her palms. The scent of the field rose all about her, pungent and layered. Somewhere a low buzzing stopped abruptly, guttered twice, then resumed its coarse monotonous tone.

When Gaaron's shadow fell over her, she smiled without opening her eyes. "Maybe it wouldn't be so bad if you sent me here for a little while," she said. "I think I'd be so lazy and sleepy all the time that I wouldn't have the energy to cause any trouble."

He didn't answer, so she squinted up at him, backlit against the slanting sun. But it wasn't Gaaron who stood over her. Too small, and sporting no wings.

For a moment, she thought it must be one of the farmers, carrying his pestilence out to infect her despite all Gaaron's precautions. She sat up, brushing her hair back and preparing to introduce herself. But once she could see clearly without the golden interference of the sun, she realized that this was no farmer. This was no one she'd ever seen before.

He was about the same height and build as Nicholas, though he held himself extraordinarily still, as Nicky could never do. His skin was darker than Susannah's, a rich brown so saturated it almost looked black. His hair was a blazing orange, bright as flame against his dark face, and his eyes were such a light blue that at first they seemed to be no color but white. He was staring at her as intently as she stared at him.

She opened her mouth as if to scream, but no sound came. She could not tell if he carried any weapons, though Gaaron had told her the Jansai girl's tale of black men with sticks of fire. She could not believe that, throughout the girl's whole recitation, she had not once mentioned that fiery hair or those unnerving eyes. But perhaps the Jansai girl had not been as close as this.

Miriam put a hand to her throat, an unconscious gesture of pure fear. "Who are you?" she whispered, but, of course, he did not reply. Her eyes dropped for a second, checking for danger, but she still could not see anything that looked like a stick. Under one arm the stranger held a round, shiny object as big as a mixing bowl. Could that be a weapon? Was he about to destroy her where she sat? "What do you want?"

He moved so suddenly that she did cry out and drop back to the ground in terror. But all he did was settle the shiny item over his head, covering both his hair and his eyes. He spoke one word, and flattened his hand across his chest.

Then he disappeared.

Miriam sat there a moment, staring at the place where he had been, sure that the thick summer air must still be vibrating with the suddenness of his passage. But there was nothing to indicate that he had been there or where he might have gone. The bees droned on. The grass continued sunning itself under the bright blue sky. The scent of hay and fertilizer pooled all around her, completely undisturbed.

She jumped to her feet and ran toward the compound with more speed than she had ever mustered in her life.

"Gaaron! Gaaron! Come quickly!" she shouted even before she got within hearing range. A worker coming up from a far field saw her wild approach and waved his hands as if to warn her away.

"Plague here!" he called. "Go back!"

She ignored him. "Gaaron! Gaaron! Come here now!"

The narrow farmhouse door burst open and Gaaron pushed himself through, squeezing his wings to his sides and ducking his head to avoid injury. "What's wrong? Stay back!" he yelled. He turned to say something to someone in the house, then jumped off the porch and came over to her on a run.

"What's wrong? Why didn't you stay where I left you?" he demanded, his voice caught somewhere between anger and fear.

"Gaaron—I saw one—in the field—he was right by me," she panted. Her hands plucked ineffectually at his arm, as if she could draw more of his attention, as if she could convey more of her alarm. "I thought it was you, but he—and then he just *disappeared*."

He stopped dragging her away from the farmhouse. "You saw who?" he said sharply.

"One of those—a black man—like the Jansai girl said."

"Here? In this field?"

She pointed to the spot. "Right over there! I was just lying there with my eyes closed, and suddenly he was standing beside me. I sat up and looked at him, and he looked at me, and then he—Gaaron, he just wasn't there anymore! I swear by Jovah's mercy, he disappeared. Came from nowhere, went to nowhere."

Gaaron stared in the direction she indicated as though he would see the ghost of that unwelcome visitor still lingering in the grass. "And he was alone? Just one?"

She nodded. "I only saw one. But I was afraid to look away. I couldn't see anything but him."

Gaaron's gaze swung back to her. "And what did he look like? A black man, that's what Kaski called him. Black clothes? Black skin? What?"

So she described him as best she could, emphasizing the bright hair and the pale eyes. "But he looked like—I mean—except for the coloring, he could have been any man you see on the streets any day," she finished up. "He looked like a mortal."

"No wings?"

"I would have mentioned it by now if he had had wings," Miriam replied sharply.

Gaaron spared a small smile for that. "Yes, I'm sure you would have." He stared down at the ground for a moment, lost in thought. "I'll have to go back inside and ask them if they've seen anything in the past few days," he said. "And to tell them to be on the lookout in case one of these visitors comes back."

"Are you going to tell them to be careful of fire?" she asked.

He trained his sober gaze on her face. "I will," he said quietly, "but I do not see how they can protect themselves against that. If indeed this man is one of the same ones who burned Kaski's camp, and from your description, he sounds as if he may be. I don't know how such a thing can be guarded against."

"But Gaaron . . ." she said, and then couldn't think of any way to end the sentence.

He nodded. "I know. Now you stay here. I'll be outside again in five minutes, and we'll go home."

She stayed where he left her, too drained by panic and her mad dash across the field to spare much energy for unnecessary movements. He was, of course, inside for longer than five minutes, and he emerged looking very somber. He headed in her direction, stopping a few yards away to bend over and scoop up something from the ground.

"What's that?" she asked immediately as he pocketed his find and came to a stop before her. "What did you pick up?"

"Medicines. In case you get sick," he answered.

She could not help a small laugh. It would never have occurred to her to be so foresighted. "Is there nothing that you don't think of?" she asked.

"Many, many things," he said. "Come on. It's late. Let me get you to the Eyrie."

She wrapped her arms around his neck and felt his arms go around her and lift her up. For a moment she felt weightless, and then—which was even better—she felt light as silk bedding, a small, easily protected scrap of a girl in the custody of an invincible protector. "Yes, please," she said. "Let's go home."

CHAPTER TWELVE

Susannah couldn't remember exactly when it was that Kaski first started sleeping in her room every night. One day Zibiah had asked if she could turn over the Jansai girl, because she would be gone overnight on a weather intercession near Castelana. Naturally, Susannah had agreed. Another evening Zibiah had had an assignation of some sort, though she did not offer details. And Susannah had gladly taken in the silent girl that night, too. And fairly soon after that, every evening, she would find Kaski awaiting her inside her room, sitting in the middle of the floor, doing nothing, staring at nothing, just waiting with that terrible patience.

"Hello, mikala," Susannah greeted her every night. "Do you plan to keep me company again? I'm so glad."

Once they had both cleaned up and climbed into the too-soft bed, Susannah would tell her stories. Mostly she spoke in the ordinary tongue that all the Samarian people shared, but once in a while she told a tale in the Edori language, so she didn't forget it. Her kinsmen felt so far away; her familiar, happy Edori existence seemed something she had dreamed of. She told Edori tales and tried to remember.

Kaski did not seem to care one way or the other what words

Susannah employed. She gave no sign of understanding either of the languages.

Yet she stayed with Susannah night after night, and Susannah was heartened by that. She had given up any hope of persuading Kaski to talk, but she did feel the little girl was beginning to trust her. For instance, she had actually allowed Susannah to take off her veils and see her pale, pinched little face. She had permitted Susannah to comb out her hair and rub cream on her dry skin. At bedtime, she would edge her small body next to Susannah's and lie there all night as if finally safe.

Meeting with the Jansai from Breven, however, had been a real setback.

At first Susannah had been encouraged—amazed—at Kaski's swift, impassioned speech as she told the older Jansai woman her story. She spoke so quickly and in such heavily accented language that Susannah could not catch every word, though the gist of the horrific tale was clear. And the fact that Kaski *would* talk, *could* talk, was proof that she could heal if given enough time and attention.

And then she had been tossed out of the wagon and rejected by her people, and Susannah had thought the little girl would literally cry herself to death.

But no. Kaski had silenced herself with a visible effort, had donned even darker and more opaque robes, and had locked herself in Susannah's room and refused to come out, even for meals.

Susannah didn't know what to do. So a week later, she did what everyone in the Eyrie did when confronted with an insoluble problem. She went to Gaaron.

He listened to her over breakfast in his room, a ritual they had fallen into enjoying once or twice a week. Susannah suspected that Esther resented these private meals between them—less because of the extra work it caused her than because it kept Gaaron away from the public eye for another two hours—but she had come to count on them as segments of rationality and peace in what were sometimes hectic days.

"And she still does not talk to you?" Gaaron asked. "Even after you heard her speaking at the Jansai camp?"

"Not a word. She'll nod. Once in a while, she'll smile. Hardly ever, now. After—you know."

He nodded. "But she listens to you?"

"Oh, yes. And I'm sure she understands me. But—she's so hard on herself. If I don't pay attention, sometimes she will go a whole day without eating. I've caught her—punishing herself. Hitting herself with a leather strap or—I watched her cut herself with a knife once. On purpose. When she saw me watching her, she put it down and let me bind the cut. But then I saw her do it again a few days later. And—there are bruises on her body. I don't know how she gets them. I'm afraid she does something to herself when I can't see her."

"You think she will try to kill herself?"

Susannah nodded. "I think she may have already tried, but she can't figure out how."

He sipped his juice meditatively. "This is beyond my experience," he said at last. "But all I can think is that she mustn't be left alone. What does she do during the day when you're not in your room?"

"I think she just stays there. Sits there. She never leaves. She never goes to Zibiah anymore."

"Not even at night?"

Susannah smiled. "I think Zibiah has found a more interesting companion for her nights."

"Huh." He sipped his juice again. "Well, this is entirely too great a responsibility for you to take on all by yourself. Clearly, she needs constant supervision, and clearly she needs more than one person to look after her. And I would guess she needs interaction as well. Something to concentrate on besides her terrors and her woes. All the children at the Eyrie attend classes. We might enroll her in some of those."

Susannah shook her head. "Not any classes with boys. She is terrified of all men. And someone like Zack—"

"Good point." He thought a moment. "Well. We will just have to organize. We will make up a schedule of her days. Perhaps she can spend a couple of hours every morning in the kitchen with Esther. At the moment, all our kitchen workers are women. We will ask the teachers to divide a couple of their classrooms into boys and girls, and she will take classes—mathematics and history classes, perhaps. Maybe an art class. Music? Does she like music?"

"She won't sing."

"Will she listen?"

"Yes, she seems to like that."

"Or—perhaps—she would like to learn an instrument," Gaaron mused. "A lap-harp, perhaps. Lydia could teach her that. She's a gentle lady."

"It seems like a lot of trouble to make everyone go to for one little girl," Susannah ventured. "They might not be so interested in rearranging so much of their lives for a stranger—and a Jansai—"

"The Librera teaches us that Jovah watches over every soul, even those who have not been dedicated," Gaaron reminded her. "We should do as much."

"We should, but so often we don't," she retorted with a smile. "Truly, I do not mind that she has become my responsibility. But I—"

"But you have other tasks to perform as well, and I believe that she will be best served by being exposed to as much activity as possible," Gaaron replied. "I believe this may pull her out of herself, return her to the world a bit."

"I think it is a good plan," Susannah admitted. She smiled, a teasing expression on her face. "No wonder everyone thinks you are so wise."

"Do they?" he said dryly. "I doubt everyone does. Not my sister."

"Your sister has been remarkably circumspect since you came back from the plague site with tales of illness and wonder."

He nodded. "She was really afraid. Not that I blame her. I am afraid—I think we should all be terrified. And yet I feel so helpless. Except for sending angels out to inform the farmers, the Edori, and the Jansai, I don't know what to do. I don't know how to guard against these marauders. I don't know who they are or what they want. It seems they do not attack large clusters of people—there have been no sightings in Breven or Semorrah or Luminaux—so I think we are safe in the cities and the holds. But so far I have had no luck convincing the Edori and the Jansai to stop their travels and stay someplace out of danger."

Susannah laughed at him. "Easier to convince Yovah to forget all of our names," she said, "than to convince the Edori to settle in one place forever."

He smiled somewhat crookedly. "You have consented to do it," he pointed out. "But at what cost to yourself, I cannot guess."

She looked away. She was never prepared for the few times he turned the conversation to personal matters. His occasional questions and observations were unexpected and shrewdly on target. "I admit to some loneliness," she said. "And—a great sense of strangeness. Sometimes as I am just—walking down a hallway or—sitting in the music chamber or—or standing on the plateau hearing the angels sing, I think, 'How has my life brought me here? Why am I so far from my people?' And I miss my friends and my family more than I can say."

"You could go back to visit them," Gaaron suggested. "I could take you to find them—or Nicholas, or any of the angels—and you could spend a week with them. Anytime you wanted."

She tried to smile. "I couldn't. That would make it too hard."

"But I don't want your life here to be one of strangeness and loneliness," he persisted. "I don't want you to have given up everything. For me."

"For the god," she corrected.

"Yes, but the god is remote and I am the one you see every day and think, 'For him I made sacrifices,' " Gaaron said with unwonted asperity. "It concerns me to be the author of such upheaval in your life. And I would do anything to keep you from being unhappy."

An interesting way to phrase it, Susannah thought. *Not "I would do anything to make you happy."* "That is kind of you," she said quietly. "I don't know what I've done to make you think I am unhappy."

"Something Miriam said."

She made herself smile. "Ah, Miriam! Well, but, Gaaron, Miriam is a mischief-maker and a romantic. Surely the least trustworthy combination you could find."

"Miriam is good at reading people's hearts. It is one of the things that makes her dangerous, that she knows what matters to you—and will either protect it or menace it, depending on her mood."

"I am not unhappy. And I do not think it would do me so much good to go off and spend time with any of my clansmen. I am doing my best to settle into my life here, Gaaron, to do what the god asked of me and whatever you continue to ask of me. It is not what I expected my life to hold. It is not what I would have chosen. But the life is new to me still. I think it will have rich rewards. I am prepared to give myself over to this new life and wait to see what it then gives back to me."

"That is generous. That is the most I could ask of you," he said formally. But she fancied she heard a note of dissatisfaction in his voice, as if he could think of other things he might ask for. She held her breath a moment, to see if he would name them, but he did not. "We are agreed, then, on the little Jansai girl? I will go to Esther and the others today, and work out some kind of schedule."

"Yes. We are perfectly agreed," she said. "I think the new program will be good for all of us."

• • •

Predictably, Gaaron was as good as his word, and by noon the next day, Kaski's life had been ordered into an entirely new routine. She was bundled off to the kitchens, to chop vegetables and clean silver under Esther's stern eye, and then she was passed between classrooms to study music and arithmetic and history. Susannah could not tell, at first, if the new regime and the constant distractions were good for the little girl or merely bewildering. But she did notice that Kaski slept better these nights, sometimes even falling asleep before Susannah did, and not waking till later in the morning. These were good signs, Susannah thought.

And there were fewer bruises and no more incidents with a knife. No time for Kaski to do harm to herself, Susannah supposed, and that, too, had to be a good thing.

Naturally, Kaski did not tell her what she thought.

Predictable, also, was the fact that the next disruption in Susannah's new life was caused by Gaaron's sister. Miriam had been altogether too well-behaved in the two weeks following her outing with Gaaron. She had stayed mostly in the Eyrie, even though Gaaron had lifted his interdiction aimed to keep her in the hold, and she had been good to everyone, even Esther. She had spent less time with Chloe and more time with Ahio, a trade Susannah approved of, and she had spent almost every night in Susannah's room, which even Kaski had seemed to enjoy. But Miriam's natural state was not one of calm, and Susannah found herself awaiting the next squall in the stormy story of Miriam's life.

The first round of thunder came very late one night, after Susannah and Kaski had already fallen asleep. Susannah was used to going to bed without Miriam in the room, and waking up with the blond girl sleeping beside her, so she did not fret when she turned out the lights and kissed Kaski on the cheek. But she felt an immediate sense of alarm when she was woken from a sound sleep by a hand on her shoulder and a whisper in her ear.

"Susannah! Susannah! Are you awake? I'm really in trouble this time."

Susannah woke completely and soundlessly, a trick she had learned years ago sleeping in a crowded Edori tent. "Miriam," she whispered back. "What's wrong?"

"I was in Velora and—oh, it's such a long story—"

Motioning to Miriam to be quiet for a moment, Susannah got out of bed carefully, to avoid jarring Kaski, and ushered Miriam to the far side of the room. She lit a couple of candles and then sank onto a pile of pillows on the floor, Miriam following suit.

"Quietly," Susannah commanded. "What happened?"

Miriam had her arms wrapped around her knees and was rocking back and forth as if to generate heat. Susannah shook out a little embroidered blanket and threw it around the girl's shoulders.

"I think someone's dead," Miriam said at last.

"What?" Susannah hissed. "Miriam, you cannot be serious."

Miriam nodded. "I am, though. I think it's my fault, but, Susannah, I didn't mean for it to happen. It didn't occur to me—I was just—and then things got out of hand—"

"Start from the beginning," Susannah said. "What happened?"

"I was in Velora. I asked Ahio to take me down in the morning, and he did, but he said he couldn't come back and get me, and I said that was fine. And I did some shopping and I had some lunch, and then in the evening I went to see Elias, even though I knew I shouldn't."

"Who's Elias?"

Miriam shrugged. "This man. He runs a freighting business. He's really nice and he has a lot of money and he doesn't lecture me all the time. I just like to be around him. But I've only see him once or twice because his wife usually doesn't—"

"His wife? He's married?"

"Yes. But he doesn't love her. And his daughters are almost old enough to get married themselves, so he—"

"Wait. How old is he?"

"I don't know. Fifty, maybe. But he—"

"Miriam are you—have you been—"

"Yes," Miriam said defiantly. "I have been. And it's not like he's the first man I've been with. First man *or* angel. Don't be so shocked. I'm nineteen years old!"

Susannah took a deep breath. She was so stunned by this revelation that for a moment she lost sight of the first, more horrific confession. "I was not that young myself, but many girls are, I know. But, Miriam, you've been seeing a married man who's thirty years older than you are and has children in the house—there is so much wrong with that. Do you know how hurtful that is to everyone involved— the wife, the children, yourself? Do you know what a knife you are wielding, and how many scars you are making?"

"I do now," Miriam whispered. "But they're not the kind of scars you're talking about."

"So what happened?"

"I went to see Elias. He told me his wife would be gone all week. She had taken their daughters and gone somewhere. Castelana, maybe. One of the river cities. She wasn't supposed to be back yet."

"And she came home . . ."

Miriam nodded. "And she came home, and she saw me, and she started screaming at him. The girls ran out of the house, I don't know where they went, and I tried to back out of the room. They weren't paying any attention to me. She was screaming and screaming, and he was angry, too, but he was calmer than she was, and I just thought it was going to be a lot of shouting. And then—I don't know—she had a knife in her hand and she stabbed him. And he started bleeding and he stopped shouting and he just looked at her. And then he crumpled over onto the floor and—and he didn't say anything else."

"What did she do?"

"She started shrieking again, kneeling on the floor by him and calling out his name."

"What did you do?"

Miriam shook her head. Her eyes were wide and haunted. They flicked all around the room, as she looked at the walls, the furniture, the sleeping girl, anywhere but at Susannah. "I just left."

"Did you tell anyone?"

Miriam shook her head again. "I just ran out in the street. Back toward the bazaar, where I knew people would be. I didn't even think any angels would be out that late, but then I saw Enoch and he said he'd bring me back. Lectured me the whole way, too, but I didn't tell him anything."

"So you left a dying man and a hysterical woman all alone in a house and ran away?" Susannah repeated. "Without going for help, without doing *anything*?"

Miriam started crying. "I was afraid," she sobbed. "It was my fault and I was so afraid. I didn't know what to do."

"It's not your fault. You didn't drive the knife home," Susannah said steadily. "But you should have gone for help. You are to blame for making a bad situation disastrous. You are to blame for a lot."

Miriam sobbed even harder. "Don't tell Gaaron," she begged. "Please. He'll never forgive me."

Susannah rose to her feet. She had never felt more wretched for someone else—or more steely with resolve. "I have to," she said. "I'm going to tell him right now."

When Gaaron opened his door—tousled, yawning, and dull with sleep—Susannah couldn't stop a stray, totally frivolous thought from crossing her mind. *What would it be like to sleep next to that big, warm body?* All he was wearing was a pair of loose cotton pants that appeared to have been hastily pulled on once the door chime sounded. Never had his chest appeared so broad or his wings so spectacular. For just a moment, Susannah wanted to step close enough to lay her head upon his shoulder, feel those cool, edged feathers settle around her; for just a moment, she wanted to surrender her own strength to someone who was clearly designed to carry burdens.

When he recognized her, his expression instantly sharpened to combat readiness. "Susannah!" he exclaimed. "What—is it Miriam?"

She nodded and stepped inside, pushing the door closed behind her. She did not know how far word of this escapade would spread; a little privacy now might save embarrassment later. It was late, but others were still astir. Even now, three voices rose and fell in a sweet melody from two stories up. Who else might be prowling about, looking for trouble?

"She's been seeing a married man in Velora," Susannah started out baldly. "Tonight, his wife came home and found them together. There was a scene. The wife pulled a blade and attacked her husband. Miriam left, but she thinks he might be dead."

With each sentence she spoke, Gaaron's face grew harder, more stony. "She didn't stop to send for help?"

"No."

"How did she get back?"

"Enoch, but she didn't tell him what happened."

"Does this man—his wife—do any of them know who she is?"

"I didn't ask her. She often tells people she is your sister—but possibly only people she wants to keep at a distance. You understand. If she wanted to spend time with this man—"

"She might keep her identity a secret."

Susannah nodded. "I don't know what we should do."

"How long ago did it happen?"

"I would guess within the hour."

He nodded. "Are you dressed to leave?"

She glanced down at the clothes she was wearing, as if, in five minutes, she had forgotten what she had put on. A skirt, a blouse that did not match it, a pair of slippers. She had dressed hastily while Miriam begged her please not to go to Gaaron now, *please*, and all she had thought about was modesty enough to navigate the hallways. She had not planned to travel.

"I could go as I am," she said.

"I'll be right out."

Ten minutes later they were on their way to Velora. Summer was finally over, and crisp autumn had marched in to snap some color and energy back into their days. The night was chilly, and even the short flight generated enough wind to leave Susannah's face and fingers red.

"How will we know where to find this man?" Susannah called to Gaaron as he coasted down, skimming over the rooftops and awnings of the city.

"Not that many murders in Velora," was his sardonic response. "There should still be a commotion at the house. And if he's a merchant, he should live in this part of town."

He proved to be right on both counts. On their first pass over the northwestern quadrant of the little city, they spotted a crowd of people gathered outside an attractive two-story house. Torches had been stuck in the grass strips lining the avenue, and gaslight inside the house poured out from every window.

"What are you going to say?" Susannah whispered as he glided to a stop, setting her gently on her feet.

"It depends on what they say to me," he answered. "We should know fairly quickly how the situation stands."

He strode forward, Susannah falling a little behind, still wondering how he would explain his sudden presence in the middle of catastrophe. But she had forgotten: He was not merely Miriam's brother, but leader of the host at the Eyrie, soon to be Archangel. Not only did everyone recognize him, they expected him to appear at crisis points, to take matters into his own hands, and to solve them. He had not even gotten through the courtyard into the front door before people accosted him.

"Angelo! Have you heard? We've had a tragedy here."

"Angelo! Come quickly! They'll want to see you."

"Gaaron—good. I did not dare hope you would still be abroad this late at night. We've got a nasty situation inside."

"What happened?" Gaaron asked briskly, turning to the last

speaker. He seemed to be some kind of dignitary—a city official, Susannah guessed, or a member of the merchant's council.

The official spread his hands. He was small and dapper—though not, perhaps, as well-groomed as he might be in the middle of the day under less dramatic circumstances—and his tangled gray hair looked as though he hadn't had a chance to comb it before running out into the night. "A domestic problem. Elias—and may Jovah strike me dead if I do not say I would never have expected it from such a steady man— appeared to be seeing a young woman. You know Elias Shapping?"

Gaaron nodded. "Know of him. Good man."

"So we all thought. And who knows what happens inside a house that makes a man look for comfort outside of it? Even so, I would not have thought . . . At any rate, this young woman was here tonight. Myra and the girls were gone to Castelana for the week. But they returned earlier than expected, and there was a fight. Myra—it seems she was carrying a weapon. She admits she grew blind with rage and attacked Elias. She says she had no intent to—to—well . . . He is dead, and that was not what she wanted. She is hysterical, but there are women with her now. I think they've given her something to keep her calm."

Three other men had gathered around Gaaron as the official's speech unfolded. These were additional councilmen, Susannah supposed, the ruling caste of the small, prosperous city. They would be the ones to mete out punishment and decide the woman's fate.

These four—and Gaaron. She kept forgetting that everyone turned to him for justice.

"What is the family's situation?" Gaaron asked, as if that was all he cared about, as if he hadn't come dashing down here to ask about the one participant in this little drama who was both guilty and missing. "Was Shapping in business for himself? Did he have partners? Are there brothers or parents who have a share in the company?"

"Myra ran the company with him," piped up one of the other councilmen. "Good head for business, too. Sharp lady." He shook his head, thinking of how a sharp lady might grow dull and stupid.

"There's a brother in Castelana," one of the others said. "I don't think he's got a stake in the business, though. It was all run by Elias and Myra."

"Children?" Gaaron asked.

"Two girls. Fifteen and seventeen. This scandal won't do them any good."

"We'll have to convene a council to review the case, but, Angelo, I don't think she's all that much at fault," the gray-haired man said. "A moment of blind passion, when she sees her husband in the arms of another woman—and who can blame her? My own wife, the sweetest-tempered woman I hope to ever meet, I think she would cleave my skull with an ax if she ever thought I had betrayed her that way."

There was a murmur of assent from his fellow council members. Susannah spared a moment to look around and try to assess the others who were present. Maybe a dozen people lingered still in the courtyard, gossiping in groups of two or three. These appeared to be neighbors or passersby who had no information to offer but who were so hopeful of further developments they could not tear themselves from the scene. Inside the house, she could see shapes flickering past the curtained windows—the daughters, she supposed, and any healers who might have been called to treat the dying man or his frantic wife. Perhaps by now the morticians had been called in as well.

Gaaron's voice brought her attention back abruptly to the small circle of men and avenging angel. "What do we know about this woman?" he asked. "The one who was here tonight?"

The councilmen looked at one another and shook their heads. "Nothing. One of the neighbor women said she was young and blond, but I don't think Myra got a very good look at her."

"Do we know her name?" Gaaron persisted.

Susannah held her breath, but the men shook their heads again. "No."

"Angelo, I didn't even know there *was* a girl, I certainly didn't know a name."

"I still can't believe it of Elias . . ."

They were still making their earnest denials and protests when one of the onlookers detached herself from a small group and made her way hesitantly over to the council. "Angelo?" she asked in a low voice. "Were you asking about the young woman who caused all the trouble?"

Magisterially, Gaaron turned to face her, the expression on his face grave but not particularly anxious. Susannah, who felt her veins jumping with alarm, wondered how he could seem so calm. "Yes, please," he said. "Do you know anything about her? Any way we can identify her?"

She shook her head. "I saw her come by once or twice before, but

I didn't think anything of it. She always had her hair covered and her face down. She was a blonde, I think. Fair-haired, anyway."

"You don't know what she looked like? Would you recognize her if you saw her again?"

Regretfully, she shook her head. "I'm sorry, Angelo, I just never paid that much attention. I thought maybe she worked with Myra and Elias. Or maybe she was a friend of his daughter's. She looked clean and respectable—you know, not the kind of woman who would arouse suspicious thoughts."

Gaaron nodded. "I don't suppose you have any idea of her name?"

The woman had just shaken her head again when there was a sudden commotion inside the house. The door burst open and a young woman came running out, waving a soft piece of cotton in her hand. She was too old to be one of the daughters, Susannah thought, and too composed to be the wronged wife.

"Angelo!" the woman cried. Her voice was excited and her expression was vengeful. "Stephen was just saying you wanted information about that slut who was here with Elias?"

Susannah's heart galloped around her rib cage and stampeded to her throat. She put her hand to her mouth to prevent any sound from escaping.

"Yes, do you know anything?" Gaaron asked, turning now to face her. Susannah came a pace nearer, wanting to see what the woman held in her hand, wanting to know what thoughtless, careless thing Miriam had done now to betray herself.

The woman was waving the cloth over her head as if it was a banner. It looked like an Edori scarf, Susannah thought, soft and multihued and designed to lend bright color to an otherwise drab wardrobe. "The girls say this isn't theirs and doesn't belong to any friend they know!" she exclaimed triumphantly. "I'll bet she dropped it, that ignorant tramp that Elias brought in, that girl who ruined this whole house with one little kiss—"

"May I see it?" Gaaron asked, and held out his hand. Reluctantly, for it was quite a prize, she laid it across his palm.

He studied it a moment, unfolding it and staring down at one of the four corners where, even by torchlight, Susannah could catch the heavy braid of embroidery. Her heart stopped bounding and now shuddered to a halt, then puffed itself up to twice its normal size so that she could not pull in breath around it. Edori women often embroidered their names on their scarves or the hems of their skirts. Miriam didn't know how to sew a stitch, but Susannah had been teaching her to embroider. She had been right when she had thought this looked like an Edori scarf . . .

Abruptly, Gaaron wheeled and passed the fabric to Susannah. She spread it out between her two hands and stared down at the embroidered pattern expertly set into the fiber. She found herself reading the letters of her own name.

Two days later, Miriam was packing for Luminaux.

They had managed to keep it a secret among the three of them—Gaaron, Susannah, and Miriam—just what kind of trouble Miriam was in this time. Nonetheless, everyone in the hold knew that something had happened, and that Gaaron was beyond fury, beyond any kind of physical or emotional retribution. He had merely said to Miriam, as he found her in Susannah's room that night, "I am sending you away." She had not protested. She hadn't even asked where she was going.

It was Susannah who had suggested, not just the city, but the venue. "There is an Edori woman who owns a bakery there, and I am friendly with her," she had told Gaaron upon their return to the Eyrie that night. It was very late, but they were both too keyed up to attempt to sleep. "I think you would like her. She is very kind but not particularly sentimental. She has raised three daughters of her own, and I don't think Miriam would surprise her much."

"Miriam surprises me every day," he said. "But if she is willing, I would be in her debt."

"I will go with her, of course, to make the introductions," Susannah said. She spoke mostly to his back, and his hunched, unresponsive wings, for he was staring out the window at the wan face of the new dawn. "Will you come, too? Or—"

"No," he interrupted. "No, I don't think I can."

Susannah took a step nearer, wanting to comfort him, but having no clue how to do it. "Gaaron, she is very young," she said softly.

"Not that young," he replied. "Old enough, in some circles, to be a wife and mother. Old enough, most definitely, to know when what she is doing is wrong. Old enough to stop trying to prove to our dead father that she can do anything she wants."

"You think this is still about him?" she asked.

He shrugged, and his wings rose and fell with an exhausted motion. "I know there are days in my own life when I am aware of my father's ghost watching over me. Gloating over my achievements or sneering at me for something I have missed. And I am older than Miriam and wiser by far."

"He sounds like a dreadful man."

Gaaron made an indecisive sound. "Dreadful? That doesn't say it precisely enough. He was an ambitious, driven, bitter man who was determined that his children would become what he could not. Nothing he did from the day I was born, nothing he said to either of us, had a root in anything except his desire to see us succeed, to win the glories he could not."

This was so alien to Edori philosophy that Susannah could not really assimilate it. "What successes? What glories?"

He finally turned away from the window, a most satirical expression on his face. "Why, the title of Archangel, of course. His own father had groomed him for that role. Had bestowed the proper name upon him. Had fostered him with the man who held the title before Adriel."

"The proper name?" Susannah interrupted. "There is such a thing?"

"Oh, yes," Gaaron said softly. "You didn't know? The Librera names the four great Archangels of the past, before the time of the founding of Samaria. Gabriel, Raphael, Uriel, and Michael. Of the twelve Archangels who have watched over us since Jovah brought us here, eight of them have been christened with one of those names. My father's name, of course, was Michael. And mine, naturally, must be Gabriel."

"So from the time you were born, he thought you—"

"From the time he was born, he thought he would be named Archangel. He thought, everyone thought, he was destined to take up the reins of power. The office rotates between the three holds, you know—or perhaps you didn't know—but not on any exact schedule. You might have one Archangel from the Eyrie, one from Monteverde, another from the Eyrie, then two from Windy Point, another from Monteverde—it is an informal schedule, yet there is a sense that no one of the angel holds can be given power too many generations in succession. And there had been three Archangels between the last one from the Eyrie and the next one to be named. And my grandfather was convinced that my father would be the next one to be called."

"But he wasn't," Susannah said.

Gaaron shook his head. "But he was not," he said very deliberately. "He was passed over, and the title went to Adriel instead. I was a boy then—nine or ten—but I will never forget my father's rage. It was as if she had stolen something from him—a birthright—something more precious than money or love. He had not been a calm man before then, but from that day on, he was possessed. He focused all his thoughts, all his energies, on turning me into the angel who would be prized above all other angels."

"Who chooses the Archangel?" Susannah wanted to know.

For the first time in this long, impossibly wretched evening, Gaaron looked at her with something of a smile. "How can it be you live in this land and do not know the answer to that question?" he asked.

She smiled tentatively back. "I have not been around angels much, and never around Archangels, so you must excuse my ignorance."

He sighed heavily and settled himself into one of those uncomfortable-looking cutaway chairs. His wings flopped on the floor behind him, listless and crumpled. Susannah sat in a rather more respectable chair and waited for his answer.

"The god chooses," he said. "He communicates his choice to the oracles, who communicate it to the rest of the world. There is no gainsaying the god. There is no lobbying to change his mind. I have always thought the system worked very well, because had it been up to men to decide—had a council of angels or mortals convened to vote on their candidates—I do believe my father would have gone on a rampage and murdered every last one of them. As it was, there was nothing he could do but rage. And make life a living hell for his children, of course."

"Did you want to be Archangel?" Susannah asked. There was stale bread and some half-filled glasses of water on the small table between their chairs. She picked up a crust and nibbled on it. She was not even hungry, but her hands were restless. She was too tense to merely sit still and talk.

Gaaron seemed to think for a long moment, and then he sighed. "I don't even know," he said. "It was as if there was no choice. Did you want to be born an Edori? The contours of your life were determined for you before you even came crying out of the womb. That is how I felt about being Archangel. About being groomed to become Archangel," he corrected himself. "There was, of course, no guarantee."

Now she sipped on the water, wondering who had last drunk from this glass and not particularly caring. "And had you not been named Archangel?" she asked. "If someone else—Neri—had been chosen instead? Would you have been disappointed? Furious? Would you have wondered then what to do with your life?"

He considered again. "I don't know. I was by then so used to the responsibilities my life held that being named Archangel was just part of the same litany. I had been chosen leader of the host by the time I was twenty-one. I was—you understand, I was a serious young man, people had gotten in the habit of relying on me. I was used to taking things on. I cannot say I wanted the glory and the glamour of being Archangel, as my father always did. What I can say is that it seems to be a hard job, given to someone who is used to doing hard jobs, and that I have done so many hard things in my life, it seemed inevitable that it would fall to me. Would I have been disappointed had the title gone elsewhere? I don't think so. I think I would have believed that some other difficult task had been reserved for me, that the god would make known in his own time."

Susannah was silent, but she felt strange. She had never heard anyone so simply and straightforwardly offer himself up for duty and rough labor. She looked at him surreptitiously, a tired man sitting lax after a devastating day, but that was not what she saw. She saw a capable man sitting in a pool of his own power, phosphorescent with will and latent force. The hard muscles of his arms were relaxed, the purposeful face was loose and weary—but a little shiver went through her. Sound an alarm, call out a warning, and those slack muscles would bunch, the fine mind would hone down to a ruthless clarity. He would not rail at a god who sent him one more crisis; he would shoulder the burden, and he would move on.

Her silence caught his attention, and he looked over at her with a little smile. "And you are thinking that one of my difficult assignments is Miriam," he said. "And you are thinking that Jovah gave me a rare task there."

"That's not what I was thinking," she said quietly.

He stretched, and those fatigued muscles rippled and lay quiet again. "I disappointed my father in every way, and I had a chance of carrying out his dream," he said. "You can imagine how he felt about Miriam, who could offer him nothing. She has lived her whole life trying to prove to him that she could be worse than he even imagined."

"I don't think he's the one she's proving it to anymore."

He thought that over and nodded. "So I have become my father in her eyes? I have tried very hard not to. But Miriam was set long ago on a path of self-destruction. And loving her does not seem to have done much to turn her feet another way."

"I think you have done as much for her as you can," she said softly, coming to her feet. "Now it is up to Miriam to decide what road to take."

He looked up at her in surprise. "You're leaving?"

"Gaaron, you look exhausted. I'm going to let you sleep for a few hours. Don't answer the door. Don't worry about anything. I'll handle Miriam and any questions that come our way."

"You're tired, too," he protested, but he did not stand. He did not look capable of standing.

She stepped around the table between them and laid her hands on his tousled hair. He had changed into reasonable clothes before they rushed off to Velora, but he had not thought to comb out his hair, tangled from sleep. For a moment he looked young and vulnerable; his resemblance to Miriam was suddenly pronounced.

"Get some sleep, Gaaron," she said quietly. "I can manage just fine for a few hours without you."

She bent down to kiss him on the top of the head, between her spread fingers. So she would have kissed Amram or Kaski or Keren or anyone who had been crying. His hands lifted hesitantly—paused in midair—settled again along his thighs. She drew back and smiled down at him.

"You're a good brother," she said. "I'll tell Miriam what you've decided. Now get some sleep."

He watched her to the door, neither rising to escort her out nor to set the lock behind her. She felt his eyes upon her back but did not turn around to look at him again before shutting the door between them. She was too tired to hurry down the hallway and around the corner, so she moved slowly, her steps measured, her face grave. At her own doorway she paused, not sure if Miriam or Kaski or anyone else would be inside. She glanced from side to side, but no one appeared to be stirring in this corner of the world.

So she pulled off her jacket there in the hallway to inspect the source of pain on the upper portion of her right arm. Not pain, exactly, but a sense of pressure, a faint hot lick of heat. She was not surprised to see the pale Kiss in her arm threaded with a glowing white coil. She put her left hand out to touch it, but the crystal dome remained cool to the touch, though the tight opal spiral in its depths still sparked and twisted. A tiny flush, a breathless exhalation of excitement; this could not, surely, be the flaring and flaming that Miriam had talked about when she told dreamy tales of Kisses igniting when true lovers revealed themselves to each other.

She pulled her jacket back on and pushed open the door.

CHAPTER THIRTEEN

Nicholas and Ahio took Miriam and Susannah to Luminaux, and never once asked why.

The trip took two and a half days and was accomplished with remarkable economy, since Miriam was not disposed to disrupt plans by sleeping late or wandering off in the mornings before everyone else was awake. She was quiet and well-behaved, a little cowed, Susannah thought, and both Ahio and Nicholas eyed her with a certain speculation as the trip proceeded. Like Susannah, they had expected more temper.

Like Susannah, they did not really believe Miriam had changed.

They stayed each night in small inns along the way, where the owners scrambled to give them the best rooms and the most sumptuous meals they could provide. Susannah was pleased to see that Miriam and both angels were gracious guests, though the standards of luxury these small-town innkeepers could meet were nothing like they were used to at the Eyrie. Nonetheless, they thanked everyone warmly and always said complimentary things about the cooking. One night, when requested, the two angels sang for the other diners, an event that seemed to leave everyone in the room blissful with disbelief. A rare treat, to hear an angel singing! Even more than the special seasonings, those songs turned the common meal into a fabulous banquet.

They arrived in Luminaux before noon on the third day. Susannah, riding comfortably in Ahio's arms for the morning, had been thinking hard about how exactly to leave Miriam behind, how to make the transition seem less abrupt. Therefore, once they had made their landing and they were all standing on their own feet again, she turned to the angels with a cheerful smile on her face.

"I'm sure the two of you know how to entertain yourselves in Luminaux," she said.

Nicholas grinned. "Anybody could."

"Then I'd like you to find something entertaining, and meet me back here tomorrow morning."

That surprised them. Ahio's blond eyebrows rose, and Nicholas made a soundless whistle. "What will you be doing all that time?" Nicholas asked cautiously. "I don't think Gaaron—"

"I think Gaaron has left this in my hands," she interrupted. "I will take Miriam, and you two will go somewhere else, and in the morning the three of us will meet back here at"—she glanced around her—"at the front of the Divinity Club, whatever that might be."

Ahio grinned. "Music bar," he said. "Good music, too."

"One would expect good music in Luminaux," Susannah said loftily.

Nicholas turned his attention to Miriam, who was looking around her with interest, though the expression on her face was not nearly as lively as it usually was. "How about you, little girl?" he asked. "Are you going to be all right here?"

She turned her dark eyes his way, a scowl across her brows. "I'm not a little girl."

Nicholas ruffled her hair. "No, you're a little hellion," he said affectionately. "We'll miss you."

She flicked him another unreadable but far from tame look. "Susannah was right," she said. "You should go now."

Ahio ignored the warning expression and stepped forward to take the blond girl into a tight embrace. He whispered something into her hair that made her laugh and squirm to get free, but she was still smiling when Nicholas also gave her a hug.

"You boys behave yourselves," she said with a hint of her old mischief, and they laughed.

SHARON SHINN

Susannah pointed. "This way," she said to Miriam, and guided her through the streets of Luminaux.

They passed meat vendors selling pies and musicians singing on the street corners; they walked by an array of little shops selling everything from jewelry to toys. The sun poured down over the blue rooflines and across the sparkling sapphire-studded marble of the buildings. Everything glittered with azure highlights, and the sky itself was a concentrated color not seen anywhere else in Samaria. It was hard to walk through Luminaux and not be happy, Susannah thought. Even Miriam appeared to be enjoying herself as they strolled along.

Frida sia Mirita had opened a small bakery along one sunny boulevard of the city more than five years ago, and today it appeared to be doing a brisk business. There were trays of glazed sweets arrayed in the display window, the tantalizing scent of bread and sugar drifting out the open door, and half a dozen customers inside, making purchases and stuffing pastries into their mouths.

"Looks like Frida would be happy to have more hands available to help," Susannah said as they entered the shop. Miriam gave her a sideways glance and did not respond.

The two girls working behind the counter were Frida's daughters, Susannah knew, though she had not met them during the summer when the Lohoras stayed near Luminaux. When Susannah approached, they looked up with the typical Edori welcoming smile.

"Is Frida here?" Susannah asked. "I have a favor to ask of her. I am Susannah of the Tachitas and the Lohoras, and she will remember my name."

Frida was elbow-deep in a vat of dough but exclaimed with delight when Susannah stepped into the back room. "Susannah! I have heard such stories of you lately! What changes there have been in your life since you were here this summer! Let me wash my hands and sit down with you for a few minutes."

"I hate to pull you away from your work, when it is obviously so successful," Susannah said with a smile. The instant she was around an Edori again, she picked up those lilting, semiformal patterns of speech. "I still cannot believe you are a businesswoman. What would your father say?"

Frida laughed and dried her hands on a scrap of cloth. "My father never slept in the same spot for two nights running," she retorted. "But my mother—she was half allali, you know. She liked to buy things and own things. She had a use for money, and she taught me some allali ways."

Susannah glanced around the kitchen, clean and well-apportioned. Here the scent of yeast was strong, and the rich smell of baking bread made her whole body yearn with hunger. "You appear to have learned very well," she said. "I am impressed."

Frida came over to give her a hug and then drew them both to a small table in the back of the cluttered kitchen. She called out directions to two young women minding the stoves, and then settled herself at the table.

"But *you* have a story these days that I am crazy to hear," Frida said. "You have left the people to go live with the angels! To be the bride of the new Archangel! Susannah, how did this come about?"

There had been no chance that that tale would not have circulated immediately among the Edori, the travelers who shared news with every other chance-met clan. In fact, Susannah had counted on Frida knowing her story before she ever set foot in the bakery.

"It is partly because of my new circumstances that I am here to see you today," Susannah said softly. "Yes, the god has directed that I go live with the angels now. And the man I am to marry has a young sister . . ."

The story was long and not quickly told, but Frida listened with genuine interest, interjecting comments from time to time. Susannah edited out any reference to Dathan, and tried to make the whole event seem less fantastical than she knew it was. By the shrewd expression on Frida's face, she could tell the older woman realized there were parts of the story she was not being told. But Frida nodded, and listened, and absorbed it all without asking difficult questions.

"So this sister—Miriam—you have brought her to Luminaux with you? I would be happy to take her in," Frida said.

Susannah smiled at this easy offer. "Gaaron thought I would have a hard time convincing you to take responsibility for her," she said. "He was afraid to ask what you might charge me for such a service! Because he can think of nothing else to do with her."

Frida brushed this off with a laugh. "Ah, he does not know the Edori ways! How many times has a daughter of the Manderras been shipped off to the Havitas because the Manderras could no longer control her? And how many Barcerra boys have gone to live with the

Chievens to learn to behave? The Edori know that we are all family, and that every hand must pitch in. I will happily take in the angel's sister for as long as he needs."

"She is wild," Susannah warned. "And I do not expect you to be able to curb that wildness. Just—just to give her a safe place to live."

Frida nodded. "I understand. And to show her a different face of love. My daughters will adore her."

Susannah smiled. "You have not even met her. You cannot know that for sure."

Frida smiled back. "*You* adore her," she pointed out. "She must be very easy to love."

Susannah came to her feet. "Come meet her," she said.

Almost to her surprise, Susannah saw that Miriam was still in the bakery, having waited patiently all this time. She'd purchased a cream-filled pastry and was eating it slowly, concentrating on every bite. She looked over at Susannah and Frida when they emerged from the back room, and the expression on her face was guarded and hard to read.

Frida marched right up to her and put her hands on both slim shoulders. "You are Miriam, and you've come to stay with me a little while," she said. "I am very happy to have you. I think you'll like Luminaux so much you won't ever want to go back to the Eyrie."

Unexpectedly, Miriam smiled at that, a brilliant, absolutely winsome smile. "I think you may be right," she said.

When most of the customers had cleared out, Frida introduced Miriam and Susannah to her daughters, explaining the story, and they all paused for an afternoon snack. But there was no such thing as a truly quiet moment at the bakery. Every few minutes someone else came in to buy bread for dinner or cake for a party, and someone had to hop up to wait on the customer and make the sale. Miriam was behaving extremely well, talking gaily with the daughters and presenting her best manners to Frida, but Susannah could tell Frida was not deceived. The Edori woman watched the angel's sister with the small smile of a woman who had raised three daughters and could map out any girl's heart without a single mistake.

They had been at the bakery for nearly two hours and were now discussing evening plans, when the door opened again and three customers stepped in. Susannah did not automatically look up, as Frida and her girls did every time someone walked in, so she did not instantly realize the newcomers were Edori. And Edori who recognized her.

Until *"Susannah!"* was shrieked into the quiet room and suddenly she was in the middle of a screaming, crying, gesticulating crowd of women. "Susannah! You're here! Susannah! *Susannah!*"

"Keren—Tirza—Claudia! Oh, I cannot believe it! You're in Luminaux! Oh, it is so good to see you! Where are you camped? Why are you back here so soon? Oh, look at you, look at your beautiful face—"

They would not answer any of her questions but demanded she tell them her own story. "To leave like that—so suddenly—and then we heard nothing more from you, not a word," Claudia said, her voice scolding and even now a little shaken. Susannah remembered with remorse that final morning in the Edori camp, the fight with Dathan, the look at Gaaron that invited him to take her, if he really wanted to take her, the leave-taking that had occurred without a single good-bye.

"Oh—such a long story—we cannot talk here, not in the middle of Frida's bakery," Susannah said, stammering a little.

"Use the back room. The other girls are gone for the day," Frida offered.

"No, no, come back to camp with us," Tirza said impatiently. "How long are you in Luminaux? Spend the night with us."

"I couldn't," Susannah said, feeling a moment's panic. "I was going to stay with Frida for the evening and leave in the morning—"

"Come back with us," Claudia said firmly. "You can stay in my tent if there is not enough room in Eleazar's. It will do you good to be with the people again for at least one night."

An unexpected voice spoke next. "Yes, Susannah, let's camp with the Lohoras tonight," Miriam said, her words clear and distinct. "I can come back to Frida's in the morning."

In the end, because she could not come up with any rational argument not to except *I want to too much*, Susannah agreed to spend the night with the Lohoras, Miriam coming along. The clan was camped just outside the city limits, where they had been for five days.

"Bartholomew has had a fever for a week or more, so we have stayed in Luminaux, where we could buy medicine from an apothecary," Tirza explained as they walked back through the city streets toward camp. They traveled erratically, detouring to pick up cheese at this stall and fresh fruit at a little shop. And, of course, they had to pause frequently to admire merchandise deemed desirable by Keren—who seemed to have formed an instant friendship with Miriam. The

two young women walked ahead of the other three, their heads together; Claudia had drifted to the other side of the street and was
eyeing the vendor carts there. Tirza and Susannah had been left more
or less alone to talk freely.

"Bartholomew is ill?" Susannah exclaimed. "He's never sick!"

"And he's much better. I think we'll leave in a day or so. But it's
made us so lazy you cannot imagine, since we haven't had to cook or
hunt for a week. We just walk into the city and buy whatever we
need." She laughed. "I think it will be *very* hard on Keren when we
pull up stakes. She has loved being here."

"How is she? How are you—how is everyone? I cannot believe—it
has been so long, it seems like a lifetime—"

"I wish you could have gotten in touch with us, Susannah," Tirza
said quietly. "We all knew where you had gone and that you must be
safe, but it was so difficult not to know how you were feeling, if you
were lonely or if you were happy. It was so hard to see you leave like
that, without even a good-bye."

I didn't have a choice, Susannah wanted to say. *Gaaron stole me
from the campsite—what could I do?* But she knew that wasn't true.
Tirza knew it wasn't true. That last night in camp, after that strange
and disturbing conversation with Gaaron, Susannah had slipped back
into Eleazar's tent to find everyone else asleep. She had picked her way
through the tangled bodies to find Tirza and shake her awake, and she
had knelt beside the other woman's pallet and whispered into her ear
the whole transcript of the conversation with the angel.

Tirza had told her to go.

Susannah had said she would not.

But, of course, the next morning, she had.

"I thought it would be easier on me, on everybody, just to be
gone," Susannah said at last. "I did not think—I did not expect to see
you now. I don't know that I am ready for it. It is so hard to leave
behind one life and embrace a new one. I thought if I did it all at once,
it would be easier."

"And has it been?" Tirza asked.

Susannah gave a small, desperate laugh. "No! I am so lonely at
times I cannot bear it. But everyone has been kind, and I think, after
I am with them for a while, I will come to love them all. Already I
love Miriam, who is the most impossible child imaginable. Think of
Keren, only multiply all her sins and all her blessings, and you might
have an idea of Miriam. She is so bad and she is so good. And the

others—I am finding them already snuggling into the empty places of my heart. I will be content there someday, I know. But for now—I miss all of you. I miss our way of life. I miss living with the rain and sun and the open land and the new adventure of every day." She put a hand on Tirza's arm. "I miss the sound of breathing around me every night. That I miss most of all."

"Do you miss Dathan?" Tirza asked.

Susannah was silent. "I try not to," she said at last. "Dathan is the reason I agreed to leave."

"He has been—I would like to say he has been faithful to your memory—" Tirza began.

Susannah shook her head. "I left to marry another man. That set Dathan free."

"And he has taken advantage of that freedom," Tirza said regretfully. "Though he is not, at the moment, tangled in any woman's charms. And I know, though he has not said so, that he thinks of you often. He will be happy to see you tonight."

"I don't want to see him," Susannah whispered. "I will sleep in Claudia's tent."

They paused under a brightly striped awning while Miriam and Keren cooed over an assortment of ribbons and bows. Claudia had ranged ahead and was earnestly talking with a vendor about some kitchen pot that looked big enough to boil a horse in. Susannah could not imagine packing that up every night and taking it on to the next campsite.

"You will have to fence Dathan out of your heart before you can invite someone else in," Tirza said seriously.

Susannah produced a small smile. "Perhaps I will not invite anyone else in. Perhaps it will be my own small solitary garden full of private flowers."

"What about this angel?" Tirza asked. "Gaaron. If you are to marry him, he may well want to smell those blossoms."

Now Susannah laughed. She had almost forgotten the easy way Edori talked about relations between men and women, how such relations were a source of constant and personal interest among the other members of the tribe. "We have not planned the wedding yet," she replied, evading.

But Tirza was not to be put off. "So how do you deal together?" she asked. "I liked him well enough when he was at the campsite, but he may have been putting on his best manners just for show."

"No, pretty much that is how Gaaron always behaves," Susannah said. "He is very serious and considerate and kind. He is completely to be trusted. Everyone in the hold comes to him with every problem, from the smallest to the gravest. He expects it. He is used to handling everything and having no one at all to help him. He is not so interested in entering a woman's flower garden and playing at love."

Tirza did not answer, and Susannah looked over at her. The other woman was watching her with a tiny frown. "That's strange."

"What is?"

"How you talk about him."

Susannah felt breathless. She thought her voice had been completely neutral. "How do I talk about him?"

"As if you are aggrieved."

Susannah laughed nervously. "Aggrieved by what?"

Tirza shrugged and shook her head, as if she could not quite define it. "By how unappreciated he is by his friends—and by how little he appreciates you."

"Don't be silly," Susannah said. "I think he appreciates me a great deal. He has told me more than once how he values my judgment, and I know he likes to talk things over with me."

"How odd," Tirza said.

"Stop saying things like that," Susannah said impatiently.

Tirza shook her head again. "He does not seem like the kind of man you would fall in love with. And yet I think you have."

Susannah looked away. "The god has decreed that I marry him," she said softly. "And I will do it. The god said nothing about love. That comes at our bidding, not Yovah's. Gaaron is a good man. I will not be unhappy with him. I do not expect more than that."

Keren came running up with a handful of red-dyed ribbons. "Look, Tirza, see, I can make a headband and wear them in my hair," she said. She held up the shiny strips of satin, and they indeed made a gorgeous contrast against her black hair. "I will make a red dress and wear it at the Gathering, and tie these ribbons around my braids," she said dreamily. "I will look so beautiful when I sing that no one will notice if I miss some of the notes."

Susannah and Tirza laughed. "Are we all done shopping now?" Tirza demanded. "It is time we got back. Everyone in the camp will be so excited to see our special guests." Her smile included Miriam in this excitement. "It is selfish of us to keep them all to ourselves."

They quickened their steps and took fewer detours as they reached the edges of the city. Susannah was feeling more apprehensive by the moment, and when they got close enough to see the Edori tents a quarter mile ahead of them, she felt her heart begin to flutter. She did not want to see Dathan again, she did not.

She did. Yovah be merciful, she did.

For a few brief, painful minutes after they arrived at the Lohora camp, no one realized she was there. The campfires cooked, sending up their pungent, familiar flavors. The children ran yelling between tents, playing some complex, ridiculous game. Voices called to one another, laughter rippled from fire to fire. Everything was so familiar, so sweet. Everything was so agonizingly lost to her forever.

Then—*"Susannah!"*—and the cry darted from mouth to mouth, tent to tent. Door flaps burst backward as bodies shot out, cook pots splashed as the cooks dropped their ladles. Never had there been such a frenzy and commotion. Susannah laughed and exclaimed as she went from one embrace to another. "You've grown so tall! You've cut your hair! Look at you, Shua, a baby on the way! Claudia must be delighted." It hurt to feel so much love at once. She could not kiss enough cheeks, could not feel enough hands upon her arms and shoulders. She was trying not to cry, but the tears came anyway.

"You should not have stayed away so long, not after leaving like that," Anna said, scolding her as Tirza had.

"No—of course I should not have—but aren't you looking well—"

She did not see Dathan, not at first. Perhaps he was out with the others, hunting, or down near the Galilee River. She did duck inside Bartholomew's tent and put her hand on the hot forehead and note the way the skin had loosened around his wrists and collarbone. But his color was not bad, and she believed him when he said he was mending.

"Seeing you will make me well before dawn," he told her with a smile.

She smiled back. "Who is tending you? Your sister?"

"At night. Most days, Anna has sat beside me and fetched whatever I needed."

Her smile grew wider. "I am happy to hear that! Did she offer, or did you ask for her?"

"She kindly offered."

Susannah bent to kiss him on the cheek. "Now you must work to reverse that," she whispered in his ear. "Have your sister tend you in the daylight, and ask Anna to lie beside you at night."

He was not a jovial man, but his face looked amused as she drew back to survey him. "I will propose that to her as soon as I have recovered my strength," he said.

When she emerged from the tent, she found Dathan waiting for her, and everyone else deeply engaged in some urgent task. She rocked back a little on her heels and stood there a moment, unable to move forward.

"Susannah," he said.

He looked beautiful as a summer morning. The slanting evening sun turned his skin to bronze and his hair a spangled midnight black. The bones of his face were elegant and severe; his dark eyes were soulful and imploring. She wanted nothing so much as to lay her hands upon his skin and soak up the very texture of his body.

"Dathan."

He stared at her as if she could not possibly be real, a woman made up of dreams and longings. Whenever she had thought of Dathan these past weeks, which was often, she had always remembered him laughing. She had forgotten how devastating it could be to have Dathan focused on her, willing her to want him, to believe him.

"I thought I might never see you again," he said.

She smiled as much as she could, which was not much. "It is too soon for me to be back here," she said quietly. "It hurts even more than I thought it would."

"Have you come back to stay?"

She shook her head. "The god has called me to a new life. I must live with the angels now."

"The god might change his mind," he suggested.

This time the smile was more real. "That does not seem to be Yovah's way."

"I've missed you," he said.

She swallowed against a tight throat. "Yes. I've missed you."

Not asking if he could, he reached out and took her arm. She felt that light grip against her skin as she might feel a brand of searing metal. "Walk with me a little bit," he said.

She could not speak, and so she nodded.

He pulled her away from the tent, away from the campsite, sliding his hand down her arm until his fingers found hers. They interlaced their hands and continued walking, heads down, mouths silent, the busily gossiping camp falling ever farther behind them. It was close to sunset now, and a brisk chill laced the air, though it was not nearly so cold here as it had been at the Eyrie. Still, no part of Susannah was completely warm except the hand held in Dathan's.

"I remember the first time I saw you," he said at last. "That time at the Gathering. You and your family had just arrived, and you were pitching your tent. And it was hot, and Paul was cross, and Linus had lost a tent peg. Your mother was too sick to help, so she was just sitting outside, looking at everything. And all of them were watching you. You were the calm, still center of that family. Every time you spoke any word, you brought peace. You found the missing stake. You gave your mother her dinner. You laughed your brother back into good humor. You kissed your father just because you loved him. And I thought, 'I want to be in that tent, with that girl. I want that peace wrapped around me.' "

Susannah smiled a little, her face tilted down so he could not see. "And the first time I saw you," she said, "you were laughing. You looked so carefree and beautiful that I thought the sun and the stars themselves must love you. I wanted to stand inside your joy and let it fill me up, let it glaze me in gold. I wanted to be one of the things that brought that happiness to your face."

He stopped and turned to look at her. He had dropped her hand, but only so that he could put both his hands on her shoulders. "You are one of those things, Susannah," he said quietly. "One of the only things that brings me happiness. I have been so sad with you gone from me."

She raised her hand so she could put her palm against his face. Dear Yovah, the smoothness of his cheek, the roughness of beard stubble along his jaw—how many times had she placed her hand just so and marveled at those subtle contradictions? She felt tears coming to her eyes and she did not know how to form any words at all, much less the ones she needed to say.

"You left because of me," he said. "No matter what call the god sent out, you did not leave at Yovah's urging. Come back because of me. I will be whatever you want."

"I want you to be the laughing man who stands at any campfire and makes it burn brighter," she whispered. "I thought I wanted to stamp that memory from my heart, but I find I want that image burned there always, a picture of joy and jubilation. I don't want you to change for me. I don't want you to change at all."

"I have changed anyway," he whispered back.

He kissed her, and the world ended. She could feel his arms around her back, his hair against her skin, his mouth upon her lips, but everything else was gone—earth, sky, scarlet sun. She kissed him back feverishly, pressing her hands against his face, against the back of his head, upon his shoulders. She dropped her hands lower, slipped them inside his shirt, her cool fingers against the warm silk of his skin. His ribs were like the carved ivory bones of some fine musical instrument; the knobs of his spine were as pronounced and delicate as spun glass globes. She touched them all, every bone of his chest, every bone of his back. She remembered each one of them.

His own hands were wandering—through her hair, down her shoulders, up again to the fastenings at the front of her blouse. How many times had they made love on some open prairie a mile or two from camp, not even trying to find a secluded spot where no one was likely to come across them by accident? She laughed as the first bow untied in his hand, laughed even harder as the second one knotted up and refused to loosen. He paused to kiss her again. When he drew his head back, she leaned her body against him, cheek against his chest, arms folded around his waist. His own arms came up and wrapped her closer, and they stood that way, embraced, till the sun finally abandoned them, slipping behind the horizon line and leaving darkness behind.

When Dathan's hands grew restless again, pushing at her shoulders and trying to find her skin, she only held him tighter. She squeezed her eyes shut and pressed her arms around his body, and would not look up or speak. He tried twice more, and then he knew. All the tension went from his body. His arms fell about her loosely, and for a moment, she was the only one holding on. Then he took a deep breath, gathered her to him more tightly, and dropped a kiss on the top of her head.

"I'm not the only one who has changed," he said.

She still would not look up. "I'm sorry," she said. "I've been afraid to come back. Afraid to see you again. For so many reasons. But this wasn't one of them."

"Do you love him? That angel?"

"Not yet," she said.

"Then—"

But she shook her head against his chest. "No," she said. "I can't. I don't understand it, but I can't. We have to go back to camp."

"All right," he said. But he did not release her, and she still clung to him. They stood there a long time, not so much embracing as leaning against each other for support, as if they had witnessed a death or a disaster, before they disentangled. They walked back to camp even more slowly and silently than they had left it, to find everyone gathered around one central campfire, already eating dinner.

"Susannah! Come sit with me! I've saved you a seat!" Amram called. Other voices called her name, invited her to try this stew or that loaf of bread, was she hungry, was she thirsty, put this shawl on against the chill. She smiled at everyone and accepted all the sudden happy embraces, but she felt hollow and strange inside. As if part of her had died, as if all of her had died and this was the wistful half-life of the dead. Tirza gave her one sharp look but said nothing, and Claudia bustled up and insisted Susannah wear her own jacket, very warm, and sit down right this minute and eat.

Everyone in the whole camp seemed to know what had just happened, down to the whispered exchange and the last averted kiss. Everyone except Miriam. She sat half a dozen seats away from Susannah and watched her with a dark, accusing stare, as if betrayed on her brother's behalf by Susannah's presumed defection. Susannah gave her a tired smile, but she had no words with which to defend herself, no words to explain what had just happened. She accepted a plate and a glass from Anna, and allowed herself the luxury, for the duration of the meal, of thinking about nothing but the food in front of her.

In the morning, essentially the same delegation headed back into Luminaux, except that Claudia did not accompany them. Susannah had indeed spent the night in Claudia's tent, claiming she wanted to be able to help should Bartholomew need aid in the night. In addition, as she pointed out, Tirza's tent was already absorbing another body, since Keren had invited Miriam to sleep beside her so they could whisper secrets in the dark. Susannah had not exactly slept. Between listening to Bartholomew's labored breathing and picturing Dathan, awake and brooding three tents over, she had had very little will to close her eyes and dream the night away.

It was with extraordinarily mixed feelings that she made her good-byes in the morning and accepted the small gifts pressed on her by

Bartholomew and Claudia and Anna. She hugged everyone once—twice—before she left again, though Dathan was nowhere in sight and so did not receive a farewell. She was sure he had absented himself to spare his own feelings, not hers, and yet she was glad he was not there.

But she missed him terribly and carried a black stone in her heart as they walked away from camp and back toward Luminaux.

They had been walking for about half an hour when Tirza said, in a cautious tone of voice that meant she was trying to sound casual, "I've been thinking."

Susannah put her hands to her heart and feigned astonishment. "Yovah rejoices! A miracle has occurred!"

Tirza ignored her. "I do not like to imagine you so lonely in that angel hold. And now with Miriam gone for some weeks, I would guess you will be lonelier than ever."

"I know," Susannah said. "But my loneliness is not the way to make decisions about Miriam's life."

"I was thinking maybe you could take Keren back with you."

Susannah was so surprised that she actually came to a full halt on the road. "Keren? Bring her back?"

"Just for a little bit," Tirza said. "A month or two. She has such envy and desire for a softer way of life. Like your Miriam, she is a good girl, but somewhat misdirected. Maybe if she got a chance to see what that other life was like, she would learn that she loves the Edori way more than she realized."

"Or maybe she will never want to return to the tent and the tribe."

Tirza shrugged. "If she is happier in the city or the hold, why should we tie her to a life of roving?"

Susannah was thinking very fast. Visitors were constantly coming in and out of the Eyrie—there was room for dozens of transients at a time. Not that Keren would take up any space at all; she would sleep with Susannah, of course. And she would love life at the angel hold—no question about that. And Susannah would be so glad to have her.

"Would she come?" Susannah asked. "Now? Today?"

Tirza nodded ruefully. "I'm sure of it. Listening to her talk to Miriam last night—all night, there was no sleeping done—I must have heard her say a dozen times how she wished she could go back with you. At first I wanted to strangle her just to silence her, but then I started thinking, 'Why not? Wouldn't everyone be made happy by this?'"

"But she'd want to return to camp, to get some of her clothes—"

"I brought them," Tirza said triumphantly, pointing at a shoulder bag she'd carried out of the tent with her. "Just a few things that I knew she'd want. I didn't want to suggest it to her unless it was a plan you approved of, but if you do—"

"Yes, I would be happy to have Keren return with me, and everyone would welcome her," Susannah said decisively. "Let's ask her."

Keren, predictably, was ecstatic at the offer—she danced in the dusty road and twirled around so fast that her skirts fanned out and the string ties of her jacket went whipping around her shoulders.

Miriam laughed. "You're excited now, but wait till the hundredth person tells you you're making too much noise or you can't behave a certain way or the dress you're wearing makes you look like a street girl from Semorrah—"

"Perhaps Keren will behave so well that no one will be tempted to say those things to her," Susannah said.

"I doubt it," was Tirza's comment.

"Oh, I will. I'll be the best girl ever. I won't even flirt!"

Everyone had to laugh at that, not even Miriam believed her. "Just act demure and shy around Gaaron, and everything will be fine," the blond girl said cynically. "You don't have to impress anyone else."

"She has to impress *me*," Susannah corrected. "The minute she gets into any kind of trouble, I'm sending her back to Tirza."

"Send her to the bakery," Miriam suggested with a flicker of humor.

"Another good idea," Susannah approved. "Though we don't want to burden Frida with too many incorrigible girls."

By this time, they had made it into Luminaux proper. Keren begged and begged Tirza to buy her a new dress so she could look beautiful as she made her debut at the Eyrie. Tirza said firmly that she didn't have a single copper on her, so she couldn't buy herself a flat of bread, but Susannah couldn't stand Keren's disappointment. Gaaron had lent her one of his bracelets so that she could take care of expenses on the road. She took Keren into a little shop not far from the bakery and let her pick out a new dress of simple cut but bright color. Susannah flashed the borrowed bracelet at the shop owner, who smiled and nodded and tallied up the Eyrie's debt in a little notebook.

Keren wore the dress out of the shop, and Miriam was extravagant in her praise. Tirza merely shook her head. "And now I'm wondering if it's really such a good idea to send her to you, if you're only going to indulge her this way?" Tirza demanded.

Susannah laughed. "Just this once," she promised. "I know how much she wants to make a good impression."

"Susannah. Keren wants to make a good impression *every day*. At least if you're talking about hair and clothes. Not if you're talking about behavior."

"She'll be fine. I'll watch her. Can't you see how happy she is? When is the last time you were so happy?"

Tirza looked at her. "When I saw you standing in Frida's shop yesterday."

Susannah smiled. "Well, and she is just that happy now."

When they arrived at the bakery, Susannah suddenly realized how hard the good-byes were going to be. "I don't know which of you I'm going to miss the most," she said, hugging first Miriam, then Tirza, then Miriam again.

Miriam accepted the embrace but didn't seem nearly as heartbroken in return. Susannah drew back a little to study the fine features and the closed, wary expression. "I can't tell what you're thinking," she said. "Maybe I should stay a few days and make sure you settle in all right."

"I'll be fine," Miriam said in a distinct voice. "You don't have to worry about me."

Susannah watched her a little longer. "All that passed between Dathan and me last night was a kiss," she said softly. "So you don't need to be angry with me for that."

For an instant, Miriam's face showed a look of surprise, and then she flashed that beautiful, brilliant smile. "I'll take that off my list, then," she said.

"I'll tell Gaaron you sent him your love," Susannah said.

Miriam laughed. "Will he believe you?"

Susannah kissed her on the cheek. "Be well, Miriam," she said. "You have no idea how much everyone loves you."

Saying good-bye to Tirza was just as difficult, though less tainted with complex emotions. "When will we see you again?" Tirza demanded. "Will you come to the Gathering, if we do not see you sooner?"

"Yes—certainly—I would not miss the Gathering for anything."

Tirza drew back. "That is too far away," she said accusingly. "Months and months."

"The time will go quickly," Susannah said. "And who knows? Perhaps I will find you again before then. And if the Lohoras make their way to northern Bethel, you can come to Velora and send me word. Why should all the burden fall on me?"

Tirza laughed shakily. "We shall do that," she said. "Maybe tomorrow we will set out in your direction."

"I'll watch for you from the circle of Yovah's arms," Susannah said, speaking the words of the traditional Edori farewell.

"And till I arrive, whisper kindly of me in his ear," Tirza replied.

Susannah turned to Keren, who had been made far more impatient than sad by the extended leave-taking. "Are you ready?" she asked.

"I've been ready for a long time," Keren said.

"Then say good-bye to Tirza," Susannah said, "and I will take you to meet some angels."

CHAPTER FOURTEEN

Susannah was only gone a week, but Gaaron missed her every day.

The first day, he wanted to tell her what Zibiah had reported about Kaski, which was that the Jansai girl appeared to be ill and refused to take Esther's medicines.

"Or maybe it's just that she won't eat," Zibiah said.

"What? She won't eat? Since when?"

"Since Susannah left."

"That's just a few hours ago. Maybe she'll be hungry by dinner-time."

Zibiah looked skeptical. "She seems pretty stubborn to me."

"What else has she done?"

Zibiah shrugged. "Nothing. I mean, she won't leave the room. She wouldn't go to the kitchen like she's supposed to, and she won't go to the classroom. I could carry her down there, I suppose, but—"

Gaaron shook his head. "What good would it do? I understand. Well, maybe it will be better tomorrow. Let me know. If we must, we'll take her down to an apothecary in Velora and see if she can help."

The second day he flew into Velora to meet with the merchants' council and decide the fate of the woman who had murdered her husband because of Miriam's presence in the house. The council was disposed to leniency, though they could not overlook the severity of the crime, and Gaaron could not help but agree with them on both counts. In the end, they decided that Myra would be allowed to keep possession of the business but that she must, for one year, be guided by the council in her major decisions, and that she must operate from her house unless escorted by one of the people whose names appeared on a hastily compiled list. In addition, they decreed that some portion of her business for the following year must be donated to a charitable cause. Myra Shapping agreeing to all these terms in a subdued, almost inaudible voice, the whole business was concluded as well as could have been expected. Better.

But Gaaron flew back to the Eyrie and wished he had someone with whom to share the news. Only Miriam and Susannah knew the whole story, and only to Susannah would he feel like expressing his sense of duplicity at concealing from the council the identity of the wayward girl. He would never have given Miriam up to the judgment of an assembly of men. He would have snatched her up in his arms, had they attempted to take her by force, and flown her to Windy Point or Mount Sinai or some other remote place of austere safety.

But still he blamed her for the whole depressing mess, and only to Susannah could he express his troubled emotions.

On the third day, he received a summons from Adriel that he and various others should meet with her at Windy Point in two days, which meant that he would have to leave immediately. He informed Esther and Enoch that he would be gone, and when he expected to be back, but he wished Susannah were there so that he could say good-bye.

Stupid. They had already said one set of cool farewells when she set out for Luminaux. It was just that he felt he had a great deal to tell her, and he was certain he would have forgotten most of it by the time he saw her again.

He packed a couple of changes of clothing, including formal dining attire, since Adriel liked to hold stately dinners whenever there was exalted company around. A satchel of food, a canteen of water, and he was ready. He took off before noon, and headed northeast toward the Galilee River.

He did not fly as high as he normally would have, only in part deterred by the coolness of the air even at lower altitudes. It was still mid-autumn, but he predicted it would be bitterly cold at Windy

Point, where the chilly seasons came faster and the warm seasons seemed reluctant to visit at all. Yet it was not the weather that kept him low; it was the thought that there might be something to see on the ground between the two angel holds. Burned campsites. Destroyed farms. A plague flag or signs of a flooded river. Any of the hundreds of signals that disaster had come and an angel's presence was required.

But he flew over miles of landscape that changed as he traveled from a faded green to a rusted autumn orange, and saw no signs of trouble at all.

He stopped for the night in a small town about fifty miles from the river. In the inn he chose, the room was small but spotless, clearly the best in the house. It was unfortunate that not a single chair in the dining room had been designed to allow for the disposition of angel wings, so, telling the innkeeper that this was how he always consumed his meals, he ate standing up. Once upstairs for the night, he found the ornate bed also precisely the wrong size to accommodate him, not narrow enough to allow his wings to trail easily off both sides, not wide enough for him to spread them out to their fullest. It was also too short for him. In the end, he slept curled up on his side, right at the edge of the bed, and let the feathered masses pool beside him on the floor.

He woke feeling unrefreshed and not particularly eager to get to Windy Point. He wondered where Susannah was at that exact moment. Still in Luminaux? On the way back? Happy to be leaving Miriam behind, or as worried about the girl as Gaaron was himself? He sighed, rose, washed, and dressed. After another quick and uncomfortable meal in the dining room, he took off again for the north.

The only real diversion of the day was passing over Semorrah, billed as the most beautiful city in the three provinces. From the air, it certainly seemed to live up to that reputation. It was only half built, or so its architects claimed, but the soaring spires and glistening white stone of the existing buildings were breathtaking and fanciful. All of it was being constructed on an island in the middle of the powerful Galilee River, making Semorrah even more magical and unattainable. Naturally, everyone wanted to go there, but only the richest could stay. Adriel said it would become the most prosperous city in the three provinces, but Gaaron thought it was a little early to be making such predictions. Still, it was a lovely, airy, whimsical town in the middle of the foaming river, and Gaaron thought that someday he would like to go there for an extended visit. Bringing Susannah with him, of course.

He would like to hear what she had to say about such a beautiful place.

He flew hard and fast for the entire day, pausing only once to break for a meal. Just as he had expected—colder here west of the Caitanas, in the inhospitable corner of Jordana that housed Windy Point. He was a man who welcomed winter for its respite from the heat that he disliked, but there was something unfriendly about this chill.

Or maybe it was just that every journey seemed seasoned with dread these days, every conference and conclave an opportunity to discuss more horrors. He wished again he had been able to bring Susannah along, for her wise words and her comforting presence and her—well, for her smile.

For no reason.

After his hasty and unsatisfying meal, he flung himself aloft again, determined to make it to Windy Point for the night. He was not particularly tired. His big wings performed their rhythmic lift and stroke with a steady, unvarying motion; his muscled body accepted the punishing buffeting of the wind with a hard indifference. His face was numb with the cold of high altitudes, but he liked the feeling, as if his cheekbones had been molded of marble and his chin from a block of ice. He could fly forever, he thought, across the whole continent, across the ocean on the eastern edge of the province, all the way to the fabled land of Ysral, if the place the Edori talked of really did exist. He might not even stop at Windy Point after all.

But he did. It was close to midnight by the time he banked over the northernmost tip of the Caitanas and dropped down toward the castle nestled in the highest reaches of the mountains. It looked liked a fortress, grim, girded, and grilled. Every window was covered with a decorative but effective grate, and the tunnel leading from the public landing ledge into the living quarters was guarded by a dropped portcullis. Not for the first time, Gaaron wondered how they'd even hauled the materials up the mountain to build the stronghold in the first place. And why they'd thought anyone who lived there would need any protection from outside enemies, who would scarcely have the energy to attack a kitten once they'd managed to make it, panting, up the steep and stony mountain.

He came soundlessly to his feet, spreading his wings until he'd caught his balance. As always after a long flight, he had a moment's disorientation, a touch of confusion about how his weight was distributed and what the muscles of his body were for. He could feel slight spasms ripple down his back, a sign that he'd probably stayed airborne for longer than he should have, and of their own accord his wings folded themselves behind him with absolutely no desire to preen.

He was glad to see that someone had been stationed at the gate, even at this late hour. Then again, Adriel was expecting company, and none of them were liable to arrive on a predictable schedule. "It's Gabriel," he called out.

"Yes, Angelo," the attendant called back. It was a young mortal man whom Gaaron could not remember ever meeting before. The son of some wealthy Jordana landowner, no doubt, invited here for the season so that Adriel could cement alliances. "How was your flight?"

"Long and cold," Gaaron said, ducking under the portcullis as soon as it had been raised far enough and stepping inside the compound. He was immediately in a high-ceilinged great hall, much more formal than the plateau at the Eyrie where visitors first arrived. "Am I the last one to arrive? Who else is here?"

"I don't know if the Archangel is expecting more visitors," the young man replied. "Neri of Monteverde and Constantine Lesh are already here, as are Solomon of Breven and James Hallomel of Jordana."

Gaaron raised his eyebrows at that, for the roster pretty much described the political elite of the three provinces. "I am glad I am not tardy," was all he said, however. "Is my room set aside for me? I know my way."

In a few minutes, Gaaron had navigated the torturous and unnecessarily complex tunnels of Windy Point to find the chamber that was always given to him whenever he stayed at the hold. It was the room that had been his when, for a five-year period, he had lived at Windy Point. He had not then been so aware of the dreariness of the place; he had been happy here. Adriel had been kind, and the entire hold had been so orderly, so well-run. In the Eyrie during those days, life had been much different. It had not taken him long to realize that Adriel's way of doing things was much preferred over his father's.

He washed off the dust and sweat of flight, and stretched himself on the ample bed, blowing out the last candle as he lay down. He stared up at the ceiling, or where the ceiling had to be; it was too dark to see anything except a faint outline of gray around the room's single window. He missed the familiar proportions of his room, the shapes of furniture against the shadows, the triple arch of windows cut into his bedroom wall. He missed the constant, reassuring sound of singers soothing away the fears of night.

He missed Susannah.

He fell asleep wondering what he was doing in Windy Point at all.

In the morning, he found out.

He was late for breakfast, but the others were still lingering at their tables when he made it down through the winding corridors to the great dining hall where Adriel insisted on having nearly every meal. Instantly he realized that the guard at the gate had somewhat understated the case. There were a number of visitors sitting around the formal tables, drinking their morning juice and engaged in lively debate—Neri and three other angels from Monteverde; the Manadavvi patriarch Lucas Karsh as well as his most constant ally, Constantine Lesh; three Breven Jansai, including Solomon; and a few of the more wealthy Jordana landowners seated alongside the contingent of river merchants. Even more surprising, there was Mahalah sitting at a table with the oracles of Mount Egypt and Mount Sudan.

Clearly this was a convocation assembled to address extremely serious matters.

"Gaaron! Come join us," Adriel called when she spotted him in the doorway. He threaded his way through the tables, nodding and exchanging greetings with various powerful individuals as he passed them. Arriving at the table filled with angels, he paused to kiss Adriel on the cheek and then settled beside her in the chair that she had obviously reserved for him.

"I'm sorry I've missed breakfast," he said. "I didn't get in till late last night."

"I'm surprised you're here at all," Neri said frankly. "The messenger came to Monteverde first, so we had a day's head start on you, and we just got here yesterday afternoon. What, didn't you stop at all?"

He spooned some cereal into a bowl and then smiled over at her. She was a dark-haired, fine-boned, intensely serious woman a few years older than he was, and she was just slightly competitive with him. She always swore she had never expected to be named Archangel, but Gaaron believed she had spent most of her years of leadership trying to prove that she would have been just as good a one as he would.

"At night I took a room that was so uncomfortable there was no need to linger," he said, "and by day I paused for food that was so dull there was no need to savor. I was determined to get to Windy Point so I didn't have to spend another night on the road."

"I was hoping you'd bring Susannah," Neri said. "I have yet to meet her."

A little murmur went around the table as the other angels echoed this comment. "Even *I* have yet to meet her, and as Archangel, I would think I would have some claim to special consideration," Adriel said humorously.

Gaaron kept his voice exceedingly pleasant, since he knew his words would sound sharp. As he meant them to. "I did not understand the nature of our gathering until just this moment, or I would have brought Susannah and Enoch and perhaps one or two others with me," he said quietly. "As it is, I see Bethel is severely underrepresented, though I am happy that someone thought to pick up Mahalah on his way."

Neri and her angels exchanged glances at that, but Adriel merely looked impatient. The Archangel's square, worn face seemed just as tired as it had the last time Gaaron had been here. Perhaps even more tired. "Nonsense, Gaaron, we are not forming up a council to cast some kind of majority vote. I just called together as many people as I could think of so we could pool our information and decide what to do."

There could only be one matter so pressing it merited the concern of the entire nation. "About the strange visitors who have been destroying settlements and camps?" he asked.

Adriel nodded. "We will all tell what we know, and perhaps, once we've shared our knowledge, we will have some kind of idea about how to proceed."

"Are we expecting anyone else to join us?"

Neri glanced rather elaborately around the room. "I wonder who else you think might be missing?"

Gaaron gave her a brief smile. "One or two of the Edori, perhaps?" he suggested. "They, too, have been victims."

Adriel nodded gravely. "Another reason we would have welcomed your Susannah's counsel. It is very hard to keep track of the Edori, or to know who they consider their leaders. We will, of course, share with them anything we learn or decide in our sessions here."

"Let me finish my breakfast, then," Gaaron said, bending over his bowl. "And we can get straight to the discussions."

As soon as the meal was done, they moved to a large conference room just down the corridor from the dining hall. Gaaron reflected that there must be many more formal discussions at Windy Point than there were at the Eyrie, where the only place big enough to hold all the residents at once was the open plateau.

It took some time for the visitors to sort themselves out and dispose themselves around the room. Gaaron made his way over to Mahalah, who had been carried here from the dining hall by one of Adriel's angels. Away from her wheeled chair and the close, comfortable setting of Mount Sinai, she looked even more frail and ancient, and Gaaron could not help but feel a stab of worry as he approached her.

"Mahalah. It is good to see you, but my instincts tell me you should not have made this trip," he said. He took the stick-thin hand she held out to him and waved aside her smile. "I'm serious. You look as fragile as a bundle of kindling."

"You, on the other hand, look as offensively robust as you always do," she retorted. "And I believe I can gauge for myself whether or not I am well enough to travel."

"How did you get here? Had I known exactly who was convening here, I would have come for you myself."

"Adriel sent one of her girls for me. We started the trip days ago and made it by easy stages, which I know very well you would not have," she replied. "I was very well looked after, I assure you. But I am sorry you did not bring Susannah. Like the Archangel, I am disappointed that I have not had the opportunity to meet with her yet."

"If you knew what my days have been like since I found Susannah, perhaps you would not be so anxious to scold me," he said ruefully. "As it is, I could not bring her, because she is off on a journey of her own."

"If we have time while we are here, you must tell me about her," Mahalah said. "Do you like her? Has the god chosen well?"

"Yes, I like her very much, and I'm sure you will, too," he said lightly. "Everyone who meets her does."

Mahalah looked like she would like to ask more questions, but at that moment, Adriel called the meeting to order. Gaaron nodded to the oracle and made his way to the front of the room, where the other angels were sitting. Adriel was standing before them, in front of a large map of Samaria that had been hastily pinned to the wall.

"Let's begin by identifying all the places where these strangers have struck," Adriel said when she had finally gotten all of them to quiet down. "Perhaps we will be able to discern a pattern in where and when they appear."

Gaaron raised his hand to get her attention. "Do you want to know only the places that they have destroyed, or are you interested in knowing also where they have made an appearance but caused no damage?"

A murmur went through the crowd at that. Gaaron turned to face those sitting behind him. "I know of two such incidents," he said quietly. "But I do not know how they choose when to strike and when to refrain."

"We're the ones who need to learn how and when to strike," someone snarled. Gaaron thought it was one of the Jansai speaking, but he could not be certain.

"We'll get to that," Adriel said, lifting her voice above the sudden swelling of commentary. "Gaaron, you know of several disasters. Why don't you start? And, yes, please tell us of any encounter with these strangers, whether they featured violence or not."

Gaaron's stories were quickly told. The destroyed Jansai camp—the two visits by disappearing men—all three tales were met with a shocked silence that was generated not by surprise, he thought, but fear. They had all heard rumors of these events, told by a peddler who'd heard it from an Edori who'd passed on the news related by a distant kinsman; the stories had seemed far-fetched and easy to discount, he supposed. But hearing them again from a credible witness who had viewed a scene of destruction with his own disbelieving eyes made all of them feel tense and uneasy in their comfortable chairs.

"And Susannah has since told me of a leveled camp that she and her clansmen encountered down by Luminaux," he added. "From the details she gave me, I can only assume the camp was burned by the same agent that burned the Jansai wagons I came across myself."

"And this camp was—?" Adriel asked, hovering by her map.

"North of Luminaux," Gaaron replied. "I'm not exactly sure."

Neri had only one story to tell, though it was clear, from the details she gave, that the tragedy in Gaza was of human origin, a farmhouse burned by carelessness and not malice. On the other hand,

Solomon could relate the details of three massacres, and Adriel added a fourth story. The river merchants repeated tales told to them by freighters, of homesteads destroyed in the sparsely populated region of southern Jordana. All of these, even the unconfirmed reports, Adriel marked on her map.

What soon became clear was that all of the incidents had occurred in the southern half of Samaria, and that the highest concentration was to be found near the coastline.

"Well, that makes sense," growled Moshe, Adriel's angelico. He was a grizzled, strongly built man in his mid-sixties who looked capable, even now, of going out and wrestling down a full-grown tree without the aid of saw or ax. "If we are under siege from enemies, it is most likely that they would be attacking us from the sea. Landing somewhere along the Jordana coast, maybe, and making their way inward."

"But—enemies coming from *where?*" Neri demanded. "There is no one on this whole world but us."

"How do you know that?" Solomon shot at her.

"Because—it says—in the Librera—" Neri floundered. She looked over at the oracles, all three of them sitting together near the back of the room. "It tells how Jovah brought us here to this world, where we could live in peace and harmony for all our lives. And our children after us, and their children after them."

Mahalah nodded. "Indeed, it does say that. And we have been on this world for more than two hundred years and never yet encountered anyone except those of us descended from those original settlers. But that does not mean that there were not, somewhere on this world, other people that we never knew existed. We have explored only this one continent, after all. Perhaps there are other stretches of land we have never seen. Perhaps these people live on Ysral or in some other place—"

There was a general murmur of dissent that drowned out anything else the oracle might have planned to say. "There is no such place as Ysral!" Solomon called. "That's a fantasy of the Edori!"

"It is mentioned in the Librera," Mahalah said mildly.

"In any case, I do not believe Jovah would have brought us here to begin with if this world was populated by other people," Adriel said. "He intended this to be our world."

"Then who are these people?" Constantine Lesh said reasonably. "If they are not us and they are not someone else?"

Adriel looked at Gaaron. "Are we sure they are not us? Some collection of rogue farmers or Jansai or Edori who have banded together to avenge some perceived injustice? Their skin is dark, you have said—as dark as an Edori's? Perhaps—"

"I have not seen one," Gaaron interrupted, "but my sister described one of the men very minutely. His skin was blacker than an Edori's, she said, and his eyes were blue, his hair a copper red. That does not sound like any of the races we have established here."

"And yet—a little hair dye, a little intermingling of bloodlines—such a look might be achieved," Constantine Lesh suggested. "And after all, Miriam saw only one of them. The others might look less fantastical—more familiar, shall we say."

"These attackers were not Edori," Gaaron said coldly. "There has never, in the entire history of the race, been any hint of violence in the Edori lifestyle."

"Jansai, then," one of the river merchants said. "Many of them are dark-skinned as well, and they're not above using force when it suits them."

Solomon came heavily to his feet, his robes billowing around his bulky body and his gold necklace bouncing against his chest. The Jansai with him also hastily rose. "We came here today in good faith, to discuss the assaults that have troubled us all," he said fiercely. "We will not stay to be maligned."

"Sit down, Solomon, no one is maligning you," Adriel said testily. "We are all agreed that the people responsible for these massacres must be outlaws that have been cast from their kin and their tribes. If they are Jansai, they are not abiding by Jansai codes. If they are Edori"—her troubled look swept over Gaaron—"then they have abandoned Edori ways. We cannot rule out anyone based on the respectable behavior of the other members of their group."

"The Jansai are not violent and lawless," Solomon said, still on his feet.

"No one said they were," Adriel said. "Please. Sit. We need your counsel on this grave matter."

Solomon stood a moment longer, as if debating, but he did eventually retake his seat. His companions once more followed suit. Gaaron had to admit privately that, if he were to pick any race from the scattered peoples of Samaria to spawn a band of violent renegades, he would first look to the Jansai. But this would not be the forum to say so.

Neri was the next to speak. "And still, I am not convinced such atrocities could be committed by anyone who has been raised, as we all have been, on the principles of harmony," she said. "I would rather believe that outsiders have found a way to visit Samaria than believe that someone who has sung beside me on the Plain of Sharon could now turn to my friends and kill them with fire."

"Yes, but if they are outsiders, where have they come from?" Moshe demanded. "I still say they have come by boat from across the water. Where else?"

"From the sky," a voice said.

Heads all craned in the direction of the oracles, where Mahalah sat there placidly, nodding her white-haired head. The speaker had been Isaac of Mount Sudan, but apparently Mahalah didn't think his comment was particularly outrageous.

Everyone else did. "*What?* The sky? Are you mad?"

"Flying? You think, like angels?"

"What do you mean, the sky? From where in the sky?"

"What did that crazy old fool say?"

Adriel held up a hand for silence and pointed at Isaac. "Oracle?" she said politely. "What did you mean?"

Mahalah was the one to speak. "We all know the story of how Jovah brought us here in his two hands," she said. She laced her fingers together and held her hands before her, cupped as the god's had been two hundred and forty years ago. "Perhaps others have been brought here the same way."

"By *Jovah?*" Neri exclaimed. "To *harm* us?"

"Perhaps by some other means," Mahalah said. "Or some other god."

There was a furious outcry at this, a babble of dissenting voices so loud and so vehement that no one argument could be heard above the din. Adriel let the outrage run on for about ten minutes and then rapped the wall behind her for silence. It was granted only grudgingly, and a few mutters could still be heard in pockets around the room.

"This is not profitable," the Archangel said. "Does it matter where these strangers have come from or who they are, whether our own malcontents or—or visitors who have been brought here from some other world? The true question facing us today is what can we do to stop them, or protect ourselves from their depredations, or both? Because so far, we and those we are sworn to guard appear to be helpless against them."

This pronouncement was greeted by a silence that was as intense, in its way, as the debate that had immediately preceded it. "Perhaps we cannot protect ourselves," one of the river merchants said. "Perhaps we can merely stay safe. The attacks seem to come only on isolated communities and small traveling bands. Perhaps we should look for safety in the cities."

"Yes, fine for those of you who never *leave* the cities," Solomon replied instantly. "But what about the Jansai, who spend more than half of their lives traveling in small bands across this continent? What would you say to them?"

"I'd say stay home, until we have found a way to protect you," the merchant shot back.

"And where would you get the goods that the Jansai ferry from Luminaux to Castelana?" Solomon wanted to know. "How would you sell the products your artisans make in your cities?"

"Who would sell food in any market across the three provinces?" one of the Jordana landowners chimed in. Gaaron recognized him as James Hallomel, Adriel's staunchest ally. "For that matter, who would grow grain and produce for all of you to eat? Since most farmers live on isolated lands with fewer than twenty people within calling distance."

"I understand that—but while this crisis holds—"

"You will all starve before you solve this crisis," the landholder said contemptuously.

"Please—some courtesy," the Archangel murmured.

"We cannot cede the land, and we cannot huddle in our cities, afraid to step foot outside their boundaries," Constantine Lesh said firmly. "We must devise weapons with which to fight back."

This time the silence was even more profound.

James Hallomel slewed around in his seat to give the Manadavvi a piercing stare. "And just how, exactly, do you propose that we fashion weapons?" he asked in a voice of withering politeness. "Have you, during these two hundred years of peace and harmony, been secretly testing *guns* and *missiles* and *bombs,* and all the other forbidden technology that is specifically proscribed in the Librera? Have you so far forgotten your heritage that you have been experimenting with the creation of destructive weapons so powerful and so terrifying that our ancestors left their home planet to escape their dangerous presence? Have you—"

"Don't be ridiculous," Lesh snapped. "Of course I haven't."

"Then how exactly do you propose to design any kind of weapon on an instant's notice? Because it seems to me we will need to deploy any defense, or any attack, as soon as possible."

"We are not stupid people," Constantine Lesh said evenly. "And there are books that the settlers brought with them—books the oracles have the keeping of—that tell of things in our past. We might find in them blueprints for the technology we have need of. And from them, we might quickly be able to fashion these *guns* and *bombs* you speak of."

This time the murmur from the crowd was speculative but, on the whole, approving.

"My father has an old book, it's been in the family forever, there's pictures in it—"

"But fire, though. Burning so hot. I don't know of any fuel we use that can get that combustion level—"

"Who would make the weapons? Who would learn how to use them?"

"No," Gaaron said.

He did not speak particularly loudly, but everyone in the room heard him, and everyone else stopped talking. He came to his feet slowly, aware as he did so of how tall he must appear, rising like a troubled man's conscience to a height too great to comfortably gaze upon. His wings arched behind him and spread out to both sides, till he was taking up more space than one man should, even one angel; he wanted no one in the room to be able to overlook him.

"No," he said again. "If we seek out weapons, we betray our god, and we forfeit his faith in us. He brought us here to escape violence. He brought us here to help us learn again how to live with each other, despite our differences and conflicts. He has promised us that he himself will destroy us if we cannot live in harmony with each other. If we construct weapons and use them, we will not have to wait for our enemies to bring us down. Jovah will do it for them."

"But, Gaaron, that's unreasonable," Neri objected. "Yes, Jovah wants us to live in harmony *with each other*, but he does not want us to be annihilated by—by strangers! He would want us to defend ourselves! If we are not turning these weapons against our own people—"

He gave her a grave look. "That has not yet been established."

"Well, if one of my own people is trying to kill me with fire, then I am damn well ready to use fire to destroy him back!" one of the river merchants shouted.

Gaaron now turned the weight of his sorrowful stare on that speaker, who instantly fell silent and turned his gaze downward, as if counting the fingers of his own hand. "Such is the philosophy that led to the destruction of the world from which Jovah rescued us," he said.

"Then we are to do nothing?" someone demanded. Gaaron could not identify the voice. "We are all to burn in our beds?"

"I believe the god will show us the way to deal with our enemies," Gaaron said. "I believe we need to work toward identifying them—discovering who they are and what they want. I believe we can find ways to appease or defeat them. But I am not willing to authorize the first steps on the short road to our self-destruction. I am not willing to devise weapons that will destroy us as surely as they will destroy our enemies. If we do, I believe Samaria will be obliterated within a generation—by the god, who will have ceased to love us, or by us, as we turn our weapons against ourselves."

Gaaron allowed himself to sit down, as slowly and impressively as he had stood up, and let the controversy rage about him for a few moments. Adriel was regarding him from the front of the room, her face expressing conflicting emotions; Neri watched him with a more considering look on her face, as if trying to gauge whether or not his will could be overcome. Moshe was the one who finally called a halt to the debate by standing and flinging his arms up for silence.

"Well, it hardly matters if Gaaron's right or not, because in fact we *don't* have any weapons, and as James said, we're unlikely to develop anything useful in the next two weeks. So does anyone else have any ideas? About how we can protect ourselves from harm?"

CHAPTER FIFTEEN

The conference went on for another three hours, but nothing conclusive was decided. The merchants did resolve that they would meet with their fellows back in their respective cities and devise ways of combining their shipments, hoping that the larger caravans would be less likely to be attacked. Solomon was willing to urge the Jansai to travel in larger packs—"Though how do I know? That may only mean that more of them are killed at once," he said cynically. All of them agreed to spread the news among the farmers and the small settlements: *Until we have overcome this crisis, consider abandoning your land and moving to one of the cities, or throwing in your lot with others so that you are harder to overcome.* Short of that, there seemed to be little they could do.

"Until we learn more, or until the god gives us the guidance Gaaron expects," Moshe said with a sideways glance at Gaaron.

"We shall ask him for his help," Isaac said.

They split up then, to pass a few hours until the formal dinner to which they had all been invited. Gaaron, who had not slept nearly enough the past two nights, headed back to his room to nap. This meant avoiding Adriel's eye and pretending he did not hear Neri call his name as he stepped from the conference room and headed through the circuitous corridors back to his room.

He drew the curtains against the sunlight and stretched out face-down on the bed. Naturally, he couldn't fall asleep. His mind played back fragments of the day's discussions, the frightening recitations of attacks by mysterious strangers, the suggestion that weapons be fashioned to meet the crisis, his own impassioned speech, and the snippets of conversation that made it clear that all of them, even the most aggressive, felt helpless and afraid. He had not thought they would solve everything by this day's convocation, but he had hoped they might leave the room with some kind of plan in mind.

But those reflections weren't all that kept him awake. Windy Point had been named for the two elements from which it seemed to be composed—the sharp slaty rock of the mountain, and the wind itself. Gaaron had been too tired last night to hear it, but now, half drowsing and far from relaxed, he could not tune out the sound. First the wind rushed against the stone walls of the fortress with a battering fury; then it whined around the turrets and crenellations like a moping beggar. It would grow quiet for a few minutes and then sidle back again, hissing along the casements and tapping at the glass. Gaaron remembered now how many nights he had lain awake when, as a teenager, he had lived at Windy Point—how many nights he had imagined the wind as some malevolent, shrieking spirit howling against the injustice of a world that could build castles that would keep it out. He had gotten used to it then—had even come to enjoy its rattling rage and supplicating moans. But not today. Today he rolled to his side and put a pillow over his exposed ear, and willed himself to an uneasy sleep.

He managed not to be tardy for dinner, though he woke up later than he expected, and he dressed himself carefully in the formal black-and-white attire that Adriel would demand. Entering the grand dining hall, he found, not to his surprise, that the Archangel had carefully arranged all the conference guests at tables set up in one corner of the room. He did pause to speak briefly to various Windy Point angels and mortals who were seated at other tables in the hall, friends from ten years ago, or allies now. There were a fair number; he had always gotten on well with the residents of the Archangel's hold.

When he made his way to the more exalted tables, he found that Adriel had chosen his dinner partners with an eye to politics. Thus he had been seated with the wealthy Jordana landowners and the powerful river merchants, all of whom would be pleased to have this chance to speak somewhat privately to the man who would next be Archangel. Gaaron summoned his most pleasant smile and took his place at the table.

The meal lasted late into the evening and was followed by entertainment in yet another of the grand chambers that took up so much of the ground level of Windy Point. Most of the program consisted of music, of course—angel choirs, young soloists, a trio of flute players whose harmony was so unearthly and so fine that Gaaron felt a little shiver pass over his spine as soon as they began playing.

"You must bring them to the Plain of Sharon this spring," he called to Adriel over the enthusiastic applause that followed their performance. "I am sure the god would like to hear them play."

"Yes, I had thought the same thing," she called back.

After the concert, there were more refreshments, and they all stood around munching on sweets and talking idly. Adriel loved to entertain—and, political creature that she was, she liked to make sure that every social opportunity also provided a chance for the country's dealmakers and power brokers to exchange ideas and promises. Gaaron himself quickly reached his limit at events such as these. He was glad that everyone was planning to leave in the morning.

"I know you consider my flying too fast and too high, but I will moderate my habits for your comfort if you would like me to return you to Mount Sinai," he told Mahalah as the party was breaking up. "I warn you, however, that I am interested in leaving as early in the morning as I can without appearing uncivil."

She smiled up at him from the overstuffed chair where someone had deposited her after the concert. "I would be happy to entrust myself to you," she said. "And I am willing to leave at dawn if it suits you. I do not do so well away from familiar things. I am eager to get home."

Gaaron spared a moment to wonder if Susannah would be back by the time he returned. Possibly—probably. He hoped so. He took Mahalah's frail hand and gave her a little bow, his wings sweeping back behind him to add even more courtliness to the gesture. "As are we all, oracle," he said. "As are we all."

It took two full days to fly in relatively easy stages from Windy Point to Mount Sinai. Gaaron would have cheerfully continued on his way to the Eyrie, since they coasted into Mount Sinai in the early evening, but Mahalah seemed so exhausted by the journey that he felt compelled to stay overnight. He dined with the acolytes, all those silly young girls, and felt older than the stones of the mountain itself as they giggled and whispered their way through dinner.

He slept pretty well, though, as he always did in Mount Sinai. As if in direct contrast to Windy Point, the oracle's retreat was a place of almost tangible serenity. Peace drifted through its muted gray corridors like the scent of summer. It was so still it encouraged even his busy thoughts to stutter and stop. He lay on the wide bed and felt all his strung muscles go lax, all his worries and questions get absorbed by the deep and ample silence.

In the morning, he rose late, unable to bear the thought of another meal with that cluster of mirthful girls, but he was happy to find Mahalah still at the breakfast table when he made it to the dining room.

"You look much better than you did last night," he said, sitting beside her once he'd filled his plate at the buffet. "I thought perhaps I should have taken the trip even more slowly than I did."

"Nonsense, you were a most considerate travel conveyance," she said brightly. "It is just that I look like paltry death whenever I grow tired. Isaac told me right before we left that I should start looking about me for my replacement. Who would be so rude? I told him I'd outlive him, though I wasn't so sure last night."

Gaaron took a bite and mulled that over. "I don't even know how an oracle's replacement is chosen," he said at last. "Is that one of the tasks that will fall to me sometime during my tenure?"

She laughed at him. "Most likely, unless you think I'll last another twenty years. Even Isaac won't be around so long."

"Then what do I need to know?"

She waved a dismissive hand. "Mostly the god takes care of it," she said. "Long before one oracle dies, it becomes clear who the next oracle should be."

"Yes, but how does it become clear?"

She shrugged, clearly unconcerned. "Someone steps forward. One of the acolytes, perhaps, or a priest. Someone who has shown a fascination with the old language, an adeptness at learning it. Someone who feels a calling. Don't worry, Gaaron, I have many good years left in me, and I am not at all concerned about finding my heir."

He smiled and sipped from his juice. "Yes, but you'll be safe and happy in Jovah's arms, and I'll be running around madly looking for able linguists," he said. "I don't think your insouciance reassures me at all."

"Well, we could go this morning and ask the god if he has considered my successor, but I warn you, Jovah's answers are sometimes not as direct as you might like."

"No, I don't think we should waste the god's time on frivolous questions when we have something far more serious to ask," Gaaron said.

Her thin white eyebrows rose. "Ah. What to do about our mysterious and violent visitors."

"If in fact they come from somewhere outside our world," he added.

"You seriously think they do not?"

"You seriously think they do?"

Mahalah spread her hands in an indecisive gesture. "I think the people of Samaria have deliberately chosen to forget everything they could about the universe outside their own backyards. And I think that universe is a pretty big thing to overlook. We know very little about where we came from—only two hundred and forty years ago. How much more will we forget as every generation passes? It is not just our dangerous technology we have chosen to put aside, but our history. I think people who choose not to acknowledge their past open themselves up to unpleasant surprises in the future."

"We know enough about our past. We know it was bloody and destructive. We know that if we re-create it, we will all die. That seems to me a good enough reason to go forward without reference to our history, forging a new personality, if you will, for our new society."

Her smile was a little crooked. "Fine, so long as there are not things you are ignoring that do not choose to be ignored," she said. "The more I know, the less I agree with some of the decisions made by Uriel and Hagar and those other early settlers. But it is too late now to voice my opinions, I suppose. I will live within the constraints imposed."

He laughed at her. "You're talking nonsense, you know."

She laughed back. "I wish I were. Come, then! Let us go question the god."

He followed her chair through the narrow corridors, as always feeling his wings brush against both walls. It was so quiet that the two noises were easily distinguished, the *hiss* of her wheels on the stone floor, the *shush* of his feathers behind her. He liked both sounds.

They went to the central room with the glowing blue faceplate set into the wall. Mahalah headed directly there and began running her fingers along the knobs before Gaaron had even fetched a chair so he could sit beside her.

"What does the god say?" he asked, sitting down.

"He has not answered yet."

"Well, what did you ask?"

"I asked what we should do about the marauders harming our farmers and traveling caravans."

"Did you ask him who the marauders are?"

"What? No. I'll ask that next. Now just be patient."

Gaaron watched in fascination as the light behind the screen seemed to ripple and re-form. Patterns appeared magically on the surface of the glass, shaped like words and sentences, though they were indecipherable to him. He leaned closer, as if he could, by the sheer power of his will, translate the message.

Mahalah seemed a little puzzled. "Perhaps I did not phrase my question clearly enough."

"What does it say?"

She put her finger to the screen, though Gaaron would have been afraid to touch it. "It says, 'I have called her. When she comes, she will make all right.' "

"Who will? What will she make right? Is he even talking about the same thing?"

"Good questions," Mahalah said, her fingers busy on the keys again. "I will ask him if he is aware that certain villages and campsites have been destroyed by enemies with fire."

This time the answer came back a little more quickly and appeared to be a single syllable.

"He says yes," Mahalah relayed. "I will ask him if he knows who these enemies are."

A slightly longer wait, and a reply that made Mahalah sigh. "What?" Gaaron demanded.

"He says, yes, he knows exactly who they are," Mahalah said. "Shall I ask him to name them?"

"You might as well. I am beginning to think the answer will not be very helpful, though."

Indeed, it was not. Mahalah scanned the new text on the screen and said slowly, " 'Their names have not been offered up to me, but I can see their movements clearly. They have not identified me, but I am aware of them.' "

Gaaron sat back in his chair with a little *thump*. His wings flounced with the movement and then lay still. "If he does not know their names . . ." he said slowly. "That means, at the very least, that they never have been dedicated. So, whoever else they are, they are not rogue angels and probably not ordinary farmers or miners. Because I have almost never come across a mortal, in any of the three provinces, who did not bear a Kiss in his arm."

Mahalah was watching him. "The Edori are rarely dedicated," she said softly. "And not all the Jansai. If you were looking for possibilities."

"I cannot believe it of the Edori," he said swiftly. "But I would not put such depredations past the Jansai! There is a race that has not entirely forgotten its violent past, mark my words."

"Jovah knows who the Jansai are, and he did not point to them for these crimes," Mahalah said.

"No, he did not tell us anything useful at all."

Now she smiled. "Yes, he did. He said he was aware of the situation and that someone—some woman—will make all right. Not a very complete answer, I will admit, but it does give me some hope that the god is watching over us and will not let us be destroyed."

Gaaron sighed and stood up, arching his wings and rolling his shoulders. "In any case, I appreciate you giving me the chance to ask," he said. "If I think of any more questions to which I would like obscure replies, I will be sure to return."

"Bring Susannah with you next time," she suggested. "I would like to meet her. We all would."

"Perhaps I should have a party," he said, not serious.

"Perhaps you should have a wedding."

He glanced down at her, startled. "We will. We just have not made plans yet."

"And what have you been doing with your time instead?"

He laughed shortly. "Mostly, running behind Miriam, smoothing over disasters."

"And how is your sister?"

He was silent a moment. "Well, I hope. I have allowed Susannah to take her to Luminaux to live for a little bit on her own. Susannah thinks that it is the great shadow of my wings over her that causes Miriam to behave, to some extent, as she does. Perhaps when she is free of attention, she will find her own way. That, or bring down the whole city of Luminaux in one blue cloud, I don't know."

Mahalah smiled. "She sounds thoughtful and wise, your Susannah. I am even more eager to meet her."

"Soon, oracle," he promised, bending over to kiss her on the cheek. "Very soon."

He was out of Mount Sinai a little before noon, loaded up with provisions that Mahalah insisted he take even though he only had a short flight ahead of him. The air was chilly in the mountains, cooler still as he climbed to a comfortable flying altitude, but the sun was a bright, happy yellow, and the flight was enjoyable. He made good time, and landed on the Eyrie's plateau without having paused once to rest.

He stood there a moment, taking stock. The paired voices of Chloe and Sela drifted down in high sweet harmony; children ran across the open area, calling out cheerful insults. Enoch stood off to one side, deep in conversation with a couple of farmers who appeared to have come to the hold to offer a petition. But nothing bespoke trouble or even urgency. It was as if his six-day absence had been unremarked.

But then Enoch broke off his conference with the petitioners and crossed the plateau to Gaaron's side. "Good, you're back," he said.

"Is anything wrong?"

Enoch jerked his head in the direction of the farmers. "A little flooding south of the Corinnis. I've sent Lydia off to take care of it."

"Any more reports of burned campsites?"

"Not that I've heard."

"Any other trouble?"

Enoch spread his hands. "Zack causing problems again. He always seems to behave worse when you're not in the hold."

"What's he done?"

"He and that other one—Jude. Took a couple of the mortal boys high up—then dropped them."

"*Dropped* them? To the ground? Sweet Jovah singing, is anyone—"

"Not to the ground," Enoch interrupted. "One of the angels dropped a kid, the other caught him. A game, maybe, except the mortal boys were screaming for help and *they* didn't seem to think it was a game. Nicholas and Ahio helped me stop them, and we've put Zack and Jude in the storerooms, away from their friends. No one knows what to do with them next, though."

Gaaron nodded and ran a hand through his hair. Knotted from

flight; he needed a haircut. "If Nicholas and Ahio are back, that must mean Susannah has returned as well," he said. He was a little surprised to hear the words come out of his mouth.

Enoch looked surprised, too, at the change of subject. "Yes, they got here the day before yesterday."

"Any word on Miriam?"

Enoch shook his head. "I haven't really talked to the angelica."

Gaaron nodded. "Well, I'll deal with Zack and Jude once I find a few free minutes. Thanks for the report."

He turned toward the tunnels, eager to find Susannah. Eager to hear of the trip, and how Miriam had settled in, and eager to tell her of all that had transpired on his end since she had left. Excited, almost, at the thought of seeing her again, of hearing everything she would have to say.

Esther caught him before he'd taken ten steps down the corridor, to repeat, though in much more lurid detail, the story of Zack's latest escapade. He kept an expression of courteous interest on his face, though he had to admit he was feeling neither courteous nor interested, and waited also through a recitation of other small woes.

"How's Kaski?" he asked, when the Jansai girl's name did not come up.

Esther sniffed. "Better now, though weak as a newborn. We could scarcely get her to eat at all while Susannah was gone, but the minute the angelica returned, the little girl seemed to come back to life. She even attended her classes again. Didn't say anything, though. I expect she never will."

"I'll need to get Susannah's assessment of that," Gaaron said, his voice grave. "Do you know where she is? The angelica?"

Esther gave a little sniff. "I suppose they're all in her room," she said. "Susannah and those girls."

Since Miriam was gone, and Chloe and Sela were singing, Gaaron could only suppose "those girls" indicated Kaski and Zibiah. He was a little disappointed. He had hoped to have a long solitary conversation with Susannah—but an informal one, something he didn't have to engineer. Well, perhaps Zibiah would offer to take Kaski off to her classroom, and he would have a free, unstructured moment with his bride-to-be.

Perhaps you should have a wedding, Mahalah had said.

Gaaron pushed the thought away, and strode purposefully down the hall. The door to Susannah's room was partway open, and even before he got close enough to see around it, he could hear laughter coming from inside. It was infectious; he couldn't help smiling. There was a soft *thud* and more laughter, as if someone had been the target of a thrown pillow. "My hair!" someone shrieked. "You've messed it all up!"

Feeling momentarily as he had while dining with all the acolytes at Mount Sinai, Gaaron sounded the door chime. More gales of laughter inside and some scrambling sounds as the women presumably assumed more decorous poses.

"Is that you, Nick?" Susannah called. "Just come on in."

Gaaron pushed the door wider and took a few steps inside. "No," he said, suddenly feeling a little ridiculous. "It's just me."

For a moment he was the target of four sets of eyes and had the distinct impression that he was completely unwelcome. He was confused himself, because there were two Edori in the room, and Susannah was the only Edori who was supposed to be at the Eyrie. Meanwhile, Kaski shrieked and dived for cover, barricading herself behind pillows and blankets so that he could not see her face. The others fluttered over her—Susannah, Zibiah, the other Edori woman—and Zibiah's lacy white wings fanned out to provide additional protection from Gaaron's eyes.

"I think perhaps I shouldn't come in," Gaaron said stiffly.

Susannah was on her feet and hurrying across the room, her hands outstretched. "No, don't be silly, she's just a little theatrical. Gaaron! I didn't know you were back."

He took the proffered hands and peered down at her, thinking she did not seem very happy to see him. At any rate, there was a look of constraint across her features, and her eyes were tired. "I just arrived. Met by Enoch and Esther with tales of disaster in the hold. But I wanted to see if you had returned safely."

"Indeed, yes, a couple of days ago."

He nodded across the room where the Edori woman was slipping behind Zibiah's wing to comfort the Jansai girl. "I see you have a friend."

Susannah looked over her shoulder toward the bed. "You remember Keren, don't you? We ran into her in Luminaux, and she was very eager to come for a visit." She turned back toward Gaaron. "I didn't think you'd mind."

He shook his head. "Not at all. Someone to keep you company."

She smiled. "You have no idea how impressed she's been by every-thing at the hold. The water room alone is enough to keep her happy for weeks. She washes her hair twice a day. I've told her it will all fall out if she keeps that up."

He was beginning to remember Keren now, the vain, pretty girl who had sat before the Edori fire and asked him about opulence at the Eyrie. She had been one of the dozens who shared Susannah's tent, along with . . .

Along with Dathan. Along with Susannah's former lover. If they had encountered Keren in the blue streets of Luminaux, no doubt they had caught up with the rest of the Lohoras as well.

He dropped her hands. "I'm glad you had a chance to see some of your Edori friends again," he said, his voice sounding stiff and for-mal even to his own ears. "She is welcome to stay as long as she likes. I hope she makes friends here."

It was not his imagination; Susannah looked as if she felt just as awkward as he did. "Yes, already Chloe and Zib and Sela have sort of adopted her, and Nicholas keeps promising to take her to Velora for a day. I'm sure I'd better go with them, though, because I'm afraid she'll persuade him to buy everything in the market for her. She could beggar the hold in one day."

He offered a perfunctory smile at that. "And how is Kaski? I heard she suffered during your absence but that she has revived upon your return."

She glanced behind her again, where whispers and giggles were beginning to emerge from behind Zibiah's spread wings. "Yes—I was very distressed to learn how poorly she did while I was gone. I'll have to work on that—making her a little more self-sufficient. But I don't know, Gaaron. She is a problem I am not certain how to solve. She doesn't belong here and she's not happy here. Although clearly she cannot return to her own home."

"We will come to a solution," he said gravely, though at the mo-ment he had little interest in Kaski, or Keren, or anyone else in the entire hold. "Not today, perhaps."

"No," she agreed. She looked over her shoulder once more, then moved toward the door, and Gaaron followed her out into the hall. "How was your own journey?" she asked in a low voice. "I hear you went to visit the Archangel."

"I and about fifteen others," he said. "To discuss the influx of murderous strangers into our midst." He shrugged; suddenly he felt tired. "We discussed it for hours and resolved nothing. Oh, except some of the Manadavvi think we should begin developing weapons so we can protect ourselves from harm."

"Weapons! What kind of weapons? Oh, Gaaron, I'm not in favor of that at all."

He smiled a little bitterly. "Neither am I, though I seemed to be the only one in the room who remembered why technology was prohibited in the first place. I do not think we are in any immediate danger of producing war toys, but I would not be surprised if Constantine Lesh returns to his estates and begins reading up on tools of destruction."

"We must find a way to stop that," she said quietly.

"There are a lot of things we must figure out how to fix," he said.

She nodded and leaned against the wall. Her hands were behind her back, as if she braced herself. Against the rosy beige stone of the corridor, her dark skin looked exotic and mysterious.

"You look tired," he said abruptly.

She attempted a smile. "Do I? I am, a little."

"Maybe you have taken on too much, bringing Keren back here and trying to mother Kaski as well. I'm sure they all sleep in the same room with you every night. That can't be restful."

"They do, but I like to have them there. I miss sleeping with all my Edori family around me at night." She paused, as if wondering how he might interpret that, and hurried on. "It's not—Keren and Kaski are not what is keeping me awake. I have—dreams—sometimes. Or rather, the same dream, all the time. I used to have it now and then, when I lived with the Edori. It's not—it's never been a frightening dream. But lately it comes almost every night, and I wake up when it ends. I find it hard to fall back asleep sometimes."

"Maybe you should talk to Esther," he said. "She acts as our apothecary here. She might have some drugs that would ease you back into sleeping."

"I know a few of those drugs myself, and I could buy them in the Velora market," Susannah said. "It's just . . ." She paused, and shrugged. "Perhaps I will," she said finally.

Her voice had been perfectly pleasant, but he felt like he had been rebuffed. As if his suggestions had no merit but she was too polite to say so. This reunion was not going at all the way he had visualized. Instead of feeling more at ease with her as the minutes passed, he felt more clumsy, more stupid. "I meant to ask much sooner," he said. "How was Miriam when you left her?"

She gave a little laugh, as if embarrassed that she, too, had forgotten the reason she had left the Eyrie in the first place. "She seemed fine. Frida was happy to take her in and treat her as one of her own daughters. Miriam behaved very well—she was quite polite—though that is no guarantee that she did not turn into a wild child the minute I left the bakery. She has promised to keep in touch, but I don't expect her to keep the promise. I expect . . ." She laughed again, a little more hopelessly. "I don't know what I expect."

"We will have to wait and see," he said. "I, at least, appreciate what you have done for my sister."

"I would do anything for her," she said. "I love Miriam."

"Yes," he said, and then his voice caught, and he had nothing more to add.

After a little pause, she said, "I'm glad you're back, Gaaron."

"Yes," he said a second time. "It is good to see you again." And then he gave her a sober smile, nodded again in a formal manner, and turned to pace down the hall. He thought he could feel her watching him, but she made no move to follow, and did not call out his name as he walked away.

CHAPTER SIXTEEN

Miriam watched Susannah stroll away, her head bent over Keren's, her laugh floating back along the cobalt cobblestones. In Luminaux, even the noises were blue; the laugh sounded azure, the color of a spring sky. It did not make Miriam feel at all mirthful.

Frida came to stand beside her. She was a generously sized woman, with the creamy brown skin and radiant black hair of all Edori, and there was a certain calm purposefulness about her. "You might find it hard to settle in, at first," Frida said. "Would you like to have this afternoon free, to look around Luminaux, or would you like to come in and learn what we do in the bakery?"

It was kind of her to offer options, Miriam thought. She turned toward the door. "I've been to Luminaux," she said, her voice indifferent but polite. "Why don't you let me see the bakery?"

So Frida took her to the kitchen and showed her where the flour was kept, the cool cistern where the butter and milk were stored, the pantry full of spices, the books full of recipes. There was also the sink full of dirty pans, and a pipe system as good as the Eyrie's for carrying water into the building and away.

"Looks like a lot of work," Miriam commented.

"It is," Frida said. "But I like it."

"Do you want me to start on the dishes?" Miriam offered. "I don't know how to mix recipes, but I do know how to clean a pot."

Frida smiled. "That would be a great help, thank you. We generally close the front of the shop in early evening, just after everyone's gone home for dinner, because we open so early in the morning. We come back here and clean up, then have our own dinners."

"You live nearby?"

"Upstairs. My oldest daughter moved away last spring, you can have her room to yourself."

"That's very kind of you," Miriam said politely.

"We're happy to have you here," Frida said.

Miriam said little more than commonplaces as she drew the hot water and filled the sink with soap. She could hear Frida moving around the kitchen behind her, wrapping up softened cakes of butter and scraping burned spills of dough from the stove. Even farther away, she could hear the voices of Frida's daughters from the front room, talking to customers and laughing with each other. It was a still and quiet place, redolent with aromas so rich they acted on her almost like wine; her mind felt relaxed and unfocused.

"What about this pan? I think it might need to soak overnight."

"It always does. Just run some water in it when you're done with the rest of the pots."

"Anything else before I dry off my hands?"

"Just this one little dish, if you don't mind."

The girls came laughing in, taking off their aprons and telling some tale of a man who, apparently, dropped by every single day for a cherry-filled pastry. "We pretended we had sold the last one, and he was so sad! He said, 'Really? But you didn't save one for me? Here, let me pay you now for the whole next week so that you will always save one for me.' Then I felt a little bad, but he looked so happy when we brought out the one that we had hidden that I stopped feeling bad."

"Why don't you girls help Miriam carry her things up to your sister's room? I'm sure she's tired, and we'll let her go straight to bed as soon as we've had our dinner."

Miriam followed the sisters up a rather narrow staircase to a pretty set of rooms on the second story of the building. None of the rooms was very big, but they were all furnished with colorful Edori scarves and rugs as well as the pottery and glassware so readily available in Luminaux. The windows overlooked the busy streets still crowded with people hurrying home to their own dinners. The sunlight was beginning to fade and the gaslights were starting to come up, and even the flames in the glass globes burned blue.

Miriam's room was tiny, barely big enough to accommodate a small bed and a somewhat dilapidated dresser, but the scarlet bedspread and flowered curtains gave it a happy air. "Oh, I like this," Miriam exclaimed. "It's so cheerful."

"My mother said that at the Eyrie, every bedroom has its own water room, but here there is only one for all of us," the oldest girl apologized.

"That should be fine," Miriam said.

"Are you hungry? We usually eat right away."

"Yes, I'm starved. Can I do anything to help get the meal ready?"

About half an hour later, the four of them ate a simple dinner around a small table wedged into one corner of the main room. The girls were still laughing and talking, though now they were talking about boys who worked at the studio down the street and not about customers with a yen for sweets. Frida appeared absorbed in daily sales reports, though she looked up once in a while to make a comment that showed she had not missed a word of the conversation.

And then, from time to time, her thoughtful gaze rested on Miriam and she considered the young hold-born girl as if none of this meekness and good nature fooled her for a minute. During those inspections, Miriam found it harder to maintain her expression of amiability and spent most of her energy finishing up the meal on her plate.

"Well, let's clear the table and then the two of you can be off, if you want," Frida remarked eventually, coming to her feet. "Miriam, feel free to go with them—they're just going down the street to meet some of their friends. They'll be happy to take you with them."

Miriam stood up, too. "No—it's been rather a long day. I think I'll just go to my room and lie down."

"Good idea," Frida said somewhat dryly. "We rise well before the sun does to start the first round of baking."

"Oh, surely *she* doesn't have to—not on her very first day," the younger girl protested. "Let her sleep in just once."

Frida shrugged. "Very well. Tomorrow morning you can sleep in, but I'll expect you down in the bakery before the sun's been up very long."

Miriam smiled at her champion. "Thank you, I'll do both of those things," she said. "And thank you for the meal. It was most delicious."

She detoured to the very cramped water room so she could clean off the dust of travel and the invisible stain of abandonment. There was a small mirror hanging above the tiny sink, and she peered into it to see if she could read anything on her face. No; her brown eyes looked perfectly calm, her fair face serene and unpinched. No one who did not know her well would be able to read anything amiss in her cheeks and eyelids. Even Susannah had not been able to tell how furious she was.

But, of course, Susannah did not care.

Back in her room, she settled herself onto the hard, narrow mattress, so different from her luxurious bed at the Eyrie, and willed herself to sleep. She was indeed tired, exhausted from three days' worth of holding in her extreme sense of rage and injustice. She had not known exactly what she would to do punish Gaaron and Susannah, but she had been sure something would occur to her—and yesterday it had. It was perfect. She just wanted to make sure Susannah was safely out of the city before she put her plan into practice.

She slept the untroubled sleep of the righteous, and woke briefly when she heard the three women gather for breakfast. She allowed herself another hour of sleep, then rolled out of bed, rested and purposeful. A quick cleaning in the water room, an even quicker repacking of all her things, and she headed downstairs with her duffel bags over her shoulders.

Frida was in the kitchen when she emerged from the stairwell; the girls were no doubt at the front counter. The Edori woman looked her up and down, taking in the luggage, the travel clothes, the mulish expression.

"I'm going out to the Lohora camp before they move on," Miriam said coolly. "I'm going to travel with them for a few months."

Frida nodded. "Is that what it is?" she said. "I knew you had something planned."

Miriam put her chin up. "I don't have to stay here."

"No. You don't."

"Although it was very kind of you to say you'd take me in."

"Do the Lohoras know you're joining them?"

"No, but they'll be happy to have me. Susannah says the Edori will take in any stray traveler and make him welcome."

"That's true. Well, let me give you some breakfast, and a few loaves of bread to take with you. Tirza appreciates my bread, I know."

Braced for a fight, Miriam felt a little deflated by Frida's cheerful acceptance of her announcement. "And if anyone comes looking for me, you can tell them exactly where I've gone," she said somewhat belligerently.

"I will, if they ask," Frida said. "Do you have a canteen with you? Plenty of water? That's the worst part of travel, you know, the thirst. Here, I've made you a little plate with some cheese and fruit. You better eat now, build up your strength."

Since it seemed stupid to refuse the food, Miriam accepted it with rather bad grace, and ate while Frida wrapped a few loaves of bread. "There. That'll go nicely with a little rabbit stew tonight," she said with satisfaction. "Be sure and give Tirza my love. And Claudia and Anna and all the rest, too, of course."

Miriam took the package and tucked it into a pocket of one of her duffel bags. "Should I say good-bye to the girls?"

"If you want. I'll tell them if you'd rather."

"All right then. I'll just go. And—well—thank you."

Frida nodded and rinsed her hands off in the sink. "I enjoyed having you under my roof the one night. Safe traveling." And she turned back to a huge roll of dough she was kneading on the counter.

Miriam picked up her suitcases and went out the back door.

The morning was cooler than she'd expected, after the heat of the bakery, so she stopped almost immediately to pull on a jacket. The suitcases were heavier than she remembered, even when she'd slung them over her back by their long leather straps. And the walk to the city limits was longer and more wearisome than it had been the other day, in the company of chattering women and free of any burdens. A few people jostled carelessly against her, apologized, and hurried on.

She was thirsty before she'd even left the city, but she couldn't remember how far the camp was and she didn't want to drink all her water before she'd made it a mile from the bakery. So she paused to buy an orange from a street vendor, flashing her wrist bracelet at him.

He laughed and shook his head. "No, lady, not for me. I don't keep no tally with the angel holds. It's coins and coppers I'll take, things I can count up at the end of the day."

Her bracelets had never been rejected before; she'd never carried cash. Embarrassed, she backed away a pace. "Oh—I'm sorry—next time, then, I guess," she said hastily.

He laughed again and tossed her one of the big bright spheres. "That's against next time," he said. "Travel safely."

She peeled and ate the orange as she walked, considerably heartened both by the friendly exchange and the taste of the sweet fruit. Still, she was frowning again soon enough. Her feet hurt, her shoulders ached, she was thirsty *again*, and the Edori camp was nowhere in sight. Could she have gone in the wrong direction? She thought not; she had paid close attention to small landmarks when she had followed Susannah and her friends here the other day. She remembered that misshapen tree and that spiky blue rock, perhaps a long-ago site of early mining efforts. She remembered that broken-down wagon, discarded years ago by its appearance, and the staved-in barrel on its side nearby. She remembered this stretch of half-dead wildflowers, giving up so early in the season before true cold had really come. She was going the right way.

But perhaps she was too late.

She was sure Tirza had said they would camp another day or two; she was sure they had wanted to give that man, that Bartholomew, a couple more days to recover. But perhaps he had grown cool and healthy in the night. Perhaps he had leapt from his pallet this morning and declared, "I'm a well man, let's move on." Perhaps they had pulled up stakes and headed off to—Breven—or northern Gaza—or western Bethel—or anywhere. Who knew where an Edori would go?

How would she find them? And if she did not find them, would she be able to find her way back to Luminaux before nightfall? Anxiously, she looked over her shoulder, but the Blue City was still visible, exuding a rich, satisfied azure glow just at the horizon line. Surely she would not walk so far that she would not be able to find her way back.

Surely the Edori were just another mile or two away.

She stopped, set down her bags, and was frozen by indecision. That way Luminaux, safe and easily reachable. The other way, the Lohora camp, or so she thought. She could return to Frida's, feeling foolish but fairly certain of a welcome; or she could keep walking until the sunlight ran out and it was clear that she had, through bad timing or bad geography, missed the Lohoras entirely. No doubt, if that occurred, she could nurse her food and her water to last her another day. She could find her way back to the Blue City before nightfall the following day.

She picked up her suitcases and moved forward.

She traveled perhaps another two miles before she saw the first silhouettes of tents against the hazy sky. She was so relieved that all her muscles loosened and she had to sit down a moment, shucking off the bags as she sank to the rocky ground. Yes, there was the meandering little streambed she remembered seeing the last time she had walked this way; this was all looking familiar. She could afford to take another swallow from her canteen. She was near water. She was near friends.

It was past noon by the time she struggled into the Edori camp, hot, thirsty, dirty, and suddenly questioning what in the god's name she had done. Would these people even remember her? Would they truly welcome her? What would she say to them? What would they hear no matter what she said?

"Miriam!" a voice called, and she dropped her bags and whirled around to face the speaker. It was Anna, she thought, Keren's older sister, the spare unsmiling one. "It *is* you. I thought I recognized your bright hair. Have you walked all this way from Luminaux?"

Her voice called Tirza from her tent and turned a few others from their cookfires. "Miriam," Tirza said in a voice of surprise. "Don't you look thirsty. Come sit down and have a drink of juice."

Miriam felt absurdly grateful, and exhausted and silly enough to want to cry. "It was farther than I thought," she said, sinking down to a mat in front of the welcome fire. "And I just finished up the last of my water."

"You can have water, too, if you like, but I think the juice will be better," said Tirza, pouring a red liquid into a chipped mug. "*Did* you walk all the way from Luminaux with your bundles in your hand?"

"They didn't seem so heavy before," Miriam said, gulping down the juice.

"All your belongings weigh twice as much at the end of the trip as they do at the beginning," Anna said with a severe smile. "Though there's only half of what you remember bringing inside each of your bags."

Tirza's gaze went to the duffel bags dropped unceremoniously at the edge of the fire. "All your belongings?" she repeated in a soft voice.

Miriam nodded, and her eyes went from one woman to the other. "I thought—Susannah wanted me to live with Frida in the city but I thought—I don't want to do that. I want to live with the Edori. Travel with you. I don't ever want to live in a city or a hold or—or anywhere ever again."

Tirza looked over at Anna, no expression to be read on either dark face. "Does Susannah know what you've decided?" Anna asked.

Miriam shook her head. "No. But I told Frida, who will tell her if she asks."

"There is so much empty space in the tent now that Keren has gone to visit the angels," Tirza said.

"Then I can stay?" Miriam asked eagerly.

Tirza looked surprised. "Of course you can. We'll be happy to have you. No Lohora ever turned away a guest or a traveler in need."

"I'll go tell Eleazar," Anna said, and moved off to thread a path through the clustered tents.

"I really can stay?" Miriam asked again.

Tirza smiled. "The Lohoras are happy to have you."

That night, eating dinner with the Edori around the campfire, warm, well-fed, and drowsy, Miriam was as happy as she remembered being at any point in her life. Neither Anna nor Tirza was much of one for fussing, but they had made her feel welcome and special, giving her extra helpings of food and water, introducing her to all the Lohoras she had not met the other day. Dathan had settled beside her and told her funny stories, flirting with her a little but in the way that Miriam understood. This was how she herself flirted with all attractive men, just because it felt good to smile and tilt her head and say things that could be interpreted two different ways. She was not surprised Susannah had been in love with him. She was surprised Susannah had been willing to leave him for Gaaron.

Of course, she would never forgive Susannah if she left Gaaron to return to this Dathan.

She might never forgive Susannah anyway.

She found it strange to sleep in the crowded tent, wedged between Anna and Amram and acutely conscious of the sounds of breathing all around her. There was a rock under her hip, but she was afraid to move and dislodge it, sure she'd wake up someone else. But she couldn't fall asleep. She wriggled to one side, hoping to edge away from its sharpest point. It remained firmly pressed against her flesh. Well, what did she care? She'd wake up in the morning with a little rock-sized bruise on her skin, but that was a small price to pay for having found sanctuary. She closed her eyes and willed herself to sleep.

She had to use the water tent.

She squeezed her eyes shut tighter. No, no, no, she would not get up in the middle of the night, pick her way through the coiled tangle of sleeping bodies, creep through the quiet camp, and try to locate the water tent (which, she had to say, she did not like even half so well as Frida's tiny water room)—all without waking up the whole camp. She would concentrate on falling asleep. She would forget about physical discomforts. She would let her mind dissolve and her thoughts turn to smoke and dreaming.

She really, really, had to find that water tent.

Pushing herself to a sitting position, she drew back her covers and came to a crouching stand. A slow process to cross the tent, putting her feet down by blankets and bodies, trying not to step on the spread masses of black hair that were hard to see in the darkness. She made it to the tent flap without mishap and stepped out into the chilly dark. It was getting cold down in the southern provinces; what would winter be like?

What would winter be like traveling in the open air and sleeping inside the rather thin walls of a tent? That had not previously occurred to her.

Shivering, she hurried through the shadowed camp to the tent set farthest from the central fires. Some small shape started and hopped away as Miriam drew closer and she had to strangle a scream. She had not thought about any dangers that might be lurking. Could there be wolves or other predators prowling just outside the camp, waiting for strays to step beyond the border of safety? She had to hope she would be quick enough to elude them.

She stepped inside the water tent, which was little more than a few shallow holes dug in the ground and a collection of jugs and bottles. Her business concluded, she hurried back to her own tent and glided inside. No one stirred, although, to her own ears, her breathing was loud and labored. She found her own pallet, remembered to move the rock, and lay down again at last.

And she smiled up at the small hole in the top of the tent, affording a tantalizing glimpse of the starry panorama overhead. It was true. She'd never been happier in her life.

In the morning, she found reason to reassess that.

She was wakened far earlier than she would have chosen by the noises of camp life going on around her—voices calling, wood being snapped in two for the fire, spoons clanking against cook pots. There were other sounds, too, that she could not identify, but somehow bigger sounds, as if important enterprises were under way. She turned her head fretfully on her flat pallet, feeling her bones ache from the un-accustomed rest on hard ground. Feeling dust in her hair and the grime of yesterday's long walk gritty against her skin.

How exactly was she going to bathe?

She stood up slowly and stepped out into the gray day, noting that the sun was losing its struggle against a low cloud cover. Tirza and Anna were arguing over the cook pot in a good-natured way, and whatever they were cooking smelled wonderful.

"Look, it's the sleepy one," Tirza greeted her with a smile. "How are you feeling this morning? You looked so tired last night."

"I feel a little stiff," Miriam admitted.

"That'll wear off after you've been walking a while," Anna said.

Miriam glanced at first one woman, then the other. "Am I to be walking somewhere?"

Tirza nodded over at the main body of the camp, where even now men and boys were circling the tents, unstringing wires and catching the big canvas coverings as they crumbled to the ground. "Bartholo-mew's so much better, and we've been here so long, that we just all decided today was the day to move on. Strike camp before noon, see how far we get before nightfall."

"Oh! Well—what can I do to help?"

"Anything you like. No shortage of tasks," Anna said.

"Very well. But first—I should like to get clean. But I don't know—I'm not sure—"

Tirza pointed at the little streambed that wound so close to their camp that it must have been the reason they chose to settle here. "About a quarter mile down, the creek deepens enough for you to go in to your waist, and it's far enough away, and late enough, that you ought to have a little privacy. I understand you allali girls are touchy about that," she added with a grin.

Miriam wasn't sure how to define "allali," but if it meant someone who didn't bathe out in the open in Bethel rivers, that was certainly her. "Won't the water be cold?" she said in a small voice.

"Not as cold as it'll be in a few weeks," Anna said unsympath-etically. "There are some who don't bathe all winter long, but I can't abide that. Once a week or I can't live with myself."

"Aren't there—can't you—I mean, you could bring water back to the camp and heat it up, maybe—"

The Edori women looked at her as if she was an apparition from a dream. "It just takes a few minutes to bathe in the river," Tirza said.

"Why, to haul water and heat it would take hours. It's trouble enough just to fetch the water for cooking."

"Well—I suppose—" Miriam said, thinking she wouldn't mind if it took her all day, if it meant she could be clean and comfortable. "Anyway, I guess today I'll just go clean up as best I can—"

"You might wash out the clothes you've got on now, if you plan to put on fresh ones," Anna suggested. "Hang them up to dry when we make camp tonight, though it still might take a day or two before they're not damp anymore."

Miriam stared at her, confronted with a new thought. Back at the Eyrie, she just dropped her clothes off at the laundry room, and they were returned to her, cleaned and pressed. She knew how to rinse out a blouse or an undergarment, of course, but she'd never actually washed her own clothes. Or thought to do it every day.

Or maybe not every day, if they didn't camp by water every night.

But if they didn't camp by water every night . . . how would she get clean every morning?

Was it possible that she would have to go a day or two, maybe more, without bathing herself, even in a medium that promised to be as unfriendly as a small riverbed?

And what about washing her hair?

"You don't have to change your clothes, of course," Tirza said, misreading her silence. "If I'm careful and don't spill anything, I can sometimes wear the same dress for a week, though I do like to have on clean underthings. And since I *hate* washing clothes, I try very hard not to spill things!"

"No, I—I guess I hadn't thought much about clothes and how to keep them clean—while I traveled," Miriam said. "I think I have six changes of clothes with me. And I was just wondering if I'd really be able to wash them out every day."

"Probably not, so wash what you can when you can," Anna said. "But hurry, now. We're going to be on the move in another hour or two."

So Miriam ducked back into the tent and pawed through her duffel bag till she found the sturdiest cotton gown in her wardrobe. It was a dark blue that rarely showed dirt; it might last her a day or two, if she didn't sweat or stain it. The outfit she had worn yesterday, a pale green skirt and blouse that she had always loved, was covered with mud and grass stains and soot from last night's fire. Clearly, every time she wore the light-colored fabric, it would require washing.

She could see she was going to have to make clothing choices much more carefully from now on.

When she emerged from the tent, Tirza handed her a cake of soap. "To wash with," she said, when Miriam looked uncertain.

"My clothes or my body?"

Tirza grinned. "Everything."

She trudged away from camp, following the curve of the creek, until she got to a place that looked both deep and private. Still, she felt a little conspicuous—and not a little cold—as she pulled off every item of clothing and stood at the edge of the water. If she waded in one foot at a time, she would never do this. She took a deep breath and plunged in, dropping to her knees as soon as she hit the center of the water.

Sweet Jovah wailing his twice-benighted prayers, but it was *cold* in the water. Miriam had never bathed so fast in her life, scrubbing the raw bar of soap along her flesh, ducking her blond hair under the water and hastily lathering it up. Quick rinse, duck, feel the mild current of the stream tug at the roots of her hair, and then rise to her feet and go running back to the bank. Damnation and isolation, she had forgotten to bring a *towel.* Shivering furiously, she dried herself on the less dirty bits of her green skirt and pulled on the clean blue dress as fast as she could. A little warmer, and a lot grimmer, she knelt at the stream's edge and washed out yesterday's clothing. She would never wear this skirt and blouse again. She would never wear *anything* that had to be washed. She would wear this blue dress for the rest of her life.

She was a little happier once the chores were done, however, and she'd wrung out the clothes so they wouldn't drip on her too much as she plodded back. There was a certain exhilaration at being clean again—or maybe the euphoria was induced by the dip in the cold river, and the quick escape. She ran her fingers through her tangled hair and hoped someone would be able to lend her a comb.

"Good, you're back," Anna greeted her. "Help me pour the rest of this porridge into some pots so we can bring it with us."

"But I haven't eaten yet," Miriam said.

"Well, you can eat while you work. And where did Dathan and Amram go? Eleazar needs someone to help him pull down the tent."

Miriam quickly crammed some sugared bread into her mouth while she distributed leftover porridge into clay pots. The pots were cleverly constructed, with wide bowls and narrow necks, and lids that fit snugly once you turned them a certain way. She imagined they traveled well. Well—they would have to. Sometimes, Susannah had told her, the Edori traveled for weeks without staying more than one night at any campsite.

Miriam was beginning to think the Edori lifestyle was a touch more demanding than she had at first envisioned.

"Miriam, where's that soap?" Tirza asked. "I'll pack it away."

Miriam turned from her stance over the packing pots. "The soap? Oh—I'm afraid I left it down at the river. I'm sorry."

"Then you'll just have to go back and get it," Tirza said impatiently. "Soap's hard to come by, you know, and I don't know how soon we'll be somewhere we can buy more."

Miriam put down the cauldron. "I'm sorry—I didn't think—"

"Finish the porridge first, then go for the soap," Anna commanded. "We don't want anything to spoil."

Feeling embarrassed, stupid, and wasteful, Miriam returned to her first task. The pot slipped in her hands a little, and some of the cereal poured down the crockery and onto the ground. Miriam looked up guiltily and saw that Anna had noticed, but the Edori woman did no more than compress her lips and glance away. Miriam tried to be very careful after that.

Finally, the cauldron was empty and the crocks were full. "As long as you're going back downstream, Miriam," Tirza said, "why don't you take the big pot with you? You can wash it out. Don't use the soap," she added. "Just rinse it very well."

"All right," Miriam said.

The cauldron was an awkward item to carry a quarter of a mile; it kept bumping against her knees when she lugged it by its handle, and it was a little too big and round for her to hold against her chest, though she tried it for a few strides. *Once it's clean,* she thought with a burst of morose humor, *I can turn it upside down and carry it on my head.*

It was also an awkward item to clean, and the whole front of her dress got splashed with cold water before she managed to get it rinsed to the standards she thought Anna would expect. Her fingers were icy, and she paused a moment to blow on them, and then tuck them under her armpits for a little warmth. When they had regained their feeling, she picked up the cauldron and headed back.

She'd gone a hundred paces before she remembered the soap.

"Cruel Jovah whispering curses," she muttered under her breath, making up maledictions as she retraced her steps. "Damnation, isolation, cremation, and despair. I hope to never see another bar of soap again as long as I live."

Finally, finally, wet, cold but victorious, she returned to the camp. To find it a camp no longer—every tent down and rolled, every horse loaded with packs and bundles. A few women fussed around wheeled long-handled carts. Miriam realized that they planned to push these in front of them for the entire journey.

She wondered if she would have to carry her duffel bags for however long they traveled today. Then, to her relief, she saw Eleazar tightening straps on a small, sturdy black pony, who was loaded with her own luggage as well as some of the paraphernalia of the tent.

"How far will we be going today?" Miriam asked Tirza.

The Edori woman shrugged. "Who knows? Sometimes we only get five miles away, or ten, and we have a reason to stop. Sometimes we travel twenty miles or more. When the weather is good and no one is sick, we might go thirty miles, but that's a long day. With Bartholomew so recently sick, and the weather starting to cool, I imagine we will go no more than fifteen miles. But we'll see."

"And where are we going?" Miriam said.

Tirza laughed. "Jovah kiss you, child, I have no idea!"

Miriam rather enjoyed the journey for the first couple of hours. Her shoes were good and sturdy, she was not carrying those damned duffel bags, and Dathan walked beside her, pointing out sights.

"Now, if you're thirsty, you can pick off a few of these leaves and chew them up, and it's as good as eating an apple," he said, twisting off a branch of a low, blue-green shrub and handing it to her. "There's a funny taste at first, but you get used to it. And you'll find your thirst disappears like that." He snapped his fingers.

Cautiously, Miriam slipped a single leaf into her mouth and ground it up. It was a little minty, a little peppery, a little something-she-could-not-identify, but the chewed leaf made a satisfying juice blob inside her mouth. Once she swallowed, she realized he was right. She'd been a little thirsty; now she felt refreshed.

"I've never even heard of such a thing before," she said. "What's it called?"

"Marrowroot. It's harder to find in Bethel," he said.

"What do you do in Bethel, then, when you can't find water?"

"Look for tosswort, but it tastes even nastier," he said with a smile. "What you really look for is water."

He showed her rabbit tracks and wolf spoor, explained why she wouldn't want to sit on a sun-warmed rock once the weather started cooling off (snakes sought the lingering heat), and named the various birds they saw flying overhead. When her hair grew hot on the back of her neck, he paused beside her for three minutes, braiding it for her and tying it with a leather strip. He asked her about life in the angel hold, said he'd never been to Velora, wanted to know what it felt like to be carried in an angel's arms and flown across the continent.

He never mentioned Susannah's name. Neither did Miriam.

When they paused for lunch, Miriam sank to the ground without even pulling out a pallet to protect her blue dress from dust. Tirza brought her some cold bread and meat, checked to make sure her canteen was full, and asked after her feet.

"I think they're fine," Miriam said. "I can't really feel them."

"I'll give you some salve tonight," Tirza promised.

The rest was short, and then they were all on the move again. The second half of the afternoon was not nearly as pleasant. Dathan wandered off to hunt or otherwise amuse himself. Miriam found herself trailing behind Anna and Claudia, who talked of people she didn't know and babies she didn't care about. Plus her feet really were beginning to hurt. There was a place on her heel that was feeling raw and rubbed, and another on the back of her ankle that she was afraid to look at. Her canteen was low, and the marrowroot leaves were not having quite the same efficacy this late in the day. She had eaten plenty of food at lunch, but she had expended so much energy just by plodding along that she was hungry again. And no one else in the caravan looked like he was on the verge of calling a halt.

Well, Miriam would not be the one to slow everybody down. She had never been the one to call it quits. She would walk on with the Edori if they didn't stop from now till Breven.

In fact, Bartholomew signaled for a rest about an hour later. Looking around, Miriam could see no reason for stopping at this particular point. They were on open ground, no river or stand of trees or windbreak of any kind nearby. But the air was cooling off as the sun slid toward an early departure and, Miriam gathered from the comments the others let fall, there was no particularly good camping ground ahead of them for another five or ten miles.

"Best not to wear everyone out," Claudia said comfortably. "Just stop for the night to sleep, and move on tomorrow."

Which meant, Miriam learned next, that none of the tents would be set up for the night, only one central fire would be built in order to conserve firewood, and the only water available was in the containers they'd carried with them.

She thought, *I could have lived this well by myself if I'd just wandered out of Velora and started walking toward southern Bethel with my arms empty.*

Still, there was plenty to do to get the clan ready for the night, as she also discovered very quickly. Amram and the other children scrounged up kindling from scrubby little bushes, while some of the men built a fire with logs dragged behind them all the way from Luminaux. Anna and Claudia and a couple of the other older women were debating what to cook in a few big pots that would feed the whole camp. Dathan and Eleazar, who had been gone for much of the afternoon, came strolling in, their hands full of treasures picked up on the road.

When she looked more closely, Miriam saw that these treasures were really dead animals. A couple of rabbits, something that looked like a squirrel, and three birds of some sort, their spread wings hanging from their limp bodies and bouncing with every step the Edori took.

Miriam looked away and for a moment she felt faint.

A few moments later, Tirza called her name. Miriam forced herself to walk over to the cook-fire, where Dathan was kneeling on the ground and Anna was giving him instructions. "Can you skin a rabbit?" Tirza asked. "Or maybe pluck a bird?"

Miriam thought she would gag. She kept her eyes turned carefully away from the sight of the corpses piled untidily beside the fire. "Skin a—no, I've never—and I've never plucked the feathers off anything," she said in an unsteady voice.

Tirza looked disappointed but unsurprised. "I can show you, but it'll take you a while to get the hang of it," she said.

Miriam's voice took on a note of panic. "I can't touch those things!" she exclaimed. "I can't—they're all bloody—and they're *dead.*"

"Well, you'd probably rather have them dead if you're going to eat them," Tirza said.

"I can't *eat* them!"

Now Tirza's expression was a little quizzical. "You ate rabbit stew the other night and did not seem to mind at all," she said. "How do you think you get meat for your table at the angel holds? Someone kills it for you. You just don't happen to see the slaughter. But here we have to do all our own tasks, both the rewarding and the not so pleasant. If we want to eat, that is. If we want to survive."

Miriam stared at her, wondering if Tirza had just told her that she would not be fed if she didn't do her share of camp chores. She wanted to shriek and run away, stomping down the dusty Jordana miles toward someplace more civilized, more sane, but she could not even do that. She could not leave this campfire. She had no idea where she was, where the nearest city was; she had no idea how to get anywhere or do anything except follow these people. She was trapped more surely, and more terrifyingly, than she had ever been when she had been forbidden to leave the Eyrie.

"I can't touch them," she whispered.

For an awful second, she waited for Tirza to say, "Fine, then you won't eat tonight," but the Edori woman merely nodded. "Well, can you peel the potatoes then?" Tirza asked. "And chop up the carrots? We're going to make three big pots to feed everyone, so we'll need a lot of vegetables."

Miriam nodded. "I can do that," she said in a small voice. "Where's a knife?"

She spent the next hour or so scraping and chopping, her hands a little clumsy but her mind completely focused. All around her, other hands were at work, kneading dough, mixing up spices, boning the carcasses and dicing meat. A few steps away from the fire, more activity was going on, as men mended harnesses and young girls sewed blouses. Even the children were busy, digging holes for the water tent and pulling out pallets for everyone to sleep on around the fire. Someone started singing an unfamiliar song in a language that Miriam didn't know, and a few other voices joined in, but idly, adding a melody line here, a harmony note there as if the workers were too busy to pause long enough to sing a song the whole way through.

Miriam herself was too exhausted to sing, even if she'd known the music.

It was full dark, and they had been at the campsite for nearly two hours, before dinner was finally ready. By this time, Miriam was so hungry that she was beginning to rethink her position; she might have snatched up a raw chunk of rabbit flesh and gulped it down, gooey bloody mess that it was, if every single bit of meat hadn't already been dumped into one of the cook pots. She almost could not wait her turn to ladle food onto her plate, and then she didn't want to take another few seconds to find a place to sit around the fire before she started eating. She dropped into the first available spot, between Amram and a teenage girl from one of the other tents, and started cramming food into her mouth. Oh, this was so good. She wasn't even sure what it was—grouse, she thought, because it didn't taste like rabbit and she didn't know what squirrel tasted like but she didn't think this was it— but it was excellent. She spooned up the stew as fast as she could, and then wiped her bowl with a crust of fresh bread. Beyond delicious. Food so good you would not be embarrassed to feed it to Jovah.

She stood up to refill her plate.

She had three helpings before she was satisfied, and then for a few moments, she felt a little sick to her stomach. That would be perfect, to get a stomach disorder out here in the middle of nowhere, with no private place to relieve herself and no ready supply of water with which to clean herself up. But no; the momentary twinges passed, and she felt just fine again. She even thought she could eat a little more if there was food left over and it would go to waste otherwise.

However, she felt too full and content even to stand up and check the contents of the cook pots.

Doubtless, everyone else felt much the same, because no one moved for a while except to shift position or lay aside a plate. No one was really talking much, either, though Bartholomew and Eleazar were murmuring about something in voices too quiet to be overheard. To- morrow's route, Miriam guessed. A course that she devoutly hoped would take them somewhere near water.

Someone began humming, a soft little lullaby, and a few other voices took up the wordless tune. Pretty soon the whole camp was singing, a swell of voices coming from around the fire, so indistinct and beautiful that for a moment Miriam entertained the fancy that the fire itself was lifting up a ragged, brilliant cry. Then someone rose to his feet—a young man named Thaddeus, Miriam thought—and began singing a real song, using real words. Everyone else fell silent to listen, though Miriam could not understand the language. Still she listened, head tilted to one side, as the liquid tenor notes rolled from his mouth. The music made her sad, made her think of bitter hours and days of mourning—made her remember her mother, who had been so quiet and so furtive and who had sometimes come into her room at night to kiss Miriam in secret.

"What's the song about?" she whispered to the girl sitting next to her, pushing the words hard past a constriction in her throat.

"It's a grieving song. His baby died a year ago. Right about this time of year."

"That's so sad!"

"Yes, but his lover is expecting another baby. They will not have to be sad much longer."

The next two to come to their feet sang much sweeter melodies, though the tunes were still wistful enough to leave Miriam depressed. She was so tired. She was so far from the people she loved. Well, she was not actually sure she loved anybody these days, but everyone she *knew* was far away and had no idea at all where she might be. She wanted to curl up in a little ball and shut her eyes against the firelight, the starlight, the chance of thinking. She came unsteadily to her feet and looked around her for a place to sleep.

Instantly, Tirza was beside her, leading her from the circle of firelight. "Over here," she said. "We've spread our pallets on this side of the camp. See? Anna is sleeping already. I knew you would be exhausted—this has been a long few days for you."

"That music is all so dreary," Miriam blurted out.

"Do you think so? They're just folk songs, little tunes about everyday life." Tirza guided her to a pallet and knelt beside Miriam as she sank to the ground.

"They're about babies dying and—and I don't know what else, but they sound like they're about broken hearts and lovers leaving and—and things like that."

Tirza pulled a cover up to Miriam's chin. "Well, babies do die and lovers do leave. That's part of life," she said. Her voice sounded amused. "But many babies live and some lovers stay around forever, and we have songs for those events, too. It is just that firelight tends to bring out the sad memories for some. But just because they are sad, that doesn't make them any less precious."

Miriam turned on her side. "I'm so tired," she said.

Tirza leaned over to kiss her on the cheek. "Sleep well, allali girl," she said. "You will have another full day tomorrow."

CHAPTER SEVENTEEN

And indeed, the next day, and next day, and the day after that, were all very much like the day that had just passed, and so were all the following days. Everyone in the camp rose early, wakened by the sun, and took just a few minutes to eat and do some desultory personal hygiene. Then they were on the move again. Some nights they camped by a riverbed, and then they took care to fill every canteen and jug and pot with water; other nights they camped by stands of trees, and then they gathered firewood against the cold nights ahead.

Sometimes when they traveled, they passed through fields of wild onions or groves of fruit-bearing trees, and so they foraged as they walked. Berries, nuts, hard little apples—all of these they found on the way. Dathan, Eleazar, Thaddeus, Bartholomew, and the other men would disappear during the course of the day, to return, if they were lucky, with rabbit or gopher or pheasant prizes. Once or twice, the men would combine their skills to bring down bigger game, and then the whole camp would feast for a day or two. It did not matter who caught the game or who found the fruit; everything was shared equally. Everyone did his or her part in readying the meals or the camp at night, and no one went to bed hungry or alone.

When there was more meat than they could eat in a night, or more fruit than they could consume for breakfast, the women carefully dried the food and packed it away in special containers. Winter was coming, even Miriam could see that; winter would be here in a month or two, and then there would be no easy hunting or foraging. They had to prepare now or die.

Miriam continued to be surprised at how hard the life was—hard in every sense—from the unyielding ground they slept on to the sheer physical difficulty of preparing every single meal from scratch, the near impossibility of keeping clean. But she was even more surprised at how quickly she adapted to it. She became adept at spotting the spiky little marrowroot shrubs before anyone else had seen them (they made an excellent addition to stew when water was scarce), and she didn't mind kneeling in a field for half a day, stripping berries from their secret places under sleek dark leaves. She learned that she was strong enough to haul heavy buckets of water uphill, and coordinated enough to spill very little. She also learned that she wouldn't die if, three nights in a row, they camped somewhere so far from water that there was no chance she'd be able to wash herself thoroughly in the morning. But this in turn taught her how happy she could be made by the simple sight of a brisk little streambed and the promise of clean hair by day's end.

She also learned that she could master a new skill if she put her mind to it. Because she had asked them to, Tirza and Amram had begun to teach her the fine art of rock-throwing. The men of the tribe hunted with a variety of weapons, including small spears and compact crossbows, but Amram was not considered old enough to handle such items without supervision. And though Tirza could handle a crossbow ("When I feel like it," she added), she and most of the other women chose not to deal with actual weapons. But, like Susannah, they could throw rocks with deadly accuracy and bring down a rabbit or, occasionally, a low-flying bird. It was a skill the young ones of the tribe also possessed, and Miriam was intrigued by it.

"As much as anything, it's practice, practice, practice," Tirza had told her. "Throw at everything, as we walk along. Pick a target, see if you can hit it. See how hard you can hit it. See if you can hit it without making any noise as you approach it. See if you can avoid swinging your arm in a wide arc that will draw the animal's attention."

All this seemed contradictory to Miriam, but she began to practice all the same. Most mornings, she would fill a shoulder bag with rocks of all sizes, and she would spend part of the day aiming these at various trees and weeds and boulders as they walked along. By trial and error, she began to learn which sizes of stones fit best in her hand, which weights and shapes were the easiest to throw. She didn't have a great deal of range, so she suspected she would never get close enough to any wildlife to put it in danger, but her accuracy improved fairly rapidly. She didn't have much strength, either, though she could knock a small stone off a big boulder if she hit it just right. Not quite like braining a rabbit and rendering it senseless. But if she lived with the Edori long enough, she was sure she would eventually get the hang of it.

She had been traveling with the Lohoras for more than two weeks before she realized, one night, that she was not completely exhausted. She was pleasantly weary, yes; her legs felt stretched and tired from her long walk, and her back ached a little from bending over bushes in a field. But those were minor sensations—welcome, actually, because they made the act of sitting that much more enjoyable. She was looking forward to settling down on her pallet, but she wasn't so drained that she almost couldn't imagine taking the twenty steps necessary to move between the fire and her bed. She felt pretty good, actually. She felt pretty happy.

So she waited until Thaddeus' pregnant lover had finished her sweet but mournful melody, and then she rose to her feet. There was a little murmur of surprise from those still gathered around the campfire, because until now, she had not once indicated any interest in singing. In fact, until this very moment, it had not occurred to her that she might ever want to do so. But she did. She wanted to sing a happy song.

"Some of you may know this. If you do, please feel free to join in," she said, glancing around at the faces looking up at her from around the fire, and feeling a fierce surge of affection for every one of them. There was Dathan with his gorgeous face and sleepy eyes; Bartholomew with his serious, watchful expression; Anna, so severe and so incapable of anything but kindness. There was Amram, even now trying to tease a smile from Claudia's daughter, five years older than he was and not interested in the attentions of younger boys. There was Claudia, sitting with Tirza, no doubt gossiping about Bartholomew and Anna, who everyone knew had shared a tent for the first time last night. There was everyone, in fact—everyone in her small world.

Miriam raised her cupped hands before her as if to catch dew or starlight; she tilted her head up toward the watchful god. When she started singing, her joy poured out of her like honey from one of Anna's spice cups. The song was an upbeat one of praise and thanksgiving, a harvest song she'd heard in the Bethel fields. Each short little dancing line was punctuated with a quick off-count handclap, and each verse ended with a different list of benefits.

"Jovah, we thank you—Jovah, we thank you—Jovah, we thank you, for giving us this day," Miriam sang. "Thanks for the sunlight, thanks for the moonlight, thanks for the starlight, shining on this day."

About a dozen Edori voices came in on the next line, changing the main word to suit themselves. "Yovah, we thank you—Yovah, we thank you—Yovah, we thank you, for giving us this day."

Miriam took the lead vocal back. "Thanks for the cornfields, thanks for the wheat fields, thanks for the bean fields, growing on this day."

Now she called him Yovah, too, a much more beautiful name, simple to say, moving through her mouth as easily as breath. Then, "Thanks for the young ones, thanks for the old ones, thanks for the sweet ones, living on this day."

Everyone was clapping along with the music now, a few of them stamping their feet. Claudia's daughter had even gotten up and started to dance. It was an irresistible song, simple though it was; it conferred liveliness and goodwill. Thaddeus jumped up before Miriam could go on to the next verse, making up his own words, as Edori were wont to do.

"Thanks for the fair ones," he sang, pointing at Miriam. "Thanks for the dark ones," he continued, sweeping his hand around to indicate the circle of Edori. Then he bent over to put his hand to his lover's swelling stomach. "Thanks for the new ones, here with us today."

That was it, Miriam knew; she would not get her song back. Laughing, she sat down as Dathan rose and offered his own thanks to the god. And after Dathan, Eleazar, and then Tirza, and then, one by one, nearly everyone in the camp. They were all giddy with silliness by the time, finally, no one could think of one more set of prayers, and the song came to a sputtering halt. Miriam let herself fall backward onto the ground behind her.

"Oh, that feels so good!" she exclaimed. "I haven't laughed that hard for—for years, maybe."

Dathan came over to push her back to a seated position, and then knelt on the ground beside her. "You should sing more often," he said. "You have a beautiful voice."

"I have a nice little soprano voice that sounds like a child's cry when you set it next to an angel's," she retorted.

"Then you should not sing with angels anymore," he said, gazing into her eyes. "You should sing only with Edori."

And, staring back up at him and willing herself to say something clever and snappy in return, Miriam found herself at a loss for words. The firelight turned him into a still, gorgeous Edori statue, all leather-brown face and midnight-dark eyes, the embodiment of freedom and beauty. It was not even Dathan she was seeing as she stared up at him, it was the collective soul of the Edori people, simple, straightforward, never at rest, always at peace.

I will never go back, she thought, unable to speak, unable to look away from him. *I will be with the Edori for the rest of my life.*

Their wanderings took them, one afternoon, to a place already set up as an Edori campsite. Miriam, pushing a cart for Thaddeus' pregnant lover, was one of the last to make it over the little rise in the land, the last to see the triangular shapes of the tents against the sky, to catch the unmistakable smell of an Edori cook-fire. She stopped a minute, scowling down at the unfamiliar faces, wanting to pick up the handles and awkwardly turn the cart around, heading back in the direction from which they'd come.

But all the other Lohoras were elated, running down the hill, calling out words of excitement and joy. Miriam saw Tirza deep in lively conversation with two young women about her age. She saw Claudia scoop up some little girl, maybe three years old, running half naked through the tents. Bartholomew and Eleazar had already threaded their way to the back of the camp and were standing with unknown men near the hobbled ponies, where they were no doubt discussing horseflesh, weather, and the availability of game.

But Miriam did not want to mingle with these strangers. They were not her Edori; they would not be her friends. She wanted the Lohoras all to herself.

Still, she could not set up her own camp, here on the crest of the hill, and pretend she was too good to take a meal with the others. Frowning even more heavily, she pushed the unwieldy cart down the hill and right to the edge of camp.

Thaddeus came running up to her, excited as a boy. "Come meet Shua's mother and father," he invited. Shua was his lover, the one expecting the baby in a few months. It was to be the first baby born to the Lohoras in a long time. "We have fallen in with the Corderras, can you believe it? Shua's family. They did not know our news and they are so delighted!"

Well, that kind of happiness it was impossible to begrudge. "Does she need anything from the cart?" Miriam asked.

"No—no—just come meet them," Thaddeus said impatiently, and grabbed her hand. He towed her through the camp, calling out greetings and insults, and shouting, "This is Miriam!" anytime someone looked with interest at his companion. "Yovah bless you, Miriam!" these new friends called as she was tugged past them, and all she could do was wave and start to laugh.

Shua's parents were hovering around their daughter, talking extremely fast and interrupting their words only to pause, stare at her in exquisite joy, and swoop in to kiss her on the cheek. So were Shua's siblings, a brace of girls and a boy about Amram's age—or maybe these were cousins or friends or simply other children of the tribe. Who could tell? Shua was flinging her arms around each voluble well-wisher, mingling her black hair with theirs for the duration of that brief hug, and pulling back to gaze with at them with heartfelt emotion.

Miriam did not particularly wish to intrude upon this reunion, but Thaddeus hauled her right into the circle. "This is Miriam," he announced. "She's been pushing Shua's cart since she got too slow and heavy to do any work."

There was a general outcry at this, but everyone was laughing, and Shua went to stand next to Thaddeus, his arm going around her. Miriam listened politely to all the Edori names, even tried to match them to faces, but she was still feeling a little sullen. She did not want to share her friends, her family, with anyone else. They were a small, perfect unit as they were, just the right number of people, just the right mix of personalities. She did not want strangers exerting their inevitable pull, changing alliances, stirring up new emotions.

Who knew, perhaps Shua would choose to sleep in her parents' tent tonight, leaving Claudia and Bartholomew and Anna lonely? And what if her sisters whispered in her ear, told tales of how much they missed her? What if Shua's mother begged her to come live with the Corderras for the winter, have her baby under the safe, watchful eyes of family? Would Shua listen to such entreaties? Would Thaddeus follow her to the Corderras? Well, of course he would. He could scarcely let Shua out of his sight as it was, he would hardly let her go off without him to bear their child. Then what would the Lohoras do, missing so many of their clan?

"I have left your cart at the bottom of the hill," Miriam said somewhat baldly to Shua. "Shall I go fetch it? Where will you be?"

Shua waved a languid hand. She was always so tired by the end of the day. "Thaddeus will get it when I need it," she said. "But won't you stay and have dinner at our fire? We will eat with my family tonight."

"No—thank you—I must go find Tirza," Miriam said, hoping she did not sound rude. "It was very nice to meet you all, of course," she added politely before turning away. She heard the chorus of replies as she stalked through the camp, looking for her own tent.

But it was hard to find anything or anyone here. The Corderras were a big tribe, twice as many as the Lohoras, and everywhere she turned, there was another strange face and another cadre of children, heedlessly careening past the fires. She could not find the Lohora section of camp—or, no, that tent looked familiar, sandwiched between two tents that she did not recognize at all. Was that it, then? The Lohoras were pitching their own tents in the spaces between Corderra campfires, deliberately trying to be absorbed into the larger group, to erase their own identity—to become, for this one night, at least, *Edori* and not merely Lohoras.

Miriam did not like it at all.

She was standing there frowning, looking about for her own tent or at least someone she recognized, when a little boy came darting out from around a cart and headed unsteadily in her direction. He tripped and fell, an action that triggered a look of incredible surprise on his solemn face. And then he screwed up his eyes and began to wail, more in anger and consternation, Miriam thought, than real pain. No young mother came instantly running. He had, it seemed, escaped all supervision in his one quick dash for freedom.

Miriam crossed over to him and caught him up in her arms, cradling him against her to stop the crying. "There now, mikale, it is not so bad," she said, swinging him from side to side in an instinctive rocking motion. "Did you hurt yourself? Or are all those tears for show, just because you do not like the way the world is ordered? I could cry just as hard as you could, you know, and for the exact same reason, but I try not to make such a spectacle of myself. I try to have a little pride."

He had stopped sobbing almost as soon as she picked him up, and now he was staring at her with great interest, his big eyes only inches from hers. He took his fingers out of his mouth and extended them, wet and sticky, to touch her cheek and then, wonderingly, her hair.

"Yes, I am a blond allali girl, not a type you've seen very often, I'll guess," she said, still rocking him, still staring down at his perfect little serious face. "But let me tell you, where I come from, more people look like me than look like you. *You* would be the strange one among my family, little mikale."

A light laugh behind her turned her around, the child still in her arms. "You would appear to have a way with children," said the young man who had come from nowhere to eavesdrop on her ridiculous conversation. He was slim and tall, with his black hair tied back in a braid and his dark eyes huge and long-lashed. "He will not sit still for me for five minutes."

"Is he yours?" Miriam asked, making no effort to return him.

"My sister's son. I was supposed to be watching him, but he escaped from me. He always does. I keep hoping she will soon stop trusting him to me, but she insists I will one day learn the knack of controlling a small evil child."

Miriam laughed and bounced the boy on her hip. He squealed with laughter. "He does not seem so evil to me," she said.

"That is because you have only known him for five minutes," he said. "But he seems to like you. You must have little siblings of your own."

"No," Miriam said, thinking briefly of the one sibling she did have. "No, I think I was always the evil child. Maybe that is why I feel such an affinity for your nephew."

"I am Daniel, by the way," the young man said. "You must have arrived with the Lohoras, but I do not remember seeing you with them before."

A polite way to put it. If she had not known better, she would have thought he was angling for information, covering up his mild astonishment at her presence among them—a blond allali girl who so clearly did not belong. But she had come to understand the Edori by now. There was nothing, not even curiosity, behind his remark.

Merely, he had never met her before. He did not think it strange that he was meeting her now.

"I am Miriam," she said. "I joined the Lohoras a few weeks back. I sleep in the tent of Eleazar and Tirza."

He glanced around. "Which I think I saw them putting up—yes, over there. Were you trying to find it?"

She laughed. "Actually, I was. I am a little lost among so many Corderras."

He started walking with her slowly through the camp, past the smoking campfires and the groups of gossiping women. Miriam continued to carry the baby. "We are a big clan," he said seriously. "I like it that way, but some of the others feel a small group is easier to travel with. We have talked of splitting up, but no one can bear the idea. Still, I think one or two tents may pull away from us once winter is over. It makes these last few months very precious."

Miriam sighed. "And I am feeling the same way, only backward," she said. He looked over at her with a smile, since her words made no sense. "I am feeling jealous of the Lohoras, with all you Corderras around to take their attention away from me," she explained. "I know that it makes no sense. But I saw your camp here, and I wanted us all to run in the other direction."

"That is because you have not been with the Edori long enough," he said. "What you will learn is that everyone loves you as much as your own clan does. You are welcome at every fire, in every tent. You will come to see a mixed camp like this as a great opportunity. You will say to yourself, 'Aha! I have not been loved enough by the twenty people in my own camp, who lavish affection on me every day. Look, now, here are thirty more people who will give me hugs and tell me I am beautiful. I will fill myself up on emotion, so much of it that even I, hungry little Miriam, will have enough.' "

She laughed, because his eyes danced even while his mouth remained prim. "That was not the way of things where I was raised," she said. "There was not enough love to go around, even when there were only one or two people in the room."

"Why, where did you grow up?" he asked, astonished.

She did not feel like giving details. "In Bethel," she said.

"And nobody loved you? I find that hard to believe."

He might have been flirting. It was hard to tell. He might just have been espousing the basic Edori philosophy. In any case, she thought about it. "Actually," she said slowly, "many people loved me.

I guess many people do still love me. It is just that I didn't know what to do with their love—or I didn't like the way their love was showed to me."

"Sometimes all you have to do is give it back," he suggested.

She smiled. "Yes, maybe that's what I should try instead."

She didn't specify what she had already tried, and he did not ask. At any rate, they had arrived at her tent, and Tirza was looking around in complete distraction. "Miriam! There you are! Can you—oh my goodness, is that Daniel? Come give me a kiss, and then go ask your sister if she has any mint leaves. I wanted to make something special for tonight, but I—Miriam, are you watching the baby? Or can you help me for a little bit?"

"I can do both," Miriam said, but Daniel took the baby from her arms.

"I will find my sister and come back with every spice in her wagon," he said solemnly. "But I will leave this little one in her hands and tell her he has worn me out."

"Tirza, can Daniel eat with us tonight?" Miriam asked.

"Of course he can! I was hoping he would."

He smiled at them both and turned the baby upside down to dangle by his feet. The boy screamed with delight. "Now I will hurry back even faster," Daniel promised.

He left and Miriam sent a swift glance around her own campfire. The tent was up, but the men were all gone, and Anna was nowhere in sight. No wonder Tirza looked so harried. Miriam pushed up the sleeves of her blue dress.

"What can I do to help?" she asked.

After the dinner, most members of both clans gathered around the central fire to trade stories and sing songs. Daniel and Miriam stood for a little while on the edge of the fire, drinking hot sweet drinks and talking, and then, by common consent, they wandered away from the firelight and the circle of their friends. The night air was downright cold, but Miriam was wearing a jacket that was too small for Eleazar, and she had begun wearing heavy socks inside her sturdy shoes, and she felt quite comfortable.

Anyway, when they spread a small blanket and sat down on it, they almost immediately began to kiss, and that combination of body heat and excitement made her warm all the way to her toes and fingertips.

They were innocent kisses, kisses that would lead to nothing else, and Miriam knew the difference. She was not sure Daniel did. She didn't think he was much older than she was, a few months maybe, and not nearly as experienced. Kissing Elias had never been like this, so full of joyous wonder at the act itself, the pleasurable exchange of softness and sweetness, without a hot impatience to follow up with the next even more intoxicating act.

Thinking of Elias made her feel small and uncertain. She pulled her mouth away from Daniel's and buried her face against his chest. But she clung to him more tightly, anxious for the reassurance of his body, the proof that he was alive and full of ageless unchanging desires.

He kissed her hair. "You're so sweet," he murmured.

She shook her head, not lifting her face. "No, I'm not."

"Maybe you aren't such a good judge."

"Maybe you don't know some of the things I've done."

Now he bent in and kissed her cheek, half exposed, though she'd tried to shake her hair over her face when she laid her forehead against his chest. "Very bad things?" he said gently. "That brought harm to others?"

She sighed. "Very, very bad things," she said. "And they brought very great harm."

He kissed her cheek again. "Did you intend the harm when you did them?"

"No."

"Would you do the same things again?"

She considered that, because she had not previously given it any thought. Would she go to the home of a married man and make love to him, knowing his wife was in another town and his daughters would be shamed by their father's actions? Would she do this even knowing that, if she were not the one in his bed, some other young girl would be, and so the fault was not really hers, or not hers entirely? Would she leave a man, covered with knife wounds and possibly dying, and run away, afraid for her own safety and good name?

Would she steal something just to see if she could do it? Would she entice a friend to run away in the night, just to prove her personal charm was so great that no one could fail to respond to it?

Would she hurt herself, just to hurt the people who loved her? Even if that was the only way she could think to prove to herself that they did, in fact, hold her dear?

"I would not do some of those things again, ever," she said slowly. "But I am not sure I am entirely reformed."

He lifted a hand to stroke her hair, and the motion was both soothing and infinitely warming. He would make a fine lover someday, a gentle and caring lover, someone who would shield his partner from the storms that raged both within her and without. But he would not be hers. "It is enough that you are trying," he said. "And that you have learned a little. And that you are willing to learn more."

She tilted her head back so she could see his face again, so he could kiss her again if he wanted to, and she was sure he wanted to. "Yes," she said. "I am very willing to learn."

They camped with the Corderras for two more days, and both days seemed, to Miriam, like the feast days and wedding celebrations she had attended at the holds and the river cities. She began to look forward to the Gathering that they talked about so much, a time when all the clans came together to recount tales of their winters apart, news of the tribes, stories of the road. To renew their deep bonds of friendship and to bask in their combined love. If the joining of just two clans could provide such joy and merriment, she could hardly imagine what the joining of all clans could produce.

She was sad, but she was ready, when, on the third day, the general consensus was reached: It was time for both tribes to move on. There were many hugs and exchanges of gifts and last-minute bits of advice given out. Daniel gave Miriam a little carved bird he had made from a stick of kindling, and she gave him a kiss, since she had nothing else. Thaddeus and Shua took clothes and gifts and good wishes from her family but did not, as Miriam had feared, decide to stay with the Corderras. No, they were Lohoras, they would travel as the Lohoras traveled and pitch their tent beside a Lohora fire. The Corderras could see the new baby at the Gathering.

And so the Lohoras moved on, turning northward now, and then west. They were somewhere in central Jordana, Miriam thought, between the Heldoras and the Caitanas, halfway between the Breven desert and the Galilee River. Actually, she had no idea where they were, and she didn't particularly care. She was happy to be on the move again, to see the landscape changing before her eyes, growing stern and cold as a disobeyed parent. Food was harder to find, though there was still some game, and Anna taught her how to dig for tubers that she never would have realized were hiding just under the surface of the ground. Their meals changed, but they never went hungry. And even on the coldest nights, when they made sure to put up the tents and sleep together, pallet to pallet, they were always warm.

They had been traveling for a couple of weeks when Tirza fell ill with a retching cough that kept her up all night and made her too weak to travel. Naturally, they made camp on the best site they could find, near water and plentiful firewood, and determined they would not travel on until she was better. A day later, Thaddeus came down with it, and moved out of his own tent to make sure Shua did not also get sick, and then Amram caught the virus, whatever it was. It did not appear to be serious, just wearisome, and everyone rallied around the stricken ones, trying to keep them comfortable.

But with so many hands missing, there was twice as much work to do for everyone who was healthy. Miriam had never hauled so much water in her life, had never chopped so many vegetables or stirred so many pots. She volunteered to launder all the clothes of the sick ones, feeling certain that *she* would not want to still be sleeping in a dress she had coughed on for three days straight, and this task took her one whole day.

Still, Anna looked harassed and Claudia and Shua looked exhausted, and Miriam was fretful, trying to find more that she could do to ease the burdens of those left healthy enough to work. Bartholomew taught her how to build a fire and Shua showed her how to do the mending, though her stitches were clumsy and the hems she set were a little puckered.

One day, Dathan came back with a trio of rabbits slung over his arm, a good bounty now that game was so scarce. Anna, who had not had time to even think about starting dinner yet, threw him a look that was both grateful and exasperated.

"Oh—excellent—I cannot get to them right now," she said. "Unless—Miriam—no, I'll finish this first and then—" She shook her head, clearly overwhelmed at all the chores before her.

Miriam went to their utensil basket and pulled out two long, wicked knives. She crouched beside Dathan where he had knelt to lay his kills on a clean board near the fire.

"Here," she said, handing him one of the blades. "Teach me how to skin a rabbit."

CHAPTER EIGHTEEN

Susannah thought it remarkable how quickly Keren adapted to life in the Eyrie when she herself was finding it even stranger than it had seemed when she first arrived.

Everything made Keren happy. The water room was a revelation and delight to her; there were mornings Susannah did not think Keren would ever emerge, but would stay inside for the rest of her life, soaping her long hair and then rinsing it out under the constantly falling stream of warm water.

The food made her happy, the effortlessly conjured meals that were laid out in the dining room three times a day (while anyone could sneak into the kitchen anytime and steal a bite or two from the cold rooms and cabinets). Keren was used to working hard for every bite she put into her mouth, but here! Like magic it appeared! There was no end to its availability or its variety. The Edori girl was enthralled.

The people made her happy, too, the endless parade of angel and mortal, resident and petitioner, all of them hurrying in one direction or another, engrossed in their own importance. She was especially happy in the company of Miriam's set of friends, for naturally she had become their little pet. Chloe and Zibiah took her anywhere she wanted to go, while Sela felt a special kinship with her—another mortal girl deposited here at the hold where so many of her friends were angels, and sometimes thoughtless. Ahio and Nicholas were never far from Keren's side, and they brought her gifts every time they came back from some errand to another part of the province. Ahio teased her with his usual quiet good humor, but Nicky was besotted with her. He would sit beside her for hours, listening patiently to her childish prattle—or maybe not listening, maybe just looking at her perfect oval face, her flawless dark skin, her braided hair, her dreamy eyes.

Indeed, Keren had always been a pretty girl, Susannah thought, but here at the Eyrie—afforded every luxury of grooming and cosmetics—she was beautiful. And her happiness made her irresistible, made even the suspicious Esther and the dour Enoch smile at her and pat her on the head when she passed by. She adored them as she adored everybody else; no wonder they were drawn to her.

Susannah felt old, watching her—old and weary and charmless and dull. Still, she couldn't help loving Keren. Nobody could.

And it was wonderful to have another Edori beside her at night, in the mornings, to whisper tales to and share reminiscences with. With Keren and Kaski beside her, the too-big bed felt just right; the silence of the night was comfortingly filled with steady, untroubled breathing. When she woke in the night—as she did, at least once, every night—Susannah put her hand out to feel Keren's reassuring presence, and her own tensions would ease. She had a sister beside her, family, someone with whom to share her nightmares. She could fall back asleep without fear.

Once in a while, that quick touch in the night would wake Keren from slumber. "What is it?" the girl would ask sleepily.

"Nothing. Just reminding myself that you're here."

"Are you having that dream again? The same one?"

"Yes."

"Shall I get you some seadrop? I know right where it is."

"No, silly thing, if I want herbs I can get up and get them myself."

"Shall I stay awake and talk to you?"

"If you like."

"I have been having my own dreams, the most wonderful dreams," Keren would say in a sleepy voice. "I am wearing a blue dress—not the blue one that I just bought, a deeper color, and it's got embroidery all around the collar, but I didn't have to do it myself . . ."

Susannah loved hearing Keren's dreams, always full of such minute detail about what she was wearing and how her hair was styled. These usually lulled her back to sleep, and more often than not, to a dreamless state. But she was beginning to dread closing her eyes at night, having the same dream over and over again.

She was in a room of white and silver, of flashing lights and strange mystical apparatuses. It was familiar from her many nighttime journeys there, but it was still an alien place, and it disturbed her to be returned there, over and over again, as if it was a place she must memorize or decipher before the dream finally left her in peace. She was not afraid while she was there, not even while that deep, insistent voice spoke to her, saying words she did not understand; but every time she woke, she found her whole body tense with protest and incomprehension.

She had not meant to mention the dream to Gaaron, but he had surprised her by commenting on her look of exhaustion. He had surprised her by showing up at her door, and looking so tall and forbidding that at first she did not think he was happy to see her. She had expected their first meeting to go a bit more formally. She would have presented herself to him at his rooms, reported on Miriam's behavior, applied for permission to allow Keren to stay with her a month or two, and behaved in every way as the model helpmeet she knew he wanted.

She had not expected to be having pillow fights with shrieking girls and looking like a bad month of travel herself.

That first meeting had been awkward, and in the subsequent days, the awkwardness had not passed. He treated her with a somewhat remote courtesy when they sat together at meals, and made no particular effort to seek her out, either to ask her advice or to share news. It was almost as if she had offended Gaaron somehow, though she could not think how, unless he was not pleased that she had brought Keren here without explicit permission.

And she could not think that was it, because he seemed as fond of Keren as everyone else in the hold was.

Which only served to remind Susannah how, when Gaaron had first told her he was looking for an Edori bride, she had thought Keren must be the one he was seeking.

She could not help but wonder if Gaaron remembered the same thing.

At any rate, included in Gaaron's counsels these days or not, Susannah had had plenty to keep her occupied since her return from Luminaux. First, of course, there was Kaski, the wretched little waif who had tried to starve herself to death while Susannah was gone. Susannah made the girl her first priority, feeding her, petting her, trying to reconnect her to the will to live. For several days, she spent every minute of her day, waking and sleeping, with Kaski, trying to reintegrate her into the regime they had devised before Susannah had left. So the Jansai girl and the Edori woman had gone together to the kitchen to work with Esther and her helpers, had attended classes together with the other hold children, and had received instruction on how to handle a small harp from Lydia. With Susannah beside her, Kaski was perfectly willing to take up these activities again—and gradually, as long as Susannah was still in the hold, Kaski was willing to pursue these exercises on her own.

So that was a victory, of a sort, but Susannah could not persuade herself that all would continue to be well.

As a result of bestowing so much attention on Kaski, she hadn't watched Keren quite as closely as she should have. So when the shipments of fabrics and dresses were delivered to her room at the hold, Susannah was speechless at the quantity and variety that were unfolded.

"Keren—Yovah bless me—child, how much did you buy in Velora?"

"As much as I could," Keren said happily, pulling bundles out of boxes and bags. "Oh, look, Susannah, is this not the most beautiful shade of gold? See, it is woven of threads all dyed different colors, but how lovely they look together."

"Yes, but how did you *pay* for all this? Did you persuade Chloe or Zibiah or Sela—"

"Well, Chloe bought me this dress—no, this one—and Sela bought me this one—with her bracelets, you know. And then one day Nicholas told me I could have whatever I wanted, and so the next time I was down with Ahio I asked him—"

"Sweet Yovah's mercy. So each of them has gotten you something, not knowing that the others—"

"Yes, and Enoch bought me the sweetest little gloves, they're red, they match my ribbons—"

"*Enoch?* But he—"

"And when I saw Esther down there one day getting vegetables at the market, she said why didn't we just walk by some of the jewelry stalls, and she got me this little ring—isn't it pretty?"

"*Esther?*"

"Everyone has been so kind to me," Keren said earnestly. "Truly, Susannah, I did not ask more than once or twice, and I didn't even *ask* Esther. Well, I thought she would say no, so wasn't it nice of her to offer?"

"Mikala—Keren—I—this is so much merchandise. I don't think— for one person—you might need to return some of it."

Keren glanced up from her spoils, spread around her like a Jansai's treasure, and looked stricken. "Oh, no, Susannah, do you think so? Because I can't bear to part with it! Any of it! I love this gold fabric so much—and the green dress—oh, and this white gown, see, it's all lace on the top but silk underneath . . ."

Appalled and embarrassed, Susannah did not know what to do. Not wanting to, but seeing no other choice, she went to Gaaron.

He was deep in conversation with Enoch when she knocked on his open door, but the look of inquiry on his face turned quickly from surprise to a sort of guarded welcome. "Come on in," he invited. "We're almost done here."

Susannah crossed to the small table where, as always, there was a tray of food set out. Somewhat spitefully, she thought, *Well, at least Esther hasn't been so wrapped up in spoiling Keren that she's forgetting to spoil Gaaron as well.* But that was mean-spirited. She sat in one of the more normally designed chairs and poured herself a glass of juice. And then, because why should it go to waste, she began nibbling on some of the sweetbread. It was quite good.

Gaaron joined her in a few moments. "You've been busy lately," was his greeting.

"Yes—I suppose," she said. "I love these pastries."

Gaaron glanced down at his plate and laughed. "Esther's newest ambition. To become a baker. Apparently Keren saw something of this sort in a Velora pastry shop and begged Esther to learn to make it. So now we are going to be treated to a succession of cakes and stollens." He took a bite of one of the sweetbreads. "I have to say, I rather admire Keren's taste in food."

"I am hoping you admire Keren's taste in clothing, too," Susannah said despairingly.

His eyebrows rose. "Something unsuitable?"

"Not exactly. Gaaron, first let me impress upon you how little she is used to having. The Edori travel six days out of seven, and they can bring almost nothing with them. A few dresses, one or two pairs of shoes, maybe an embroidered blouse that they've made for special days. And Keren, as must be obvious, loves things. Beautiful things. And she has—and, you see, everyone seems to be indulging her, because she is really quite sweet and so beautiful—"

"Too many gifts from Velora?" he interrupted. "All my angels are buying her presents?"

"Gaaron, my room almost cannot hold the packages that have begun to arrive. Dresses and shoes and gloves and hats and scarves and—I didn't even stay to see them all opened. I know she must send some of them back, but she—and I know the hold pays for all the charges accrued to it, but I don't perfectly understand the system. What must I tell her? And how can we stop the others from buying for her everything her mercenary little heart desires?"

He was, thank the god, smiling—but then, of course, he hadn't seen quite how many bundles were being unwrapped on the floor of Susannah's room. "The Eyrie is rich enough to pay for a few pretty things for a pretty girl," he said. "None of the angels—or mortals— no one who lives here would spend so rashly that we could not cover the expenses. I'm sure you're right. I'm sure they have given her more than she should expect. But it won't hurt her to be indulged for once in her life. I'll put the word out quietly that Keren will be quite adequately clothed for the next few weeks, and perhaps you can explain to her that there are spending limits. But you don't have to send anything back. I would hate to see her made unhappy."

Susannah's mouth almost dropped open from the surprise, but she clamped her jaws shut and swallowed instead. "That's very kind of you, Gaaron," she said. "I will tell her how generous you are."

He laughed. "And it would not be inappropriate for you to spend a little on yourself now and then," he said almost gaily. "Perhaps you could accompany Keren on her next trip into Velora, and she could pick out a few gowns for you as well."

How mortifying. He disliked her dark colors, her sensible though highly appropriate skirts and blouses. He wanted her to be more vivid, more colorful . . . more like Keren. "Perhaps I'll do that," she said quietly, coming to her feet. "Thank you, Gaaron. Keren will be quite happy."

Now he frowned up at her, as if aware that she had taken something amiss, but not at all sure what. "I hope that you are happy, too, Susannah," he said gravely.

She nodded. "I'm sure the purchase of a few new outfits will have the desired effect," she said, something of an edge in her voice. Before he could offer up a reply to that, she turned and headed for the door. She didn't say good-bye as she passed into the hallway, and he made no other remark before she left.

But she hadn't taken him up on the suggestion right away. It would seem too odd if, after that uncomfortable conversation, she rushed right down to Velora and began designing a new wardrobe. She did start to wear, with more frequency, the more colorful items in her closet—a fuschia blouse, a flame-and-yellow dress, a scarlet vest that looked rather nice over a black skirt. Once or twice she thought she saw an approving look in Gaaron's eyes, but he said nothing.

When she could free herself from Kaski and Keren and her other responsibilities, she spent some time in the music rooms. Ahio had put together a selection of masses for her—all of them, he said, adaptable to harmony and relatively easy to transpose—and she was intent on listening to each one over and over until she found the piece that lingered in her mind and became a part of her mental repertoire. They were all so complicated; that was part of the problem. They were not like little folk songs that she could learn after two verses. They were instead composed of distinct and individual melodies—Ahio called them movements—each with its own tone, rhythm, and complex lines of music. She had been intrigued to learn, however, that every mass consisted of the same choral responses sung at approximately the same place in the piece. No matter what mass the angelica chose, the angels and the mortals and all the others attending the Gloria would be sure to know their parts.

She remembered Miriam's suggestion that Susannah learn the Lochevsky *Magnificat,* and so she sought it out when it did not appear among Ahio's selections, but the very first few minutes of listening convinced her that this was a piece well beyond her ability to learn. Still, she loved Hagar's breathtaking swoops and leaps of sound, particularly the three-and-a-half octave jump that occurred in the first soprano solo. Susannah was not a soprano—but she found herself, from time to time as she went about her daily business in the hold, humming that particular measure of music. In her own key, of course. About one entire octave below Hagar.

But she would fail at the *Magnificat* if she tried to perform it, so she dutifully turned back to Ahio's suggestions. She found herself drawn more and more often to a much simpler *Eleison,* sung, at least on this recording, by a light tenor voice of great clarity and sweetness.

She didn't know who the singer was, but she had become familiar enough with Uriel's voice to know it wasn't the Archangel, and the woman who joined her solos to his was not Hagar. Two anonymous angels from the founding of Samaria, serenading Susannah as she sat, rapt and motionless, on the floor of the room they had probably helped construct. It seemed strange to her that it did not seem stranger, what she was hearing and how she was hearing it. Perhaps her whole life had become so unfamiliar that she couldn't pick out the truly miraculous events anymore.

Gradually, she stopped playing the other possibilities and instead played the *Eleison* over and over, sometimes twice a day if she could spare the four hours. It became the music in her head almost constantly, though as a rule almost any tune could be jostling about in there, ready to come out in a snatch of song when she was preoccupied by something else. Now, there was no room for anything but the *Eleison*—the tenor solo, the soprano solo, any part of it from supplication to amen. Sometimes it even served as the background music to her dreams, accompanying her through the chrome-and-white corridors of her nighttime visitation.

And even that, when she woke at night and considered it, did not seem so odd.

Without even making the conscious attempt, she began creating her own harmonies to the *Eleison*, for a while experimenting as the mood struck her, but gradually settling on a more permanent score. On the opening movement, her harmonic line matched the solo one note for note, though some of the intervals were creative and not a few were dissonant, just for a beat or two. On the first soprano solo, she crafted a descant that was so radically different in tempo and mood that it sounded like an entirely separate song, though it was quite hauntingly beautiful when sung against the main melody. With the two duets she was obedient, tamely accepting the harmonies of the composer, but on the final tenor solo, she played with the music a little, embroidering a little here, echoing a little there. She liked the way it sounded.

She was not, however, confident enough of her own musical ability that she would even consider performing her own versions without first getting Ahio's approval. So one afternoon, she invited him to join her down in the music rooms to hear what she'd accomplished.

"You've already written the harmony?" he asked, amused. "I thought I was going to do that for you once you'd picked the piece."

"Oh—that's right—well, you can probably come up with something even better than I have," she said in a rush, because she greatly respected Ahio's abilities and she truly had forgotten.

He was grinning. "Probably not," he said. "At any rate, I can't wait to hear what you've dreamed up. I'll come down this afternoon. I have to finish this for Enoch first, though."

"I'll leave the door open for you," she said.

Which was how it happened that she was sitting on the floor in the music room, out of sight of the hallway, and momentarily in silence as she hunted for a new disk to insert in the machine, when Gaaron came down the hall with Zack and Jude in tow. Normally, of course, anyone using a music room would shut the door to perfect the acoustics, so it was entirely natural that Gaaron would assume the entire hall was empty.

"I see both of you boys are none the worse for wear from your three weeks helping Enoch," Gaaron said, his voice pleasant.

Zack growled something unintelligible and Susannah frowned, trying to remember what exactly had happened. Oh yes—a dreadful thing. Zack and Jude carrying mortal boys up into the air and then dropping them, taking care to catch them before putting them nonchalantly on the ground. It had been the talk of the hold until Susannah arrived with Keren, happening during both her absence and Gaaron's. Gaaron had told Enoch to have the boys labor in the storerooms until he came up with a suitable punishment, a word that caused Susannah to shiver.

Then again, she had flown in an angel's arms, and she knew just how petrifying it was to look down and realize that only chancy luck and unshakable goodwill were keeping her from plunging headfirst onto the ground. She could not imagine being the mortal boys terrorized by the angels in such a way.

But she hated to think of Gaaron being unmerciful.

"I've given some thought to what I can do to impress upon you that what you did was not only wrong and dangerous, it was harmful to you and Jude as well," Gaaron said.

There was a sharp crack of laughter from Zack. "Didn't hurt *me* any," he said scornfully. "Didn't hurt them, either. Stupid babies. Afraid to fly."

"There are many things I'm afraid of," Gaaron said. "Flying doesn't happen to be one of them. I'd hate to be dropped in the middle of the ocean, though, trying to find my way to shore. I think my wings would drag me down and I'd drown. I think you would, too," he added thoughtfully. "If you were set down in the ocean, I'd think you'd find the water as unfamiliar an element to survive in as Silas and Mark found the air."

There was a moment of dreadful silence. "You're going to drop us in the *ocean*?" Jude demanded in a squeaky voice. "To *drown*?"

"You can't do that," Zack said quickly, but not as if he entirely believed it. "You can't."

"No, I can't," Gaaron said. "But I know I have to do something to teach both of you how serious your actions were—and how fragile and precious life is. Even the life of someone unlike you. Even the life of someone you do not like."

"Silas isn't precious," Zack muttered.

"He is to someone," Gaaron said.

"Well, so what is it that you're going to do?" Zack demanded.

"I'm sending you on a journey."

Susannah felt a certain dismay shiver through her. He had threatened once to do that, to send Zack and Jude to Breven—and, after all, she had put the thought in his head when she suggested he send Miriam to Luminaux. But Breven was so far away, and full of such unreliable citizens. She was not sure she would turn anyone over to the Jansai.

Zack made a little offhand grunt, accompanied, she was sure, by a characteristic careless toss of his unkempt black hair. "Yeah, Breven," he said. "You said that before."

"Manadavvi country," Gaaron corrected.

Everyone within hearing distance was surprised, including Susannah, who should not have been listening.

"What would we want to go there for?" Jude asked.

"You'll be accompanying two women and two babies who are taking a trip from the Eyrie to Constantine Lesh's estate," Gaaron said. "I can provide you with maps, but I believe the women know the way. They were born there, though both of them have lived at the Eyrie for many years. They'll be coming back after their visit home."

"I can't carry a woman and a baby," Jude protested. He was taller than most mortal boys his age, but skinny; he probably didn't have Susannah's body mass, and *she* certainly couldn't have carried a mother and a child anywhere.

"*I* can," Zack said.

"Oh, you won't be flying," Gaaron said. "You'll be walking alongside them. Or riding, if you can find a horse to carry you, but generally they shy at our wings. You'd be thrown five times a day. Walking's probably safer. More comfortable."

There was another short silence. "You want us to walk from here to northern Gaza?" Zack said. "It'll take—weeks! We'll—why would we do that? Someone else can fly them there. *You* could do it."

"I could, but I'm too busy," Gaaron said. His voice was perfectly calm, perfectly reasonable, but absolutely unyielding. "They need to bring a cart with them, full of possessions to return to Constantine. Something about a piece of furniture that has been in the Lesh family for generations. That really needs to be transported over land."

"So? Why does it have to be me and Jude?" Zack wanted to know.

"Because as leader of the hold I am asking you to perform a task for me. As you grow older and more responsible, I will often have missions that I will send you on—to pray for rain, to pray for plague medicines. I have to know now if you can be entrusted with those important duties, that will determine if the people of Bethel live or die. If you cannot be, of course, then you cannot be useful members of the hold, and you will not be permitted to live here."

Now the silence was awful.

"That's one reason," Gaaron said, still speaking in that reasonable, inflexible voice. "Another reason is that I realize I am partially at fault for your recent actions. I have not trusted you, Zack, or you, Jude, with the tasks that any angel should be expected to perform. I have thought you were too young, too immature—with the result that you acted irresponsibly and cruelly. But I believe that if I give you a chance to perform a hard task, you will perform it well. You will see that the lives of four other people are completely dependent on you. I am certain that, under your guidance, they will make it safely to Gaza, and that they will be fed with the food you gather, and that they will be kept warm by the fires you build along the road, and the water that you fetch for them when you make camp too far from a riverbed."

"I don't know how to make a fire," Jude said.

"Don't you? Then you'd better learn. You leave in two days."

"Two days!" Zack exclaimed. "But we—you can't just—"

"And the third reason I want you to accompany these women on the journey," Gaaron said, raising his voice to drown out Zack's, "is that I believe they would both like a chance to get to know you better. Silas' mother and Mark's aunt. They came to me and asked what kind of people could be so cruel as to torment these boys. I thought a journey of some weeks would give them a chance to learn more about each of you—and you to learn about them. As I said, Silas and Mark are precious to someone. As you are precious to someone. I thought it would not hurt to remind you that love is a powerful force in this world, invisible though it seems."

Again, not a word from either of the boys. Susannah herself was not sure she could have spoken, had she been sitting nearby and invited to participate in the conversation. What a risk, but a glorious one, to send these two wild boys off on such a tricky mission! Surely Gaaron had built safeguards into his plan—surely he or one of his other angels would fly overhead from time to time, to monitor the progress of the traveling band and make sure the angel boys did not desert the very vulnerable women. There was a devious kind of elegance to his solution, offering both boys a chance to be so good, if they didn't take the much easier course of being bad. Was he right? Or would this difficult journey prove them to be as incorrigible as it sometimes seemed they already were?

"What if we won't go?" Zack asked finally. "Will you send us to Breven then?"

"Oh, no," Gaaron said coolly. "I'll set you out on the streets of Velora to do as you will. You'll be no more responsibility of mine or the hold's. But I'm sure you'll be able to take care of yourselves."

"You can't . . ." Jude breathed, but he did not finish his sentence. Zack said nothing at all.

"So, you understand the terms?" Gaaron said briskly. "You need to pack your own clothes for the journey—winter gear, I'd imagine, since it's getting cold. You need to consult with Esther about what kind of food to bring, though you'll have to obtain more food on the road. I can help you map out your route, there are plenty of small towns on the way. You shouldn't have to camp out more than every other night, and I'd think you could buy enough food in any small town to see you through a few days' travel. And you will have to learn to build a fire."

"*Nobody* knows how to build a fire!" Jude burst out. "Nobody living in the hold, anyway!"

"I think the angelica does," Gaaron said. "Why don't you go ask her? She might even have some other tips you'll find useful for long-distance travel."

Now Susannah had to hide her mouth in her sleeve to muffle the sound of her laughter. Sweet Yovah singing, she could terrify them by the hour, describing the horrors they might encounter upon the road. Of course, Gaaron was right; a trip between the Eyrie and Manadavvi country was filled with enough small towns and large farming settlements that they would not really have to live the rough life of the Edori, but she could paint a picture of enough privation to make them grateful for even the meanest shelter on a cold night.

"So you'd best go seek out Susannah sometime today or tomorrow," Gaaron continued, "and then pack your gear."

"I don't want to go to Manadavvi country," Jude said.

There was a ruffling sound; Susannah imagined Gaaron shrugging his great arched wings. "Fine," he said. "You will still need to pack your belongings for your move to Velora."

"But you can't—"

"Jude!" Zack hissed. "Shut up!"

"Maybe you'll want to think it over," Gaaron said. "I'll be happy to discuss the whole journey with you later, but right now I've got to meet with a petitioner. You can come find me tomorrow morning and tell me what you've decided."

"You can't really turn us out of the hold," Jude said.

Again, that sound of rustling silk; Gaaron had shrugged again. "It is interesting that you believe I cannot," he said. "I must go. We'll talk tomorrow."

And there was another soft sound of feather and stone, as Gaaron turned and headed away down the corridor. The two boys almost immediately began arguing, Zack's voice rough and angry, Jude's high and frightened. They were only a few paces behind the angel, and their tense, excited voices faded within a few minutes.

Susannah stayed where she was on the floor of the music room, her knees drawn up to her chest, her arms wrapped so tightly around her folded legs that every muscle in her body ached from cramp. Her ankles hurt, her bent knees hurt, the sinews in her stretched arms burned with protest. She was dumbstruck by Gaaron's bold and perilous plan. She was left breathless by the man himself.

She remembered Gaaron telling her how he was used to accepting hard tasks. How he did not view the role of Archangel as a position of privilege but as a grave responsibility, hedged about with obligation and difficult choices. She had always thought him a good man, though a little dull—strong, but devoid of ardor. He had no glamour, this Gabriel Aaron, and none of that quick joy that had characterized Dathan, that had drawn her to Dathan like a cold hand seeking sparkling flame. But how had she missed the great roaring fire of Gaaron's passion? How had she failed to see the controlled but inextinguishable blaze that was Gaaron's obsession for justice and honor—the great light of his soul that shone through the measured sentences, the thoughtful silences, the quiet decisions? His was a flame that would not burn out, that would struggle valiantly against any darkness, till it found a way to sear away malevolence and reignite hope. His was a flame that would not falter, that could be trusted to offer both heat and light on the grimmest night at the darkest hour.

She wanted to put her hands out and warm them at that fire.

Instead, she held herself more tightly, almost rocking there on the chilly stone floor, feeling heat course through her as revelation tingled across her skin. Dathan (poor Dathan) had asked if she was in love with Gaaron, and she had said *not yet*; and that was still true, she was sure that was still true. She was in awe of him, she thought that described it better. She was in awe of him and she was a little afraid of him, and she thought she might, as all the people of his hold did, feel some adoration for this man, this angel. But that was not love. That was not love as she remembered it.

She squeezed her arms more tightly around her body, and her whole body protested, fire at her sharply bent knees, fire at both strained shoulders. So she slowly unlocked herself, unkinked her muscles and bones, and pulled herself to a standing position, though it caused a few twinges of pain. Her left leg was clenching and relaxing with a recurring spasm and she stamped her foot a few times to try and relieve it. A muscle in her right arm flared and knotted in protest as well, and she lifted her left hand to rub away the sharpness and the pain.

But her hand touched, instead of coiled muscle, hard glass, and she realized at once what knife was poised with its crystal tip against her skin. She did not strip away her woolen shirt to inspect the colors that she knew would be rioting in her Kiss; she did not want to witness the dance of flame and fever. She knew a god's hallucinatory celebration when she saw one, and this one she did not need to see.

Chapter Nineteen

It seemed to Gaaron that every time he turned around, there was Keren.

Every time he went to the dining room, she was seated there with her ever-expanding circle of friends, lingering over breakfast, enjoying a luxuriously long lunch, taking a second or third course at dinner. When he signed up for a mid-afternoon shift to sing the harmonics, Keren was there before him, performing a duet with Sela or joining a chorus that included Nicholas and Ahio. If he happened to go into Velora for the day, she was strolling the streets with Zibiah or Chloe, looking wistfully at the fabric she had been forbidden to buy, and accepting, with a look of happiness so incandescent that even Gaaron couldn't begrudge her, the illicit small purchase that her friendly companion would make on her behalf.

Naturally, anytime he went to seek out Susannah, Keren was at her side. Keren and Kaski and any number of other miscreants who had nothing better to do than create worries for the angelica-to-be.

It was not as though he minded having Keren at the hold. He didn't. She was like a drift of summer darkness, scented with herbs and honeysuckle, adorned still with the last affectionate kiss of sunset. To sit with her for an hour was to grow both relaxed and restless, to be both stirred up and reminded of satiety. Everything about her— everything, from her narrow dark face to her lustrous black hair, to her quick hands and easy laugh—blended innocence and sensuality to such a degree that it was impossible to overlook either trait.

He no longer wondered why the Lohoras had been willing to send her so far away, to live with strangers and take up allali ways. He wondered instead how one tribe had ever been able to contain her.

But she was a good-hearted girl, completely unself-conscious. She would turn that flirtatious smile on a woman as well as a man. Flirtatious might be the wrong word, he thought. It was instead an inviting smile, an inclusive one, a smile that said, *Oh, I can tell you like me, and isn't that fun? Because I like you, too.* Maybe that was, after all, what made Keren so seductive: her genuine happiness.

It amused Gaaron to see Nicholas so caught up in the Edori's spell, for Nicholas was the most easygoing of lovers who could not have told you, if you'd asked him, how many girls he had kissed. He had always taken love quite lightly—unlike Ahio, who had had a few serious affairs, and seemed quite shaken whenever they ended—and any girl who had ever loved Nicky talked about him warmly still. Nicholas neither reaped hearts nor broke them, and love had always made him charming and careless. But then, everything made Nicky charming and careless; no reason love should be any different.

Except it was different this time.

Gaaron kept wanting to ask Susannah what she thought of Nicholas and Keren, did she notice, was she worried, had she given any thought to what might happen when Keren left the hold to return to her tribe? But it seemed he never saw Susannah unless Keren was nearby, and, of course, he could not ask her then. He did not want to summon Susannah to see him privately—what a strange thing, that an affianced man and woman did not naturally find themselves alone together, talking, if nothing else—merely so they could discuss Keren.

Though he did wish there would be an excuse to see Susannah privately.

She had approved of his handling of the mess with Zack and Jude. That he knew, because she had told him. It was at dinner the next night, and their table was full with the hold residents who took turns seating themselves with the Archangel-elect. Susannah shared the table with him, of course, and this night so did Keren and Nicholas and a few of the mortals who had lived there since before his father's time. The Edori women were laughing.

"Those two boys will be stuffing themselves till they are sick today and tomorrow," Susannah said gaily. "You should have heard Keren! Telling tales about eating raw horsemeat on nights when it was too cold to build a fire."

"Well, *you*." Keren hooted. " 'One night it was so cold that I made a blanket of snow, and crawled beneath it, and it was warmer than the outer night air.' No one sleeps under *snow*," she added, as if the hold residents were so dense and so inexperienced that they might actually find such a story credible.

"If you're that cold, you sleep with the horses," Susannah added.

"If you're that cold, you move down to southern Jordana and camp for the winter," Keren retorted.

"Did you, in fact, teach them how to build a fire?" Gaaron asked.

"Yes, and they caught on to it quite quickly," Susannah said. "They were so enthralled with their new skill, in fact, that when they return to live in the Eyrie, I'm afraid you might have to worry about them burning the place down."

"If they return to the Eyrie to live, I am hoping they will no longer be the kind of boys who burn things down," Gaaron said.

He caught Susannah's look, brimming with some emotion, and he was sure she wanted to tell him something. But she glanced around the table at all their listeners, and she did not. Anyway, she wouldn't have had a chance to speak, since Keren immediately began telling some new story, not about Zack and Jude, and everyone at the table was laughing. Even Susannah was laughing. Gaaron turned his eyes to Keren and smiled, though he had not heard a word of the tale. When he glanced back at Susannah, she was looking at him again, but she was no longer smiling.

So that was one missed opportunity, and there were others. And some days there were no opportunities at all. This was a busy season for Gaaron, for all the angels, because Samaria never made the transition easily through the seasons. The autumn harvests could so quickly be ruined by rain, the early winter crops could be so completely devastated by drought, that weather intercessions were almost a daily requirement. Gaaron sent his angels off on as many of these missions as he could, but he was traveling much of the time himself, singing the prayers for rain or the prayers for sun. He enjoyed the work; he liked the strong sense of connection he felt when he prayed to the god for a change in climate. He could feel it, as if it were a rope woven of glitter and breath. The prayer itself rooted in the sere winter soil, twisted upward like an aerobic vine, coiled once around his torso, and spiraled up some unimaginable distance to wrap itself around the wrist of the god. Thus they were all laced together, god, angel, and Samaria itself, through the medium of prayer and the force of conviction. Every time Gaaron left the site of a successful weather intercession, he felt energized, radiant, flushed with the god's approval.

He would do a weather intercession every day, for just that sensation, except that there was too much else to do.

He had given his angels strict instructions, which he followed himself, to fly low to the ground when they were on their way to any corner of Bethel, and to watch what went on below. Did they see dark-skinned strangers lurking under the yellowing leaves of the cornstalks? Did they spot smoke from a catastrophic fire—or the blackened remains of a leveled farmhouse? Did they notice anything unusual at all?

For the past few weeks, such incidents had been nonexistent, and both Neri and Adriel reported perfect calm in their realms as well. Maybe the marauders had reached the end of their fury, or their resources; maybe, if they were visitors, they had moved on. But unease flew with Gaaron everywhere he traveled, perched on his spine between his working wings, and worry wrapped her cold little hands around his throat and whispered in his ear as he flew.

During this time Gaaron was also, as always, in high demand among the merchants of Velora. He met regularly with the governing council, and informally with the more powerful retailers and wholesalers who ran the city. The matter of Myra Shapping seemed to have been settled to everyone's satisfaction. Her business was struggling a little, but everyone was sure that, in a year's time, she would have recovered both her poise and her financial independence. But there were other matters to discuss, trade agreements with the river merchants, deceptive practices attempted by the Jansai, the higher prices set by the Bethel farmers because of a corn blight that had affected many crops. Gaaron found these details less interesting but equally crucial to the success of life in the province, and so he attended meetings, and listened gravely to arguments, and never failed to give his considered opinion, even when it was not popular.

"Well, I hate to say it, but you're right," one of the councilmen said to Gaaron one afternoon as they wrapped up a session. "Though it makes my very bones ache to think of giving the same price to a Semorrah merchant as a Luminaux craftsman."

"The day will come when a Semorran stamp will be as valued as one from Luminaux," Gaaron said with a smile. "Or more so."

The man shook his head. "I can't see it. Stupid place to live, anyway, in the middle of the river. Stupid place to build a city. My son and I went out there just last month. Almost drowned trying to cross the Galilee. I don't think I'll be trading there quite so often."

"Your choice, of course," Gaaron said. "I confess I find it a strange place myself. But that won't stop it from becoming the trading capital of the three provinces."

They talked a few more minutes before Gaaron headed outside. The merchantman had a shop in the heart of the bazaar district, a place that Gaaron rarely went because he rarely felt the need to purchase anything. But he remembered that he had encouraged Susannah to buy herself something new, a gift for herself, and that she had consequently started wearing a little more color. Perhaps she would appreciate a gift from his hand, some gesture of—affection, he might call it. Friendship.

Perhaps she wouldn't, but now that the idea was in his head he would at least have to look at the merchandise.

So he turned down one long row of stalls, skipping the arrays of fruits and vegetables and going directly for the fabrics. He really didn't know much about buying clothing for women. The times he'd purchased something for Miriam, she'd selected it herself. He couldn't remember buying gifts for others.

Still, he found he liked pausing in front of a vendor's table and picking up a bolt of cloth, imagining it against Susannah's dark skin and black hair. Some of the brighter, busier patterns struck him as too jarring for her taste, but he was drawn to a length of figured coral cotton, and he stretched it between his hands to examine it.

"Oh, that is *just* the prettiest color. I was admiring it this morning but I couldn't convince Ahio to buy it for me," said an excited voice in his ear. Keren, of course. He should have come here looking for her. "But, see? Isn't it perfect against my hair?" And she took the fabric from his hands and swathed her head with it. He had to admit it looked beautiful.

The shopkeeper (probably familiar with Keren by now as the best customer he'd had in a decade) hurried over with a smile on his thin face. "All Edori women look their most gorgeous in these deep, dark colors," the man purred. "See, and here is an apricot-gold silk—also most alluring against that skin and that hair."

Keren obligingly unwrapped a few yards of the apricot silk and draped this over her shoulders like a shawl. The two colors, gold and coral, did not look so well together, but Gaaron liked them both equally. He pulled the cotton from Keren's head and studied the effect of the unadorned silk.

"How much would someone need to make a dress?" he asked.

"It depends on the dress," Keren said promptly. "Several yards, at least. Were you thinking of buying some for me?"

"No, you wretch, I was thinking of buying some for Susannah."

She clapped her hands together and looked just as pleased as if he'd offered to buy out the stall for her pleasure. "Oh, that will make her so happy! Susannah is quite a seamstress, you know, but she doesn't have much time to sew these days."

"We have seamstresses at the hold who can make clothes for her."

Keren turned back to the vendor's table and began sorting through piles. "Well, I would definitely get both the gold and the coral, but I saw something the other day that I think she would like. It was red, but a very dark red, almost wine-colored, but redder than that. I wanted it, but then I decided I already had two red dresses, I didn't need more."

Gaaron grinned, because that was patently untrue, and watched as she deftly separated out the inferior fabrics from the preferred ones. "Aha!" she exclaimed, and pulled out a folded scrap of red. Even Gaaron could tell there was not enough fabric there to make a dress or even, probably, a shirt, but it was a gorgeous color, somewhere between flame and sunset. It was woven of some heavy thread that Gaaron (no seamstress) could not identify, but it felt heavy and substantial in his hands.

"What would she do with this—this little piece?" he asked.

Keren took it from him. "Oh, she could make a scarf, or a belt, or a headband. She could sew it into a panel of another dress, here, right at the bodice, wouldn't that be pretty? Or she could just fold it up and lay it across her pillow at night, because I think it would give her happy dreams to put her head on such a lovely color."

He could not help it; her fanciful words made him smile. "And you think she would like it?"

"Yes, *and* the gold silk *and* the bolt of cotton. You must buy all three so she is really impressed."

"I could wrap them for the angelo now," the vendor interposed.

Gaaron spread his hands, and his bracelets flashed sapphire sparks as they caught the late-afternoon sunlight. "Very well. All of the red cloth, and enough of the other two fabrics to make a suitable dress from each."

Keren clapped her hands together again, and then flew over to give him a kiss on the cheek. He laughed down at her. "I haven't bought *you* a present," he teased.

"Yes, but Susannah will let me borrow her dresses or at least she will give me all the leftover scraps, so it is just as if you have bought me something," she replied earnestly.

He laughed again and tousled her hair. She gave a little shriek and pulled back, crying, "Don't muss me up!" He laughed harder and ruffled her hair even more. She laughed, too, and backed away from him, one hand on top of her head, the other extended as if to fend him off. But when the vendor reappeared with the packages neatly wrapped in brown paper and twine, she extended both hands with alacrity.

"Thank you, sir. And thank you, Gaaron," she said primly.

Before he could say, "Don't forget that those are not for you," her attention was caught by something just ahead of them down the row of stalls.

"Susannah! Susannah!" she cried, and went skipping forward toward the other Edori woman, whom Gaaron had not even noticed coming toward them. His head snapped around and he had a smile at the ready—but it was clear she had seen them first, and she was nowhere near smiling. Momentarily confused and disappointed, he felt his mind do a quick backward scan of the most recent few minutes, and realized that she must have thought he was buying gifts for Keren, someone who did not need any more gifts from anyone. How to explain that away without looking ridiculous?

But in this, at least, Keren was his ally. "Look what Gaaron has bought you!" Keren was exclaiming, tearing back an edge of the paper to show off the apricot silk. "Oh, and there's more, this lovely sort of orange color and a red square. I wanted the red for me, but he said I could not have it," Keren added artlessly. "But I told him you would give me any pieces that were left over, and you will, won't you?"

Now Susannah's face was a little flushed, and some confusion showed in her own expression as well. "What? Oh, of course, you can have what you—but are you sure Gaaron intended this all for me?"

By this time Gaaron had arrived beside them, and he bestowed a serious, searching look upon his intended. "I know your years of Edori frugality have made you reluctant to spend money recklessly," he said, attempting to invest his words with some humor. "So I thought I would nudge you along a little. Keren helped me choose the items, and I trusted her taste more than mine."

"Thank you—they are quite beautiful—no, Keren, I do not believe there will be even a ribbon's length of red left over for you," Susannah said. She, too, seemed to be attempting lightness, though that confusion and—could it be?—embarrassment still lingered at the corners of her eyes and made her voice somewhat unsteady. "How kind of you, Gaaron. You chose quite well."

"I am *so* thirsty," Keren announced. "There is a little shop, up around the corner, do you know it? We could get something to drink."

"I'm sure Gaaron has much to do—"

"No, I am at your disposal," he interrupted. "Keren's right. Let's get something to drink."

So Susannah smiled and acquiesced, and they walked the three blocks through the bright awnings to the little coffee shop that enjoyed Keren's patronage. But Gaaron could not rid himself of the sensation that Susannah was not happy with something that had transpired, though she pretended to be at ease and in her usual good humor. It took some of his own pleasure out of the purchase and the chance-met encounter, and it made Keren's aimless chatter grate on his nerves much more than it usually did. He considered handing over to her his sapphire bracelets and inviting her to go buy whatever she liked, if she would only leave him alone with Susannah for ten minutes, but he was afraid that that gesture, like the purchase of the fabric, might be misconstrued. So they had a pleasant little respite, sipping drinks, eating pastries, and talking over the events of the day—but of the three of them, although all of them laughed and smiled, only Keren was truly merry.

CHAPTER TWENTY

Once the coughing sickness finally left their camp, the Lohoras packed their tents and moved on. They were following the backbone of the Caitanas now, the looping mountain range caught all the humidity of the cloud masses as they swept east across Samaria and dumped it out as rain before it could reach the desert around Breven. So it was wet, and it was cold, and Miriam was thoroughly miserable the first day that they were back on the road.

They camped for the night, intending to move on in the morning but putting up tents anyway just for shelter against the weather. The wood burned badly, so supper was slow, and no one really had the heart or the energy to sing after the meal. Miriam was one of the first to turn in, though her tentmates followed within the hour. She scooted over close to Tirza to soak up a little of the other woman's body heat, and Tirza reached out to pat her on the shoulder. The small gesture of comfort helped send Miriam off the ledge into a floating sleep.

The morning dawned absolutely clear and absolutely frigid. The flat brown stalks of grass around the camp were weighed down with patterns of frost; the air itself felt spiked with pinpoints of ice. Miriam stepped from the tent and inhaled great cold gusts of air while the sun stared down at her, mercilessly bright, and she smiled. Beautiful morning, spectacular day. She could not wait to set out into that limitless light and see what the world might offer.

Tirza emerged to stand beside her, and she, too, lifted her face to the hard sunlight and took in deep breaths of that cleansed, cold air. The older woman turned to her, smiling, but all she said was, "Have you had time to start the fire?"

"Not yet," Miriam said, striding forward. "I'll get to it now."

The weather held fine for the next two days, though it continued cold. Miriam learned how to dress for walking against the wind, and she also learned—rather to her surprise—how quickly she could adapt to the lower temperatures. In fact, she rarely felt cold while they were on the move, since her layers of woolens and outer garments trapped her body heat and kept her skin almost rosy. Her toes and fingers grew numb, but once she complained about this, Anna lent her a pair of wool socks for her feet and made her a pair of gloves for her hands. And after that, the only weather she minded was the rain, and everybody hated traveling in the rain.

They were still heading north and west, aiming for the great circle of mountains that ringed the Plain of Sharon. Miriam had trouble envisioning their route, so one evening after they'd camped, Dathan drew it out for her, using a stick to scratch lines and ovals in a patch of dirt. She was rather impressed by the distance they had covered, more than half the length of Jordana. She would not have thought she would be able to walk so far.

"If we turned east, we'd pass Windy Point and then, eventually, come upon the ocean," Dathan told her, sketching in these details as well. "And if we could build boats and sail across the sea, eventually we'd come to Ysral."

Miriam laughed at him. "Ysral does not exist," she told him. "It's a place the Edori have made up."

He grinned at her. His stick made undulating lines in the dirt by the coastline; she supposed these were meant to indicate the waves of the ocean. On the other side of the squiggly lines he drew a roundish mass, roughly half the size of Samaria. "It exists," he told her. "It is right here. We think. Or maybe a little north. Or a little south. But if we built boats and sailed for days, we would eventually find it. And someday we *will* build boats and sail away, all the Edori, and live in the land that Yovah has set aside especially for us."

She shrugged and came to her feet, brushing the mud from her knees. "I figure I'm having quite enough travel as it is, just moving around Jordana with the Lohoras," she said. "I don't need to go off in any boat and try to find some mythical continent. But you go ahead and look for it."

He smiled and reached out a hand so she could pull him to his feet. "Someday," he said with mock solemnity. "Someday you will see."

She laughed and left him, going down to the river to wash herself as thoroughly as the cold weather would allow. They had camped by water for two days running, but they might be a day or two on the road before they intersected their next major waterway—the Galilee River—and Miriam wanted to bathe while the chance was there. She'd become a pretty efficient washer, able to get herself and her clothes clean in something under fifteen minutes, though to really wash her hair took a little longer. Keeping in mind the scarcity of opportunities in the upcoming week, today she took the extra time to soap and rinse her hair, then braided it back still wet to keep it out of her face.

It was getting so long. She had always worn her hair a little past shoulder length, but now it was more than halfway down her back. And a great nuisance, even when it was clean, when she let it hang free while they were traveling, so mostly she kept it in a single braid. She wondered every once in a while how the severe style suited her face. She was used to curling her hair and arranging it carefully so that it framed her face just so. But she didn't have a mirror. She had no idea what she looked like. Good enough for the Lohoras to like her; good enough for Daniel to kiss her. That was enough for Miriam.

They made it to the Galilee River three days later. They were a little north of Semorrah, which disappointed Miriam. She had rather wanted to see the fabulous, fanciful city again, for, from the stories she had heard, amazing new architecture was being added every day, changing the skyline and the legendary status of the city almost as you watched.

But the Edori avoided cities, except for Luminaux, preferring to trade in small towns used to itinerant travelers and unpretentious goods. Semorrah was too fine for them. Miriam looked down at her now rather ragged blue dress, sighed, and had to agree.

They camped by the great river that more or less bisected Samaria, the one it would take a couple of rafts and maybe a day to cross here so close to its source. Down by Luminaux it was broader and gentler, though still not an easy ford. There were only a few places along its whole single-minded southward course that the Galilee was an unadventurous river to cross. The Lohoras had navigated it once just a few days outside of Luminaux; they might not pass over it again until spring, preferring to stay in Jordana for the winter.

Then again, they just might traverse the Plain of Sharon, exit into eastern Gaza, and meander on down the western coast of Bethel. They hadn't decided yet. They would camp a few days here, camp a few days near Mount Galo, and talk things over. Eventually a plan would emerge, and they would all be happy with it, and they would move forward as they had agreed—until a chance-met band of fellow travelers, or an unexpectedly good campsite, or illness, or some other random factor occurred to change their plans again.

They set up their tents a little distance from the river, but its incessant self-important rumbling was still audible in the camp. It sounded like nothing so much as a council of Manadavvi come to tell Gaaron what they had decided about something stupid, Miriam thought. The idea amused her; she had never given the river, *any* inanimate thing, a personality before.

Her disdain for the river's personality did not keep her from heading downstream immediately, however, to get herself completely clean and, in the process, completely chilled.

She hurried back up the riverbank, slipping a little on the icy mud, and dressed herself with hands that felt numb to the bone. As usual, she had taken her bath alone, since she couldn't quite overcome the modesty of her early training enough to strip down in front of everyone else in camp. No one seemed to think it strange; in fact, Anna often took advantage of the fact that Miriam bathed earlier or later than the others to have her fetch back another bucket of water or wash out just one more forgotten shirt.

Her cold feet felt too lumpish to fit back into her shoes but she forced them, and then tied the laces with clumsy fingers. She was more tired than she had realized, or maybe the cold water had made her tired. She almost didn't want to go to the effort of putting back on every layer of clothing, retying her shawl around her waist, settling her empty bag over her shoulder and using it to hold whatever interesting items she might gather as she trudged back to camp. But this much she had learned during her two months traveling with the Edori: Never leave anything behind that you might someday want again, and never miss an opportunity to pick up something that might be useful in the future.

So she knotted the shawl at her hip and settled the bag over her shoulder, and dumped in a handful of river rocks, since she was there and they were there and they were the smooth, round kind that she liked best. And—what a find, at this time of year—there was a little stubby shrub of marrowroot, its leaves shriveled and brown by now but still (she had discovered) tasty in stew. So she stripped the branch and tucked the leaves into a small pocket on the outside of the bag. Not ten steps from the river and she'd already picked up a couple of treasures. Always on the lookout. That was the Edori way.

She walked back slowly, hoping some sensation would come back into her feet, picking up a couple more throwing stones and the dry spiny skeleton of a dead sapling. It would make good kindling, something else that was always useful, though it was a rather cumbersome item to carry. She hooked one of the spindly little branches through the knot at her waist and let the sapling dangle down her side. Now she had both hands free again. Another Edori goal. As long as you had one hand free, you could pick up one more item. The very thing you might discover that you needed the most.

The only other thing Miriam found on her way back, though, was another rock, hard and black and sharp-edged, but shaped perfectly for her hand. She didn't immediately put it in her bag, but walked along holding it so she could admire its glittery color and jagged contours. She would have to ask Dathan where it came from, or what special minerals it contained. He often knew the answers to questions like that. He could tell her if a stone was good enough and hard enough to chip down to a spear point, or if it was too soft to make into a useful weapon. This one looked like a weapon, she thought. Dathan would like it.

She was only a dozen yards from camp, and still admiring her rock, when she looked up and saw the black strangers spying on the Lohoras.

She came to a dead halt before her mind had even processed the picture. Three black-clad men in strange shiny hats, kneeling behind a boulder and watching the Lohoras put up their tents. They sat so still that they looked like shadows crouched behind the rock, just as insubstantial, just as harmless. She did not even know why she had bothered to glance over at them, what abbreviated gesture or glint of sunlight on unfamiliar material had caught her attention. For they made no motion. They made no sound. They merely sat and watched.

As Miriam stood and gaped.

She remembered the stranger she had seen in the farmland in Bethel, dressed just like these were, who had watched her just a moment and disappeared. But these three showed no signs of disappearing. She remembered, too, Kaski's story of marauders who lifted long thin sticks of metal and shot fire at the unsuspecting Jansai.

Were these three merely watching, or did they intend to attack? What could she do? *What could she do?*

She could not believe that no one saw her. Not one of the three black men sensed her presence, thirty feet away, and whirled around to crisp her with flame. No one in the busy camp caught sight of her and called out, "Miriam! You lazy allali girl! Come help with supper!" Everyone seemed completely oblivious, the Edori unaware of the strangers, the strangers blind to Miriam's presence—and Miriam, agonized and frozen, acutely aware of them all.

One of the black men, the one in the middle, leaned in as if to whisper to his companion. The man he had addressed edged away, slowly, careful to make no sudden movements. The man in the middle, moving with equal caution, brought his right arm up to rest it on the boulder. In his hand was a long thin stick of metal, pointed directly at the heart of the camp.

Miriam did not even feel herself move. It was as if her whole body had become as numbed and icy as her feet and she could not tell if her nerves and muscles obeyed her. She did not will herself to scream. But still a great wailing cry broke from her throat, and her feet carried her forward, and she threw her glittering black rock as hard as she could, and the whole world exploded.

The second rock was in her hand, and thrown, and then the third rock, before she was even aware of her actions. The three black strangers had scattered in a sparking arc of fire, one of them crying out in a fierce howl as flame ripped across his chest. The other two fell low to the ground, and rolled, and came to their knees to stare at her.

The Edori in the camp shouted and scattered, some flattening themselves to the ground, some dashing to one side, some to the other. Three came running straight for Miriam—and the waiting black strangers.

"*Noooo!*" Miriam shrieked, throwing another rock, and another one, though rocks were stupid, rocks were useless, against men who could throw incendiary fire. "Go *back!* Go *back!* Run away!"

But Dathan was racing toward her, five paces ahead of Bartholomew, and Thaddeus was right behind them. She saw, because it seemed she saw everything with a desperate clarity, one of the black-clad strangers lift a hand to his throat.

And then two of them disappeared.

Miriam kept scooping rocks out of her bag and pelting them at the single remaining visitor, who lay strangely motionless on the ground. And she kept screaming at the oncoming Edori, "Go back, go back, go *back!*" But Dathan and Bartholomew and Thaddeus still ran toward her, not breaking stride, and the stranger still lay on the ground, unmoving.

Dathan reached her first and wrestled her down, as if to protect her from any danger that might be about to shatter her from a low height. Bartholomew and Thaddeus, she saw, had little crossbows in their hands—weapons that could fell a deer and so might reasonably be expected to kill a man, except that no Edori would ever consider turning a weapon upon another human being.

"She's safe!" Dathan shouted over his shoulder. "See what's out there!"

"It was them—the black men—but they disappeared," Miriam moaned, knowing she sounded incoherent, knowing he could not possibly understand her. "The ones who burn the camps—I saw them before—they were here, but they disappeared—"

"There's one that didn't disappear," Dathan said grimly. He was crouched over her, his hands pinning her in the grass, his body angled to shield her from any harm that might come from the direction of the boulder. But his head was turned to watch Bartholomew's progress. "Looks like he might have gotten hurt." He glanced down at her with a flicker of a smile. "One of your rocks, I guess."

She shook her head, hard to do flat on her back. "The fire," she whispered. "His friend lifted the stick to send fire at you, and I knocked his hand, I think. The fire went over this one instead."

Dathan was silent a minute, no doubt watching Bartholomew's cautious approach toward the fallen enemy. In a moment, he allowed a little hiss to escape between his teeth. "Here's an interesting gift from Yovah," he breathed. "This one is still alive."

• • •

They made their camp around the injured man. Dathan and Bartholomew and Miriam had been tacitly chosen to deal with this stranger, this invader, and they had none too gently hauled him into the circle of tents while the others continued building up fires and cutting up vegetables and in general preparing for the oncoming night.

At first, Miriam did nothing except watch. Bartholomew had dumped the black man onto an unused pallet, letting his arms flop to the ground and not taking any care to make sure his head was out of the mud. Then the two men had crouched beside the stranger and begun their examination. First to go had been the shiny hat, which revealed bright coppery hair that was neither as bright nor as fiery as the hair on the man Miriam had seen in a Bethel field. They had pulled off his black clothes to reveal that strange, lustrously dark skin beneath—not so dark as his outer garments, but deeper than the Edori brown—and to reveal also a deep wound across his chest. It was blackened and blistering, though oozing red, and it was hard to tell how deep it went. This was the effect of the fire-throwing stick, Miriam thought, turned at close range upon a friend.

This was the effect of a rock-throwing allali girl traveling with Edori and reacting with pure and terrified instinct.

Bartholomew and Dathan consulted in low voices, and Miriam crept closer to hear. "Breathes like a man," Bartholomew said.

"Bleeds like one, too," Dathan concurred.

"Let's see the rest of him," Bartholomew said, and began to pull down the stranger's lower garments.

For a moment, Miriam turned away, instinctively granting privacy, but curiosity turned her back again. Yes—he appeared to be a man in all the familiar ways, covered with more hair on his genitals and thighs than she was used to, though she understood that even among ordinary men, that sort of thing varied. She let her eyes wander over his whole body, seeking similarities to the men she had known, seeking differences. Except for the skin and the hair, he seemed formed like the humans living on Samaria; he was built no differently than Gaaron or Nicholas or Elias.

Bartholomew laid a hand just above the ugly curve of the wound. "Feels like a heartbeat," he said.

Dathan tilted his ear over the slack mouth. "Breath moving in and out," he said. He straightened. "You can see the blood running under his skin. He is patterned like we are."

"He is not one of us."

Dathan shook his head. "But he is in some sense a brother."

"In the sense that Jansai are brothers," Bartholomew said, with a morbid pass at humor.

Dathan responded with a sharp crack of laughter. "Yes, in just that way," he said.

Miriam edged even nearer, till she, too, crouched on the ground, her shoulder brushing against Dathan, her eyes still studying the naked, unconscious man. This close, she could hear the faint, laboring sound of his troubled breathing. "What are you going to do with him?" she asked.

Bartholomew looked at her across the prone body. "What would you do with him?" he asked.

"What would I—it's not my decision!" she exclaimed.

"It is the whole clan's decision," Dathan explained. "Your words are to be weighed as carefully as Bartholomew's, or mine."

Miriam looked now at the dark face, pinched in an expression of pain and confusion. The coppery hair was matted with sweat, though the air was so cool; the heavy hat must be hot to wear. His skin looked so smooth, even across his cheeks and jaw. Either he was almost too young to shave, or men in his tribe did not grow hair on their faces. She wondered suddenly if his beard would be as red as the hair on the top of his head. She glanced again at his pubic hair. Almost dark as an Edori man's, but with a coppery glint in its tangled curls.

She looked again at his face.

He was pretty, with prominent cheekbones and a small, modeled nose; his mouth, open to draw in more air, was wide and generous. She wondered if his eyes were the same startling green she had seen on that stranger in Bethel. If he died of his wounds tonight, she would never know.

"He was not the one who lifted the stick of fire," she said at last. "It was the man next to him."

Bartholomew nodded seriously. "He does not appear to have any weapons on him at all. At least that I can identify as weapons."

"He looks like a boy," Dathan said.

"Too young to stand against his tribe, or to know that the path his clan follows is violent and harsh," Bartholomew added.

"He looks cold," Miriam said.

There was a moment's silence. "Get a blanket," Bartholomew said.

She rose to her feet and flew through the camp, bumping into half a dozen Edori and apologizing breathlessly. She dove inside her own tent and took the blanket from her own pallet, sure that Tirza or Amram would share with her when the night became too cold. In a few moments, she was back beside Bartholomew and Dathan, and they allowed her to cover up the comatose stranger.

"What about his wound?" she asked.

Bartholomew shrugged. "I don't know how to dress it. Not much you can do for a burn, anyway, except keep it clean."

Dathan nodded. "Looks cauterized. Just let it heal."

Miriam watched the dark face gather in a spasm of pain, then the stranger gave a little cough, made a strangling sound, gasped twice—and then resumed his difficult breathing. "He might be thirsty," she said.

"A risk to give him water," Bartholomew said. "He could choke on it."

"Just a little bit," Miriam said.

Bartholomew nodded. "Get a rag. Dip it in a cup. Squeeze a few drops into his mouth. We'll see how he does with that."

Miriam came to her feet again and then paused, looking down at the three men. "Does that mean you're going to help him live?" she asked.

Bartholomew glanced up at her. "It's up to the clan," he said.

CHAPTER TWENTY-ONE

Dinner that night was a largely silent affair, as each small group gathered around its own fire and ate quickly and efficiently. Tirza asked Miriam once if she was feeling all right, since the blond girl only picked at her food and took a few sips of water, but Miriam merely nodded. She was overwhelmed with thoughts—unpleasant thoughts—terrifying ideas.

What if she had come back from the river five minutes later, to find the campsite a charred, smoking circle of catastrophe? What if she had been stranded out here, miles from anywhere or anyone she knew, completely alone and helpless? Or what if she had arrived just in time to scream in horror, and draw the attention of the murderous strangers, and be scorched to cinders in turn? She could be dead right now. Everyone in this circle of tents could be dead—everyone she had come to love so very deeply, all could have disappeared in an instant. Five minutes—one minute—some random combination of seconds could have coalesced and completely altered the course of her life.

What if her aim had not been so true? What if she had not had the rock in her hand? What if the stranger holding the stick of fire had not been distracted, and turned to face her, and so injured his companion? What if he had decided to destroy her first and then turn his weapon back on the Lohoras?

Why had he spared them? Why had she been so fortunate as to arrive in time to slow his hand?

Was this Yovah's work? Was Yovah guarding them so closely that he would not allow the fire to fall upon the Lohoras? Then why had he allowed it to fall on the other camp—the Carhansons, it was widely believed, for no one had seen them in months? Why was one tribe saved and another tribe sacrificed? Where was the god's hand in that?

She could not get past the fact of her own mortality. She could not get past the fact that she had been so close to death that she had literally stared it in the face. She could not imagine what Gaaron's emotions would be upon learning that his sister had disappeared, that she had not only left the sanctuary he had provided for her, but deliberately put herself into the path of danger—and been destroyed by it. She could have died today and he would not have known for weeks, maybe months, that she was dead.

All the Lohoras could have died, and no one who loved them would have known.

She could not get her mind to absorb and accept this information.

"Here. Let someone who'll enjoy it eat your stew," Tirza said, taking her bowl from Miriam. "I'll save you a few chunks of bread. You'll be hungry later tonight, and bread's always easiest, even on a stomach that's turned at the sight of tragedy."

Miriam stared up at her kind, calm face, knowing that desperation peered out of her own eyes. "Tirza," she said in a small voice. "Everybody almost died."

Tirza nodded. "I know," she said. "I know."

Miriam wanted to say more, to put the whole shocking haphazardness of the event into words, but she could not think how. Tirza placed her palm against Miriam's pale cheek.

"Not an easy thing, to look at death and see him looking right back at you," she said quietly. "Not an easy thing to see death stalking your friends. It shouldn't be an easy thing. Go ahead and tremble."

Miriam nodded and then she shook her head. She would not be a weakling, she would not be the only Lohora who was not calm and strong. "I'll have some of that bread now," she said in a determined voice. "I find I am a little hungry after all."

• • •

They held the council meeting around Bartholomew's fire, because Bartholomew was the one they all most admired, even if each of them planned to speak up with an opinion that every other one would listen to. Miriam sat between Tirza and Bartholomew, cross-legged on a folded pallet to keep away the chill of the damp ground. When Tirza reached over to take her hand, Miriam allowed her to hold it. For comfort, and for strength.

"Let us begin with a prayer," Bartholomew said quietly. He sang the opening lines of a song that was new to Miriam, and all the others joined in a few beats later. It was a solemn piece that sounded like a plea for wisdom and courage. Miriam could not tell for sure, because the words were Edori, and she had, in all this time, only learned a little bit of their language. But she hummed along when she could catch the melody, and she added a high little harmony to the "amen" at the end.

When the song was through, Bartholomew glanced around the fire, touching each individual face with his gaze, drawing them all together in a sense of strong purpose. "As you all know, we have been very blessed this day," he said in a low, clear voice. "We were approached by enemies, and we were saved by the hand of Yovah. Our enemies are gone, and we are alive. It is a day of thanksgiving."

"Alleluia," the Edori murmured.

"Now we must ask ourselves, what was the god's purpose in showing us such mercy? Are we merely to thank him for his great gift of our lives? Or are we to ask him, Yovah, what truth did you reveal to us? For what purpose did you spare us? What are we to do now?"

"What is the state of the strange man who was left behind?" asked Claudia's lover, Adam.

"Grave," Bartholomew said. "He breathes and sleeps, but neither his breath nor his sleep is easy. He will die without tending."

"He should die," Anna said. "He wanted to kill us."

"But he did not kill us," Adam reminded her.

"It was not his conscience, nor even Yovah's hand, that saved us," she retorted. "It was Miriam's scream and Miriam's quick action."

A low murmur of assent went around the camp at that. "I believe Yovah's hand wrapped itself around Miriam's hand," Bartholomew said gently. "Or none of us would be alive now."

"Yes, and we thank Yovah profusely for interceding," Eleazar said. "But it was not this one's intent to spare us. There is no reason for us to spare him."

"It is not the Edori way to kill any creature, except to hunt for food," Bartholomew said.

"We don't have to kill him," Eleazar said. "We merely let him die. As he would have let us die."

"Miriam says his was not the hand that held the weapon."

"Yes, but his was not the hand that struck down the weapon. He stood aside. Let us stand aside. Let the god make his disposition."

"What if he was spared for a reason—as we were spared for a reason?" Bartholomew asked.

Eleazar shrugged. "What reason could that be?"

"I do not presume to read the ways of Yovah's heart."

"He's a boy," Dathan spoke up. "He does not look evil."

"The corvain root does not look evil, and yet it will kill you if you so much as touch it," Eleazar said with some heat.

Dathan spread his hands. Miriam could not remember ever seeing that laughing face so serious. *Susannah would be proud of him,* she thought, and then she wondered where that thought had come from. "I have traveled with the Lohoras all my life," Dathan said. "I have never seen them turn away a stranger in need. I have never seen them leave a wounded creature to die. I have never seen them refuse a gift from Yovah. I agree with Bartholomew. This man was sent to us for a purpose. Perhaps that purpose is nothing grander than Yovah testing us to see if we will be kind to our enemies. And perhaps it is greater. I think we are meant to care for him, and perhaps return him to his tribe recovered. Perhaps that will convince his brothers and his uncles and his friends that they should no longer wage war on such a gentle people."

"Perhaps that will convince him that we are so gentle he can murder us all in our tents one night," Eleazar said angrily.

"That might be so," Bartholomew said. "But I will not be able to vote for him to die."

There was a small silence. Tirza spoke up. "I have not yet gotten a close look at this young and hostile stranger," she said. "I have sometimes been a fair judge of a person's heart by the outward shape of his face. I would like to look at him now, while he lies there sleeping, and then I will know how to cast my vote." She glanced around the circle of firelit faces. "I think we should all look at his face before we cast our votes."

This idea finding universal favor, Tirza came quickly to her feet and headed off into the darkness. She returned shortly, and Eleazar rather angrily retraced her steps. He was gone longer than she was; his face looked thoughtful when he rejoined the others at the fire. One by one, the other Edori came to their feet and turned in the direction of the sleeping man. Even Amram went, even Claudia's daughter.

Even Miriam, though she had already had a good look at their wounded stranger. She knelt beside him and tucked the blanket a little more tightly around his shoulders, and then she dipped the cloth in the bowl of water and dribbled a few more droplets into his mouth. His fine coppery brows were drawn down in a scowl of pain; she thought his breath sounded even more strained. She hated to leave him to go back to the fire, but she came to her feet and returned to the others, taking her place silently next to Tirza. The other woman reached out to squeeze her hand and then drop it.

Dathan and Bartholomew were the last two to go take a look at the stranger. When they returned, there was a moment's silence while everyone thought over the situation. Then Bartholomew said, "My vote is to let the man live, and to care for him as best we can to ensure that he does not die. Dathan?"

"I vote with Bartholomew."

They went around the fire that way, name called, answer given, everyone's voice listened to with an equal solemn attention. Miriam held her breath when Anna's name was called, but the older woman simply bowed her head. "It is the Edori way to offer shelter to anyone who appears at their campfire," she said in a subdued voice. "I vote with Bartholomew."

Eleazar, Tirza, and Miriam were the last three to express their opinions. Eleazar no longer sounded angry, but he did not sound happy. "I do not agree with the tribe, but I will not vote against it," he said. "And I will abide by the decision of the clan."

Bartholomew nodded. "Tirza?"

"He must be allowed to live."

"Miriam?"

She looked over at him, feeling as alien as the dark stranger, she with her bright hair and her pale skin among this cohesive and unified group. Maybe that was why she so desperately wanted to save this outsider, wanted to bring him into the warm haven that was the Edori clan—to deliver him from himself—to rescue someone else as she had herself been rescued. "I vote with the tribe," she said. "But I will do more, if you will let me. I will tend him. You will have to help me, because I don't know how to nurse a sick man, but I will care for him, and feed him, and bind his wound. I will help him live again."

"So be it," Bartholomew said, and the council came to an end.

They set up a tent around him, carefully, a small spare one that Bartholomew carried against the ever-present possibility of unexpected guests. Though no guest could have been more unexpected than this one. The wind had picked up, and its icy razor edge cut through even Miriam's layers of clothing. She went to Bartholomew's tent to borrow another blanket from Anna.

"You're a good girl, Miriam," Anna said, taking her in a quick hug. Anna was not as generous with casual affection as most of the Edori, and so the gesture caught Miriam by surprise. "Here. A bowl of broth. If you think your invalid can swallow it."

"Thank you," Miriam said gravely. "I think he'll have to eat something. Eventually."

The tent was up and Tirza was inside it when Miriam returned. There was a second pallet unrolled next to the black man, piled with its own blankets. "I thought we would take turns watching him and sleeping," Tirza explained. "At least for this first night."

Miriam knew better than to protest, because Tirza always did whatever she thought was right. "Thank you," she said. "I hope you can teach me how to care for him. I've never tended anyone who was sick or injured."

Tirza was kneeling beside the unconscious stranger, placing a small pillow under his head, straightening his blankets, in general trying to make him more comfortable. "Who watches the sick ones at your angel hold, then?"

Miriam shrugged. "Angels are never sick. The rest of us—oh, Esther acts as apothecary, and some of the other mortal women take turns doing the nursing. I don't know. I was never sick, either."

"Well, I'm not sure there's much we can do for this one except keep him warm. I've ground up a little manna root to spread on his wound. That ought to ease his pain a bit. Bartholomew said you'd given him some water?"

"Yes, and Anna gave me some broth. If you think—"

"Well, he hasn't spit the water back up. Let's try just a taste of the soup. It will be a good sign if he can take it."

Miriam held the man's head up while Tirza tipped two spoonfuls of broth down his throat. He choked a little, turning his head from side to side, and Miriam felt a moment's panic. But then he subsided, sighing as she laid his head back on the pillow.

"Good. If he keeps that down, we'll give him some more in a couple of hours," Tirza said. "Let's take a look at the wound."

She peeled back the blankets and studied the ugly burn for a few moments. She very gingerly spread its red edges with a thick white paste, then just as carefully covered him back up. "Maybe that will help," she said. "But it's going to take some time for a burn like that to clear up."

"Is he going to die?" Miriam asked fearfully.

Tirza looked over at her. She'd lit four big fat candles and set them all around the tent. They didn't supply much warmth, and their light was unreliable, but it was enough for Miriam to see Tirza's face by. "I don't know," she said. "I don't know how his body is built and how much he can withstand. I don't know how deep the burn went, or what vital parts of his body it might have wounded. He is alive now. So we will help him as much as we can."

"You sleep first," Miriam said. "I will watch him."

Tirza nodded and lay on the second pallet. She had a gift that Miriam greatly envied, the ability to fall asleep within minutes, no matter what the hour or temperature or situation. True to form, she appeared to fall asleep instantly, her breathing as soft and regular as the stranger's breathing was uneven and cluttered. Miriam sat there, knees updrawn, body very still, listening to the interior sounds of the tent and the exterior sounds of the camp, until there were hardly any sounds at all.

She moved very little for the next couple of hours, only rearranging a ragged blanket underneath herself to keep away the chill of the ground. When the wounded man stirred, she leaned forward and squeezed a little more water down his throat. She thought his lips looked dry, so she fished a little container out of her pocket, filled with a balm made of fat and herbs that Anna had given her, and she smeared a little across his mouth. She laid her palm gingerly across his cheek and thought his skin felt hot. But maybe the heat was generated by the intense dark pigment of his flesh, a color so rich and deep it made her think of Manadavvi soil and the onyx quartz mined near Luminaux. She wondered if he had a fever. She wondered if there would be anything Tirza could do about it if he did.

After Tirza had been asleep for just over two hours, Miriam

dipped her rag in the bowl of broth. It was harder to feed him all by herself, but she edged around in the small tent until she was kneeling at his head, and then she carefully lifted his head and laid it upon her knees. She dripped a little of the broth down his cheek, but he took most of it, not seeming to cough or choke so much this time. She thought that was a hopeful sign.

Miriam had already decided she would not wake Tirza when her turn came, but the Edori woman woke on her own about an hour after that. "How is he?" she asked in a low voice, pushing herself to a sitting position and seeming to be wide awake on the instant.

"A little restless. I gave him more broth about an hour ago."

"And he kept it down? Good."

"And I just gave him a little more water ten minutes ago."

"Excellent. Why don't you lie down now? I'll watch for a while."

Miriam wanted to protest—she wanted to be the one to care for this stranger, this violent, helpless, unwelcome creature sent into their midst. But she was so tired she did not think she would be able to keep her eyes open much longer. She and the Edori woman traded places, Miriam snuggling with a certain sensuous delight into the blankets warmed by Tirza's body.

But before she closed her eyes, she had one more question. "Tirza. What happens tomorrow?"

"What do you mean?"

"When we move out. I don't think he's well enough to travel."

"He's not. We'll make camp here for a few days."

"Good," Miriam said drowsily, and let her eyelids droop. But a new thought almost immediately flicked them open again. "But Tirza," she said more urgently. "What if his friends come back for him? They might. *I* would. If we're still here, they'll find us for sure. They'll set the whole camp on fire!"

Tirza was running a wet cloth over the man's cheeks and forehead. Obviously, she thought he was too hot, too. "If they come looking for their friend, they'll find him right here in our tent. And I don't think they'll set us on fire if they want him back."

"But Tirza—"

"As the god wills," she said with calm certainty. "They will come or not come. They will burn us or not burn us. We cannot move until he is well enough to travel. Yovah will abide by his plan."

Miriam closed her eyes, but she was not entirely reassured. This was the same god who had let other tribes be scorched to ashes. She was not convinced he was watching over all of them as carefully as he might. But Tirza was right. There was nothing they could do about it, tonight, anyway. She turned over on her side, put her hands beneath her cheek, and slept.

In the morning, Tirza looked exhausted and the stranger looked no better. His skin was so dark that it was hard to tell if he was either flushed or pasty, but somehow he did not look *right*. His breathing, which had smoothed out during the night, was labored again, and his skin was so hot to the touch that it was impossible not to worry about fever.

"You should have woken me," Miriam said remorsefully as she looked at Tirza's weary face. "I meant to only sleep a couple of hours."

Tirza shrugged this off. "I think we'll need some hellsbane to try to bring his temperature down," she said. "I don't know who might have some. There is none in my stores, I know."

"He needs plague medicine," Miriam said.

Tirza smiled in a tired way. "Such as the angels pray for? I hear there are all different kinds and the god always knows what to send."

Miriam shrugged. "He sends what you ask for. There are different prayers for different medicines."

"Well, I suppose we could run up a plague flag and see if an angel drops by in response," Tirza said. It was an attempt at humor; the Edori never asked the angels for help. "Though I don't know if they would be as willing as the Lohoras have been to aid an enemy."

"No," Miriam said, unable to think of a single angel from any of the three holds who would not view her with horror if she stepped out of an Edori tent here by the Galilee River. "We don't want angels here."

Before Tirza could respond to that, the tent flap folded back and Anna stepped inside. "How is he? I've brought some mashed fruit. He might be able to eat that."

"He might," Tirza agreed. "He's done very well with your broth. But he seems worse this morning. I don't know that he'll be able to take anything at all."

Anna's sharp gaze went from Tirza's face to Miriam's. "You two go back to your tent," she ordered. "I'll sit with him this morning."

"No," Miriam protested. "I'm the one who said I'd watch him. I meant it. It's my duty."

Tirza had already gotten to her feet, and now she picked her way past the sleeping man to place a hand on Miriam's head. "And it was a generous offer to make," she said kindly. "But no one person can do all the nursing for a sick man. We will take turns. We always do. You can just take more turns than the rest of us."

"Now go back and get some sleep," Anna said gruffly. "You can come see him as soon as you're rested."

They stepped outside into a dull sunlight that was still brighter than the murky tent, and Miriam had to squint for a minute until her eyes adjusted. The air was incredibly crisp, sweeping down from Mount Galo with fresh armloads of snow that it was considering dropping. Miriam took a few deep breaths, emptying her lungs of stale air and candle smoke.

"I'll come to the tent in a moment," she told Tirza. "Right now I have to go down to the river and bathe."

"You bathed yesterday, don't you remember?" Tirza asked with a tired grin. "You coming back from the river is what saved us all."

Miriam smiled back. "Then I should bathe every day that we are here so that our luck holds just as good."

She took a bucket with her (never miss a chance to gather more water) and a change of clothes. After she cleaned herself as quickly and thoroughly as she could, she washed out the dress she had worn yesterday and the day before. She was so tired that the thought of walking back to camp, wet bundle in one hand and bucket in the other, was almost more than she could bear. So she sat for a moment at the water's edge, far enough back to keep from soiling her dress on the muddy bank, and stared at the muscular, impatient river charging past.

And then she began to sing.

At first she kept her voice soft, because this was not a song any mortal should know—certainly not a song any mortal should offer up to the god, expecting the god to hear. But she had learned in the last two months that the Edori felt just as comfortable offering prayers to Yovah as the angels did offering prayers to Jovah. She had been shocked the first few times she had heard the Lohoras beseech or thank the god as casually and as confidently as the angels addressed him— as if certain he heard them, whether or not he chose to reply. And why not? He watched over all of them, did he not? He graced every dedicated mortal with the mark of his favor, the Kiss; he did not reserve that particular honor only for angels. He cared about every one of them, angel, mortal, Jansai, Manadavvi. Perhaps he even cared for this violent and misguided stranger. He had saved the man, after all. Perhaps he would be willing to do even more to make him well.

So Miriam strengthened her voice, tilted her head back, and imagined the words of her song boring up through the heavy clouds and straight to Yovah's ear. They were so close to the Plain of Sharon, the place where, every year, the angels raised their voices in the Gloria. Surely, if the god could hear her anywhere in the three provinces, he could catch her voice from here. She came slowly to her feet, her voice even more forceful now, offering once more the simple, repetitive prayer that asked for alms of relief and healing. She could feel her thin soprano gain color and roughness as she sang the piece one more time, the notes rasping against her throat grown raw from too much music. But the song poured out of her, powerful and supplicating; her hands lifted of their own volition in a gesture of submission and entreaty. Her head was thrown back as if she would watch the sky for a sign of Yovah's mercy, but her eyes were closed. She could feel the weak sunlight against her eyelids, sense the movement of the sullen clouds, boiling above her as if to hurl down an insult of rain. She dropped her hands and finally halted her voice, too hoarse to try for another note. But she stood still with her head tipped back and her eyes closed, as if asking to catch the first raindrops on her upturned cheeks.

And, indeed, something small and pelletlike hit her face and bounced away, and then another pellet, and then a small shower of them, needlelike and frenzied. She opened her eyes and instinctively crouched down, throwing her arms over her head to protect herself from the hail. But it continued to fall in quick, sharp bursts, a strangely colored blue outburst of precipitation—and it was, after all, not hail.

With a little cry, she began gathering up the small tablets, as many as she could find in the brown grass and the sticky ooze of the river mud, and tossing them in her shoulder bag where yesterday she had carried rocks. Yes, handfuls and handfuls and *handfuls* of drugs from Yovah—enough to heal the injured stranger and to allow the Edori to hoard them against sickness for months or maybe years to come.

As quickly as it had come, the shower passed. Miriam, on her knees in the dry grass, glanced up at the sky to see even the scowling clouds beginning to part and roll away. The thin winter sunlight streamed down to envelop her in a private circle of affection. She could not help herself. She lifted her arms up as if to ask for a hug, and then she laughed for the sheer joy of being alive.

CHAPTER TWENTY-TWO

Never a fan of surprises, Gaaron was far from pleased when Adriel and Neri showed up at the Eyrie one day, eager to meet his bride-to-be.

It had been a relatively calm week, holding no major crises, but he had been busy almost every minute. The Velora merchants had held a series of meetings to discuss a controversial new set of trading guidelines being sponsored by the Manadavvi and the river merchants, and they had found themselves in the strange position of being allies with the Jansai, who were heartily against the new regulations. So Gaaron's presence had been requested at all these discussions, and he had tried to devote his complete attention to the arguments and counterarguments that were presented. His best suggestion was that they bring in a contingent of Luminaux artisans and get their input, and that plan was instantly put in motion. Gaaron sent Enoch south to request a visit from a convocation of Luminauzi. He considered going himself, and swinging by a little Edori bakery to check on his sister. But then he decided against it.

But then he thought about it some more.

But he ultimately chose to let it go. When Miriam wanted to communicate with him, she would. He had, in fact, gotten two scrawled letters from her, sent by some godlessly circuitous route via Jansai and Edori caravans. It was hard to tell when she had written them or how long the letters had been on the road, and he learned no real news from them. Just that she claimed to be well and happy enough. "Someday I will have much to tell you," she concluded in one letter, and he read that a few times with a sense of foreboding. But he decided to take her at her word, and to believe that she *was* well and happy enough. That should be good enough for anyone.

By that criteria, he thought with a certain unaccustomed wistfulness, *how am I doing?* Physically, he was well, of course; he was always healthy. But was he happy? Relations had continued to be strained between him and Susannah, though he could not put his finger on what was wrong. She always ate dinner with him, and shared his table at any other meal when he happened to be present (which was rarer and rarer these days). If he asked her a question, she responded immediately and thoughtfully; she was always gracious in conversation. But the feeling persisted that she was angry at him—or withdrawn from him—or mistrustful of him, and he did not know why, and he did not know how to ask her.

He was pleased to see that she seemed to have wholeheartedly accepted the gifts of fabric he had purchased for her in Velora. She had made a point of modeling for him a quite beautiful gown she had had made from the apricot silk, "though it is too fine for everyday wear," she said with a sigh. "I shall have to wear it only on special occasions."

The coral cotton she had made into a skirt and blouse, and these she wore several times, accenting them with a wide embroidered belt that he thought she might have made herself. The scrap of red she had worked into a quilted patchwork vest that was colorful and casual, and so she wore this most of all. And seemed pleased enough in the fabric of Gaaron's providing.

But she still did not seem entirely happy. Well enough, but not happy. He wondered what she would write to Miriam if she were to sit down and pen a letter to his sister.

He had not been able to come up with the words that would enable him to ask her if anything was wrong by the time Adriel and Neri showed up, smug and pleased with themselves and entirely unwelcome.

They were blown in by a snowy wind that had cleared the outdoor plateau quite early in the afternoon and kept everyone inside the lab-yrinth of the Eyrie's corridors. The luckless souls who had signed up for harmonics shivered around a brazier set up in the open-air cupola; even their voices sounded frosty, drifting down through the star-chilled air.

The angels arrived as the dinner hour was just ending, strolling into the dining room with their faces rouged with cold, their wings fanned out to warm their feathers. They were both laughing.

"Gaaron! I hope you don't mind that we've decided to pay you a visit," Neri greeted him with a gaiety contrary to her usual seriousness.

"I hope this is not a bad time for us to drop by," Adriel added.

Gaaron came quickly to his feet, astonished to see them, not at once understanding why they were here. "Is something wrong? Do you have news?" he asked sharply.

Adriel shook her head. "No, all has been quiet for weeks now. Even on the southern shores. I think our unfriendly visitors are gone."

"We've come here to celebrate," Neri added.

"And to meet your bride," Adriel said. "We grew tired of waiting for an invitation."

Now Gaaron's face flushed as red as theirs. "You must forgive me for my rudeness," he said, hoping that by using the word he would convey to them just what he thought of their own behavior. "Naturally I am happy to have you both here for however long you choose to stay."

He turned with an assumed composure to include Susannah in the conversation. Susannah had risen to her feet as soon as the women started speaking—guessing, more quickly than he had, what was afoot. She was wearing today the coral outfit and the embroidered belt, and she looked both exotic and at ease. Her hair was braided back from her face, strands of gold and orange and red plaited into the black, and her dark, smooth skin showed no hint of a blush.

"Susannah," he said as majestically as he could. "This is Arch-angel Adriel of Windy Point. A dear friend of mine and someone from whom I have learned a great deal. And this is Neri, leader of the host at Monteverde. Another good friend."

Susannah smiled and held out her hand. "Gaaron has spoken of both of you quite often," she said. "We have been discussing what kind of event we should have to introduce me to all the leaders of the provinces. But I confess I am not very comfortable around crowds of strangers, so it is so much better for me to have you drop by this way."

Neatly said, Gaaron thought in admiration, and he could see that Neri, too, thought it a very good speech, though probably a lie. Adriel seemed more focused on Susannah's face than her words.

"But you're quite lovely!" she exclaimed, putting her hands up to Susannah's cheeks. "Gaaron spoke of your insightful mind and your strength of character, but he did not say how attractive you were."

Susannah, who could easily have been offended by such a remark, instead looked amused. "Perhaps he thought you would be more impressed by principles than by prettiness," she said.

"I don't know. My Moshe is a thoughtful man, but I would not have married him if he was not good-looking," Adriel said frankly, and they all laughed.

Gaaron gestured at the table, half covered with used dishes, which some of the kitchen girls were hastily clearing away. Esther had gotten one look at the exalted company walking in the door and hurried off to take care of things. "Are you hungry? Would you like something to eat? Sit down a while and tell me of your flight. And how you hatched your little plan to come calling," he added.

In a few minutes, the four of them were seated at the table and the new arrivals were enjoying a meal. Susannah had asked for a cup of hot tea, but Gaaron had required wine, and he was sipping that.

"We met in Sinai and flew on together. Mahalah said she would come visit some other time," Adriel reported.

"I must say, she has those girls remarkably well trained," Neri broke in. "When I go to Sudan, Isaac's boys are running around like ill-trained mongrels. But it is very calm and peaceful at Mount Sinai."

"I don't know. I find her acolytes a little silly and—giggly sometimes," Gaaron said. He was not sure why all the women at the table laughed at him.

"So, Susannah! Tell us a little about yourself," Neri invited. "What do you think about life in an angel hold?"

"It is quite pleasant," Susannah said promptly. "I particularly admire the water rooms, which are a grand luxury when you're used to bathing in the open river. My friend Keren—an Edori girl who is visiting me here—enjoys the benefits of the kitchen. We are used to finding and cooking all our own food, you know, which is sometimes a chore that can take all day, when there's snow on the ground and game is scarce. And the proximity to the markets of Velora is a daily delight for both of us."

Neri looked fascinated, Adriel just a little repulsed. "You gathered and cooked your own food—yes, I suppose you must have," the Archangel said in a faint voice. "I have never—but then, I suppose someone is out there slaughtering the meat I eat every day without thinking about it."

"You have more important things to think about," Neri excused her.

Susannah's smiled widened. "Although, trust me, when you're hungry and you've eaten the last of your dried meat and you can't even find a skinny rabbit to go in the stew, you do think there aren't many things too much more important than dinner," she said.

"And so you've always been an Edori?" Neri asked, and then her face flamed as soon as she realized what a stupid question it was. "I mean—you've always traveled as the Edori have?"

Susannah nodded. "Yes, I have friends who have chosen to settle in Luminaux or one of the river cities—because it *is* a hard life, you know, and when you're older, or infirm, or simply tired, it is easier just to stay in one place. But this is the first time in my life I haven't been on the move."

"That must be a relief," Adriel said.

Susannah looked at her. "I miss it," she said. "I miss the intimacy of the seasons—feeling winter creep closer day by day, waking up in the morning and knowing, before I even set foot outside the tent, exactly how much sun I'll see before night falls again. I miss being in motion, always on the lookout for *something*—a good campsite, a patch of berries, deer tracks so we know we can hunt for game that night. I miss the constant awareness of the world. I miss being so thirsty that when I finally come to a stream and can take a drink, the water actually tastes sweet. And I miss being so tired that I can sleep the minute I lie down, and sleep the whole night through, and not wake even when I'm disturbed by unquiet dreams."

She fell silent. The two women stared at her. Surely the poetry was deliberate, Gaaron thought, an antagonistic but lyrical response to the angels' smug assumption that their lives were so much more civilized than the Edori's. But it might also have been aimed at him. *You have wondered why I have not been happy in your household. Because these are the things you have taken from me.*

Although he still had not asked her why she was not happy in his household.

"Well. I see. I have been told the Edori are all quite passionate about their lifestyles, and now I suppose I can understand why," Adriel said. "You speak quite beautifully."

"There is much more about the Edori life that is wonderful," Susannah said calmly. "The camaraderie—the closeness of the clans—those things are impossible to describe. I have made good friends among the angels and their kin, but I have not found anything to equal the companionship I have experienced among the Edori."

Adriel cast a quick, troubled look at Gaaron, and he read that as a question about the relationship between the Archangel-to-be and his designated bride. As well she should question it. Certainly he had not offered Susannah much camaraderie. Although he had thought she had managed to find that on her own.

"It always takes some time to settle in to a new place," Adriel said, peering into Susannah's face with her kind, worried eyes. "You have only been here a few months. Do not give up so soon on the chance to make lifelong friendships that matter deeply to you."

Susannah's smile seemed a bright rejection of the Archangel's proffered concern. "Oh, I do not intend to give up," she said. "I have committed my life to the course the god has chosen."

"Yes, and that was one of the questions we had to ask you," Neri spoke up. "When is the wedding to be? You must be married before the Gloria, you know, and that is only three months away."

Even more tactless than he would have expected, even from the blunt Neri, Gaaron thought. But to this challenge, as well, Susannah was more than equal. "I am so glad you are here to help advise me on that very point!" she exclaimed. "The Edori do not marry, as you may know, so I am not conversant with the customs that are required. I have not particularly wanted to ask Esther's help, and Miriam is so extravagant I was sure I could not trust any of her suggestions. But while the two of you are here, perhaps you could give me some recommendations about what I should wear and what I am supposed to do. As for a day to choose—how much notice should we give? Who must be invited? You can help me with all those decisions."

Adriel gave her a doubtful look, as if unsure whether Susannah's response was sincere, but Neri nodded briskly. "We'll be happy to. In the morning, maybe, we can get out a calendar and make some plans. I don't think you want to wait too much longer, but you're right, you must give your guests a certain amount of notice. We'll make lists for you. We can get it all in order."

"Well, then, if that's settled—" Gaaron began. But before he could finish his sentence, Sela came up to the table and whispered in Susannah's ear. Susannah nodded and rose to her feet.

"Forgive me. There is a small girl who depends on my attentions, and it looks as if she needs me," she said, smiling in a winning way. "If I don't see you again this evening, I will be happy to meet with you in the morning. We'll have a great deal to talk about then."

And as quickly as that, talking quietly with Sela as she left, Susannah was gone.

"Well," Adriel said a little blankly. "She is not at all what I expected. Though to tell the truth—I have no idea what I expected."

"She has a daughter? Is that what she said?" Neri demanded. "I did not think Jovah paired up Archangels with spouses who already had other children. Adriel, have you ever heard of that before?"

"It's not her daughter," Gaaron said briefly. He did not bother to add that Susannah could have easily had a daughter, could have had any number of children, had had a whole life and set of lovers and a satisfactory existence before he had swooped down on her campsite to change everything. He was sure Sela had come over at some invisible signal from Susannah, to rescue her from an unendurable conversation, and he frankly was just as glad to see her go. "It is a Jansai girl who has become her responsibility."

"A Jansai girl!" Neri exclaimed. "Gaaron, what strange people you seem to have gathered together. What exactly has been going on at this hold?"

So he talked to them a while longer of the events that had transpired, not going into much detail about Miriam's troubles but giving them a brief outline so that they could draw their own conclusions. After that, talk segued easily into gossip about the angels at the other holds, and Gaaron actually began to enjoy the conversation. They talked fairly late into the evening, till the dining room was completely empty and even the workers in the kitchen had finished cleaning up the evening meal.

"You must be tired," Gaaron said at last. "I'm sure Esther has had your usual rooms made up while we've been talking. I'll see you both in the morning."

"No, we'll be making bridal plans with Susannah," Neri corrected. "But I'm sure we'll be free by lunchtime."

"Maybe we'll go down to Velora," Adriel said.

Gaaron nodded in a courtly way. "As the day unfolds," he said.

He walked them to the bedchambers always reserved for their use, tarried long enough to make sure Esther had really put the rooms in order, and then headed back to his own suite.

Where he found Susannah before him, pacing up and down, and looking absolutely furious.

"This can't be good," he said, and closed the door.

She turned on him, her dark eyes snapping, her smooth cheeks flushed with more color than he had ever seen. "I am so angry, but I will start with an apology if you like, because none of this was your fault," she burst out. "I am usually better behaved, and I know I must do everything to be civil to your friends, but Yovah love me if I can sit there meekly and hear them say insulting things about the Edori—"

He smiled faintly. "Don't bother apologizing to *me*," he said. "I thought you handled it all magnificently. I wasn't even sure you were angry, though once or twice I had an inkling, and Adriel suspected something was wrong."

" 'Have you always been an Edori?' " Susannah said, mimicking Neri's voice. " 'Oh, it must be so nice for you to live here away from the savages!' How can they say such things to me? Don't they realize that we are all Yovah's people, every one of us, and that he loves us all equally? And even if he did not," she added, "we would still be good enough for her and her angel friends."

Gaaron could not help but laugh. This was a side of Susannah he had not seen before. "You must realize that the Edori seem exotic to us," he said. "I did not know what to expect the first time I came to land beside an Edori campfire. That they were friendly to me, and welcomed me with great graciousness, was due more to the Edori nature than any attempts I made, and I found that a humbling experience."

"Yes, well, Adriel and Neri could stand a humbling experience or two," Susannah fumed.

It was so unlike her that Gaaron laughed again. "No doubt. Neri especially. Perhaps you can be very rude to them tomorrow, and that will teach them a lesson."

"No! I can't!" she exclaimed in dismay. "I am quite incapable of it! Sometimes I can manage a nasty comment or two, but I always phrase it in such a delicate way that no one ever knows they have been insulted!"

Now he laughed even harder. "Well, perhaps that is not such a bad trait to have," he said in a placating way. "Your generosity of spirit wins you many friends. It is not so terrible to have Neri and Adriel thinking you like them. They can be powerful allies."

"Yes, but Gaaron, aren't *you* angry?" she demanded. "For the affront was to you as much as to me. Assuming you were too doltish to pick your own bride, or at any rate a bride that was worthy of you—"

"I was a little displeased when they showed up," he conceded. "Although I view their motives a little differently. I think they were proving to me that I was mishandling my own courtship, that *I* had done *you* a dishonor by appearing to think you were unworthy of meeting them. And if that is the perception that really does exist, then I am the one who needs to apologize to you. For that is not what I intended, and that is not how I feel."

That little speech had a remarkable effect on her, seeming to calm her completely. She stopped in her pacing, and stood a little apart from him, turned half away, half toward him. Her face was furrowed in a frown. "But Gaaron, you have always treated me with the utmost courtesy," she said. "And—well, I must confess—I have been glad that you haven't brought a parade of people through here to come stare at me and decide if I was worthy to be your bride. I have wanted to get a little used to everybody here before I started to show myself off to strangers."

"Yes, and we have had so many troubles here, there has not seemed to be a good time to sit down and plan a party," he agreed. "But they are right, you know. Sooner or later you must meet everyone—and sooner or later there *is* the wedding to plan."

Now she was silent for a moment. "Yes," she said at last. "I have given no thought at all to the wedding. But I suppose we must marry."

He felt a sudden intense clench of sadness at her words, at her tone. "Although I have thought lately," he said, in a gentle tone of voice, "that you were less and less pleased at the idea of marrying me."

Her eyes came swiftly to his face. "Why? What have I done? I am sorry if I—I know I have been very involved with Kaski, perhaps there are other crucial matters that I have overlooked—"

He held up a hand and she fell silent. "No. As always, you have been a model for civility and kindness. It is just that I—I have worried about you a little bit. I cannot forget that you were coerced here, to some extent. And you have seemed—" He paused, feeling trapped in dangerous phrases, unable to find words that seemed truthful without being hurtful. "For a while, it seemed as though you and I were friends of a sort," he said in a rush. "And lately that does not seem to be true. And I don't know what I have done, or what has happened, to change you. Or perhaps I am the one who has changed without intending to. I live in great fear of you becoming unhappy, you see. For I know it will be my fault if you do."

Now her face seemed alive with color; she put her hands up over her cheeks as if to hide her blush from his eyes. "Oh, Gaaron," she said, her voice muffled by her hands. "Not everything that happens in this whole world is your fault and your responsibility to correct."

He smiled faintly at that. "Indeed? That is the first I have heard of it."

She dropped her hands and turned to face him head-on, wearing a look of resolution. "The truth is—the truth is I have been afraid that you have been regretting being forced to take me as your bride," she said. "The truth is, I have thought that if we postponed the wedding long enough, you would come to realize that you would rather marry elsewhere—and you would be able to convince Yovah that a different wife was in your best interests. I have tried to keep out of your way somewhat, so that you could think things through and consider who you would marry."

He was smiling again, and he knew the expression on his face was quizzical. "But who else would I want to marry?" he asked. "I scarcely have time to see you, let alone go out to study the charms of other women."

"Well—Keren," she said.

"Keren!"

"She is quite young and beautiful, and she is so joyous that everybody loves her," Susannah said defensively. "And you seem to enjoy her company, and I always thought she would make a better angel's bride than I would—"

Now he laughed out loud. "I have had more than my share of beautiful and self-centered girls," he said. "The god spare me the agony of a lifetime married to one. Give me a reasonable and levelheaded woman any day over someone as volatile as Keren or my sister."

An expression so swift that he could not be sure of it flitted across her face; he had the sense he had displeased her again. "Yes," she said rather flatly. "I am reasonable and levelheaded."

He took a step nearer. "And kind, and intelligent, and possessed of a lovely smile," he added. "Mahalah tells me I am inept at complimenting women. You should consider that a fault of mine, and not a reflection of any defects of your own."

Now the lovely smile came, swiftly, and then was hidden away again. "An ability to flatter women would come low on the list of virtues I would look for in a man," she said. "It is very well by firelight, but it does nothing to fill the dinner pot."

"*Excuse* me?"

She laughed out loud, her hands back to her hot cheeks. "Oh— an Edori saying—it just popped right out of my mouth!" she exclaimed. "It means—well—"

"I can tell very well what it means," he said, amused. "I will take it as a compliment in turn that you consider I have some useful skills."

"Oh, I admire you greatly," she said. "I am like everyone else."

"Then we are agreed?" he said, his voice a little stern. "We will be friends again, and we will go forward with this wedding, and we will not each secretly be thinking the other one is unwilling?"

She held out her hand and he took it. "We are agreed," she said. "But tell me now. Should I put myself completely in the hands of Adriel and Neri? Or are there arrangements you would like to make? None of this is familiar territory to me, so I have no ideas about how to plan a ceremony."

"You can turn your life over to them or not, but they will go ahead and plan it anyway, so you may as well give them free rein," he said. "I think you can trust their taste, at any rate."

Her face was solemn but her eyes were laughing. "Ah, but I have already gotten advice from your sister and her friends about what I should wear at the wedding," she said. "Surely Adriel and Neri could have no objections to their suggestions?"

He gave a little groan, and then he laughed. "Yes, that is exactly the tack to take if you want to bedevil Adriel and Neri," he said. "Neri in particular admires Miriam, as you might imagine. She will take the news especially well."

She laughed. "Yes, I know just how to go about it," she said. "I'm sure I shall enjoy myself immensely in the morning."

He smiled down at her and brought her hand up to his heart, giving it a small squeeze. He thought perhaps he should give her a hug, or drop a kiss upon her dark hair, but they had reestablished a fragile friendship and he did not want to jeopardize the truce. "Plan a very nice wedding," he said. "Tell me all about it tomorrow."

• • •

But the next day, they were not talking about weddings. They were talking about deaths.

Gaaron did not see Susannah again until the noon meal. He was already seated at his customary table, Enoch beside him and Esther perched on an empty chair, complaining about the quality of the baker's bread, when Susannah, Adriel, and Neri came in together. Susannah looked prim and innocent, while the two angels looked ruffled and confused, so he supposed the morning had gone more or less the way Susannah intended. But the three women had barely made it to the table before there was a commotion across the room, and Nicholas swept in.

He looked exhausted and somehow thinner, as if he had expended a year's worth of energy in one quick physical action, and cold clung to his skin and feathers. "Gaaron," he said breathlessly as he charged across the room. Gaaron came to his feet, braced for disaster.

"What it is? Can you stand? Should you sit?"

Nicholas shook his head and gasped for air. "A farm settlement. Almost at the Gaza border. It's been burned to the ground."

A cry of surprise and dismay went up from the people sitting near enough to hear. "What?" Adriel said sharply.

Nicholas looked over at her, not even registering surprise at her presence. "Farming community. Big one—maybe fifty people lived there. All gone. Leveled. The ashes were cold, so I don't know when it happened. I flew over it two days ago and all was well."

"They haven't left, then," Gaaron said to Adriel. "We had hoped—there've been no reports—and this is bad."

"They've never attacked a place so big before," Neri said.

"That we know of," Gaaron corrected.

Adriel shook her head. "I've sent out patrols every day. Everything's been safe."

"Nothing's safe," Gaaron said grimly.

"I've got to get back to Monteverde," Neri said.

"Can you give me coordinates?" Gaaron asked Nicholas. The younger angel nodded.

"Draw you a map," he said.

Susannah stepped forward before Gaaron could speak again, putting a hand on his arm. "Zack," she said.

His head snapped back; he had actually forgotten. "Sweet Jovah singing," he swore. "Enoch—find Chloe and Zibiah, and meet me on the plateau in half an hour. We've got to pick up Zack and Jude and the women they're traveling with. Pack for a journey to Monteverde."

"If you're coming my way, I can travel with you, and carry one of them back," Neri offered.

Gaaron shook his head. "We'll move too slowly. You just go."

"What should I do?" Nicholas asked.

"Make me a map, and then sleep," Gaaron said.

"I can't stay," Adriel said.

Gaaron leaned over to kiss her soft cheek. Again, she looked haggard, as she had from time to time in the past year. Not nearly as carefree and pleased with herself as she had appeared last night. He would infinitely prefer the laughter of the previous night to the seriousness of this hour. "Go," he said. "Stop in the kitchens and take food. I am gone from here within the hour."

The Archangel turned to the Edori, holding her hands out. Susannah ignored them, and instead threw her arms around Adriel, giving her a warm hug. "You are a delightful girl," Gaaron heard Adriel murmur into the black hair. "We will meet again soon, and next time there will be no disasters to end our visit this way."

Susannah also hugged Neri, though Gaaron suspected the embrace was a little less fervent. It was much easier to like Adriel. "Soon," Neri promised Susannah. "It was good to meet you at last."

They scattered, Gaaron hurrying to his room to put on his heaviest flying gear and pack a couple of changes of clothes. How could he have been so stupid as to put the young boys of the hold in such danger? Yes, he had made sure that his own patrols followed the travelers' slow progress, and all had appeared to be well, at least from the air, but the possibility of true danger had never really occurred to him. He had thought the worst thing that could happen would be that Zack and Jude would desert their charges, though the two women were resourceful enough to make the rest of their journey alone. He had not considered that they might be in actual peril. Like Adriel, he had begun to hope the marauders had left Samaria—and they had never struck this far north before.

But he should have known, he should have thought more carefully, he should never have sent boys out to face hazards so great. He would never forgive himself if one of them came to harm.

Gaaron was on the plateau before the others had assembled, though he thought perhaps Neri had left already, not even bothering to collect her belongings. He was confident that Esther would magi-

cally appear, food packed for all four of the Eyrie angels—but instead
it was Susannah who came hurrying out of the corridor, her hands
filled with packages and her face furrowed with concern.

"For all of you," she said, handing him the leather pouches. "The
women and their babies as well."

"I'll probably be gone five days or more," he said.

She nodded, then she shook her head. "Don't be stupid, Gaaron,"
she said, her voice low and forceful.

He was taken completely by surprise. "Don't—what?"

She put her hands up to his arms, as if what she really wanted to
do was take his shoulders and give him a good shake. "Don't be stupid—don't blame yourself. You could not have foreseen this," she said
swiftly.

So she had read the self-condemnation on his face, or perhaps she
knew him better than he thought. "I am to blame," he said bitterly.
"I knew there was danger in the realm. Terrifying danger. And I sent
them out into it—unprepared—alone—"

"The danger did not exist where you sent them. The circumstances
changed," she said. "This is not your fault."

He stared bleakly down at her. "Tell me that when I return and
they are all still alive."

Now she did try to shake him, her fingers closing hard on his
muscles. "You are not responsible for the well-being of every single
soul in Samaria! You cannot direct every life and protect every life!
You are one man! And you are doing the best job you can."

"But this was an ill-done job," he said, pulling away from her.
Enoch broke onto the plateau, dressed in heavy flying leathers, and
Chloe and Zibiah were right behind him. Everyone looked worried.

"Where were they seen last?" Chloe said. "Do you know?"

Gaaron nodded. "Ahio made his report yesterday. They can't have
gotten too far from that point."

"I think we're ready," Enoch said.

Gaaron nodded, but Susannah's hand on his arm tugged his attention back to her. She hugged him, as she had hugged the angels,
and he was surprised at the strength and energy he derived from her
quick embrace. Her arms were sinewy and strong; he could feel the
smoothness of her cheek pressed against the fabric of his shirt.

"Do not forget to take care of yourself while you are taking care
of the rest of the world," she said, in a voice so low it was almost a
whisper. She drew back from him before he could reply, and gave all

of them a quick, comprehensive look. "Travel safely. Yovah hold you in his arms."

Chloe kissed Susannah on the cheek. "Back soon," she said. A few more desultory good-byes, and the angels flung themselves aloft.

They flew low to the ground in a spread-out formation, just close enough to call out to the nearest angel should any of them spot anything. Flying was rougher, this close to the surface, but Gaaron didn't want them to miss anything. A burned campsite, a broken body, an overturned cart filled with useless, splintered furniture.

They had not reached the travelers' latest campsite by the time early darkness fell, so they stopped for the night. It would be too easy to miss Zack and the others in the dark. Gaaron hated to stop, but he hated even more to take the blind risk. They found a small inn in a tiny town and bespoke two uncomfortable rooms for the night. Enoch slept poorly, which Gaaron knew because he didn't sleep at all. In the morning, the young women looked heavy-eyed and exhausted. No one said much as they ate a hasty meal and set out again.

The air was cold; it was the start of true winter. There would most certainly be snow up around Monteverde, possibly even farther south. That would make the travelers easier to spot, if they were still on the move. It would make the remains of their bodies more difficult to find, if they were not.

Gaaron shook his head, trying to dislodge the image.

By noon, they had encountered neither snow nor wreckage, and they halted for a quick meal. "How much farther ahead are they, do you think?" Chloe asked.

"I'd guess, no more than another thirty miles," Gaaron said. "Depending on how much ground they were able to cover yesterday. I would hope we'd find them in the next hour."

"Couple of little towns east of here," Enoch mentioned. "If one of them fell sick or they got scared at something, they may have taken shelter there."

Gaaron nodded. "If we don't find them on the road, we'll double back and check out the towns."

"Are we going to swing by the settlement? The one Nicky saw?" Chloe asked.

Gaaron shrugged, feeling his wings lift and settle behind him. "No reason to," he said quietly. "We've seen those sights before."

Back aloft into the frigid wind. Shards of sleet sliced through the air and across their skin. Gaaron could almost fancy he was collecting an assortment of tiny cuts all along his face and unprotected forearms. His fingers were numb, since he hadn't remembered to bring gloves, and even his feet, usually so comfortable in his leather boots, felt chilled and shrunken.

Better cold and shivering than burned to ashes.

After they had been flying for about twenty minutes, Zibiah, positioned at the westernmost edge of the formation, gave a little cry. They all canted over in her direction to see what she'd spotted. Gaaron's first reaction was one of severe disappointment: It was a large caravan moving at a plodding pace across the hard ground. The travelers were probably Jansai, though Gaaron thought he caught sight of some of the flags of Castelana among the carts and wagons. Gypsies and river merchants choosing to travel together—now that was a rare occurrence. Maybe they were heading to Manadavvi country to work out some mutually agreeable trading contract, or maybe the hard weather had encouraged them to pool their energy and their food stores. Gaaron counted twenty-two separate wagons before he lost track.

Beside the slow-moving twenty-second wagon, he spotted the diaphanous white arch of folded angel wings.

He gave a shout and pointed, immediately angling down for a landing. He was enough in the lead that he was on the ground and striding forward before any of the other three had landed.

Zack—for it was Zack that Gaaron had noted from the air—had seen Gaaron descend, his great wings spread and his big body casting a shadow across the wagon. The younger boy stopped walking, letting the carts and other conveyances roll past him, and he stood there waiting for Gaaron. His shoulders were tense and his head was thrown back; he looked braced for anger, or punishment, or anything.

"Zack!" Gaaron greeted him, his voice sounding stern even to his own ears. "Where are the others—Jude—the women?"

Zack jerked his head in the direction of the wagons. "Clara and Lena are riding with some of the merchants. Jude's gone off to the river to bring back more water. His third trip today."

The nearest river, if Gaaron remembered his map, was about ten miles northeast. A hike for a man on foot, but an easy distance for an angel to cover. And an angel, blessed with phenomenal body strength, could haul a lot more water back than a solitary man.

"How long have you been traveling with the caravan?" Gaaron

asked. He saw the other three angels land and head their way, but with a quick shake of his head, he sent them over toward the caravan. Enoch began to pace alongside one of the wagons, asking the driver questions.

"We met up with them yesterday morning. We couldn't—we saw—I didn't know what to do," Zack burst out. "We hadn't gone very far yesterday when we came across a campsite—all burned, all cinders—looked like just a few travelers, maybe a family. I knew we weren't safe, but the nearest town was a day's walk away, maybe more. So when the caravan came through—there haven't been any attacks on big groups, at least that I'd heard about—I thought we should pitch in with them."

Gaaron nodded, keeping his expression neutral. "Jansai and a few Castelana traders?" he asked, and Zack nodded. Gaaron continued, "Not the friendliest group, I'd imagine. But they just took you in? Let the women pick a wagon?"

Zack looked even more defensive. "No. We had to negotiate. That's why Jude's going for the water, and I'm taking first watch tonight."

Gaaron nodded again, the thoughtful expression on his face masking his quick surge of elation. Crisis and resolution, and Zack had handled it beautifully. Gaaron never would have expected it. "Did you think about just picking the women up and carrying them the rest of the way to Monteverde?"

"Thought about it," Zack said. "And I would have if the caravan hadn't come along—I'd have left the furniture behind, too, I didn't care. But the babies don't do well when we fly—we tried it a couple nights when it was late and we were too far from a town. They wouldn't have made a long journey. The caravan seemed safer."

"I almost didn't see you as we flew overhead," Gaaron said.

Zack was scanning his face, trying to read his tone. "I'm sorry if you don't like it, Gaaron," he said. "But I didn't know what to do."

Gaaron took a step nearer, putting his heavy hands on the boy's shoulders. "I'm proud of you," he said softly. "You've done well."

For a split second, it was as if Zack hadn't heard him. Then his face flushed, and he ducked his head, and he looked away. "Now, tell me," Gaaron said, dropping his hands. "How was your trip until yesterday?"

"Hard enough," Zack said in a strained voice. "The first few days were—they hated us, and the babies hated us, and we hated them. And we didn't make it to a town till late, and then no one wanted to leave the next day because everyone was sore. I had to just go outside and pick up the cart handles and start walking. I figured, the sooner I got to Monteverde, the sooner I could get back. And they all followed me." He shrugged a little. "And every day it got a little easier."

"Clara's a nice woman," Gaaron said. The caravan was a good thirty feet beyond them now, so he started walking slowly in its wake. Zack fell into step beside him. "Lena's harder to get to know."

"But Lena doesn't give up, and sometimes Clara does," Zack said with some energy. "Silas is just like his mother, too, that's why he gives up. I told her she had to be tougher with Matthew."

"Matthew?"

"The baby. She better raise him right."

Gaaron was sure the last person on earth Clara would want child-rearing tips from was Zack. But, amazingly, there seemed to have been some kind of deal struck, some kind of bond woven, among this little group during the span of their adventure.

"So how badly do Matthew and the other baby take to flying? How far can you go before they—start crying or whatever?"

"Before they start throwing up," Zack said with a certain bitterness. "About fifteen minutes."

"That's unfortunate," Gaaron said.

"Why?"

"Because we're here to fly the whole group to Monteverde. You made a good decision, joining the caravan, but you were wrong. You weren't safe here, either. Nicholas just flew back with news that a big settlement had been burned down not seventy-five miles from here."

Zack's face paled. "How big?"

"Maybe fifty people." Gaaron swept his arm out to indicate the slow-moving mass ahead of them. "If they can destroy fifty people at a time, they can destroy a hundred."

"What do you want to do?" Zack asked.

Gaaron glanced down at him. "What do *you* want to do?"

Zack thought about it. "I'd rather have vomit all over my shirt than be burned up," he said. "If we wait till both babies are asleep, we can probably go some distance before they get sick. We could try it, anyway."

"What about the furniture?" Gaaron asked.

Zack squinted at the caravan ahead. "Pay someone to haul it," he suggested. "They're going to Monteverde anyway. Someone would be willing to bring it."

Gaaron clapped him on the shoulder. "Excellent!" he approved. "I'll let you make the arrangements."

Zack stared up at him as if astonished. Gaaron realized that it might have been the first time he had ever offered the boy approval of any sort, and that maybe Zack was having trouble recognizing the expression on his face. "You did well," he said again. "I'm proud of you."

CHAPTER TWENTY-THREE

Kaski had not been happy about the visit from the angels. It was hard sometimes to determine what fueled the little girl's moods, but this time the cause and effect seemed pretty clear. She hated that Susannah had spent the entire morning with Neri and Adriel, and she ignored Susannah that night as the two of them prepared for bed.

As always, Susannah talked to her in a kind, encouraging voice, as if they were having a normal conversation. "Adriel has decided that I should get married while it is still winter, when all the world is old and dry and covered in snow," she said, combing out her hair in front of the mirror. Kaski lay curled up in a ball on the big bed and appeared not to be listening. "She says that this means my marriage will blossom along with the buds and new leaves that arrive with spring. I don't actually think this would have been her first choice," Susannah continued with a laugh. "She really wanted me to marry about a month before the Gloria, when spring is just about to arrive. But I told her that the Gathering would be held then, and that no silly marriage to any no-account Archangel would prevent me from attending the Gathering, so she decided to move the date up a little."

Susannah laid her brush down and moved through the room, extinguishing all lights except a small one near the water room. Then she climbed into bed beside the small stiff bundle of disapproval. "You can attend my wedding, won't you like that?" Susannah whispered into the back of the child's head. Her hair was scented with fresh herbs and soap, and her skin had a little-girl smell. "Perhaps we can buy you a new gown and you can parade across the plateau tossing out dried rose leaves and manna seeds. I'll make a garland for your hair and embroider a handkerchief for you to carry."

But this elicited no response from Kaski, either, unless the small body shrinking even farther way could be considered a response. Susannah sighed, kissed the dark hair, and rolled over to face the other way.

She missed everybody. She missed Miriam, who used to come here at least once a week and spend the night with her and Kaski; she missed Chloe and Sela and Zibiah, who would often spend the last two hours of the day in this room, gossiping about recent events, before seeking their own beds. And she missed Keren, who had slept in this bed every night since she arrived at the Eyrie . . . until a week ago, when she had begun spending her nights in Nicholas' bed instead.

Susannah sighed again and tried to mold her pillow into a comfortable shape. She had done her best to fit into the lifestyle at the angel hold. She had made true friends and she believed that Gaaron valued her. But she was so lonely sometimes. Everyone was so polite and distant; there was not that casual affection, the quick hug, the kiss in passing, that she was used to and still craved, every day. Yovah had sent her here and she accepted her duty. She would serve the god and the Archangel with every scrap of intelligence she could muster. But she missed the emotion. Her soul was crying out for love.

She twisted over to lie on her back. Keren had found love, of course; Keren always did. Susannah could not decide what she thought about this union of angel and Edori girl, mostly because it was not clear to her which one of them would suffer most when the relationship came to an end. As it had to, didn't it? Surely Nicholas was expected to marry well, bring in a high-caste Manadavvi girl with whom he could sire more volatile, warmhearted angels? And surely Keren was too restless to stay here more than a season, flirting with the luxuries of life but true, at heart, to her Edori origins.

Susannah was a great believer in letting people make their own choices, and their own mistakes, but she could not help worrying a little about both of them. They seemed so much in love. She remembered that great swooping emotion, so giddy and so intense, and she envied them—but she feared for them, too. Equally as great would be the sense of loss and betrayal; no matter how grand the world seemed now, it would feel small and bleak and desolate when the love affair ended. She knew. She had lost just such a love herself.

She told herself she would settle for companionship now. But here she was, alone with a sulky child, not even a friend to share her night with. She refused to cry or feel sorry for herself, but her face grew tight with the effort of holding back tears, and she was so tense that it was an hour or more before she could fall asleep.

The next few days were no less dreary, gray and damp outside the hold, anxious and silent inside it, as everyone awaited news about Zack and Jude. When the whole flock of angels finally reappeared—everyone safe, the whole venture a success—relief sent the entire hold into a festive mood. Esther cooked up a feast, and after the meal they all gathered outside in the cold, wet air to sing songs of celebration. Susannah wanted just five minutes alone with Gaaron to ask him for details of the trip and to make sure he wasn't still punishing himself for sending the boys away in the first place. But everyone, it seemed, wanted to be close to Gaaron this night. There was no time for a private conversation.

And in the morning he was gone, off to the southern settlements to warn the farmers of fresh dangers. She thought she had risen early enough to wish him farewell, but he had left before true dawn. It was not certain when he would return.

The news put her in a gloomy mood, which she made some effort to push aside. It was a pretty day, cold but clear. *Never waste a gift from Yovah,* Anna used to say on brilliant winter days, and Susannah had always tried to take the advice to heart. Particularly now—there was no need to sulk inside the Eyrie just because she was feeling low. She would take advantage of the sun.

Accordingly, she rounded up Chloe and Zibiah and even Kaski, and headed down to Velora to shop. The little Jansai girl sometimes enjoyed the open marketplace and sometimes did not, and Susannah had long ago given up trying to figure out what made her like Velora and what turned her against it. Today she was quite content to wander from stall to stall, admiring the silk and gold and spices, her eyes crinkling up happily behind the severe mask of her veil.

"Traditionally, of course, a bride wears gold," Chloe said, fingering a long bolt of yellow satin. "Not quite this color, though."

"Lady Anne wore blue at her wedding last year," Zibiah said.

"Oh, well, in *Semorrah*, what do you expect?" Chloe said scornfully. "The angel brides wear gold." She picked up a length of figured silk and held it up to Susannah's face. "A good color for you. The darker, the better. Bronze, I think, not true gold."

"With an embroidered collar," Zibiah added.

"I could do the embroidery myself," Susannah agreed.

"Did Adriel have a style of dress in mind?" Chloe asked.

"She said she would send me a few patterns."

"Well, she had better act quickly! If the wedding is only to be a couple of months away—do you realize how much is to be done?"

Susannah shook her head. "I don't know, it seems very strange to be planning a big, important event when we are—we are under *attack*! Surely no one will be interested in attending this wedding when they are all in fear for their lives."

"Nonsense, the god would have to strike them all dead before anyone would miss Gaaron's wedding," Chloe said, trying another bolt of cloth against Susannah's hair. "Oh, I like that. What do you think?"

"Very rich," Zibiah agreed. "She could wear scarlet accents with it—a little ribbon around her wrists—"

"Everyone loves Gaaron, you know," Chloe added, pushing Susannah toward the long mirror set up in the back of the stall. "Everyone wants to see him settled in place. They want a chance to celebrate with him."

Susannah stared at the image reflected back, a dark woman with her head wrapped in crimson-shot gold, her face serious, her eyes tired. "Yes, but do they want to see him marry *me*?" she asked in a small voice.

Chloe clouted her on the head with a large roll of lace. "If they know you, they do. Hey, what do you think of this, Zib? Too blond? I like the pattern, though."

"Buy some for yourself," the other angel suggested. Talk went that quickly from wedding gowns to day gowns, and Gaaron's name didn't come up again for the rest of the morning.

His name came up again the next day when Esther insisted that she and Susannah discuss the menus for the various meals that had to be planned for the wedding. There would be a light lunch for guests arriving early, a formal dinner following the evening ceremony, and a less formal but still imposing breakfast the next morning. Esther had already taken the trouble to compose some traditional courses, she informed Susannah. If only the angelica would look over the possibilities and indicate which ones she liked the best?

Esther was always tricky. She could be an ally or an enemy, pretty much in the same five-minute space, and learning to handle her had been one of Susannah's first chores upon arriving at the Eyrie. This one was easy, though. "Oh, Esther! I don't have any idea what would be best for a wedding feast!" Susannah exclaimed in dismay. "I know you have too much to do as it is, but—well—what would *you* suggest?"

Esther preened a bit at that. "Well, of course, beef and lamb would be the *proper* dishes to serve, but what with you being an Edori, I didn't know if there were special meats you'd like to have. And my girls and I can cook anything, we just have to have time to prepare."

"To tell you the truth, I've never eaten anything at an Edori campfire that was half as good as the meals you serve on the most casual days," Susannah said. "There's nothing special I'd ask for—except that fruit pie. I love that. Is that appropriate for a wedding?"

Esther seemed even more pleased at that compliment. "Not for the wedding, no, but for the luncheon—now, that would be just the right touch to end up the meal. I'll add that to the list here."

It took another two hours to confirm that every one of Esther's suggestions was perfect and that no bride could expect to have a better chef overseeing her celebratory meals. Kaski, who had accompanied Susannah to this conference, grew bored and began building huts and cottages out of silverware, linen napkins, and a few stray plates. Naturally, one of these unsteady constructions fell to the floor with a loud crash and the sound of shattering china.

"Now—! You troublesome child, haven't I told you before—oh, look at this mess. Not an hour before lunch and I've got this disaster on my hands to clean up—"

"I'll help you," Susannah offered. "I think only a couple of plates broke—"

Esther was on her knees, picking up the biggest pieces and sweeping the chips into a pile with the edge of her hand. She gave a quick irritated glance at Kaski, standing beside the table with a look of apprehension and contrition on her face. "Honestly. That girl is always into something."

"It's my fault. I should have given her something to keep her occupied while we were talking."

"It's not your job to entertain her every hour of the day! And night," Esther added, for she heartily disapproved of Susannah's habit of sleeping with the Jansai girl. "She'll have to find herself a new bed as soon as you marry Gaaron, and that will be better for everyone, as far as I'm concerned. Let her grow used to the idea now, that she can't have every minute of your time."

"Esther," Susannah reproved.

"Well, she can't. Better for you if she *had* gone back with those Jansai when they came to Velora. She belongs with her own people if she's not going to make any effort to fit in here."

It took Susannah a few more moments to calm Esther down—there was nothing the mortal woman hated so much as disarray—but once the broken plates were cleaned up, Esther rather grudgingly said Kaski was generally a pretty good girl and it wasn't such a bother to have her around. By that time, however, Kaski was nowhere in sight.

It was true: Susannah did not have to keep Kaski in view every minute of every day. But a vague sense of uneasiness made her hunt for the Jansai girl throughout the Eyrie, checking Kaski's usual hiding places and asking everyone she ran across. "Have you seen Kaski? Sometime within the last twenty minutes . . . the last half hour . . . the last hour . . ."

But she was not there. Increasingly more frantic, Susannah began to suspect that the little girl had found someone to take her down to Velora, though she had never known Kaski to leave the hold on her own before. She ran back to her room to put on a warm jacket and then headed out to the plateau, where a glowering sky and bitter wind promised rain in the near future.

She was in luck: Zibiah and Ahio were just landing, and calling out laughing greetings to each other over the cold wind. Susannah hurried over, waving them closer. "Have you just been to Velora? Did either of you see Kaski down there?" she demanded.

Ahio shook his head. "I've just come from southern Bethel with Gaaron."

Susannah's mood instantly lightened. "Gaaron's back?"

"Not yet. About an hour behind me."

"Is Kaski missing?" Zibiah asked.

"I can't find her anywhere. I know she's upset. She heard Esther and me talking and Esther said—well, you know how she is—"

"We know," Ahio said.

"And I think Kaski may have run away. I can't find her in the hold, but I can't imagine who would have taken her down to Velora without telling me—"

"We'll come help you look," Ahio said.

Susannah hesitated. "Unless—unless she *is* still here and I just haven't found her," she began.

Zibiah nodded. "I'll stay here and look for her. You two go down to Velora."

Within minutes, Susannah and Ahio were on their way. It had been cold enough on the somewhat sheltered plateau; the short airborne trip was almost unendurable. Susannah was shivering when Ahio set her down.

"Where do you want to look?" he asked.

She spread her hands. "She likes the sweets and pastries, so maybe down by the food stalls? I guess we should split up."

"I'll head down toward the shops. You take the market," he said. "Shall we meet back here in an hour?"

Susannah thought it might take longer, but she wasn't thinking too clearly. She was having trouble putting together sentences. "An hour—do you think—I guess so. I'll see you then."

She set off through the open market, blundering against people and making constant apologies as she craned her neck to see into as many stalls and alleyways as she could. Many of these vendors knew her and her entourage from the Eyrie, of course, so she asked them, "Have you seen Kaski? She's missing."

"That little girl? Sure haven't. I'll keep my eyes open, though."

One matronly vendor said she *thought* she'd seen someone who *looked* like Kaski, but then the girl had turned around and she wasn't even Jansai. "Funny how people look alike," the woman said.

Susannah didn't think it was funny at all. "Yes—well—thank you," she said and moved on, feeling even more desperate.

It was more than an hour later, and she'd forgotten all about the promised rendezvous with Ahio, when she spotted a small, heavily veiled little girl a few rows ahead of her in the crowded market. She had been beside herself with worry, for she had almost reached the last row of stalls—beyond were only a few blocks of dreary commercial buildings and then the rocky plains and hillocks that spilled away from the mountain. Nowhere else to look, unless Ahio had found her.

Or Susannah had. "Kaski!" she called, waving her arms and trying to find the best route through the close-packed stalls. "Kaski! Come over here."

The small figure turned, suspicion in every line of its draped and hooded body. Kaski, all right. "Kaski!" Susannah called again.

But Kaski took off running.

Susannah tore after her, bumping into people and knocking merchandise off of tables in her haste. "Kaski! Kaski, wait! Kaski, please let me talk to you!" But the little girl did not slow down, just ran with a demon speed through the staring buyers and the pointing sellers, slipping out of the last row of stalls and into the gray business district of the city.

Susannah ran behind her, calling her name, and feeling more frightened and helpless with each step she took. Kaski was not just hurt and angry, she was inconsolable. Susannah did not see how she would be able to calm the little girl, even if she caught up with her. "Kaski! Please, please, let me talk to you!" she cried, but there was no answer. Just a few blocks ahead of her, a small scurrying figure breaking free of the overhung shadows of the buildings and racing out into the untracked land surrounding the city.

Once out into the open, Kaski's pace slowed a little, into a fast, determined walk that could cover the miles with efficiency. Kaski was Jansai, used to hard travel and punishing wear on the feet and body. But Susannah was Edori, and she could walk all day, two heavy sacks over her back and a rock in her hand. She could keep up; she would not wear down before this little girl.

Accordingly, Susannah, too, fell into a familiar long-legged stride, her eyes fixed on the small figure before her, her hands tucked under her arms to keep them warm. Sweet Yovah singing, but it was cold. The clouds bunched together, arguing and angry; the sky grew blacker with irritation. The wind sheering straight down from the north slapped against her face like wet linen, leaving her cheeks streaked with red.

After she had been following Kaski for an hour, it began to rain.

"Kaski!" Susannah called out again as the first big, cold drops began to fall. She was beginning to tire—all those months of soft allali living were making it harder than she had expected to chase after Kaski this way—and it was an effort to gather enough breath to shout out. "Kaski, come back! Let's find shelter!"

In response, Kaski began to run.

Awkwardly, painfully, Susannah began to run behind her. Now the rain was lashing down in wicked, wind-driven sheets. The ground was turning swampy and treacherous; it was hard to find footing, it was hard to see. Plus it was so cold. The icy rain had completely soaked through Susannah's heavy jacket and her woolen clothes beneath. She was wet to the skin. How would she and Kaski even make it back to Velora? She panted for air, and her breath made a foggy exhalation against the wet wind.

"Kaski! Please come back!" she called, but her voice was drowned out by the ill-tempered snarl of thunder. The god protect them, this storm was about to get worse. *"Kaski!"*

Ahead, the terrain altered, swelling into a series of low foothills, still rocky and inhospitable this close to the mountain range. Another grumble of thunder and Kaski seemed to slow down, throwing her head up as if to track the source of the noise. Then the little girl looked around rather wildly, as if wondering where to seek refuge. Susannah, who had not slacked her pace, almost caught up with her.

"Kaski! Over there! By the hill—"

Either Kaski heard her, or she had drawn her own conclusions, for she veered to the left and an unpromising little mound of rocky earth. Cold, soaked, gasping for air, Susannah arrived beside her, skidding to a halt in the clotted dirt. "Kaski—oh baby, you had me so worried . . ."

Now, finally, miles from the city and equally as far from any hope of succor, Kaski turned to her, panicked and sobbing. Susannah crouched down against the small hill, wrapping the shaking, hysterical body in her arms, and trying to take the brunt of the rain and the wind on her back. "It's all right, it's all right, it's all right," she crooned into the buried hair.

Though it was not all right. The wind picked up force, screeching like a child in a tantrum, and the rain fell with a sudden fierce fury. Lightning cracked across the sky like a welt of fire, causing both of them to cry out, and the ominous crash of thunder that followed sounded like the world splitting in half.

When the lightning flashed again, Susannah saw the great silhouette of doom stretched above her, the terrifying shadow of winged death. She shrieked and hugged Kaski closer.

When the lightning sparked again, the shadow was beside her, and it was Gaaron.

"Gaaron!" she cried, but the roar of wind and rain was too strong; she could not even hear her own voice. His mouth opened as if he, too, was shouting a greeting, but she could not understand him over the flash and rattle of the heavens. The rain came down even harder, seeded with pods of hail, and Susannah crouched lower over Kaski, trying to shield the small shoulders with her own body.

And then, though the storm still raged about them, the rain stopped.

Susannah lifted her head, but she could not see. It was too dark, she was encased in darkness. Lightning flared and gave her a quick glimpse of a white, quilled tent stretched above her; then blind darkness again. Another pulse of lightning—another dreamlike vision of a broad, feathered canopy spread from over Susannah's head straight to the ground. One shadow at the center, like a tent pole made of oak.

Gaaron had made a shelter of his own body, his own wings, and braced himself against the onslaught of the storm to protect them.

"Gaaron!" Susannah cried again, but he could not have heard her. He had not ducked his face beneath the laced mesh of his wings. He had, no doubt, lifted his head to the oath and pummel of the storm, gauging its strength and rage. Or—she didn't know—perhaps he was even now trying to tame it, meeting fury with calm, beating back the wild violence of weather with a steely lullaby. Just because Susannah couldn't hear him singing didn't mean the god could not.

But he might not be singing. He might be merely enduring, knowing the storm would wear itself out and that even he did not have the strength to challenge it. They were not safe here—any venomous slash of lighting could strike them at random—but neither would they be safe attempting to take off for the Eyrie in such weather.

Kaski turned in Susannah's arms with a little mewling cry, and Susannah hugged her closer. "I know, baby, I know," she murmured into the child's hair, not sure if Kaski could hear her, could hear anything, over the anger of the storm. Another streak of lightning and Gaaron's wing looked like nothing but tendon and bone above them, skeletal and insubstantial. Another nasty yowl of thunder. Kaski cried out again. "I know, mikala, I know."

The storm lasted another half an hour, Susannah judged, and even when the worst of the battle moved on, the rain still fell steadily. Not only were Susannah and Kaski thoroughly soaked, their clothing was covered with the mud that had formed under them as the rain poured down. Yovah's tears, how far was it back to the Eyrie? Would they hold together that long? Susannah was so tired and so cold and so wet that she felt herself shivering with an uncontrollable ague, and Kaski merely lay in her wet lap and cried.

The white curtain above them parted and Gaaron peered down. There was enough milky light overhead to allow her to see his face through the ghostly aura of his spread wings. "Is she all right? Are you?" he called over the lingering rumble of thunder.

"I don't know! I think she'll recover once we get her to shelter. Gaaron, how did you find us? We would have died out here without you."

Rain ran down his jawline and dripped onto Susannah's upturned cheeks. "Ahio told me what had happened. I circled the whole area a couple of times. You'd gotten farther than I expected."

"I was never so glad to see anyone in my life."

A faint smile crossed his face, hard to see in the pale light. "You looked frightened when you saw me."

"You looked frightening," she retorted. "Oh, but Gaaron, if you had not come along—and sheltered us—I was so afraid—"

He nodded once and withdrew his head, as if glancing up to check the clouds again. Perhaps he did not want to be thanked; perhaps he did not want his expression to reveal how frightened he, too, had been. He poked his face back through the overlapping weave of feathers.

"I think we can risk taking off now," he said. "It's still raining but the wind isn't as strong. You'll get wet."

She couldn't help a laugh. "We're already wet. And miserable and *cold.*"

He folded back his feathers, and she was instantly covered with a light, chilly rain. "Can you stand?" he asked.

He reached down as if to take Kaski from her arms, but the little girl, who had seemed almost comatose for the past few minutes, shrieked and writhed away. Gaaron straightened, a look of deep displeasure on his face.

Susannah stared up at him. "Perhaps you should go back and get Zibiah," she said hesitantly. "We'll be all right here a little while, now that the rain's stopped. I don't think Kaski will let you take her in your arms."

His expression tightened still more. It took Susannah a moment to realize that he was furious, probably had been furious this whole time, and not at Susannah. "She damn well will let me take her in my arms and fly both of you back to the Eyrie," he said deliberately. "You can hold her so that she is not—contaminated—by my touch, but I am done indulging her at your expense. I will *not* leave you here another minute to freeze or be swept away. Can you stand with her in your arms, or shall I help you?"

"I can stand," Susannah said softly. It was a struggle to come to her feet and then gather the shaking, weeping child in her arms, but she managed it, somewhat gracelessly. Gaaron bent and, with one quick movement, picked them both up and cradled them against him. Kaski cried out once more and buried her head in Susannah's chest, but she did not fight to get free.

"Gaaron," Susannah exclaimed involuntarily. "You're so warm." For the heat of his body radiated through her wet clothes and his own, unbelievably powerful and comforting.

A smiled flickered across his face. "Angel blood," he said. "Nothing cools it."

"Can you carry us both all that way?" she said.

Now he actually laughed. The falling rain looked misty around his face. The drenching had left his hair plastered against his skull, so that the bones of his head and his cheeks and his jaws stood out, stubborn and unrelieved. He looked intransigent as a mountain, as impossible to destroy. No wonder the storm had battered itself uselessly against his body and then moved on.

"I could carry the two of you from here to Luminaux and not notice the burden," he said lightly. "Do not be concerned for me."

If she had not had to hold on to the miserable bundle of Kaski, she would have thrown her arms around his neck. "Oh, Gaaron," she said, "I am only so grateful that *you* have been concerned for *me*."

At that, he smiled again but made no reply. His arms tightened around her but that was no lover's signal; he was preparing for flight. His great wings clawed through the air, seeking a purchase, as he ran forward, light as a deer through the sucking mud of the field. Susannah gasped as his forward motion flung them all into the air—they were too heavy, even his wings were not strong enough, there was no way they would not pitch forward again, back to the dull, heavy earth. And yet they were flying, gaining altitude with every wingbeat, pushing through the soggy air with nothing but brute determination. Back to the Eyrie. Back to safety and home.

Susannah wrapped her arms more closely around Kaski, murmuring endearments into the wet veil. She was glad of her own clothes, soaked and uncomfortable as they were—glad especially of the heavy jacket, made of dark material so dense that nothing would show through it. She knew that the sharp, steady pain on her arm was the result of no injury sustained from that mad dash through the treacherous terrain. She had tripped and fallen once or twice, but she had not landed in such a way as to bruise that arm. No, if she were to strip off the jacket, she would find no wound, just a pulsating, insistent light in the opal depths of her Kiss.

It would look much like the Kiss glittering and exulting on Gaaron's arm, naked to the world for all to see. He did not act as if he noticed either the color or the pain, and she thought it was very likely that he did not. No one had told her that rage could set sparks in the heart of a Kiss, but perhaps it was so; that was the only emotion he had shown this afternoon, and even that he had kept banked down. She did not understand him—she was only beginning to understand herself—and in any case, she was too exhausted to think about it now. She rested her head against the welcome warmth of his chest, and closed her eyes.

Two days later, Gaaron informed Susannah that he had made arrangements for Kaski.

"Arrangements?" she said blankly. "What do you mean?"

He had been gone for most of these two days, and she had missed him. When he had sent for her, late on that second night, she had been a little fluttery and excited at the thought of seeing him again. *Stupid and girlish!* she thought, but she had changed her shirt so she could wear the vest with red accents, and she had combed her hair out again before hurrying down the hall.

To learn that he wanted to talk about Kaski.

"She can't stay here," he said. He had offered Susannah a chair and then failed to sit down himself, so that she sat, small and stationary, while he paced the floor. He smelled like winter starlight; he must have just this minute landed on the plateau after a long flight. "She is too disruptive. She takes too much of your time, and Esther's and

Chloe's and Zibiah's—she cannot be trusted—and she is not happy. For everyone, it seems better if she were placed elsewhere."

"But—*where?*" Susannah demanded. "The Jansai won't take her and she is afraid of every man she sees—"

He turned to face her, but his attention seemed elsewhere. "There is a place where only women live," he said. "At Mount Sinai, with the oracle and her acolytes. It is true that men visit there from time to time, but the compound is big, and the visitors stay mostly in one small part. I think she would feel safe there, among people she could trust. And Mahalah has kindly consented to take her in."

"Mahalah?" Susannah repeated, because at the moment she could not think who belonged to the name.

"The oracle. It is time you met her, anyway. I would like you to come with me tomorrow when I take Kaski to her. It will ease Kaski's transition to have you present, and it will give you some time to meet one of the most gracious women of all Samaria."

Susannah shook her head and came to her feet, feeling outmaneuvered and a little angry. "But Gaaron, I am not convinced that this is the right thing to do! It is true that Kaski is troublesome, but she is a lonely, frightened child—"

"Who needs special care that you cannot provide."

"But I *want* to provide it! I am very fond of her! You cannot just—you cannot just take her from me like an ill-mannered pet—or treat *me* like a child who does not have the sense to take care of her own playthings."

He stopped in his pacing to look at her seriously. "Is that what you think? This is not about any failure on your part. You could take in any Jansai or Edori in the three provinces, and have them run wild at the Eyrie, and let them tear the place down to the floorboards every night, and I would not complain. But this girl has put you at risk, and because you allow yourself to love her, she will continue to put you at risk, and I will not have you endangered. I won't. End of discussion. I have found a place for her that I think is safe, that you can get to without much trouble, so that you can keep her in your life if you so choose. But she is going to Mount Sinai tomorrow. I hope you will come with us, but even if you don't, that is where she is going."

Susannah stared at him, not knowing how to answer. All she could think was that he was still angry—even angrier than she had realized as they huddled against the hillock—and that reason never won any skirmish with rage. She remembered arguments between Tirza and Eleazar, arguments over trivial matters, sometimes, and how Tirza would simply walk away, saying, "No." Whatever it was that Tirza refused to do would not ever get done. In some situations there were no compromises, and Susannah recognized such a situation now.

"What time do you want to leave?" she asked in a low voice.

"As soon as we've eaten. Tell Kaski or not, it is up to you."

"And you alone will take us all that way?"

"I have asked Zibiah to come with us. I think that will be more comfortable for Kaski."

Susannah nodded dumbly and turned for the door. She thought Gaaron might stop her on her way out, call her name, at least, but he did not. Not until she stepped into the hall and shut the door behind her did she realize that she was shaking.

Mahalah indeed was one of the most gracious women Susannah had ever met. Also the frailest, the smallest, the tiniest wisp of a woman. It seemed a wonder to Susannah that she could ever summon the strength to take her next breath, since her body did not seem constructed to withstand such abuse.

"Ah, the new angelica," Mahalah greeted her, taking her hand. The oracle's grip was more compelling than Susannah would have expected, and her black eyes were keenly watchful. "We must have time to sit and visit while you're here, just the two of us."

"Don't let her tell you unkind things about me," Gaaron said to Susannah. "She does not hold me in high esteem."

"Nonsense. I value you just as I should. It is just that I know so much more than you do, and have such greater wisdom, that I cannot always accept your pronouncements the way your host does at the Eyrie."

"Everyone always does exactly what Gaaron says," Zibiah offered. She was standing a little to one side of the main group, allowing Kaski to rest her veiled head against her flying leathers.

"I'll wager that you do not," Mahalah said, sending Susannah a shrewd look. The oracle was still holding on to the angelica's hand, and Susannah was surprised at the heat in the thin fingers. "The Edori are rather a wayward lot, and you do not have a look of submission about you."

Susannah smiled. "I have tried to be docile and accommodating," she said demurely.

"Do not tell me that you do not have a stubborn streak," the oracle exclaimed. "I can read it in your face."

Susannah's smile widened. "I have not had an opportunity to show it," she said, her voice still prim. "I would have to be very hard to please if I did not find life at the Eyrie satisfactory."

Mahalah released her hand and turned to Gaaron. "Watch that one," she advised him. "She is not so trouble-free as she looks."

Clearly this conversation was not much to Gaaron's taste. "And yet, it is not Susannah whom we have come here today to discuss," he said pleasantly. "May we introduce Kaski to you? She is, as you see, a Jansai girl who has fallen under our protection."

Zibiah gently pushed Kaski the few yards over toward Mahalah, who sat patiently unmoving in a high-backed wheeled chair. Kaski moved along with the angel, but she would not look up, even when Zibiah encouraged her to say hello.

"Yes, this one is very damaged," Mahalah said in a soft voice— and then added something in a language none of them could understand. Susannah saw Gaaron give the oracle a sharp look, and she was surprised herself. The words sounded Jansai, though she had never heard of anyone who was not Jansai being taught the secretive, complex language.

At any rate, the speech had the effect of lifting Kaski's head and spinning her around to face the oracle. She actually responded, issuing a few sharp, suspicious words that sounded like a question. Mahalah nodded and gave her an emphatic answer, making her hands into two fists for emphasis. Now Kaski launched into a torrent of words, she the silent child of no speech, and the three other visitors stared at her in wonder. Mahalah answered her, and then turned her attention back to the angels and the Edori.

"Yes, I think Kaski will do quite well here," she said serenely. "I am glad you have brought her to me."

Although Susannah could tell that Gaaron was eager to get back to the Eyrie, it was clear that it would be too rude to leave Mount Sinai minutes after delivering their bundle, so the two angels and the Edori stayed for another few hours. Susannah accepted the offer of a tour through the tunnels, which Mahalah narrated while she led the way in her wheeled chair.

"Here's one of the guest rooms. If you ever come to spend the

night, you'll stay someplace like this. It's nice, isn't it? My own rooms
look much the same, only a little bigger. . . . Down this hall are the
dorm rooms where the girls sleep. I would show them to you, except
they are embarrassingly messy, and I don't want you realizing what a
slack housekeeper I am. . . . That's the audience chamber, you saw that
when you came in. . . . The kitchens are that way, but even *I* don't go
into them, since I can't cook. I bet you can cook, though, can't you?"

"Camp food," Susannah said. "Nothing fancy."

"I can't even do that much. Couldn't roast a rabbit to save my
life!"

"But you can speak Jansai, which makes up for your other defi-
ciencies," Susannah said demurely.

Mahalah cackled with laughter. "I can speak Edori, too," she said,
switching to that tongue. "And the old language, the one the settlers
used when they first landed. And I've seen texts of other languages that
came from that world we used to live on, and I can understand a few
of those words, too. I'm good with words. Some people are good with
math. Some people are good at cooking rabbits."

"You speak Edori very well," Susannah said. "You must have had
a native teacher."

"I did," Mahalah admitted, but didn't give specifics. She had
wheeled into a large, high-ceilinged room. It was cluttered with books
and furniture but otherwise gave the appearance of light and openness,
though it was an interior room with no windows. Or perhaps that was
a window against the far wall, looking onto a blue vista like sky or
water. Susannah walked that way, drawn by the mesmerizing brightness of the rectangle of color.

Mahalah rolled up beside her. "That caught your attention, didn't
it? It's the interface."

"The what?"

"The interface. The device through which I communicate with the
god." Mahalah laid her hand against the glowing glass, and her flesh
took on a strange appearance, dark and dull and outlined in black. "I
use this keyboard here to write to the god, and his words appear to
me on the screen."

Susannah shook her head. "What?" she said again, a small smile
on her face.

Mahalah laughed. "I know. Old technology. It doesn't make any
sense to us these days. But it is like—oh—writing letters to the god
through the medium of this device. And having him write letters back."

"I think I would be nervous if I received a message from Yovah," she said. "Terrified, more likely. I would not want to misinterpret what he had to say."

"And it is easy to do," Mahalah agreed, dropping her hand back into her lap. "His words are cryptic at best."

Susannah came a step closer. "May I touch it?"

"Certainly! Just lay your hand across the screen like so."

Cautiously, Susannah put her palm against the cool glass, feeling a tingle like a charge of static against her skin. Nothing else. No vibration, no heat, no streak of shock. "It's so curious," she observed at last. "I have seen—technology—like this before."

"You have? Have you been to one of the other oracles, then? Or— I know—the music machines at the hold are rather like this, aren't they?"

Susannah shook her head. "In my dreams, sometimes. I dream that I am in a room filled with—what did you call them?—screens and keyboards, just like these. And some that are a little bit like this, but different, too. Rooms and rooms full of them."

Now Mahalah was looking at her sharply. "How long have you had these dreams? How often?"

"Since I was a child. At first I did not have them more than once every month or two. Lately—almost every night." She smiled. "I don't know, maybe the god *is* trying to give me a message, if he sends me dreams about his machinery."

"Kneel down here for a moment," Mahalah said imperiously. Wondering, but not for a moment hesitating, Susannah obediently went down to her knees in front of the oracle. "Bend your head forward—I want to see—" And without explanation, Mahalah began to run her small hands over Susannah's scalp. "There must be—otherwise I don't understand—but if you are having dreams—"

In moments, the probing fingers found the second Kiss embedded behind Susannah's ear. "Aahhh," Mahalah said on a long sigh. She kept one hand on the little nodule, and with the other tilted Susannah's head up. "You have been doubly Kissed, did you know that?"

Susannah nodded carefully, so as not to dislodge the hands, but Mahalah released her anyway. "Yes. It is rare, I know."

Mahalah leaned back in her chair. "So rare almost no one knows that such a thing can even occur," she said.

"What does it mean? Something special?" Susannah asked. "Was the second Kiss the reason I was named angelica?"

"Perhaps. Perhaps that is part of the reason, I don't know. As I said, Jovah is often mysterious. What I do know is that, once every three generations, according to the instructions the priests have lived by since the time of the original settlers, someone living in Samaria must be outfitted with this second Kiss. As I understand it, the choice is entirely arbitrary. No one knows in advance which priest will draw this rare Kiss, or on whom he will bestow it. No one knows what makes the Kiss special, or why its installation is required. Only that once every three generations, someone living in Samaria bears it."

Susannah sat back on her heels, fingering the knob behind her ear. "And you think this second Kiss sends me dreams?" she asked.

"I think that the god tracks us all by the Kisses we bear in our arms," the oracle said, seeming to choose her words with care. "I would assume he uses this special Kiss to communicate with you in some way. Dreams might be the way."

Susannah was silent a while, thinking everything over, and then she smiled and stood up. "Well, then," she said, "I will just have to try harder to understand what he has to say in these dreams."

"Perhaps you might—" Mahalah began, but she was interrupted by an influx of angels into the room.

"Here you both are!" Gaaron exclaimed, striding forward. Zibiah trailed behind him. "You have been missing for an hour."

"I was giving Susannah a tour," Mahalah said.

"And I'm sure she enjoyed it, but we have to be heading back," Gaaron said.

"Perhaps Susannah could stay with me a day or two," Mahalah suggested. "I would enjoy her company, and I think Kaski would be glad to have her here."

Susannah looked neutrally at Gaaron, wanting to read his face before committing herself one way or the other. True, she was worried about Kaski and she would like to see the little girl settled in, but she did not particularly want to spend a few days at Mount Sinai. She was tired; she had woken with a cough this morning, no doubt the result of shivering in the rain for half a day. And Mount Sinai was a strange place. She was getting used to living at the Eyrie, but she was not sure she wanted to try to understand the stone and silence of another mountain hold.

"Some other time, perhaps," Gaaron said, answering for her. "These are rather perilous times, and I want to keep my angelica close by me at the moment."

Mahalah turned back to Susannah. "But you will come visit me again—very soon, I hope," she said in an unmistakably urgent voice. "Together I think we may be able to interpret some of the god's wishes."

"Of course," Susannah said, bending to give the old woman a kiss on the cheek. "Let me know how Kaski does."

A few more farewells, a quick walk through the serene corridors, and they were back on their way to the Eyrie.

CHAPTER TWENTY-FOUR

When the stranger was well enough to travel, the Lohoras moved. They were too exposed, there on the flank of the river, and there was a place practically within the Galo mountain itself where they would be sheltered from weather and able to rest for a while. The Lohoras had been making for this spot, in their typically circuitous way, for weeks now. It was protected on three sides by an overhang of precipitous mountain and was situated close to water that bubbled up warm from underground fires. As often as they could be found anywhere during the winter months, they could be found here—though, from time to time, making their way here, they had been sidetracked by the discovery of other delightful winter spots, or the chance encounter with a friendly band of Karditas, and turned from their purpose.

This year, nothing occurred to keep them from their chosen destination. Indeed, the recent events made them more eager than ever to find a place where they could settle in till spring.

They moved slowly, though. Not only did they carry a wounded man in their midst—healing, but slowly, and not able to walk on his own—but snow had fallen two days in a row, and much of the land was impassable. The men led the horses at the front of the caravan, to break through the drifts and create a trail of sorts for the women behind, but even so the going was rough. The trampled snow hid treacherous patches of rutted earth, where an unwary walker could turn an ankle. The snow itself was hard to walk on, slick as ice in spots and offering no safe footing. Those pushing carts in front of them moved even more warily, blundering through unbroken snowbanks and catching their rough wheels on buried obstructions.

Plus they were all cold. Dathan had made a pair of leather outer boots for Miriam, and she wore these over her shoes, stuffing layers of cotton between them for added warmth. But her feet were always frozen. She walked with her blanket draped around her to cover her head, her shoulders, and her torso, but the wind was wicked and knifed its way through to the unprotected flesh beneath. She had wrapped her hands in two pairs of gloves, but this only made her fingers clumsy, and did not keep them warm, so eventually she went back to one pair and paused every once in a while to blow on her fingers. Her lips were chapped; her cheeks, when she laid a palm to them, felt smooth and hard as river ice.

Yet most of the time she did not think about herself. All her concentration was on the dark stranger she had come to think of as her responsibility. The tablets that Yovah had sent down—was it a week ago now? she kept losing track of time—had effected a miraculous recovery in the burned man. Within two days, his fever was gone, he was sitting up in bed, and he was able to take care of his own bodily functions, though he was too weak to move far. He had eaten ravenously, though once or twice some Edori ingredient had made him so sick he vomited everything back up. Still, it was clear he was much better—and a little afraid of all of them.

Before he was well enough to walk, the Lohoras decided that they had to move on, and how to transport the injured man had been one of their chief points of concern. Ultimately, it had been decided that the contents of one of the carts could be redistributed, and that he could ride in the wagon, and that the men would take turns pushing it. Miriam had offered to take this duty sometimes, but Tirza had shaken her head. "It will be too heavy for you," the Edori woman had said—and, once she tried it, Miriam realized this was true.

So she contented herself with foraging for the injured man. He seemed to have no trouble eating the tuber roots and dried nuts that could still be found by a careful seeker even at this time of year, at this latitude. So Miriam ranged well away from the bulk of the caravan, looking for the telltale signs of bushes and stalks poking up above the snowline. She dug up everything she could find, anything that looked edible, and took it back to Claudia and Anna to see if they could identify it. Most times, what she retrieved could be added to the cook pots, and the older women praised her for her good eye and hard work. Miriam always shared her finds with every cook in the camp— but she kept some of the best samples back to make into an evening meal for the stranger.

They had tried, at one point, to integrate him into the tent shared by Tirza, Eleazar, Miriam, and the others, but he had refused to lie still or settle. He had, in fact, crept out of the tent in the middle of the night, to be found the next morning curled in the snow before the dead fire, his wound reopened and his temperature dangerously high. So wherever he was from, the Lohoras concluded, kinsmen did not sleep together in warmth and comfort—or it was taboo to do so, or only citizens of the lowest classes disposed themselves in such a way. In any case, he did not like it. So they pulled out Bartholomew's small, spare tent, and set it up close to the fire so he could have whatever warmth was available while the fire still burned; and that seemed to content him.

While they were on the road, Miriam went to this tent every night with an offering of food. The exertions of the day always had worn him out, and she would find him already stretched on his pallet, his black face looking strained and used up, his eyes closed. But he would sit up when she entered, take the food from her hungrily, and say something to her in a completely unintelligible language. She imagined he was thanking her, or perhaps thanking his god. Though she really thought his next actions constituted a prayer to his deity, for he would come to his knees, painfully, and hold the bowl up at about eye height. He would speak a few more words in a singsong voice, lay the bowl on the tent floor, touch his fingers to his mouth and his heart, and sit motionless for another few seconds, his eyes closed. Only then would he pick up the bowl and begin eating.

Miriam always waited in respectful silence while he went through this ritual. She was very sure that the god he prayed to was not the god she worshiped, and she wondered what Yovah thought of this strange man offering thanks to a god who could be found nowhere in the vicinity of Samaria. But she had learned, while traveling with the Lohoras, that the Edori were rather more liberal than the angels in their conception of divinity. They trusted their hearts and bodies to

Yovah, but they did not think Yovah was the only god to be found anywhere in the universe. Dathan had taken Miriam aside one night, and pointed at all of the stars overhead, and informed her that, for every star, there was a god created specifically to guard that point of light, that planet, and any of the creatures that might live there. Over all the gods—and over all the stars and planets that they could see, and even the ones that they couldn't see—ruled one great, benevolent spirit that the Edori knew only as the nameless one. His was the hand that had created all the worlds, and all the gods who watched over them—and he, no doubt, was familiar with the god to whom this stranger prayed, and he approved.

What Miriam wanted more than anything in the world was a way to communicate with the stranger.

During the first few days of their excruciatingly slow journey, the injured man had no strength left over at night to do anything but pray, eat, and lie back on his pallet before Miriam had even cleared away the used dishes. So Miriam made no attempt to speak to him, beyond greeting him civilly when she came in and saying a good-bye to which he did not respond as she left the tent.

"Don't worry about it," Tirza told her one evening as Miriam returned with the empty bowl and rather despondently ate her own dinner at the communal fire. "When he is whole again, he will become curious and energetic. He will be interested in what you have to say then."

"Or he will become violent and unpredictable," Anna said with a little sniff. She had agreed with the other Edori to take this man in and shelter him, but she had never entirely lost her mistrust of him, and neither had Eleazar. Eleazar watched the stranger night and day with hooded, unfathomable eyes. Miriam was sure that if the black man made any sudden moves of hostility, Eleazar would be right there ready to club him into insensibility.

"A sick man is not himself," Tirza said, spooning more stew onto Miriam's plate. "And a young girl who worries herself to death over a stranger is not herself, either. You better eat up, allali girl, or you won't have the strength to walk to Galo."

So Miriam ate, and took her place in the crowded tent at night, and willed herself to sleep so that she would be strong enough in the morning to gather more food for the hurt man. And the next day they packed up and moved on, breaking through another five miles of snow, or maybe ten. And Mount Galo loomed higher and higher on the horizon, a big-shouldered, stolid peak set among the low, placid ring of mountains that circled the Plain of Sharon. Miriam set her eyes on it as she walked, willing it to become bigger, closer, so close that they could nestle against its blue side, and finally come to rest for the winter.

They had been traveling for a week when the stranger finally began to recover some of his strength. On that sunny but frigid day, as they stopped for a noon break, he rolled himself shakily out of his cart and stood there a moment, looking around. The Edori, who prided themselves on showing no curiosity, did not stare at him or behave as if this action was at all unexpected, but busied themselves with the usual pursuits of melting snow and mixing up food for the noon meal.

The black man put one hand to the side of the cart, as if to keep his balance, and watched them, a dazed but determined expression on his face. He was much taller than Miriam had realized, and extremely slender. Bartholomew's borrowed clothes were both too big and too short for him, and a thin stick of a bare arm protruded from the cuff of the sleeve as he held on to the cart. He turned his head slowly from side to side, the sun catching in his matted copper hair and kindling it to a pretty glow, filthy as it was. His face looked narrow, the cheekbones high and prominent, the chin a sharp point at the end of a long jawline. His eyes were a bright blue, like bits of winter sky ripped from overhead and tucked in place between his night-dark lids. He glanced around, blinking a dozen times, and then carefully released his hold on the side of the cart.

Miriam held her breath as he took his first shaky steps away from the safety of the wagon, but he did not topple over or even skid on the snow. He did not seem to have a destination in mind, just an action: He wanted to see if he could walk, and if so, how far. His steps were slow and measured, his face tight with concentration, and his balance imperfect. But he made it about ten steps away and ten steps back without mishap. Then he stood for a while at the side of the cart, panting a little as if from a great exertion.

Bartholomew brought him a bowl of food and made no comment. The stranger ate it, still standing on his feet, and seemed to relish every bite. When he was done, he glanced around, but no one was close enough to take the bowl that he was ready to hand back. Miriam, watching from a few yards away, moved as if to stand up, but Tirza's hand on her arm kept her in her kneeling position.

"Let us just see what he will do next," Tirza said, though her eyes were trained on the task before her and she did not appear to be watching the stranger at all. No one in the whole camp did. Miriam forced herself to stay where she was.

The black man hesitated a moment, then pushed himself away from the cart, where he had been leaning his hips while he fed himself. He took a few shaky steps from the path they had traveled, coming to a patch of unsoiled snow. There he knelt and, scooping up the snow with one hand, cleaned the bowl with it as thoroughly as he could. Carefully he eased himself to a standing position and turned back toward the cluster of wagons. Moving cautiously but with great determination, he carried the bowl back to Bartholomew, who stood a few yards distant, his back to the stranger but his alert stance announcing that he was aware of every move the other man made.

"Toteyosi," the black man said, or something that sounded like *toteyosi*, and handed the bowl to Bartholomew.

"Thank you," Bartholomew said gravely, and took it. The Edori made no move to aid the other man in his painful trek back to the cart, a journey that seemed slower and more perilous with every step. But the black man made it, reaching out to clutch the side of the cart with an unsteady hand. He stood there shaking for a few minutes before he gathered the strength to haul himself back in over the side.

None of the Edori said anything to him. They continued busying themselves with making, eating, and cleaning up their noon meal, chattering amongst themselves. But Bartholomew turned his head just enough to catch Miriam's eye, and he smiled at her.

That night the injured man was almost too exhausted to eat when Miriam arrived with his food. He did murmur a word when he took the bowl from her hand—she thought it was *toteyosi* again, the word that must mean "thank you" in his language—but his fingers were trembling as he lifted the spoon from the bowl to his mouth. She was so frustrated and impatient. She had thought that his successful attempt to move under his own power must mean that he was better, that he was well, and yet it appeared he had spent all his fragile strength on those two circuits through the camp. He set the bowl down before he had even eaten all its contents and lay back on his pallet, his eyes closed before his head touched the ground. Miriam gathered up the bowl and spoon, and left in silence.

The next day was much the same, except that the weather was worse and the noon stop even briefer. The stranger did climb out of the cart again, though he did not walk as far and did not seem as tired when he pulled himself back in. And he seemed a little more alert that evening when Miriam came to bring him his evening meal.

"Toteyosi," he said as she placed the bowl on the ground between them.

"You're welcome," she said, as she always said. Even when he had been too weak to speak, or even to notice if she spoke to him, she had talked to him. He had never responded, making her wonder from time to time if he might be deaf—or if he perhaps could not comprehend that the noises she was making represented language.

But today he looked over at her in curiosity when the sounds tumbled out of her mouth. "Ska?" he said.

It sounded like a question. "You're welcome," she said again.

He watched her a moment more with interest. His eyes were blue enough to seem vivid even here in the semidarkness of the tent. He had a fine coppery stubble all along his jawline, but it was not the full beard that a mortal man would acquire if he had gone this long without shaving. Maybe men of his tribe did not grow beards; or maybe he was so young that he could not produce a beard if he tried.

He spoke again, a long string of incomprehensible syllables that sounded like a mix of questions and statements. Miriam laughed and spread her hands, wondering what that gesture might mean to him.

"Ska?" he said again, more insistently, and now he pointed at her. "Ska?"

She had thought it meant merely *what?*, but perhaps it meant *who?* or *who are you?* or *what's your name?* Her name was what she would give him, in any case. She put her hand to her chest. "Miriam," she said.

"Ska?"

"Miriam. Meer-ee-um."

"Meer*imuh*," he said very carefully.

She could feel a smile of great delight throw dazzling lights across her face. "Yes!" she exclaimed. "Miriam."

"Meerimuh," he said again.

Good enough. She put her hand out now and pointed it at his chest, not quite having the nerve to touch him. She had bathed and tended him while he was unconscious, and she had seen every inch of his naked skin, but she did not know how the healthy man would feel about casual contact. "Ska?" she asked.

He seemed startled that she had used the word, so perhaps she had used it incorrectly; but then his face sharpened to even more interest. He touched his collarbone and said, "Jossis."

For a moment she thought he said *Joseph,* and a little shiver went through her, that the name of this utter stranger could sound so much like a name from the Librera. "Ska?" she asked, merely to hear him repeat it.

"Jossis."

"Jossis," she said, and he smiled.

He had not smiled before. She had not thought about it, what a smile might mean. Not only did it transform his severe, sharp face, it conveyed emotion—emotion that she understood, happiness or approval or pleasure—and it made him look, for a moment, familiar. It made him look, even more than the shape of his body, like he was one of them, a clansman from a far distant tribe.

Who are you? she wanted to demand. *Where did you come from, you and your brothers? Are you like we are, children of Yovah, brought here from a distant world? What do you want from us? Why do you hurt our people? If we can make you understand us, will you stop hurting us? Or will you peacefully go away?*

But she did not know how to say any of it, and so she merely smiled back at him. Then she picked up the bowl of food that sat on the floor between them, and handed it to him.

"Eat your food, Jossis," she said, in a language he clearly would not be able to understand. "Regain your strength. We will have much to talk about in the coming days."

Three days later, the Lohoras were ensconced in their winter home. It was a good campground, right up against the mountain in a shallow bowl of valley through which a thin stream of heated water made a wandering pass. Eleazar and Adam grumbled a little about feeling closed in, surrounded by stone, but Miriam liked the feeling. She had grown up sheltered by mountain, after all. She liked the sense of walls and ceiling holding her close at night.

The problem with settling in one place for any length of time, of course, was food. When the tribe was on the move, it could catch a little wildlife here, harvest a few fruits and grains there, and move on before everything was picked clean. But if they were to stay here for two or three months, they would, within a short period of time, dig up every root and tuber and scare away all the game. Not only that, it would not take them long to gather all the firewood within easy reach. Thus virtually all their waking hours were dedicated to laying in food and fuel for the winter.

Hunting parties went off for days at a time so the men could bring back sizable hauls of game, and the women would spend the next week drying and salting the meat. The older children were sent out to scour the countryside for timber, and Amram made quite a stir the day he tied himself and two other boys to a huge fallen tree that they dragged all the way back to the camp. When the women weren't dressing meat, they were out on gathering expeditions, digging through the snow and hard earth for edible products below the surface of the soil.

Miriam was a little amazed at how much could be accomplished during the day when the sole goal was survival. Until now, the Edori had expended much of their energy on moving from place to place, and although she had thought they were efficient and productive then, she saw that the travel itself had been a task, and one that ate most of their time. Now, as the Lohoras readied themselves for winter, they became a different people altogether: focused, practical, and disinclined to waste time or energy.

Miriam threw herself into all the camp tasks with great willingness. She still was not good enough with a rock to bring down more than the unluckiest game hen, so she concentrated on gathering the roots and tubers that she had become good at identifying. She preferred this work to cutting and drying animal meat—she even preferred the task of gathering up the week's laundry and carrying it down to the hot spring for washing, so she often took care of this task for her tent. The water was so steamy, even when the air was raw, that she would climb right in with the laundry and immerse herself to the chin. Sometimes these dips in the stream were the only moments all day that she was truly warm.

She did so much washing that her hands became red and chapped, but Bartholomew made her a salve of animal fat and herbs, and it helped put some of the suppleness back into her skin. It smelled dreadful, of course, but after a while she didn't even mind that. Between digging in the dirt and slapping around dead animal carcasses, none of them smelled too good by day's end, and not everyone was as fastidious as Miriam was about cleaning up every day.

Jossis, too, could often be found down at the river, bathing.

By the time they had settled in to the mountain camp, Jossis had recovered well enough to move on his own and care for himself completely. Miriam suspected he was not up to full strength, but he was able to walk for most of a day, his hand often resting on the cart for support, and he was no longer a burden to his caregivers. He surprised everyone by putting up his own tent the day they arrived at the mountain encampment. He must have been watching Dathan and Bartholomew more closely than they knew to be able to reproduce the complex actions of intertwining pole and guy.

That same day, he joined the others at the central campfire, instead of waiting in his tent for Miriam to bring him food. There were five cauldrons set up, two holding meat stew, one a vegetable medley, and two some combination of ingredients that the cooks had decided to try for the night. Miriam walked with him from pot to pot, helping him avoid the foods that might make him sick.

"Yes," she said, pointing at the vegetable cook pot. She had been at some pains over the past few days to teach him "yes" and "no," and while she wasn't positive how he had translated the words, he did seem to associate the meanings *good* and *bad* with the appropriate syllables. "Yes. No. No. No."

"Toteyosi," he said, and spooned up food from the cauldrons that she had indicated were safe.

As he always had while in the seclusion of his tent, Jossis observed a ritual before eating his food. But he was not oblivious to the Edori rituals, either. That first night he ate with them, he appeared to listen closely as Bartholomew sang the prayer of thanksgiving. The next two evenings, he did not begin to eat his own meal until this song had been performed by some member of the tribe. Miriam was not sure that anyone noticed this but her.

When they had been camped under the mountain for three days, Miriam went down to the little stream to wash a mound of clothes—and herself—with the strong soap that Tirza had been hoarding all season. It was a chilly day, but not as bitter as it had been, so Miriam only minded a little that the dripping clothes held tight against her chest were soaking her right through, and making her even colder. She had just made it to her own tent and dropped the clothes to the ground, when Jossis materialized beside her.

"Tatsiya?" he asked, emphasizing the last syllable, as he so often did.

"Ska?" she replied, pushing back her damp hair and looking up at him. He was so tall, and still so bony, that it was almost painful to look at him. His eyes never ceased to startle her, often though she looked into them.

"Tatsiya," he said insistently. He pointed down at the wet clothes, then reached out a hesitant finger to touch her wet hair. "Notebie? Tatsiya?"

"I don't have the faintest idea what you're talking about," Miriam told him, spreading her hands. Between them, this gesture had come to mean *I don't know*.

He looked around as if to find a prop, but whatever he wanted was not immediately visible. Instead, he cupped one hand before him, and with the other, mimed the action of pouring something into it. "Tatsiya," he said firmly. Then he pointed, first to the clothes, then at Miriam's hair. "Tatsiya." Now he pretended to be splashing air into his face, and scrubbed his hands down his cheeks. "Notebie?" he added, and looked at her hopefully.

"Do you mean *water*?" she demanded. "Yes, water nearby. Come and I'll show you."

The stream wasn't far, but hard to see if you weren't looking for it, so she was not surprised that Jossis had not stumbled across it. It hissed and bubbled up from a cracked hole at the base of the mountain, paused to make a little stone pool about a quarter mile from the camp, and then wound away past the outflung fingers of Mount Galo. The Lohoras got all their drinking water from the stone pool, so they washed themselves and their clothes some distance downstream.

They had to clamber over a few pointed boulders to make it to the edge of the stream, but then they were practically standing in the warm water. "Tatsiya?" she asked, pointing down.

But Jossis was already on his knees, no doubt cutting his thin flesh on those quartz-studded rocks, and happily dipping his hands into the steaming water. He leaned over and practically thrust his face into the stream, using his hands to gouge up great sprays of water to cover his head and his hair. Miriam could sympathize. She wished she had thought to bring soap with them, and a change of clothes so he could fully savor the experience of getting thoroughly clean.

She touched him carefully on the shoulder, and he looked up from his hedonistic union with the water. Drenched and flat to his head, his copper hair looked brown and unremarkable, but his eyes glittered out from a falling veil of water.

"Yes," she said, aiming her finger at the water where he now splashed. "No," she added, pointing upstream to the place where they drew all their drinking water.

"Yes," he said, mimicking her actions. "No."

She smiled and touched her finger to her chest, and then gestured back at the camp. "Miriam go," she said, though she was not sure he had deciphered the word *go* yet.

"Toteyosi," he replied.

"You're welcome."

She left him at the water's edge to give him some privacy and headed back to tell Tirza the news. At first, when the rhythms of the camp had dictated that Jossis would be left alone for a little while, Miriam had fretted. "What if he leaves?" she had asked.

Tirza had shrugged. "And what if he does? He is not our prisoner. He is our guest."

"No, but he could get lost, he could get hurt—"

"He could find his friends and direct them back to us," Tirza had said. "I cannot do anything about that. I have too much to do to sit and watch a stranger every day and make sure he does not bring harm or come to it. And so do you."

But it was still hard for Miriam to leave Jossis alone at the pool and not worry about what might happen next.

He was fine, of course. He returned in about thirty minutes, soaking from head to toe and smiling so widely that no one who saw him could help smiling back. He came up to Tirza and Miriam where they stood around the cook pot and loosed a torrent of unintelligible words. The women could not help but laugh, for he was so clearly explaining how good it felt to be clean, how miserable it had been to be so dirty for so long, how fresh the water felt, how kind the god was.

"Yes," Miriam said, for she knew no other syllable of approval that he would understand. "Yes. You're welcome."

After that, Jossis could be found down at the stream almost as often as Miriam. Miriam was surprised at the difference a good thorough cleaning made in the stranger's appearance. The matted copper hair took on a fineness and a bright radiance that made it look milkweed-soft and fire-red. His skin was still black as good dirt, but it glowed with a smooth ebony luster that made her think of fine wood sculpture crafted by the Luminauzi carpenters. His face seemed more expressive, now that it was clean—although that might be, instead, the effect of returning health and boundless curiosity.

Everything interested him. He would walk around the camp and examine every pack, every carton, every cauldron, every tent. If anyone was nearby and looked agreeable, he would pelt them with questions, "Ska?" and "Yes?" coming out of his mouth most often. If someone took the time to give him a word, and repeat it to him often enough, Jossis would stand there for nearly an hour, repeating it over and over until he had the inflection right. Thus he learned *fire, tent, stew, boot, rabbit, marrowroot, Tirza, Claudia, Anna, Amram, Dathan, Bartholomew, knife, crossbow, blanket, pot* and any number of other words that surprised Miriam when she had her own conversations with him.

Tirza had decided to make use of his affinity for water and teach him how to fetch buckets of it from the stone pond. Miriam was doubtful about this, because if Jossis really was their guest, was it fair to put him to work? But he seemed happy enough to perform this task for Tirza, once he understood exactly what it was she wanted of him. He even learned a new word, and would come up to her often during the day to ask, "Bucket?" He kept her so well-supplied with water that eventually no one else had to make a trip to the stream at all.

It was clear he was restless, and used to physical activity, so Miriam began to take him with her on expeditions to hunt for food. Once she had identified for him the shapes of the leaves and twigs that denoted edible plants, he was an indefatigable assistant, digging with great patience and concentration through the rockiest and most impenetrable soil. Now and then his zeal led him to dig up a plant that she did not recognize, and he would hold it up to her and inquire, "Ska?" She would spread her hands in a gesture of uncertainty and then say, "Yes," and they would bring it back for Anna or Claudia to identify. If it was something they could eat, Miriam and Jossis would continue to look for it in the following days. If it was not, she would tell him "No," and he would never accidentally dig up that tuber again.

Jossis was not really interested in women's work, though; that she could tell. Every day as the men left for the hunt, he would watch them, his bright eyes a little duller, a despondent expression on his face. But Eleazar had argued vociferously against teaching him the uses of the crossbow, and everyone else had been forced to see the wisdom of this stance. Jossis could *say* "knife" and "crossbow," but he was not allowed to handle either one. And he did not seem to question this, he just looked sadly after the instruments and occupations of men, and knew they were not for him.

"Wherever he comes from, I think he must be really smart," Miriam said to Tirza one day as they cut up dried vegetables for the simmering cook pot. "He catches on so quickly! He seems to understand even the things that are hard to explain."

Tirza looked at her with a little smile. "You have not been around young children much, have you?"

"No," Miriam said a little defensively.

"Jossis reminds me of a two-year-old. He knows a few words, he knows how to convey when he is hungry or sick. He understands what is forbidden, though he may not like it, and he understands that there is more to the world than he has been able to grasp somehow, and he is determined to learn it."

"He is much smarter than a two-year-old!"

"There are few things in this world craftier than a small child just figuring things out," Tirza said mildly. "I agree with you. I think he is very intelligent. But perhaps they are all intelligent where he comes from. I do not know how to judge him."

"Well, and I think he must be more good-natured than the others of his tribe," Miriam said defiantly. She could have no way of knowing this, either, but she was certain it was true. "He is so willing to help. He works very hard. Have you noticed how often he smiles? When he was sick, he didn't smile at all. It makes him look very happy."

Tirza reached for another tuber, a brown misshapen form that was grotesque on the outside but quite delicious on the inside, and began chopping it up for the pot. "Yes, he seems like a good-hearted young man," she agreed, but her voice did not hold enough enthusiasm for Miriam.

"I thought you liked him," the younger girl challenged.

Tirza looked over with a faint expression of astonishment. "I do! He seems to have many good traits. He works hard and is determined not to be a burden on us. I admire that. He is easy to care for and eager to learn. But, Miriam, he arrived with men intent on killing us. I do not think he is such an innocent as you would like to believe."

Miriam had already worked this out to her own satisfaction. "He's very young, you see," she explained. "You can tell, because of how thin he is and how his beard does not grow. He is very young, and this was the first time the men of his tribe took him out into—into battle. And he was shocked at what they intended to do. And—you know, I always thought that I caught the other man off-guard when I threw my rock, but maybe that's not what happened. Maybe Jossis had already turned to grab the other man's arm, to push aside the fire stick. Because his good heart would not allow his kinsmen to kill us in such a fashion."

Tirza put down her knife and her brown tuber and laid both her hands on the blond girl's shoulders. "Miriam," she said softly. "When I was a little girl, my tribe came across the body of a dead wildcat, mauled by some other hunting animal. And beside that dead wildcat was a kitten, crying and starving for milk. I begged my father to allow me to keep that baby wildcat, and he agreed, and I fed it scraps of meat and let it sleep beside me in my tent. And it would follow at my heels when I left camp to do laundry or gather roots. And it would come to my hand when I called its name. But one day, when it was about six months old, it saw a rabbit scooting through the high grass, and it dashed out and with one swipe of its paw, it brought that rabbit down. And two days later, it was gone from camp, and I never saw it again."

Miriam looked away, too angry to speak, but Tirza's hands tightened on her shoulders. "You can bring a wild thing to your side, and you can think you've tamed it, but it will always be the wild thing it was born," Tirza finished up in a gentle voice. "You may think you have made this man your friend, but he is a stranger here, and his allegiances lie elsewhere. Be prepared to see him hurt you, and the ones you love, and be prepared to let him go when the time comes. He is what he was fashioned to be, and only Yovah knows what shape he will finally take."

Tirza was not the only one to speak of Jossis with an air of caution. Claudia—who liked him, and who would save special treats for him when she was making the evening meal—told Tirza within Miriam's hearing that the allali girl should not be allowed to spend so much time with the stranger. "You can just see she'll form an attachment for him and break her heart," Claudia said. Eleazar, of course, had never relaxed his vigilance and would never say anything remotely kind about Jossis, though Miriam tried over and over to make the Edori confess that Jossis was not a monster.

"He's a banked coal ready to burst into flame," was all Eleazar would say, which sounded enough like the baby wildcat theory that Miriam finally gave up.

Eleazar, in fact, was the one to cause a little flare-up that came after they had been camped beside the mountain for nearly three weeks. The men had been out hunting the day before and had come back with a good haul of meat, and they had left again in the morning to look for more. All the women had gathered around yesterday's carcasses to begin skinning and dressing the animals. It was still a job for which Miriam had no love, but she could do it, and rather competently, too. So she had settled in beside Tirza and reached for the nearest rabbit.

In a moment, Jossis was beside her, crouched down flat on his feet in a pose he could hold for hours. "Ska?" he said.

Miriam pointed to the various dead bodies. "Rabbit. Grouse. Deer. And—something, I can't recall what Eleazar called it."

"Furdebeest," Tirza supplied. "Fairly rare, and I hate to see it brought down to fill our cook pots, but . . ." She shrugged and went on with her skinning.

"Raaaaa*bit*," Jossis said, putting out his hand to touch the bloodied side of the smallest animal. Then he pointed to the deer again. "Ska?"

So Miriam went through the litany again, and this time he had them all. Next he touched an unused knife lying on the ground before the women. "Jossis help?" he asked.

Miriam was so surprised she dropped her own knife. She had already discovered how hard it was to teach someone verbs, and she had no idea where he had learned this one. *Walk* and *run* were fairly easy to demonstrate, of course, and even *sleep* and *eat* had been simple to simulate. But *help* was a concept more complicated than any of those and one she couldn't imagine anyone taking the time to teach him. Perhaps he had picked it up on his own.

What was even more surprising than his word choice was his offer.

"Jossis help?" he asked again, his voice a little more insistent. He gestured again at the knife.

Miriam glanced at Tirza, who had not paused in her own work, and the older woman merely shrugged. So Miriam picked up the extra knife, handed it to him, and said, "Yes. Jossis help."

She expected to have to demonstrate skinning, but it was clear as soon as his fingers closed around the hilt that he knew how to handle a small weapon. And when he tugged a small furdebeest out of the pile, it was also clear that he knew how to dress game, because he set the sharp blade to the animal's throat and slit the fur down the belly in one quick slice. Then he turned to Miriam for confirmation. "Yes?" he asked.

"Yes."

She glanced over at Tirza, who only shrugged again and kept on with her own work. Claudia, however, came to her feet and wiped her bloody hands on a rag. "You've got enough hands here you don't need me for a while," she remarked. "I'll go start the bread."

Jossis worked beside them happily for the next hour, clearly finding this chore a little more to his taste than the other women's work. Maybe in his tribe, men both hunted for game and cut it up afterward. The question seemed too complicated to ask.

They were still working on the carcasses from the day before when the men returned with a much smaller haul, mostly game birds. Miriam was talking quietly to Tirza and did not pay much attention when Eleazar came striding over, two dead pheasant swinging from his fingers.

She noticed instantly when he gave a shout, dropped the birds, and sprinted across the pile of skins to snatch the knife from Jossis' hand. Jossis scrambled to a low crouch, but Miriam jumped to her feet, all the while astonished by the sound of Eleazar yelling.

"Are you *mad*? Has Yovah struck you dumb? Giving a knife to this man, our enemy! How long has he sat here today with a blade in his hand, trying to decide which of you to kill first? Is all of this animal blood, or has one of your sisters been killed while you sat here smiling?"

Miriam immediately launched her own attack, so angry that she actually reached out and shoved Eleazar's arm. "Don't you say such things! He is not our enemy! He is our friend—at least, he *wants* to be our friend, and yet you, with your bitter mind—"

"My bitter mind may yet keep us all alive. Stupid allali girl, who would have thought you would be so trusting?"

"I am not stupid—it is you who are stupid, you who are unkind and unwelcoming, like no Edori I have ever met—"

"Yes, now lecture me upon the Edori—"

"Stop it. Both of you," Tirza intervened, moving between them as if with her body she could cut the cord of anger that bound them. "Eleazar is right, Miriam, we have been a little too trusting to put a weapon in the hand of our enemy."

"But he is *not*—"

"And Miriam is right," Tirza said, turning her shoulder in Miriam's face and staring at her lover with calm eyes. "He does seem to want to be our friend. He has only offered to help us. Since he has been in our camp, he has not been angry or violent or cruel. We Edori have been taught to judge the individual, and even then not harshly. This individual has done nothing to hurt us."

Eleazar stared back at her with an unrelenting fury. "This *individual* would have killed us all," he said coldly. "You cannot call him harmless."

"He is a boy," Tirza said. "And he can be taught better ways."

"We will not live to be the ones to teach him."

"If he—" Tirza began, but she did not get a chance to finish. Jossis, who had stayed in a crouch all this time, now slowly rose to a standing position. Moving carefully—as if trying not to alarm Eleazar, Miriam thought—Jossis took the few steps necessary to put himself next to the angry Edori. Both Eleazar and Tirza turned to look at him, Eleazar frowning, Tirza questioning. Jossis did not look at them. He had his head bowed, his eyes trained on the ground at his feet. Now he put his hands out, slowly, and turned them palms up, showing his hands empty of anything except animal blood. Keeping his arms out and his head down, he slowly sank to his knees in a gesture of submission and docility that was impossible to mistake. He stayed that way, unmoving, almost unbreathing, while everyone in the camp stared down at him.

Finally, Eleazar spoke, his voice low and hard. "I don't know what you want from me," he said.

Jossis still did not look up, and his voice, when it came, was muffled and soft. "Friend," he said.

"I do not trust you," Eleazar said flatly.

"Friend," Jossis repeated.

"You are no friend of mine," Eleazar said, and turned on one heel and stalked away.

Jossis stayed where he was, head down and hands outstretched. Tirza dropped to her knees beside him and put her hands on his shoulders. "You are my friend," she said softly.

Others had come over to watch the drama, some curious, some troubled. Disharmony was rare among the Edori, rarer still between lovers, and no one liked to see anyone as angry as Eleazar was. But this man was their guest; they had taken him in. Most of them could not summon the mistrust Eleazar had exhibited—they had no practice with it.

"Friend," Bartholomew said, stepping close enough to lay his hand on Jossis' head, and then stepping back.

"Friend," said Thaddeus, and Shua, and Dathan, and Anna, mimicking Bartholomew's action. One by one, the other Lohoras came forward, repeated the word, then backed off to make room for another kinsman.

Miriam was the last one to make her declaration. Like Tirza, she knelt before Jossis, face-to-face with him on the blood-soiled ground. She put her hand out and placed it under his chin, turning his face up so she could look into his jeweled eyes. "Friend," she said, and leaned forward to kiss him on the cheek.

There was absolute silence in the camp as she drew back. Jossis was staring at her—but then, so was everybody else. She still had her fingers under his chin, and now he lifted both of his dirty hands and wrapped them around her wrist. His grip was strong and the pressure of his hands took hers down to rest on his knees. He was still watching her with those bright eyes, and she could not look away.

"Meeri*muh*," he said at last. "Friend."

Neither Eleazar nor Tirza attended the communal dinner that night, but Miriam thought that might be a good thing. She had seen Tirza prepare two bowls of stew and carry them away from the campfire, and she thought perhaps the quarreling lovers were going to take some private time to discuss their differences. The tent would be empty while the others were at dinner; they might find their problems easy to resolve in the oldest and most traditional manner.

Miriam had wanted to sit beside Jossis at the evening meal, to reaffirm her championship of him, but apparently all the other Edori had had pretty much the same idea. In any case, Jossis was between Amram and Shua when the meal began, and Miriam did not have the heart to intrude. Amram was showing Jossis some rock he had found down by the river. It did not look particularly interesting from where Miriam sat, but examining it seemed to occupy the man and the boy for a good twenty minutes before the meal began.

The meat stew was good, and there was enough of it, for a change, that no one felt compelled to stick with a single serving. So they were all full and happy by the time the plates had been collected. The fire was warm, and the tents standing a few yards away were not, and no one made a move to leave once dinner was truly over.

Shua was the first to lift her voice in song, a pretty and rather happy melody that sounded good on this deep winter night. Claudia's daughter and Amram then tried a duet that faltered in a few places when Amram's voice unexpectedly broke, but all the listeners applauded anyway. Miriam took her turn, rising to her feet to offer a heartfelt prayer of thanksgiving to the god. She could not have said exactly what she was thanking Yovah for on this cool and starry evening—a good meal, clear night skies, her Edori friends, Jossis' continued presence in her life, her very existence—but she was filled with an overwhelming sense of gratitude and well-being and the only way she knew to express her emotion was in song. The others gathered around the campfire listened appreciatively, and when she sat down, Claudia leaned over to wrap her arm around Miriam's shoulders.

The next one to stand up, offering to sing, was Jossis.

Everyone fell silent, for he had never lifted his voice in all the weeks he had been with them, and there had been singing almost every night. It was hard to see him, his skin so dark against the darkness of the night, his hair like a ragged branch of flame suspended in midair. He moved, and the shadows that were his hands spread before him in a gesture of supplication. No one else in the circle shifted or spoke or breathed.

He began singing and his voice was sweet and pure, not a boy's voice, but not that of a full-grown man, either. The melody was complex, dipping to baritone range and then jumping to a near falsetto, but he produced it easily, flawlessly, not even seeming to need to catch his breath between notes. All of the words were incomprehensible, words in his native language, but there was no doubt of the intent of the piece—thanks to the god for great gifts received or great danger averted.

All the Edori applauded madly when the piece was ended, and Jossis gave an impish little bow and sat down again, smiling widely. But Miriam did not clap and she could not bring herself to smile. She had not understood a word of the song, but she had heard it before, and often: It was a prayer to Jovah that the angels sang, though none of the other races of the three realms performed it, and Jossis could not have learned it anywhere in Samaria.

CHAPTER TWENTY-FIVE

It was crowded in Velora. Well, *crowded* didn't begin to cover it, Susannah thought—it was impossible. Every inn and hotel was full to bursting, with families all crammed into one room and solitary strangers bedding down on pallets in the halls. Tents had been set up along every city street that had an open lot or a small park, and on the outskirts of the city a veritable second town had grown up, composed of carts and wagons and more tents. Everywhere you looked, there were people—farmers, miners, Jansai, Edori. The city was overrun.

News of the latest depredations on large settlements had sent a wave of panic through the people of all three provinces, and during the past month, there had been a wholesale emigration to the cities. Adriel and Neri were reporting the same tale, that of small towns swelling to three times their sizes as residents of outlying settlements and isolated farms migrated to the relative haven of urban areas. Luminaux, Castelana—even the waterbound Semorrah—all had become refuges for these frightened country dwellers. Any town that had boasted a population of more than a thousand now could lay claim to three times that many residents.

Not, Susannah thought, *that anyone was safe, even in the swollen cities.* How could any of them be certain that marauders who could destroy fifty people with a single weapon couldn't also destroy a hundred and fifty, or five thousand, or ten? True, Susannah couldn't understand the construction of a weapon with such capability, but she could not conceive of killing a single person with intent. But once a race began engaging in wholesale slaughter, she did not see how sheer numbers could be expected to daunt them.

She sympathized with the farmers and the miners, though, the ones who lived on far-flung homesteads where they were completely at the mercy of malicious intruders. And she worried about all the Edori clans, camped out on the open prairie, maybe aware of their danger and maybe not, completely unprotected from a sudden onslaught of fire and death. Was her father safe, were her brothers and her nephews? What about the Lohoras, every single one of them so precious to her? Had they thought to take shelter in Luminaux or one of the bigger towns that dotted Jordana? Or were they—as she was sure most Edori were—happily setting up their winter camps, oblivious to danger or fatalistic about it, putting their lives in the hands of Yovah?

She could not stand not knowing, but there was no way to get information. Though that had not stopped her from trying.

"When you have a free minute, could you take me down to Velora?" she had asked Chloe that morning, and the angel had obligingly carried her down to the city a couple of hours later. Now Susannah stood in the middle of chaos and wondered which way to turn.

The town was too small to handle this many people, that much she could tell at once. Merchants and innkeepers appeared quite delighted with their sudden surge in business, but surely even they realized that space, food, and water could quickly run out. She knew, because Gaaron had told her, that the city council was hastily trying to throw together laws about sewage and waste disposal, which also required them to construct systems that would enable the populace to comply with the laws. But their efforts had come a little late, and there was a faint smell of rotting garbage and human waste that overhung certain sections of the city. There appeared to be plenty of food for now—merchants always stocked up against the meager supplies to be had during the winter—but how quickly would those stores be depleted when there were so many more mouths to feed? So many people living in such close proximity also generated other problems—theft, violence, plague. Susannah was fairly certain the city council had not looked far enough ahead to counter those troubles before they arose.

But she was not there to lead the reordering of Velora. She was there to see if any of the Edori tents on the outskirts of town were sheltering any clans she knew.

So she made her way through the mobs of people, trying to be gentle about it. There were more Jansai than she had expected. Why hadn't they all taken refuge in Breven? Children ran past her, screaming and playing. Someone bumped her hard into a stone wall, offered only a muttered "sorry," and hurried on. She paused to steady herself by taking a deep breath, regretting it instantly as she inhaled the mingled smells of close-packed bodies, cooking food, animal fur, sweet perfume, churned-up mud, and piles of garbage.

She moved on a little more carefully, holding her arms close to her body with the intent of making herself as small as possible. There was no walking on the crowded sidewalk, so she stepped off into the street, where milling pedestrians and impromptu vendor carts were making the way impassable for horse-drawn vehicles. Everyone was shouting—the happy vendors, the angry carters, the lost travelers. Susannah wanted to press her hands to her ears and run away from the confusion and noise, but there was nowhere to run to escape the crowds.

Eventually she made her way to the tattered edge of town, where the Jansai and the Edori had set up camps as far from each other as the limited space would allow. She counted dozens of Jansai wagons as she picked her way past, and there were maybe fifty Edori tents set up on the grass in front of her.

Too many, was her first thought. There was not enough water or game available this close to the city to support that many people. How would they get through the winter, how would they all survive?

But how would they all survive alone in the Bethel grasslands, easy target for malicious intruders who killed without mercy?

Susannah stepped into the first circle of tents, looking for familiar faces. To some extent, every Edori was familiar—she had met most of them at some Gathering or another over the past twenty-five years, and even the clans she did not know well she had heard news of from other clans that were kin. But there were only a hundred or so Edori that she considered close friends, and none of them appeared to be among the group camped here.

That did not prevent the first women who spotted her from offering a warm welcome. They were standing beside their cook pot, arguing good-naturedly over a packet of seasonings, when Susannah approached.

"Hello!" the oldest one greeted her. "Are you from the Malitas? I did not see you this morning when I came over to inspect your tent."

"Did you need more marrowroot?" the younger woman said. She was thin and childlike, but obviously more than a few months gone in pregnancy, so she could not be quite as young as she looked. "You can borrow as much as you like."

"Thank you, no—no marrowroot and I'm not a Malita," Susannah said with a smile. "I'm Susannah of the Lohoras—or I was. I've come to live here now."

She left it deliberately vague, for it was certainly possible that an Edori woman would choose to live in Velora, following a lover or electing to leave the nomadic lifestyle. There was no need to introduce herself as Susannah, bride-to-be of the Archangel-elect.

"The Lohoras—now, I've never had many dealings with them, but my sister's lover's daughter, she followed a man of the Corderras, who are friends with the Lohoras," the older woman said.

"So I take it they aren't camped among the tents here today," Susannah said. She knew they weren't; Tirza would have sent word to her if she was anywhere near the Eyrie. But she *had* hoped for more recent information. "Or the Tachitas? That was the clan I left to follow the Lohoras."

No, these women had no information about either of the clans so close to Susannah's heart. "But the Corderras are here," the older woman added helpfully. "They arrived three days ago—"

"Four days," the pregnant girl corrected. "Because they came the day it snowed, you remember? And I walked into town with Daniel and his nephew and I ruined my shoes."

"I told you not to wear those shoes," the older woman said.

The young woman shrugged. "They were old anyway. I bought a new pair." She turned to Susannah with a happy smile. "Did you know that you can buy anything you need here in the Velora markets? Leather shoes and warm gloves and coats and food and *everything*. I don't have much money, though," she added regretfully. "But I would spend it all if I did."

Susannah spared her a quick sympathetic smile, though she was impatient to move on to someone who might have information for her.

"Yes, I quite like living in Velora," she said. "Though it does not really compare to Luminaux, of course."

They talked a few more minutes before Susannah felt she could, without rudeness, make her farewells and move on. It took her a few more tries to locate the Corderras—who might be friends of the Lohoras but who had not often come Susannah's way in the years that she had been traveling with that clan. Clan friendships sometimes extended back for twenty or thirty years and were maintained by goodwill, not actual contact, if the tribes did not happen to meet often during their travels.

But she recognized several of the Corderra women and was recognized by them, and there was a joyous reunion over the communal cook pot. They had heard her news, of course. No putting them off with evasive comments about "living here."

"Tell me what life is like there in the angel hold," demanded Baara, a kind-faced, stoop-backed older woman who sat before the fire and made no attempt to help with dinner preparations. "How can you bear it, to be all shut in like that? How can you breathe at night?"

Curious; just a couple of weeks ago she was defending the Edori to the angels, and now she must defend the angels to the Edori. "I rather like the life," she replied with a smile. "It is much easier than the Edori way, I must say! I am growing quite soft." She held out her hands so Baara could examine her pink palms. "See? No calluses. I do no work at all. But I am busy every day."

So then she had to recount for them tales of the people in the Eyrie, and say suggestive things about her husband-to-be (for no Edori woman would believe she and Gaaron had not shared a bed by now). "I have heard that this Gaaron is a very large man," Baara said, and Susannah replied archly, "Oh yes, *quite* large," which made everyone within hearing distance laugh.

"And he values you, I hope," Baara added.

That Susannah could speak to with more certainty. "Yes, he admires me greatly and says so," she answered. "And I find that I admire him more every day. It is a good union."

More of this talk was required before she could ask her own questions. *Have you, in any of your recent travels, come across the Tachitas or the Lohoras? Are they safe for the season? Do you know where they have chosen to winter?* Not so baldly stated, of course. The Edori were nothing if not roundabout.

"The Tachitas . . . no, I have had no news of them," Baara said thoughtfully. "But the Lohoras—yes, we camped with them for two days not three months ago."

Susannah's heart leapt. "You did? And they were all well?"

"All of them," Baara confirmed. "Let's see now. Bartholomew had been sick, but he was healthy by the time we saw him. And Anna had begun to share a tent with him—"

"That is big news!" Susannah exclaimed.

"She was still shy about it, but she seemed happy." Baara went through the tribe person by person, remembering something about each one in order to give Susannah the most personal update possible. Even something so small as "Amram kissed one of the girls in my clan, I think it may have been for the first time" was an indescribably precious scrap of information to Susannah. She found that she was hugging herself with excitement, actually shaking a little—though some of that could have been from cold as well.

"And the allali girl—she did not look happy that first night we all camped together, but she had grown to like us by the time the tents parted," Baara finished.

Susannah's eyebrows rose. "Allali girl? In a Lohora tent?"

Baara nodded. "Yes, did you not know her? I don't think she had been traveling with them very long, though she was as tired and dirty as the rest of them. A pretty girl, though. She was sleeping in Tirza's tent, I believe, and Tirza seemed quite fond of her."

Susannah found herself unreasonably jealous at the thought that an outsider had slipped into her place so easily that no one even noticed she was gone. Sleeping in Tirza's tent, indeed! No doubt this girl was flirting with Dathan, too, and going off to pick berries with Amram.

"What was this allali girl's name?" she asked with remarkable composure.

Baara couldn't remember, and neither could any of the women gathered around the fire. "Daniel will know, he went off courting with her," someone said, and all the women laughed.

"Yes, and wasn't he stupid-struck for three days after she left?"

"Still, she was a pretty girl."

"Mischievous, I thought."

"Well, that's an allali for you."

Someone went off to fetch Daniel, he who had been so stupid-struck by the charms of a city girl, and Susannah resigned herself to a wait. She consented to taste the stew, pronounced it quite good, and listened for a while to Baara's tale of their travels across Bethel. Much sooner than she had expected, one of the women returned with a tall, slender young man who could not have been more than nineteen or twenty. His smile was engaging, though he looked a little shy.

"This is Susannah of the Tachitas, who used to travel with the Lohoras and who lives with the angels now," Baara said by way of introduction.

"The Lohoras! We just camped with them a few months ago," Daniel exclaimed.

"Yes, and I have just given her all their news," Baara said. "We really only called you over so you could tell her the name of that other girl. The one who was traveling with them."

"The blond girl," someone else put in. "You must remember, you courted her for two whole days."

Daniel looked embarrassed but he replied without hesitation. "Of course I remember! Her name was Miriam."

Susannah made her way back through Velora slowly, her head in an even greater state of confusion than the city itself. This time, she scarcely even noticed the children careening into her or the adults pushing past her, cursing under their breath.

Miriam was traveling with the Lohoras—was not, as they had believed all this time, safely settled in Luminaux and learning to live a calm, productive life. Susannah had not been able to hide her shock at Daniel's revelation, so they had made her sit for a while, and drink a little wine, and explain what it was that troubled her about Daniel's announcement. "She is a girl I care for a great deal, and I had not realized where she was," was all Susannah managed to say. So Daniel had gone to some trouble to assure her that Miriam was safe, well-treated, well-behaved, and happy, and he had reproduced enough snippets of her conversation to make Susannah believe that he had truly spent a good few hours with this troublesome girl.

Hard as it was to believe, it sounded like Miriam had at last found a place where she could fit in. According to Daniel, she had helped watch the children, volunteered to prepare the food, joined in the singing, been thoughtful to her tentmates, and generally behaved like any good-hearted Edori girl. At any other time, Susannah would have been glad at the news that Miriam had run off to the Edori and found herself made over.

But knowing that the fierce strangers were roaming the entire countryside of Samaria, wantonly destroying any camp or settlement they came across, Susannah was nearly paralyzed with fright. Miriam *might* have been safe in Luminaux, though even that seemed doubtful these days, but what risks did she run encamped with the Lohoras on the open plains of Jordana? Susannah could not bear thinking about it.

She must tell Gaaron.

Then again, what could Gaaron do?

There was no telling where any particular tribe would be camped at any point in time. At the Gathering, the clans would recite for one another the routes they had taken during the previous year, and the trails they planned to follow in the coming months, but no one ever stuck to these plans. A tribe might go for three years running to the edge of Breven on the cusp of spring, and then never wander back to the outskirts of the Jansai city again. Tribes that made plans to meet every summer on the cool northwestern tip of Gaza would always add "As the god wills," because so often one or the other group would get distracted or slowed down and never make the rendezvous. That was why the Gathering was so important—it was the one place, one time, every clan made sure to come together as planned.

Susannah might tell Gaaron that Miriam was somewhere traveling with the Lohoras, but that information would be sure to make him crazy. He could spend the next six months seeking her out, crisscrossing the three provinces, and never find her. And then would he worry less, thinking her safely hidden somewhere in some remote valley—or worry more, thinking her lost to him forever?

Hard as it would be, she must keep this secret till spring. When the Gathering came around, she would entreat Gaaron to accompany her, and there they would find Miriam, safe and happy.

Please Yovah, sweet Yovah, let us find her safe and happy.

It was nearly dinnertime when Susannah made her way to the heart of Velora and spotted Enoch, who agreed to take her back to the Eyrie. Enoch was not one of her favorite angels, and Susannah had much on her mind anyway, so they did not speak during the short flight back.

She was also quiet over dinner, unable to summon her usual animation, and she noticed both Gaaron and Keren watching her with concern. She waited for the question to come, though. She had decided on the tack she would take, and there was a certain reserve that was required.

"Are you feeling well?" Gaaron asked her in a low voice as she toyed with her dessert, a sweet confection of berries and cream. "You hardly touched your dinner."

"Oh—yes—I'm sorry," she said, looking up at him with a half-hearted smile. "It's just—I spent the day in Velora, you know."

"All those people!" Keren exclaimed. "I could not get through the market to even *look* at new fabrics."

"You have no need at all of new fabrics," Gaaron responded automatically, then returned his attention to Susannah. "Perhaps you picked up some illness when you were around so many people."

"No, I . . ." She shrugged. "I went down to the Edori camps to see if I knew anyone there. And I did—a few—but none of them were the ones I was looking for."

"The Lohoras would never camp near a city for the winter," Keren said.

"No, nor the Tachitas," Susannah agreed. "I had hoped for news."

"You miss them," Gaaron said in a steady voice.

She gave him a straight look. "I worry about them. They are so unprotected."

"The Lohoras are probably not unprotected," Keren said. "Don't you think they are camping by Galo this year? It is very nice and comfortable under the mountain."

Susannah glanced over at her. "By Galo? We never wintered there while I traveled with the clan."

"Yes, but we always did when I was little," Keren said. "Every year, it seemed! It was very boring. And I know Bartholomew was talking about it last summer. I'm sure that's where they are."

"Where by Mount Galo?" Susannah asked. "On the Gaza side?"

Keren rolled her eyes. "Oh, no, the east side. Not far from Windy Point." She made a little sketch on her plate from the remains of her sauce. "See? Here is the mountain, and here is the ocean and Windy Point is here—or here, maybe—anyway, these would be the Caitanas. The Lohoras are right here." She pushed a bit of fruit over to indicate the Edori camp. "Unless they are not at Galo," she added. "They might have gone back to Luminaux, especially if Bartholomew was sick again."

"Baara said he was well."

"Or they may have stayed in the Caitanas. We did that a few times, too, and it was not quite as boring."

"The Caitanas are what I remember," Susannah said.

"Did you want to go visit the clan?" Gaaron asked. "I could take you there, but I don't think I would want you to stay. It is so dangerous on the open land."

She smiled at him, for it was a kind offer, but the last thing she wanted was for Gaaron to fly her to an Edori camp where Miriam was making her home. "No, thank you," she said in a quiet voice. "I will just worry about them from here."

Still, over the next few days, she thought about it almost incessantly. There might be a way to get to Miriam without letting Gaaron know. Chloe or Zibiah would take her up to Mount Galo without telling Gaaron their destination, though they would need a good excuse for making a trip in this weather, during this hazardous season. Nicholas or Ahio would also be willing to fly her somewhere, though they could not be counted on to keep secrets from Gaaron; the women could.

But then Susannah risked putting the angels in danger, too, and she would never forgive herself if something happened to anyone in the hold because of her. She did not know what to do.

She fretted about it for the next few weeks, trying not to let her preoccupation keep her from her normal daily tasks. Much of these centered on planning the wedding, for Esther simply would not make a decision about food or decorating without soliciting Susannah's opinion—or, rather, Susannah's approval and extravagant praise. Chloe, Zibiah, and Sela were happy to gather with her for a little while every day, working on a quilt they had decided they would make for her as a gift, while Susannah embroidered the sleeves and bodice of the gold dress that was being made into her wedding gown.

"You must rearrange Gaaron's quarters, too, and find things of your own to hang on the walls," Chloe told her. "It is so spare and masculine in there! The room must have feminine touches."

"Perhaps Gaaron will not like my touches," Susannah said.

Chloe gave a little sniff. "Perhaps it does not matter what he likes."

Gaaron, of course, was gone most of this time, returning every other night looking strung with fatigue. Susannah always made a point of dining with him, or dropping by his rooms on the nights he came back very late, if only to exchange a few words. His news was never good.

"We found a small farm in southern Bethel—all burned," he told her one night. "Probably thirty people had lived there." Another time it was a story about a tiny river town, obliterated. The roads were deserted; many of the smaller settlements had been completely abandoned. The bigger towns had become cities, and the cities were overflowing.

"Adriel said there was a fight in Semorrah—a riot, really—when two groups started arguing over a supply wagon. Too many people crowded into the cities, looking for safety, but now the cities are starting to feel the pinch, and I don't know how long the situation can last."

"Is there enough food for everyone?" Susannah asked when he told her this story. It was close to midnight, and he was eating a late meal in his rooms. Or, rather, picking at it, since he seemed to have no appetite. Esther would not be pleased when she collected the nearly full plates in the morning.

"For now. All the harvests are in, and we would be living on stored grain anyway at this time of year. But spring is not so far away, and then what? If no one is willing to go back to the farms and work the fields, we will all starve within a season. These—these marauders will kill us off as surely as if they had burned us all to the ground."

"I am surprised no one has talked about building weapons again."

Gaaron ran his hand over his face. "They have. Adriel and Moshe were most adamant about it when I saw them two days ago. I am against it still—I cannot say how strongly I oppose the idea—but I think they are too afraid to listen to me. I am sure there is someone in Semorrah working on a projectile weapon even as we speak. But I cannot imagine such a thing can be developed soon enough, and powerfully enough, to give us an edge in a battle with our enemies."

"Then what do we do?" Susannah asked.

He stared at her. His broad, serious face looked thin with worry; his whole big body seemed compacted with stress and effort. She could not possibly tell him news that would add to his troubles. "I don't know," he said at last. "Every day I try to answer that question, and every day I fail to find the answer."

Susannah came to her feet, and he watched her rise. "You're so tired," she said. "I'm going to let you get some rest. You will solve it, Gaaron—I know you will. But not if you're too exhausted to think."

She had made it as far as the door before he spoke again. "Not so tired that I don't appreciate your company and your belief in me," he said. "It is good of you to wait up for me."

"Why, Gaaron, I am always happy to see you."

"You don't look so happy. I have noticed that lately."

"I think you have more things to concern yourself with right now than my happiness."

"I will always be concerned with your happiness."

She smiled and did not answer directly. "Sleep, Gaaron. We'll talk again in the morning."

But in the morning, of course, he was gone.

She did not see him for another two days—bleak days, for her. Chloe and Zibiah were gone, also Ahio and Nicholas, carrying messages between holds and cities. Keren spent a day with her in Velora, but did nothing but talk rapturously of Nicholas and his many virtues. Susannah was pleased for her, of course, and could wholeheartedly agree that Nicholas was a sweet man, a handsome one, quite loving and beautiful; but it was not a particularly stimulating conversation as far as Susannah was concerned. And she was—well, she hated to think it, hated to admit it—but she was jealous, a little, of Keren's sublime joy. Not that she would wish such delight to be taken away from Keren, oh no; she just would wish for a little love and happiness to come her own way.

At dinner that night, Susannah's unfortunate lot was to draw as dinner companions Esther and Enoch, her two least favorite people at the hold, and a thin, stringy mortal woman who never said much and whose role at the Eyrie was unclear to Susannah. Susannah made an effort to be gracious to everyone, but she didn't have much energy, so the meal was hardly a success.

"Come back in about an hour, after I've got all the dishes cleared away, and I'll show you a new recipe for the wedding breakfast," Esther commanded as the meal finally wound up. "I think you'll like it."

"Oh—all right," Susannah said without much enthusiasm. She was so tired she wanted to go straight to her room and directly to bed. But this was important, she reminded herself—definitely important to Esther, and it should be important to her.

She didn't really care what she ate at any meal from now till she died, let alone what she had for breakfast on the day she married Gaaron. Life was so strange now that she could not imagine a wedding making things any better, so it was hardly something she wanted to celebrate, or even think about. She just wanted to sleep.

Still, after an hour of dutifully singing harmonics in the chilly cupola, she returned to the kitchen to see what Esther had come across now.

"I got it from a chef in Luminaux—a good friend of mine," Esther said a little smugly. "It is practically nothing but sugar and butter, but, see, the recipe calls for a touch of cream, very rich and delicate—"

"I can't tell much from a recipe," Susannah apologized. She had said those exact same words about thirty times in the past few weeks, but Esther continued to insist on handing her a list of ingredients as if it was the most wonderful treat in the world. "I'm sure it will be delicious."

"But, Susannah, you must *decide*," Esther said. "This pastry or the almond-nut one? We could do both, but I think that might be too much dough, since we're also having the fresh-baked bread and the cherry tarts—unless you don't want the tarts, and I think that would be a mistake, and you can't not have *bread* with the meal."

"Esther! I simply don't care!" Susannah exclaimed. "Serve what you like! Plan the entire menu! It doesn't matter to me if we eat dried meat and raw prairie grass! I—just—don't—care."

Esther was staring at her. The few women left in the kitchen, still wiping down stove and ovens, gaped at one another and then back at her. Susannah put her hands to her cheeks, which should have been hot with mortification. But instead they were cool and dry, waxy with indifference and exhaustion.

"I'm sorry," Susannah said abruptly. "I'm not—I'm not feeling well. I have a great deal on my mind, and food for the wedding is not something I worry about much. Because I know whatever you choose will be perfect. Now you must excuse me . . ." And making no attempt to add anything to that inadequate apology, she blundered from the kitchen and through the hallways to her room.

Where she burst out crying and did not think she could ever stop.

Stupid, stupid, stupid. So many things in the world that mattered more than her own lonely heart. It was small-minded and self-indulgent to feel sorry for herself because nobody loved her and this sham of a marriage would only underscore that. It was stupid to think now of Dathan, who was merry and faithless, and whom she had not loved or even thought about for weeks now. It was stupid to think of Gaaron, big and blind and awkward with women, but so *good,* so strong and so steady and so kind to her, but so oblivious, completely unable to read the emotions that Susannah felt must be painted on her face.

She crossed to her window and opened the glass, letting the cold starlight rush in. If Miriam were only here—if Miriam were only *safe*—if Chloe or Zibiah or Keren or even Kaski were here—she would not feel so alone and worthless. She missed the warmth of a second body in the bed, the sound of breathing in the night. She missed—Yovah, she missed being loved.

She knew the god loved her, for the god loved everybody, but sometimes that simply was not enough.

She remembered standing here, in this room, at this window, the first week she had been brought to the Eyrie. A thousand years ago, that seemed, and much had changed since then. But that day she had been depressed by solitude and crushed by loneliness, and tonight she felt at least as abandoned and betrayed as she had felt then. She folded her elbows on the sill, and rested her head on her arms, and let the winter air turn her teardrops to ice.

When the chime sounded at the door, she was too stiff and frozen to turn and call a welcome. No need to, since the chime was immediately followed by the door being thrown open and Gaaron striding in.

"Susannah? Are you here? It's late, I hope you're not sleeping—"

She straightened quickly and stepped away from the window. She had only two candles lit, and the room was dark, but light enough for her to see the excitement on his face. Too dark, she hoped, for him to see the frost on hers. "What is it?" she said, trying to make her voice sound normal. "Good news?"

He laughed. "I hope so! Though it doesn't sound like good news to begin with. There was another attack—"

"Oh no!"

"On one of the towns on the western coast. Small place, but maybe five hundred people. They'd been alerted, of course—everyone has been—so they had men standing guard, even at night."

"But—against men with those fire sticks—what could they do even if they were standing guard, unless they had weapons of their own?"

"That's just it! They had crossbows—well, not crossbows, exactly, but something like them that they use to catch big fish off the coast. So they were standing guard, and these black men showed up and aimed their fire sticks at them. And the men shot back with their crossbows, and wounded some of the invaders, and there was a lot of noise and yelling, but then the *best* part. One of the arrows from the cross-bow hit one of the fire sticks and caused it to explode or something. Huge fireball right in the middle of the crowd of black men, and some of them burned up and they were all screaming. And then the rest of them disappeared," Gaaron added. He was speaking so fast it was hard to understand all his words, but he was clearly thrilled. "So the town held fast! They turned back the enemy! It was such good news I could hardly believe it."

Susannah stepped closer to him. Even her feet were numb; she must have stayed at the window longer than she realized. "Gaaron, that's wonderful," she said as warmly as she could. "Perhaps if these black men learn we can fight back, they'll go away and leave us alone. Have you told Adriel and the others? Because certainly there are men and women throughout the provinces who can use a crossbow."

"No, I just found out this afternoon. I'll be off for Windy Point in the morning. Yes, this is news I'll be happy to spread—though it might just have been a lucky shot, and maybe all fire sticks don't explode like that, but it's something to try. It gives us a defense."

"Does it change your mind about weapons?"

"No," he said seriously. "What I have not wanted is the technology for destruction. I do not want us to develop an appetite for firepower. I do not like where that hunger leads. But this is something simple, and useful, and designed for another purpose, and so it does not seem chancy to me." He smiled a little, the faint expression hard to read in the shadowed room. "I don't know, perhaps that makes me inconsistent. I just do not want to develop weapons that we will some-day turn upon ourselves."

"Well, it's excellent news, Gaaron," she said. "I hope this gives you some reprieve from your worries."

Now he was the one to come a few steps closer. "Yes, but—you do not look like *you* have had any reprieve from worries," he said unexpectedly. "You look worn and tired."

She smiled a little. "I *am* tired," she said. "For no reason, really. I do not have the cares weighing on me that weigh on you."

"It is not that you look tired, exactly," he said. "You look more as if you have been crying."

Even more unexpected. "Oh—I was feeling a little sad tonight," she said, trying to make her response airy and careless, but sensing that her voice sounded dull and heavy. "Sometimes moods catch up with me. It doesn't mean anything."

He came closer still. "It means something to me," he said quietly. "What has made you sad? I know you are worried about your Edori friends."

"Yes—but there are so many people to worry about, throughout Samaria—it is not only my people who are not safe."

"And it is not just the Edori who are your people now," he said. "You will be the angelica for all the races."

"Yes—very soon now—" she said somewhat at random, for she was not sure how to answer that. The angelica for all races, indeed. What was that supposed to mean? She didn't even have a single friend, and now she was supposed to be a figure of hope and comfort to every malcontent in the three provinces? That hardly seemed fair.

"Is that what troubles you?" he persisted, peering down through the dark as if trying to read the secrets on her face. "Your responsibilities when you become angelica?"

"No—Gaaron—nothing troubles me. I am just—tired and sad and lonely. It does not matter, it—"

"Lonely?" he interrupted. "There is an entire hold full of people here, all of whom admire you greatly. There is Keren, and Chloe and the girls, and Nicholas and Ahio are your friends, too—you have a connection with all of them—"

"Gaaron, you do not know what true *connection* is if you think that!" she exclaimed, suddenly able to hold back her emotion no longer. "I am used to sleeping five or ten in a tent that is maybe twice the size of this bed—I am used to mornings where five people kiss me before I've even had breakfast. If I was sad, I could sit beside any of twenty people and have them put their arms around me and comfort me with the feel of their pulses matched to mine. Now I—I am so isolated. No one touches me. Miriam is gone, Kaski is gone, Keren has gone to Nicholas' bed, and I cannot sleep at night for the loneliness and the dreams. There is—every night—I wake up with dreams in the middle of the night, but there is no one to wake up beside me and tell me I am safe. I cannot make you understand me. I am not a bad angelica by daylight, but at night I am a frightened Edori woman who has no one to hold on to."

He stepped even closer. "Susannah—"

But she had turned away. She was shaking uncontrollably now, and the tears had started again, hot enough to melt the rime of frost on her cheeks. She wanted to tell him to go away, to not worry, to leave her until this mood passed, if it ever did, but she could not force any words past her closed throat. She put her hand over her eyes and felt the sobs increase in force.

"Susannah," he said again, and put his arms around her, and wrapped his wings around them both.

She had been cold; now she was enveloped in warmth. The heat of his body was so great it was as if she had stepped inside a gentle fire burning at a pitch just high enough to raise her temperature by a degree. The feathers of his wings lay against her flesh like bolts of the finest satin, layer after layer unrolled from the merchant's hand. She stirred a little, just to feel the delicious sweep of texture against her skin, and found herself turning in his arms, laying her cheek against his chest, letting her arms go around his back. He was so warm; he was a steady generator of heat and power and security. She pressed herself closer against him to absorb even more of his heat, and found herself inhaling his complex, musky odor. He smelled like sweat and far distances, high-altitude night skies, leather, winter, and skin. She took a deep breath, and then another.

She had stopped trembling. She felt as she always had, first thing in the morning, lying warm and cozy in the center of a Lohora tent, surrounded by love.

"I will sleep beside you tonight, if you like," Gaaron murmured into her hair. "It has not seemed to me—clearly I have been wrong—it has not seemed to me you had much need of me beside you, since you had so many who shared your time. But I would not want you lying here lonely when I can lie beside you."

She stirred a little, enough to lift her head but not enough to pull away from his delicious warmth. "Gaaron—I do not want to be one of your many burdens," she said.

"You are not a burden," he said. "You are a thing I care about."

"You care about all your burdens," she retorted.

She could hear the smile in his voice. "Not Zack so much," he said. "Not Esther."

She giggled. "I'm afraid I made Esther mad tonight."

"You can apologize in the morning."

"Gaaron, I—"

"Shhh," he whispered. "Don't talk about it. Don't worry about it. Just relax and go to sleep."

"I'm so tired," she admitted.

"I know," he said. "Let's just go to sleep."

It was not as smooth as that, of course. They both had to make quick trips to the water room, and then there was the strange business of climbing into the big bed next to someone who had never lain in that bed before. Some of Susannah's nervousness had returned by the time she settled herself next to Gaaron, her face scrubbed and her hair combed and her thoughts in turmoil. But he merely moved to one side, making a space for her, and she snuggled against him, fitting the curve of her body to the curve of his. He had pushed the blankets to the foot of the bed, and it was clear she would not need them since the heat of his body instantly made her warm.

He shifted, and the darkness in the room was momentarily swept with eerie light as one of his white wings unfolded and drifted down to cover her. Again, that sensation of serrated satin against her skin. She shivered a little at the sheer sensuousness of the contact.

"Are you cold?" he asked instantly.

"No—no—" she said, a little breathless. "I'm—thank you—you're so warm. This feels so nice—"

"Very nice," he said, a smile sounding in his voice. "It will be something pleasant to get used to."

She lay tentatively against him, knowing that much more could happen between them than this simple sharing of body heat, unsure if she should make the first overture, unsure of what he wanted, too happy with this much to risk it all by asking for more. She was still tired, but she was not at all sleepy. She could turn to him now, and press a kiss against his full mouth, show him what she knew and explain to him what she wanted.

The thought made her giddy and, for a moment, weak. It had been so long since she had loved a man, and she had never felt for Dathan what she felt for Gaaron. She had loved Dathan—she had thought she had loved Dathan—but that emotion had been girlish and shallow compared to what she felt for Gaaron. Dathan had energized her and frustrated her and delighted her and disappointed her; half of the time she had wanted to fold herself into him, and half the time she had wanted to change him. But Gaaron put her in awe. She would follow him barefoot from Luminaux to Mount Galo, dumbly doing any task he requested, because she believed in him so passionately, because he was so brave and so good, because she simply wanted to be with him. Because she loved him so much. He had come to occupy her thoughts so often that it was like she shared the space of her mind with another person; there were two people inside her skin. She did not know how to separate herself from him. She did not want to.

But she did not know how to present herself to him so that he would feel the same way about her. He cared for her—that she could not question. He had stated it as plainly as a man with few eloquent phrases could state it. But did he love her? At least as she wanted him to love her? How could she discover that—and if he did not, how could she bring such a thing about? Cautiously, she thought, for Gaaron was not a man who was adept at romance. Unlike Dathan, he did not look for lures and signals; he did not expect to be loved.

She could change all that. But slowly. Not tonight.

She settled against him a little more closely. His arm came up and rested on her waist. Susannah smiled but said nothing. She closed her eyes and allowed happiness to waft her into dreaming.

The first thing she noticed when she woke in the morning was that she was shivering. There was no other thought in her head except *I'm cold,* and she felt for the cast-off covers before even opening her eyes.

It was while her hands were groping for the blankets that she remembered why these blankets had not been spread over her to begin with, and she opened her eyes to see why Gaaron was not still lying beside her.

He had not left the room. He had not been that thoughtless, to spend the night beside her and leave without warning. But he was standing apart from her, staring out the window, and his face looked as remote as the mountain reaches of the Caitanas.

"Gaaron," Susannah said, sitting up and pulling the covers around her shoulders. He turned at the sound of her voice, and she could see that the window was open before him. No wonder she was freezing.

"I'm sorry—are you cold?" he asked courteously, shutting the glass. "I should have covered you up."

"What's wrong? What woke you?" she asked directly. "Is there bad news?"

His face looked pinched and wintry. If she had not known better, she would have said that he, too, was cold. "No—no news. I merely woke and—I got up."

She felt a frown flicker across her face. This distant and dispassionate person was not the kind man who had shown such concern for her last night. "Was it me?" she asked with a nervous laugh. "Keren and Kaski often told me I woke them with my dreams."

Now his face grew even more masklike. "Yes, I assume you were dreaming," he said.

"What did I say?" she wanted to know. She had not, last night, had that frequent vision of the white-and-chrome room; there had been no sonorous voice calling out her name. She tried to remember what she *had* dreamed about. Happy things, she thought. Edori dreams. "I'm sorry if I woke you."

"I was sorry not to be the one you dreamed about," he said stiffly.

"What?" Pulling the blanket more securely about her shoulders, Susannah got out of bed and crossed the room to his side. Dearest Jovah, but the stone floor was icy against her bare feet. "Gaaron, I don't even remember who or what I dreamed about. What did I say?"

"You called out names," he said, as if reluctant to speak at all.

"I did? Whose?"

He looked down at her, and she was shocked at the hurt expression on his face. She had seen Gaaron angry, she had seen him worried, she had seen him baffled, but she had never seen him devastated. He did not answer, but he did not have to.

"Dathan," she guessed. "You heard me say his name."

He nodded wearily and turned away. "I have to leave as soon as I can for Windy Point," he said. "You know the news I must share with Adriel. After that, I will probably go to Monteverde. I may not be back for three or four days."

"Gaaron." She put her hand on his arm to stop him; he was already stepping toward the door. He turned back to her, but his face was guarded, as if he did not want to hear what she had to say. "Gaaron, I don't even remember seeing his face in my dreams. It has been months since I have wanted to see his face in the flesh. You are the one I wanted to be with last night—and for all the nights to come. Please don't be angry because of a name I might have spoken when I was sleeping."

"I am not good with women," he told her. "Mahalah and Adriel have said that to my face, and I have always known it—and it must be obvious to you. I do not know how to flatter and say pretty things. I do not know how to express what I want. I have tried to think how to say those things to you, when the time was right—and I have thought the time would be right when you were happy here, when you no longer missed your Edori friends and your—your Edori lover. But I see I was wrong. You will never forget those friends and lovers, you will never be at ease here. I have expected too much to expect you to change that far. You have been gracious in consenting to live here, and you came at the god's behest, but you will not become one of us.

You will not become mine. I will release you from the burden of my hoping for such a thing."

"Gaaron!" she exclaimed, and she shook the arm that she still had hold of. "Gaaron, do not say such things! I am here of my own free will, I have committed myself to you. I will—"

He pulled back a pace and released himself from her hand. "I know. You will do as the god directs, and so will I. But I will not expect more from you than that."

"But Gaaron, I will give you more! I will ask for more! If I had had to settle for a loveless marriage with an indifferent man, I would have accepted it, if it was the god's will. But we can create something better than that, you and I—we *can* love each other, we can believe in each other. We—"

"I am not good at love, and you clearly love elsewhere," he interrupted. "That's as close to heartbreak as either of us needs to come. I must go. I am out of words for the moment."

And he swept away from her, his spread wings seeming to brush across every surface of the room as he stalked to the door and stepped through it. Susannah stared after him, feeling shocked and rebuffed and confused.

But not entirely hopeless. Only a man with his heart engaged would have any fear of harming it. Perhaps she had been wrong about Gaaron, last night; perhaps, after all, he already loved her.

She would have to wait four or more days to find out.

CHAPTER TWENTY-SIX

Miriam sat with Jossis in the mud and played with dolls.

It was a fine winter morning, brilliant, cold, and beautiful, and they had crept away from the camp before all the work was done merely to enjoy the sunshine. Tirza had seen them go, however, and had done nothing to stop them, so Miriam didn't feel too bad about it. They had wandered along the northern edge of the mountain, clambering over rocks and skidding from time to time into shadowed banks of gray snow, and they had laughed and pointed things out to each other and generally had a grand time.

When they had come to a sun-warmed little alcove punched into the rock, they had instantly settled into it, safe from the inquisitive breeze and almost comfortable with the built-up heat stored in the stone. Miriam pulled out a packet of dried food while Jossis melted snow in a bowl, and they ate a companionable lunch under the noon sun. From time to time, Jossis would point at something he had not seen before—though there was little, here on the upper reaches of the Galo range, that he had not come across by now—and ask the inevitable "Ska?" When she knew, Miriam told him. When she did not, she spread her hands and laughed.

Today she had decided to work on counting, so once the meal was done, she gathered a handful of twigs and rocks, then settled back down on their spread blanket. Jossis crouched beside her, instantly on the alert; there was nothing he loved so much as a new lesson. Miriam held up a single twig.

"One," she said.

He nodded, still waiting, not sure if that was the name of the object or some other piece of knowledge that he would only comprehend as the lesson unfolded. She picked up a second twig and held it with the first. "Two."

She went all the way to ten before repeating the exercise with the rocks, which was when she could tell Jossis began to catch on. Excited, he jumped to his feet and returned with a handful of empty seed pods, all more or less alike.

"Wuh," he said, separating a single pod from the pile. "Tooooo. Theee."

"Yes, yes! That's it!" Miriam said, clapping her hands with excitement. She extended her index finger. "One."

He held up both of his own index fingers, side by side. "Toooo."

He got stuck after three, so she had to repeat the whole sequence for him several times. She made him match the word to the actual amount the first few times—one finger, two rocks, three twigs, four seed pods—so that the sound and concept became synonymous. But after that she just allowed him to recite the series of syllables over and over so that he would memorize the phonetics.

"Very good," she approved when she was sure he had it. Once he learned something, he never forgot it. He would integrate the most unexpected words into his limited conversations.

"More?" he suggested.

She laughed. "Well, you already know your colors and every object we own in the camp, and now you can count. I wish you could tell me more about *you*, that's what I really want to know."

"More?" he repeated.

She frowned at him a moment, thinking. What else could she teach him, how could she get him to teach her? She gathered up the twigs again and signaled for a new game.

"Miriam," she said, holding up one of the twigs. "Tirza. Eleazar. Bartholomew." She said a name for everyone in the camp, and Jossis nodded. "The Lohoras."

"Lo-ho-*rah*," he said obediently.

She planted the collection of twigs in the hard mud, then made a little mound of snow and dirt and rocks and pointed at the peak of Mount Galo. "Here," she said, for that was a concept he had mastered a few days ago. "Lohoras here."

He nodded again, though whether or not he truly understood was anybody's guess. Now she picked up a stick and moved to a flat wash of mud that had settled beside a boulder, and she began drawing a map. "Mountain here," she said as she sketched in Galo. "River here. Lohoras here." She stuck a small rock at the base of her pointed mountain. "And here's the rest of Samaria." She added the outline of the coasts, a long squiggle for the Galilee River, and more triangular shapes to represent the Caitanas and the Velo range. "Samaria," she said, then tapped her chest. "My world."

He was crouched flat-footed before her map, studying it intently, and she had no idea how much he was absorbing. She didn't think she would understand if the situation were reversed and he was trying to explain his world to her. But then, as she had told Tirza, she thought Jossis was very intelligent—smarter than she was, smart enough to understand anything he was shown.

"Stick?" he said, holding out his hand, and she passed him her stylus. He bent lower and began scratching a few more designs into the dirt, and Miriam had to repress a smile. He had not understood her, after all. He thought she was demonstrating drawing techniques or basic topographical distinctions. When he was done making improvements, he picked up a few pebbles and embellished his finished masterpiece with carefully placed rocks. "Samaria," he said, gesturing proudly.

Still smiling, Miriam bent over to have a look at what he'd done. But her smile faded almost immediately. For with the stick he had sketched in more mountains—the Heldoras in Jordana, the Corinnis in southern Bethel, the few ragged peaks that housed Mount Sinai and Mount Sudan and Monteverde. With his rocks, he had marked the most prominent cities of the three provinces—Luminaux, Breven, Semorrah, Castelana—as well as the exact placement of all three angel holds. Each stone, each pointed peak, was as precisely placed as the imperfect limitations of Miriam's map would allow.

"Meerimuh?" he asked, when she did not speak. "Meerimuh?" He crouched even lower, bending around to try and peer into her averted face. "Samaria, yes? Meerimuh?"

She nodded, feeling her throat tighten to the point where words were difficult. Eleazar was right, of course. Jossis was a member of a clan that had come here to destroy them. Here was the evidence, a detailed and meticulous surveying of her entire world, more accurately drawn than she managed herself. Mountains here, rivers here, unprotected city dwellers there . . .

"Meerimuh? Sad?" he asked now, reaching out to touch her shoulder. *Happy* and *sad*. Those were two words she had taught him, for those had been easy enough emotions to convey. *Terror*, that would be a harder one, though not impossible, with the right look of horror and fear. *Betrayal*. She was not sure how to explain that one.

"Meerimuh?" he said, his voice and his hand both more insistent. He tugged her around to look at him, now putting his hand under her chin to tilt her face up. "Sad?"

She let him turn her, let herself meet his gaze, the whole while examining his face. He looked so innocent and so hopeful, his blue eyes blazing with the excitement he always showed upon mastering a new skill, but his mouth pursed, his eyebrows drawn down, in an expression of concern for her. "Sick?" he asked now.

She shook her head. "Not sad," she said. "Not sick." She spread her hands in the *I don't know* gesture, this time meant to convey *I can't explain*. It was his turn to explain something. She came slowly to her feet, crossing back to where she'd left all the twigs stuck in the ground. He rose and followed her. She passed over all the sticks except one, which she held up in front of him. "Jossis," she said, shaking the twig a little. Then she handed him that one as well.

He looked down at the bundle in his hand, frowning, but not as if he was confused—more as if he was trying to decide how to create a concept that she would understand. He nodded, then bent to lay all the twigs on the ground and went off in search of more props. He returned a few minutes later with a whole pile of kindling in his hand and motioned her over. He had found another level place on the ground, next to the map that represented Samaria, and he smoothed away the rocks and small debris that had piled on top of the mud.

"Meerimuh—Samaria," he said, pointing first at the woman, then to the map. "Jossis—Mozanan," he added, pointing at himself and then the outline he was producing in the soil. Miriam nodded.

He didn't trouble with many details this time. Clearly, he was not so interested in showing her the arrangement of lakes and oceans on his home world. As soon as he had roughed in what looked like three or four large land masses, he began poking sticks and twigs into the mud. He bunched them so closely together that soon he could thrust more sticks into the forest and they would not even need to reach the mud to stay in place. More sticks—more—an overcrowded, claustrophobic, chaotic representation of a world.

He looked at Miriam seriously and spoke a few words. She nodded, though she didn't understand him, but she knew what he meant. There were too many people in his home, wherever his home was. There was not enough room for everybody.

"Now, Jossis," he said, and plucked one of the twigs from the stand of sticks. He reeled off more names and drew more sticks from the mud, then bundled them together with a length of dried grass. Then, holding this package between his hands and making silly whistling noises, he made the bundle fly through the air, up and down, in the direction of the map of Samaria.

Miriam nodded again. Some of this was taking shape for her. She knew, though only vaguely, that the original settlers of Samaria had come from some other world, both overpopulated and prone to violence, and that Jovah had brought them to Samaria to start anew. How they had traveled here was unclear—the Librera claimed that Jovah had carried them in his hands—and Miriam had never really given it much thought. But that men could move through the starlit alleys from one world to another she had always accepted on faith, and it seemed like Jossis and some of his companions had done just that.

She had another thought, but it was hard to get her mind around it. Had Jossis come from the *same* planet as the original settlers had? Could that explain the familiarity of his shape, his expressions, the fact that he looked very much like every other man she had ever encountered? True, there were some superficial differences in hair color and skin color—but even among Samarians, there were several races, all with some differences, all with great similarities. Could Jossis have come from another race that had not been among those to emigrate to this new world—until now? Was his history a shared history with hers? Could that explain the song he had sung at the campfire the other night, a song that the angels had brought with them from their home world, and that Jossis had learned on that same planet? Was he tied to her even more closely than she had thought?

And if he had *not* come from that world . . . then how many worlds were there, populated by people who looked enough alike and thought enough alike that they must be related in some way? Had they all been created by the hand of the same god and scattered throughout the planets of the universe? Or had the nameless one placed them all on one homeland and allowed them to move, in slow stages as the mood took them, to fresh worlds warmed by newer stars? Miriam could not grasp all the implications of this theory; she could not get her mind to comprehend the logistics.

Jossis was looking at her, hopeful again, wanting her to acknowledge that she understood. She nodded and repeated the gestures. "Samaria," she said, pointing to the map of her own world. "Mozanan." There was another word he knew; maybe he would grasp it in this context. "Far?" she asked, pointing again between the two worlds.

He nodded emphatically, then frowned a little, trying to figure out how to convey distance to her. Then he ran over to the blanket to pick up one of the seed pods, and handed it to Miriam. "Samaria," he said, and she nodded. He held up a second pod. "Mozanan."

She nodded again, and he took off running. They were in a semi-enclosed space, so he could not get far before he ran out of level land, but then he began climbing. He clambered up a few tumbles of rock, awkwardly, using only one hand to pull himself up because he still had the seed pod grasped in his other.

"Jossis!" Miriam called, because this was dangerous; she did not want him to hurt himself.

He turned to face her, still waving the pod in his hand. "Far!" he exclaimed, and threw the pod away from him as hard as he could. Miriam watched, but she could not see where it landed. Nonetheless, the message was clear. Jossis' home world was so far from this one that the distance was unimaginable. She could not guess how he had gotten here, but she was beginning to understand why he—and his people—had come.

Two days later, Miriam and Jossis played with more sophisticated toys. Miriam had spent a couple of evenings using rags and string to create dolls with a little more personality, though Tirza had laughed when she showed them to her.

"That's supposed to be me?" the older woman said. "I like my hair." It was a single swatch of black fabric culled from the ragbag and tacked to the doll's cotton head.

"Mine isn't much better," Miriam said. She had cut a few scraps of yellow fabric into strips and sewed each of these to a misshapen head. "But I'm not going to try to sell these in a Luminaux market, you understand. I'm just trying to get a point across. And learn something."

"And when you've learned, what else will you know that you don't know now?" Tirza said with a shrug. But she didn't stop Miriam from proceeding with her project.

The days had been too busy to allow two working members to skip out and play games, so Miriam didn't have a chance to show Jossis the dolls until after dinner that night. They sat a little outside the common circle, listening to the Edori sing, and letting the flickering firelight illuminate their charades.

"Miriam, Tirza, Eleazar, Bartholomew, Anna, Claudia, Adam," Miriam said, naming the dolls she had constructed. She had also made a whole family of black-skinned dolls to represent Jossis and his people, and these lay before him while he watched her with narrowed eyes. "Tirza and Eleazar," she said, and mimed the two dolls holding hands, kissing each other on the face, dancing together to simulate joy. "Happy," she said.

Bartholomew and Anna were also seen to be happy together. Then Miriam created the whole clan as a cheerful unit, insufficient rag arms around one another, cotton kisses pressed to cotton cheeks. "All happy." She picked up the doll that represented Jossis and brought him into the circle. Bartholomew's thin arm went around Jossis' dark neck; Tirza put her embroidered lips to his black cheek. "Happy," she said again.

Then she induced the Jossis doll to dance across the blanket to his fellows piled up before Jossis himself. "Happy?" she asked when the character was reunited with his clan.

But Jossis shook his head vehemently. "Sad," he said.

He took the Jossis doll and set it aside, midway between the two camps, and frowned down at the pile of bodies before him. Then, with a sudden furious action, he dove his hands into the mass of dolls and flung them into the air. He grabbed one of the bigger dolls and used it to beat on the smaller ones, then the smaller ones turned on one another in equal violence. Snatching up a stick from the ground, Jossis held this to the hand of one of the figures and manipulated it so that it lashed across the faces of the others. But this didn't satisfy him. He looked around, his face still creased in a scowl. While Miriam sat watching in some stupefaction, he leapt to his feet, hurried over to the circle of Edori around the fire, and dipped his stick into the flames. The tip was burning when he came back to sit beside Miriam again.

"Mozanan," he announced, and set several of the dolls on fire.

"Jossis!" Miriam exclaimed, but he sat there calmly, watching each little black hand, each crude face, go up in flames.

Then he reached for the doll that represented him and danced it back to its homeland. "Jossis," he said, and set himself on fire.

A shadow fell over them. "What's going on here? What's he doing?" Eleazar's voice demanded. "Are you trying to burn down the camp?"

Miriam stared up at him, so stunned at Jossis' actions that she was having trouble recalling speech patterns. "He's—he's showing me what life is like at home among his clan," she said stupidly.

Eleazar made a sound like a grunt. "Well, that can't surprise you much. It's what his clan is like here, too."

"I think they war against each other, not just us," she said.

"Violent men are violent all the time," Eleazar said. "That's what I've been saying about your little friend here."

But Miriam shook her head emphatically. Jossis had not looked up, even when Eleazar came striding over. He was watching his friends, his family members, himself, burn away to cinders and ash. "Not Jossis," she said. "He's different."

Three days of bitter cold kept everyone in the camp, desperate for the warmth of the fire. They took turns keeping a nighttime watch so that someone could feed logs to the fire all night long and they would not have to wake to absolute zero. Even so, the mornings were almost unendurable. Miriam was, every day, the last one to leave the tent, the one most reluctant to pull herself from the shared warmth of friendly bodies and thrust herself out into the hostile chill of the day. She would cling to Tirza's hand when the older woman tried to rise, or grab Amram's foot and wrestle him back to the ground beside her, murmuring, "Heat, heat, heat, heat." She only got up when the whole tent was empty and it was scarcely any warmer inside than out.

But she was worried about Jossis.

He still was sleeping solitary in a small tent that, even close to the fire, had no interior warmth. He would freeze to death, she was sure of it. She would go in one morning and find him a curled black stone of a man. She had procured extra blankets for him, which he accepted willingly, but he refused to go to any other tent at night.

She had tried to pantomime for him the benefits of communal sleeping. She had kept her dolls, and made another one to represent

Jossis, and one morning she made little tents for them out of leftover fabric. The Jossis doll, lying solitary under his canvas, shivered and could not sleep. When he crept over to Miriam's tent, though, and slipped between Amram and Tirza, he sighed and grew warm and instantly fell asleep.

Jossis smiled when she enacted this play for him, but he shook his head. "Why?" Miriam demanded in frustration.

Jossis picked through the dolls to find a particular one she had named early. "Eleazar," he said, holding it up. Eleazar then confronted Jossis, shaking in a way that connoted anger. "Eleazar not happy Jossis."

Miriam snatched all the dolls back and renamed them. "Anna, Bartholomew, Thaddeus, Shua," she said, and walked the Jossis creation over to that shared tent. "Jossis sleep Bartholomew. Warm."

But Jossis just shook his head. "No," he said.

Tirza, when appealed to, did not seem too worried about it. "He hasn't died yet," was what she said when Miriam expressed her chief worry. "Let him live the way he chooses to live, Miriam."

"But his way is wrong!"

Tirza laughed at her. "And here I thought you were turning into a true Edori."

Which made Miriam furious, but she realized the underlying criticism was true. She could happily camp year-round with a tribe of clansmen, travel the length and breadth of Samaria with them, living off the land, doing her share of the chores, celebrating the change of seasons—but she would never truly think like an Edori. She had too many opinions and was willing to express them too strongly; she had no deep well of tolerance to draw on, and not a great deal of patience, either.

"If a true Edori would let a fellow clansman die out of sheer stubbornness, then I suppose I am not one," Miriam said sullenly.

Tirza laughed again. "But you will not let him freeze. I am very sure of that."

Thinking that over, Miriam realized there was a way to save Jossis from himself.

Accordingly, that night after the campfire songs, she rounded up the ever-willing Amram, and they pulled their pallets and blankets from their accustomed tent. "Where are *they* going?" Eleazar demanded.

"Elsewhere, for a little change," Tirza said mildly, and Eleazar did not ask further questions.

Jossis appeared to have just wrapped himself in his own blanket when Miriam pulled back the tent flap and peered in. "Jossis?" she said, just to announce herself. "Miriam and Amram sleep here. Warm."

"Ska?" he said, sitting up on his pallet, clearly unsure, at least for a moment, what this invasion meant. But Miriam pushed her way inside the small space, Amram behind her, and they proceeded to arrange themselves on either side of the other man.

"Meerimuh," Jossis said in a scolding voice. He unleashed a torrent of words that sounded both disapproving and slightly panicked, but Miriam and Amram ignored him.

"Will you be warm enough there?" Miriam asked the boy. "Would you rather sleep between us?"

"I think we'd better keep him in the middle, or he'll sneak out before midnight," was Amram's response.

Miriam stifled a giggle. "If he gets up in the middle of the night, you scream and grab his ankle."

"What if he's just going to the water tent?"

"Then I guess he'll be embarrassed, won't he?"

They both laughed at that. Jossis was still talking to them earnestly, trying to explain something that clearly they were not going to understand. Miriam knelt beside him on her own pallet and gave him a serious look.

"This is the Lohora way," she said.

And she put her palm flat against his chest and pushed him back to his pallet. At first he resisted, still talking, but a little more half-heartedly. "Sleep now," Miriam said firmly. "Warm."

"Jossis Mozanan," he said, but he sounded less convinced. "Not Lohora."

"Lohora now," Miriam said, and pushed some more.

He lay down with a sigh, flat on his back and staring up at the top of the tent. Miriam glanced over at Amram, who nodded. As soon as Miriam lay on her own pallet and pulled her blanket up to her chin, she and Amram both scooted over, to press Jossis between their two bodies. He yelped out some word of distress in his own language, but they laughed and stayed where they were. Miriam could feel the tension in his body, through her own blanket, through his, but she did not roll away. He would lie awake all night, alarmed and unhappy, or he would sleep; and if he slept, he would sleep warm; and if he did not sleep, he would be so tired that the next night he would have no choice but to fall asleep between them. He would have to accept their ways, which were good ways. He was an Edori now.

For the next three nights, Amram and Miriam joined Jossis in his small tent. After the first session, which seemed to pass for Jossis in a sort of ecstatic terror, the Mozanan man seemed to relax and actually enjoy the company. This might have been because, one night, Miriam and Amram began tickling and teasing each other, in the process climbing over Jossis and kneeing him in the ribs or—accidentally, of course— tickling him, too. This might have been because Amram hid a rabbit skull in the bottom of Miriam's blanket or because Miriam crushed highly perfumed dried seeds over Amram's pallet. In any case, there was much merriment inside that small tent for those three days, and Jossis could not help but join in the laughter.

On the fourth night, Amram elected to sleep in Bartholomew's tent. Miriam elected to sleep beside Jossis as usual.

They had both stayed at the campfire circle as long as the circle held, lifting their voices on the group songs and listening quietly when someone rose to perform a solo. Over the past couple of weeks, Jossis had learned the harmonies to a few of the more common melodies, and had acquired the ability to produce the words at least phonetically, so he always sang along on the pieces he knew. Miriam liked to sit beside him and listen to his voice tentatively skip to the note he was not sure of, then strengthen when he realized he had it right. Conversely, she also liked to sit across the fire from him so she could watch his face shift between concentration and delight. He had not offered to sing a solo again. She thought perhaps he was shy about his voice, which was sweet but not particularly well-trained. She thought that perhaps that would be the next thing she would teach him: formal music.

There was so much to teach him. She was impatient for him to learn the words that he would need to acquire all the other knowledge he must have.

The singing hummed to a close and the circle began to drift apart. Miriam watched Amram go off to Bartholomew's tent, first pausing to speak a few words to Thaddeus, who would mind the fire for the early evening shift. She waited till most of the tents were full for the night, and there were not many observant eyes turned her way, before going to the only tent with a single occupant.

Jossis was already lying on his pallet by the time she crept in, and he instinctively moved over to make room for her. She was settled in next to him, her back against his stomach, before he seemed to realize that something about the night was different.

"Amram?" he asked.

"Bartholomew's tent," she replied.

There was a moment's silence, then Jossis spoke again, more urgently. "Amram? Now?"

"Not now," Miriam said.

"Meerimuh!"

She hunched her shoulders in the dark, letting him feel the motion of the shrug. He knew that gesture well enough. "It doesn't matter," she added for good measure. "Warm."

But this made him tense, and she could feel his coiled body refusing to relax against her. She mentally reviewed all the reasons he would find it unacceptable to be alone at night with a woman. First, of course, there seemed to be some privacy issues among the people of the Mozanan clan, and perhaps her mere closeness was a taboo that he did not know how to explain. Second, the aura of intimacy was impossible to mistake, and he might have all sorts of objections to sexual context: He might be a virgin, he might be celibate, he might be promised to some girl back on Mozanan and true to his vows.

Or he might simply be too young to be comfortable with the thought of sleeping next to a woman. She didn't think that was it, though. She hadn't had a chance to try to explain the concept of "years" and "age" to him, but she did not think, even in his own culture, he could be as young as Amram. For one thing, he had been conscripted to serve with his fellow clansmen on this perilous journey. Surely he must be a man by his people's standards, though a young one. For another thing . . . well, she had seen him stretched out and naked, and he looked like an adult to her.

Of course, there could be another reason she made him uneasy: He might find her unattractive, and the idea of how he might be expected to relate to her might repulse him.

That was a dreary thought to sleep with on a cold winter night, she thought, closing her eyes. She decided that she would ignore all his fears, while simultaneously ignoring all the possibilities of the moment, and merely provide for him what she had set out to provide: warmth against the killing cold. She did not wriggle closer, but she did not move away, as she finally drifted off to sleep.

In the morning, Jossis seemed troubled and watchful; there was no move Miriam made that he missed. She guessed that he, too, was wishing they had progressed a little further in their ability to communicate so that he could ask her pressing questions or explain implacable restrictions. She could not imagine that her dolls would be much help here, though the thought of what she might demonstrate with them made her grin involuntarily.

"Did you find out what you wanted to know last night?" Tirza asked her as they worked over the cook pots.

"Not unless what I wanted to know was that Jossis is afraid of me," Miriam replied glumly.

Tirza went off into a peal of laughter. Miriam added, "Or finds me too hideous to contemplate."

"That, at least, is not the case," Tirza answered, regaining her composure. "He watches you every minute of the day."

"Because, after last night, he is afraid of what I might do next."

"No, he has always watched you. Since he first opened his feverish eyes while he lay helpless on a sickbed. This is not a man who finds you disagreeable."

Miriam made a gesture. "Anyway, I am not sleeping in his tent in the hopes that he finds me attractive. I am sleeping in his tent to keep him warm."

"A great kindness," Tirza said solemnly, but Miriam thought she was still laughing. "Surely *that* is not something that might be rejected."

The day passed in the usual labor of staying alive. More men were dispatched to gather firewood than to hunt, since they were low on fuel but fairly well-stocked with game. Anna and Claudia pulled down their tent to repair a rip, then put it back up again. Miriam spent the day cooking with Tirza. Jossis went off with Amram and the other young members of the tribe to forage for additional wood.

That night, after the meal and camp songs, Amram joined Miriam and Jossis in the little tent. Miriam had snagged one of the short, smelly candles that Tirza sometimes made from tallow and string, and brought it lit into the tent with them. The practice was widely frowned upon, due to the risk of fire. Amram's eyes grew wide at the infraction, but Miriam smiled and put a finger to her lips, enjoining silence.

"I'm not sleepy," she said.

Amram pulled a sack of smooth stones from his pocket and proceeded to lay them out in the sequence of a gambling game that the Edori boys were fond of. Jossis gave a low exclamation of delight, for he had mastered these rather complex rules after a couple of sessions around the circle. Miriam smiled and took up her third of the stones. She was not very good at the game, but she understood it well enough to keep her place for half an hour. Jossis and Amram were still playing when she lay on her pallet and went to sleep.

The next day was a copy of the previous one, down to the session of gambling in the tent; and so was the following day, except that Amram slept in Eleazar's tent that night.

Jossis did not seem so alarmed this time when he found himself alone with Miriam and a fresh tallow candle. He had watched her closely these past few days, though the look of trouble on his face had been replaced by a more speculative expression. She had made no attempt to be alone with him, or spend any more time with him than she did with anyone else. And so when she turned up in his tent, unaccompanied, she was able to be both friendly and neutral, as she would have been to Adam or Bartholomew or any of the women.

"Candle," she named it for him again before setting it in a small earthenware dish.

"Cannel," he repeated.

She glanced around for diversions, and found that Amram had left his gambling sack behind. "Stones?" she asked, picking up and shaking the bag so its contents rattled.

Jossis took the sack from her but laid it aside. "Talk," he said.

Miriam made her expression as encouraging as she could. "Ska?"

He was sitting cross-legged on his pallet, his spine straight, his face furrowed; he seemed to be thinking very hard. Miriam, by contrast, was quite relaxed, half reclined, leaning on one arm and stretching her legs out comfortably.

He held up his hands in loose fists as if to represent two separate entities. "Man, woman," he said. She nodded. He brought them together slowly, so the knuckles touched. A kiss, perhaps; an embrace. "Good?"

She nodded emphatically. "Yes, very good. *Good* good."

He flung his hands apart as far as they could go, the fingers still curled in balls of meaning. "Man, woman—bad?"

Was he asking if the separation of the sexes was always a bad thing, or if it was bad only if the separation occurred after a man and woman had come together? If a union was always taboo—or if it was merely wrenching when it failed? She did not know how to convey concepts so complex.

She had her little pile of sticks with her. She almost always carried them now, whenever she thought she might see Jossis. Sitting up so she could arrange them before her, she made a little grouping on her blanket. "Tirza and Eleazar—Anna and Bartholomew—Claudia and Adam," she said, and he nodded. She picked up the sticks that posed as Tirza and Eleazar. "Tirza and Eleazar—happy." They danced through the air to express their joy. "One day—Tirza and Eleazar apart." She made the two sticks walk away from each other in slow dejected hops.

"Bad?" Jossis asked intently.

Miriam shrugged. "Sad," she corrected. She laid the sticks down so she could be more expressive with her hands, putting her fingers to her cheeks to wipe away pretend tears, sniffling and sobbing like a brokenhearted woman.

"Sad bad," Jossis pointed out.

Miriam couldn't help smiling. She picked up the Tirza stick and let it sojourn back to its circle of friends, where new twigs had been added to the Lohora camp. "Tirza—new man," she said. She picked up Eleazar and did the same. "Eleazar—new woman. Happy again." And all the sticks danced together across her blanket.

He sat there a long time, watching the candlelight make patterns on her hands as she skipped the sticks up and down the coverlet. He appeared to be absorbing her little drama, both what she had said, and what it meant to him. *A man can love a woman. The love can go away. They will both grieve, but they will mend. They are free to love again.* And its corollary: *I can love a woman of Samaria, and I can go away when I must. She will grieve for a short time, but she will love again* . . .

She wondered how such matters were handled in his own clan. Even among the other races of Samaria, relations between the sexes were not quite so simple. Love might result in marriage, which was not quite so easily dissolved when one or the other of the parties wished to "go away." And failed love could result in violence. She had heard that tale often enough, though she had never witnessed it among the angels. At the holds, love was a fairly carefree thing. The angels mated where they would—were encouraged to be promiscuous, in fact, in the hopes that their unions would produce more angel children— and even the angels who married were rarely entirely faithful.

Gaaron will be faithful, came the thought unbidden to her mind. She pushed it away. This was certainly not a time when she wanted to be thinking about her brother.

Jossis himself seemed lost in thought, so perhaps her little demonstration had not entirely reassured him. Miriam picked up two more sticks.

"Jossis," she named the first one, and made it travel through the air to land beside the second one. "Woman? In Mozanan? Jossis and woman?"

He started at that, his eyes intent on hers as if amazed that she could read his mind. She wished she could. All she could tell was that he was thinking something over very carefully. "Yes," he said at last. "Taralin."

Miriam was surprised at what a blow this was. She felt literally sick to her stomach. But she tried to keep her expression open and smiling. She set the two sticks to dancing side by side. "Jossis and Taralin happy?"

He shook his head violently. "No. No, no, no." He snatched the sticks from Miriam's hands and then sat there, staring at them, as if unable to figure out how to show her just what made Taralin so terrible. At last he just laid them on the ground. "Not happy," he said.

Then don't go back to her, Miriam wanted to say, but even that collection of one-syllable words was too complicated to utter. She didn't even know how to ask him what his exact relationship with Taralin was. Were they merely promised to each other, or were they already married? Did he hate her because she was stupid or because she was cruel? Why had he accepted her if he did not like her, or was the marriage arranged and entirely out of his hands? That he felt some duty to her was clear. Nothing else was.

She spread her hands and smiled at him, a gesture intended to be both helpless and reassuring. *I can do nothing about this, but it's all right,* she meant to say. *I still like you more than I can say.*

"Sleep now," she said, reaching for the candle. "Talk tomorrow."

But he took the candle from her hand before she could blow it out and set it back on the ground. "Merrimuh," he said, and reached out both of his hands to frame her face.

His touch was so gentle that it was not even pressure, it was a mere hovering sensation of skin next to skin. She could feel the coolness of his fingertips, though his palms were still warm from the hour before the fire. She could smell the scent of strong soap on his skin. They had both bathed in the river that morning, passing each other as she left the hot spring and he arrived. Soap and woodsmoke and leather and snow; he smelled of all of these things, and something richer that she could not identify. Himself.

She lifted her own hands to trace the bones of his face, the high cheekbones, the curved jawline, the elegant dome of his skull. Her fingers lost themselves in the crisp radiance of his hair, and he smiled as she made fists inside his curls and tugged. "Where could you possibly get hair this color?" she asked in a whisper.

He replied in an equally incomprehensible sentence, and then laughed at whatever it was he had said. "Don't make fun of me," she said sternly. "I'm the only true friend you have here."

"Friend," he repeated, catching the word, and shook his head. "Not friend." He cocked his head to one side. "Ska?"

She could not help laughing. This was not a word she had thought to introduce into his vocabulary. "Ska?" she repeated innocently.

"Tirza and Eleazar. Claudia and Adam. Not friend. Ska?"

"Lover," she said.

"Lover," he repeated, and bent in to kiss her on the mouth.

For a moment she thought the candle had gone out; she was lost in darkness and sensation. Her hands went automatically to his shoulders, as his had gone to her back. He was pulling her closer with an unthinking insistence, cradling her against him with a motion that was both protective and demanding. The heat of his mouth was extraordinary, or perhaps it was the heat of her own body, for she felt herself flush from toes to eyebrows.

Whatever else they considered taboo on Mozanan, they certainly knew how to kiss.

She pulled away long enough to resettle herself more comfortably on his lap, then pressed her whole body against him when she kissed him again. He cooperated enthusiastically but not quite single-mindedly, for his hands were already going to the buttons and ties that held together her shirt. She giggled and drew back to help him, pulling off first the outer layer of her clothing, and then the soft cotton shirt beneath.

Half nude, she presented herself to him by the flickering light of a single candle. His expression was both awestruck and eager, and he loosed a torrent of words that only made her laugh and shake her head. He reached for her, but she pulled back.

"Now you," she said.

He lost no time divesting himself of everything, jacket, shirt, trousers, socks, so while he was disrobing, she pulled off the rest of her own clothes. Still on their knees, they paused to admire each other a moment. Sweet Jovah singing, he had filled out in these past few weeks. He was muscled and lean as any outdoorsman, with a fine keyboard of ribs showing through the glistening black skin of his chest. His flesh was so dark that she could not resist the temptation to spread her hand across the region of his heart merely to enjoy the stark contrast of colors. They were like snow and shadow, noon and midnight.

"Beautiful," he said, another word she had not known he knew, and then he kissed her again.

She strained against him and they toppled over, laughing as they landed in a muddled heap on his pallet. "I'm *cold!*" she squealed and dove beneath the blanket, Jossis right beside her.

"Jossis warm," he offered.

She pressed herself against him, her whole body against the length of his, and kissed him hard. "Very warm," she agreed. "My lover."

He responded very tenderly in words she could not decode, but she replied anyway. "I wonder what you know that is different from what I know," she whispered. "I want to learn it. Show me now."

And he showed her. And she learned, to her great satisfaction, that what they knew was very much the same.

In the morning they were silly, as all new lovers were silly. The whole camp watched them with indulgent smiles as they emerged from the tent and tried not to look self-conscious. Tirza came over right away with a pair of buckets, thus sending them to the river together where they could share a few more kisses and incidentally get clean. Anna made a great show of bringing them an extra set of blankets, saying, "I'm sure you must have been cold last night, only two bodies in the tent. That can't be enough for proper warmth," and everyone listening laughed. Bartholomew only winked at Miriam and slapped Jossis on the back, but did not make any knowing comments. Eleazar scowled at Jossis, but then he smiled at Miriam, and she was sure he was not entirely displeased.

"I will make an Edori of him yet—you'll see," she murmured when she bumped against Eleazar at the noon meal.

"The allali and the foreigner—yes, those are true Edori," he retorted, but he was still smiling.

"I will show you," she promised. "You will be proud to know me."

Unexpectedly, for he was not the most demonstrative man, he leaned over and hugged her. "Ah, Miriam," he said roughly. "I am proud of you every day."

"I think you should—" she began, but she was interrupted by a scream from across the camp.

She spun around. Eleazar whirled and dropped into a hunting crouch, his hand going to the knife on his belt. Another scream. The noise seemed to be coming from the head of the camp, the place that they passed through to get into the sheltered land against the mountain. Miriam and Eleazar ran forward, along with Amram and Anna and Bartholomew, to find everyone else bunched up at the narrow place in the mountain that led to open land. Shua was screaming and pointing, and everyone else was staring, frozen in terror or dread.

"What is it? What is it?" Eleazar was shouting. He had paused somewhere in their mad dash across the ground to snatch up a crossbow.

But it would do no good. Anyone could see it would do no good. Facing them across the narrow divide was a line of foreign marauders, dressed in their black suits and shiny hats, and leveling an array of fire sticks at the Edori camp.

CHAPTER TWENTY-SEVEN

Gaaron took off from the Eyrie with all of his bones feeling so heavy that he was not sure he could muster the strength to fling his body into the air. Indeed, it took more energy than he could ever remember expending to flex his wings for each separate downbeat that would drive him higher into the atmosphere. His body seemed made of bronze, cold and heavy; his feathers were made of enamel, showy and useless. The winter air glided against his skin like a cold and eager serpent.

What did it matter, after all, if his bride did not love him? If she loved another man? She was still a good woman; she would be an excellent angelica. She would superbly carry out all the tasks for which she had been selected. Jovah had consulted, not Gaaron's heart, but his own grand scheme for Samaria when he cast his eyes over the women of the world and laid his hand upon this one. It was stupid to feel so betrayed.

It was wrong to feel such anger at the god.

The thing was, Gaaron was not sure he would be able to unlove Susannah. He had not really given much thought to love itself, even when Mahalah had told him he must take a wife, even when he had brought that wife home. It had been his duty, one of his large collection of duties, and he had accepted it along with the other responsibilities that had piled up on him. The god said, "Marry," and he had found a bride. He had not thought the command would be, "Fall in love." He had had no practice with that.

Which was why, perhaps, this love for Susannah had hit him so hard. He did not know what to do with it; it was awkward and unwieldy, it made him clumsy with words and actions. But it was such a big thing, and such a pervasive one. It took up so many of his scattered thoughts, occupied such a large region inside his chest. He could not fold it down small enough to make it a comfortable burden, something he could slip inside a pocket and take out only when he wanted to admire it.

Now, of course, it was even worse. His sense of black betrayal was even larger than his secret love; it was so big it engulfed him, covered him from wingtip to wingtip. He could not fly fast enough to outpace it, or far enough to leave it behind. It would be awaiting him, panting and sly, on the high peak of Windy Point, and it would accompany him all the way to the icy hills of Monteverde.

For this, the god had sought him out and marked him. For all his service to Jovah, this was his bitter reward.

Adriel was happy to see him and had news of her own. "Four of my angels were flying from Luminaux to Semorrah," she told him. "Carrying a large marble slab, maybe six feet by eight feet. You can imagine how awkward, one of them at each corner."

A little amusement seeped through his black mood. "Why would they be given such a commission?"

"Because Colton of Semorrah wanted it, of course, and he couldn't wait! He's such a pompous ass. And none of the Luminaux drivers would agree to transport it, for fear of being attacked on the road. So after he harassed me for three weeks, I agreed to have my angels act as carriers—although they were not, I can tell you, exactly thrilled about it."

"So then what happened?"

"They were flying north along the Galilee, and they came across a band of marauders in the act of burning down a Jansai camp. They were flying low, of course, because the marble was heavy and they were making many stops, and so they could see everything most clearly. One of them let out a yell, and they were all so startled, they dropped the slab. Which landed in the middle of the invaders and *crushed* them all to death. Well, not all of them," Adriel amended, "but several of them. The rest all did that thing where they disappear."

"Excellent!" Gaaron approved, feeling actually quite happy at the news. "What did the angels do next?"

"They landed, of course, to see if there was anything they could do for the Jansai. Some of the travelers were severely hurt, so my angels took them back to Luminaux. None of the Jansai had been killed, though five of the invaders were."

"And what did they do with those bodies?"

Adriel gave him a look of revulsion. "What would you expect them to do with the bodies? They were left for the wild dogs."

Gaaron shrugged. Too late, then. "I would have thought—we could have examined them to see in what ways they might differ from us. If nothing else, look at their clothes and their weapons and see what we might learn."

"None of their weapons were left behind," Adriel said positively. "My angels did look. The ones who disappeared took everything."

"And what happened to Colton's marble slab?"

Adriel could not help a smile. "Destroyed. Shattered into a dozen pieces upon impact."

"Is it possible I can imagine Colton's reaction to this?"

"Quite possible, I would think. I have told him the hold will absorb the cost, and the Luminaux craftsmen will undertake to make him a second one at all speed. Apparently it takes some months to get the carving done just right, however, so Colton is not happy with me for using his marble as a weapon."

"That's public-spirited," Gaaron said dryly.

Adriel smiled. "I'm sure he would have been happier to contribute to the cause if it had been a merchant caravan that we had saved from destruction. But he doesn't have much use for Jansai."

"Well, this is good news," Gaaron said thoughtfully. "I wonder . . . I know you have people working on weapons of our own. And I know you know how I feel about that. But—while we are still debating that—perhaps we can insure that all angels go armed? We cannot fly about carrying large blocks of marble, of course, but—rocks? Other heavy objects? If all angels carry a sack of stones across their shoulders whenever they fly a patrol, they could provide some firepower if they came across an attack in progress. You can kill a man with ease if you drop a stone on his head from a hundred feet."

Adriel looked intrigued. "It would certainly create a disturbance.

And from what we have seen so far, these marauders do not seem inclined to stage a pitched battle. At the first sign of resistance they"— she snapped her fingers—"vanish. So a few well-aimed rocks just might scare them off. Temporarily, at any rate."

Gaaron came to his feet. He had only been there a couple of hours and already he was restless. He wanted to go back to the Eyrie, see Susannah again. Tell her nothing, of course, make no speeches or accusations—be only civil and polite—but *see* her. That would be enough for him. "We must carry the word to Monteverde," he said.

Adriel watched him. "Yes, we will. I will send someone out right now. But *you* do not have to leave right this moment. Sit down, Gaaron. Tell me what is going on at your hold."

Reluctantly, he sat again, though he didn't exactly relax against the thin back of the chair. "It is chaos in Velora," he said. "My merchants are doing what they can to impose some kind of order, but the city is too full and the tensions are too high. We cannot exist this way for long."

"Breven has become a nightmare city," she responded, nodding. "There is a murder a day there between one gypsy chief or another. Solomon assures me that he can control the Jansai, but he has not been too successful so far. I worry about what happens when the hot weather comes. Tempers will run even higher. We will not have to wait for the invaders to attack us. We will destroy ourselves."

Gaaron shook his head. "We must solve it before then. Before the Gloria. How can we sing to the glory of the god if we are looking over our shoulders, waiting to be attacked?"

"But if have *not* solved it by then—"

"We will."

She hesitated, then shrugged and smiled. Nothing to be gained by arguing. "We must solve it much sooner," she said, her voice grown playful. "By your wedding day. Everyone must feel safe to come to that. How do the plans go on?"

"Quite well, or so I assume," he said. "Susannah and Esther are handling most of the details."

"Have the invitations been sent out?"

"As I said—"

"You don't know," she finished up for him. "I will have to rely on receiving word from Susannah. I liked her a great deal, you know."

"She is quite a favorite with everyone," he said in a wooden voice.

Adriel leaned forward, her soft-face lined with concern. Blessed

Jovah, she had aged in this past year. She should not be so gray and faded; she was only in her mid-fifties. "Is there trouble between you and the angelica?" she asked in a gentle voice.

Gaaron drew back as far as his chair would allow. "I assure you, we are working out the details of our lives to our own satisfaction."

Adriel shook her head. "She is a good girl, Susannah. She would be a good wife to any man—she would understand that the god mixes the good with the bad, and that she could not expect her life to be nothing but happiness. She would try very hard before she would give up. But I don't think you should underestimate her, Gaaron. I think she is quite capable of walking away if her situation is bad enough. I don't think this is a woman who will tolerate any abuse."

He was offended. "And what leads you to think that I would abuse *anyone* in my care?"

She made a careless motion with her hand. "Perhaps that is the wrong word. There are ways to treat someone badly without actually harming her. I would be very careful, if I were you, to treat Susannah well. You do not want her to leave you."

He thought about Susannah as he had first seen her, living with the Edori and deeply in love with her unfaithful lover. She had left Dathan without a single farewell. And had only spoken his name again in dreaming. "She can't leave me," he said stiffly. "It is the god's will that she serve beside me."

"Perhaps she does not interpret the god's will quite as you do," Adriel said dryly.

"In any case," Gaaron said, "there is no need for you to trouble yourself about Susannah."

"I am more worried about you."

"And less reason for you to worry about me. Now, would I be rude if I asked you to feed me? I have flown all morning, and I'm starved."

They ate, and then they spent a few hours clambering over the treacherous broken ground that lay all around Windy Point, looking for suitable rocks. Half a dozen of the other angels joined them, calling out jokes to one another and seeming to find the whole thing something of a lark, but Gaaron was deadly serious. He experimented with different weights and sizes of stones, heaving them off the mountain peak to see how they felt as they left his hand. Adriel had lent him a sturdy burlap bag, and he filled it to the top, hefting it from time to time to see if he would still be able to carry it. But it was no heavier than many of the burdens he had carried from one end of the province to another—his sister, his angelica, other mortals. He would manage just fine.

He lingered a day at Windy Point because Adriel asked him to, though the stay made him restless. She had sent angels on to Monteverde with their combined news, so there was no reason for him to push on west, and there was certainly no reason to hurry home. But he had trouble sleeping and his thoughts would not settle, and he did not want to be anyplace but at the Eyrie. So when he rose the next morning, he would not let Adriel convince him to stay another day.

"I will see you soon enough," he promised, kissing her on the cheek. "At the wedding, if not before."

"Fly carefully," she admonished. "Give Susannah my love."

He smiled. "I will do both those things."

But as it turned out, he did neither. He flew low to the ground, seeking out trouble, a rock in his hand ready to be thrown. He traveled later than he should have, and then had trouble finding a suitable town to stop in for the night, and he even considered making a cold camp somewhere on the Bethel side of the Galilee. But he certainly did not want to die a solitary death on the open field at the hands of armed marauders, so he kept on till he found a town that boasted an impressive collection of inns. The bed was unexpectedly comfortable, and the breakfast the next morning surprisingly good, and he was actually in a cheerful mood as he headed for home.

Where it turned out he could not give Susannah any greetings from Adriel, because she was not there.

No one seemed to have any precise knowledge about where she had gone, or why, or how long she would be gone. All they could tell him was when she had left.

"You had only been gone a few hours," Esther informed him. "Jesse came in from Monteverde looking for you, but you weren't here, so he left a letter in your chambers. I haven't read it, of course," she said, which made him think it had been closed with a seal, "so I don't know what it was about."

"What does Jesse have to do with Susannah?"

"She left with him."

He frowned. "She wanted to go to Monteverde?"

Esther frowned in turn. "I'm not sure Monteverde was where he was going next. He said he had several stops to make. Perhaps he was going somewhere else Susannah wanted to visit."

"Yes, but where would that have been?" Gaaron asked patiently.

She shrugged. "She didn't tell me anything."

She hadn't told Keren much, either, or Chloe or Sela or Zibiah—though Keren, at least, would speculate. "Oh! I know! Perhaps she went to see the others."

"What others?"

"The Lohoras. You know she was worried about them."

"I thought you weren't sure where their winter camp might be."

Keren shrugged. "No, of course I'm not *sure,* but they are so often by the Galo mountain. You remember, we talked about it one night at dinner."

He did remember it, quite distinctly, for he had had to choke down a most unworthy feeling of jealousy as Susannah had spoken with such concern of her missing families. "Can you show me again?" he said. "I may want to go find her."

Keren shrugged. "But they might not be there."

"But then, where would Susannah be?"

"Somewhere else, looking for them. Or for the Tachitas."

She could, in fact, be anywhere, and his chances of finding her appeared smaller and smaller as the day wore on. But he would look for her, nonetheless. How could he leave her alone and unprotected on the open Samarian plains? This was a season too dangerous to allow for a show of rebellion. When the marauders were turned back—when Samaria was safe again—then she could leave the Eyrie for any destination she chose, for as long as she liked. But not now.

Naturally, he could not, as he would have liked, leave right away to hunt for Susannah. Esther had questions—visiting petitioners had questions—the Velora merchants had left an urgent request for him to come join them at his earliest convenience—and Neri's letter (some trifling trade question) had to be answered. So it was morning before he could annoy Esther and leave the rest of the hold somewhat mystified by announcing he was leaving again and did not know when he would be back.

It took even longer to get to Mount Galo than it had taken to get to Windy Point. The air was icy, blowing straight down from the oceans north of the Plain of Sharon and following the course of the Galilee River south to the end of the world. Pinpricks of sleet needled his cheeks and his arms as he headed straight into the wind, and he could feel a film of frost forming in his hair. The current was against him, so he did not make very good time, and he elected to stop in Semorrah for the night, though he would have liked to push on farther.

If he had been the diplomat Adriel was, he would have gone to the house of Lord Colton and asked to spend the night. His very presence would confer quite a cachet on the lord's house and make up for whatever inconvenience his sudden appearance might cause. But Gaaron was not the easy social talker that Adriel was—and he did not particularly like Lord Colton. He headed instead to one of the more genteel hotels that catered to an affluent clientele. There, an unctuous concierge ushered him personally to the grandest room in the building, a white, spacious, cool, and exceptionally comfortable room fitted with furniture meant for an angel. Gaaron thanked him gravely and settled in for the night.

It was already dark, and once he had cleaned himself up, he strode to the window to look out at the city. By night, Semorrah was even more magical than it was by day, filled with a thousand fairy lights and decorated with mysterious swoops of shadowed white architecture. Although it did not seem quite so magical this night as Gaaron opened his window and looked down. There were crowds in the street even this late—workers laboring by torchlight to erect yet another building in this city that could not build fast enough—wealthy revelers returning home late from some elegant party—dispossessed farmers and miners bedded down in the streets, shouting out insults at the merchants as they passed. In the half hour that he watched, Gaaron witnessed two altercations between separate groups, each of which deteriorated into physical violence. Both were stopped quickly and effectively by Semorrah's night watchmen.

Gaaron pulled back inside, latched the window, and laid himself on the bed. Samaria was in danger from without and within. If they did not take care of the menacing strangers, they would all turn on one another and be destroyed anyway. It was a not a comforting thought to take to bed with him.

The next morning was neither as clear nor as cold, and the heavy cloud cover helped hold a little of the sun's heat. Gaaron had left at first light, determined to make it to Galo before sundown so that he could search the entire plain if he had to. He had settled into his customary mode of fast travel, his wings working so rapidly that he was not even aware of each separate lift and downstroke. Today, he did not have to fight the wind. He was merely aware of the air as an element he must pass through, feeling it slick and silken against his skin.

He was just south of the mountain when hunger forced him to make a quick landing. He ate rapidly and threw himself aloft again, driven by impatience and something like dread. What would he say to Susannah when he found her—when he insisted that she return with him—when he said, in effect, that he did not care if she was lonely or unhappy as long as she was beside him and safe? There would have to be a better way to put those words. He would have to make her understand.

He came in from straight south and veered a little right to circle the east side of the mountain. That was where Keren had said the camp would be situated, sheltered a little from the punishing winds that blew off the northern coast. He dropped low enough to be able to read the terrain, low enough to see massed tents and moving figures, if there were any, but high enough to catch the currents of the air and gain some altitude when the surface wind made flying treacherous this close to the ground.

When he rounded one of the low shoulders of the mountain, he saw a tableau spread below him, and a single glance was enough to let him take it in.

To the left, an Edori camp. To the right, a line of black-clad marauders. What he had mistaken for an Edori campfire was a burning tent. What looked like snippets of red ribbon were shots of fire streaking from the invaders' weapons into the Edori camp.

He hovered, for a moment too stunned to react. He could see the frantic figures below, running, ducking, trying to find shelter from the malicious flames. Why had the invaders not destroyed the whole camp with a single blast? Why did they stand there, faces pressed to the long thin barrels of their weapons, careful shots darting out at individual targets? What was there within this Edori campsite that the strangers wanted to recover or preserve?

No time to wonder. No time to think. He had left his sack of rocks behind at the Eyrie, but he still had a weapon of his own, and it was a dire one. Driving his wings down hard against the brittle air, he arched his head back and began to sing.

The prayer poured from his mouth, the music harsher and thinner the higher he climbed. His beating wings created a bellows of air that fed through his chest and erupted in malevolent song. He sang and he sang, the music streaming behind him as he arrowed upward, boring through the thin clouds and the layered atmosphere to a place so elevated it offered no air to breathe. He was so high now he could no longer see the camp below him, with its dark dots of bodies and snatches of flame. He himself was small, a starling buffeted by the god's own breath, for he was so high that he must be almost at Jovah's front door. He sang the prayer again, desperately, hopelessly, his booming confident voice a child's pleading whisper. The prayer that no one ever sang, the request that no angel ever made, the song that he had never, in his entire life, sung straight through . . .

The air split before him in a seam of light. Gaaron tumbled backward as the world broke in pieces, then crashed back together with a noise of falling boulders. Again, an explosion of light followed by a crack of thunder. The air smelled like ozone and sulphur—the god's perfume, lingering from where he had touched his finger to the earth . . .

Gaaron beat his wings madly, regaining control, regaining altitude, trying to catch his breath. Then he folded his feathers back and dove, crazy to see what was happening. In a few short moments, the earth loomed up below him, alarmingly close, and he spread his wings to halt his careening descent. He hovered a moment, scanning the scene. Four or five bodies lay strewn upon the ground, and the earth itself was seared black by the force of the lightning bolts. There was no other sign of invaders. The Edori themselves were running back and forth between their fallen enemies and their burning camp, shouting out information and instructions. From what Gaaron could see, their camp was only partially destroyed, and there were plenty of Edori left. Perhaps there had really been a miracle. Perhaps none of the Edori had been killed.

He stretched his wings and tilted his body, catching a current that would send him down slowly. Someone glanced up and saw him, and then there were more shouts, followed by another quick gathering of Edori. They came together on their ruined field to witness the sight of the avenging angel come down to give them tidings.

He settled his feet on ground still hot from the lash of the god's anger and stared about him. Four dead invaders, their black skin singed even darker by fire. Maybe twenty Edori, running toward him, questions on their lips and terror or excitement in their eyes. His gaze went quickly from one face to another, seeking out the only person whose fate truly mattered to him, praying to find her alive and whole among the circle of her friends.

He was more surprised than he had ever been in his life when, among the figures hurrying his way, he saw, not his angelica, but his sister.

CHAPTER TWENTY-EIGHT

Miriam raced into his arms, headlong, burying her face against his chest and clinging to him with a child's frenzy. "Oh, Gaaron!" she sobbed. "Merciful Yovah, I was so afraid! They had their fire sticks, and they were shooting at us, and there was nothing we could do, *nothing*, and everyone was screaming—and then the thunderbolt, and everything exploded, and how did you know? How did you come to be here? How did you know where I was?"

It was instinct, at first, to calm her, to enclose her in his arms and murmur soothing phrases. How many times had he comforted her in just this way over the past nineteen years? But there were so many questions to be asked, and he had more than she did. When she had stopped shaking and stopped pouring out her incoherent phrases, he pulled back a little and looked sternly down at her.

"Miriam," he said. "Why are you here with the Edori? We thought we left you safe in Luminaux."

She looked up at him, wariness instantly chasing away the relief and gladness on her face. How many times, too, had he watched that change in her expression as he scolded her for one of her misadventures? "I didn't want to stay in Luminaux," she said sulkily. "I wanted to be with my friends."

"Your friends! You don't even know any Edori."

"Susannah took me to meet the Lohoras. I wanted to stay with them, and they were happy to have me. Gaaron, let all that go! I have so much to tell you! But first, you tell *me*. What are you doing here? How did you know I was here?"

He released her and looked around at the ruined camp. The Edori who had headed his way when he landed seemed to have dispersed as soon as they realized who he was—and whom he had found in their camp. They had managed to put the fires out, but half a dozen tents were still smoldering. The men were standing in one huddled group, conferring, while the women were examining cook pots and calling out useful finds to the others in the camp. He thought he recognized a few faces from his brief sojourn with the Lohoras, nearly six months ago, but no one looked over in his direction. No one appeared to be listening to this conversation.

"I didn't know you were here," he said distinctly. "I thought you were in Luminaux. I was looking for Susannah."

"Susannah! But she's not here. She's not at the Eyrie?"

"Obviously not. She left a few days ago while I was at Windy Point. No one seems to know where she's gone."

"And she didn't tell you? Didn't leave you a note or something?" Miriam's sharp eyes fixed themselves on Gaaron's face. "Did you argue with her? Gaaron, what's happening?"

"We didn't argue," he said, though he could feel the heat rise in his cheeks. To have to explain himself to Miriam! That would be the height of embarrassment. "There may have been—a misunderstanding. But it is dangerous on every road these days, and I wanted to see her returned to safety."

"Well, she's not here. Maybe she went to the Tachitas."

A couple of months with the Edori and already she was talking like one. Gaaron took another moment to survey her. Was this really his spoiled and wayward sister? She was dressed in a somewhat ragged jacket thrown over a shapeless dress, and the shoes she was wearing could not have come from any fashionable cobbler. Her glorious hair was braided away from her face and didn't look as if it had been washed in a day or so, and her face was smudged with soot. She looked thinner than he remembered but healthy, he thought. Her dark eyes were snapping with interest.

"I don't know where she went," he said slowly. "But I am glad, even if I have lost her for the moment, that I have found you. Had I known how much danger you were in these past few months, I don't believe I would have slept a single night. Miriam, there have been so many deaths upon the road—so many Edori and Jansai killed, and even small towns sent up in smoke. You have no idea how lucky you are that you are still alive. And to think that I happened to arrive just as your whole camp was about to be destroyed—"

"For the second time," she interrupted.

"*What?*"

She nodded. "We were attacked before by a group of raiders, but we were lucky then, too. I frightened them, and they accidentally shot at each other—oh, it's a long story. But I don't think this group today was trying to destroy us. They could have killed us all in five minutes, but they didn't. I think they wanted something from us."

"Wanted—what could they possibly—"

She took a step away from him and motioned in the direction of the camp. He had been so focused on his sister's face that he had not been paying much attention to the people a dozen yards away, trying to set the camp to rights. Now he saw that one of them had stepped close enough to hear their discussion: a black-skinned, flame-haired, and absolutely motionless young man, watching Gaaron with the still intentness of a predator.

"Miriam," Gaaron breathed, but the sight of the nearby invader did not discompose her.

"I think they came back looking for Jossis," she said.

Over the protests of the Edori, Gaaron had insisted on raising a plague flag to call the attention of any passing angel. "There is no plague here," he was informed very politely by the burly man he was reintroduced to as Bartholomew. "And Edori are not used to asking for help from angels."

"But I am used to it," Gaaron said, "and I need some aid. Let's just see who might come down and investigate."

He had offered to pitch in and help, but Miriam had caught him the by arm and pulled him to one side. "No," she said. "You come talk to me. They'll come get us if they need us."

"It seems rude," he protested as she tugged him away from the main activity of the camp.

"Everyone will understand."

They settled finally about fifty yards away from the camp, sitting on a couple of tattered tarps that Miriam had brought with her. Gaaron spread his wings carefully behind him, not exactly pleased with the sensation of feathers in snow but otherwise not particularly discomfited by the cold. Miriam made sure to sit in a patch of sun, but seemed comfortable enough in her oversize jacket and heavily padded shoes.

"Now tell me," he commanded. "What in the name of the god above is going on here?"

Miriam leaned forward, her face a study in excitement and intensity. "I told you. Our camp was attacked—oh, fifty miles south of here. Or more. I don't know. We were able to frighten off the attackers, and most of them just disappeared, but one of them was injured almost to the point of death. And so we nursed him back to health."

"Of all the stupid, unthinking, disastrous—"

"Yes, but Gaaron, he's just a boy—my age, I think, or something like it. And we've learned so much from him! I helped take care of him, and I started to teach him words, and I've learned a little bit about the world he came from. I think it's—"

"The world he came from," Gaaron interrupted. "You're certain he and his friends aren't from somewhere close? From another part of this world?"

"I know it's incredible, but I think they traveled here from some other place—much like the original settlers did—"

Gaaron nodded. "That's a theory Mahalah proposed a few weeks back at Windy Point. We haven't been able to prove it or disprove it."

"It's what he told me. And the world he comes from is full of violence and hatred, and Jossis was happy to get away, but he did not realize that violence and hatred would come with them to a new place—"

"He's told you all that? You are able to understand his language?"

"Well—not entirely. I have learned a few of his phrases and we act some things out—but the part about the violence, that I'm sure of—"

Gaaron thought privately that the concepts she was discussing would be hard to convey through gestures, but he was willing to believe Miriam had established a kind of rough communication with the foreigner. If anyone could, Miriam could. "Why have they come here? Did he tell you that?"

She shook her head. "I cannot tell if they are looking for a new world to live on—"

"As the original settlers did here."

"Yes. Of if they are just—the kind of men who like to go places and hurt other people. Who just like to destroy things. There are people like that, even in Samaria."

He nodded. "And what did you say his name was?"

She looked even more excited. "Jossis. And, Gaaron, isn't that odd? It sounds almost like Joseph. And every once in a while he says a word that sounds familiar to me, or I say one to him and he is nodding before I can even define it. And—this was the strangest thing—one night before the campfire, he sang the Bacha *Ode*. Note for note. Where could he have learned something like that?"

He looked at her for a long time without speaking, the thoughts spinning in his mind so quickly it was hard to pin them down. Well. They had always known there must be other humans, other creatures like them, somewhere in the universe. Jovah had plucked them from one world and placed them on another; wasn't it possible that he had done the same for other races, other communities? The Librera hinted that, after Jovah took them away from their first world, that world had destroyed itself with its excess of rage, but Jovah may have rescued hundreds, thousands, of others before that planet burned itself up. On Samaria, they had chosen to turn their backs on technology, to ignore both its siren lure and its demon fire, but others might not have chosen the same path. They might have left a life of violence and re-created it in a new place. They might have learned nothing from their past at all.

"Gaaron," Miriam said, when she finally got tired of his silence. "Don't you see? I think we must be in some way related to Jossis. To all of them."

He nodded slowly. "I think you could very well be right," he said. "That does not mean we are in any less danger from them, however. And I think you have been unforgivably reckless in attempting to make friends with someone so unpredictable—"

She shook her head impatiently, not even willing to take the time to argue. "Jossis will not hurt any of us. You have to talk to him, you will see how much you can learn from him—and you'll like him, I know you will—"

He could not help but smile at that. There was no likelihood he would like a bloodthirsty young invader who had been dropped by chance into his lap. "I seriously doubt that I will be able to converse with him well enough to learn any useful information," he drawled. "But I think I know someone who can."

Miriam looked instantly suspicious. "Who?"

"Mahalah. If he speaks any language derived from the settlers' speech, she will be able to understand him."

Miriam stood up. "Then go get her. Bring her here."

Gaaron stood as well. "Oh, no. I will take him to Mount Sinai."

"You can't! You can't take him away from me!"

Gaaron spared a moment to wonder just how deep this supposed new "friendship" had gone, and then decided he did not want to know. And that it didn't matter. "I can and I will. But I'm not leaving you here with the Lohoras to be murdered in your sleep."

She crossed her arms and gave him a mulish look. "So there. You can't take both of us away. Even you couldn't carry two of us all the way to Sinai."

"That's true," he agreed. "We'll just have to wait."

"Wait for what?"

"For whoever spots the plague flag and comes down to investigate."

Naturally, that sent Miriam stomping straight back to camp to try to haul in the flag. It was a makeshift signal, a ripped red shirt tied to a fire-shortened guy line, and Gaaron had tied it to a tree halfway up the mountainside. Miriam was furious when she couldn't make enough headway through the tumbled stone to get close to the tree. Gaaron watched her thrashing up the mountain—saw the flame-haired Jossis go hurrying after her—and turned his attention back to the Lohoras and their ragged camp.

They'd made remarkable progress in the thirty minutes he and Miriam had been in consultation. Not every tent had been burned, it seemed, not every cook pot demolished. He returned to a small but bustling little enclave where tarps were being thrown over freshly cut poles and unusual ingredients were being mixed into cauldrons. Everyone seemed hard at work and no one seemed too devastated by their recent brush with annihilation.

The bodies of the dead men had been dragged somewhere out of sight, and no trace of blood remained in the snow.

Gaaron approached a woman who looked familiar, though he

could not recall her name. "May I help you in any way?" he asked formally. "I am Gaaron, you know. I met your tribe once before."

She looked up from her pot and gave him a ready smile. Her face was broad and peaceful, though it was hard to guess her age. She looked like she had lived a life in which every day was crammed tightly with event. "When you came for Susannah. Yes, I remember," she said. "I'm Tirza. Susannah shared my tent."

He nodded, not sure what to say to that. He did not particularly want to be asked about Susannah's whereabouts again, so he turned the subject. "Is there anything I can do to help?" he repeated.

She held up a spoon, dripping with broth. "You could taste that and tell me if it's any good. We just threw everything we had into the pot. We might be sorry."

This was not at all what he had meant by making the offer, but he carefully sipped the liquid from the spoon. "Very tasty," he said. "You will not be ashamed to serve that tonight."

She laughed out loud and returned to her stirring. "So, Gaaron, why have you come here? Is it to take Miriam away? I am surprised you let her linger with us so long, though we have come to love her dearly. I will be sorry to see her go."

"She is in danger here," he said quietly. "You all are. If you would take my advice, you would retreat to Castelana or Monteverde and shelter with the crowds until the invaders are gone."

She shrugged. "How can you be sure the invaders will ever be gone? I do not understand them and I don't know why they're here, but what makes you think they will leave?"

"They must," he said. "We will have to drive them away."

Her expression was full of polite disbelief. "And I hope you do," she said. "But we are not going to change our lives because of them. We will stay here until the winter ends and it is time to move on."

"Miriam will not," he said flatly.

She nodded. "No, I can understand that you would want to take her to safety. But I will be surprised if she is willing to go."

"I do not much care if she is willing or not."

Now her expression was carefully neutral. "That is the allali way, I suppose," she said. "If she was my sister, I would let her make her own decision."

"I am used to making decisions for people who do not choose well on their own."

"Perhaps that is why they choose badly," she said.

He flung up a hand. No point in arguing. "And I will take this Jossis with me as well," he added.

Now Tirza looked troubled. "He seems to be a good man," she said. "I know it would be hard for you to trust him. But we have lived with him for several weeks now, and he is—we have all come to care for him. If you could, please treat him kindly."

"I will take him to the oracle," he said stiffly. He was growing a little tired of being urged to kindness and tolerance. Was he so unkind and intolerant in general? And was everyone else too stupid to see when ruthless action was required? "There we will decide what to do with him."

"You will stay for dinner first, surely," she said. "And we would be happy to have you spend the night with us. The tents will be crowded, because we lost two, but there will be room for you—"

"I appreciate the hospitality," he said. "And indeed, I must stay until someone responds to my signal. I cannot take both my sister and her new friend with me at once."

"Then while you are awaiting another angel, perhaps you would like to take the time to get to know Jossis," she said. "I think you might be surprised."

He glanced to the side of the mountain again, where Miriam had given up the attempt to pull down his flag. Jossis and Miriam were standing very close, almost embraced. His hands were upon her shoulders and her face was tilted up to his, dramatic intensity in every line of her body. What in the world could she be telling him? What words could she possibly be using? "And to think I believed that Miriam could no longer surprise me," he said wearily.

Tirza smiled again. "Would it surprise you to learn that she can build a fire, skin fresh meat, cook a meal from scratch, care for a sick friend, and, indeed, willingly learn any new task that would be helpful to her clan?"

Gaaron looked at her a long time. "It would not surprise me to learn that she *could* do these things," he said at last. "Miriam has always been extremely capable, when she chose to be. It surprises me that she *would* do them. And willingly."

"She is made of pure gold, that one," Tirza said softly. "If I were a Luminaux craftsman, and I had made her mold, I would cast it over and over again. No matter the trouble she caused me and the burns I received when the liquid metal leaked onto my fingers. I would know that I would never again make a product quite so fine."

"Miriam has been lucky," he said quietly, "to fall in with friends as good as you."

"No," said Tirza. "We were the lucky ones."

Dinner was quiet, at least during the actual meal. Afterward, there was a great deal of informal singing. Most of the songs were in the Edori language, so Gaaron was not sure what the prayers meant, but he was certain they included words of thanksgiving and praise. Because he, too, was feeling overwhelming gratitude to the god, when there was a little break in the music, he rose to his feet and offered his own prayer. He kept it simple, for this did not seem the venue for one of the complex sacred pieces, but it was heartfelt nonetheless. *Thank you, Jovah, for protecting my sister—for leading me to her side in time—for responding to my urgent entreaty. Thank you, Jovah, for watching over us all.*

When he sat down again, Tirza regarded him with eyes so wide her expression was almost comical. "Yovah bless me," she said. "You *do* have the most beautiful voice in the three provinces. I have never heard anything like it."

He smiled in the dark. Miriam had refused to sit anywhere near him, taking her place between Jossis and some pole-thin young boy who had talked to her restlessly all night. But Tirza had plopped herself right next to him with every appearance of friendliness. He could not help but like her. "It is why the god has named me Archangel," he said gravely. "For my voice."

"And perhaps your temperament?"

"There are days I am not as sure of that as I once was."

She smiled a little, but her expression was serious. She was watching him as closely as the unreliable flames would allow. "Susannah has great faith in you and your ability to lead men," she said.

"Does she?" he said, and even he could hear the wistfulness in his voice. "That is kind of her."

"Why haven't you once mentioned her name to me?" she asked softly. "Didn't you come here to find her?"

He looked at her quickly. Had she guessed that, or had Miriam repeated that choice bit of gossip? "I did not want to worry you with news that I was uncertain of her whereabouts," he admitted.

"Why would she have left you uncertain about that? Would she have had any reason for not wanting you to know?"

Every reason. No reason. Gaaron turned his gaze across the fire, where the gorgeous young man named Dathan had just risen to his feet to begin a song. His voice was supple and beautiful, and even when he sang he seemed to laugh. Where could Susannah have run to if not to this woman, this man, these people? "We do not always get along as well as we could," he said at last. "I am sure that is my fault, but the god made a difficult choice this time. We are not much alike, Susannah and I. I had hoped to bridge our differences better than this. I had hoped we could be friends."

"Friends!" she exclaimed. Her voice was so low that he was sure no one else could hear it, but the disdain in it was impossible for him, at least, to miss. "I do not think Susannah is interested in being *friends* with you."

"Indeed, that is how it appears," he said dryly.

She leaned forward and whispered in his ear. "I think she would prefer that you love her."

The night was cold and uncomfortable, as Gaaron politely refused the invitation to share a tent with fourteen other people. He did not see where Jossis bedded down, but Miriam disappeared inside the tent that held Eleazar and Tirza and what could have been a dozen others. Every time he woke in the night—which was often—Gaaron built up the fire again, but it did little good. Even he was chilled straight through by the time the sullen sun came up.

Its welcome arrival was followed within the hour by a second, even more welcome visitor: Nicholas, circling down in response to the red shirt. He seemed bemused to see Gaaron among the Edori, and even more bewildered when Miriam came tearing up from the river's edge to fling herself into his arms. Automatically wrapping her in a brotherly embrace, Nicholas looked over at Gaaron with a question in his eyes.

"What's going on? Why didn't you pull down the plague flag once you arrived?"

"He put the stupid flag up," came Miriam's voice, muffled against Nicky's chest.

Nicholas raised his eyebrows at Gaaron, who nodded. "I needed another angel, and I wasn't about to leave her alone here while I went to fetch help," he said. "I need you to take her back to the Eyrie while I go on to Mount Sinai.

Nicholas nodded, but Miriam wrenched free of his absentminded hold and whirled on Gaaron. "No! I won't go back to the Eyrie! I'm going to Sinai with you and Jossis!"

"Who?" Nicholas said.

"You're going home," Gaaron said, calm but unyielding.

Miriam stamped her foot, though the gesture wasn't too impressive in the dirty snow. "I won't! And if you make me, I'll just leave again. You can't ever keep me away from Jossis."

"Who's Jossis?" Nicholas asked.

"Jossis?" Gaaron repeated, his voice so reasonable it was a parody of reason. "Jossis is Miriam's new friend. One of the invaders who's been attacking Samaria for the past few months. Miriam has formed an attachment to him."

Nicky turned to survey Miriam with some misgiving. "He's teasing me, right?"

She looked like she wanted to stamp her foot again, but remembered the snow, so instead she crossed her arms on her chest and scowled at both of them. "He's my friend, and nothing you say can change that, and if you would only *listen* you might learn something from him—"

"Why are you taking this guy to Mount Sinai?" Nicholas asked next.

"So he can keep me away from him!"

"So Jossis can talk to Mahalah. If he can," Gaaron answered. "Miriam seems to think that some of this man's words are the same as our words. And if so—Mahalah might be able to interpret."

Nicholas nodded, that quickly accepting the whole unlikely situation. "Sounds good. When do you want me to take Miriam back?"

Miriam took three quick steps over and clasped her brother's arm. "Gaaron, please," she begged. "Let me go with you to Mount Sinai. He will be so alone and so afraid. I can help you, I can help him—don't make him go away alone with strangers."

Gaaron opened his mouth to refuse her again—and then something made him hesitate. Involuntarily, he looked away from her pleading face, over to the circle of Edori eating breakfast around the fire. Most of them showed their usual indifference and lack of curiosity, but Tirza was watching them with no attempt to disguise her interest. She was too far away to hear what was being said, but something in her expression made Gaaron think she had read their faces and gestures clearly enough. She did not nod or shake her head or show any change in her expression, but Gaaron knew she was sending him some kind of message. Or watching him to see if he had learned anything at all from Miriam's flight and sudden, dramatic reappearance.

"Very well," he said abruptly. "You can go with us to Mount Sinai, as long as you promise not to leave there until I return for you."

Her face was transformed. She squealed and jumped up to kiss him on the cheek. "Thank you! Thank you thank you thank you! I will be packed and ready to go in five minutes."

She tumbled away from them, and Gaaron was left staring at the other angel. "What's going on here?" Nicholas asked again. "Why isn't Miriam in Luminaux?"

"Because Luminaux is where I wanted her to be." Gaaron sighed. "So naturally, that is where she is not."

"And who's this—Jossis? Why is she so crazy about him?"

Gaaron shrugged. "That I have yet to discover. But we'll have a couple days on the road. Maybe we'll find out."

But there was little to learn from the dark-skinned, jewel-eyed stranger. He appeared to be afraid of Gaaron—and of Nicholas—awed by their impressive wingspans and not exactly keen on flying. Gaaron carried him as neutrally as he would have carried a sack of clothing, but Jossis never relaxed in his arms. The angel could feel the stranger's taut-strung muscles for every mile of that long flight.

They had to sneak Jossis into the inn they'd chosen in the small town where they stopped for the night. Everyone in Samaria knew by now the description of danger, and Jossis matched it. They could not risk him being mobbed. Nicholas went and fetched food for all of them once they were safely ensconced in their rooms, and they ate in relative silence. Miriam, who could out talk any of them, stayed focused on Jossis, who seemed withdrawn and ill at ease. He answered her when she addressed him—he even smiled at her once, as if in reassurance—but there was none of this vaunted conversation of which she had bragged. Jossis said hardly a word the whole time Gaaron watched him.

But that there was a connection between his sister and the invader Gaaron had no doubt. She laid a hand upon his knee, he brushed his elbow against her arm—they sat as close as lovers when they ate their meal. Surely that could not be true, surely even Miriam could not have gone so far, merely to spite Gaaron, merely to hurt him? And yet the smile she directed at that closed, dark face was full of private meaning; the hand she lifted to brush through her hair came to rest, for just a moment, against the young man's cheek.

Sweet Jovah singing, she loves him, Gaaron thought, and the realization struck him so dumb that he could not summon another thought for the duration of the evening.

Sinai was crowded with more petitioners than Gaaron had ever seen crammed into the small audience chamber. A result of the depredations of the invaders, Gaaron guessed, as people came to the god looking for answers, or looking for sanctuary. After some discussion, he and Miriam and Nicholas had decided to veil Jossis as heavily as a Jansai bride so that they could bring him into the chamber without alarming any penitents who might be present. They still drew their share of curious stares while they waited for the acolytes to announce them to Mahalah, but at least no one ran screaming down the stone hallways in terror.

"Angelo. Please, will you and your guests follow me?" asked Mahalah's young acolyte, reappearing in the doorway. "She will be very happy to see you immediately."

"Thank you," Gaaron said, and led the small procession down the hall. Mahalah was sitting before her mysterious blue glass plate, but she wheeled around to face them as they entered.

"Ah, Gaaron, I know why you are here," she said with a smile. "I am surprised it has taken you so long to come."

He bent to take her frail hand in his and kiss her lightly on the cheek. "I am astonished that you have been expecting me," he answered. "How did you know what I had to bring you?"

But now her eyes went past the arch of his wings, and for the first time she saw his companions. "Miriam! What are you doing here? And Nicky—why, Gaaron, what is this? And who is your friend? Have you brought another Jansai girl to me for safekeeping?"

"Something even more exotic, I think," Gaaron said as soon as Nicholas and Miriam had murmured quick greetings. "Be calm, for I think he will surprise you."

"I am too old to feel much surprise," she retorted. "What have you brought me?"

Gaaron nodded at Miriam, who tugged the veils off of Jossis' face. For a long moment, there was a profound silence in the room.

"I see," Mahalah said quietly. "You have captured one of our enemies. But why have you brought him to me?"

"Miriam thinks he may know a language that you understand," Gaaron said. "A language that our ancestors knew, at any rate."

Mahalah's brows went up. "Indeed? That would mean . . ."

"I know," Gaaron said, as her words trailed off.

"Let him speak to me, then," she said.

Gaaron looked over at Miriam, who put a hand on Jossis' arm and urged him forward. She spoke a few words to him, so quietly that Gaaron could not understand what she said, and she stayed close beside him as he stepped up to the oracle's chair.

"Toteyosi," Jossis said, or syllables that sounded something like that, and then he loosed a whole string of words that Gaaron could not divide into sounds or sentences.

But Mahalah was nodding, her face drawn into a frown of concentration, her hand lifted to ask him to slow down. "Ska?" she said once, and then a few more unintelligible words.

Jossis repeated something in a voice that sounded insistent.

Mahalah replied in a long, careful sentence.

A new voice sounded at the doorway. "Mahalah—" said a woman, and then she gasped. Gaaron looked over in irritation, not wanting this delicate interview to be interrupted by the hysterics of an acolyte.

But it was no giggly young girl who stood framed in the door, staring at the unlikely tableau inside the chamber. It was Susannah.

CHAPTER TWENTY-NINE

Susannah had two shocks to withstand within fifteen seconds: the sight of Gaaron standing in the oracle's chamber, and the force of Miriam's body as the girl threw herself in the Edori's arms.

"Susannah! Oh, I'm so glad you're here! Gaaron said he didn't know where you were, but I have so much to tell you, and you have to meet Jossis and—can you imagine?—I have been with the Edori all this time. But Susannah, why *are* you here? Is something wrong?"

Susannah kept her eyes on Gaaron's face a moment longer, trying to read his expression. Relief—concern—surprise—and then a shutting down of all emotions. Whatever had drawn him to Mount Sinai, it had not been her presence here.

Summoning a smile, she looked down at Miriam, giving the blond girl a quick hug before letting her go. "*I* came to check on Kaski," she said lightly. "Nothing more alarming than that. But you! Traveling with the Edori! And what are you doing here?"

"I came with Jossis."

Susannah's eyes lifted again, taking in the sight of the black-skinned man with the iridescent hair. Impossible as it seemed, he appeared to be deep in a halting conversation with Mahalah, though a lot of repetition and hand gestures seemed to be required for him to make his meaning clear. "You have made friends with one of our enemies," she said softly. "But of course you have. If anyone could, it would be you."

"He is not an enemy. He is a good man. He got hurt and he has lived with us for more than two months, and he has told me so much—"

"But which tribe did you travel with as you lived among the Edori?" Susannah interrupted, although she knew. She just did not want Gaaron to know she knew any part of this story.

"The Lohoras," Miriam said defiantly.

Susannah took a step back to ostentatiously look over the younger girl. "Yes, you certainly seem to bear the stamp of the Lohoras. I would swear Claudia embroidered that belt for you."

"She did. And this is a shirt that was too small for Tirza. Dathan made the gloves for me."

At the name, Susannah started, and then hoped no one else had noticed her reaction. Blessed Yovah, Miriam and Dathan. That would be a combination likely to set the whole prairie on fire.

But no. Miriam was here with the dark-skinned man, claiming him as her friend and watching him closely even as she hovered next to Susannah. Miriam had not made the calamitous choice of falling in love with Dathan. She had made an even worse one.

"You're right. We have much to talk about," was all Susannah said. "Perhaps later—when we've sorted all this out—"

"Well, I'm staying here as long as Jossis stays here," Miriam said. "So we can talk after Gaaron is gone."

Mention of the name turned Susannah's eyes in the angel's direction again. He was standing beside Mahalah and the stranger, but he was watching his sister and his angelica. Nicholas had wandered out of the room shortly after entering it, muttering something about food.

So it was just the five of them.

"How did Gaaron happen to find you with the Lohoras?" Susannah asked, keeping her gaze on him.

"He was not looking for me. He was looking for you."

And that Gaaron must have heard, because he finally walked over to greet her. His expression was still impassive, maybe a little stern. "No one knew where you had gone," he told her. "I thought you might have sought out your Edori friends. Keren reminded me where they might be."

"I'm sorry to have worried you," she said, speaking as coolly as he had. "I thought I would be back before you returned. But Kaski was so happy to see me that I decided to stay a week or two."

"I would have appreciated a note of some sort."

"I will be sure to let you know all of my future movements."

Miriam turned her head from side to side, watching each of their faces as they spoke. "You've argued about something," she declared.

"No," Gaaron and Susannah answered in unison.

"I hope it wasn't about me," Miriam said.

Gaaron laughed. "I would not spend the energy on something so insignificant," he told her.

Before Miriam could reply to that, Mahalah called out. "Miriam! Come here and help me with this." And the blond girl skipped away, to leave Susannah and Gaaron face-to-face.

"What is the story here?" Susannah asked. "With Miriam and this man? Surely she cannot—but it seems—"

"With Miriam, there is no 'surely,' " Gaaron replied with faint humor. "She has taken it upon herself to befriend him—though to what extent I cannot be certain."

"I will talk to her later and see what she will tell me."

Gaaron looked at her. "You plan to stay here longer, then? I thought Nicky and I could take you back to the Eyrie."

"I am not ready to go back to the Eyrie just yet," she said.

He watched her a while in silence. She could read the trouble on his face—read also his thought that this was not the time and place to discuss it. "I wish you wouldn't be gone very long," he said at last.

She smiled a little. "I have things to think about. I have found that this is a good place for thinking."

"If you can get away from all the silly girls," he said.

"I like the silly girls. But I also like the silence, and I have found an abundance of it here."

"I must go back," he said. "Tonight, or in the morning."

She nodded. "Will you take Miriam with you?"

"I promised to leave her with Jossis," he answered somewhat bitterly. "And I do not think I can break my promise."

"Then I will watch her for you as best I can."

That was the last private conversation they had, which was both a relief and a frustration to Susannah. Part of her wanted to rail at him, weep at him, beat him on the shoulders and force him to pay attention to what feelings lay between them. Part of her wanted to step back, as cool and remote as he, and say, "Very well. You have closed your heart to me. I can close mine to you. Let us see how long it takes you to realize that you are bound to me more tightly than you thought."

Instead, they joined Nicholas, Jossis, Miriam, Mahalah, the three older women who helped her run the retreat, and a dozen gossiping girls for a tasty but somewhat tempestuous dinner. Every five minutes, one of the acolytes would burst into laughter, or shrink down in tears—two girls jumped up and left the table at different points during the meal—and one came in late, obviously moping. Mahalah treated them all with cheery kindness, though now and then she rolled her eyes at Susannah, impatient with all the display of temper. Susannah could only smile.

Kaski had elected to eat with the cooks in the kitchen, since there would be men present at the meal. Susannah had been amazed at how quickly Kaski had blossomed under Mahalah's care—the sullen child had become a shy but smiling little girl who would even talk now and then, in quick mumbled sentences. She had made friends with a few of the younger acolytes and positively adored Mahalah. There was no question that this had been the right place to bring her.

And when she was feeling more friendly toward Gaaron, Susannah would tell him so.

After the meal, Miriam dragged Susannah off to relate to her, in harrowing detail, the story of her last four months. They sat on the comfortable bed in the room that had been assigned to Susannah, blankets wrapped around their shoulders to chase away the chill. The tales of cold, hunger, and hard work were familiar to Susannah, and she could not help but see how well Miriam had functioned under the rough Edori lifestyle—but she was shocked by the reports of fending off attacks from invaders.

"You could have been killed—merciful Yovah—"

"Well, I wasn't," Miriam said briskly, and went on with her recital. She rather delicately conveyed her interactions with Jossis, dwelling on the slow understanding that had built up between them, emphasizing his intelligence and his thoughtfulness, but Susannah could hear all the words that were not being said.

"I will have to make sure to spend some time trying to get to know this young man," was Susannah's comment at the end. She took care to keep her voice noncommittal, so that Miriam did not think she either approved or disapproved of this development.

"I think Mahalah has him now. They went away together right after dinner."

"Have you thought," Susannah asked gently, "what happens to Jossis now? You say how well he fit in with the Lohoras, but—does he want to stay with them? With us? Doesn't he want to go back with his own people?"

"He doesn't like his own people," Miriam said sharply, but there seemed to be a touch of fear in her voice nonetheless. "He wants to stay here."

"But what do his friends want? If they came to the camp to find him that second time—surely they were trying to recover him—"

"He doesn't want to go with them. He'll continue to hide from them."

"For how long?"

"Until they go away."

"But what will make them go away? Has he told you that?"

Somewhat fearfully, Miriam shook her head. "Maybe, if he can talk to Mahalah, he will tell her," she said hopefully.

"He may not want to betray his friends."

"They are not his friends! They are violent and cruel, and they have hurt him," Miriam burst out. "He wants to stay here on Samaria, with the Edori and—and with me."

Susannah nodded. "Well, then, we'll see if we can make that happen," she said quietly. "We'll talk about it some more in the morning. Right now it's late, and time for bed. Kaski has been sleeping with me. Would you like to spend the night with us? Or . . ." She hesitated and could not bring herself to ask the words. *Or would you like to spend the night with Jossis instead?* It was ridiculous, she knew. Miriam had as good as forced them all to acknowledge that she was an adult woman, capable of caring for herself and making the decisions that would please her, if they pleased no one else, and yet still Susannah could not help looking at her as a rather willful child. And she could not bring herself to condone this new relationship, however intelligent and wonderful Jossis might be. "Or perhaps you would rather sleep alone tonight," she ended lamely.

Miriam gave her a smile full of all the wickedness in the world, and impulsively leaned over to throw her arms around Susannah. "I will share the bed with you and Kaski tonight," she whispered in Susannah's ear. "But not every night that we are here. Though I am thinking there might be another bed you should be sleeping in."

Susannah drew away, blushing deeply. Yes, not only a woman, but an Edori woman; Miriam had grown up a great deal. "And I don't think the issue of where I sleep is of much concern to you," she said.

Miriam regarded her with a teasing half-smile. "Just ask me," she invited. "I can tell you how to handle Gaaron."

Susannah sighed. "You can only tell me how to push him away," she said. "I want to bring him closer."

Miriam bounced once on the bed and then came to her feet. "Let's go say good night to him right now," she said.

Susannah rather unwillingly stood up. "It's late. He may already be in bed."

"All the better."

"Miriam!"

"We'll just say good night. He said he was leaving in the morning. And then we'll get a snack and say good night to Jossis and find Kaski."

Although Susannah was still protesting, they left the room to put this plan in action. The long, cool corridors were finally quiet—it *was* late, and most of the whispering, chattering girls had already gone to bed. Susannah had not thought she could learn to love any place of stone and silence, but she was at peace in Mount Sinai. It reminded her of the great mountain chapels where the Edori camped from time to time. Every rock, every seam between hallway and floor, seemed alive with the mystical presence of the god.

But she still did not want to live here. She wanted to be back in the Eyrie, if there was some sort of life she could work out with Gaaron—or among her own people, away from any shelter at all.

They found Mahalah in the great central chamber, but she was alone. "I sent Jossis to bed," she told them. "He found both the trip here and the effort of speaking with me so exhausting that he could not concentrate anymore."

"Where is he?" Miriam asked.

Mahalah shook her head. "He is sleeping," she said gently. "You can see him in the morning."

"Have you learned anything from him?" Susannah asked.

Mahalah regarded her a moment with her eyes narrowed. "Many things," she said at last. "Not all of them, I think, should be repeated. Forgive me while I take some time to think through what I know."

"Well, that's not fair!" Miriam exclaimed. "Anyway, it doesn't matter if you won't tell us anything. He'll tell *me* what he told you."

Now Mahalah studied Miriam with that same close attention. "Perhaps he will," she said slowly. "But perhaps you won't understand it as well as I do, or you—well, we will see. I need to talk to Gaaron."

Miriam looked around the room, where Gaaron obviously was not. "Is he asleep, too?" she asked somewhat scornfully.

"Oh, no," Mahalah said. "He's gone."

Gaaron had left Mount Sinai mostly because he wanted to stay. When he had looked up and seen Susannah standing there, he had been suffused with the strangest sensation—his whole body had tingled with shock. It had taken him a moment to remember that he had been searching for her—and why he had been searching for her—and the circumstances of their last meeting. And then the pleasant, unfamiliar tingling sensation went away, and he felt leaden and stupid and cold.

He had found it hard to talk to her, which was strange, since for the past week all he had wanted to do was talk to her. When he did manage to speak, his words ranged from the commonplace to the accusatory, which made him believe he would have been better off not speaking at all. It had been a relief to go into dinner and be surrounded by all those histrionic girls.

And another relief to see Miriam drag Susannah away for what was sure to be a long conference.

He'd turned to Mahalah. "I have to go," he said.

She looked up in surprise. She'd been giving instructions to one of the women who worked with her, and her mind was clearly elsewhere. "Go? Go where?"

"Back to the Eyrie."

"You mean, right now?"

He nodded. "I'll leave Nicholas here for a day or two, in case you need to get word to me, or in case Susannah wants to return. But I'll come back when I can." He smiled. "Because, at some point, we'll have to decide just what to do about Miriam's new friend—and about Miriam."

"He has told me some appalling things."

"Which I hope you will share with me."

Mahalah meditated. "If I can. Some of them—I do not know how to explain this—there are some things the god has made it very clear that he wants only the oracles to know. But Jossis knows them. And if I repeat them to you—I do not know how that changes your relationship with the god. I do not know that I want to be responsible for changing that relationship. I don't know how to say it any more clearly than that."

"Has he told you yet how we can defeat his people?" The look on her face was troubled, and he smiled somewhat grimly. "I thought not."

"Jovah knows about his people," she replied in a low voice. "And Jovah has a plan. But it—for him to carry it out—I am not sure how this can be accomplished . . ."

Too many secrets, too much hesitation and misdirection. Gaaron found himself edgy and restless. He must have action or explode. "You tell me what you can, when you can," he said. "I'm off for the Eyrie."

"Can you fly that far by night?" she asked gravely. "Gaaron, be sensible. You flew half the day today already."

But he was already on his feet, and glancing around for any items he may have shed in this room when they first arrived. No, he had not been carrying much—besides Jossis. "It's only three hours, and I am wide awake," he assured her.

"What will I tell Miriam? And Susannah?"

"I'll be back in two or three days. We'll talk then."

And though she argued halfheartedly for a few more minutes, he was determined to go. She followed him down the still hallways, the hissing of her chair wheels making a faint counterpoint to the *shushing* sound of his feathers against the walls. He kissed her good-bye and then dove into the star-stained night.

After the warmth of the retreat, the cold outside was a shock against all his senses. The air was icy as river water against his skin; the wind smelled like snow. He felt both weightless and motionless, as if his wings merely ruffled the breeze for no purpose but decoration, and he hung suspended in a limitless black expanse of frigid night. It was too dark to see the landscape unfolding below him, too cold to gauge his progress by changing currents of wind against his flesh. He imagined himself just another small star pinned against the black ceiling of the heavens, fixed eternally in place and only intermittently visible.

And yet he flew west and south at a steady, confident pace, aware of the sweep and motion of his wings, the calm intake and exhalation of his breath, the slow but certain passage of time. It was an hour or so before midnight; he would make it to the Eyrie well before the arrival of dawn.

His muscles warmed up as the exertion of flying created a pleasant heat along his veins. Now he could differentiate his body from the ambient air just by the variation in temperature, and he liked the way it felt. The night stroked cool fingers along his spine, ran diaphanous hands through his heavy hair. He glistened with sweat and starlight, phosphorescent against the night.

And still the miles fell behind him like children too slow to keep up. Midnight approached and passed; the sky was still a layered, impenetrable black. Gaaron was almost sorry to think that he would be at the Eyrie within the hour. He felt strong enough to fly to Luminaux and back—to Ysral, if it existed—to the god's stronghold, so high above him that he could not guess the distance. He could fly all those places in a single night, and then back to Mount Sinai, where his heart lay.

He was closer now—a few minutes from the familiar home mountain range—and he began dropping down to a more reasonable altitude. The closer he grew to the ground, the more his mind began to fill with earthbound thoughts. He needed to get word to Adriel and Neri about their acquisition of an invader; he needed to consult with Esther on the plans for the wedding (so soon now! And he and Susannah had not even discussed it). He needed to decide what in the god's name he would do with Miriam. And then there was the Gloria, scarcely two months away. He needed to consult with his own angels about how that event would be orchestrated, for it was more than a single mass sung under the shadow of Mount Galo. It was a whole day's worth of feasting and entertainment, and there was much planning that had to be done to make sure the event went smoothly.

But all these concerns went out of his head as he descended even closer to the ground. He was hovering a few hundred feet above the Eyrie and below him he could see—clearly delineated against the rich blackness of the night—that Velora was on fire.

CHAPTER THIRTY

Susannah woke with a start in the middle of the night. Her heart was hammering and her breath came too fast. She must have been dreaming, though she had no memory of a nightmare. She sat up carefully, trying not to jostle her sleeping companions, and took in deep breaths of air.

But she still felt troubled and panicked, too restless to sleep. There had been times in the Lohora camp—and, before that, the Tachita tents—that she had been roused from sleep in the middle of the night, and always with some cause. The fire had grown mischievous, a child had cried out, there was some danger approaching on silent feet. Had there been a noise or a scent, here in the slumbering halls of Mount Sinai, that had jerked her awake and put all her senses on alert?

Shivering a little in the cold, she slipped out of bed and threw on a robe, then crossed to the door and stuck her head out. No sounds, no odors, nothing to rouse her to fear.

But something had wakened her.

She paused only long enough to add slippers and a lighted candle to her ensemble, and then she quietly left the room. The untenanted halls were ghostly and full of whispers, though there was no feel of menace in the dorm wards or the women's halls, as Susannah made her way quietly through the living quarters. Nothing disturbing in the kitchens or the dining room. No aura of danger in the public chambers. No sense of trouble at all.

But when she glanced down the long corridor that led to Mahalah's workroom, she saw a faint light at the end of the hall.

Soundlessly, she stepped along the stone floor, using her hand to shield her candle flame from the wind of her passage. She listened intently, but she could hear nothing coming from the big central room—no voices, no sound of weeping, no noise of working. She paused a moment at the open doorway, and then stepped in.

Mahalah was sitting in front of the interface, making unreadable words appear on the glowing blue screen. There was no one else in the room.

Susannah had made no sound, but Mahalah wheeled her chair around the instant that she entered. The oracle was smiling. "Susannah," she said. "What keeps you up so late at night?"

"I'm sorry," Susannah said at once. "I didn't mean to bother you."

"No bother," Mahalah said. "I'm often up at all hours. But I usually have every inch of Mount Sinai to myself when it's this late."

"Something woke me up," Susannah said. "I thought I would check and see if there was anything amiss. But I've been through every hall and found nothing disturbed."

Mahalah smiled at her kindly. "I think you might be dreaming," she suggested.

Susannah put a hand to her forehead. Indeed, she felt strange, almost disembodied. She could feel her fingers against her brow, but they seemed disconnected from her body. "I think you might be right," she agreed.

"But I'm glad you've come here tonight," Mahalah said. "There's something I've been wanting you to see, and you can only see it if you're dreaming."

That made no sense, but no one ever made sense in a dream. "What is it?" Susannah asked, stepping closer.

Mahalah gestured toward something in the middle of the room. "Do you see that little box lying there on the floor? Go stand by it, and then wait for a few moments. I'll tell you when to close your eyes."

Stranger and stranger, but now that she knew she was dreaming, Susannah was at peace. Obediently she crossed the few yards to the spot that Mahalah had indicated. She stooped to examine the box, a small wooden container inlaid with rows of ebony. "What's in this?" she asked.

"The box means nothing. It merely marks the place," Mahalah said. "Now, close your eyes and count to—to fifty, I think. That should be long enough. And don't be afraid. You will be quite safe."

"I'm not afraid," Susannah said, and closed her eyes.

She began counting, not very fast because she felt too sleepy and languorous to hurry through her numbers. Her skin felt alive with static, as if a storm was about to pass through, and her robe stirred around her as if there was a breeze in Mahalah's chamber. But she kept her eyes closed and continued counting.

Suddenly her whole body was seized with magic. It was as if her skin turned inward and her bones turned outward, as if her lungs shrank down while her head expanded. She kept her fingers curled around her candle, except she could no longer feel the candle; she could no longer feel her fingers, or her elbows, or her toes. Keeping her eyes tightly shut, she kept on counting, though it seemed she had been counting for centuries. When she reached the number fifty, she opened her eyes.

She was in a place of glass and ivory and silver.

Pivoting on one heel, she turned slowly to take in the whole picture. Oh, this was nothing new—she had been here hundreds of times before. There was the wide, blank screen with the flickering lines; there was the incomprehensible map laid across a translucent surface. At stations scattered throughout this brightly lit chamber were variations of the interface that Mahalah used in her own chamber, and that Susannah had seen so many times in her dreams. Even the chairs and the vents high on the walls looked familiar. Even the floor, tiled in smooth, unbroken white. Even the hallways that branched invitingly away.

"Mahalah was right," she said aloud, though quite softly. "I am merely dreaming."

She set down her candle, because there was no need of it in this well-illuminated place. Besides, the flame had gone out sometime while she was counting.

"I have been here so many times before," she said. "I wonder what I am supposed to be looking at now?"

"Susannah," said a voice so deep and resonant that she imagined it was what winter would sound like, but so well-known to her that it was almost comforting to hear it now. "You have come to visit me at last."

She almost laughed. "I have come to visit you *again*," she said. "Surely I have been here many times before in my dreams."

"Many times," he agreed. "But this time I can actually see you."

"Is it Yovah who has sent me the dreams of this place?" she asked. "For I do not feel afraid, and yet this place is somewhat fearsome."

"Yes, Jovah has communicated with you," the voice replied. "For there is a task that must be done, and only you can do it."

"I will be happy to do whatever the god wishes," she said obligingly. "But why am I the only one who can perform this duty?"

"Mahalah is too frail, and everyone else too frightened," he said.

She shook her head, for it seemed she would get no direct answer; but again, that was the way of dreams. "What would you like me to do?" she said.

"Do you see the corridor directly before you? The one with the triple lights at the end of the hall."

She looked in two wrong directions before she spotted the markers he indicated, and then she stepped forward. The white tile looked so smooth and cool that she wanted to take off her slippers merely to feel it beneath her feet, but she wasn't sure where she was and she didn't want to be disrespectful, so she kept her slippers on. "What next?" she asked when she reached the designated intersection.

"Now turn to your left, and walk until you reach a door marked with a numeral two."

Again, she followed his directions and came to the location he had described. "Go down the stairwell and exit through the door at the bottom."

The stairwell was like nothing she had ever seen before, a single spiraling twist of open steps made of metal or glass or—what it really looked like—frozen foam. She kept her hand on the reed-thin railing and descended cautiously. She was relieved to step through the door and out into another corridor that was constructed and lit just as the hallways above were.

"And now?"

"Down this hallway before you, toward the row of blinking red lights. Stop when you get to the door marked with this word—" And he spoke something that she didn't understand. It came to her, in a quick fanciful thought, that Jossis might have used such a word. The arrangement of vowels and consonants sounded like the invader's speech, or what little she had heard of it.

"I didn't understand," she said.

"Just walk slowly forward. I will tell you when to stop."

So she traversed the corridor, which seemed lined with windowless doors that guarded who knew what collection of secrets. Many of the doors bore small placards that announced their names, or perhaps what lay inside, but Susannah could read none of the words.

"Stop here," the voice directed. "Open the door on your left."

She tried, but the door stayed shut. "I think it's locked," she said.

"Do you see the flat metal plate above the handle?" he asked. "Lay your palm on that until you feel the metal heat up. Then lift your hand very quickly."

Wondering, because this had never been part of the dream before, Susannah did as he bid her. The metal plate was as cool and smooth as she imagined the white tile would be, and she did not think the temperature of her hand would be enough to warm it. But sure enough, after she had stood there less than a minute, she felt a fever surge through the flat metal, and she hurriedly withdrew her hand.

"Enter the room," the voice said, and she did so.

Rarely had her dreams contained any vision like this, and for a moment she was afraid to step forward. It was as if she had skipped up a street made of moonbeams to come to rest on an avenue of stars. One quarter of the room was nothing but glass, and it all seemed to overlook the constellations. She felt faint and dizzy, as if she was on top of Mount Galo—on top of a mountain ten times higher than Galo—and as if she stood on the very peak of the mountain and looked up into the sky. She stayed very close to the doorway, where the floor and the walls were solid, and hesitated before asking for her next directive.

"Now what would you like me to do?" she said at last in a small voice.

"I need you to reposition my artillery."

For a moment, Gaaron felt himself freeze into place above the mountain. For a moment, he could not actually comprehend what he was seeing. It was not the entire city that was on fire, but bits and pieces—the southern perimeter was completely ablaze, as well as most of the eastern bazaar. Here and there, a residential district was in flames, or a solitary building, or a low patch of land that might have been a park. But all the fires were growing, leaping higher, spreading out searching tendrils of flame to the next block, the next building. Soon enough, there would be nothing of the city left.

As he watched, still stunned, a fresh tongue of flame licked out and darted into the safe heart of the city.

Which was when he realized invaders were below, sending their bolts of fire into Velora.

A cry ripped from his throat, and he suddenly remembered to breathe. And, as suddenly, remembered how to work his wings, to dive closer to the ground so that he could see the marauders and gauge how many of them there were.

There appeared to be hundreds, their dark bodies illuminated by their own trail of luminous destruction. The whole southern half of the city was ringed by massed black figures, two and three deep. The Edori tents and Jansai wagons that had stood here only a day ago were gone, leveled to ashes. The invaders marched slowly forward, fire sticks pointed before them, scuffing through the cinders of the ruined camps.

One of the strangers saw Gaaron's shadow against the night sky and shouted. Instantly, half a dozen fire sticks veered Gaaron's way. He banked sharply and then strained forward, hoping to escape the range of their venom. Heat licked along his bare arm but he saw no arrow of fire; the flame must have evaporated inches from his skin.

He darted deeper into the city, away from the advancing terror, desperate to see how matters lay. A few of the bigger buildings were on fire, burning with a frenzied intensity that promised to leap to the neighboring awning and the roof across the alley. By their light, he could tell that the streets were filled with milling, screaming people, everyone running for safety, everyone maddened with fear. Gaaron was close enough to see a small girl standing alone on a corner, eyes closed, fists clenched, her mouth open in a perpetual shriek. Even over the din of fire and shouting, Gaaron thought he could single out her thin, wild cry.

"Gaaron!" A harsh voice called his name and he wheeled around to see one of the Velora merchants waving both arms to him. The man was grimy and flushed; he looked as if he had barely escaped from the falling timbers of a blazing house. "Gaaron, do something!" the man shouted up at him.

"I will," Gaaron called back, and drove his wings down hard against the hot air of the burning city.

He had not risen a hundred feet above the ground when rocks began raining down from the sky.

"Gaaron!" a new voice cried just as he jerked himself upward, beating his wings frantically to escape this fresh danger. Suddenly, the air around him was seething with the flexing of many angel wings. The currents were so rough from their random beating that it was hard to keep himself aloft.

"Gaaron!" someone else shouted, and he found himself in a circle of maybe twenty angels, hard to see in the dark by the starlight above and the firelight below. "They're attacking Velora!"

"How long have they been here?" he shouted back.

"I don't know!" the voice replied. He thought it was Enoch, but the speaker was so hoarse that he couldn't be sure. "We've brought— we just flew out here a little while ago—we've got bags and bags of rocks, we've been throwing them down—"

"Good!" he called. "Have you managed to hit any of them?"

"Too far away to tell," came another voice. Ahio, he thought. "But I've seen some of their fire sticks shooting astray, and I think that's because we've knocked someone over."

"You'll have to get closer," Gaaron said. "Aim for their heads as best you can. But not too close—you don't want them to turn their fire sticks on you."

"Gaaron, what else can we do?" Chloe.

"Nothing yet," Gaaron replied tersely. "First I must pray for thunder."

There was a general exclamation at that and a moment of rough air almost impossible to negotiate as all the angels crowded closer to hear more. But Gaaron pushed himself a yard or two higher, away from their questions and their dangerous wingbeats.

"Ahio, come with me," he directed. "The rest of you—closer to Velora, and don't stop flinging down your stones. I do not know how long it will take the god to respond to our prayer."

"But Gaaron—"

"But can you be sure where the lightning will strike?"

"Gaaron, the city will be leveled in half an hour!"

"Gaaron—"

"But, Gaaron—"

He ignored them all, left them all behind with a determined downbeat of his wings. The god was so far above them that he could not see the danger that threatened. Gaaron must go practically to Jovah's doorstep to ensure that the god could hear.

He pointed his chin upward and followed his own trajectory as high as he could go, up through the black heavens and into the regions that belonged solely to the god. It was so cold that his feathers turned to frost; the blood in his veins iced over. The air was so thin that his head pounded with pain, and a thin soprano shrieking began sounding in his ear. He could barely breathe this high up. He was not sure he could sing.

He hovered a moment, investing great energy in each drag and uplift of his wings, letting his lungs accustom themselves to the knife-thin air. He was so light-headed that he had forgotten Ahio was to follow him, and so he was astonished to see a pale, fluttering shape materialize beside him in the uninhabited reaches of space.

"Gaaron," Ahio said, and his beautiful voice sounded tinny and faraway. "This is too high."

"We will sing from here," Gaaron said, and opened his mouth to begin his prayer.

The notes fell out of him like sparks or fireflies—tiny, beautiful, and winged with fire. He saw them drift away from him and spiral upward, as if wafted by invisible smoke on summer air. He sang one entire verse before Ahio's voice dropped in, dark and smooth as polished amber. Their voices blended, and the images faded, and now the world around Gaaron was turned to music. The stars sent up faint trumpet blasts; the wind soughed through with an oboe plaint; and the braided voices of the angels gained force and beauty as they chorused their way up the chilly ramps of the atmosphere to the dark, vaulted chambers of the god.

They sang for an hour, their voices growing more powerful with every melodic line. Their lungs filled up on this insufficient air and their hearts beat in quick, metronomic strokes to send the blood racing more industriously through their bodies. Ahio's voice glided under Gaaron's, providing a structure, a place to gather; Gaaron's voice leapt upward from the springboard of Ahio's strength. They flung their prayer to the god's attention, and felt it go crashing through the windows of Jovah's house.

Yet, no thunderbolt fell. No lightning erased the stars.

Once again—singing the prayer over again from the beginning. Gaaron felt himself starting to tire. His wings were woven of icicles; the feathers tinkled together like crystal quills. He weighed a thousand pounds, two thousand. If he folded his wings and plummeted to the earth, his impact would destroy Velora and every invader within fifty miles. He was so cold he could not distinguish any sensation, internal or external. He was cold enough to be the source of winter itself.

But he kept on singing, and Ahio sang beside him.

And the lightning did not snarl down, and the god remained silent.

"Gaaron!" Ahio cried, suddenly breaking off his dark harmony. "Gaaron, *look*!"

And Gaaron, who was already staring upward at the stars, stared even higher.

Above them, so high they could not possibly fly that far, the heavens were riddled with fire. Streaks of light flew from an invisible source to an unseen target, and then it was as if the stars themselves exploded. Sheets of light turned to coruscating color, then a great aureole of glittering particles shimmered and disappeared. Again, the bright, soundless, blooming illumination of the sky—the cascading run of colors, from violet to emerald—then the shattered halo of light—then darkness.

Surely it was his imagination that from below them came a desperate outcry of terror and alarm?

"Keep singing!" Gaaron shouted, pausing long enough to take one deep breath. And then he plunged back into prayer, invigorated and determined. He had no idea what that convulsion of light signified, but that it was the work of the god, he was certain. And that it had come in response to his supplication, he had no doubt.

Once again, he prayed for a thunderbolt. Once again, the heavens opened up into an opal devastation, and sparks rained down like ruined stars.

And then the air grew dense, or else so starved that it was impossible to take it in. Gaaron could not breathe, could not produce a note, and as if from far away, he heard the sound of Ahio choking.

"Down!" Gaaron coughed out, and folded his wings and dropped.

He was a bolt from the god, he was an arrow from a crossbow. He fell like a creature with no restraints. Down, down, down, a descent so rapid that his skin heated up and his frozen wings began to curl with smoke. He could see the mountain taking shape below him, see the fires that marked Velora separate into their individual towers of flame. The sounds of destruction and lamentation rose in a faint cacophony to his ears. He unfurled his wings so sharply they made a snapping sound, and he felt his whole body jerk backward. He lashed the air until he had stabilized high above the city of Velora.

The invaders appeared to be gone.

More prudently, he dropped closer to the ground, trying to reconstruct what had occurred. The fires still raged all around the city, but no new ones flared up while he watched. He could see small shadowy shapes hurrying in all directions below—residents seeking water to put out the flames, mothers searching for their lost children, couriers bawling out their news. But these were all figures crisscrossing one another inside the city limits. No massed marauders were huddled outside Velora, mapping out a new strategy or preparing a new assault. All of Jossis' friends seemed to have disappeared.

Gaaron dropped lower, trying to read even more of the story. Littered around the burning city were dark shapes broken on the ground—the bodies of dead invaders, Gaaron guessed, brought down by his angels' primitive weapons. But surely the angels could not have killed all of the invaders who had been here. There had not been enough rocks in their arsenal. There were not enough bodies on the ground.

Perhaps they had seen the detonations in the sky and been frightened away by the god's display of might. Perhaps they knew, if they torched one more city or leveled one more town, they, too, would be annihilated with divine fire.

But Gaaron could not really understand it.

The air rocked around him, and he was once again in a circle of angels, all beating their wings at once. "What happened here?" he called out. "Where did they all go?"

"Gaaron, did you see the light in the heavens?" Zibiah cried.

"Yes—three times—like the sky was on fire."

"They saw it, too—it frightened them," someone else took up the story. "Some of them saw and pointed, and then they—and then half of them disappeared."

"Some of them stayed, and pointed more fire sticks at Velora—"

"But then the light in the heavens came again—"

"And again—"

"And more of them disappeared each time."

"But they kept *pointing*," Enoch added. "After that first flash of light, they kept pointing, and crying, as if something they wanted was up there in the sky. As if they thought it was in danger and they had to rescue it."

"That makes no sense," Chloe said impatiently.

"I know it doesn't, but that is what I saw—"

"Peace, we may never understand it," Gaaron interrupted, throwing his hands out to signal for silence. "Wherever they have gone, they are not here now."

"But Gaaron, will they come back?" Zibiah asked, her voice fretful. "We held them off today, but not very well, and Velora is almost destroyed."

"I don't know if they'll be back," Gaaron said soberly. He was watching a winged shape meander down from overhead, at a more leisurely pace and a better angle than he had chosen. Ahio, come to join the conference of angels. "But they are gone now. Let us do what we can for Velora."

"What can we do?" Zibiah demanded, and it was Ahio's hoarse, thready voice that answered.

"Pray for rain," he said.

Susannah huddled on the white floor in the white room, and prayed for stillness. She was sick with incessant motion. The chamber she was in seemed to dart and dive and whirl from side to side in random bursts of energy. Outside the oversize windows, the constellations seemed to jump and collide. Small flashes of light sizzled past her field of vision and disappeared. Twice she saw the whole black canvas of the heavens blanch to white, and then she closed her eyes and did not look again. She was sick from motion and apprehension.

But she did not pray aloud or expect the god to hear her. She could not imagine that even Yovah could see past these sudden blinding spasms of light, or catch up to the spinning, plunging, rolling chamber in which she sat. She just said the words over and over again in her head, and hoped with all her strength that she would soon wake up.

And then the motion ceased. The room seemed to shudder to a halt and then fell into a silence so immense that it made her wonder what noise had been present before. She had the sense of a predator waiting, a feeling that impossibly delicate senses were alert and attuned to scents or sounds that she would never discern. Even the wall behind her seemed strung with anticipation; the floor seemed coiled and ready to pounce.

She stayed tumbled where she was and did not move.

At last a great sigh seemed to travel through the room—or perhaps it was not a sigh—there was a hiss of air and a low hum like one she had sometimes heard in the music rooms at the Eyrie. As if a machine had been turned on and was waiting for the next hand upon the dial.

At least it seemed as if the rocking and the spinning had stopped for the moment. And the huge, thin windows showed only the same placid stars they had showed before. Cautiously, Susannah pushed herself to a seated position. When the world did not dissolve into motion again, she stood up.

"I hope," she said aloud, but very softly, "it is time for me to leave this place."

For some reason, she had not expected the voice to reply, but it did. "Indeed, you have been most useful, but it is time to return you to your proper existence," came the welcome words. "You must do one more task for me, and then I will send you home."

She was not so sure about this task, but she was eager to go home, so she said, "Tell me what I must do."

"Reverse my artillery to its former position," he said. "I will talk you through the exercise."

This was not so hard as it sounded, as it had not been so hard the first time, though it involved pushing a stubborn lever from one slot to another and punching a number of buttons in the sequence that the voice called out. Three times she had to wait while a deep, grinding noise seemed to originate in the floor beneath her feet, and then she had to flip a series of switches. None of this made any sense; she followed the crazy, colorful logic of a dream. And waited for what the voice required next.

"There. Main artillery realigned, auxiliary guns realigned, shield engaged in self-repair," the voice announced. "I thank you, Susannah. Your hands have performed functions that all my circuits could not."

"You're welcome," she said, because it seemed the polite thing to say. "May I go home now?"

"Do you remember the route you followed to this room?"

She glanced at the door, somewhat surprised to find it, after all this commotion, in roughly the same spot it had been when she entered. "I'm—not sure."

"I will direct you."

And so she went through the door, and down the hallway, and up the stairs, and down another hallway, and at last emerged into the room of white and silver with which she was most familiar. And here, look, the candle that had been in her hands when she arrived, marking the very spot where she had first stood. With a little cry, she ran the last few remaining steps and snatched it up. It felt like the only thing in this whole vast, alien place that was natural or real.

"Good. Stand where you are," said the voice. "I will return you."

"Should I close my eyes?" she asked, remembering how she had arrived.

"If you wish."

"I will," she said, and dropped her lids. The voice had not told her to count to fifty, but she began to tell off the numbers anyway, hoping that by the time she reached the highest one, this nightmare would finally be over. She was in the silent space between "nine" and "ten" when she felt the magic take her over again, rustling along her bones and turning her skin to silver.

She was on her knees and had forgotten to keep counting when she heard Mahalah's voice call her name.

CHAPTER THIRTY-ONE

"Here, drink this. Yes, I know you think you aren't thirsty, but drink this anyway," Mahalah insisted. The oracle had made no attempt to move Susannah from her crumpled posture on the floor, but wheeled over with a glass of wine in her hand and pressed it into Susannah's cold fingers.

"I can't—I think I'm still dreaming," Susannah said. Her hands were shaking so much she didn't think she could get the glass to her mouth—and anyway, food and drink were always wasted in a dream.

"Yes—well—you've been sleepwalking, I believe," Mahalah said quickly. Susannah had the impression that the oracle was improvising. "But you're awake now, I'm quite sure of it, and I think you'd better have the wine. It will help you sleep better once you get back to your own bed."

"I'm not sure I want to sleep again if my dream will come back," Susannah said with an attempt at humor.

"I don't think it will," Mahalah said softly. "I think that is the last time you will be dreaming of that particular place."

Susannah wondered how the oracle could be sure of that, but she didn't have the strength to ask. She could smell the wine, sweet and fruity; and when she finally put the rim to her lips, she could taste the wine as well. So she was awake, at last, and she must have been walking in her sleep to have come this far from her bed. She drained the glass and put it on the floor.

It was then she looked beyond Mahalah and saw Jossis standing a few feet behind her. His dark face looked blank with shock. He had his arms wrapped around his chest, as though to ward off cold.

"What is he—why is he—Jossis—" Susannah managed to say.

Mahalah glanced at him over her shoulder and then returned her attention to Susannah. "Like me, he could not sleep," she said gently. "We have much to talk about, Jossis and I."

"But he looks—Mahalah, I think he has been crying."

"Yes," Mahalah said. "This has been a hard night for him as well. He has lost so much."

None of it made any sense. Despite the taste of wine in her mouth, Susannah was sure she must still be asleep.

"I'm so tired," she said. She thought, if she tried very hard, she might be able to stand. She put her palms against the floor and pushed.

"Yes. I think you should go to your room now," Mahalah said. "Sleep well into the morning. We can talk then. You can tell me about your dream, and I can tell you that it means nothing. Only the mind sending out pictures and asking unanswerable questions."

Susannah was on her feet now—shaky but, she thought, mobile. "Will Jossis be all right?"

"I will talk to him until he is," Mahalah said. "But send Miriam to me in the morning. She will help me heal him."

"Good night, then," Susannah said. Her head spun a little, but her feet moved forward well enough, and she cleared the door with no mishap. Once in the hallway, she balanced herself against the wall with one hand and kept on walking. One corridor, one turn, another corridor, another turn, a few more steps, and she was in her door.

A few more steps, and she was in her bed.

Kaski stirred and moved over without waking up. Miriam's head came up from the pillow, ghostly blond in the filtered moonlight. "Susannah?" she asked. "Where have you been? I woke up and you were gone."

"Mahalah says I have been walking in my sleep," Susannah said.

"You're so cold! Here, have my blanket, it's all warm."

"Thank you," Susannah said, snuggling down between the other two and burrowing under the covers. "Oh, Miriam, I have had the strangest dream! I'll tell you about it in the morning."

"Tell me now. You won't remember it in the morning."

The heat, the relief, the sweetness of Miriam's concern were combining to make Susannah sleepy and relaxed. "I think I'll remember," she said, closing her eyes. "I don't think I'll ever forget."

In the morning, Miriam was the first one awake and too restless to wait patiently as the others sauntered yawning from their dreams. She leaned over to kiss Susannah on the cheek, patted Kaski on the head, and climbed out of bed. In a few minutes, she was washed, dressed, and out the door.

The acolytes, it appeared, had all gotten up before her, because the halls were full of their thin, tense figures and the echoes of their cries and laughter. She made her way to the dining hall, where the servants were already clearing away the breakfast dishes, but one of the cooks smiled at her and gave her a late meal. She ate slowly because she couldn't imagine what she would do with herself once the meal was over. She had no idea how anyone passed the time in an oracle's retreat.

She could find Jossis, though. Since he was a man, he had been assigned special quarters somewhere in this labyrinth, but he had been allowed to spend the night. She was pretty certain that, wherever he was bedded down, she would make that her own living quarters for the duration of her stay.

Before she had taken her last sip of juice, however, one of the acolytes approached her—a pretty girl, with the high, narrow cheekbones that bespoke a Manadavvi lineage. "Miriam?" the girl asked in a quiet voice. "The oracle has directed me to look for you and ask you to come see her as soon as you have a free moment."

This was much like being summoned by the Archangel; one really didn't delay. "Tell me where she is," Miriam said. "I'll come right now."

Mahalah was in the large, windowless interior room where she had been when they arrived. Once again, the older woman was seated before that flickering blue glass panel set into the wall, but she turned quickly at Miriam's entrance.

"You're awake early," the oracle said.

"My brother often tells me I have too much energy," Miriam said demurely. "It sometimes causes me to wake up before everyone else."

"Well, good. I wanted to see you this morning to tell you . . ." The oracle hesitated, and her eyes searched Miriam's face. The younger woman waited with unwonted patience. "I wanted to ask you a little about Jossis," Mahalah said at last.

Miriam felt a stirring of fear. "Is something wrong? I didn't see him after dinner last night. Is he sick?"

"Heartsick, I think," Mahalah said. "And you can help him. But you—"

Miriam was halfway to the door. "Where is he? Where are the quarters for the men?"

"Miriam, sit down," Mahalah said, and her voice was so firm that without even planning to, Miriam turned back into the room and seated herself before the oracle's wheeled chair. "I have much to explain to you before you go off seeking him, and a few things to ask you as well. May I have your word that anything I tell you will remain confidential between the two of us? That you will tell no one—not Gaaron, not Susannah, none of your angelic or Edori friends—what we are going to talk about?"

Miriam felt her whole face grow loose with astonishment. The few other people who had sworn Miriam to secrecy had been less than twenty years old and about to tell of misdeeds. She was not used to making solemn oaths to respectable elders. "Yes," she said at last. "I swear I will tell no one what you say to me."

Mahalah glanced at her bright blue screen, as if to check that the god was still present in the room. "You know, because Jossis told me that you knew, that he comes from a different world. And that his ancestors are probably the same as ours—another branch of the same colonizing family that settled on Samaria."

"The settlers who came to Samaria were brought here in Jovah's hands," Miriam said automatically. She found herself instinctively using the allali pronunciation of the god's name when speaking dogma.

"Be that as it may, Jossis' ancestors took to the skies in machines that allowed them to move between worlds. And their goal, or so it appears, was to settle on as many planets as they could—maybe ten, all told, in the past two hundred years."

Miriam felt the surfaces of her brain quivering; her skull seemed to be expanding and contracting as Mahalah talked. "Wait—these machines—and these other planets—how many worlds are there? Besides ours, and the one we came from, and the one that Jossis came from?"

"I don't know. Fifteen? Twenty? Dozens? Just because Jossis and his people located and explored a few does not mean there aren't other worlds that other men might be living on—or creatures that are not men. But that is a discussion for another day! Jossis' people have taken their conquests and their wars to five or ten other worlds, and they arrived on Samaria about six months ago, intent on overtaking us as well."

Miriam nodded, for that much she had more or less pieced together. "And they have weapons we don't have."

"They have a great deal of technology that we don't have," Mahalah said. "And they could have easily destroyed us. But we have destroyed them instead. They are all gone now—all but Jossis."

Now Miriam's head was whirling again. Half of what Mahalah said made no sense at all. "How can you know that? We don't even know where they have been in hiding. They can appear and disappear at will—did you ask him about that? They may have disappeared for now, but they will show up again with their fire sticks aimed at us—"

Mahalah put up a hand and Miriam fell silent. "They have been living on these machines I mentioned to you. Machines that can travel through the heavens. When they were not on Samaria, they were living in these machines above the earth. Last night," she said, appearing to choose her words with exceptional care, "they attacked Velora. But Jovah was able to turn his thunderbolts upon their airborne machines, and he destroyed them all."

"How do you know this?" Miriam whispered.

"Your friend Chloe arrived early this morning with a description of the battle, though she did not understand the story she told. But I knew it last night, because Jovah informed me as the action occurred. And Jossis, it seems," she added, "has had, all along, a way to communicate with his friends. When I asked him to confirm for me that they were dead, he tried to reach them, but could not. He has been feeling some anguish as a result of this. I believe you know that he does not relish the life that his clansmen live—but he cannot help but care for some of them. And they are all dead now."

Miriam nodded. She knew too well how easy it was to love someone who was not perfect. "I must go to him at once," she said, but she stayed seated in her chair.

"Not only are all of Jossis' friends dead," Mahalah continued, "there is now no way for him to leave Samaria. These traveling machines are destroyed, and his communications devices will not range so far as to allow him to contact anyone in his home world. He is here now for the rest of his life."

"Poor Jossis!" Miriam exclaimed, although she was not really sorry. Sorry for whatever sadness he might be feeling, but otherwise feeling no regret at all.

"I believe," said Mahalah, "that there is much he can do for us on Samaria, if he chooses to embrace it as his new home. And there are indications that, once his grief passes, he will be happy to settle here. He seems, at least, genuinely attached to you. I do not wish to pry into the secrets of your heart—"

"I love him," Miriam said instantly. "I will never leave him. I knew I could not follow him if he chose to go back to his own world, but for as long as he is on my world, I will stay by his side."

Mahalah smiled and settled back into her chair. "Good. That is what I was hoping to hear. But such a decision will require some sacrifices on your part. For one thing, I do not think Jossis would do well in an angel hold. He—"

"We will live with the Edori," Miriam interrupted. "The Lohoras will happily take us in."

"That may do for now, for a short time," Mahalah said meditatively. "But eventually, he must live in Mount Sudan. And in time, of course, he must live here."

Miriam stared at her.

"There are things I know, as oracle, that no one else on Samaria knows," Mahalah said. "As oracle of Mount Sinai, I know things that not even the other oracles have been taught. But Jossis knows these things. He understands them. And I want him to be the steward of this knowledge once I am gone."

"How can he know these things?" Miriam whispered.

Mahalah waved a hand as if to convey that the answer was too complex to attempt to put into words. "He understands how to communicate with the god, for one thing," Mahalah said.

"So do the other oracles!"

"Yes, but he—he knows things about the god that even they do not know," Mahalah said. "About what the god is capable of. I cannot explain it any better than that. But I want him here when I am dead. And to learn to become the next oracle, he must study somewhere. And since *I*," she said, displaying a small fit of temper, "have been forced to surround myself only with girls, I think I must send your Jossis up to Isaac for training. Where he can study among men."

Miriam was rapidly making the corollary deductions. "So then I must go to Mount Sudan, too?"

"Well, you may visit there, but I do not think you'll be allowed to stay. You could live nearby, I would think."

"At Monteverde? I won't! Neri is worse than Gaaron. And I refuse to stay with the Leshes or the Karshes. And even if you tell me to, I won't do it. And even if Gaaron tells me to—"

Mahalah's face grew very stern. "Miriam," she said. "Don't act the spoiled brat with me. You are a brave and intelligent woman who has it in her power to influence the next thirty or forty years of Samarian history. You have bits and pieces of knowledge that make you both powerful and dangerous. You could do so much good, you could do so much harm. *Think* a minute! Until this point in your life, you have wasted almost all of your energy in spite and childish games. Do you realize how much more you could accomplish? Do you realize the opportunity that lies before you? What kind of woman do you want to be when you turn my age and look back on your life? You are strong enough to shape your own destiny. I cannot control you, and neither can your brother. But choose wisely, or you will drag disaster in your wake."

Never in her life had anyone spoken to Miriam like that. Never had she felt so small and immature—and never, at the same time, so filled with a sense of purpose and resolve. Indeed, she had always done just exactly what she wanted, and no one had ever been able to stop her—but until now, she had never really wanted something worth having.

"I will—I will do wise things—good things," Miriam said, stammering a little because she was not used to having conversations like this. "I will go with Jossis, and I will make Gaaron and Neri understand. And I will do what you tell me to," she added humbly. "Because I don't really see my way clear yet."

Mahalah smiled and laid a frail hand on Miriam's shoulder. "You will," she said. "Every day it will be more clear."

They stayed that way a moment longer, Miriam with her head bowed, still in an attitude of supplication. "I should go to him now," she said.

"I think you should," Mahalah said, and dropped her hand, and wheeled her chair a few feet back.

Miriam stood up, surprised to find herself as shaky as if she had just witnessed a scene of terror. "Where is he?"

"Down the corridor that branches to the left by the kitchens. I told him to wait there this morning until someone came for him. All these bothersome girls! I can't allow men to roam around at will."

Miriam nodded. "Do you want me to bring him here?"

Now Mahalah smiled and gave Miriam a wicked look. "Oh, not right away," she drawled. "I will not expect you for another hour or two."

Miriam blushed and then she laughed. "And where were you raised, an Edori tent?" she asked politely, heading toward the door. "One would think it by your lack of modesty."

"Miriam," Mahalah called right before Miriam stepped outside. Miriam turned back. "Were you considering—had it occurred to you to think about whether or not you might want to have children? With Jossis?"

Miriam had literally never stopped to consider the issue one way or the other, when she had been with Jossis or any other man. "I suppose I will—I don't know—I never thought—"

"I think you should not," Mahalah said gently. "Let Jossis' heritage die with him, many years from now. I believe Jossis is a good man, but he was bred of violent stock, and the last thing we want to introduce to Samaria is trouble of that variety. You will make your own decision, of course, but that is my advice. There are always many children to care for if you cannot bear children of your own. You never need to be at a loss for love."

"I'll think about everything you've said," Miriam replied gravely, because surely she was not expected to give an answer now. "And I will repeat nothing of what you've said. And I thank you for everything you've said. I will not soon forget this day."

Mahalah nodded and turned away. Miriam ducked into the corridor and hurried quickly down a series of hallways. She was almost running by the time she arrived at the men's quarters, a suite of four or five bedrooms that clearly did not see much use. She knocked on two of the closed doorways before a voice bade her enter.

She stepped inside to find Jossis standing at the window, looking out. He turned when she entered but did not cross the floor to take her in an embrace. His dark face seemed aged by five years or more; sorrow set creases between his eyes and his lips. Even his bright hair seemed scarred and grieving, even his brilliant eyes.

"Jossis," she said and flung herself across the room. He was sobbing as he put his face down to hers and she could not understand his short, guttural cries of mourning. But she held him against her, rocking him as if he were a child, murmuring the words that every lover knew, that required no language and never went amiss. He leaned upon her as if there was no other support anywhere in the world, and she held him as if she would undertake no other task for all eternity.

CHAPTER THIRTY-TWO

Susannah stirred the pot once, then brought the spoon to her mouth and tasted. Edible, but rather lacking in spices—which she could have said of the other five meals she'd had since arriving in the Edori camp two days ago. Thank the god they were on the ragged tail-end of winter now. Another few weeks and it would be time for the Gathering. A few weeks after that and it would be true spring. Then the game would be plentiful, the spices would be in bloom, and there would be other things to worry over than putting together a tolerable meal.

Although, these days, she was just as happy when the only real worry she had was whether or not dinner would taste good.

Ruth came up behind her with the sleeping baby in her arms and her almost-two-year-old at her heels. He had grown so much that he was a sturdy little storm of a boy, an inquisitive, insistent, cunning, self-centered creature of destruction. There was never a moment when he could go unwatched. "Now, that smells better than my stew from last night," Ruth commented, setting the sleeping girl in a basket before the tent and picking up her son. "Where did you find marrowroot? Mine's all gone."

"I got some in Luminaux before I came to find you," Susannah said. "They never use it at the Eyrie, and I missed it. That's the last of it, though," she said ruefully, looking down into the pot. "So you'd *better* appreciate it."

"You shouldn't have to waste your spices on us."

Susannah gave her a lofty look. "Well, I plan to eat some, too."

Ruth smiled but she did not look entirely amused. All the other Tachitas had been delighted when Susannah strolled into camp the day before yesterday, carrying only a few bundles of clothes and the handful of herbs she'd purchased in the Blue City. Her father had wept into her hair as he hugged her. Paul and Linus had nearly crushed her with their fierce embraces—Paul because he was so happy to see her, Linus to prove that he could, now that he had grown another two inches and gained ten more pounds. One by one the other Tachitas had come forward to kiss her on the cheek or hug her around the shoulders, and in those quick exchanges she had been told the story of the tribe's last six months.

"Abi is expecting a baby."

"Judith may follow the Morostas after the Gathering."

"Micah is not doing so well—his foot, you know."

But Ruth had put down the baby, and come over to hug Susannah, and then pulled back and asked, "What are you doing here?"

"I have come to see if my father and my brothers are safe," Susannah had answered. "There has been such trouble in the three provinces, and I hoped the Tachitas had taken shelter near Luminaux. So I took a chance and came to the Blue City, and here you are. I am so relieved and happy to find you all whole and well."

This was the truth, as far as it went. Chloe had come to Mount Sinai with the news that Velora was rescued, and Mahalah had—although in the most mysterious fashion imaginable—offered the revelation that Yovah had succeeded in routing all the invaders. Their war, if that was what it could be called, was over.

And Gaaron was still in Velora. Susannah was tired of thinking about what she would say to him when she saw him next, and so she decided to make him think about that a little bit, too. So she asked Chloe to bring her to Luminaux, because Chloe would do it and Nicholas might not, and she left a note behind to tell Gaaron where she had gone. And she had been lucky in that the Tachitas had been camped right where she most hoped they would be. They never roamed far from Luminaux during any winter. During this one, which had been bad for so many reasons, they had camped right outside the city limits. Susannah had bid Chloe a cheery good-bye and the Tachitas a tearful hello. She had been just as happy when the tribe pulled up stakes and moved out the very morning after she arrived. The Gathering was to be in northeastern Jordana in a few weeks, after all. It was time to begin the slow, drifting move in that direction.

But Ruth seemed to think there was more to the story. Although until this afternoon, they had had no chance to talk in private.

"You are certainly welcome to any meal at our campfire, whether or not you have helped cook it," Ruth said now. "But I have to think there are other places you should be instead."

"What other places?" Susannah said lightly. She handed the spoon to Ruth and took the toddler in trade. He squealed in her ear and then gave her his fat and happy smile.

"Aren't you supposed to be marrying soon?"

Susannah gripped her nephew's ribs and held him over her head, twisting him back and forth. That made him shriek even more loudly. "Why, Ruth, I didn't know you listened to allali gossip."

"Living all season in Luminaux, I have heard all manner of tales about the angels and their consorts," Ruth said. "And your wedding date is set for ten days from today."

"Is it?" Susannah asked. She folded her arms so suddenly that she gave the boy the sensation of a plummeting fall, but she caught his weight before he had reached the ground. That elicited another shriek and caused him to wave his bunched fingers. "Perhaps I don't care that much about my wedding."

Ruth took the child from her and rested him against her shoulder. This meant Susannah had overexcited him, and Ruth wanted him calm enough to eat his dinner. "You care," Ruth said. "You are so angry that you must care even more than I thought."

Startled, Susannah looked at her straight on. The quiet, determined girl had always seemed so shy but had proved, in the past few years, to be so strong. More than once, Susannah had envied this woman her place in the tent beside Paul and Linus and all the men of Susannah's own family. Not begrudged that place to her, but envied her because of it.

"I am not so angry that I am disrupting the peace of my brother's tent, I hope," Susannah said.

"It is you I am worried about, not us," Ruth said. "Did you quarrel with the angel? Is that it?"

The pot did not need stirring, but Susannah swirled the spoon through it again, just for something to do. "He does not want to marry me," Susannah said. "So I do not want to marry him."

"As I understood it, the marriage between the Archangel and his— what is that word—"

"His angelica."

"Is not a marriage of love, anyway. It is a political union, arranged by the god. So perhaps it should not matter if he does not want to marry you."

Susannah watched the whorls form in the bubbling stew, following the slow path of the spoon. "Wouldn't it matter to you?" she asked.

"Only if I loved him," Ruth said.

Susannah kept stirring and did not answer.

The meal was highly praised, despite its lack of flavor, probably because it was seasoned with so much contentment. Susannah sat between Linus and her older nephew, now nearly three and determined to speak whole conversations, though his vocabulary was small and his understanding of grammar only rudimentary. Between his sweetness and Linus' jokes, she could not stop smiling through the whole meal.

Afterward, of course, there was music. "Sing with me, Susannah," Linus commanded, pulling her to her feet before anyone else had a chance to rise. She obliged, placing her sure voice against his changing and uncertain one so that their harmonies were creative but well-received. Everyone applauded, and then everyone else had a turn calling out her name.

"Susannah—remember that lullaby about baby Emma? Can we sing that?"

"Susannah, I wrote this piece but I haven't had time to come up with the harmony. Will you improvise?"

"Susannah, we've been practicing our duet for the Gathering, but won't you sing the middle part?"

And so she did. It felt good, it felt wonderful, to be again among people who loved her without reservation. Who did not find it necessary to conceal the fact that they cared for her. Who knew that the best way to win love was to show it first.

She sang all night with them, but the music did not lift her spirits.

• • •

In the morning, a day or two before she had actually expected him, Gaaron arrived.

He came slanting down from overhead like late-spring sunshine, his wings extended to their fullest, most impressive reach. Even the Edori could not help staring a little and exclaiming out loud at his grandeur. He landed a few yards from the camp and came forward, his wings folded behind him and the expression on his face courteous, but he did not look like any ordinary man come unexpectedly to the Tachita campfire, hoping for hospitality.

He looked like the Archangel, searching Samaria for a missing prize.

Paul and a couple of the clan elders went over to greet him and reintroduce themselves, for it had been several months since he had seen them last, and he was a busy man who might have forgotten their names. Susannah busied herself with the baby, a cooing, happy girl who divided her time between sleeping and smiling. But she glanced up from time to time to see if she could gauge what the conversation between the Tachitas and the angel might be about.

"Have you made up your mind what you might say to him?" Ruth asked, coming up behind her.

"He might not have come here to see me," Susannah replied.

Ruth stared at her. "Are you a want-wit?" she demanded. "Why else seek out the Tachitas?"

Susannah swung the baby up to nestle against her shoulder. "Perhaps he is seeking out all the Edori, to tell them that the invaders are gone."

"Perhaps he is seeking out all his wives to tell them to come home," Ruth retorted, and Susannah could not help laughing.

But her face was smooth and serious when Paul brought Gaaron over to their campfire. Ruth smiled at him and showed him the new baby, only two months old and sweeter than tree-warm honey. Gaaron also spoke grave hellos to both the boys, though the younger one hid his face for fear of the broad wings, and the older one was struck dumb by the sight. A few words with Susannah's father followed next, and then Gaaron turned to his angelica.

"Susannah," he said. "Will you come walk with me a little way? I have a great deal of news, and I don't want to interfere with the daily work around the campfire."

How could she refuse such a carefully worded request? She did not look him full in the face as she nodded, laid aside the spoon and spices she had taken up, and gave Ruth one quick, rueful glance. Ruth kept her face neutral, but her eyes were full of interest.

"Let's walk over this way," Susannah said, picking up a couple of the camp buckets, "and we can bring back water."

Gaaron took one of the buckets from her and they strolled away from the tent in silence. Edori as a rule never allowed themselves to show curiosity, but Susannah could feel her family staring after her before turning to look at one another and wondering aloud what might be going on.

Gaaron was the first one to speak. "So you've heard the news from Velora," he said.

She nodded. "Chloe told us. Is the city completely destroyed?"

"About half of it. But enough of it remains standing that there is shelter for everyone, and the rebuilding has already begun."

"How many lives were lost?"

"We have not counted them all yet," Gaaron said. "A couple of hundred at least, or so it seems. Many of them burned beyond recognition, so it is a grim task to assess who is lost and who is merely missing."

"How many of Jossis' people were killed?"

"A few dozen that we found. We also found, beside their bodies, a few of those fire sticks that they used to burn the towns and villages."

"I don't think those should be left lying about," Susannah said in some alarm.

He shook his head. "I have sent them on to Adriel. She says she has a room at Windy Point where she can keep them—a room that only the Archangel has access to. They will be safe there."

"So much to do and to decide," Susannah said. "You must be very busy."

"With many things," he agreed. "Messages from Neri and Adriel come every day—and so do offers of food and other aid. The Manadavvi and the river merchants have sent food and clothing and money. Solomon of Breven has offered help," he added with a cynical note creeping into his voice, "but he wants payment for it. So far we have managed to do without his assistance."

"Do you think the invaders are truly gone?" she asked.

"That is what Mahalah says. And there has been no sign of them for four days now. But I don't know how we can be certain that they will never return. I'm not even certain what happened to drive them away."

"Mahalah says they were frightened away by Yovah."

"Mahalah has not been specific enough to satisfy me."

"What else can you do but watch and wait?" she asked.

He shook his head. "Nothing. Go on with the day-to-day governing of the realm. Rebuild Velora. Plan for the Gloria. Proceed with my own wedding."

She kept walking, but she said nothing.

"Which means you must return with me to the Eyrie today," he added.

"I'm not going to marry you," she said.

Gaaron stopped and put his bucket down. She had thought his response might be a quick flare of anger, but he seemed composed. "Then we must talk about that," he said.

She put her own bucket on the ground and faced him. She was more tense than she had thought she would be. When she had imagined this scene, as she lay awake in Mount Sinai, she had been serene and reasonable. "I have decided not to be your angelica after all," she said.

"And why is that?"

"You have asked me often what it would take to make me happy at the Eyrie—among the angels—in your life," she said. "And I had thought I could be happy enough doing the work of the god. Becoming your angelica because he asked me to. But I have realized that is not enough for me. If I am to marry you, I have to love you."

"And you do not love me," he answered steadily.

"I do love you," she said, and she saw the shock on his face. "I just have not said so."

"Susannah—"

"And I have not said so, because you have not said that you love me. And I will not marry you unless you do."

There was a long silence. Gaaron turned his head as if to look meditatively into the distance; he had quickly hidden his astonishment behind the usual mask of calm. But she was beginning to be able to read his face, even the texts he did not want to make public. "Susannah," he said. "We were such good friends before. Can we not find a way to mend this breach and be friends again?"

"*I* can't," she said flatly. "I cannot be married to the man I love and pretend that I want nothing more from him than kindness and companionship. I do not want to—I do not *intend* to—spend my days yearning for you. If I cannot have you as my lover, then I will not have you in my life at all. I will stay here with the Tachitas, or perhaps go back to the Lohoras, or perhaps find a place with some other clan, and go on with my life."

"The god wants you beside me," he said, still looking away.

"The question is, do you?"

Now he looked down at her, and there was some kind of repressed emotion in his face. His eyes smoldered with it, but she did not think it was anger. Fear, perhaps, a fear even deeper than he knew how to analyze.

"My life has been bounded by so many restrictions that I have not been allowed very many freedoms," he said slowly, as though the words were being tortured out of him. "I consider all emotions to be a kind of distraction, and love to be the most irresistible distraction of all. It is all very well and good when it is going smoothly, but when it fails? When one person loves and the other does not? Or when one person still loves and the other turns away? I know myself well enough to know that I would not lightly endure such devastation. I know myself well enough to realize that I would not emerge intact. I have too many other things to do to allow myself to be broken by love. And so I have sworn to myself that I would not love you."

"You may have sworn not to *say* it," Susannah answered softly, "but you do love me."

"I cannot afford love," he said, and bent to pick up his bucket.

Susannah caught up her own pail and hurried after him. "Then you cannot afford an angelica," she said in a conversational tone. "And you will have to cancel this wedding when you return."

"You have to be at the wedding," he said, still walking.

"No. And I don't have to be at the Gloria, either," she said.

That stopped him dead in his tracks. "Don't have to—of *course* you have to be at the Gloria!" he exclaimed, finally roused to emotion. "If the Archangel and the angelica do not lead the masses in prayer—if representatives of all the people of Samaria are not gathered together to sing on the Plain of Sharon—"

"I know," Susannah said. "The god will smite the mountain, and then he will smite the river, and then he will destroy the world."

Gaaron started walking again. "So don't be so foolish as to say you will not come to the Gloria."

"Well, I won't."

He whirled around, exasperated and disbelieving, but she stood her ground. "I won't," she said again. "I won't come sing at your side at the Gloria unless I am married to you, and I won't marry you unless you say you love me."

"This is ridiculous," he snapped. "To say you would risk the demolition of the entire world—"

"Miriam told me," Susannah said, "what Mahalah told you. That Yovah picks for every Archangel the spouse who is his perfect complement. So that if the Archangel is impetuous, the angelica will be wise. And if the Archangel is arrogant, the angelica will be humble. And you thought, because you are stubborn, that your angelica would be docile and easily swayed.

"But what you didn't realize," she continued slowly, "is that I am even more stubborn than you are. Yovah picked me because you cannot wear me down. I will not do what you want unless you do what I want. And I want to live with a man who loves me."

"But Susannah—you cannot seriously tell me—you would not really let the god loose his wrath upon Samaria—"

She shrugged and stepped forward again. At this rate, they would never make it to the river. "I think the god knows my heart better than you do," she said over her shoulder. "And he will understand why I refuse to sing."

"But Susannah—"

She kept walking, letting him catch up with her, and attempt to argue with her, and receive nothing from her but silence in return. They made it to the riverbed, a quick, shallow stream that fed into the Galilee not a mile from here, and she dipped her pail into the clear water.

"Fill your bucket," she directed as she stepped away from the bank, for he had stood there this whole time haranguing her.

He did so hastily, but she didn't wait, starting back on the rocky path toward camp. He hurried so much to keep up with her that water sloshed out of his bucket onto his leather boots and her cotton dress.

"That's *cold!*" she exclaimed.

"Susannah, wait. Listen," he said. He had set down his pail again and now he caught her by the arm to make her stay in place. Obediently, she waited, placing her bucket carefully on the ground beside her feet. "You cannot mean what you say," he went on.

"Which part of it?" she said.

"Any of it."

She put her hands on her hips and frowned up at him, like any virago giving a scold to her errant husband. "And now you're accusing me of lying?" she demanded.

"What? I didn't say that. Susannah—"

"I tell you that I love you, and you don't believe me. That means you think I'm lying."

"It means," he said, and his voice sounded tired, "that I think you love someone else more. Or someone else, too. It means that I don't trust your love, anybody's love, to be there when I need it most. And I have too many people relying on me for *me* to rely on supports that will not hold."

Her face softened. She came a step nearer and reached up so she could lay a hand against his cheek. He had shaved that morning and his skin was free of whiskers, but it seemed roughened by other things: worry, work, wonder. She wanted to smooth away every line, refresh every tired pore with a kiss.

"But you see," she said softly, "I am the support you can count on. You have so many people to care for. I want to be the one who cares for *you*. I want to be the sweet voice in the dark that answers only to your call. I want to be your place of warmth and safety, your refuge and your home. I want to be the one you think of when every other thought is gone."

"You are that thought," he said, very low. His head was bent down; his eyes were closed. It was as if he wanted to be conscious of nothing but the feel of her fingers against his cheek. "You are that place. You are that voice."

She put her other hand up and guided his face down toward hers. "Then say it," she whispered.

"Susannah, I love you."

"And the world did not end," she said, and kissed him.

His arms went around her first, bulky and uncertain; it was like being taken in the massive embrace of an oak, unused to clasping humans. Next his wings enfolded her, more cautiously, settling down on her with the weight and color of sunlight. She kissed him—or he kissed her—there was, in the whole world, nothing but mouth and cheek and feather and arm. He held her so tightly that there was not even air to breathe, but she did not need air. She had Gaaron, and that was enough.